PETER ROBINSON grew up in Leeds, Yorkshire. He emigrated to Canada in 1974 and attended York University and the University of Windsor, where he was later Writer in Residence. He received the Arthur Ellis Award in 1992 for *Past Reason Hated*, in 1997 for *Innocent Graves*, and in 2001 for *Cold Is the Grave*. *Past Reason Hated* also won the 1994 TORGI Talking Book of the Year Award, and in 2001, Robinson won the Edgar Award for best short story. Seven additional Inspector Banks novels have all been published to critical acclaim. He lives in Toronto.

Other Inspector Banks mysteries published by Penguin:

PETER ROBINSON

Meet Inspector Banks

INSPECTOR BANK'S EARLY CASES

Gallows View

A Dedicated Man

A Necessary End

Penguin Books

PENGUIN BOOKS

Published by the Penguin Group

Penguin Books Canada Ltd, 10 Alcorn Avenue, Toronto, Ontario, Canada M4V 3B2
Penguin Books Ltd, 27 Wrights Lane, London W8 5TZ, England
Penguin Putnam Inc., 375 Hudson Street, New York, New York 10014, U.S.A.
Penguin Books Australia Ltd, Ringwood, Victoria, Australia
Penguin Books (NZ) Ltd, cnr Rosedale and Airborne Roads, Albany,
Auckland 1310, New Zealand

Penguin Books Ltd, Registered Offices: Harmondsworth, Middlesex, England

Gallows View first published in Viking by Penguin Books Canada Limited, 1987.
Published in Penguin Books, 1988.

A Dedicated Man first published in Viking by Penguin Books Canada Limited, 1988.
Published in Penguin Books, 1989.

A Necessary End first published in Viking by Penguin Books Canada Limited, 1989.
Published in Penguin Books, 1990

Published in Penguin Books, 2000

10 9 8 7 6 5 4 3 2 1

Gallows View © Peter Robinson, 1987
A Dedicated Man © Peter Robinson, 1988
A Necessary End © Peter Robinson, 1989

Manufactured in Canada

NATIONAL LIBRARY OF CANADA CATALOGUING IN PUBLICATION DATA

Robinson, Peter, 1950 –
Meet Inspector Banks

Contents: Gallows view — A dedicated man — A necessary end.

ISBN 0-14-100816-4

I. Title II. Title: Gallows view.   III. Title: A dedicated man.   IV. Title: A necessary end.

PS8585.O35176M43 2001   C813'.51   C2001-0337X
PR9199.3.R62M43 2001

Visit Penguin Canada's website at www.penguin.ca

CONTENTS

GALLOWS VIEW

For my father, Clifford Robinson,
and to the memory of my mother, Miriam Robinson,
1922–1985.

Now winter nights enlarge
    The number of their houres,
And clouds their stormes discharge
    Upon the ayrie towres;
Let now the chimneys blaze
    And cups o'erflow with wine,
Let well-tun'd words amaze
    With harmonie divine.
Now yellow waxen lights
    Shall waite on hunny Love,
While youthfull Revels, Masks, and Courtly sights,
    Sleepes leaden spels remove.

Thomas Campion
The Third Booke of Ayres

Town of
Eastvale

East Side Estate

Railway

Glue-Sniffers'
Ginnel

Mick's
House

The Green

Jenny's
House

Pathway

River
Falls

Terraced

River

Gardens

Pathway

Formal
Gardens

Pathway

River Swain

Excavated
Pre-Roman
Site

Bus
Station

Castle
Hill

York Road

Nat West
El Toro

Joplin's

Eastvale
Community
Centre

Church

Market
Square

Queen's
Arms

Golden
Grill

E

N   S

Police
Station

Market Street

W

Town
Hall

Eastvale
Comprehensive

King Street

Banks's
House

Elmet Street

The
Oak

Cardigan Drive

Carol
Ellis

Leaview Estate

Fields

Andrea (4)
Wooller (6)
Sharps (8, 10)

Alice (2)

Gallows
View

Fields

ONE

I

The woman stepped into the circle of light and began to undress. Above her black, calf-length skirt she wore a silver blouse with dozens of little pearl buttons up the front. She tugged it free of the waistband and started undoing the buttons from the bottom very slowly, gazing into space as if she were recalling a distant memory. With a shrug, she slid the blouse off, pulling at the left sleeve, which stuck to her wrist with static, then lowered her head and stretched her arms behind her back like wings to unclasp her bra, raising one shoulder and then the other as she slipped off the thin straps. Her breasts were large and heavy, with dark, upturned nipples.

She unzipped her skirt down the left side and let it slide to the floor. Stepping out of it and bending from the waist, she picked it up and laid it neatly over the back of a chair. Next she rolled her tights down over her hips, buttocks and thighs, then sat down on the edge of the bed to extricate herself from each leg, one at a time, careful not to make runs. As she bent over, the taut skin folded in a dark crease across her stomach and her breasts hung so that each nipple touched each knee in turn.

Standing again, she hooked her thumbs into the elastic of her black panties and bent forward as she eased them down. As she stepped out of them, she caught the waistband with her left foot and flicked them into the corner by the wardrobe.

At last, completely naked, she tossed back her wavy blonde hair and walked towards the dresser.

It was then that she looked towards the chink in the curtains. His whole body tingled as he watched the shock register in her eyes. He couldn't move. She gasped and instinctively tried to cover her breasts with her hands, and he thought how funny and vulnerable she looked with the triangle of hair between her legs exposed....

As she grabbed for her dressing-gown and dashed towards the window, he managed to drag himself away and run off, scraping his shin and almost falling as he jumped the low wall. He had disappeared into the night by the time she picked up the telephone.

II

"Where on earth did I put that sugar bowl?" Alice Matlock muttered to herself as she searched the cluttered room. It was a birthday present from Ethel Carstairs—a present for her eighty-seventh birthday three days ago. Now it had disappeared.

Alice was having trouble remembering little things like that these days. They said it happened when you got older. But why, then, should the past seem so vivid? Why, particularly, should that day in 1916, when Arnold marched off proudly to the trenches, seem so much clearer than yesterday. "What happened yesterday?" Alice asked herself, as a test, and she did remember little details like visiting the shop, polishing her silverware and listening to a play on the radio. But had she really done those things yesterday, the day before, or even last week? The memories were there, but the string of time that linked them like a pearl necklace was broken. All those years ago—that beautiful summer when the meadows were full of buttercups (none of those nasty new bungalows, then), the hedgerows bright with cow-parsley ("gypsy" she always called it, because her mother had told her that if she picked it the gypsies would take her) and her garden full of roses, chrysanthemums, clematis and lupins—Arnold had stood there, ready to go, his buttons reflecting the sunlight in dancing sparks on the whitewashed walls. He leaned against the doorway, that very same doorway, with his kitbag and that lopsided grin on his face—such a young face, one that had never even seen a razor—and off he marched, erect, graceful, to the station.

He never came back. Like so many others, he was destined to lie in a foreign grave. Alice knew this. She knew that he was dead. But hadn't she also been waiting for him all these years? Wasn't that why she had never married, even when that handsome shopkeeper Jack Wormald had proposed? Down on his knees, he was, by the falls at Rawley Force; got his knees wet, too, and that didn't half vex him. But she said no, kept the house on after her parents died, changed things as little as possible.

There had been another war, too, she vaguely remembered: ration books; urgent voices and martial anthems on the radio; faraway rumblings that could have been bombs. Arnold hadn't come back from that war either, though she could imagine him fighting in it like a Greek god, lithe and strong, with a stern face, a face that had never seen a razor.

Other wars followed, or so Alice had heard. Distant ones. Little wars. And he had fought in them all, an eternal soldier. She knew, deep down, that he would never come home, but she couldn't lose hope. Without hope, there would be nothing left.

"Where on earth did I put it?" she muttered to herself, down on her knees rummaging through the cupboard under the sink. "It must be somewhere. I'd forget my head if it was loose."

Then she heard someone running outside. Her eyes were not as good as they used to be, but she was proud of her hearing and often ticked off the shop-girls and bus conductors who assumed that they had to shout to make her hear them. After the sound of running came a gentle knock at her door. Puzzled, she stood up slowly, grasped the draining-board to keep her balance, and shuffled through to the living-room. There was always a chance. She had to hope. And so she opened the door.

III

"Perverts, the lot of them," Detective Chief Inspector Alan Banks said, adjusting the treble on the stereo.

"Including me?" asked Sandra.

"For all I know."

"Since when has making artistic representations of the naked human form been a mark of perversion?"

"Since half of them don't even have films in their cameras."

"But I always have film in my camera."

"Yes," Banks said enthusiastically, "I've seen the results. Where on earth do you find those girls?"

"They're mostly students from the art college."

"Anyway," Banks went on, returning to his scotch, "I'm damn sure Jack Tatum doesn't have a film in his camera. And Fred Barton wouldn't know a wide-angle lens from a putting iron. I wouldn't be at all surprised if they imagined you posing—a nice willowy blonde."

Sandra laughed. "Me? Nonsense. And stop playing the yahoo, Alan. It doesn't suit you. You don't have a leg to stand on, acting the idiot over photography while you're inflicting this bloody opera on me."

"For someone who appreciates artistic representations of the naked human form, you're a proper philistine when it comes to music, you know."

"Music I can take. It's all this screeching gives me a headache."

"Screeching! Good lord, woman, this is the sound of the human spirit soaring: 'Vissi d'arte, vissi d'amore.'" Banks's soprano imitation made up in volume what it lacked in melody.

"Oh, put a sock in it," Sandra sighed, reaching for her drink.

It was always like this when he found a new interest. He would pursue it with a passion for anywhere between one and six months, then he would have a restless period, lose interest and move on to something else. Of course, the detritus would remain, and he would always profess to be still deeply interested—just too pushed for time. That was how the house had come to be so cluttered up with the novels of Charles Dickens, wine-making equipment, twenties jazz records, barely used jogging shoes, a collection of birds' eggs and books on almost every subject under the sun—from Tudor history to how to fix your own plumbing.

He had become interested in opera after seeing, quite by chance, a version of Mozart's *Magic Flute* on television. It was always like that. Something piqued his curiosity and he wanted to know more. There was no order to it, neither in his mind nor in his filing system. He would plunge into a subject with cavalier disregard for its chronological development. And so it was with the opera craze: *Orfeo* rubbed shoulders with *Lulu*; *Peter Grimes* was *Tosca*'s strange bedfellow; and *Madama Butterfly* shared shelf-space with *The Rake's Progress*. Much as she loved music, opera was driving Sandra crazy. Already, complaints from Brian and Tracy had resulted in the removal of the television to the spare room upstairs. And Sandra was forever tripping over the book-sized cassette boxes, which Banks preferred to records, as he liked to walk to work and listen to Purcell or Monteverdi on his Walkman; in the car, it was generally Puccini or Guiseppe Verdi, good old Joe Green.

They were both alike in their thirst for knowledge, Sandra reflected. Neither was an academic or intellectual, but both pursued self-education with an urgency often found in bright working-class people who hadn't had culture thrust down their throats from the cradle onwards. If only, she wished, he would take up something quiet and peaceful, like beekeeping or stamp collecting.

The soprano reached a crescendo which sent involuntary shivers up Sandra's spine.

"You're surely not serious about some people in the Camera Club being perverts, are you?" she asked.

"I shouldn't be surprised if one or two of them got more than an artistic kick out of it, that's all."

"You could be right, you know," Sandra agreed. "They're not only women, the models. We had a very nice Rastafarian the other week. Lovely pector—"

The phone rang.

"Damn and blast it." Banks cursed and hurried over to pick up the offending instrument. Sandra took the opportunity to turn down the volume on *Tosca* surreptitiously.

"Seems that someone's been taking unasked-for peeks at the naked human form again," said Banks when he sat down again a few minutes later.

"Another of those Peeping Tom incidents?"

"Yes."

"You don't have to go in, do you?"

"No. It'll wait till morning. Nobody's been hurt. She's more angry than anything else. Young Richmond is taking her statement."

"What happened?"

"Woman by the name of Carol Ellis. Know her?"

"No."

"Seems she came back from a quiet evening at the pub, got undressed for bed and noticed someone watching her through a gap in the curtains. He took off as soon as he realized he'd been spotted. It was on that new estate, Leaview, those ugly bungalows down by the Gallows View cottages. Great places for voyeurs, bungalows. They don't even need to shin up the drainpipe." Banks paused and lit a Benson and Hedges Special Mild. "This one's taken a few risks in the past, though. Last time it was a second-floor maisonette."

"It makes my skin crawl," Sandra said, hugging herself. "The thought of someone watching when you think you're alone."

"I suppose it would," Banks agreed. "But what worries me now is that we'll have that bloody feminist group down on us again. They really seem to think we haven't bothered trying to catch him because we secretly approve. They believe all men are closet rapists. According to them, our secret hero is Jack the Ripper. They think we've got pin-ups on the station walls."

"You do. I've seen them. Not in your office, maybe, but down-stairs."

"I mean pin-ups of Jack the Ripper."

Sandra laughed. "That's going a bit far, I agree."

"Do you know how difficult it is to catch a peeper?" Banks asked. "All the bugger does is look and run away into the night. No finger-prints, no sightings, nothing. The best we can hope for is to catch him in the act, and we've had extra men and women walking the beat in the most likely areas for weeks now. Still nothing. Anyway," Banks said, reaching out for her, "all this talk about naked bodies is exciting me. Time for bed?"

"Sorry," answered Sandra, turning off the stereo. "Not tonight, dear, I've got a headache."

TWO

I

"And where the bloody hell do you think you were till all hours last night?" Graham Sharp roared at his son over the breakfast table.

Trevor glowered into his cornflakes. "Out."

"I know you were bloody out. Out with that good-for-nothing Mick Webster, I'll bet?"

"What if I was? It's my business who I hang out with."

"He's a bad 'un, Trevor. Like his brother and his father before him. A rotten apple."

"Mick's all right."

"I didn't raise you all these years with my own hands just so you could hang about with hooligans and get into trouble."

"Well, if you weren't such a bleeding little Hitler my mum might not have run off."

"Never mind that," Graham said quietly. "You don't know nothing about it, you was only a kid. I just want you to do well for yourself," he pleaded. "Look, I've not done much. Never had the opportunity. But you're a bright lad. If you work hard you can go to university, get yourself a good education."

"What's the point? There's no jobs anyway."

"It's not always going to be like this, Trevor. I know the country's going through a bad time right now. You don't need to tell me that. But look to the future, lad. It'll be five or six years by the time you've done your 'A' Levels and your degree. Things can change a lot in that time. All you need to do is stay in a bit more and do your homework. You never found it hard, you know you can do it."

"It's boring."

"Look what happened to Mick, then," Graham went on, his voice rising with anger again. "Left school a year ago and still on the bloody dole. Sharing a hovel with that layabout brother of his, father run off God knows where and his mother never home to take care of him."

"Lenny's not a layabout. He had a job in London. Just got made redundant, that's all. It wasn't his fault."

"I'm not going to argue with you, Trevor. I want you to stay in more and spend some time on your schoolwork. I might not have made much out of my life, but you can—and you're bloody well going to, even if it kills me."

Trevor stood up and reached for his satchel. "Better be off," he said. "Wouldn't want to be late for school, would I?"

After the door slammed, Graham Sharp put his head in his hands and sighed. He knew that Trevor was at a difficult age—he'd been a bit of a lad himself at fifteen—but if only he could persuade him that he had so much to lose. Life was hard enough these days without making it worse for yourself. Since Maureen had walked out ten years ago, Graham had devoted himself to their only child. He would have sent Trevor to a public school if he'd had enough money, but had to settle for the local comprehensive. Even there, despite all the drawbacks, the boy had always done well—top of the class, prizes every Speech Day—until last year, when he took up with Mick Webster.

Graham's hands shook as he picked up the breakfast dishes and carried them to the sink. Soon it would be opening time. At least since he'd stopped doing morning papers he got a bit of a lie-in. In the old days, when Maureen was around, he'd had to get up at six o'clock, and he'd kept it going as long as he could. Now he couldn't afford to employ a flock of paper-carriers, nor could he manage to pay the assistant he would need to deal with other business. As things were, he could just about handle it all himself—orders, accounts, stock checks, shelf arrangements—and usually still manage to come up with a smile and a hello for the customers.

His real worry was Trevor, and he didn't know if he was going about things the right way or not. He knew he had a bit of a temper and went on at the lad too much. Maybe it was better to leave him alone, wait till he passed through the phase himself. But perhaps then it would be too late.

Graham stacked the dishes in the drainer, checked his watch, and walked through to the shop. Five minutes late. He turned the sign to read OPEN and unlocked the door. Grouchy old Ted Croft was already counting out his pennies, shuffling his feet as he waited for his week's supply of baccy. Not a good start to the day.

II

Banks reluctantly snapped off his Walkman in the middle of Dido's lament and walked into the station, a Tudor-fronted building in the town centre, where Market Street ran into the cobbled square. He said "Good morning" to Sergeant Rowe at the desk and climbed upstairs to his office.

The whitewashed walls and black-painted beams of the building's exterior belied its modern, functional innards. Banks's office, for example, featured a venetian blind that was almost impossible to work and a grey metal desk with drawers that rattled. The only human touch was the calendar on the wall, with its series of local scenes. The illustration for October showed a stretch of the River Wharfe, near Grassington, with trees lining the waterside in full autumn colour. It was quite a contrast to the real October: nothing but grey skies, rain and cold winds so far.

On his desk was a message from Superintendent Gristhorpe: "Alan, Come see me in my office soon as you get in. G."

Remembering first to unhook the Walkman and put it in his desk drawer, Banks walked along the corridor and knocked on the superintendent's door.

"Come in," Gristhorpe called, and Banks entered.

Inside was luxury—teak desk, bookcases, shaded table lamps— most of which had been supplied by Gristhorpe himself over the years.

"Ah, good morning Alan," the superintendent greeted him, "I'd like you to meet Dr Fuller." He gestured towards the woman sitting opposite him, and she stood up to shake Banks's hand. She had a shock of curly red hair, bright green eyes with crinkly laugh-lines around the edges, and a luscious mouth. The turquoise top she was wearing looked like a cross between a straight-jacket and a dentist's smock. Below that she wore rust-coloured cords that tapered to a halt just above her shapely ankles. All in all, Banks thought, the doctor was a knock-out.

"Please, Inspector Banks," Dr Fuller said as she gently let go of his hand, "call me Jenny."

"Jenny it is, then," Banks smiled and dug for a cigarette. "I suppose that makes me Alan."

"Not if you don't want to be." Her sparkling eyes seemed to challenge him.

"Not at all, it's a pleasure," he said, meeting her gaze. Then he remembered Gristhorpe's recent ban against smoking in his office, and put the pack away.

"Dr Fuller is a professor at York University," Gristhorpe explained, "but she lives here in Eastvale. Psychology's her field, and I brought her in to help with the Peeping Tom case. Actually," he turned a charming smile in Jenny's direction, "Dr Fuller—Jenny—was recommended by an old and valued friend of mine in the department. We were hoping she might be able to work with us on a profile."

Banks nodded. "It would certainly give us more than we've got already. How can I help?"

"I'd just like to talk to you about the details of the incidents," Jenny said, looking up from a notepad that rested on her lap. "There's been three so far, is that right?"

"Four now, counting last night's. All blondes."

Jenny nodded and made the change in her notes.

"Perhaps the two of you can arrange to meet sometime," Gristhorpe suggested.

"Is now no good?" Banks asked.

"Afraid not," Jenny said. "This might take a bit of time, and I've got a class in just over an hour. Look, what about tonight, if it's not too much of an imposition on your time?"

Banks thought quickly. It was Tuesday; Sandra would be at the Camera Club, and the kids, now trusted in the house without a sitter, would be overjoyed to spend an opera-free evening. "All right," he agreed. "Make it seven in the Queen's Arms across the street, if that's okay with you."

When Jenny smiled, the lines around her eyes crinkled with pleasure and humour. "Why not? It's an informal kind of procedure anyway. I just want to build up a picture of the psychological type."

"I'll look forward to it, then," Banks said.

Jenny picked up her briefcase and he held the door open for her. Gristhorpe caught his eye and beckoned him to stay behind. When Jenny had gone, Banks settled back into his chair, and the superintendent rang for coffee.

"Good woman," Gristhorpe said, rubbing a hairy hand over his red, pock-marked face. "I asked Ted Simpson to recommend a bright lass for the job, and I think he did his homework all right, don't you?"

"It remains to be seen," replied Banks. "But I'll agree she bodes well. You said a woman. Why? Has Mrs Hawkins stopped cooking and cleaning for you?"

Gristhorpe laughed. "No, no. Still brings me fresh scones and keeps the place neat and tidy. No, I'm not after another wife. I just thought it would be politic, that's all."

Banks had a good idea what Gristhorpe meant, but he chose to carry on playing dumb. "Politic?"

"Aye, politic. Diplomatic. Tactful. You know what it means. It's the biggest part of my job. The biggest pain in the arse, too. We've got the local feminists on our backs, haven't we? Aren't they saying we're not doing our job because it's women who are involved? Well, if we can be seen to be working with an obviously capable, successful woman, then there's not a lot they can say, is there?"

Banks smiled to himself. "I see what you mean. But how are we going to be seen to be working with Jenny Fuller? It's hardly headline material."

Gristhorpe put a finger to the side of his hooked nose. "Jenny Fuller's attached to the local feminists. She'll report back everything that's going on."

"Is that right?" Banks grinned. "And I'm going to be working with her? I'd better be on my toes, then, hadn't I?"

"It shouldn't be any problem, should it?" Gristhorpe asked, his guileless blue eyes as disconcerting as a newborn baby's. "We've got nothing to hide, have we? We know we're doing our best on this one. I just want others to know, that's all. Besides, those profiles can be damn useful in a case like this. Help us predict patterns, know where to look. And she won't be hard on the eyes, will she? A right bobby-dazzler, don't you think?"

"She certainly is."

"Well, then." Gristhorpe smiled and slapped both his hands on the desk. "No problem, is there? Now, how's that break-in business going?"

"It's very odd, but we've had three of those in a month, too, all involving old women alone in their homes—one even got a broken arm—and we've got about as far with that as we have with the Tom business. The thing is, though, there are no pensioners' groups giving us a lot of stick, telling us we're not doing anything because only old people are getting hurt."

"It's the way of the times, Alan," Gristhorpe said. "And you have to admit that the feminists do have a point, even if it doesn't apply in this particular case."

"I know that. It just irritates me, being criticized publicly when I'm doing the best I can."

"Well, now's your chance to put that right. What about this fence in Leeds? Think it'll lead anywhere with the break-ins?"

Banks shrugged. "Might do. Depends on Mr Crutchley's power of recall. These things vary."

"According to the level of threat you convey? Yes, I know. I should imagine Joe Barnshaw's done some groundwork for you. He's a good man. Why bother yourself? Why not let him handle it?"

"It's our case. I'd rather talk to Crutchley myself—that way I can't blame anyone else if mistakes are made. What he says might ring a bell, too. I'll ask Inspector Barnshaw to show him the pictures later, get an artist in if the description's good enough."

Gristhorpe nodded. "Makes sense. Taking Sergeant Hatchley?"

"No, I'll handle this by myself. I'll put Hatchley on the peeper business till I get back."

"Do you think that's wise?"

"He can't do much damage in an afternoon, can he? Besides, if he does, it'll give the feminists a target worthy of their wrath."

Gristhorpe laughed. "Away with you, Alan. Throwing your sergeant to the wolves like that."

III

It was raining hard. Hatchley covered his head with a copy of *The Sun* as he ran with Banks across Market Street to the Golden Grill. It was a narrow street, but by the time they got there the page-three beauty was sodden. The two sat down at a window table and looked out at distorted shop-fronts through the runnels of rain, silent until their standing order of coffee and toasted teacakes was duly delivered by the perky, petite young waitress in her red checked dress.

The relationship between the inspector and his sergeant had changed slowly over the six months Banks had been in Eastvale. At first, Hatchley had resented an "incomer," especially one from the big city, being brought in to do the job he had expected to get. But as they worked together, the Dalesman had come to respect, albeit somewhat grudgingly (for a Yorkshireman's respect is often tempered with a sarcasm intended to deflate airs and graces), his inspector's sharp mind and the effort Banks had made to adapt to his new environment.

Hatchley had got plenty of laughs observing this latter process. At first, Banks had been hyperactive, running on adrenalin, chain-smoking Capstan Full Strength, exactly as he had in his London job. But all this had changed over the months as he got used to the slower pace in Yorkshire. Outwardly, he was now calm and relaxed—deceptively so, as Hatchley knew, for inside he was a dynamo, his energy contained and channelled, flashing in his bright dark eyes. He still had his tempers, and he retained a tendency to brood when frustrated. But these were good signs; they produced results. He had also switched to mild cigarettes, which he smoked sparingly.

Hatchley felt more comfortable with him now, even though they remained two distinctly different breeds, and he appreciated his boss's grasp of northern informality. A working-class Southerner didn't seem so different from a Northerner, after all. Now, when Hatchley called Banks "sir," it was plain by his tone that he was puzzled or annoyed, and Banks had learned to recognize the dry, Yorkshire irony that could sometimes be heard in his sergeant's voice.

For his part, Banks had learned to accept, but not to condone, the prejudices of his sergeant and to appreciate his doggedness and the sense of threat that he could, when called for, convey to a reticent suspect. Banks's menace was cerebral, but some people responded better to Hatchley's sheer size and gruff voice. Though he never actually used violence, Hatchley made criminals believe that perhaps the days of the rubber hosepipe weren't quite over. The two also worked well together in interrogation. Suspects would become particularly confused when the big, rough-and-tumble Dalesman turned avuncular and Banks, who didn't even look tall enough to be a policeman, raised his voice.

"Hell's bloody bells, I can't see why I have to spend so much time chasing a bloke who just likes to look at a nice pair of knockers," said Hatchley, as the two of them lit cigarettes and sipped coffee.

Banks sighed. Why was it, he wondered, that talking to Hatchley always made him, a moderate socialist, feel like a bleeding-heart liberal?

"Because the women don't want to be looked at," he answered tersely.

Hatchley grunted. "If you saw the way that Carol Ellis dressed on a Sat'day night at The Oak you wouldn't think that."

"Her choice, Sergeant. I assume she wears at least some clothes at The Oak? Otherwise you'd be derelict in your duty for not pulling her in on indecent exposure charges."

"Whatever it is, it ain't indecent." Hatchley winked.

"Everybody deserves privacy, and this peeper's violating it," Banks argued. "He's breaking the law, and we're paid to uphold it. Simple as that." He knew that it was far from simple, but had neither the patience nor the inclination to enter into an argument about the police in society with Sergeant Hatchley.

"But it's not as if he's dangerous."

"He is to his victims. Physical violence isn't the only dangerous crime. You mentioned The Oak just now. Does the woman often drink there?"

"I've seen her there a few times. It's my local."

"Do you think our man might have seen her there, too, and followed her home? If she dresses like you say, he might have got excited looking at her."

"Do myself," Hatchley admitted cheerfully. "But peeping's not my line. Yes, it's possible. Remember, it was a Monday, though."

"So?"

"Well, in my experience, sir, the women don't dress up quite so much on a Monday as a Sat'day. See, they have to go to work the next day so they can't spend all night—"

"All right," Banks said, holding up his hand. "Point taken. What about the others?"

"What about them?"

"Carol Ellis is the fourth. There were three others before her. Did any of them drink at The Oak?"

"Can't remember. I do recollect seeing Josie Campbell there a few times. She was one of them, wasn't she?"

"Yes, the second. Look, go over the statements and see if you can find out if any of the others were regulars at The Oak. Go talk to them. Jog their memories. Look for some kind of a pattern. They needn't have been there just prior to the incidents. If not, find out where they do drink, look up where they were before they were ..."

"Peeped on?" Hatchley suggested.

Banks laughed uneasily. "Yes. There isn't really a proper word for it, is there?"

"Talking about peeping, I saw a smashing bit of stuff coming out of Gristhorpe's office. Is he turning into a dirty old man?"

"That was Dr Jenny Fuller," Banks told him. "She's a psychologist, and I'm going to be working with her on a profile of our peeper."

"Lucky you. Hope the missis doesn't find out."

"You've got a dirty mind, Sergeant. Get over to The Oak this lunchtime. Talk to the bar staff. Find out if anyone paid too much attention to Carol Ellis or if anyone seemed to be watching her. Anything odd. You know the routine. If the lunchtime staff's different, get back there tonight and talk to the ones who were in last night. And talk to Carol Ellis again, too, while it's fresh in her mind."

"This is work, sir?"

"Yes."

"At The Oak?"

"That's what I said."

Hatchley broke into a big grin, like a kid who'd lost a penny and found a pound. "I'll see what I can do, then," he said, and with that he was off like a shot. After all, Banks thought as he finished his coffee and watched a woman struggle in the doorway with a transparent umbrella, it was eleven o'clock. Opening time.

IV

It was a dull journey down the A1 to Leeds, and Banks cursed himself for not taking the quieter, more picturesque minor roads through Ripon and Harrogate, or even further west, via Grassington, Skipton and Ilkley. There always seemed to be hundreds of ways of getting from A to B in the Dales, none of them direct, but the A1 was usually the fastest route to Leeds, unless the farmer just north of Wetherby exercised his privilege and switched on the red light while he led his cows across the motorway.

As if the rain weren't bad enough, there was also the muddy spray from the juggernauts in front—transcontinentals, most of them, travelling from Newcastle or Edinburgh to Lille, Rotterdam, Milan or Barcelona. Still, it was cosy inside the car, and he had *Rigoletto* for company.

At the Wetherby roundabout, Banks turned onto the A58, leaving most of the lorries behind, and drove by Collingham, Bardsey and Scarcroft into Leeds itself. He carried on through Roundhay and Harehills, and arrived in Chapeltown halfway through "La Donna è Mobile."

It was a desolate area and looked even more so swept by dirty rain under the leaden sky. Amid the heaps of red-brick rubble, a few old houses clung on like obstinate teeth in an empty, rotten mouth; grim shadows in raincoats pushed prams and shopping-carts along the pavements as if they were looking for shops and homes they couldn't find. It was Chapeltown Road, "Ripper" territory, host of the '81 race riots.

Crutchley's shop had barred windows and stood next to a boarded-up grocers with a faded sign. The paintwork was peeling and a layer

of dust covered the objects in the window: valves from old radios; a
clarinet resting on the torn red velvet of its case; a guitar with four
strings; a sheathed bayonet with a black swastika inlaid in its handle;
chipped plates with views of Weymouth and Lyme Regis painted on
them; a bicycle pump; a scattering of beads and cheap rings.

The door jerked open after initial resistance, and a bell pinged
loudly as Banks walked in. The smell of the place—a mixture of
mildew, furniture polish and rotten eggs—was overwhelming. Out of
the back came around-shouldered, shifty-looking man wearing a
threadbare sweater and woollen gloves with the fingers cut off. He
eyed Banks suspiciously, and his "Can I help you?" sounded more like
a "Must I help you?"

"Mr Crutchley?" Banks showed his identification and mentioned
Inspector Barnshaw, who had first put him onto the lead. Crutchley
was immediately transformed from Mr Krook into Uriah Heep.

"Anything I can do, sir, anything at all," he whined, rubbing his
hands together. "I try to run an honest shop here, but," he
shrugged, "you know, it's difficult. I can't check on everything people bring in, can I?"

"Of course not," Banks agreed amiably, brushing off a layer of dust
and leaning carefully against the dirty counter. "Inspector Barnshaw
told me he's thinking of letting it go by this time. He asked for my
advice. We know how hard it is in a business like yours. He did say
that you might be able to help me, though."

"Of course, sir. Anything at all."

"We think that the jewellery the constable saw in your window
was stolen from an old lady in Eastvale. You could help us, and help
yourself, if you can give me a description of the man who brought
it in."

Crutchley screwed up his face in concentration—not a pretty
sight, Banks thought, looking away at the stuffed birds, elephant-
foot umbrella stands, sentimental Victorian prints and other junk.
"My memory's not as good as it used to be, sir. I'm not getting any
younger."

"Of course not. None of us are, are we?" Banks smiled. "Inspector
Barnshaw said he thought it would be a crying shame if you had to do
time for this, what with it not being your fault, and at your age."

Crutchley darted Banks a sharp, mean glance and continued to probe his ailing memory.

"He was quite young," he said after a few moments. "I remember that for sure."

"How young, would you say?" Banks asked, taking out his notebook. "Twenty, thirty?"

"Early twenties, I'd guess. Had a little moustache." He gestured to his upper lip, which was covered with about four days' stubble. "A thin one, just down to the edge of the mouth at each side. Like this," he added, tracing the outline with a grubby finger.

"Good," Banks said, encouraging him. "What about his hair? Black, red, brown, fair? Long, short?"

"Sort of medium. I mean, you wouldn't really call it brown, but it wasn't what I'd call fair, either. Know what I mean?"

Banks shook his head.

"P'raps you'd call it light brown. Very light brown."

"Was the moustache the same?"

He nodded. "Yes, very faint."

"And how long was his hair?"

"That I remember. It was short, and combed-back, like." He made a brushing gesture with his hand over his own sparse crop.

"Any scars, moles?"

Crutchley shook his head.

"Nothing unusual about his complexion?"

"A bit pasty-faced and spotty, that's all. But they all are, these days, Inspector. It's the food. No goodness in it, all—"

"How tall would you say he was?" Banks cut in.

"Bigger than me. Oh, about . . ." He put his hand about four inches above the top of his head. "Of course, I'm not so big myself."

"That would make him about five-foot-ten, then?"

"About that. Medium, yes."

"Fat or thin?"

"Skinny. Well, they all are these days, aren't they? Not properly fed, that's the problem."

"Clothes?"

"Ordinary."

"Can you be a bit more specific?"

"Eh?"

"Was he wearing a suit, jeans, leather jacket, T-shirt, pyjamas—what?"

"Oh. No, it wasn't leather. It was that other stuff, bit like it only not as smooth. Brown. Roughish. 'Orrible to touch—fair makes your fingers shiver."

"Suede?"

"That's it. Suede. A brown suede jacket and jeans. Just ordinary blue jeans."

"And his shirt?"

"Don't remember. I think he kept his jacket zipped up."

"Do you remember anything about his voice, any mannerisms?"

"Come again?"

"Where would you place his accent?"

"Local, like. Or maybe Lancashire. I can't tell the difference, though there are some as says they can."

"Nothing odd about it? High-pitched, deep, husky?"

"Sounded like he smoked too much, I can remember that. And he did smoke, too. Coughed every time he lit one up. Really stank up the shop."

Banks passed on that one. "So he had a smoker's cough and a rough voice with a local accent, that right?"

"That's right, sir." Crutchley was shifting from foot to foot, clearly looking forward to the moment when Banks would thank him and leave.

"Was his voice deep or high?"

"Kind of medium, if you know what I mean."

"Like mine?"

"Yes, like yours, sir. But not the accent. You speak proper, you do. He didn't."

"What do you mean he didn't speak properly? Did he have some kind of speech impediment?" Banks could see Crutchley mentally kicking himself for being so unwisely unctuous as to prolong the interview.

"No, nothing like that. I just meant like ordinary folks, sir, not like you. Like someone who hadn't been properly educated."

"He didn't stutter or lisp, did he?"

"No, sir."

"Fine. One last question: had you ever seen him before?"

"No, sir."

"Inspector Barnshaw will want you to look at some photos later today, and he's going to ask you to repeat your description to a police artist. So do your best, keep him in focus. And if you see him again or think of anything else, I'd appreciate your getting in touch with me." Banks wrote down his name and number on a card.

"I'll call you, sir, I'll do that, if I ever clap eyes on him again," Crutchley gushed, and Banks got the distinct impression that his own methods appealed more than Barnshaw's.

Banks heard the sigh of relief when he closed his notebook and thanked Crutchley, avoiding a handshake by moving off rather sharply. It wasn't a great description, and it didn't ring any bells, but it would do; it would take him closer to the two balaclava-wearing thugs who had robbed three old ladies in one month, scared them all half to death, vandalized their homes and broken the arm of one seventy-five-year-old woman.

THREE

I

The white Cortina skidded to a halt outside Eastvale Community Centre, splashing up a sheet of spray from the kerbside puddles. Sandra Banks jumped out, ten minutes late, pushed open the creaking door as gently as she could, and tiptoed in, aware of the talk already in progress. One or two of the regulars looked around and smiled as they saw her slip as unobtrusively as possible into the empty chair next to Harriet Slade.

"Sorry," she whispered, putting her hand to the side of her mouth. "Weather. Damn car wouldn't start."

Harriet nodded. "You've not missed much."

"However beautiful, majestic or overwhelming the landscape appears to your eyes," the speaker said, "remember, you have no guarantee that it will turn out well on film. In fact, most landscape photography—as I'm sure those of you who have tried it know—turns out to be extremely disappointing. The camera's eye differs from the human eye; it lacks all the other senses that feed into our experience. Remember that holiday in Majorca or Torremolinos? Remember how wonderful the hills and sea made you feel, with their magical qualities of light and colour? And remember when you got the holiday snaps developed—if they came out at all!—how bad they were, how they failed to capture the beauty you'd seen?"

"Who's this?" Sandra whispered to Harriet while the speaker paused to sip from the glass of water on the table in front of him.

"A man called Terry Whigham. He does a lot of pictures for the local tourist board—calendars, that kind of thing. What do you think?"

It wasn't anything new to Sandra, but she had more or less dragged poor Harriet into the Camera Club in the first place, and she felt that she owed it to her not to sound too smug.

"Interesting," she answered, covering her mouth like a schoolgirl talking in class. "He puts it very well."

"I think so, too," Harriet agreed. "I mean, it all seems so obvious, but you don't think about it till an expert points it out, do you?"

"So the next time you're faced with Pen-y-Ghent, Skiddaw or Helvellyn," Terry Whigham continued, "consider a few simple strategies. One obvious trick is to get something in the foreground to give a sense of scale. It's hard to achieve the feeling of immensity you get when you look at a mountain in a four-by-five colour print, but a human figure, an old barn or a particularly interesting tree in the foreground will add the perspective you need.

"You can also be a bit more adventurous and let textures draw the viewer in. A rising slope of scree or a field full of buttercups will lead the eye to the craggy fells beyond. And don't be slaves to the sun, either. Mist-shrouded peaks or cloud shadows on hillsides can produce some very interesting effects if you get your exposure right, and a few fluffy white clouds pep up a bright blue sky no end."

After this, the lights went down and Terry Whigham showed some of his favourite slides to illustrate the points he had made. They were good, Sandra recognized that, but they also lacked the spark, the personal signature, that she liked to get into her own photographs, even at the expense of well-proven rules.

Harriet was a newcomer to the art, but so far she had shown a sharp eye for a photograph, even if her technique still had a long way to go. Sandra had met her at a dreadful coffee morning organized by a neighbour, Selena Harcourt, and the two had hit it off instantly. In London, Sandra had never been short of lively company, but in the North the people had seemed cold and distant until Harriet came along, with her pixyish features, her slight frame and her deep sense of compassion. Sandra wasn't going to let her go.

When the slide show was over and Terry Whigham left the dais to a smattering of applause, the club secretary made announcements about the next meeting and the forthcoming excursion to Swaledale, then coffee and biscuits were served. As usual, Sandra, Harriet, Robin

Allott and Norman Chester, all preferring stronger refreshments, adjourned to The Mile Post across the road.

Sandra found herself sitting between Harriet and Robin, a young college teacher just getting over his divorce. Opposite sat Norman Chester, who always seemed more interested in the scientific process than the photographs themselves. Normally, such an oddly assorted group would never have come together, but they were united in the need for a real drink—especially after a longish lecture—and in their dislike for Fred Barton, the stiff, halitoxic club secretary, a strict Methodist who would no more set foot in a pub than he would brush the dandruff off the shoulders of his dark blue suit.

"What's it to be, then?" Norman asked, clapping his hands and beaming at everyone.

They ordered, and a few minutes later he returned with the drinks on a tray. After the usual round of commentary on the evening's offering—most of it, this time, favourable to Terry Whigham, who would no doubt by now be suffering through Barton's fawning proximity or Jack Tatum's condescending sycophancy—Robin and Norman began to argue about the use of colour balance filters, while Sandra and Harriet discussed local crime.

"I suppose you've heard from Alan about the latest incident?" Harriet said.

"Incident? What incident?"

"You know, the fellow who goes around climbing drainpipes and watching women get undressed."

Sandra laughed. "Yes, it's difficult to know what to call him, isn't it. 'Voyeur' sounds so romantic and 'Peeping Tom' sounds so *Daily Mirror*ish. Let's just call him the peeper, the one who peeps."

"So you have heard?"

"Yes, last night. But how do you know about it?"

"It was on the radio this afternoon. Local radio. They did an interview with Dorothy Wycombe—you know, the one who made all the fuss about hiring policies in local government."

"I know of her. What did she have to say?"

"Oh, just the usual. What you'd expect. Said it was tantamount to an act of rape and the police couldn't be bothered to make much of an effort because it only affected women."

"Christ," Sandra said, fumbling for a cigarette. "That woman makes me mad. She's not that stupid, surely? I've respected the way she's dealt with a lot of things so far, but this time..."

"Don't you think you're only getting upset because Alan's involved?" Harriet suggested. "I mean, that makes it personal, doesn't it?"

"In a way," Sandra admitted. "But it also puts me on the inside, and I know that he cares and that he's doing the best he can, just as much as he would for any other case."

"What about Jim Hatchley?"

Sandra snorted. "As far as I know they're keeping Hatchley as far away from the business as possible. Oh, Alan gets along with him well enough now they've both broken each other in, so to speak. But the man's a boor. They surely didn't let him talk to the press?"

"Oh no. At least not as far as I know. No names were mentioned. She just made it sound as if all the police were sexual deviants."

"Well that's a typical attitude, isn't it? Did she call them the 'pigs,' too?"

Harriet laughed. "Not exactly."

"What do you think of this business, anyway?"

"I don't really know. I've thought about what...what I would feel like if he watched me. It gives me the shivers. It's like someone going through your most private memories. You'd feel soiled, used."

"It gives me the creeps, too," said Sandra, suddenly aware that the others had finished their own conversations and were listening in with interest.

"But, you know," Harriet went on slowly, embarrassed by the larger audience, "I do feel sorry for him in a way. I mean, he'd have to be very unhappy to go around doing that, very frustrated. I do think it's a bit sad, don't you?"

Sandra laughed and put her hand on Harriet's arm. "Harriet Slade," she said, "I'm sure you feel sorry for Margaret Thatcher every time another thousand people lose their jobs."

"Have you never thought that we're most likely to find the culprit among ourselves?" Norman suggested. "That he's probably a member of the club? Everyone's a voyeur, you know," he announced, pushing back a lock of limp, dark hair from his pale forehead. "Especially us. Photographers."

"True enough," Sandra agreed, "but we don't spy on people, do we?"

"What about candids?" Norman replied. "I've done it often enough myself—shoot from the hip when you think they're not looking."

"Women undressing?"

"Good Lord, no! Tramps asleep on park benches, old men chatting on a bridge, courting couples sunbathing."

"It really is a kind of spying, though, isn't it?" Robin cut in.

"But it's not the same," Norman argued. "You're not invading someone's privacy when they're in a public place like a park or a beach, are you? It's not as if they think they're alone in their own bedrooms. And anyway, you're doing it for an artistic purpose, not just for a sexual thrill."

"I'm not always sure there's much of a difference," Robin said. "Besides, it was you who suggested it."

"Suggested what?"

"That it might be a member of the club—that we're all voyeurs."

Norman coloured and reached for his drink. "I did, didn't I? Perhaps it wasn't a very funny remark."

"Oh, I don't know," Sandra said. "I could certainly see Jack Tatum staring through bedroom windows."

Harriet shivered. "Yes. Every time he looks at you, you feel like he can see right through your clothes."

"I'm sure the peeper's someone much more ordinary, though," Sandra said. "It always seems the case that people who do the most outlandish things live quite normal lives most of the time."

"I suppose a policeman's wife would know about things like that," Robin said.

"No more than anyone who can read a book. They're all over the place, aren't they, biographies of the Yorkshire Ripper, Dennis Nilsen, Brady and Hindley?"

"You're not suggesting the peeper's as dangerous as that, are you?" Norman asked.

"I don't know. All I can say is that it's a bloody weird thing to do, and I don't understand it."

"Do you think he understands it himself?" Robin asked.

"Probably not," replied Sandra. "That's why Harriet feels sorry for him, isn't it dear?"

"You're a beast," Harriet said and flicked a few drops of lager and lime in her direction.

Sandra bought the next round and the conversation shifted to the upcoming club trip to Swaledale and a recent exhibition at the National Museum of Photography in Bradford. When they had all said their goodbyes, Sandra dropped Harriet off and carried on home. Turning into the driveway, she was surprised to hear no opera coming from the front room, and even a little angry to find Brian and Tracy still up watching a risqué film on Channel 4. It was almost eleven o'clock and Alan wasn't back yet.

II

If you picture the Yorkshire Dales as a splayed hand pointing east, then you will find Eastvale close to the tip of the middle finger. The town stands at the eastern limit of Swainsdale, a long valley, which starts in the precipitous fells of the west and broadens into meandering river-meadows in the east. Dry-stone walls criss-cross the lower valley-sides like ancient runes until, in some places, the grassy slopes rise steeply into long sheer cliffs, known locally as "scars." At their summits, they flatten out to become wild, lonely moorlands covered in yellow gorse and pinkish ling, crossed only by unfenced minor roads where horned sheep wander and the wind always rages. The rock is mostly limestone, which juts through in grey-white scars and crags that change hue with the weather like pearls rolled under candlelight. Here and there, a more sinister outcrop of dark millstone grit thrusts out, or layers of shale and sandstone streak an old quarry.

Eastvale itself is a busy market-town of about fourteen thousand people. It slopes up from Swainsdale's eastern edge, where the River Swain turns south-east towards the Ouse, rises to a peak at Castle Hill, then drops gradually eastwards in a series of terraces past the river and the railway tracks.

The town is certainly picturesque; it has a cobbled market square, complete with ancient cross and Norman church, tree-shaded river-fulls, sombre castle ruins, and excavations going back to pre-Roman times. But it has some less salubrious areas that tourists never visit—among them the East Side Estate, a sprawl of council housing put up in the sixties and declining fast.

A visitor sitting in the flower gardens on the western bank of the River Swain would probably be surprised at some of the things that go on across the river. Beyond the poplars and the row of renovated Georgian houses stretch about fifty yards of grass and trees called The Green. And beyond that lies the East Side Estate.

Amid the graffiti-scarred walls, abandoned prams and tires, uncontrolled dogs and scruffy children, the inhabitants of the over-crowded estate try to survive the failure of the town's two main indus-tries outside of tourism—a woollen mill on the river to the northwest, and a chocolate factory near the eastern boundary. Some are quiet, peace-loving families, who keep themselves to themselves and try to make ends meet on the dole. But others are violent and angry, a mixed bunch of deadbeats, alcoholics, wife-beaters, child-abusers and junkies. Drawing the "east side beat," as it is known in the police sta-tion, is a duty most young constables do their utmost to avoid.

Of course, there had been protests over the council's plan, but the sixties was an era of optimism and new ideas, so the houses went up. It was also a period of rank political corruption, so many councillors enjoyed holidays abroad at the expense of various contractors, and a great deal of tax-free money changed hands. Meanwhile, the ten-ants, crammed into their terrace blocks, towers and maisonettes, just had to put up with the flimsy walls, inadequate heating and faulty plumbing. Many thought themselves lucky; they were living in the country at last.

The railway track, raised high on its embankments, ran north to south and cut right through the estate, giving its passengers a fine view of the overgrown back gardens with their lines of washing, tiny greenhouses and rabbit hutches. Several low, narrow tunnels ran under the tracks to link one part of the estate to another, and it was in one of these that Trevor Sharp and Mick Webster stood smoking and discussing business.

The tunnel had been christened "Glue-Sniffers' Ginnel" by the estate's residents because of the great numbers of plastic bags that lit-tered its pathway. It was a dark place, lit at one end by a jaundiced streetlamp, and it reeked of glue, dog piss and stale vomit. Locals avoided it.

Mick Webster, whatever one might call him, was not one of the glue-sniffers. Naturally, he had tried it, along with just about everything else, but he had decided it was for the birds; it dulled the brain and made you spotty, like Lenny. Not that Lenny sniffed glue, though—he just ate too much greasy fish and chips. Mick preferred those little red pills that Lenny seemed to possess in abundance: the ones that made his heart race and made him feel like Superman. He was a squat, loutish sixteen-year-old with a pug nose, a skinhead crop and a permanent sneer. People crossed the street when they saw him coming.

Trevor, on the other hand, was not the kind of boy that the average townsperson would take for a bad sort. He was quite handsome, like his father, and was a slave to fashion in neither clothing nor haircut. Because he was regarded as an exceptionally hard case, nobody ever ragged him about his neat, conservative appearance.

The 10:10 from Harrogate rattled overhead and Trevor lit another cigarette.

"Lenny says it's time we stopped it with the old dears and got onto something a bit more profitable," Mick announced, kicking at some shards of broken glass.

"Like what?"

"Like doing houses. Proper houses where rich folk live. When they're out, like. Lenny says he can let us know where and when. All we got to do is get in, pick up the gear and get out."

"What about burglar alarms?"

"They ain't got burglar alarms," Mick said scornfully. "Peaceful little place this is, never have any crime."

Trevor thought it over. "When do we start?"

"When Lenny gives us a tip."

"Lenny's been taking too much of a cut, Mick. It hardly makes it worth our while. You'd better ask him to give us a bigger percentage if we're gonna get onto this lark."

"Yeah, yeah, all right." It wasn't a new subject, and Mick was getting tired of Trevor's constant harping. Besides, he was too scared of Lenny to mention anything about it.

"How are we going to break in?" Trevor asked.

"I don't fucking know. Window. Back door. Lenny'll give us what we need. It'll be people on holidays or away for the weekend. That kind of thing. Dead easy. He keeps his ear to the ground."

"Got the money for that last lot?"

"Oh, nearly forgot." Mick grinned and pulled out a wad of bills from his hip pocket. "He said he only got fifty for the gear. That's ten quid for you and ten for me."

Trevor shook his head. "It's not right, Mick. That's sixty percent he's taking. And how do we know he only got fifty quid for it? Looked like it was worth nearer a hundred to me."

"We believe him 'cos he's my fucking brother, that's why," Mick said, getting nettled. "And without him we wouldn't be able to get rid of any of the stuff. We wouldn't get nothing, man. So forty percent of what he does is better than a hundred percent of fuck all, right?"

"We could fence it ourselves. It can't be that difficult."

"How many times do I have to tell you? You need the contacts. Lenny's got contacts. You can't just walk into one of those wanky antique shops on Market Street and ask the geezer if he wants to buy a pile of stolen jewellery or a fancy camera, can you?"

"I just don't think it can be all that difficult, that's all."

"Look, we've got a nice little racket going here, let's leave it the way it is. I'll try and get us up to fifty percent, all right?"

Trevor shrugged. "Okay."

"Did I tell you Lenny's got a shooter?" Mick went on excitedly.

"No. Where'd he get it from?"

"Down The Smoke. This bloke what owns a club in Soho. Big fucker it is too, just like on telly."

"Does it work?"

"Of course it works. What good's a shooter that don't work?"

"Have you tried it? Do you know it works?"

"Of course I haven't fucking tried it. What do you expect me to do, walk downtown on market day and start fucking target practice?"

"So you don't know for sure if it works?"

Mick sighed and explained as if to a small child. "These blokes down The Smoke, they don't give you dud shooters, do they? Wouldn't be in their interest."

"What kind is it?"

"I don't fucking know. A big one, like the ones on telly. Like that one Clint Eastwood carries in those Dirty Harry flicks."

"A Magnum?"

"That's right. One of those."

"Powerful shooter," Trevor said. "'Seeing as this is a forty-four Magnum, the most powerful handgun in the world, and can blow your head clean off, you gotta ask yourself, punk, do I feel lucky today? Well, do ya, punk?'"

The Dirty Harry impersonation went down very well, and the two traded shooting noises until the 10:25 to Ripon clattered overhead and drowned them out.

III

"Look, before we start," Jenny Fuller said, "I'd like to tell you that I know why I was chosen to help on this case."

"Oh," said Banks. "What do you mean?"

"You know damn well what I mean. Don't think I didn't notice that eye contact between you and Gristhorpe this morning. There are at least two male professors in the area better qualified to deal with this kind of thing—both experts on deviant psychology. You wanted a woman because it looks good in the public eye, and you wanted me because I've had connections with Dorothy Wycombe."

They were lounging comfortably in armchairs by the crackling fire, Banks cradling a pint of bitter, Jenny a half.

"It's not that I mind," she went on. "I just want you to know. I don't like being taken for a fool."

"Point taken."

"And another thing. You needn't imagine I'm going to go reporting to Dorothy Wycombe on everything that goes on. I'm a professional, not a snooper. I've been asked to help, and I intend to do my best."

"Good. So now we know where we stand. I'm glad you said that, because I didn't feel too happy about working with a spy, whatever the circumstances."

Jenny smiled and her whole face lit up. She really was an extraordinarily beautiful woman, Banks thought, feeling rather distressing tugs of desire as he watched her shift her body in the chair. She was wearing tight jeans and a simple white T-shirt under a loose lemon jacket. Her dark red hair spilled over her shoulders.

Banks himself had paid more attention than usual to his appearance that evening: at least, as much more attention as he could without giving Sandra cause for suspicion. Over a hasty supper, he had told her he would be spending the evening with Dr Fuller discussing the psychological angle of the peeper case. Getting ready, he had resisted the temptation to apply some of the unopened cologne a distant relative had bought him several Christmases ago, and settled instead for a close shave and a liberal application of Right Guard. He had also taken care to smooth down his short, black hair, even though it was always cut so close to the skull that it never got a chance to stand on end.

He had arrived at the Queen's Arms at least ten minutes before Jenny was due—not simply because he didn't believe in keeping a woman waiting, but because he didn't like the idea of her waiting alone in a pub, even a place as congenial as the Queen's Arms. When she walked in five minutes late, all the heads at the bar turned in her direction.

"So where do we start?" he asked, lighting a cigarette and opening his notebook.

"Oh, put that thing away," Jenny protested. "Let's keep this informal while we build up some kind of a picture. I'll give you a full report when I've got things worked out."

Thus admonished, Banks put away his notebook.

"What are your own ideas?" she asked. "I know I'm supposed to be the expert, but I'd like to know what you think." There was a slightly taunting tone in her voice, and he wondered if she was trying to draw him out, make a fool of him. It was probably just her seminar manner, he decided. Like doctors have bedside manners, teachers have classroom manners.

"I'm afraid I wouldn't know where to begin."

"Let me help. Do you think the women ask for it, by the way they dress?"

It was a loaded question, exactly the one he had expected.

"They might well be inviting someone to try and pick them up in a normal, civilized way," he answered, "but of course they're not inviting voyeurs or rapists, no."

He could tell that she approved by the way she looked at him. "On the other hand," he went on, just to provoke her, "if they walk in dark alleys after ten o'clock at night dressed in high-heels, mini-skirts and low-cut blouses, then I'd say they were at least being foolish, if not asking for something."

"So you do think they ask for it?" she accused him, green eyes flashing.

"Not at all. I just think that people, especially women, ought to be more careful these days. We all know what the cities are like, and there's no longer any reason to think a place like Eastvale is immune from sex offenders."

"But why shouldn't we be able to go where we want, when we want and dressed how we want?"

"You should. In a perfect world. This isn't a perfect world."

"Well, thank you for pointing that out to me. Bit of a philosopher, aren't you?"

"I do my best. Look, is this what you want, some kind of sparring match over women's issues? I thought you were playing straight with me. All right, so I'm a man, guilty, and I can never in a million years fully understand what it's like to be a woman. But I'm not a narrow-minded hypocrite, at least I don't think I am, so don't treat me like one."

"Okay. I'm sorry. I'm not really a shrill virago, either. I'm just interested in men's attitudes, that's all. It's my field—male and female, masculine and feminine psychology, similarities, differences. That's why they thought I was the next best thing to a brilliant, ideally qualified man for this job."

She laughed at herself and Banks laughed with her. Then she held out her hands as if holding up a clapper-board, snapped them together and said, "Banks and Fuller: *Co-operation*, Take Two. More drinks first, though. No, I'll get them this time."

Enjoying the slow, feline grace of her movements, Banks watched her walk to the bar and lean on it as the barman drew the beer. When she got back, she smiled and put the drinks on the table.

"Right," she said. "Down to business. What do you want to know?"

"A great deal."

"Well, that'll take a long time."

"I'm sure it'll be time well spent."

Jenny smiled in agreement. "Yes," she said, "I do believe you're right."

To cut through the silence that followed, Banks put his first question: "Is there any chance of this peeper moving on to more violent sex acts?"

"Mmmm," Jenny said. "I'm afraid I'm going to seem as noncommittal as any scientist on some of these matters. According to most of the evidence, voyeurism in itself isn't regarded as a very serious disorder, and it's unlikely to spiral into other forms."

"But?"

"But it's only 'unlikely' according to existing evidence. All that means is that we don't have many documented cases of voyeurs becoming rapists—peeping is usually about as far as they can go. It doesn't mean there are no cases, though, and it doesn't mean that your man might not be one of them. Something could snap. If just looking ceases to give him what he needs, he could either break down or turn to other, more aggravated forms of sexual violence. I'll see if I can look up some case histories for you."

"You call it violence, but he hasn't physically hurt anyone."

"I call it violence purposely, because that's what it is. Look at it this way. We all like to watch the opposite sex. Men more than women—and I think I can safely say that your peeper's definitely not a woman. So why do men do this? There's always the sense, in childhood, of not being permitted to look at a woman's body, so it becomes mysterious and desirable. You don't need a degree in psychology to figure out why men like breasts, for example—they're one of the first sources of love and nourishment we ever experience. Okay so far?"

Banks nodded.

"So we all like to look. You look at women in the street. They seem to dress just to make you look at them. And why not? It makes the world go round, keeps the race going. But at what point does looking, the kind we all do—and women these days now and then glance at a man's bum or the bulge in his pants—become voyeurism?

In the streets, in pubs, in all public places, it's fine, there's an implicit permission to look. We even have special places such as strip-clubs which legitimize the voyeuristic impulse—all quite legal. But when a woman is in her bedroom getting undressed for bed, unless she's doing it for her husband or lover, she doesn't want anyone to watch. Often enough, she doesn't even want her husband to watch. The permission is no longer there, and to look then is an act of sexual violence because it's an intrusion, a violation, a penetration into her world. It degrades her by turning her into an object. Am I making myself clear?"

"Very," Banks said. "What does the voyeur get out of it, then? Why does he do it?"

"They're both very difficult questions to answer. For one thing, he's getting power over her, a certain triumph in dehumanizing her, and perhaps he's also getting revenge for some past wrong that he imagines women have done him. At the same time, he's re-enacting a primal sexual scene, whatever it was that first excited him. He just keeps on repeating himself because it's the only way he can achieve sexual pleasure. You see how complicated it is? When the voyeur penetrates his victim's privacy, then he dominates her, and the element of risk, of 'sin' involved only endows that act with a special intensity for him. Does your man masturbate while he's watching?"

"I don't know. We haven't found any traces of semen."

"Have you looked?"

"The lab boys have been brought in on every incident. I'm sure if it was there they'd find it."

"Okay. It doesn't really matter. I suppose his pants would act as a prophylactic—either that or he stores the image and masturbates later."

"What kind of person are we talking about?"

"His personality?"

"Yes."

"Again, I'm going to have to be a bit vague. He could be an introvert or an extrovert, tall or short, thin or fat..."

"That's certainly vague."

Jenny laughed. "Yes, it is. Sorry, but there's no one type. In a way, it's much easier to describe the true psychopath—a sex murderer, for example. A voyeur—the scientific term is scopophiliac, by the way—is not simply a grubby loner in a dirty mac. Our man's actions are caused by frustration, basically. Intense frustration with life in general and with relationships in particular. It might be that the most meaningful early sexual experience he had was voyeuristic—he saw something he shouldn't have seen, like his parents making love—and since then everything's been a let-down, especially sex. He'd certainly have difficulty handling the real thing.

"What makes voyeurism, or 'scopophilia,' what we call 'abnormal' is simply that the scopophiliac gets all his gratification from looking. Nobody would deny that looking is an integral part of the sex act. Lots of men like to watch their partners undress; it excites them. Plenty of men like to go to strip-clubs too, and whatever the women's movement thinks of that, nobody would seriously consider such men to be clinically abnormal. The scopophiliac, though, gets stuck at the pre-genital stage—his development gets short-circuited. Whatever relationship he's living in—alone, with a wife or a dominating mother or father—it's essentially a frustrating one, and he probably feels great pressure, an intense desire to break through.

"It's unlikely that he's married, but if he is, there are serious problems. In all probability, though, he's living alone. His sexuality wouldn't be mature enough to deal with the demands of a real, flesh-and-blood woman, unless she's a particularly unusual person herself."

"I see," said Banks, lighting a cigarette. "It doesn't look like it's going to be easy, does it?"

"No. It never is when it comes to people. We're all such incredibly complex beings."

"Oh? I always thought of myself as simple and straightforward."

"You're probably one of the most complex of the lot, Alan Banks. First off, what's a nice man like you doing in the police force?"

"Earning a living and trying to uphold the law. See? Simple."

"Would you uphold a law you didn't believe in?"

"I don't know."

"What if the law said that anyone caught stealing a loaf of bread should lose his or her hand? Would you actively go looking for people stealing bread?"

"I think that, in that kind of society, I wouldn't be a policeman."

"Oh, what an evasive answer!"

Banks shrugged. "What can I say? At least it's an honest one."

"All right, what about the drug laws? What about students smoking pot?"

"What are you asking me?"

"Do you pester them? Do you think people should be prosecuted for smoking pot?"

"As long as it's against the law, yes. If you want to know whether I agree with every law in the country, the answer's no. There's a certain amount of discretion allowed in the enforcement, you know. We don't tend to bother students smoking pot so much these days, but we are interested in people bringing heroin up from London or the Midlands."

"Why shouldn't a person take heroin if he or she wants to? It doesn't hurt anyone else."

"I could well ask why shouldn't a man go around watching women get undressed. That doesn't hurt anyone, either."

"It's not the same thing and you know it. Besides, the woman is hurt. She's shocked, degraded."

"Only the ones who know."

"What?"

"Think of it this way. So far, four incidents have been reported. How many do you think have gone unnoticed? How many times has he got away with it?"

"I never really thought of that," Jenny admitted. "And by the way, I'm not going to forget our discussion of a few moments ago, before you so cleverly sidetracked me back to work." She smiled sharply at him as he went off to buy two more drinks.

"I suppose," she said when Banks returned, "that he could actually do it every night, though I doubt it."

"Why?"

"Most sexual activities, normal or perverted, require a kind of gestation period between acts. It varies. The pressure builds again and there's only one way to relieve it."

"I see. Would once or twice a week be too much?"

"For who? You or me?"

"Don't distract me. For our man."

"No. I'd say once a week might do him fine, two at the most." She broke into a fit of laughter and covered her mouth with her hand. "Sorry. I get a bit gigglish sometimes. I think you must make me nervous."

"It comes with the job. Though I sometimes wonder which came first. A chicken or egg thing. Do I make people nervous because I've learned to do it unconsciously through dealing with so many criminals, or was I like that in the first place? Is that why the job suited me?"

"Well?"

"I didn't say I knew the answer, only that I wonder sometimes. Don't worry, when you get to know me better it won't bother you."

"A promise?"

"Let's get back to business."

"All right." Jenny wiped her eyes, full of tears of laughter, sat up straight and once again broke into a laughing fit. Banks watched her, smiling, and soon the others in the pub were looking. Jenny was turning as red as her hair, which was shaking like the fire in the grate. "Oh, I'm sorry, I really am," she said. "Whenever I get like this it's so hard to stop. You must think I'm a real idiot."

"Not at all," Banks said drily. "I appreciate a person with a sense of humour."

"I think it's better now," she said, sipping cautiously at her half of bitter. "It's just all those *double entendres*. Oops," she said, putting her hand to her chest. "Now I've got hiccups!"

"Drink a glass of water in an inverted position," Banks told her. "Best cure for hiccups I've ever known."

Jenny frowned at him. "Standing on my head?"

"No, not like that." Banks was just about to demonstrate to her, using his pint glass, when he sensed a shadow over the table and heard a polite cough. It was Fred Rowe, the station desk-sergeant.

"Pardon me for bothering you, sir," Rowe said quietly, pulling up a chair, "but there's been some trouble."

"Go on," Banks said, putting down his glass.

"It's an old woman, sir, she's been found dead."

"Cause?"

"We can't say yet, sir, but it looks suspicious. The friend who reported it said the place had been robbed."

"All right. Thanks, Fred. I'll get right over. Address?"

"Number two, Gallows View. That's down by—"

"Yes, I know it. Look, get onto Sergeant Hatchley. He'll be in The Oak. And get Dr Glendenning and the photographer out there, and as many of the Scene-of-Crime boys as you can rustle up. Better get DC Richmond along too. Does the super know?"

"Yes, sir."

"Fine. Tell him I'm on my way, then."

Sergeant Rowe returned to the station and Banks stood up to leave, making his apologies to Jenny. Then he remembered that Sandra had taken the Cortina.

"Dammit," he cursed, "I'll have to go over and sign out a car."

"Can't I drive you?" Jenny offered. "I know where Gallows View is."

"Would you?"

"Of course. You're probably over the limit, anyway. I've only been drinking halves."

"You'll have to keep out of the way, stay in the car."

"I understand."

"Right, then, let's go."

"Yes, sir," Jenny said, saluting him.

FOUR

I

It had stopped raining only an hour earlier, and the air was still damp and chilly. Trevor held his jacket collar tight around his neck as he set off across The Green thinking over what Mick had said. Past the Georgian semis, he crossed the fourteenth-century bridge and spat in the water that cascaded over the terraced falls. Then he strode through the riverside gardens, and took the road that curved around Castle Hill to the market square.

Sometimes Mick scared him. Not his physical presence, but his stupidity. There would be no increased percentage from Lenny, Trevor was certain, because Mick wouldn't even dare ask him. Trevor would. He wasn't frightened of Lenny, gun or no gun. The gun didn't really interest him at all; it seemed more like a silly toy for Mick to show off about.

It was the pills, most likely. Them and natural stupidity. Trevor was sick of seeing Mick sweating and ranting on, hopping from one foot to the other as if he wanted to piss all the time. It was pathetic. He hadn't tried them himself, though he thought he might do one day. After all, he wasn't Mick; they wouldn't affect him the same way.

He hadn't tried sex either. Mick kept boasting about having it off with some scrubber up against an alley wall, but Trevor was unimpressed. Even if it was true, it wasn't the kind of fun he was interested in. He would do it all: drugs, sex, whatever. All in his own sweet time. And he would know when the time was right.

As for the new idea, it made sense. Old people seemed to have nothing worth much these days. Probably had to pawn all their old keepsakes just to keep them in pabulum. Trevor laughed at the image. The first time it had been fun, a change from dipping, or mugging the odd tourist—"Just doing my bit for the Tourist Board, your honour, trying to make the New Yorkers feel at home"—it was exciting being able to do whatever you wanted in somebody else's house, break stuff, and them too feeble to do a thing about it. Not that Trevor was a bully; he would never touch the old women (more out of disgust than kindness, though). That was Mick's specialty—Mick *was* a bully.

This would be something different. The old folks' houses all smelled of the past: lavender water, Vicks chest rub, commodes, old dead skin. This time they would be in the classy homes, places with VCRs, fancy music centres, dishwashers, freezers full of whole cows. They could take their time, enjoy it, maybe even do some real damage. After all, they wouldn't be able to carry everything away. Best stick to the portables: cash, jewellery, silver, gold. He could just imagine Mick and Lenny being stupid enough to try and sell stolen colour tellys and videos at Eastvale market. These days everyone wrote their bloody names and postcodes on everything from microwaves to washing-machines with those ultraviolet pens, and the cops could read them under special lights. He hoped Mick was right about burglar alarms, too. It seemed that people were becoming very security-conscious these days.

He crossed the south side of the deserted market square and walked through the complex of narrow, twisted streets to King Street. Then he cut through Leaview Estate towards Gallows View. The terrace of old cottages stood like a wizened finger pointing west to the Dales.

As he passed the bungalows and crossed Cardigan Drive to the dirt track in front of the cottages, Trevor noticed some activity outside the first house, number two. That was where the old bag, Matlock, lived. He walked by slowly and saw a crowd of people through the open door. There was that hotshot copper from London, Banks, who'd got his picture in the local paper when he'd got the job a few months back; that well-known local thug, Hatchley, who looked a bit unsteady on his pins; and the woman standing in the doorway. What on earth was she doing there? He was sure it was her, the one who lived in the fancy Georgian semis across The Green from the East Side Estate, the one Mick was always saying he'd like to fuck. Maybe she was a cop, too. You never could tell. He walked into number eight to confront his father once again over homework not done.

II

Jenny, who had disobeyed Banks's orders and stood unobserved in the doorway, had never seen a corpse before, and this one looked particularly bad. Its wrinkled bluish-grey face was frozen in a grimace of anger and pain, and pools of dark blood had coagulated under the head on the stone flags of the room. Alice Matlock lay on her back at the foot of a table, on the corner of which, it appeared, she had fractured her skull while falling backwards. These were only appearances, though, Jenny realized, and the battery of experts arriving in dribs and drabs would soon piece together what had really happened.

Despite the horror of the scene, Jenny felt outside it all, taking in the little details as an objective observer. Perhaps, she thought, that was one of the qualities that made her a good psychologist: the ability to stand outside the flux of human emotions and pay careful attention. Outside looking in. Perhaps it also made her not so acceptable as a woman—at least one or two of her lovers had complained that however enjoyable she was in bed and however much fun she was to be with, they felt that they couldn't really get close to her and were always aware of themselves being studied like subjects in a mysterious experiment. Jenny brushed aside the self-criticism; if she didn't conform to men's ideas of what a woman should be— fainting, crying, subjective, irrational, intuitive, sentimental—then bugger them.

The house was oppressive. Not just because of the all-pervading presence of death, but because it was absolutely cluttered with the past. The walls seemed unusually honeycombed with little alcoves, nooks and crannies where painted Easter eggs and silver teaspoons from Rhyll or Morecambe nestled alongside old snuff boxes, delicate china figurines, a ship in a bottle, yellowed birthday cards and miniatures. The mantelpiece was littered with sepia photographs: family groups, stiff and formal before the camera, four women in nurses' uniforms standing in front of an old-fashioned army ambulance; and the remaining wall space seemed taken up by framed samplers, and watercolours of wildflowers, birds and butterflies. Jenny shuddered. Her own house, though structurally old, was sparse and modern inside. It would drive her crazy to live in a mausoleum like this.

She watched Banks at work. As she had expected, he was professional and efficient, but he often seemed distracted, and sometimes a look of pain and sadness crossed his features when he leaned against the wall and gazed at the old woman's body. The photographer popped his flash from every angle. He looked far too young, Jenny thought, to be so matter-of-fact about death. The doctor, one of those older, cigarette-smoking types who pay house calls when you have flu or tonsillitis, busied himself with thermometers, charts and other tools of his trade. Out of decency, Jenny turned away and tried to name the wildflowers depicted on the walls. She felt invisible, standing by the doorway, arms folded across her breasts. Everyone seemed to think she had come with Banks. Nobody even paid her the slightest bit of attention; no one, that is, except the slightly squiffed detective she had seen earlier on her visit to the station, who occasionally cast lecherous glances in her direction. Jenny ignored him and watched the men at work.

Also in the midst of this routine, robotic activity sat Ethel Carstairs, who had discovered the body. Though trembling and white with shock as she sipped the brandy a police constable had brought her from Alice's medicinal bottle in the kitchen, she had regained enough control to talk to Banks.

"Alice was supposed to call on me this evening," said Ethel in a weak, shaky voice. "She always comes on Sundays and Tuesdays. We play rummy. She's not on the phone, so when she didn't come there wasn't much I could do. As time went on I got worried, then I decided to walk over and see if she was all right. She was eighty-seven just last week, Inspector. I bought her that sugar bowl broken on the floor there."

It looked as if someone had pulled all the drawers out of the old oak sideboard, and a pretty, rose-patterned sugar bowl lay in several places on the flags.

"She always did have a sweet tooth, despite what the doctor told her," Ethel went on, pausing to wipe her eyes with a lace-edged handkerchief.

"Is this exactly how you found her?" Banks asked gently.

"Yes. I didn't touch a thing. I watch a lot of telly, Inspector. I know about fingerprints and all that. I just stood in the doorway there, saw her and all the mess and went to the box on the corner of Cardigan Drive and phoned the police."

Banks nodded. "Good, you did exactly the right thing. What about the door?"

"What?"

"The door. You must have touched it to get in."

"Oh yes, silly of me. I'm sorry but I did have to open the door. I must have smudged all the prints."

Banks smiled over at Vic Manson, who was busy dusting the furniture with aluminium powder. "Don't worry, Mrs Carstairs," Manson assured her. "Whoever it was probably wore gloves. The criminals watch a lot of telly these days, too. We have to look, though, just in case."

"The door," Banks went on. "Was it ajar, open, locked?"

"It was just open. I knocked first, then when I got no answer, I tried the handle and it just opened."

"There's no sign of forced entry, sir," added Detective Constable Richmond, who had been examining the doorframe beside Jenny. "Whoever it was, she must have let them in."

Hatchley came down from his search of the upper rooms. He wasn't irredeemably drunk, only about two sheets to the wind, and like most professionals, he could snap back into gear in a crisis. "It's been gone over pretty thoroughly," he said to Banks. "Wardrobe, drawers, laundry chest, the lot."

"Do you know if Mrs Matlock owned anything of value, Mrs Carstairs?" Banks asked.

"It's Miss Matlock, Inspector. Alice was a spinster. She never married."

"So she has no immediate family?"

"Nobody. She outlived them all."

"Did she own anything valuable?"

"Not really what you'd call valuable, Inspector. Not to anyone else, that is. There was some silverware—she kept that in the sideboard cupboard, bottom shelf." The cupboard door gaped open and there was no sign of cutlery among the bric-à-brac scattered on the flags. "But her most valuable possessions were these." Ethel gestured towards the knick-knacks and photographs that filled the room. "Her memories."

"What about money? Did she keep much cash in the house?"

"She used to keep a bit around, just for emergencies. She usually kept it in the bottom drawer of her dressing table."

"How much did she have there, as a rule?"

"Oh, not much. About fifty pounds or so."

Banks glanced at Hatchley, who shook his head. "It's a mess up there," he said. "If there was any money, it's gone now."

"Do you think our man, or men, knew where to look?"

"Not by the looks of it," Hatchley answered. "They searched everywhere. Same pattern as the other break-ins."

"Yes," Banks said quietly, almost to himself. "The victims always let them in. You'd think older people would be more careful these days."

"Prosopagnosia," announced Jenny, who had been listening carefully to all this.

"Pardon?" Banks said, seeming as surprised to see her there as she was by the sound of her own voice. The others looked around, too. With an angry glance, Banks introduced her: "Dr Fuller. She's helping us with a case." Everyone smiled or nodded and went back to work. "Can you explain it, then?" Banks asked.

"Prosopagnosia? It's the inability to recognize faces. People sometimes get it after brain damage, but it's most common in senility."

"I don't quite see the connection."

"Alice wasn't senile, young lady," Ethel Carstairs cut in, "but it's true that she was beginning to forget little, day-to-day things, and the past was much closer to her."

Jenny nodded. "I didn't mean to be insulting, Mrs Carstairs. I just meant it's part of the aging process. It happens to us all, sooner or later." She turned back to Banks. "Most of us, when we see a face, compare it with our files of known faces. We either recognize it or we don't, all in about a split second. With prosopagnosia, the observer can see all the components of the face but can't assemble the whole to check against memory files. It makes elderly people vulnerable to strangers, that's why I mentioned it."

"You mean she might have thought she recognized whoever it was?" Banks asked.

"Or thought she *should* have and not wanted to be rude. That's the most common problem. If you're a kind, polite person, you'll want to avoid giving offence, so you'll pretend you know who it is. It's like when you forget the name of an acquaintance and find ways of avoiding having to say it, only this must be much worse."

Dr Glendenning packed up his battered brown bag, lit a cigarette—strictly forbidden at the scene of a crime, but generally overlooked in his case—and shambled over to Banks and Jenny. "Dead about twenty-four hours," he said out of the corner of his mouth in a nicotine-ravaged voice with a strong trace of Edinburgh in it. "Cause of death, fractured skull, most likely inflicted by that table edge there."

"Can you tell if she was pushed?"

"Looks like it. One or two bruises on the upper arms and shoulders. That's just preliminary, though. Can't tell you more till after the autopsy. But unless the old dear was poisoned, too, I shouldn't imagine there'll be much more to tell. You can get her to the morgue now. There'll be a coroner's inquest, of course," he said, and walked out.

Everybody had finished. Manson had plenty of fingerprints to play with, most of them probably Alice Matlock's, and the other two Scene-of-Crime boys had envelopes filled with hairs, fragments of clothing and blood scrapings.

"You can go now, Mrs Carstairs," Banks said. "I'd appreciate it if you'd drop by the station in the morning and give a formal statement." He called Detective Constable Richmond to drive Ethel home and instructed him also to pick her up in the morning and take her statement.

"Right, then. I'm off home, too," Banks said in a tired voice. "It's up to you now, Sergeant. See there's someone posted here all night. Deal with the ambulance. And you might as well start talking to the neighbours. They'll still be up. Curiosity's a great cause of insomnia. Do Gallows View and the six end bungalows over the street here. The rest can wait till tomorrow. Remember, the doctor puts the time of death at about twenty-four hours ago—let's say between ten o'clock and midnight last night. Find out if anyone saw or heard anything. Okay?"

Hatchley nodded glumly. Then his expression brightened when he saw Richmond leading Ethel Carstairs outside. "Don't be long, lad," he said, baring his yellow teeth in what passed for a smile. "I've got work for you to do."

Banks and Jenny left. She was surprised that he didn't vent his anger at her disobedience, but they broke the silence in the car only to arrange another meeting to work on the profile later in the week, then she dropped him off and drove home, unable to get the image of Alice Matlock's body out of her mind.

III

Detective Constable Philip Richmond was almost as pleased with his recent promotion to the CID as he was with his new moustache: the latter made him look older, more distinguished, and the former, more important, successful. He had worn the uniform, driven the Panda cars and walked the beat in Eastvale for as long as he cared to, and he had an intimate knowledge of every alley, snicket and back-street in the town: every lover's lane, every villain's hangout and every pub where visiting squaddies from Catterick camp were likely to cut up a bit rough at closing time.

He also knew Gallows View, the cottages at the far western edge of the town. Developers had petitioned for their demolition, especially when Leaview Estate was under construction, but the council, under pressure from the Parks and Monuments Commission, had reluctantly decided that they could stay. There were, after all, only five cottages, and two of those, at the western end of the street, had been knocked together into a shop and living quarters. Richmond had often bought gob-stoppers, Tizer and lucky-bags there as a lad, later graduating to cigarettes, which the owner would often trade him for his mother's coupons giving threepence off Tide or Stardrops.

Richmond stood in the street, drawing his raincoat tighter to keep out the chill, and cursed that damned slave driver Hatchley to himself. The bastard was probably guzzling the dead woman's medicinal brandy while his junior paid the house calls in the rain. Well, blow him, Richmond thought. Damned if he's going to get credit for anything I come up with.

Resigned, he knocked on the door of number four, which was opened almost immediately by an attractive young woman holding the lapels of her dressing-gown close around her throat. Richmond showed his identification proudly, stroked his moustache and followed her indoors. The place might be an old cottage, he thought, but by heck they'd done a good job on the inside: double-glazing, central heating, stucco walls, nice framed paintings, a bit abstract for his taste, but none of your Woolworth's tat, and one of those glass-topped coffee tables between two tube-and-cushion armchairs.

He accepted her offer of coffee—it would help keep him awake—but was surprised at how long she took to make it and at the odd, whirring noises he heard coming from the kitchen. When he finally got to taste the coffee, he knew; it was made from fresh-ground beans, filter-dripped, and it tasted delicious. She put a coaster on the low table in front of him—a wild flower, wood sorrel, he guessed, pressed between two circles of glass, the circumference bound in bamboo—then, at last, he was able to get down to business.

First he took her name, Andrea Rigby, and discovered that she lived there with her husband, a systems analyst, who was often away during the week working on projects in London or Bristol. They had lived in Gallows View for three years, ever since he had landed the well-paying job and been able to fulfill his dream of country living. The woman had an Italian or Spanish look about her, Richmond couldn't decide which, but her maiden name was Smith and she came originally from Leominster.

"What's happened?" Andrea asked. "Is it Miss Matlock next door?"

"Yes," Richmond answered, unwilling to give away too much. "Did you know her?"

"I wouldn't say I *knew* her. Not well, at any rate. We said hello to each other and I went to the shops a few times for her when she was ill last year."

"We're interested to know if you heard anything odd last night between ten and midnight, Mrs Rigby."

"Last night? Let me see. That was Monday, wasn't it. Ronnie had gone back down to London...I just sat around reading and watching television. I *do* remember hearing someone running in the street, over in Cardigan Drive. It must have been about eleven because the news had finished and I'd been watching an old film for about half an hour. Then I turned it off because it was boring."

"Someone running? That's all?"

"Yes."

"You didn't go to the window and look out?"

"No. Why should I? It was probably just kids."

Richmond jotted in his notebook. "Anything else? Did you hear any sounds from next door?"

"I thought I heard someone knocking at a door after the running, but I can't be sure. It sounded muffled, distant. I'm sorry, I really wasn't paying attention."

"How long after the running?"

"Right after. The one stopped, then I heard the other."

"Did the running fade into the distance or stop abruptly?"

Andrea thought for a moment. "More abruptly, really. As soon as people or cars or anything pass the corner of our street you can't hear them anymore, so it doesn't mean much."

"Did you hear any sounds at all from Miss Matlock's, next door?"

"No, nothing. But then I never do, not even when her friend comes to see her. I can hear knocking at the door, but nothing from inside. The way these old places were built the walls are very thick and we both have our staircases back to back, so there's quite a gap, really, between her living-room and mine. I sometimes hear the stairs creak when she's going up to bed, but that's all."

Richmond nodded, closing his notebook. "You haven't noticed anyone hanging around here lately, have you? Kids, a stranger?"

Andrea shook her head. Richmond couldn't think of any more questions, and it was getting late—he still had others to talk to. He thanked Andrea Rigby for her excellent coffee, then went to knock at number six.

The door opened a crack and a man wearing thick glasses peered out. Once Richmond had gained entry, he recognized Henry Wooller, the branch librarian, a bit of an oddball, loner, dry stick. Wooller's house was a tip. Scraps of newspaper, dirty plates, worn socks and half-full cups of tea with clumps of mould floating in them were strewn all over the room; and the place stank: an acrid, animal smell. Richmond noticed the corner of a pornographic magazine sticking out from under the *Sunday Times* Review section, where it had probably been hastily hidden. It was one he recognized, imported from Denmark, and the *UNCY* of its name, *BIG'N'BOUNCY*, was clearly visible. Wooller made a pretence of tidying things up a bit and was careful to hide the magazine completely.

Richmond asked the same questions he'd put to Andrea Rigby, but Wooller insisted that he had heard nothing at all. It was true that he was one cottage further from Cardigan Drive, which ran at right angles to the easternmost end of Gallows View, along the western edge of Leaview Estate, but Richmond didn't think the distance was a factor. He felt not only that Wooller didn't want to get involved, a common enough reaction to police enquiries, but also that he was hiding something. The expression behind the distorting glasses, however, remained fixed and deadpan; Wooller was giving nothing away. Richmond thanked him cursorily and left, making a note of his dissatisfaction.

The entrance to the living quarters of the shop was what used to be the door to number eight. Hearing voices raised, Richmond paused outside, hoping to learn something of value. He could only catch the odd word—the door must have been thick, or perhaps they were in the back—but it didn't take long to work out that a young lad was being told off for staying out too late and for not spending enough time on his schoolwork. Richmond smiled, feeling an immediate sympathy for the boy. How many times had he heard the same sermon himself?

When he knocked, the voices stopped immediately and the door was opened abruptly. Graham Sharp looked worried when he found out that a policeman wanted to see him. Everybody did, Richmond reflected, and it usually meant nothing more than an outstanding parking ticket.

"No, I didn't know her well," he said. "She came in here to do some of her shopping. It was convenient for her, I suppose. But she kept herself to herself. What happened to her?"

"Did you hear anything around eleven o'clock last night?" Richmond asked.

"No, nothing," Sharp answered. "I was watching telly in the room upstairs. We've converted one of the old bedrooms into a kind of sitting-room. It's right at the western end, as far as you can get in Eastvale without being in a field, so I wouldn't be able to hear anything from Cardigan Drive way."

"Noticed anything odd lately? Any strangers, kids hanging about?"

"No."

"No newcomers in the shop? Nobody asking questions?"

"Only you." Sharp smiled tightly, clearly relieved to see Richmond pocketing his notebook.

"Could I speak to your son for a moment, sir?" Richmond asked before leaving.

"My son?" Sharp echoed, sounding nervous again. "What for? He's just a young lad, only fifteen."

"He might be able to help."

"Very well." Sharp called Trevor from upstairs and the boy slouched down moodily.

"Where were you at about eleven o'clock last night?" Richmond asked.

"He was here with me," Sharp butted in. "Didn't I already tell you? We were upstairs watching telly."

Richmond flipped back through his notebook—mostly for effect, because his memory was good. "You told me that *you* were upstairs watching television, sir. You didn't say anything about your son."

"Well, that's what I meant. I just took it for granted. I mean, where else would he be at that time?" He put his arm around Trevor's shoulder. The boy winced visibly.

"Well?" Richmond addressed Trevor.

"It's like he says, we were watching telly. Not much else to do around here, is there?"

Richmond thanked them both and left, again jotting down his reservations in his book, and also noting that he thought he recognized Trevor Sharp from somewhere. All in all, it wasn't turning out to be a bad evening's haul. Already he was enjoying the responsibility of interrogation and feeling less vitriolic towards Sergeant Hatchley.

Nobody was at home in the first two houses on Cardigan Drive. Residents of two of the others had been out late at a club fundraiser the previous evening, and the remaining two had heard somebody running past at about eleven, but neither had looked out of their windows nor heard anyone knocking on Alice Matlock's door.

Richmond, who had thought to show some keenness by doing more than the first six houses, was beginning to tire a little by then, and as he'd done his duty, he decided to report back to Hatchley.

He found the sergeant sitting in Alice Matlock's armchair, his feet up on the stool, snoring loudly. The body was gone and all that remained were the chalk outline on the worn flags and the pools of dried blood. The place was still dusty with Manson's aluminium powder. The level in the brandy bottle had dropped considerably.

Richmond coughed and Hatchley opened a bloodshot eye. "Ah, back already, lad? Just thinking about the case, taking in the atmosphere. Done all the houses?"

Richmond nodded.

"Good lad. I think we'd better be off now. You'll need your beauty sleep for all the report writing you've got to do in the morning."

"Inspector Banks said to leave someone on duty here, sir."

"Did he? Yes, of course. One of the uniformed blokes. Look, you hang on here and I'll call the station on my way. Someone should be down in about fifteen minutes. All right, lad?"

Weary, cold and wet, Richmond mumbled, "Yes, sir," and settled down to comfort himself with thoughts of the beautiful Andrea Rigby not more than about seven or eight feet away from him through the wall. Taking out his notebook, he thought he might as well draft the outline of his report, and he began to look over his small, neat handwriting to see how it all added up.

FIVE

I

Wednesday was a difficult morning for Banks. His desk was littered with reports, and he couldn't get Jenny Fuller out of his mind. There was nothing wrong with his marriage—Sandra was all, if not more than, he had ever expected in a partner—so there was no reason, Banks told himself, why he should find himself interested in another woman.

It was Paul Newman, he remembered, who had said, "Why go out for hamburger if you can get steak at home?" But Banks couldn't remember the name of the subversive wit who had countered, "What if you want pizza?"

At thirty-six, he surely couldn't have hit middle-age crisis point, but there was no doubt that he was strongly attracted to the bright, red-headed Doctor of Philosophy. The sensation had been immediate, like a mild electric shock, and he was certain that she had felt it, too. Their two meetings had been charged with a strong undercurrent, and Banks didn't know what to do about it. The sensible thing would be to walk away and avoid seeing her anymore, but his job made that impractical.

He slugged back some hot, bitter station coffee and told himself not to take the matter so seriously. There was nothing to feel guilty about in fancying an attractive woman. He was, after all, a normal, heterosexual male. Another mouthful of black coffee tightened him back into the job at hand: reports.

He read over Richmond's interview statements and thought about the young detective's reservations for a while before deciding that they should be pursued. He also remembered Trevor Sharp, who had been a suspect in a tourist mugging shortly after Banks had arrived in Eastvale. The boy hadn't been charged because his father had given him a solid alibi, and the victim, an "innocent abroad" from Oskaloosa, Iowa, wasn't able to give a positive identification when the case relied solely on his word.

Hatchley had wasted his time at The Oak. He had talked to the bar staff and to the regular customers (and would no doubt be putting in a lengthy expenses claim), but nobody remembered anything special about Carol Ellis that night. It had been a quiet evening, as Mondays usually were, and she had sat at a corner table all evening talking to her friend, Molly Torbeck. Both had left before closing time and had, presumably, gone their separate ways. Nobody had tried to pick either of them up, and nobody had spent the evening giving them the eye.

The sergeant had also talked to Carol, Molly and the three other victims. When it was all added up, two of the four, Josie Campbell and Carol Ellis, had been in The Oak on the nights in question, and the other two in pubs at opposite ends of Eastvale. It wasn't the kind of pattern Banks had been hoping to find, but it was a pattern: pubs. Jenny Fuller might have something to say about that.

Skipping his morning break at the Golden Grill, Banks tidied up his own report on the interview with Crutchley and left the file in his pending tray to await the artist's impression.

He missed his lunch, too, looking over the preliminary post mortem report on Alice Matlock, which offered no new information but confirmed Glendenning's earlier opinions about time and cause. The bruises on her wrists and arms indicated that there had been a struggle in which the woman had been pushed backwards, catching the back of her head on the table corner.

Glendenning was nothing if not thorough, and he had a reputation as one of the best pathologists in the country. He had looked for evidence of a blow by a blunt instrument prior to the fall, which might then have been engineered to cover up the true cause, but had discovered only a typical *contre-coup* head injury. Though the skull had splintered into the brain tissue at the point of impact, the occipital region, there was also damage to the frontal lobes, and that only occurs when the body is falling. The effect, Glendenning had noted, is similar to that of a passenger bumping his head on the windscreen when a car brakes abruptly. If, however, the blow is delivered while the victim's head is stationary, then the wound is restricted to the area of impact. The blow that killed Alice Matlock was the kind of blow that could have killed anyone—and she was old, her bones were brittle—but it wasn't necessarily murder; it could have been accidental; it could have been manslaughter.

A red-eyed Richmond brought in Ethel Carstairs' statement. Again, there was nothing new, but she had given an itemized description of the missing silverware. Manson had found only two different sets of fingerprints in the house: one belonged to the dead woman herself and the other to Ethel, who had been good enough to offer hers for comparison.

At about two-fifteen, Superintendent Gristhorpe stuck his head round the door. "Still at it, Alan?"

Banks nodded, gesturing to the papers that covered his desk.

Gristhorpe looked at his watch. "Go get a pie and a pint over the road. I think we'd better have a conference about three o'clock and I don't want your stomach rumbling all through it."

"A conference?"

"Aye. A lot's been happening. The peeper, the break-ins, now this Alice Matlock business. I don't like it. It's time we threw a few ideas around. Just me, you, Hatchley and Richmond. Have you read the young lad's reports, by the way?"

"Yes, I've just finished."

"Good, aren't they? Detailed, no split infinitives or dangling modifiers. He'll go far, that lad. See you at three in the boardroom."

II

The "boardroom" was so called because it was the most spacious room in the station. At its centre was a large, shiny, oval table, around which stood ten matching, stiff-backed chairs. The set-up looked impressive, but the conference was informal; a coffee pot sat on its warmer in the middle, surrounded by files, pencils and notepads.

There were no ashtrays, though; unless he was in a pub or a coffee shop, where it was unavoidable, Gristhorpe didn't approve of people smoking in his presence.

"Right," the superintendent announced when they had all arranged their papers and helped themselves to coffee. "We've got four break-ins—all at old people's houses—involving one assault and one death. We've also got a Peeping Tom running around town looking in any window he damn well pleases, and we've got hardly a thing to go on in either case. I reckon it's about time we pooled what brainpower we've got and let's see if we can't come up with some ideas. Alan?"

Banks coughed. He needed a cigarette but had to content himself by fiddling with a paper clip while he spoke. "I think Detective Constable Richmond should speak first, sir. He conducted interviews with the dead woman's neighbours last night."

Gristhorpe looked at Richmond, inviting him to begin.

"Well, sir, you've all seen copies of the report. I don't really have anything to add. We had a uniformed man on duty all night, and another made inquiries all the way down Cardigan Drive. A couple of people heard someone running, but that was all."

"We know who that someone was, don't we?" Gristhorpe asked.

"Well, not his identity, sir. But, yes, it was that chap who's been looking in on women getting undressed."

"Right," Gristhorpe said, turning over a page of the report in front of him. "Now, Andrea Rigby says that she heard running, then a knock at a door. Never mind the alternative explanations for the moment. Could there be any possibility that it was the peeper, not a burglar, who killed Alice Matlock? Maybe she knew him, maybe he came for help or protection, or to confess—she threatened to report him, they struggled and he pushed her? Manslaughter."

"The place had been gone over just like the others, sir," Sergeant Hatchley pointed out.

"And no prints."

"No prints, sir."

"Couldn't it have been made to look like it was a burglary?"

"How would the peeper know to do that?" Banks asked.

"Surely he must read the papers?" Gristhorpe suggested.

"It doesn't fit, though. It's all too deliberate. If it happened as you say, then it was probably an accident. He probably just panicked and ran."

"People have been known to cover their tracks after crimes of passion, Alan."

"I know, sir. It just doesn't seem to fit the profile we have so far."

"Go on."

"Dr Fuller"—there it was again, so formal. Why couldn't he call her Jenny in front of others?—"Dr Fuller said we're dealing with a very frustrated man who's probably going about as far as he dares in peeping through windows. No one can be certain, but she said it's unlikely that a voyeur would progress to more serious sex crimes. On the other hand, as the pressure builds in him, he might feel the need to break out. It's a trap he's in, a treadmill, and there's no predicting what he'd do to escape it."

"But this wasn't a sex crime, Alan. Alice Matlock, thank the Lord, hadn't been interfered with in any way."

"I know, sir, but it still doesn't fit. The peeper does what he does when pressure or tension builds up and he can only find one way of releasing it, watching women undress. It wouldn't even really work for him in a strip-club—the women would have to be unaware of him, he would have to get that feeling of power, of dominance. When he's done it, though, the pressure's released. A personality like that is hardly likely to go running to an old woman and confess, let alone murder her just after he's satisfied himself."

"I see your point, Alan," Gristhorpe agreed. His bushy eyebrows joined in the middle and drew a thick grey line over his child-like blue eyes. "Perhaps the best thing to do would be to rule it out by checking into who Alice Matlock knew."

"She seemed to be a bit of a loner, sir," Richmond chipped in. "Most of the neighbours didn't know much about her, not much more than to say hello if they met in the street."

"I knew Alice Matlock," Gristhorpe told them. "She was a friend of my mother's. Used to come to the farm for fresh eggs when I was a kid. She always brought me some boiled sweets. But you're right, lad, she was a bit of a recluse. More so as she got older. Lost her young man in the first war, as I recall. Never did marry. Anyway, look into it. See if she's been at all friendly with a likely young peeper."

"There is one other thing."

"Yes, Alan?"

"Even if it wasn't the same person, if it was the usual lot did the break-in and the peeper just looked and ran, they might have seen each other."

"You mean, if we get one we might get a lead on the other?"

"Yes."

"But right now we've very little on either?"

"That's right."

"Where do you think our best chance lies?"

"The break-ins," Banks answered without hesitation. "I'll be getting an artist's impression of the man who fenced the stuff in Leeds any time now. I've already got a fairly good description but it doesn't check with any of the local villains I know. Sergeant Hatchley and Constable Richmond don't recognize him either."

"So maybe he's not local. New in town?"

"Or been away," Richmond suggested. "Only here every now and then."

"Possible. Know anyone who fits that profile?"

Richmond shook his head. "Only Andrea Rigby's husband. He's a computer whizz and he spends a lot of time away. But I saw a photo of him on the mantelpiece and he doesn't fit the description. He wouldn't be the type, anyway. From what I could see, he gets plenty of money from fiddling about with computers."

"Ask around, then," Gristhorpe advised. "See if you can come up with anything. You mentioned Wooller in your report, Richmond. He seemed suspicious. Anything in particular?"

"Well, no, sir." Richmond felt flustered, caught out on a hunch. "There was the dirty magazine, sir, that's in the report."

"Yes," Gristhorpe said dismissively, "but most of us have looked at pictures of naked women now and then, haven't we?"

"It's not just naked women, sir," Richmond pressed on, realizing only when it was too late that he had walked right into it. "Some of them are tied up, sir..." His voice faltered. "...and they do it with animals."

"Well," Gristhorpe said, beaming at him, "I can see you've been doing your homework, lad. But even if the stuff is illegally imported there's not a lot we can do. What exactly are you getting at?"

"Just that he seemed suspicious, sir. Completely uncommunicative, shifty, acted as if he was hiding something."

"Think he might be our peeper, do you?"

"Could be, sir."

"Alan?"

Banks shrugged. "I've not had the pleasure of meeting him, but I've been told that our man could take any size, shape or form. Certainly if he lives a frustrated existence and gets his kicks from bondage and bestiality magazines, then there's a chance."

"All right," Gristhorpe said, making a note. "Keep an eye on him. Drop by for a chat. Nothing heavy, though." He glanced sternly at Hatchley, who looked down at his notes and straightened his tie.

"The kid, sir. Trevor Sharp," Richmond said.

"Yes?"

"There was something funny about that, too. I heard them arguing about him being late all the time and neglecting his homework, and when I asked about the night before, his father only mentioned himself at first, sir. Said he was watching telly, right at the far end of the block. Then, later, when I asked, he said the kid was with him, too."

"Think he was lying?"

"Could be."

"We had the kid on suspicion of mugging four months ago," Banks added. "No case."

"Well," Gristhorpe said, "seeing as the only information we've got on the burglars so far is that they're young, we might as well follow up. Maybe you could talk to them, Alan? Father and son together. See if you get the same impression as Richmond here."

"All right," Banks agreed. "I'll drop by after school today."

"Might be a good idea to have a word with the head, too. You never know, some of 'em keep tabs on the kids. What school is it?"

"Eastvale Comprehensive, sir," Richmond answered. "Same place I went to."

"That'll be old Buxton, right?"

"Yes, sir. 'Boxer' Buxton we used to call him. He must be close to retiring age now."

"He's been at that school going on for forty years. Been head for twenty or more, since back when it was Eastvale Grammar School.

He's a bit of a dodderer now, lost in his own world, but have a word with him about young Trevor anyway, see if he's been acting strangely, playing truant, associating with a bad crowd. Is there anything else?" Gristhorpe turned to Sergeant Hatchley. "Anything for us, Sergeant?"

"I can't seem to find a pattern to the peeper's operation, sir," Hatchley said. "Except that he always picks blondes."

"What do you mean?"

"How he chooses his victims, sir, how he latches onto them, knows who to follow."

"The women weren't all single, were they?" Gristhorpe asked.

"Bloody hell, no, sir," Hatchley said. "One of 'em had her husband right there in bed dozing off while our chap was doing his bit through the curtains."

"He must do some reconnaissance first," Banks added. "He knows which window to look through, knows the layout of the house. Even picks the best time to be there."

"So he chooses his victims well in advance?"

"Must do."

"They'd all been in pubs the nights they were peeped on," Hatchley said. "But I couldn't find any evidence that they were being watched."

"That would explain it, though, wouldn't it?" Banks said. "If he already knew who he was going to spy on, he'd know something about their habits. If he'd watched the houses, he'd know when a woman comes home from the pub and how soon the bedroom light goes on. He'd know if the husband stayed downstairs or took a bath while she undressed. He must do his groundwork."

"Fair enough, Alan," Gristhorpe said, "but it doesn't help us much, does it?"

"We could warn people to make sure they're not being followed, to keep an eye out for strangers hanging about the street."

"I suppose we could." Gristhorpe sighed and ran his hand through his hair. "Anything's better than nothing. You talked to the victims again, Sergeant Hatchley?"

"Yes, sir. But I didn't find out anything new, just that all the incidents had occurred after a night out."

"Maybe it makes him feel that they're sinners or something," Banks guessed. "It's possible that he needs to feel like that about them. A lot of men don't like the idea of women smoking or going to pubs. They think it cheapens them. Maybe it's like that with him; perhaps he needs to feel that they're impure in the first place."

Gristhorpe scratched his neck and frowned. "I think you've been talking to Dr Fuller too much, Alan," he said. "But maybe you've got a point. Follow it up with her. When are you meeting again?"

"Tomorrow."

"Evening?"

Banks felt himself begin to flush. "We're both too busy during the day, sir."

Hatchley suppressed a guffaw by covering the lower half of his face with a huge dirty handkerchief and blowing hard. Richmond shifted uneasily in his seat. Banks could sense their reactions, and he felt angry. He wanted to say something, to tell them it was just bloody work, that's all. But he knew that if he did, they would think he was protesting too much, so he kept quiet and seethed inside.

"Put it to her, then," Gristhorpe said, ignoring the others. "Ask her if there could be any connection between the peeper and Alice Matlock's death, and find out if it's likely our man has a thing about women in pubs."

"She'll probably laugh at me," Banks said. "We all seem to fancy ourselves as amateur psychologists at one time or another."

"Not surprising, though, is it, Alan? We'd be a pretty bloody incurious race if we didn't think about our nature and behaviour once in a while, wouldn't we? Especially us coppers. Is that all?" he asked, rising to end the meeting.

Everyone kept silent. "Fine, then, that's it. Follow up Wooller and the Sharp kid, get that drawing circulated soon as it comes in, and check with Ethel Carstairs about any other friends Alice Matlock may have had."

"Should we say anything to the press?" Banks asked. "A warning to women about keeping their eyes open for strangers?"

"It can't do any harm, can it? I'll take care of that. Off you go, then. Meeting adjourned."

III

Graham Sharp rolled off Andrea Rigby and sighed with pleasure: "Ah, Wednesdays. Thank God for half-day closing."

Andrea giggled and snuggled in the crook of his arm. He could feel the weight of her breasts against his rib cage, the nipples still hard, and the sharp, milky scent of sex made them both warm and sleepy. Andrea traced a line from his throat to his pubic hair. "That was wonderful, Gray," she said dreamily. "It's always wonderful with you. See how much better you feel now."

"I was just a bit preoccupied, that's all."

"You were all tense," Andrea said, massaging his shoulders. Then she laughed. "Whatever it was, it certainly made you wild, though."

"When are you going to tell him?"

"Oh, Gray!" She snuggled closer, her breasts crushed against his chest. "Don't spoil it, don't make me think about bad things."

Graham smiled and caressed her hair. "Sorry, love. It's the secrecy. It gets me down sometimes. I just want us to be together all the time."

"We will be, we will," Andrea murmured, rubbing against him slowly as she felt him begin to stiffen again. "Oh God, Gray." She breathed hard as he took hold of her breast and squeezed the nipple between thumb and forefinger. "Yes...yes..."

Graham knew, in his more rational moments, that they would never be together all the time. Whatever Andrea thought about her husband, he wasn't such a bad sort really. He didn't beat her, and as far as Graham knew, he didn't cheat on her either. They got on well enough when he was around, which wasn't often, and, perhaps more important than Andrea would have cared to admit to herself—especially now, as she was nearing orgasm—he made a lot of money. Soon, in fact, she had told Graham sadly, they would be moving from their first country home into something a bit more authentic: an isolated Dales cottage, or perhaps somewhere in the Cotswolds, where the climate was milder. Why he wanted to live in the country, Andrea said she had no idea—he was hardly ever there anyway—but she had found Eastvale a great deal more interesting than she had expected.

Graham also knew deep down that Trevor would never accept

another mother, especially one who lived two doors away and was, at twenty-four, closer to the age of an older sister. There was the money, too. Graham could hardly make ends meet, and if he really thought about it (which he tried not to) he couldn't see Andrea as a shop-keeper's wife: not her, with her Paris fashions, original art works, and holidays in New York or Bangkok. No, just as he knew that Trevor would never accept her, he also knew she would never give up her way of life.

But they were both romantics at heart. At first, Andrea had come to the shop more and more often, just for little things like a packet of Jacob's Cream Crackers, some fresh Baps or perhaps a bottle of tar-ragon vinegar, and if there had been no other customers around she had lingered a little longer to talk each time. Over a week or two, Graham had come to know quite a lot about her, especially about how her husband was away so much and how bored she got.

Then, one evening, one of her fuses blew and she had no idea how to fix it. She went to Graham for help, and he came along with torch and fuse wire and did it in a jiffy. Coffee followed, and after that an exciting session of kissing and groping on the sofa, which, being one of those modern things made up of blocks you can rearrange any way you want, was soon transformed into an adequate approximation of a bed.

Since then, for about two months, Graham and Andrea had been meeting quite regularly. Theirs was a circumscribed life, however: they couldn't go out together (though they did once spend a nervous evening in York having dinner, looking over their shoulders the whole time), and they had to be very careful about being seen in each other's company at all. Always Graham would visit Andrea, using the back way, where the high walls of the back yards kept him from view and muffled the sound of his passing. Sometimes they had candlelight din-ners first; other times they threw themselves straight into lovemaking. Andrea was more passionate and abandoned in bed than anyone Graham had ever known, and she had led him to new heights of joy.

It was easier at first. Trevor spent three weeks in France on a school trip, so Graham was a free agent. On the boy's return, though, there were difficulties, which was why half-day closing was such a joy. Weekends were out, of course. That was when Andrea's husband was around, so the most they could manage was the occasional evening when Trevor was allowed to go out to the pictures with his mates, to the youth club or a local dance. Lately, though, with Trevor being out so often and taking so little notice, Graham had spent much more time with Andrea.

When they had finished, they lay back and lit cigarettes. Andrea blew the smoke out of her nose like an actress in a forties movie.

"Did they talk to you last night?" she asked.

"The police?"

"Yes."

"What do you think happened?"

"The old woman, Alice Matlock. She's dead."

Andrea frowned. "Was it murder?"

"They must think so or they wouldn't waste their time asking everyone what they were doing and where they were."

He sounded irritated. Andrea stroked his chest. "Don't worry about it, darling. It's nothing to do with us, is it?"

"No, 'course not," he said, turning and running his palm over her damp stomach. He loved Andrea's body; it was so different from Maureen's. She had had smooth skin, smooth as marble and sometimes as cold. He had hardly dared touch it, fearing it would be some kind of violation. But Andrea's skin had grain to it, a certain friction you could feel when you ran your hand over her buttocks or shoulders, even when they were moist as they were now.

"What did they want to know?" he asked her.

"Just if I heard anything the night before last."

"And did you?"

"After you'd gone, yes. I heard someone running along Cardigan Drive, then someone knocking at a door."

"The same person?"

"Could have been."

"There was a woman peeped on in Cardigan Drive Monday evening," Graham told her. "I read about it in the paper."

"Another of those Peeping Tom things?"

"Yes."

Andrea shivered and nestled closer. "So they think it might be the same person?"

"I guess they must," Graham said.

"What did they ask you?"

"Same thing. If I heard anything. And they asked Trevor where he was."

"They're always picking on kids, Gray, you know that. It doesn't mean anything. Since all that unemployment they automatically think kids are delinquents these days."

"True enough."

"What did you tell them?"

"That he was home with me, of course."

"Oh, Gray, should you have? I mean what if someone saw him somewhere else? It could make things really bad."

"He didn't do it, Andrea, he's not that kind of a lad, and I'm damned if I'm going to let the police get their hooks into him. Once they latch on they never let go. It was bad enough last time; it's not going to happen again."

"If you think it's best, Gray."

Graham frowned at her. "I know you don't think he's worth it," he said, "but he's a good lad, he'll turn out well in the end, you'll see."

Andrea put her arms around him. "I don't think ill of him, really I don't. It's just that you seem to dote on him so much. He can't do any wrong in your eyes."

"I'm his father, aren't I? I'm all he's got." He smiled and kissed her. "I know what I'm doing, love. Don't worry." He looked at his watch on the bedside table. "Bloody hell, I'd better be going. Trevor'll be home from school any minute."

Andrea moved away from him sadly. "You know I hate it when you leave, Gray," she said. "It's so lonely and boring being here all by myself in the evenings."

Graham kissed her lightly on the lips. "I know. I'll try and get back later if I can. I don't know what Trevor's got planned for tonight."

Graham slipped into his trousers, as Andrea watched from the bed.

"I'm getting a bit worried about Wooller, Gray," she said, just before he left.

"What about him?"

"I don't know if I'm being paranoid or feeling guilty or what, but it's just the way he looks at me, as if he *knows*. And worse, it's as if he's thinking about what to do with what he knows. Do you know what I mean? I feel like he's seen all of me, all of us."

"Don't worry about it," Graham said, sitting down on the edge of the bed and taking her hand. "You're probably overreacting. We've been discreet. The walls are very thick—I'm sure he wouldn't be able to hear a thing. And I'm always careful when I call. Really, love, don't worry about it. Must rush." He patted her hand and kissed her on the forehead. Andrea yawned and stretched, then turned over and lay in the impression his body had made. The bed still smelled of his Old Spice. She pulled the sheets around her shoulders and waved goodbye lazily as he slipped out through the door.

IV

It was six o'clock when Banks pulled up outside number eight Gallows View. He had decided to take on the Sharps himself and leave Wooller to Hatchley.

"Good evening," he said politely, introducing himself, as Graham Sharp opened the door, a forkful of sausage in his hand.

"We're just having dinner, can't it wait?"

"Won't take long," Banks said, already inside. "Just carry on eating."

The room wasn't exactly a living-room, it was more of a storage place full of boxes of tinned goods and crisps that could be easily carried into the shop. At the back, though, was a fairly modern kitchen, complete with a microwave oven, and Banks guessed that the real living quarters must be upstairs, spread out over the two adjoined cottages.

Graham and Trevor sat at the formica-topped table finishing what looked like bangers and mash with baked beans. Big white mugs of tea steamed in front of them.

"What is it, then?" Graham asked, polite enough not to talk with his mouth full. "We talked to one of your chaps last night. Told him all we knew."

"Yes," Banks said. "That's why I'm here. I just want to clear up a few things in the statement. Detective Constable Richmond is new to the job, if you know what I mean. We have to keep a close eye on new chaps, see that they get it right, go by the book."

"You mean you're here because you're doing some kind of job performance check on the young bloke?" Sharp asked incredulously.

It wasn't in the least bit true, but Banks thought it might put the Sharps at ease for as long as he wanted them to let their guards down. After that, of course, there were ways of putting them on the defensive again, a position which often turned out to be much more illuminating.

"Well, I never!" Sharp went on. "You know, I never really thought about the police force as a job like any other. I suppose you get wages as well and complain about pay-rises and poor canteen food?"

Banks laughed. "We don't have a canteen, but, yes, we complain a lot about pay-rises, or the lack of them." Innocently, he took out his notebook. "Detective Constable Richmond tells me that you heard nothing at around eleven o'clock on Monday night. Is that correct?"

"It is."

"Where were you?"

"Watching television in the sitting-room." He pointed towards the upstairs. "Far end of the house. Have a look if you want."

"Oh, I don't think that will be necessary, thanks all the same. You said you were watching television all evening?"

"Well, from about eight o'clock to midnight, anyway."

"Good," Banks said, peering into his notebook. "It looks like our man did a good job. You wouldn't, of course, hear anything from as far away as Cardigan Drive, or even number two Gallows View, if you were in the sitting-room with the television on, would you?"

"Nothing. You can try it if you want."

Banks waved aside his offer, then turned sharply to Trevor. "And where were you?"

Trevor, taken by surprise halfway through a mouthful of sausage and beans, spoke through the mush of semi-masticated food. "With him," he mumbled, pointing his fork at his father.

"Mr Sharp," Banks said, returning to Graham and frowning, "DC Richmond says that when you first told him you were watching television you made no mention of your son whatsoever. It was all in the first person, as if Trevor wasn't even home."

"What are you getting at?" Sharp said belligerently, putting down his knife and fork.

"Just checking up on the constable's statement, sir. Want to see if he got it right. He was a bit curious about this one point. He put a question mark by it."

Sharp glared at Banks for a few moments while Trevor went on chewing his food. "If you're insinuating that my Trevor had anything to do with this, you're barking up the wrong tree. He's straight as a die, always has been. Ask anyone."

"I'm not insinuating anything, Mr Sharp. I'd just like to know why the constable should mention this."

"It was a way of speaking, I suppose," Sharp said. "You don't always think you're going to have to account for the person who was with you, do you? I mean if someone asked you what you did last night and you stayed home watching telly, you probably wouldn't say 'My wife and I...blah-blah-blah...' would you?"

"You've got a point there, Mr Sharp. I probably wouldn't. So let me get this straight. You and Trevor spent the whole evening, from about eight till midnight, watching television, and you neither heard nor saw anything unusual. Am I right?"

"That's right. Only Trevor went to bed about eleven. Needs his sleep for school."

"Of course. What did you watch, Trevor?" Banks asked casually, turning to the boy.

"We watched—"

"I'm asking Trevor, Mr Sharp. What did you watch, son?"

"Don't really remember," Trevor said. "There was one of them American cop shows. You know, all car chases and shoot-outs." He shrugged. "Half the time I was reading my book and not paying attention."

"What book was that?"

"Now, look here," Graham burst out, the vein on his temple pulsating with anger. "You can't just come in here and interrogate my son like this, accuse us of lying to you. I told you, Trevor was with me all evening until he went to bed at about eleven o'clock."

"What was he reading?"

"Eh?"

"The book. What was he reading?"

"It was *The Shining*," Trevor answered, "Stephen King. Do you know it?"

"No," Banks said, smiling at Trevor. "Any good?"

"Yeah. Better than the film."

Banks nodded and packed away his notebook. "Well, I think I've got all I need. I'll let you finish your meal in peace. No, don't bother," he said, putting out his arm to stop Graham from standing up. "I can see myself out."

And with that he was gone. The Sharps ate the rest of their dinner slowly, in silence.

SIX

I

Thursday morning hit like a cold shower in the dumpy form of Ms Dorothy Wycombe. She was in Gristhorpe's office when Banks arrived at the station, and the superintendent called him in the moment he snapped off his Walkman. Gristhorpe clearly had no idea how to deal with her. For all his learning and compassion, he was a country gentleman and was not used to dealing with crusaders like Ms Wycombe. He looked lost.

Some people are susceptible to environment, but Dorothy Wycombe was not. Gristhorpe's office was a cosy, lived-in room with a studious air about it, but she might just as well have been standing on a platform at Leeds City Station waiting with her arms crossed for the 5:45 to King's Cross, glaring at everything within her field of vision. The dominant expression on her face during the meeting that followed was one of distaste, as if she had just eaten a particularly sour gooseberry.

"Er...Miss...er...Ms Wycombe, meet Detective Chief Inspector Banks," Gristhorpe muttered by way of introduction.

"Pleased to meet you," Banks said apprehensively.

No reply.

Through his job, Banks had come to realize that it was unwise to expect stereotypes; to do so only led to misunderstandings. On the other hand, he had also been forced to admit the existence of stereotypes, having met more than once, among others, the lisping, mincing homosexual, the tweedy retired colonel with handlebar moustache and shooting-stick, and the whore with the heart of gold.

So when Dorothy Wycombe stood before him looking like every-man's parody of a women's libber, he could hardly claim surprise. Disappointment, perhaps, but not surprise.

"Seems there's been a complaint, Alan," Gristhorpe began slowly. "It's about Sergeant Hatchley, but I thought you ought to hear it first." Banks nodded and looked at Dorothy Wycombe, whose chins jutted out in challenge.

That she was unattractive was obvious; what was not clear was how much of this was due to nature itself and how much to her own efforts. She had fizzed all the life out of her colourless hair, and the bulky sack that passed for a dress bulged in the most unlikely places. Above her double-chin was a tight, mean mouth, lined around the edges from constant clenching, and a dull, suet complexion. Behind the National Health glasses shone eyes whose intelligence, which Banks had no doubt she possessed, was glazed over with revolutionary zeal. Her speech was jagged with italics.

"I have been informed," she began, consulting a small black notebook for dramatic effect, "that while questioning the victims of your *Peeping Tom*, your sergeant's attitude was flippant, and, furthermore, that he expressed the desire to commit a similar act of violence against one interviewee in particular."

"Those are serious charges," Banks said, wishing he could smoke a cigarette. "Who made them?"

"I did."

"I don't remember you ever being a victim of the scopophiliac."

"Pardon?"

"I said I don't recall that you ever reported any invasion of your privacy."

"That's not the point. You're simply trying to obscure the issue."

"What issue?"

"Your sergeant's *lewd* and *lascivious* suggestions—an attitude, might I add, that reflects on the entire investigation of this whole scandalous affair."

"Who made the charges?" Banks repeated.

"I told you, *I'm* bringing them to your attention."

"On whose authority?"

"I represent the local women."

"Who says so?"

"Inspector Banks, this is infuriating! Will you or will you not listen to the charges?"

"I'll listen to them when I know who made them and what gives you the authority to pass them on."

Dorothy Wycombe moved further away from Banks and puffed herself up to her full size. "I am the chairperson of WEEF."

"Weef?"

"W.E.E.F., Inspector Banks. The Women of Eastvale for Emancipation and Freedom. WEEF."

Banks had often thought it was amusing how groups twisted the language so that acronyms of organizations would sound like snappy words. It had started with NATO, SEATO, UNO and other important groups, progressed through such local manifestations as SPIT, SHOT and SPEAR, and now there was WEEF. It didn't seem to matter at all that "Women of Eastvale" sounded vaguely mediaeval or that "Freedom" and "Emancipation" meant more or less the same thing. They simply existed to give birth to WEEF, which sounded to Banks like an impoverished "woof," or the kind of squeak a frightened mouse might utter.

"Very well," Banks conceded, making a note. "And who brought the complaint to your attention?"

"I'm not under any obligation to divulge my source," Dorothy Wycombe snapped back, quick as a reporter in the dock.

"Yesterday," Banks sighed, "Sergeant Hatchley spoke to Carol Ellis, Mandy Selkirk, Josie Campbell and Ellen Parry about their experiences. He also spoke to Molly Torbeck, who had been with Carol Ellis in The Oak on the night of the incident. Would you like me to interview each in turn and find out for myself? I can do that, you know."

"Do what you want. I'm not going to tell you."

"Right," Banks said, standing up to leave. "Then I've no intention of taking your complaint seriously. You must realize that we get a lot of unfounded allegations made against us, usually by overzealous members of the public. So many that we've got quite an elaborate system of screening them. I'm sure that, as a defender of freedom and emancipation, you wouldn't want anyone's career to suffer from injustice brought about by smear campaigns, would you?"

Banks thought Dorothy Wycombe was about to explode, so red did her face become. Her chins trembled and her knuckles whitened as she grasped the edge of Gristhorpe's desk.

"This is outrageous!" she shouted. "I'll not have my movement dictated to by a fascist police force."

"I'm sorry," Banks said, heading for the door. "We just can't deal with unidentified complainants."

"Carol Ellis!" The name burst from Dorothy Wycombe's tight mouth like a huge build-up of steam from a stuck valve. "*Now* will you sit down and listen to me?"

"Yes, ma'am," Banks said, taking out his notebook again.

"It's *Ms* Wycombe," she told him, "and I expect you to treat this matter seriously."

"It's a serious charge," Banks agreed, "as I said earlier. That's why I want it fully documented. What exactly did Carol Ellis say?"

"She said that Sergeant Hatchley seemed to treat the whole Peeping Tom business as a *bit of a lark*, that he seemed either *bored* or *amused* whilst interviewing her, and that he made certain *suggestions* about her body."

"Bored or amused, Ms Wycombe? Which? They're very different, you know."

"Both, at different times."

"Certain suggestions about her body? What kind of suggestions? Lewd, offensive?"

"What other kind are there, Inspector? He hinted that the Peeping Tom must have had *quite a treat*."

"Is that all?"

"Isn't it enough? What kind of—"

"I mean are there any other allegations?"

"No. That's all I wanted to say. I hope I can trust you, Inspector, to see that *something* is done about this."

"Don't worry, Ms Wycombe, I'll get to the bottom of it. If there's any truth in the charges, Sergeant Hatchley will be disciplined, you can be sure of that."

Dorothy Wycombe smiled grimly and suspiciously, then swished out of the office.

Gristhorpe took a deep breath. "Alan," he said, "when I made that joke about throwing your sergeant to the wolves the other day, I didn't mean it bloody literally. Whatever we might think about Ms Wycombe and her manner, we've got to concede that she's got a point. Don't you agree?"

"If what she says is true, yes."

"You think it might not be?"

"We both know how the truth gets twisted in emotional situations, sir. Let me get Hatchley's version before we go any further."

"Very well. But let me know, Alan. Are you getting any further?"

"No, but I'm seeing Jenny Fuller again today. Perhaps she'll have a bit more light to shed on things. If we can narrow the field down a bit, we might at least be able to start checking around."

"What about Alice Matlock?"

"Nothing yet."

"Get a move on, Alan. Too many things are piling up for my liking."

II

Back in his office, Banks found a note from Inspector Barnshaw accompanying a police artist's drawing of the man that the Leeds junk dealer, Crutchley, had described. He had recognized none of the file photographs, but the sketch was a good realization of the description Banks had taken.

He lit a cigarette, tidied the files on his desk, and sent for Sergeant Hatchley, who arrived about five minutes later.

"Sit down," Banks said, his abrupt tone foreshadowing the bollocking the sergeant was in for.

Banks decided not to beat about the bush. Instead, he told Hatchley exactly what Dorothy Wycombe had said and asked him for his version of what had happened during the Carol Ellis interview.

Hatchley blushed and scratched his chin, avoiding Banks's glance.

"Is it true?" Banks pressed. "That's all I want to know."

"Well, yes and no," Hatchley admitted.

"Meaning?"

"Look, sir, I know Carol Ellis. I'm a bachelor and she's not married

either, and I'm not denying I've had my eye on her for some time—
long before this business ever started."

"Go on."

"When I talked to her yesterday, she'd got over what happened.
After all, it was just a bit of a shock. Nobody got hurt. And she was
even joking about it a bit, wishing she'd worn her best underwear,
given a better show, that kind of thing. 'Appen she was saying it to
cover up her nerves, or maybe she was embarrassed. I don't know.
But, like I told you, I know her and I quite fancy her myself, so I might
have joked along, you know, made things a bit more personal."

"'Might have'?"

"All right, I did."

"Were you bored?"

"With Carol Ellis around? You must be joking, sir. A bit casual,
maybe. It's not like interrogating someone you don't know, or a
villain."

"Did you suggest that the peeper must have had quite a treat?"

"I don't rightly recollect. I might have joked along with her, like.
When she said about wearing her best undies, I probably said she'd
look fine to me in any underwear. You know, just like a compliment.
A bit cheeky, but..."

Banks sighed. It was clear to him what had happened, but it was
equally clear that it shouldn't have. The worst he could accuse
Hatchley of was tactlessness and allowing personal affairs to come
before police work. Whatever Carol Ellis had said to Dorothy
Wycombe had probably been said in a spirit of fun, and was no doubt
grossly distorted.

"I don't need to tell you that it was a bloody stupid thing to do, do
I?" he said to Hatchley, who didn't reply. "Because of your actions,
we're in for a lot more bad publicity, and we've got to spend time pla-
cating Dorothy bloody Wycombe. I do wish you'd learn to keep your
urges to yourself. It's one thing to chat the woman up in a pub, but
quite another to do it while you're interviewing her about a crime.
Am I making myself clear?"

Hatchley pressed his lips together and nodded.

"Are you sure that Carol Ellis took your remarks in the spirit they
were intended?"

Here, Hatchley beamed. "She's going out with me on Saturday night, sir, if that's of any account."

Banks couldn't help but smile. "Something must have got twisted in the communication network, then," he muttered. "I'll talk to her myself and straighten it out. But be bloody careful in future. I don't need the aggro, and the superintendent certainly doesn't. You'd better stay out of the peeper case in future. And you'd better stay out of the old man's way for a day or two, as well."

"What do you want me to do?"

"Concentrate on the break-ins and the Alice Matlock killing." He passed Hatchley the drawing. "Get copies done of this and spread them around. Help Richmond find out if Alice Matlock had any younger friends, any lame ducks, lonely hearts, that kind of thing. Did you see Wooller, by the way?"

"Yes, last night."

"Anything?"

Hatchley shook his head. "Nah. He's an odd one all right, but I'm pretty damn sure he didn't see or hear anything."

"Did you get the impression he was holding something back?"

"Lots of things. He's a dark horse, sure enough. But nothing about the Matlock case, no. I still reckon he's worth keeping an eye on for the other business, though. You definitely get a kind of dirty feeling, talking to him."

"Okay," Banks said. "But you're off that. And if the press get hold of Dorothy Wycombe's story, which I'm sure they will, I want no comments from you. None at all. That understood?"

"Yes, sir. Bit of an Amazon, eh, that Dorothy Wycombe?"

"Off you go, Sergeant."

Hatchley left and Banks relaxed, glad it was over. He didn't mind yelling at the sergeant in the course of duty, but he hated the formality of the official reprimand. It was easy to see why Gristhorpe had passed the buck to him in the first place; the superintendent was diplomatic enough, all right, but he was also too soft-hearted when it came to his men. He looked at his watch. It was just after eleven. He decided to take his coffee and toasted teacake alone this morning, and leave Hatchley to lick his wounded pride for a while.

III

Eastvale Comprehensive used to be called Eastvale Grammar School. In the old days it was a respectable institution attended by promising children from miles around, many of whom gained scholarships to Oxford or Cambridge, or went on to the northern red-brick universities closer to home.

The building itself was Victorian, attractive in a Gothic way from the outside, with turrets, a clock and a bell tower, and full of high gloomy corridors within. A number of "temporary" classrooms, trailers propped up on bricks, for the most part, had been added to the original building in the early seventies, and they looked as if they were definitely there to stay.

Things changed for the school when the comprehensive system was turned loose on the country. Now teachers struggled with overcrowded classes of such mixed abilities that it was impossible to nurture the bright and do justice to the slow. Often the children had to suffer inept teaching by fools who knew more about athletics and rugby than Caesar's conquest, Shakespeare, or the square roots of negative numbers.

Banks knew the place, though he had never set foot inside the main building before. Both Brian and Tracy went there, and the tales they told did a lot to undermine Banks's faith in the comprehensive system.

As a working-class boy in Peterborough, he had always felt a strong aversion to any kind of elitism, yet as a moderately well-educated man with a taste for knowledge, he had to admit that no amount of special treatment and mollycoddling could turn a lazy, hostile slob into a star pupil; far from it, too many mediocre minds could do nothing but discourage exceptional students from doing their best. At school, he remembered, kids want to belong; they do not want to be ostracized by their peers, which happens if they excel at anything other than sports.

As far as natural abilities went, he had no real opinion. Perhaps some were born with better brains than others. But that wasn't, to him, the issue—the point was that everybody should be given the chance to find out, and the idealistic basis of the comprehensive system seemed to grant just that possibility. In practice, it didn't seem to be turning out that way.

In his own education, he had been very lucky indeed. After failing his "eleven-plus" exam, he had been condemned to the local secondary modern school, there to be moulded into an ideal electrician, bricklayer or road sweeper. He had nothing against manual occupations—his own father had been a sheet-metal worker until angina forced an early retirement—except that he wasn't interested in any of them.

Fortunately, because he did well at his studies, he got a shot at the "fourteen-plus." He worked long and hard, passed, and found himself a new boy, an outsider at the grammar school. It seemed that all the relationships had been formed already during the three years he had spent in exile, and for the first two terms he despaired of making any friends. It was only typical schoolboy stand-offishness, though. As soon as the others found out that he was a terror in a scrap, owned the toughest conker in the school, and made perhaps the finest rugger scrum-half the team had ever seen, he had no problem gaining acceptance.

It had been a cruel process, though, he reflected. The first exam split his groups of friends in the most divisive way: grammar school kids rarely talked to secondary modern boys, no matter how many games of commandos or cricket they had played together in their childhood; and his next exam accomplished much the same thing in reverse. This time, however, the friends that Banks had made at the secondary modern school never spoke to him again because they thought he had betrayed them. Entering the gates of Eastvale Comprehensive somehow brought back the good and the bad of his own schooldays.

When Banks walked through the yard it was lunchtime; the children played hand-tennis or cricket against stumps chalked on the wall in the yard, or smoked behind the cycle sheds, and the teachers lounged in the smoky staff room reading the *Guardian* or grappling with the *Sun* crossword. The head, however, was in his sanctuary, and it was into this haven that Banks was ushered by a slim, pretty secretary, who looked hardly older than school-leaving age herself.

The institutional-green corridors were half glass, so that any-one passing by could look into the classrooms. Now, the desks stood empty, and the blackboards were still partly covered in indecipherable scrawl. Many of the desks, Banks noticed, were just as desecrated with the carved initials of girlfriends and the names of famous cricketers, footballers and rock-and-roll bands as they had been in his own schooldays. Only the names had changed. And the place smelled pleasantly of bubble gum, chalk dust and satchel leather.

The head was sipping tea in his panelled office, a well-thumbed copy of Cicero on the desk in front of him. He greeted Banks and turned sadly to the book. "Latin, Inspector. Such an elegant, noble language, quite easily capable of sustaining lengthy flights of poetry. Nobody, it seems, has any use for it these days. Anyway," he sighed, standing up, "you've not come to hear about my problems, have you?"

The head, like his book, looked as though he had seen better days. His face was haggard, his hair grey, and he had a pronounced stoop. His most noticeable feature, however, was a big red nose, and it didn't take much imagination to guess what nicknames the kids had for him. Though he wore a bat-like cape, there was no mortar-board in sight. The study looked so much like Banks's old headmas-ter's lair that he felt the same quiver of adrenalin as he had all those years ago while waiting for the cane.

"No, sir," Banks smiled, slipping easily into the language of respect. "I came to ask a few questions about one of your boys."

"Oh, dear. Not been getting himself into trouble, has he? I'm afraid, these days, it's very difficult to keep track of them, and there are several bad elements in the school. Do sit down."

"Thank you, sir. It's nothing definite," Banks went on. "We're just faced with one or two discrepancies in a statement and we'd like to know if you can tell us anything about Trevor Sharp."

There was no flash of recognition in Buxton's expression. Obviously he had long since given up trying to keep track of all his pupils. He got up and walked towards his filing cabinet, from which, after much muttering and tut-tutting, he pulled out a sheaf of papers.

"Reports," he said, tapping the papers with a bony finger. "These should tell us what you want to know. I'd appreciate it, though,

Inspector, if this got no further than you and me. These are supposed to be confidential. . . ."

"Of course. In return, I'd be pleased if you didn't mention my visit, especially to the boy himself or to anyone who might tell him."

The head nodded and started turning the pages. "Let me see . . . 1983 . . . no . . . winter . . . summer . . . 1984 . . . excellent . . . ninety per-cent . . . very good . . ." and he went on in this fashion for some time before returning to Banks. "A bright boy, young Master Sharp. The name suits him. Look at this." And he passed Banks the reports for the previous year. They were full of "excellents" and high marks in all subjects except Geography. About that, his teacher had said: "Does not seem interested. Obviously capable, but unwilling to work hard enough."

As it turned out, that lone failure foreshadowed the more recent reports, which were scattered with remarks such as "Could do better," "Does not try hard enough" and "Takes negative attitude towards sub-ject." There were also several complaints from the teachers about his absences: "If Trevor were in class more often he would attain a better grasp of the subject," wrote Mr Fox, his English teacher, and "Failure to hand in homework and to appear in class have contributed greatly towards Trevor's disappointing performance in History this term," commented Mr Rhodes.

"What this adds up to, then," Banks said, "is a promising pupil who seems to have lost his way."

"Yes," Mr Buxton agreed sadly. "It happens so often these days. There seem to be so many distractions for the boys. Of course, in most cases it's a phase they have to go through. Rebellion. Have to get it out of their systems, you know."

Banks knew, but the transformation from star pupil with a great career ahead into truant and slacker was certainly open to other inter-pretations.

"Who are his friends?" Banks asked. "Who does he hang around with?"

"I'm afraid I wouldn't know, Inspector. It's so hard to keep track. . . . His form master, Mr Price, might be able to tell you." He picked up his phone, handling it as if it were a severed limb. "I'll ask Sonia to bring him in."

When Mr Price arrived, he looked both annoyed at having been disturbed on his dinner break and apprehensive about the purpose of the call. The head soon put him at ease, and curiosity then gained the better edge, turning him into a garrulous pedant. After trying to impress both Banks and the head for several minutes with his modern approach to language teaching and his theories on classroom management, he finally had to be brought around to the point of his visit.

"I've come to inquire about one of your students, Mr Price—Trevor Sharp."

"Ah, Sharp, yes. Odd fellow, really. Doesn't have much of anything to do with the other lads. Rather sullen and hostile. One simply tends to stay away from him."

"Is that what the other boys do?"

"Seems so. Nobody's actively against him or anything like that, but he goes his way and they go theirs."

"So he has no close friends here?"

"None."

"Is he a bully?"

"Not at all, though he could be if he wanted. Tough kid. Very good at games. He always dresses conservatively, while the others are trying to get away with whatever they can—purple hair, mohawk cuts, spiky bracelets, studded leather jackets, you name it. Not Sharp, though."

"The others don't make fun of him?"

"No. He's the biggest in the class. Nobody bothers him."

"I understand from his school reports that he's been absent a lot lately. Have you talked to him about this?"

"Yes, certainly. In fact, last parents' day I had a long chat with his father, who seemed very concerned. Doesn't seem to have done much good, though; Sharp still comes and goes as he pleases. Personally, I think he's just bored. He's bright and he's bored."

There was nothing more to say, especially as Banks had no concrete grounds on which to investigate Trevor. He thanked both the headmaster and Mr Price, repeated his request for discretion, and left.

IV

As Banks was shuffling through the reports in the headmaster's office, Trevor himself was about a mile away. He had gone out of bounds to meet Mick at a pub where the question of drinking age was rarely broached, especially if the coins kept passing over the counter. They sat over the last quarters of their pints, smoking and listening to the songs that Mick had chosen on the jukebox.

Trevor kept sucking and probing at his front teeth, pulling a face.

"What's the matter with you," Mick asked. "It's driving me bleeding barmy, all that fucking around with your gob."

"Don't know," Trevor answered. "Hurts a bit, feels rough. I think I've lost a filling."

"Let's take a look."

Trevor bared his teeth in an evil grin, like a horse with the bit in its mouth, while Mick looked and pronounced his verdict. "Yeah, one of 'em's getting a bit black round the edges—that little one next to the big yellow one. I'd see a fucking dentist if I was you."

"I don't like dentists."

"Fucking coward!" Mick jeered.

Trevor shrugged. "Maybe so, but I don't like them. Anyway, you said we'd got two jobs on?" he asked when the music had finished.

"That's right. One tonight, one next Monday."

"Why tonight? It seems pretty short notice to me."

"Coming back from 'oliday tomorrow, aren't they? And Lenny says the pickings'll be good."

"What about next Monday?"

"Bird always goes to her country club Mondays. Lenny's heard she always keeps quite a bit of jewellery around the place. Rich divorcée, like."

"Has Lenny given you any idea about how we get in?"

"Better." Mick grinned pimplishly. "He's given me this." And he opened his parka to show Trevor the tip of what looked like a crowbar. "Easy," he went on. "Just stick it between the door and the post and you're home free."

"What if someone sees us?"

"Nobody will. These are big 'ouses, detached like. And we'll go in the back way. All quiet, nobody around. Better wear the balas to be on the safe side, though."

Trevor nodded. The thought of breaking into a big, empty, dark house was frightening and exciting. "We'll need torches," be said. "Little ones, those pen-lights."

"Got 'em," Mick said proudly. "Lenny gave us a couple before he split for The Smoke."

"Fine, then," Trevor smiled. "We're on."

"We're on," Mick echoed. And they drank to it.

SEVEN

I

Jenny laughed at Banks's theory about the peeper spying on female pub *habitutées*: "Only been working for me three days and already coming up with ideas of your own, eh?"

"But is it any good?"

"Might be, yes. It could be part of his pattern, like his fixation on blondes. On the other hand it was perhaps just the most convenient time. A time when nobody would miss him or see him. Or a time when he could depend on his victims going to bed after a few drinks. He wouldn't have to hang around too long to get what he came for."

"Now you're doing my job."

Jenny smiled. They sat in deep, comfortable chairs by the crackling fire and looked as if they should have been drinking brandy and smoking cigars. But both preferred Theakston's bitter, and only Banks puffed sparingly at his Benson and Hedges Special Milds.

"How many pubs are there in Eastvale?" Jenny asked.

"Fifty-seven. I checked."

Jenny whistled through her teeth. "Alcoholic's paradise. But still, you must know which areas he operates in?"

"Random so far. He's spread himself around except for picking two from the same pub, so that doesn't help us much, but we do have some evidence that indicates a possible link between our peeper and the Alice Matlock killing. Could it be the same person?"

"Do you expect a yes-or-no answer?"

"All I want is your opinion. Is it likely that the peeper, after watching Carol Ellis get undressed, ran down the street, knocked on Alice

Matlock's door and, for some reason, killed her either intentionally or accidentally?"

"You want an answer based purely on psychological considerations?"

"Yes."

"I'd say no, then. It's very unlikely. In the first place, he would have no reason to run to Alice Matlock's house. If he'd been spotted, his impulse would be to get as far away as possible, as quickly as possible."

"You're still doing my job."

"Well, dammit," Jenny said, "they're so close. What do you want me to say?"

"I don't know. Something about a peeper not being the murdering kind."

Jenny laughed. "Primary-school psychology? You won't get that from me. I've told you it's unlikely and I've given you one good reason. If he got the release he needed from watching Carol Ellis, I doubt that he'd be emotionally capable of murder immediately afterwards."

"That's what I said to the superintendent."

"Well, why the bloody hell. . . ." Jenny started, and then began to laugh. "We really are doing each other's jobs, aren't we? But seriously, Alan, I say it's unlikely but it's not impossible."

"Would he go to her to confess, perhaps?"

Jenny shook her head. "I don't think so. Not to an old woman. Doesn't fit at all. Offhand, I'd say you're looking for a bald, short-sighted, middle-aged man wearing a plastic mac, bicycle-clips and galoshes."

"If only."

"Stereotypes do exist, you know."

"Oh, I know. Believe me, I do."

"What do you mean?"

"Dorothy Wycombe."

"Ah," Jenny said. "Had a visit, have you?"

"This morning."

"Ah, yes. Dorothy's quite a formidable opponent, don't you think? I find her a bit hard to take, myself."

"I thought you two were friends."

"Acquaintances. We've worked together on one or two projects,

that's all. We don't really have a lot in common, but Dorothy is ener-
getic and very good at her job."

"WEEF?"

"Yes, WEEF. Pretty pathetic, isn't it?"

Banks nodded.

"Anyway," Jenny went on, "Dorothy is an intelligent woman, but
she lets her dogma get in the way of her thinking. What was it all
about, if it's not private?"

"It is a bit delicate," Banks told her, then gave an abbreviated
account, not mentioning any names, and they both had another
laugh.

"The poor man," Jenny sympathized. "He was just trying to chat
her up."

"Not so much of the 'poor man,' if you please. He should have
known better."

"But why did she report him to Dorothy?"

"She didn't. I popped round to see her on my way here, and she
was very annoyed by what had happened. Apparently Ms Wycombe
had been visiting the victims—rather like some Victorian lady visiting the poor, I should imagine—and trying to gather some ammuni-
tion against us. The woman chatted in quite a friendly way to Ms
Wycombe and joked about my man's visit. She'd actually been quite
flattered as she'd had her eye on him for a while and wondered when,
if ever, he was going to make his move. Anyway, Dorothy Wycombe
twisted the information to suit her purposes and marched in demand-
ing blood."

"What a job you do."

"I know. It's a dirty job—"

"—but somebody's got to do it. Talking of dirty jobs," Jenny went
on, "I've dug out a couple of case histories for you."

"I'm listening."

"Ever heard of Charles Floyd or Patrick Byrne?"

Banks shook his head. "I'm afraid my history of crime's not what it
should be. Tell me."

"Patrick Byrne murdered a girl in the Birmingham YWCA in 1959.
He was a labourer on a building site near the hostel, and one
afternoon he got sent back to the yard by his foreman for returning

to work drunk after lunch. He'd often peeped on the girls undressing in the hostel, but this time he went in and strangled a girl. After that, he undressed her, raped her, then cut off her head with a table knife. He also made an attempt to eat one of her breasts with sugar."

"That's not a very encouraging tale, is it?"

"No. Apparently Byrne had had sadistic fantasies, including cutting women in half with a circular saw, since he was about seventeen. He said he wanted to get his own back on women for causing him nervous tension through sex. Before that, he'd been content with simply watching girls undress, but because he was drunk and upset by being told off by his foreman, he went beyond everything he'd ever done before. He also left a note that read, 'This was what I thought would never happen.'"

"Is the other case just as heartening?"

"Yes. About the only consolation is that it happened in Texas in the forties. Charles Floyd started by watching women get undressed. Then he waited till they went to sleep, killed them and raped them, in that order. There was one woman who never closed her curtains, and he watched her for several nights before he finally climbed in after she fell asleep. He battered her to death, then wrapped her head in a sheet and raped her. After that, he spent the rest of the night in bed with her. He killed other women, too, and when he got caught he admitted he'd been a Peeping Tom who turned to murder and rape when the sexual excitement got too much for him."

"The woman didn't close her curtains?" Banks commented. "Surely that was asking for it in a way?"

Jenny shot him a cold glance. "We've already been through that."

"And I did say that women should be careful not to appear to be inviting men to sex."

"And I said that we should be able to dress how we like and go where we damn well please."

"So we agree to differ."

"It looks like it. But please understand, I'm not condoning the woman leaving her curtains open. It was probably a very stupid thing to do. All I'm saying is that what Floyd did was an act of violence more than of sex, and that such things will happen anyway, whatever we do, until more men start to see women as people, not as sex objects."

"I don't believe the solution is as simple as that, admirable as it sounds," Banks said. "Yes, they are acts of violence, but it's violence that is highly sexual in nature. I think it's true that at least one of the reasons for the rise in sex crimes is the increase in stimulation—and that includes fashions, pornography, advertising, films, TV, the lot."

"And who determines women's fashions?"

"Mostly men, I should imagine."

"That's right. You dress us the way you want us, you create us in the image you desire, and then you have the gall to accuse us of asking for it!"

"Okay, calm down," Banks said, concerned at seeing Jenny so hurt and angry. He put his hand on her shoulder and she didn't brush it off. "I understand what you're saying. It's a very complex subject and it's hard to portion out blame. I'm willing to take my share. How about you?"

Jenny nodded and they shook hands.

"What conclusions have you drawn from those cases?" Banks asked.

"None, really. Only the most obvious ones."

"I must be thick, nothing's obvious to me."

"Until we know our man's motivation, we can't know whether some kind of trigger might exist for him, or how close he is to reaching it."

"Look," Banks said, glancing at his watch, "it's almost ten o'clock. Can I get you another drink?"

"Yes, please."

"Right you are. And while I'm at the bar, think about this. Is there any indication at all, from what little we know already, that our man might cross the same borders as Floyd and Byrne did?"

II

The area around the lock splintered easily when Mick pushed on the crowbar, and the two of them broke into the dark, silent house in no time. The light from their small torches criss-crossed the kitchen, picking out the gleaming appliances: fridge, washing machine,

microwave, dishwasher, oven. Quickly, they moved on; only the poor
kept their money in jam jars in the kitchen.

Down a short hallway was the split-level living-room, and Mick
cursed as he tripped over the divide. It was a big room, sparsely furnished as far as they could make out. Their torches picked out a
three-piece suite, TV and video on a stand, and a music centre. By the
door stood a tall cabinet full of china and crystal glasses. Mick
opened the lower doors and found it full of booze—scotch, gin,
vodka, brandy, rum, everything under the sun—and he grabbed a
bottle of Rémy Martin by the neck. He slugged it back greedily and
began to cough and splutter. Trevor told him to keep quiet.

Trevor was awed just to be in the place. Already he'd forgotten
what they came for and was trembling with the excitement of violation. This was someone's home, someone's "castle," and he wasn't
supposed to be in it. It felt like a vast cave full of possibilities, one of
those boat rides through dark tunnels he used to take as a child at
Blackpool Pleasure Beach—a ghost train, even, because he did feel
fear, and each tiny detail his light picked out was a surprise: a wall-
lamp curving upwards like a bent arm holding a torch; an ornate standard lamp with carved snakes winding around its column; an antique
pipe on the mantelpiece. And his light caught occasional images from
the big framed paintings on the walls: a giant bird terrorizing a man;
some naked tart standing on a seashell. He could hear his heartbeat,
his breathing, and every movement he made was a further violation
of somebody else's silence.

Mick finished with the cognac and dropped the bottle on the
floor. Wiping his lips with the back of his hand, he tapped Trevor on
the shoulder and suggested that they look around upstairs. In the
master bedroom, their eyes, now accustomed to the dark, picked out
the outlines of bed, wardrobe and dresser. The gleam of a streetlamp
through the net curtains helped visibility, too, and they turned off
their pen-lights.

Trevor began searching through the drawers, using his light again
to illuminate the contents. He found dark, silky underwear: bras,
panties, tights, slips, camisoles. They were soft and slippery in his
hands, charging him with static, and he rubbed them against his face,
smelling the fresh, lemony scent of the woman. He also found an old

cigar box in a drawer full of the man's socks, string vests and under-pants; inside it were a set of keys and about a hundred and fifty pounds in cash.

Mick found what looked like a jewellery box on the dresser. When he opened it up, a ballet dancer began spinning to tinkling music. He dropped the box and spilled the jewels on the floor; then, cursing, he bent and scooped them up.

Trevor looked around for any locked cabinets that the keys might fit, but he found nothing. The two of them went back downstairs, feet sinking luxuriously into the deep pile carpeting, and, shining their torches again, had another look around the living-room. There, in a corner, set into the wall, was what looked like a safe. Trevor tried his keys but none fit. Mick tried the crowbar but it bent. Eventually, they gave up.

"Let's take the VCR," Mick whispered.

"No. It's too heavy, too easy to trace."

"Lenny'll get rid of it in London."

"No, Mick. We're not taking big stuff like that. It'll slow us down. You've got the jewels and I've got a hundred quid. It's enough."

"Enough!" Mick snorted. "These people are fucking rolling in it. We've not got much more than we get from the old bags."

"Yes, we have. And people are more careful these days—we're bloody lucky to have got so much."

Reluctantly Mick gave up the idea and agreed to leave. Trevor was still enjoying just being there, though, still tingling, and he wanted to do something. Finally, he unzipped his fly and started to urinate over the TV, VCR and music centre, spraying lavishly on the carpet, paint-ings and mantelpiece, too. It seemed to go on forever, a powerful, translucent stream glittering in the pen-light's beam, and with it, he felt himself relax, felt a delicious warmth infuse his bones.

Not to be outdone, Mick lowered his pants and dropped a steam-ing pile on the sheepskin rug in front of the fireplace, giggling softly to himself as he did it.

When they'd both finished, they left the way they came, pausing only briefly to check the kitchen drawers and cupboards, just in case.

III

"There's no evidence that we've got a Byrne or a Floyd on our hands," Jenny said, sipping her half of bitter. "I think that if we had, something would have happened before now. The trouble with psychology is that it works best when you know all the facts. It's hard to make guesses in the dark. It's also unscientific."

"Police work's the same," Banks added. "There's nothing like facts, but I've always found that occasional guesses, or some kind of hunch based on limited knowledge, can often work well. It gives you a bit of room for the intuition, imagination."

"That's surprising, coming from you," Jenny said, looking at him as if all her earlier theories had been wrong.

"Why?"

"It just is. I suppose I've been used to you asking for facts, looking for evidence."

"It's important, I'm not denying it. But more often than not forensic evidence is only useful in getting a conviction. First you have to catch the criminal, and he's as cunning and imaginative as can be. Some aren't, of course, some are plain stupid. But they're the easy ones."

"I should think your peeper is probably quite intelligent. Again, this is mostly guesswork, but he has avoided capture so far, and he's got his system worked out quite well. It remains to be seen how adaptable he is. He's certainly not a fool."

"Back to my original question," Banks said. "You don't think he'll escalate?"

"I said I didn't think we had a serious sex criminal on our hands. I don't think he's likely to move on to necrophilia or eating breasts, with or without sugar, but I wouldn't be too sure that merely peeping will keep him happy for much longer. It might be getting too easy for him, especially if he's intelligent. If he stops getting his thrills that way...then..." She shrugged. "At best he might turn to exhibitionism, at worst some kind of attack, molestation."

"Rape?"

"Ultimately. Although it might not be rape in the legal sense.

There may be no penetration; he might simply force women to strip. I don't know, I'm just trying to project the pattern. He might feel the need for greater danger, more risk; he might need to see and absorb the fear of his victims. Yes, it could happen. Especially the closer he gets to his original impulse."

"What do you mean?"

"If he finds someone who reminds him of his mother, or whoever he was first struck by, then the stimulus might be too much; it might cause him to push through to another level."

"What can we do with what we've got so far, then?" Banks asked.

"You want me to tell you your job?"

"Why not? You've not done so badly at it so far."

"All right. What I'd do is this: find out how many men between the ages of about twenty and thirty-five are either living alone or with a single parent, most likely a mother."

"Why?"

"It's just what the statistics show. Not completely reliable of course, but better than a slap in the face with a wet fish, wouldn't you say?"

"I would. I was just wondering about the single-parent business."

"I think there's generally more stability with both parents around, unless the marriage is in a really bad way. It's what the stats show, anyway. Shall I go on?"

"Yes."

"There shouldn't be all that many in Eastvale, I don't think. Most people move away or get married. Next I'd 'stake out' selected pubs, as they say on the telly."

"I've told you how many pubs there are in Eastvale. We don't have anything like the manpower."

"Use what you have. He's tried the same pub twice. Why not a third time? There's one you can cover. And you must have some pretty policewomen around who'd be happy to work overtime to help get rid of this particular criminal, surely?"

Banks nodded. "Go on."

"As far as the other two pubs are concerned, you can cover them, too. If he struck lucky once he might try for a second time."

"So you suggest that we cover the pubs he's already operated in?"

"Yes."

"Good. We're already doing that."

"Bastard!" Jenny laughed and slapped his arm playfully. "You've got to admit, though, I was on the right track, wasn't I?"

"Definitely. Any time you need a job. Is there anything else?"

"You might check around the pornographic bookshops—if there are any in Eastvale—and the strip-clubs. I don't mean that you should pester everyone who enjoys seeing a bit of tit and ass now and then, but make your presence felt. Maybe if you put the wind up him he'll make a mistake."

"You think he's likely to hang around such places?"

"It's possible. After all, it's looking, isn't it? Even if it's not as thrilling as the other kind. By the way, are there places like that in Eastvale?"

"One or two. We keep an eye on them, but I'll do as you recommend, push a bit harder."

Jenny nodded. "Excuse me for asking," she said, "but how did you get that scar?" And she leaned forward and touched the small scar by Banks's right eye.

"Accident," he said tersely. "Years ago."

"How disappointing. And I thought you must have got it in some heroic struggle with a knife-wielding maniac, or perhaps from a gun that went off as you grappled to save someone's life."

"You've got quite a romantic imagination for a psychologist."

"And you've got none! Come on, where did you get it?"

"I told you, an accident."

"What kind of accident?"

"I fell off my tricycle."

"Liar. You're only doing this because you think it makes you mysterious, aren't you?"

"And you're only teasing me because you've had too much to drink."

"Ooh, I haven't."

Banks laughed. "Perhaps not. But if you drink any more you will have, and then I'll have to book you for drunken driving."

"I haven't got my car. I walked up to town before we met and spent an hour or so in the library."

"I've got mine today—and I haven't had too much to drink. Come on, I'll give you a lift."

It was raining fast again, and Banks drove carefully around the base of Castle Hill, down the narrow, winding streets, crossed the river, and pulled up outside Jenny's house by The Green about five minutes later.

"Coming in for a coffee?" she asked.

"Just a quick one."

IV

Trevor and Mick sat in the front room sharing out the money. Trevor had already palmed about fifty pounds, and he then managed to persuade Mick to tell Lenny that they'd only found fifty. He knew that Lenny would make up his profit by selling the jewellery, anyway.

Mick was restless. He'd taken some uppers before going out and some downers when they got back, just to take the edge off. Now the drugs were clashing and fighting it out in his body. He couldn't settle and listen to music or watch telly, and Trevor, bored with him, was getting ready to go. They looked out of the window at the rain. Across The Green, they saw a car pull up outside one of the old houses.

"It's that bird," Mick said. "The redhead with the long legs. Ooh, I'd like to feel them wrapped around my waist. Who's she with? Some fucking wanker for sure."

"I think it's that copper," Trevor said, recognizing Banks. "Funny, that, I saw him with her the other night at the old bag's house."

"Maybe she's a cop, then. Waste of a good screw, if you ask me. Nice pair of tits she's got, though."

"Maybe he's just knocking her off," Trevor said. "He's going in, anyway."

"Lucky bastard."

"It's funny, though, seeing them twice like that."

"What's so funny? I see her all the time. She only lives across The Green, you know."

"I mean seeing them together like that."

"He's probably poking her. Fucking hell, wouldn't I just like those long legs wrapped around my waist."

But Mick was fast slipping into the arms of Morpheus. The amphetamine, already mostly burned up, was losing to the barbiturate, and he felt as if his brain was slowly turning to cotton-wool and his senses were closing like valves. The light around the edges of his eyes dimmed, and he could hear a gentle whooshing, like the ocean, in his ears; his tongue felt too tired and too heavy to speak.

Trevor recognized the signs, put on his coat and left. It had been a good night, one of the best in years, and he felt, as he walked home through the quiet town reliving the excitement, that he could hardly wait for next Monday.

EIGHT

I

The sudden creaking of rusty hinges broke the silence in the cool church. Sandra and Harriet looked around and saw Robin Allott coming in, followed closely by Norman Chester.

"So this is where you're hiding," Norman said, as he shut the heavy door behind them. "We were wondering where the lovely ladies had got to." His voice echoed from the stone walls.

"What are you doing?" Robin asked.

"Waiting for the sun," Sandra replied. "I want to get a good shot of the stained-glass window here."

"It shouldn't be long," Robin said, walking down the aisle towards them. "The clouds seem to be breaking up and the wind's pushing them along nicely. It is quite beautiful, isn't it?"

Sandra nodded, glancing up again at the east window. They stood in the Parish Church of St Mary, Muker, one of the places the Camera Club was visiting on its trip to Swaledale. Most club members were out walking along Ivelet Side putting Terry Whigham's ideas on landscape photography into practice with shots of the spectacular view of Oxnop, Muker Side and the dark mass of Great Shunner Fell. Harriet and Sandra, however, had stuck to the village itself, photographing the craft centre, village store and old Literary Institute, before approaching St Mary's.

"It's supposed to depict the landscape outside," Robin went on, pointing to the window. "You can see Christ the Good Shepherd there, leading his flock and carrying a lamb—real horned Swaledale sheep. The hill is Kisdon, that big one out there, and you can see the River Swale to the right and Muker Beck to the left."

"You seem to know a bit about it," Sandra said. "Have you been here before?"

"Once or twice."

Norman's footsteps echoed as he wandered around examining the font and chalice.

"It is a wonderful church, though," Robin said. "And the cemetery's interesting, too. It's the kind of place I wouldn't mind being buried in."

"How morbid."

"Not at all. They used to have to carry people in wicker coffins ten or fifteen miles away to Grinton church before this place was built. They took the old Corpse Way along Ivelet Side. People wanted to be buried on consecrated ground. I'd hope for a long and healthy life first, though, like poor Alice Matlock."

"Alice Matlock?"

"Yes. The old lady they found dead in her cottage the other day. Surely your husband must have mentioned her?"

"Yes, of course," Sandra said. "I was just surprised to hear you talk about her, that's all."

Robin looked up at the dim stained glass. "I knew her, that's all. I was a bit shaken to hear that someone who'd lived through so much should have died so violently. Does your husband have any clues?"

"None that he's told me about. How did you come to know her?"

"I suppose I'm exaggerating a bit. I haven't seen her for a few years. You know how it is; we lose touch with the old so easily. She was a friend of my grandmother's, my father's mother. They were about the same age and both of them worked as nurses at Eastvale Infirmary for years. My gran used to take me over to visit Alice when I was a kid."

"Haven't you thought that you might be able to help?" Sandra asked.

"Me?" said Robin, startled. "How? I said I hadn't seen her for years."

"Alan says it's frustrating not to know much about her background. Most of her friends are dead. Anything you could tell him might be a help."

"I don't see how."

"When you've lived with a policeman for as long as I have," Sandra said, "you don't ask how. Would you be willing to see him?"

"I don't know...I...I can't see how it could help."

"Come on. Alan won't eat you. You said you were upset about her death. Surely it's not too much to ask?"

"No, no, I don't suppose it is. If you think it'll help, of course..."

"It might."

"Very well."

"Good. I'll tell him, then. If I see him. He's not home much these days. Still, we are supposed to be going out tonight, if he hasn't forgotten. When's a good time? I'm sure he won't want to inconvenience you."

"I don't know. This weekend sometime? I should be home."

"Fine." Sandra took Robin's address and turned her attention back to the stained-glass window. "Come on, come on," she urged the sun.

They stood there a full minute or more until, slowly, the glass brightened and the red of Christ's robe, the blue of the rivers at his feet and the purple, orange and green of the hills behind began to glow. Sandra selected a wide aperture and let the built-in exposure-meter set the shutter speed.

"It's strange," Robin said, watching, "but it sometimes seems to me as if we're looking outside through a clear window at some idealized image."

"Yes, it does," Harriet agreed. "Like a vision. Ooh, look how the colours are shining on us!"

"Vision indeed," Norman sneered, walking over from the north-west window. "A right lot of romantics, you are." And he joined them as they took it in turns to capture the stained glass on film.

II

Friday brought a lull in affairs at the Eastvale station. Nothing had come of the previous evening's pub surveillance, and Richmond said that he'd shown the artist's impression of their one suspect in the robberies to some of the lads on the beat, but nobody had recognized him. After sending the detective constable to the Town Hall to check on the statistics of young men living alone or with single parents, Banks found himself with little to do. No Dorothy Wycombe marched in to liven up the day; no Jenny Fuller; nothing.

He had plenty of time to think, though, and spent the rest of the morning puzzling over the three cases, whose outlines had become blurred in his mind. There was a Peeping Tom in Eastvale, that was clear enough. Also, two young thugs had robbed defenceless old women. But had any of them killed Alice Matlock?

On the evidence so far, it looked like it: she had been old and alone, her home had been left in a shambles, and money and silverware had been stolen. It was certainly possible that she had tried to struggle with them and had fallen or been pushed backwards, catching the back of her head on the sharp corner of the table.

There was still room for doubt, though, and Banks found himself wondering if it could have happened some other way for some other reason. He had ruled out the peeper after what Jenny had said, so the next step was to try and discover if anyone had a motive for getting rid of Alice Matlock, or at least for engaging in such a violent confrontation with her.

According to Sergeant Hatchley, Ethel Carstairs had said that Alice had kept herself to herself over the past few years, and that she had not been the type to take in strays or befriend strangers. If the two young tearaways were not responsible for her death, then who was, and why?

Unfortunately, the slow afternoon allowed Banks more time than he would have liked to reflect on the events of the previous evening. Sandra had been asleep when he got home, so he was spared a telling off, but she had been very frosty in the morning, reminding him that they had arranged to go out that evening with Harriet Slade and her husband, who had already booked a sitter, and that he'd promised to take the kids up to Castle Hill on Saturday morning. It was her way of hinting that he wasn't spending enough time with his nearest and dearest, whatever else he might be up to.

Though he certainly felt pangs of guilt, he hadn't really been up to anything much at all.

His first move, after Jenny had led him into her front room, had been to remark on the expensive stereo system and the lack of a television.

"I used to have one," she said, heading for the kitchen, "but I gave it to a colleague. Without it I get much more done—reading, listening to music, going out, seeing films. When I had it I was terribly lazy; I always take the line of least resistance."

"It doesn't look much like a professor's living-room," Banks shouted through. There were only a couple of recent psychology journals and a folder of notes on the table.

"The study's upstairs," she yelled back. "I *do* work hard, honestly, Inspector. Milk and sugar?"

"No, thanks."

Banks squinted at the framed print on the wall. It showed an enormous dark mountain, more steep than broad, completely dominating a small village in the foreground.

"Who did this?" he asked Jenny when she came into the room carrying two mugs of coffee.

"That? It's an Emily Carr."

"I've never heard of her," said Banks, who had gained a basic knowledge of art through Sandra.

"That's not surprising; she's a Canadian. I spent three years doing postgraduate work in Vancouver. She's a West Coast artist, did a lot of totem poles and forest scenes. Oddly enough, I saw that painting in a gallery at Kleinburg, near Toronto. I fell in love with it right away. Everything looks alive, don't you think?"

"Yes, in a dark, creepy kind of way. But I'm not sure it would pass my simple test for paintings."

"Don't tell me!" she said, imitating a Yorkshire accent. "'Ah don't know much about art bu'rah knows whar'ah likes.' Not bad for a Leicester girl, eh?"

Banks laughed. "Better than I could do. Anyway, that's not my test. I just ask myself if I could live with it on my living-room wall."

"And you couldn't?"

"No. Not that."

"What could you live with? It sounds like a very hard test."

Banks thought back over some of the paintings Sandra had introduced him to. "Modigliani's *Reclining Nude*, maybe Chagall's *I and the Village*. Monet's *Waterlilies*."

"Good lord, you'd need an entire room for that one."

"Yes, but it would be worth it."

With the coffees, Jenny also poured out generous measures of cognac, giving Banks no time to refuse, then she put some music on the cassette deck and sat down beside him.

"This is good music," he said. "What is it?"

"Bruch's violin concerto."

"Mmm, I've never heard it before. Are you a classical music buff?"

"Oh, no. I mean, I enjoy classical, but I like a bit of everything, really. I like jazz—Miles Davis and Monk. I still love some of the old sixties stuff—Beatles, Dylan, Stones—but my old copies are a bit scratched up by now."

"For a psychology teacher you seem to know a lot about the arts."

"English was my second subject, and my father was a bit of an amateur artist. Even now I seem to spend more time with the arts faculty than the sciences. Most psychologists are so boring."

"Do you like opera?"

"That's one thing I don't know very well. My sister took me to an Opera North performance of *La Traviata* once, years ago, but I'm afraid I don't remember much about it."

"Try some. I'll lend you a couple of tapes. *Tosca*, that's a good one."

"What's it about?"

"An evil chief of police who tries to coerce a singer into sleeping with him by threatening to have her lover killed."

"That sounds cheerful," Jenny said; then she shivered. "Someone just walked over my grave."

"The music's good. Some fine arias."

"All right. Here's to opera," said Jenny, smiling and clinking glasses. "Do you think we did a good evening's work?"

"Yes, I think so. We didn't expect miracles. That's not why we brought you in."

"Charming! I know why you brought me in."

"I mean why we brought a psychologist in."

"Yes. I know that, too."

"Why?"

"You were all afraid that this was going to spiral into a rash of rapes and sex-murders, and you wanted to check on the evidence."

"Partly true. And given that, we also wanted to make damn sure we had a better chance of stopping him before he went too far."

"Are you any closer?"

"That remains to be seen."

As they sat in silence, Banks could feel his heart beating faster and his throat constricting. He knew he shouldn't be there, knew there could only be one interpretation of his accepting the offer of coffee, and he was nervous about what to do. The music flowed around them and the tension grew so strong it made the muscles in his jaw ache. Jenny stirred and her scent wafted towards him. It was too subtle to be called a perfume; it was the kind of fresh and happy smell that took him back to carefree childhood trips to the country.

"Look," Banks finally blurted out, putting down his coffee and facing Jenny, "I'm sorry if I've given you the impression that . . . the wrong impression . . . but I'm married." Then, having confessed in what he felt to be as graceless a manner as possible, he started to apologize and rephrase, but Jenny cut in.

"I know that, you fool. You think a psychologist can't spot a married man a mile off?"

"You know? Then . . ."

Jenny shrugged. "I'm not trying to seduce you, if that's what you mean. Yes, I like you, I'm attracted to you. I get the impression that you feel the same way. Dammit, then, maybe I am trying to seduce you. I don't know." She reached out and touched his face. "No strings, Alan. Why must you always be so serious?"

Immediately, he felt himself freeze, and it shocked her so much that she jumped away and turned her face to the wall.

"All right," she said, "I've made an idiot of myself. Now go. Go on, go!"

"Listen, Jenny," Banks said. "You're not wrong about anything. I'm sorry, I shouldn't have come."

"Why did you, then?" Jenny asked, softening a little but still not facing him.

Banks shrugged and lit a cigarette. "If I went to bed with you once," he said, "I wouldn't want it to stop there."

"You don't know till you try it," she said, turning and managing a thin smile.

"Yes, I do."

"I might be lousy in bed."

"That's not the point."

"I knew you wouldn't do it, anyway."

"You did?"

"I'm a psychologist, remember? I've spent enough time with you to know you're not frivolous and that you're probably a very monogamous person."

"Am I so transparent?"

"Not at all. I'm an expert. Maybe you were testing yourself, taking a risk."

"Well, they do say there's no better test of virtue than temptation."

"And how do you feel now?"

"Intolerably virtuous."

Jenny laughed and kissed him swiftly on the lips. It was a friendly sort of kiss, and instead of increasing Banks's desire it seemed to diffuse it and put things back on a simpler, more relaxed level.

"Don't go just yet," Jenny said. "If you do I'll think it's because of all this and it'll keep me awake all night."

"All right. But only if I get another black coffee—and no more cognac."

"Coming up, sir."

"By the way," Banks asked as Jenny headed for the kitchen, "what about you? Divorced, single?"

"Single." Jenny leaned against the doorpost. "Marriage never happened to me."

"Not even almost?"

"Oh, yes, almost. But you can't be almost married, can you? That would be like being a little bit pregnant." And she turned to go and make the coffee, leaving a smile behind her which faded slowly like the Cheshire cat's.

Banks snapped out of his reverie feeling half-remorseful for having gone so far and half-regretful that he hadn't seized the moment and abandoned himself to Eros. He put on his headphones, rewound *Dido and Aeneas* to the lament, "When I am laid in earth," and left the building. Abandoned by her lover, Queen Dido sang "Remember me, remember me..." It sent shivers up and down Banks's spine.

III

The evening out with Harriet and David went well. They drove along the Dale on the road by the River Swain, which was coursing high and fast after the recent rains. Beyond the sloping commons, dark valley sides rose steeply on both sides like sleeping whales. At Fortford, David took an unfenced minor road over the hills and down into the village of Axeby. The Greyhound, an old low-ceilinged pub with walls three feet thick, held a folk night there every Friday that was so well respected it even drew people from as far afield as Leeds, Bradford and Manchester.

They were early enough to find a table for four near the back, which provided a relatively unobstructed view of the small stage. David brought the first round and they drank to a good evening. Though Banks thought David, an assistant bank manager, a bit of a bore, he made an effort to like him for Sandra's sake, and the two of them got on well enough. But Banks still found himself wondering what such a lively and interesting woman as Harriet saw in her husband.

The music was good; there were none of the modern, whining protest songs that got up Banks's nose. You could usually depend on The Greyhound for solid, traditional folk music—"Sir Patrick Spens," "The Wife of Usher's Well," "Marie Hamilton," "The Unquiet Grave" and the like—and that night there was nothing to spoil Banks's joy in the old ballads, which he loved almost as much as opera. The "high" and "low" or "culture" and "folk" distinctions didn't concern him at all—it was the sense of a story, of drama and tension in the music, that enthralled him.

Because it was David's turn to drive that night, Banks was allowed more than his usual two pints, and as the beer at The Greyhound— brewed on the premises—was famous for its quality, he indulged himself freely. He could take his drink, though, for a small man, and the only signs that he'd had one or two too many were that he smoked and talked more than usual. Sandra stuck to gin and tonic, and drank slowly.

The day, which had been heavy with disturbing feelings for Banks, seemed to be ending well. This evening out with Sandra and the Slades, good music and good beer, was driving Jenny from his mind. Looking back from a distance of four or five pints, what he had done didn't seem so bad. Many men would have done much worse. True, he had sounded terribly moral and sanctimonious—but how else can you sound, he asked himself, if you have to say no to a beautiful, intelligent woman?

As he reached for a cigarette, Sandra glanced over from her conversation and they smiled at each other.

IV

It was a good position on the sloping roof because, lying down, he seemed to melt into the slates, but it was very uncomfortable and he was getting tired of waiting.

He'd done his reconnaissance well enough—not hanging around the front, especially as the street was a cul-de-sac, but just passing by occasionally, watching from the unlit alley at the back, nothing more than a narrow dirt track between fenced back gardens. Ideal. He'd slipped through the fence, climbed the pipe up the side of the wall—it was an addition to the house, a kind of storeroom or workshop attached to the back—and found himself just on a level with the bedroom window. He knew it was the right one because he'd seen the children's wallpaper in the front rooms as he'd passed by one day. He also knew that she tended to go to bed first. The husband would often stay up in the front room and listen to music or read for a while.

What was keeping her? They'd been home half an hour and still no sign. Finally the bedroom light came on and he took his position by the chink at the bottom of the curtains. The woman tied back her straight blonde hair and reached behind her back for her zipper. Slowly, she pulled it down and slipped the black, silky dress from her pale shoulders, letting it fall all the way to the carpet, then picked it up and hung it carefully in the wardrobe.

There she stood, the dark V of cleavage clear at the front of her bra, the inviting curve in at the waist and out again, softly, at the hips.

Her figure was slight; there was nothing out of proportion, nothing in excess. It was what he had been waiting for, what had first stirred his feelings and had eluded him ever since. He felt himself getting more and more excited as she sat at the dressing table and removed her makeup before undressing any more. He could see her reflection, her concentration as she applied the tufts of cotton wool. It was just like he remembered. Almost unconsciously he rubbed himself as he watched, not wanting her to finish, willing it to go on for ever.

Finally she stood up again and pulled her nightdress out from under the pillow. Facing him, she unclipped her bra and he watched her small breasts fall slightly as it loosened. He was rubbing himself all the time, faster and faster, and then it happened. What he'd been waiting for. She saw him.

It all happened in slow motion. One moment she was taking off the bra, the next a look of shock spread across her face slowly, like spilled milk on a table, as she caught his eye. At the same moment he climaxed, and the spasms shook his body with pleasure. He slid off the roof, dropped to the garden and shot out through the fence before she could even open the curtains.

V

Sandra couldn't say exactly how or at what moment she knew she was being watched. It was sudden, a feeling of not being alone. And when she looked she saw an eye. It seemed disembodied, just hanging there in the gap in the curtains, but as she ran forward, yelling for Alan at the same time, she caught a glimpse of a figure in a dark raincoat slipping through the gap in the fence and making off down the back alley.

Banks came running up and then left Sandra to calm down the children, who had heard her cry out, while he gave chase. There was nobody in the alley, and it was too dark to see clearly anyway. First, Banks ran up to the main road end, but there was nobody in sight. Then he walked slowly and quietly in the other direction, wishing he'd had the foresight to bring a torch, but he saw nothing move in the shadows, and however still he stood, he couldn't hear breathing or rustling—nothing. All he managed to do was disturb a cat, which darted across his path and almost gave him a heart attack.

He walked as far down as the narrow gap at the far end that led to the park, but it was pitch black. There was no point in going any further. Whoever it was had melted back into the darkness, another victory. Banks cursed and kicked the rickety fence hard before storming back indoors.

NINE

I

On Saturday morning, as promised, Banks stood high on the castle battlements and looked out over his "patch," or "manor," as he would have called it in London. It was a sharp, fresh day and all the clouds had gone. The sky was not the deep, warm cerulean of summer, but a lighter, more piercing blue, as if the cold of the coming winter had already wormed its way into the air.

Banks looked down over the cobbled market square. The ancient cross and square-towered church were almost lost among the makeshift wooden stalls and the riot of colour that blossomed every market day. The bus station to the east was full of red single-decker buses, and in the adjacent car park, green and white coaches dwarfed the cars. Small parties of tourists ambled around, bright yellow and orange anoraks zipped up against the surprising nip in the air. Banks wore his donkey-jacket buttoned right up to the collar and the children wore kagoules over their woollen sweaters.

To Tracy, Eastvale Castle represented a living slice of history, an Elizabethan palace where, it was rumoured, Mary Queen of Scots had been imprisoned for a while and a Richard or a Henry had briefly held court. Ladies-in-waiting whispered royal secrets to one another in echoing galleries, while barons and earls danced galliards and pavanes with their elegant wives at banquets.

To Brian, the place evoked a more barbarous era of history; it was a stronghold from which ancient Britons poured down boiling oil on Roman invaders, a citadel riddled with dank dungeons where thumb-screws, rack and Iron Maiden awaited unfortunate prisoners.

Neither was entirely correct. The castle was, in fact, built by the Normans at about the same time as Richmond, and, like its more famous contemporary, it was built of stone and had an unusually massive keep.

While the children explored the ruins, Banks looked over the roofs below, chequer-board patterns of red pantile, stone and Welsh slate, and let his eyes follow the contours of the hills where they rose to peaks and fells in the west and flattened into a gently undulating plain to the east. In all directions the trees were tinged with autumn's rust, just like the picture on his calendar.

Banks could make out the town's limits: beyond the river, the East Side Estate, with its two ugly tower blocks, sprawled until it petered out into fields, and in the west, Gallows View pointed its dark, shrivelled finger towards Swainsdale. To the north, the town seemed to spread out between the fork of two diverging roads—one leading to the northern Dales and the Lakes, the other to Tyneside and the east coast. Beyond these older residential areas, there were only a few scattered farmhouses and outlying hamlets.

Though he saw the view, Banks could hardly take it in, still troubled as he was by the events of the previous evening. He hadn't reported the incident, and that nagged at his sense of integrity. On the other hand, as he and Sandra had decided, it would probably have been a lot more embarrassing and galling all round to have reported it. It was easy to imagine the headlines, the sniggers. And even as he worried about his own decision, Banks also wondered how many others had not seen fit to tell the police of similar incidents. If women were still reluctant to report rape, for example, would many of them not also balk at reporting a Peeping Tom?

For Banks, though, the problem was even more involved. He was a policeman; therefore, he was expected to set an example, to follow the letter of the law himself. In the past, he may have occasionally driven at a little over the speed limit or, worse, had perhaps one drink too many before driving home from a Christmas party, but he had never been faced with such a conflict between professional and family duty before. Sandra and he had decided, though, over a long talk in bed, and that decision was final. They had also told the children, who had heard Sandra's scream, that she had thought someone was trying to break in but had been mistaken.

What bothered Banks was that if there was no investigation, then valuable clues or information might be sacrificed. To put that right as far as possible, Sandra had offered to talk to the neighbours discreetly, to ask if anyone had noticed any strangers hanging around. It wasn't much, but it was better than nothing.

So that was that. Banks shrugged and watched a red bus try to extricate itself from an awkward parking spot off the square. The gold hands against the blue face of the church clock said eleven-thirty. He had promised that they would be home for lunch by twelve.

Rounding up Brian and Tracy, who had fallen to arguing about the history of the castle, Banks ushered them towards the exit.

"Of course it's an ancient castle," Brian argued. "They've got dungeons with chains on the walls, and it's all falling to pieces."

Tracy, despite her anachronistic image of the period, knew quite well that the castle was built in the early part of the twelfth century, and she said so in no uncertain terms.

"Don't be silly," Brian shot back. "Look at what a state it's in. It must have taken thousands of years to get so bad."

"For one thing," Tracy countered with a long-suffering sigh, "it's built of stone. They didn't build things out of stone as long ago as that. Besides, it's in the history book. Ask the teacher, dummy, you'll see if I'm not right."

Brian retreated defensively into fantasy: he was a brave knight and Tracy was a damsel in distress, letting down her hair from a high, narrow window. He gave it a long, hard pull and swaggered off to fight a dragon.

They wound their way down to the market square, which, though it had seemed to move as slowly and silently as in a dream from high up, buzzed with noisy activity at close quarters.

The vendors sold everything from toys, cassette tapes and torch batteries to lace curtains, paintbrushes and used paperbacks, but mostly they sold clothes—jeans, jackets, shirts, lingerie, socks, shoes. A regular, whom Banks had christened Flash Harry because of his pencil-thin moustache, flat cap and spiv-like air, juggled with china plates and cups as he extolled the virtues of his wares. Tourists and locals clustered around the draughty stalls handling goods and hag-

gling with the red-faced holders, who sipped hot Oxo and wore fin-
gerless woollen gloves to keep their hands warm without inhibiting
the counting of money.

After a quick look at some children's shoes—as cheap in quality
as they were in price—Banks led Brian and Tracy south along
Market Street under the overhanging second-floor bay windows.
About a quarter of a mile further on, beyond where the narrow
street widened, was the cul-de-sac where they lived. It was five to
twelve.

"Superintendent Gristhorpe called," Sandra said as soon as they
got in. "About fifteen minutes ago. You're to get over to number 17
Clarence Gardens as soon as you can. He didn't say what it was
about."

"Bloody hell," Banks grumbled, buttoning up his donkey-jacket
again. "Can you keep lunch warm?"

Sandra nodded.

"Can't say how long I'll be."

"It doesn't matter," she said, and smiled as he kissed her. "It's only
a casserole. Oh, I almost forgot, he invited us to Sunday dinner
tomorrow as well."

"That's some consolation, I suppose," Banks said as he walked out
to the garage.

II

"It's a bloody disgrace, that's what it is," Maurice Ottershaw
announced, hands on hips. Banks wasn't sure whether he meant the
burglary itself or the fact that the police hadn't managed to prevent
it. Ottershaw was a difficult character. A tall, grey-haired man, deeply
tanned from his recent holiday, he seemed to think that all the public services were there simply for his benefit, and he consequently
treated their representatives like personal valets, stopping just short
of telling Banks to go and make some tea.

"It's not unusual," Banks offered, by way of meagre compensation
for the mess on the walls, carpet and appliances. "A lot of burglars
desecrate the places they rob."

"I don't bloody care about that," Ottershaw went on, the redness of his anger imposing itself even on his tan. "I want these bloody vandals caught."

"We're doing our best," Banks told him patiently. "Unfortunately, we don't have a lot to go on."

Richmond and Hatchley had already talked to the neighbours, who had either been out or had heard nothing. Manson had been unable to find any fingerprints except for those of the owners and their cleaning lady, who had been in just the other day to give the place a thorough going-over. There was no way of telling exactly on what day the robbery had taken place, although it must have happened between Tuesday, the day of the cleaner's visit, and the Ottershaws' return early that Saturday morning.

"Can you give me a list of what's missing?"

"One hundred and fifty-two pounds seventy-five pence in cash, for a start," Ottershaw said.

"Why did you leave so much cash lying around the place?"

"It wasn't lying around, it was in a box in a drawer. It was just petty cash for paying tradesmen and such. I don't often have cash on me, use the card most of the time."

"I see you're an art lover," Banks said, looking towards the large framed prints of Bosch's *Garden of Earthly Delights* and Botticelli's *The Birth of Venus* hanging on the walls. Banks wasn't sure whether he could live with either of them.

Ottershaw nodded. "Just prints, of course. Good ones, mind you. I have invested in one or two original works." He pointed to a rough white canvas with yellow and black lines scratched across it like railway tracks converging and diverging. "London artist. Doing very well for herself, these days. Not when I bought it, though. Got it for a song. Poor girl must have been starving."

"Any pictures missing?"

Ottershaw shook his head.

"Antiques?" Banks gestured towards the standard lamp, crystalware and bone china.

"No, it's still all there and in one piece, thank the Lord."

"Anything else?"

"Some jewellery. Imitation, but still worth about five hundred pounds. My wife can give you descriptions of individual pieces. And there's all this of course. My wife won't watch this TV again, nor will she touch the hi-fi. It'll all have to be replaced. They've even spilled the Rémy."

This last remark seemed a bit melodramatic to Banks, but he let it slip by. "Where is your wife, sir?" he asked.

"Lying down. She's a very highly strung woman, and this, on top of being stuck at the bloody airport for a whole night . . . it was just too much for her."

"You were supposed to be home yesterday?"

"Yes. I told you, didn't I? Bloody airport wallahs went on strike."

"Did anyone know you were away?"

"Neighbours, a couple of friends at work and the club."

"What club would that be, sir?"

"Eastvale Golf Club," Ottershaw announced, puffing out his chest. "As you probably know, it's an exclusive kind of place, so it's very unlikely that any criminal elements would gain access."

"We have to keep all possibilities open," Banks said, managing to avoid Ottershaw's scornful glare by scribbling nonsense in his notebook. There was no point in getting involved in a staring match with a victim, he thought.

"Anyone else?"

"Not that I know of."

"Would your wife be likely to have told anyone?"

"I've covered everyone we know."

"Where do you work, sir?"

"Ottershaw, Kilney and Glenbaum."

Banks had seen the sign often enough. The solicitors' offices were on Market Street, just a little further south than the police station.

"Who's going to clear all this up?" Ottershaw demanded roughly, gesturing around the disaster area of his living-room.

The faeces lay curled on the rug, staining the white fibres around and underneath it. The TV, video and stereo looked as if they'd been sprayed with a hose, but it was quite obvious what had actually happened. Amateurs, Banks thought to himself. Kids, probably, out on a lark. Maybe the same kids who'd done the old ladies' houses, graduating to the big time. But somebody had told them where to come, that the Ottershaws were away, and if he could find out who, then the rest would follow.

"I really don't know," Banks said. Maybe forensic would take it away with them. Perhaps, with a bit of luck, they'd be able to reconstruct the whole person from the faeces: height, weight, colouring, eating habits, health, complexion. Some hope.

"That's fine, that is," Ottershaw complained. "We go away for a ten-day holiday, and if it's not enough that the bloody wallahs choose to go on strike the day we leave, we come home to find the house covered in shit!" He said the last word very loudly, so much so that the lab men going over the room smiled at each other as Banks grimaced.

"We're not a cleaning service, you know, sir," he chided Ottershaw mildly, as if talking to a child. "If we were, then we'd never have time to find out who did this, would we?"

"Shock could kill the wife, you know," Ottershaw said, ignoring him. "Doctor said so. Weak heart. No sudden shocks to the system. She's a very squeamish woman—and that's her favourite rug, that sheepskin. She'll never be able to manage it."

"Then perhaps, sir, you'd better handle it yourself," Banks suggested, glancing towards the offending ordure before walking out and leaving the house to the experts.

III

The Oak turned out to be one of those huge Victorian monstrosities—usually called The Jubilee or The Victoria—curving around the corner where Cardigan Drive met Elmet Street about half a mile north of Gallows View. It was all glossy tiles and stained glass, and it reminded Banks very much of the Prince William in Peterborough, outside which he used to play marbles with the other local kids while they all waited for their parents.

Inside, generations of spilt beer and stale cigarette smoke gave the place a brownish glow and a sticky carpet, but the atmosphere in the spacious lounge was cheery and warm. The gaudy ceiling was high and the bar had clearly been moved from its original central position to make room for a small dance floor. It now stretched the whole length of one of the walls, and a staff—or what looked more like a squadron—of buxom barmaids flexed their muscles on the pumps and tried to keep smiling as they rushed around to keep up with the demand. The mirrors along the back, reflecting chandeliers, rows of exotic spirits bottles and the impatient customers, heightened the sense of good-natured chaos. Saturday night at The Oak was knees-up night, and a local comedian alternated with a pop group whose roots, both musical and sartorial, were firmly planted in the early sixties.

"What on earth made you bring me to a place like this?" Jenny Fuller asked, a puzzled smile on her face.

"Atmosphere," Banks answered, smiling at her. "It'll be an education."

"I'll bet. You said there's been a new development, something you wanted to tell me."

Banks took a deep breath and regretted it immediately; the air in The Oak wasn't of the highest quality, even by modern pollution standards. Fortunately, both the comedian and the pop group were between sets and the only noise was the laughter and chatter of the drinkers.

When Banks had phoned Jenny after he'd left the Ottershaws' house, he hadn't been sure why he wanted her to meet him at The Oak, or what he wanted to say to her. He had brought the *Tosca* cassettes that he had promised to lend her, but that wasn't excuse enough in itself. She had been obliging, but said she had to be off by nine as there was a small party honouring a visiting lecturer at the university. Banks also wanted to be home early, for Sandra's sake, so the arrangement suited him.

"Last night we had a visit from the peeper," he said finally. "At least Sandra did."

"My God!" Jenny gasped, wide-eyed and open-mouthed. "What happened?"

"Not much. She spotted him quite early on and he ran off down the back alley. I went out there but he'd already disappeared into the night."

"How is she?"

"She's fine, taking it all very philosophically. But she's a deep one, Sandra. She doesn't always let people know what her real feelings are—especially me. I should imagine she feels like the others—hurt, violated, dirty, angry."

Jenny nodded. "Most likely. Isn't it a bit awkward for you as far as your job's concerned?"

"That's something else I wanted to tell you. I haven't reported it."

Jenny stared at Banks far too long for his comfort. It was an intense, curious kind of look, and he finally gave in by going to the bar for two more drinks.

The crowd was about five deep with what looked like at least two local rugby teams, and Banks was smaller and slighter than most of the men who waved their glasses in the air and yelled over the heads of others—"Three pints of black and tan, Elsie, love, please!"... "Vodka and slimline, two pints of Stella, Cherry B, and a brandy and crème de menthe,"..."Five pints of Guinness...Kahlua and Coke, and a gin-and-it for the wife, love!" Everybody seemed to be placing such large orders.

Fortunately, Banks spotted Richmond, tall and distinctive, closer to the bar. He caught the constable's attention—the man was on duty, after all—and asked for one-and-a-half pints of bitter. Surprised but immediately compliant, Richmond added it to his own order. Rather than demand waiter service of his young constable, Banks waited till Richmond had got the drinks, paid him and made off.

"What are you thinking?" he asked, sitting next to Jenny again.

Jenny laughed. "It wasn't anything serious. Remember the other night?"

So the ice was broken; the subject wasn't taboo, after all. "Yes," he answered, waiting.

"I said I knew how you'd behave, even though I hoped it would be different?"

"Something like that."

"Well, I was just trying to work out where I'd have placed my bet. Reporting or not reporting. I think I'd have been wrong. It's not that I think you're a slave to duty or anything like that, but you like to do things right...you're honest. I'd guess that if you don't do things the way you know they should be done, you suffer for it. Conscience. Too much of it, probably."

"I never asked for it," Banks replied, lighting his second cigarette of the evening.

"You weren't born with it, either."

"No?"

"No. Conditioning."

"I didn't ask for that either."

"No, you didn't. None of us do. You've surprised me this time, though. I'd have guessed that you would report the incident no matter how much embarrassment it might cause."

Banks shook his head. "There would be too much unfavourable publicity all round. Not only for Sandra but for the department, too. That Wycombe woman would just love to get her hands on something like this. If it were made public and we solved the case quickly, according to her it would only be because a policeman's wife was among the victims. No, I'd rather keep it quiet."

"But what about interviews, questioning people?"

"Sandra and I will do that locally. We'll ask if anyone has seen any strangers hanging around."

Jenny looked at him quizzically. "I'm not judging you, you know. I'm not the authorities."

"I know," Banks said. "I needed to tell someone. I couldn't think of anyone else who'd..."

"Automatically be on your side?"

"I was going to say 'understand,' but I suppose you're right. I did count on your support."

"You have it, whether you need it or not. And your secret's safe with me."

"There is something a bit more technical I want to ask you, too," Banks went on. "This new incident, the fact that it was Sandra, *my* wife. Do you think that means anything?"

"If he knew who it was, and I think he probably did, then yes, I do think it's a development."

"Go on."

"It means that he's getting bolder, he needs to take greater risks to get his satisfaction. Unless he's some kind of hermit or human ostrich, he must have read about reactions to what he's been doing, probably with a kind of pride. Therefore, he must know that you've been heading an investigation into the case. He does a bit of research on you, finds you have an attractive blonde wife—"

"Or knows her already?" Banks cut in.

"What makes you think that? He could simply have watched the house discreetly, seen her come and go."

"It's just a feeling I've got."

"Yes, but what basis does it have? Where does it come from?"

Banks thought as deeply as he could, given that the pop group had started its set with a carbon copy of the ancient Searchers' hit, "Love Potion Number Nine."

"We were talking about the Camera Club Sandra belongs to," he answered slowly. "Sometimes they have nude models, and I said that most of the men probably don't even have films in their cameras. It was just a joke at the time, but could there be any connection?"

"I'm not sure," Jenny replied. "A Camera Club does grant permission for its members to look at the models, though if someone really didn't have a film in his camera, it might give the illusion of peeping, of doing something vaguely wrong. That's a bit far-fetched, I'm afraid, but then so is your theory. We can at least expect our man to be interested in naked women, although it's spying on them that gives him his real thrills. What happened about this other fellow you got onto?"

"Wooller?"

"If that's his name."

"Yes, Wooller. Lives on Gallows View. We did a bit of very discreet checking, and it turns out that he was on a two-week library sciences course in Cardiff when two of the incidents took place. That lets him out, however much pornography he's got hidden away."

"Sorry," Jenny said, glancing at her watch, "but I've got to dash. The department head will have apoplexy if I'm not there to greet our eminent visitor." She patted Banks's arm. "Don't worry, I think you made the right decision. And one more point: I'd say that our man's recent actions also show that he's got a sense of humour. It's a bit of a joke to him, leaving you with egg on your face, wouldn't you say? Call me after the weekend?"

Banks nodded and watched Jenny walk away. He noticed Richmond glancing over at him and wondered how bad it looked— a Detective Chief Inspector spending Saturday evening in The Oak with an attractive woman. He saw Jenny in his mind's eye just as she had looked on Thursday night after telling him she knew he wouldn't sleep with her. Was it being predictable that annoyed him so much? If so, he could console himself with thoughts of having won a small victory this time. Or was it guilt over what he had really wanted to do? Maybe he would do it anyway, he thought, sauntering out into the chilly October evening. It wasn't too late yet. Surely a man, like a woman, could change his mind? After all, what harm would it do? "No strings," Jenny had said.

Banks turned up his collar as he walked back to the Cortina. He needed cigarettes, and fortunately there was an off-licence next door to the pub. As he picked up his change, he paused for a moment before pocketing it. Hatchley might have questioned the barmaids at The Oak, but he hadn't said anything about talking to the local shopkeepers.

Banks identified himself and asked the owner's name.

"Patel," the man answered cautiously.

"What time do you close?"

"Ten o'clock. It's not against the law, is it?" Mr Patel answered in a broad Yorkshire accent.

"No, not at all. It's nothing to do with that," Banks assured him. "Think back to last Monday night. Did you notice anybody hanging around outside here during the evening?"

Mr Patel shook his head.

It had probably been too early in the evening for the peeper and too long ago for the shopkeeper to remember, as Banks had feared.

"A bit later, though," Mr Patel went on, "I noticed a bloke waiting at the bus stop for a bloody long time. There must have been two or three buses went by and 'ee were still there. I think that were Monday last."

"What time was this?"

"After I'd closed up. 'Ee just sat there in that bus shelter over t'street." Banks looked out of the window and saw the shelter, a dark rectangle set back from the road.

"Where were you?" he asked.

"Home," Mr Patel said, turning up his eyes. "The flat's above t'shop. Very convenient."

"Yes, yes indeed," Banks said, getting more interested. "Tell me more."

"I remember because I was just closing t'curtains when a bus went by, and I noticed that bloke was still in t'shelter. It seemed a bit odd to me. I mean, why would a chap sit in a bus shelter if 'ee weren't waiting on a bus?"

"Why, indeed?" Banks said. "Go on."

"Nothing more to tell. A bit later I looked again, and 'ee were still there."

"What time did he leave?"

"I didn't actually see him leave, but 'ee'd gone by eleven o'clock. That were t'last time I looked out."

"And the time before that?"

"Excuse me?"

"When was the last time you looked out and saw him?"

"About 'alf past ten."

"Can you describe the man?"

Mr Patel shook his head sadly. "Sorry, it were too dark. I think 'ee were wearing a dark overcoat or a raincoat, though. Slim, a bit taller than you. I got the impression 'ee were youngish, some'ow. It was 'ard to pick him out from the shadows."

"Don't worry about it," Banks said. At least the colour of the coat matched the description that Sandra and the other victims had given. It had to be the man. They could talk to other people in the street: shopkeepers, locals, even the bus drivers. Maybe somebody else would have noticed a man waiting for a bus he never caught on Monday night.

"Look," Banks said, "this is very important. You've been a great help." Mr Patel shrugged and shook his head shyly. "Have you ever seen the man before?"

"I don't think so, but how would I know? I couldn't recognize him from Adam, could I?"

"If you see him again, or anyone you think looks like him, anyone hanging about the bus stop without catching a bus, or acting oddly in any way, let me know, will you?" Banks wrote his number on a card and passed it to Mr Patel, who nodded and promised to keep his eyes skinned.

For the first time in days, Banks felt quite cheerful as he drove home to the delightful melodies of *The Magic Flute*.

TEN

I

On Sunday morning, Banks paid his visit to Robin Allott, who lived in his parents' modest semi about ten minutes walk away.

A tiny, bird-like woman answered his knock and fluttered around him all the way into the living-room.

"Do sit down, Inspector," she said, pulling out a chair. "I'll call Robin. He's in his room reading the Sunday papers."

Banks looked quickly around the room. The furniture was a little threadbare and there was no VCR or music centre, only an ancient-looking television. Quite a contrast from the Ottershaws' opulence, he thought.

"He's coming down," Mrs Allott said. "Can I make you a cup of tea?"

"Yes, please," Banks said, partly to get her out of the way for a while. She made him nervous with her constant hovering. "I hope I'm not disturbing you and Mr Allott," he said.

"Oh no, not at all." She lowered her voice. "My husband's an invalid, Inspector. He had a serious stroke about two years ago and he can't get around much. He stays in bed most of the time and I look after him as best I can."

That explained the badly worn furnishings, Banks thought. Whatever help the social services gave, the loss of the breadwinner was a serious financial setback for most families.

"It's been a great help having Robin home since his divorce," she added, then shrugged. "But he can't stay forever, can he?"

Banks heard footsteps on the stairs, and as Robin entered the room, Mrs Allott went to make the tea.

"Hello," Robin said, shaking Banks's hand. He looked an almost unnaturally healthy and handsome young man, despite the unmistakable signs of his chestnut-brown hair receding at the temples. "Sandra said you might call."

"It's about Alice Matlock," Banks said. "I'd just like to find out as much as I can about her."

"I don't really see how I can help you, Inspector," Robin said. "I told Sandra the same, but she seemed quite insistent. Surely you'll have found out all you want to know from her close friends?"

"She only had one, it seems: a lady called Ethel Carstairs. And even they haven't been friends for long. Most of Alice's contemporaries appear to have died."

"I suppose that's what happens when you reach her age. Anyway, as I said, I don't know how I can help, but fire away."

"Had you seen her recently?"

"Not for a while, no. If I remember correctly, the last time was about three years ago. I was interested in portrait photography and I thought she'd make a splendid subject. I have the picture somewhere—I'll dig it out for you later."

"And before that?"

"I hadn't seen her since my gran died."

"She and your grandmother were close friends?"

"Yes. My father's mother. They grew up together and both worked most of their lives in the hospital. Eastvale's not such a big place, or it wasn't then, so it was quite natural they'd be close. They went through the wars together, too. That creates quite a bond between people. When I was a child, my gran would often take me over to Alice's."

Mrs Allott appeared with the tea and perched at the opposite end of the table.

"Can you tell me anything about her past?" Banks asked Robin.

"Nothing you couldn't find out from anyone else, I don't think. I did realize later, though, when I was old enough to understand, what a fascinating life she'd led, all the changes she'd witnessed. Can you imagine it? When she was a girl cars were few and far between and people didn't move around much. And it wasn't only technology. Look at how our attitudes have changed, how the whole structure of society is different."

"How did Alice relate to all this?"

"Believe it or not, Inspector, she was quite a radical. She was an early struggler for women's rights, and she even went so far as to serve with the International Brigade as a nurse in the Spanish Civil War."

"Was she a communist?"

"Not in the strict sense, as far as I know. A lot of people who fought against Franco weren't."

"What were your impressions of her?"

"Impressions? I suppose, when I was a child, I was just fascinated with the cottage she lived in. It was so full of odds and ends. All those alcoves just overflowing with knick-knacks she'd collected over the years: tarnished cigarette lighters, Victorian pennies and those old silver three-penny bits—all kinds of wonderful junk. I don't imagine I paid much attention to Alice herself. I remember I was always fascinated by that ship in the bottle, the *Miranda*. I stared at it for hours on end. It was alive for me, a real ship. I even imagined the crew manning the sails, doing battle with pirates."

Mrs Allott poured the tea and laughed. "He always did have plenty of imagination, my Robin, didn't you?"

Robin ignored her. "How did it happen, anyway? How was she killed?"

"We're still not sure," Banks said. "It looks like she might have fallen over in a struggle with some kids come to rob her, but we're trying to cover any other possibilities. Have you any ideas?"

"I shouldn't think it was kids, surely?"

"Why not?"

"Well, they wouldn't kill a frail old woman, would they?"

"You'd be surprised at what kids do these days, Mr Allott. As I said, they might not have killed her intentionally."

Robin smiled. "I'm a teacher at the College of Further Education, Inspector, so I'm no great believer in the innocence and purity of youth. But couldn't it have happened some other way?"

"We don't know. That's what I'm trying to determine. What do you have in mind?"

"Nothing, I'm afraid. It was just an idea."

"You can't think of anyone who might have held a grudge or wanted her out of the way for some other reason?"

"I'm sorry, no. I wish I could help, but..."

"That's all right," Banks said, standing to leave. "I wasn't expecting you to give us the answer. Is there anything else you can think of?"

"No. I can dig out that portrait for you, though, if you're interested."

Out of politeness' sake, Banks accompanied Robin upstairs and waited as he flipped through one of his many boxes of photographs. The picture of Alice, when he found it, was mounted on mat and still seemed in very good shape. It showed a close-up of the old woman's head in semi-profile, and high-contrast processing had brought out the network of lines and wrinkles, the vivid topography of Alice Matlock's face. Her expression was proud, her eyes clear and lively.

"It's very good," Banks said. "How long have you been interested in photography?"

"Ever since I was at school."

"Ever thought of taking it up professionally?"

"As a police photographer?"

Banks laughed. "I didn't have anything as specific as that in mind," he said.

"I've thought of trying it as a freelance, yes," Robin said. "But it's too unpredictable. Better to stick to teaching."

"There is one more thing, while I'm here," Banks said, handing the photograph back to Robin. "It's just something I'm curious about. Do you ever get the impression that anyone at the Camera Club might be...not too serious...might be more interested in the models you get occasionally than in the artistic side?"

It was Robin's turn to laugh. "What an odd question," he said. "But, yes, there's always one or two seem to turn up only when we've got a model in. What did Sandra say?"

"To tell the truth," Banks said, "I didn't like to ask her. She's a bit sensitive about it and I've probably teased her too much as it is."

"I see."

"Who are these people?"

"Their names?"

"Yes."

"Well, I know..." Robin said hesitantly.

"Don't worry," Banks assured him, "you won't be getting them into trouble. They won't even know we've heard their names if they've done nothing wrong."

"All right." Robin took a deep breath. "Geoff Welling and Barry Scott are the ones who spring to mind. They seem decent enough sorts, but they hardly ever turn up and I've never seen any examples of their work."

"Thank you," Banks said, writing down the names. "What do they look like?"

"They're both in their late twenties, about my age. Five-ten to six feet. Barry's got a bit of a beer belly but Geoff seems fit enough. What's all this about? That Peeping Tom business?"

"Robin!" Mrs Allott shouted from the bottom of the stairs, "Can you come and take your dad up his tea and biscuits?"

"Coming," Robin yelled back, and followed Banks down the stairs.

"Another cup of tea, Inspector?" Mrs Allott asked.

"No, I won't if you don't mind," Banks said. "Have to get home."

As he walked the short distance back home, Banks tried to pinpoint exactly what it was that Robin had said to increase his uneasy feeling about the Alice Matlock killing.

II

Apart from the immediate shock, which had made her scream, Sandra felt very calm about her experience. One minute she had been undressing for bed, as she had done thousands of times before, absorbed in her own private rituals, and the next moment that world was in tatters, would probably never really be the same again. She realized that the idea of such permanent ruin was melodramatic, so she kept it to herself, but she could think of no other way to express the complex sense of violation she had experienced.

She wasn't scared; she wasn't even angry after the shock had worn off and the adrenalin dispersed. Surprisingly, her main feeling was pity—Harriet's compassion—because Sandra did feel sorry for the man in a way she found impossible to explain, even to herself.

It was something to do with the unnaturalness of his act. Sandra had always been fortunate in having a healthy attitude towards sex.

She had neither needed nor wanted the help of manuals, marital aids, awkward positions or suburban wife-swapping clubs to keep her sex life interesting, and it was partly because of this, her own sexual healthiness, that she felt sorry for the pathetic man who could only enjoy sex in such a vicarious, secretive way. Her pity was not a soft and loving feeling, though; it was more akin to contempt.

That Sunday morning as she rang Selena Harcourt's doorbell, which played a fragment of "Lara's Theme" from *Doctor Zhivago*, she thanked her lucky stars for the hundredth time that she had managed to persuade Alan not to report the incident. It had gone against all his instincts, and the task had required all of Sandra's rhetorical expertise, but she had done it, and here she was, about to fulfill her part of the bargain.

"Oh, hello, Sandra, do come in," Selena said in her cooing voice. "Excuse the mess."

There was, of course, no mess. Selena's living-room was spick and span, as always. It smelled of pine air-freshener and lemon-scented disinfectant, and all the souvenir ashtrays and costume-dolls from the Algarve, the Costa del Sol and various other European resorts simply glowed with health and shone with cleanliness.

The only new addition to the household was a gloomy poodle, called Pépé, who turned around slowly from his spot by the fireplace and looked at Sandra as if to apologize for his ridiculous appearance: the clippings and bows that Selena had inflicted on him in the hope that he might win a prize in the upcoming dog show. Sandra duly lavished hypocritical praise upon the poor creature, who gave her a very sympathetic and conspiratorial look, then she sat uneasily on the sofa. She always sat uneasily in Selena's house because everything looked as if it were on show, not quite real or functional.

"I was just saying to Kenneth, we haven't seen very much of you lately. You've not been to one of our coffee mornings for simply ages."

"It's the job," Sandra explained. "I work three mornings a week for Dr Maxwell now, remember?"

"Of course," Selena said. "The dentist." Somehow or other, she managed to give the word just the right shade of emphasis to imply that although dentists might be necessary, they were certainly not desirable in respectable society.

"That's right."

"So what else have you been up to since we last had a little chat?"

Sandra couldn't remember when that was, so she gave a potted history of the last month, to which Selena listened politely before offering tea.

"Have you heard about this Peeping Tom business?" she called through from the kitchen.

"Yes," Sandra shouted back.

"Of course, I keep forgetting your hubby's on the force. You must know all about it, then?" Selena said as she brought in the tray bearing tea and a selection of very fattening confectionery.

"On the force, indeed!" Sandra thought. Selena knew damn well that Alan was a policeman—in fact, that was the only reason she had ever talked to Sandra in the first place—and her way of digging for gossip was about as subtle as a Margaret Thatcher pep speech.

"Not much," Sandra lied. "There's not much to know, really."

"That Dorothy Wycombe's been having a right go at Alan, hasn't she?" Selena noted, with so much glee that the lah-de-dah inflection she usually imposed on her Northern accent slipped drastically around "having a right go."

"You could say that," Sandra admitted, gritting her teeth.

"Is it true?"

"Is what true?"

"That the police aren't doing much. Now, you know I'm no women's libber, Sandra, but we do get treated just a teeny bit unfairly sometimes. It is a man's world, you know."

"Yes. As a matter of fact, though, they're doing quite a lot. They've brought in a psychologist from the university."

"Oh?" Selena raised her eyebrows. "What's he supposed to do?"

"*She* helps tell the police what kind of person this peeper is."

"But surely they know that already? He likes to watch women undress."

"Yes," Sandra said. "But there's more to it than that. Why does he like to watch? What does he do while he's watching? Why doesn't he have a normal sex life? That's the kind of thing the psychologists are working on."

"Well, that's not much use, is it?" Selena observed. "Not until they've caught him, anyway."

"That's what I came to see you about," Sandra said, forging ahead. "They're worried that he might not stop at looking—that might be just the beginning—so they're really stepping up the investigation. They've already got enough information to know that he checks out his areas before he strikes, so he knows something about the layout of the house. He probably finds out when people go to bed, whether the woman goes up alone first, that kind of thing. So I suggested that it would be a good idea if we all kept our eyes open for strangers, or anyone acting strangely around here. That way we could catch him before he did any real harm."

"Good lord!" Selena exclaimed. "You don't really think he'd come around here, do you?"

Sandra shrugged. "There's no telling where he'll go. They've not found any rhyme or reason to his movements yet."

Selena's hand shook slightly as she poured more tea, and she bit her bottom lip between her teeth. "There was something," she started. "It was last week—Wednesday, I think—it startled me at the time but I never really gave it much thought later."

"What was it?"

"Well, I was walking back from Eloise Harrison's. She lives on Culpepper Avenue, you know, two streets down, and it's such a long way around if you go right to the main road and along, so I cut through the back here. There's a little snicket between the houses in the next street, you know, so I just go out of our back gate into the alley, then cut through the snicket, cross the street, do the same again, and I'm right in Eloise's back garden.

"Coming back on Wednesday, it was quite dark and wet, a nasty night, and when I cut into our back alley I almost bumped into this man. It was funny, I thought, because he looked like he was just standing there. I don't know why, but I think if we'd both been moving we'd have really bumped into each other. Well, it made me jump, I can tell you that. There's no light out there except what shines from the houses, and it's a lonely sort of place. Anyway, I just hurried on through the back gate and into the house, and I never really thought much more of it. But if you ask me, I'd say he was just standing there, loitering."

"Do you remember what he looked like?"

"I'm sorry, dear, I really didn't get a good look. As I said, it was dark, and what with the shock and all I just hurried on. I think he was wearing a black raincoat with a belt, and he had his collar turned up. He was wearing a hat, too, because of the rain, I suppose, so I couldn't have seen his face even if I'd wanted to. It was one of those ... what do you call them? Trilbies, that's it. I think he was quite young, though, not the dirty-old-man type."

"What made you think that?"

"I don't know, really," Selena answered slowly, as if she was finding it difficult to put her instincts and intuitions into words. "Just the way he moved. And the trilby looked too old for him."

"Thank you," Sandra said, anxious to get home and make notes while it was all still fresh in her mind.

"Do you think it was him?"

"I don't know, but the police will be thankful for any information about suspicious strangers at the moment."

Selena fingered the plunging neckline of her dress, which revealed exactly the right amount of creamy skin to complement her peroxide curls, moon-shaped face and excessive make-up. "If it was him, then he's been watching us. It could be any of us he's after. Me. You. Josephine. Annabel. This is terrible."

"I shouldn't worry about it that much, Selena," Sandra said, taking malicious pleasure in comforting the woman for worries that she, herself, had raised. "It was probably just someone taking a short cut."

"But it was such a nasty night. What normal person would want to stand out there on a night like that? He must have been up to something. Watching."

"I'll tell Alan, and I'm sure the police will look into it. You never know, Selena, your information might lead to an arrest."

"It might?"

"Well, yes. If it is him."

"But I wouldn't be able to identify him. Not in a court of law, or one of those line-ups they have. I didn't really get a good look."

"That's not what I mean. Don't worry, nobody's going to make you do that. I just meant that if he's been seen in the area, the police will know where to look."

Selena nodded, mouth open, unconvinced, then poured more tea. Sandra refused.

Suddenly, at the door, Selena's face brightened again. "I keep forgetting," she said, putting her hand to her mouth to stifle a giggle. "It's so silly of me. I've got nothing to worry about. I live right next door to a policeman!"

III

Sunday afternoon at Gristhorpe's farmhouse was a great success, though it did little for Banks's emotional confusion. On the way, he was not allowed to play opera in the car and instead had to put up with some dull, mechanical pop music on Radio One—mostly drum-machine and synthesizer—to keep Brian and Tracy happy. It was a beautiful day; the autumn sky was sharp blue again, and the season's hues glowed on the trees by the riverbank. In daylight, the steep dale sides showed a varied range of colour, from the greens of common grazing slopes to the pink, yellow and purple of heather and gorse and the occasional bright edge of a limestone outcrop.

Gristhorpe greeted them, and almost immediately the children went off for a pre-dinner walk while the three adults drank tea in the cluttered living-room. The conversation was general and easy until Gristhorpe asked Banks how he was getting on with the "lovely" Jenny Fuller.

Sandra raised her dark eyebrows, always a bad sign as far as Banks was concerned. "Would that be the Dr Fuller you've been spending so much time with lately, Alan?" she asked mildly. "I knew she was a woman, but I'd no idea she was young and lovely."

"Didn't he tell you?" Gristhorpe said mischievously. "Quite a stunner, our Jenny. Isn't she, Alan?"

"Yes," Banks admitted. "She's very pretty."

"Oh, come on, Alan, you can do better than that," Sandra teased. "Pretty? What's that supposed to mean?"

"All right, beautiful then," Banks growled. "Sexy, sultry, a knock-out. Is that what you want?"

"Maybe he's smitten with her," Gristhorpe suggested.

"I'm not smitten," Banks countered, but realized as he did so that he was probably protesting too forcefully. "She's being very helpful," he went on quickly. "And," he said to Sandra, "just so that I don't get accused of being chauvinistic about this, let me put it on record that Dr Fuller is a very competent and intelligent psychologist."

"Brains and beauty?" Sandra mocked. "How on earth can you resist, Alan?"

As they both laughed at him, Banks slumped back into the armchair, craving a cigarette. Soon the talk changed direction and he was off the hook.

The dinner, presented by a proud Mrs Hawkins, was superb: roast beef still pink in the middle, and Yorkshire puddings, cooked in the dripping, with exactly the right balance of crispness outside and moistness within, smothered in rich gravy.

After a brief post-prandial rest, Brian and Tracy were off playing Cathy and Heathcliffe again on the moorland above Gristhorpe's few acres of land, and Sandra took a stroll with her camera.

"Do you know," Gristhorpe mused as they stood in the back garden watching Sandra and the children walk up the grassy slope, "millions of years ago, this whole area was under a tropical sea? All that limestone you see was formed from dead shellfish." He swept out his arm in an all-embracing gesture.

Banks shook his head; geology was definitely not his forte.

"After that, between the ice ages, it was as warm as equatorial Africa. We had lions, hyenas, elephants and hippopotami walking the Dales." Gristhorpe spoke as if he had been there, as if he was somehow implicated in all he said. "Come on." He took Banks by the arm. "You'll think I'm turning into a dotty old man. I've got something to show you."

Banks looked apprehensively at the embryonic dry-stone wall and the pile of stones to which Gristhorpe led him.

"They amaze me, those things," he said. "I can't imagine how they stand up to the wind and rain, or how anyone finds the patience to build them."

Gristhorpe laughed—a great booming sound from deep inside. "I'll not say it's easy. Wall-building's a dying art, Alan, and you're right about the patience. Sometimes the bugger runs me to the end of my tether." Gristhorpe's voice was gruff and the accent was clearly North Yorkshire, but it also had a cultured edge, the mark of a man who has read and travelled widely.

"Here," he said, moving aside. "Why don't you have a go?"

"Me? I couldn't," Banks stammered. "I mean, I wouldn't know where to start. I don't know the first thing about it."

Gristhorpe grinned in challenge. "No matter. It's just like building a case. Test your mettle. Come on, have a go."

Banks edged towards the heap of stones, none of which looked to him as if it could be fitted into the awesome design. He picked some up, weighed them in his hand, squinted at the wall, turned them over, squinted again, then picked a smooth, wedge-shaped piece and fitted it well enough into place.

Gristhorpe looked at the stone expressionlessly, then at Banks. He reached out, picked it up, turned it around and fixed it back into place.

"There," he said. "Perfect. A damn good choice."

Banks couldn't help but laugh. "What was wrong with the way I put it in?" he asked.

"Wrong way around, that's all," Gristhorpe explained. "This is a simple wall. You should have seen the ones my grandfather built—like bloody cathedrals, they were. Still standing, too, some of them. Anyway, you start by digging a trench along your line and you put in two parallel rows of footing stones. Big ones, square as you can get them. Between those rows you put in the hearting, lots of small stones, like pebbles. These bind together under pressure, see. After that, you can start to build, narrowing all the time, two rows rising up from the footing stones. You keep that gap filled tight with hearting and make sure you bind it all together with plenty of through-stones.

"Now, that stone you put in fit all right, but it sloped inwards. They have to slope outwards, see, else the rain'll get in and soak the hearting. If that happens, when the first frost comes it'll expand, you see." He held his hands close together and moved them slowly apart. "And that can bring the whole bloody thing tumbling down."

"I see." Banks nodded, ashamed at how such basic common sense could have been beyond him. Country wisdom, he guessed.

"A good dry-stone wall," the superintendent went on, "can stand any weather. It can even stand bloody sheep scrambling over it. Some of these you see around here have been up since the eighteenth century. Of course, they need a bit of maintenance now and then, but who doesn't?" He laughed. "You and that lass, Jenny," he asked suddenly. "Owt in it?"

Surprised at the question coming out of the blue like that, Banks blushed a little as he shook his head. "I like her. I like her a lot. But no."

Gristhorpe nodded, satisfied, placed a through-stone and rubbed his hands together gleefully.

That evening, back at home, Alan and Sandra shared a nightcap after they had sent Tracy and Brian off to bed. The opera ban was lifted, but it had to be quiet. Banks played a tape of Kiri te Kanawa singing famous arias from Verdi and Puccini. They snuggled close on the sofa, and as Sandra put her empty glass down, she turned to Banks and asked, "Have you ever been unfaithful?"

Without hesitation, he replied, "No." It was true, but it didn't feel true. He was beginning to understand what Jimmy Carter's predicament had been when he said that he had committed adultery in his mind.

ELEVEN

I

By midday on Monday, DC Richmond had not only discovered from the Eastvale census records and electoral lists that there were almost eight hundred men aged between twenty and thirty-five living either alone or with a single parent, but he also had a list of their names.

"Marvellous what computers can do these days, sir," he said to Banks as he handed over the report.

"Keen on them, are you?" Banks asked, looking up and smiling.

"Yes, sir. I've applied for that course next summer. I hope you'll be able to spare me."

"Lord knows what'll be going on next summer," Banks said. "I thought I was all set for the quiet life when I came up here, and look what's happened so far. I'll bear it in mind, anyway. I know the super's keen on new technology—at least as far as the workplace is concerned."

"Thank you, sir. Was there anything else?"

"Sit down a minute," Banks said as he started reading quickly through the list. The only names he recognized at first glance were those he had heard from Robin Allott the previous day: Geoff Welling and Barry Scott.

"Right," he said, shoving the papers towards Richmond. "There's a bit more legwork to be done. First of all, I want you to check into the two names I've ticked here. But for God's sake do it discreetly. I don't want anyone to know we're checking up on private citizens on so little evidence." He grinned at Richmond. "Use your imagination, eh? First thing to find out is if they have alibis for the peeping incidents. Clear so far?"

"Yes, sir."

"The next job might take a bit more doing." Banks explained about Mr Patel's observations, hoping that he might also relieve any anxieties Richmond had about his being in The Oak with Jenny on Saturday evening. "Someone else might have seen him in the area, so talk to the residents and local shopkeepers. Also, see if you can find out who the bus drivers were on the routes past The Oak that night. Talk to them, find out if they noticed our man. All right?"

"Yes, sir," Richmond said, a bit more hesitantly.

"What is it, lad?"

"I'm not complaining, sir, but it's going to take a long time without help."

"Get Sergeant Hatchley to help you if he's not too busy."

When Richmond hardly appeared to jump with joy, Banks suppressed a smile. "And ask Sergeant Rowe if he can spare you a couple of uniformed boys."

"Yes, sir," Richmond said more cheerfully.

"Right. Off you go."

Banks had no great hopes for the enquiry, but it had to be carried out. It was the same with every case; thousands of man-hours seemed to amount to nothing until that one fragment of information turned up in the most unexpected place and led them to the solution.

He remembered his mental note to visit Alice Matlock's cottage again and see if he could nose out what it was that had bothered him since his talk with Robin.

As it was a pleasant, if chilly, day, he put on his light overcoat and set off. Turning left into the market square, then left again, he walked through the network of old cobbled streets to King Street, then wound his way down through Leaview Estate to Gallows View.

Alice Matlock's house was exactly as the police had left it almost a week ago, and Banks wondered who was going to inherit the mess. Ethel Carstairs? If there was anything of value, would it have been worth killing for? No will had been discovered so far, but that didn't mean Alice hadn't made one. She had no next of kin, so the odds were that at some point she had considered what to do about bequeathing her worldly goods. It was worth looking into.

As he stood in the small, cluttered living-room, Banks tried to

work out exactly what it was that bothered him. Again, he made the
rounds of the alcoves, with their hand-painted figurines of nursery-
rhyme and fairy-tale figures like Miss Muffet and Little Jack Horner,
their old gilt-framed sepia photographs and teaspoons from almost
every coastal resort in Britain.

He picked up a glass-encased Dales scene and watched the snow
fall on the shepherd and his sheep as he shook it. Moving on, he
found an exquisitely engraved silver snuff-box, dented on one edge.
Opening it up, he noticed the initials A.G.M. on the inside of the lid.
Alice? Surely not. Still, Robin Allott had said she was a radical, a
fighter for women's rights, and Banks had seen photographs of pio-
neer feminists smoking cigars or pipes, so why not take snuff, too?
On the other hand, he was certain she had no middle name, but there
had been a boyfriend who had died in the Great War. Perhaps the
snuff-box had been his. The dent might even have been caused by
the bullet that killed him, Banks found himself thinking. There was
something about Alice's house that made him feel fanciful, as if he
were in a tiny, personal museum.

Next he peered closely at the ship in the bottle. Banks could easily imagine a young boy populating the ship with sailors and invent-
ing adventures for them. Its name, *Miranda*, was clear on its side, and
all the details of deck, mast, ropes and sails were reproduced in miniature. There was even a tiny figurehead of a naked woman with
streaming hair—Miranda herself, perhaps.

As he moved back to the centre of the room and looked around
again at Alice's carefully preserved possessions, he realized exactly
what it was that had been nagging away at the back of his mind.

When Robin had mentioned the ship, Banks had visualized it
clearly, just as he had been able to remember many of the other articles in the room. True, the place had been a mess—cupboards and
sideboards had been emptied and their contents scattered over the
floor—but there had been no gratuitous damage.

One of the features of the Ottershaw burglary that led Banks to
believe it was the work of the same youths who had been robbing the
old women was the wanton destruction of property: the urine and
faeces that had defaced Ottershaw's paintings, music centre, television and VCR.

It was slim evidence to base a decision on, Banks realized, but it confirmed the hunch he already had about the Matlock killing. If the same youths had been responsible, they would, according to form, have smashed the ship in the bottle, the snowstorm and any other fragile object on display. But no, this thief had only made a straightforward utilitarian search for cash and such things as could be easily translated into money; the gratuitous element was entirely missing.

Pulling his collar up against the breeze, Banks set off, deep in thought, back to the station.

II

"I'm worried, Gray," Andrea said as they dipped into a dessert of cherry pie and ice cream after a main course of lasagne and salad. It was Monday evening—Andrea's husband was off in Bristol for the week and it was Trevor's youth-club night—so Graham and Andrea could actually have dinner together like a normal couple. The romantic peace of their candle-lit dinner was spoiled, however, by her obvious distress.

"What is it?" Graham asked, spooning up another mouthful of pie. "Don't tell me Ronnie's getting suspicious?"

"No, it's not that," Andrea reassured him quickly. "But it could lead to that."

She looked beautiful across the table. Her breasts pushed at the tight black blouse, which revealed tiny ovals of olive skin between the buttons, and her glossy hair, equally black, swept down across her shoulders and shimmered every time she tossed her head. Her red lipstick emphasized her full lips, and her dark eyes reflected the candle flames like brightly polished oak. Graham was excited, and Andrea's preoccupied mood irritated him.

"What's happened, then?" he asked, sighing and putting his spoon down.

Andrea leaned forward on the table, cupping her chin with her hands. "It's that man next door."

"Wooller?"

"Yes, him."

"What about him? I know he's a bit of a creep, but…"

"Remember last week I told you I thought he'd been looking at me funny?"

"Yes."

"Well, he actually spoke to me this morning. I was just going to the shops and he caught up with me at the end of the street and walked along beside me."

"Bloody cheek! Go on," Graham prompted her, curious. "Did he try to pick you up?"

"No, it wasn't like that. Well, not really like that." She shivered. "He makes my skin crawl, those thin, dry lips of his, and that weird smile he's always got on his face, as if he knows something you don't. He knows about us, Gray, I'm sure of it."

"Did he say so?"

"Not in so many words. He wasn't direct about it. First he just went on about how lonely it must be with my husband away so much, then he said it was so nice that I'd found a friend, that nice Mr Sharp from the shop. He said he'd seen you coming and going out of the back window, and he thought it was so good of you to keep me company, especially when you had a son to look after, too. It was the way he said it, though, Gray. His voice. His tone. It was dirty."

"Is that all he said?" Graham asked.

"What do you mean?"

"About seeing me visit you."

"Yes. I told you, it wasn't what he said but the way he said it, as if he knew much more."

"Go on." Graham started chewing on his bottom lip as Andrea continued her story.

"He said that not everyone was as sympathetic as him, and maybe my husband wouldn't be so understanding—he might worry about people talking, for example, even though there was nothing really going on. But he was leering at me all the time, as if he was nudging me and saying, 'We both know there's something going on, don't we?' I just ignored him and tried to walk faster, but he kept up with me and even turned the corner when I did. He went on about what a pity it would be if my husband did find out and wasn't understanding—then I'd be all lonely again, and I'd never have any nice friends again, however innocent their intentions were. I asked him to get to the point, to tell me what he was getting at, and he pretended to take offence."

"What does he want?" Graham asked impatiently. "Money?"

"I don't think so, no. I think he wants to go to bed with me."

"He what?"

"He wants me himself. I couldn't bear it, Gray. I'd be sick, I know I would." She was almost in tears now.

"Don't worry," Graham comforted her. "It won't come to that, you can be certain. What did he say?"

"He just said that there was no reason why I shouldn't have another friend, like him, for example, and what a good friend he could be and all that. He never really said anything, you know, explicit, nothing you could put your finger on. But we both knew what he was talking about. He said how pretty he thought I was, what nice legs I had, and I could feel his eyes crawling all over my body while he spoke. Then he said we should all have tea together soon, and he'd be happy just to sit there and watch us—Oh, he's disgusting, Gray! What am I going to do?"

"You're not to worry," Graham said, moving his chair next to hers and stroking her hair. "I'll take care of him."

"Will you?" She turned her face so that it was close to his. He could smell the cherries on her breath. "What will you do?"

"Never you mind about that, love. I've told you I'll deal with him. Don't I always keep my word?"

Andrea nodded.

"Then you've nothing to worry about, have you? You won't hear anything from him again. He won't even so much as glance in your direction if he sees you in the street, I promise you that."

"You won't hurt him, will you Gray? I don't want you to get into trouble. You know what that might lead to."

"At least then," Graham said wearily, "we'd be out in the open. We could go away together."

"Yes," Andrea agreed. "But it wouldn't be a good start, would it? I want things to be better than that for us."

"I suppose so," Graham said, sitting back.

"But you'll really deal with him, will you? And not make any trouble?"

Graham nodded and smiled at her. Andrea caught his look and stood up to clear the table. "Not yet, you goat," she said. "Wait till I've cleared the dishes."

"They can wait," Graham said, reaching out for her. "I can't."

She moved away playfully and his hand caught the collar of her blouse. As she stepped back, the material ripped down the front and the buttons flew off, pinging against wine glasses and plates. The blouse hung open, revealing Andrea's semi-transparent black brassiere, the one that stood out in clear relief against her pale skin and exposed a great deal of inviting cleavage.

Graham froze for a second. He didn't know what her reaction would be. Perhaps it was an expensive blouse—it felt soft, like silk— and she would be angry with him. He was all set to apologize and offer to buy her another when she laughed and reached forward to pull at his shirt.

"Come on, then," she said, smiling at him. "If you really can't wait." And they rolled to the floor, laughing and tearing at each other's clothes.

Afterwards, sweaty and out of breath, they lay back and laughed again, then went up to the bedroom to continue making love in a more leisurely way for another two hours.

Finally, it was time to go. Trevor was due back in about half an hour, and Graham had promised to drop in on Wooller on his way home.

"Remember," Andrea said, kissing him as he left, "no trouble. Ask him nicely. Tell him there's nothing in it."

III

Graham Sharp knocked softly at the door of number six Gallows View, and a few seconds later, Wooller peered around the chain, squinting through his thick glasses.

"Mr Sharp!" he exclaimed. "What a pleasant surprise. Come in, come in!"

The messy room smelled of old socks and boiled cabbage. Wooller, obviously thinking that Sharp had come to make some arrangement about Andrea Rigby, scooped some newspapers from a straight-backed chair and bade him sit down.

"Tea? Or perhaps something a little stronger?"

"No, thanks," Graham said stiffly. "And I won't sit down either. I'll not be stopping long."

"Oh," said Wooller, standing in the kitchen doorway. "Sure I can't persuade you?"

"No," Sharp said, walking towards him. "You can't bloody persuade me. But I think I can persuade you."

Wooller looked puzzled until Graham grabbed him by the front of his pullover, bunching the wool in his fist and half-lifting the frail librarian from the floor. Sharp was much taller and in far better physical shape. He began to shake Wooller, gently at first, then more violently, against the kitchen door jamb. Each time Wooller's back hit the wood, Graham spat out a word. "Don't...you...ever... threaten...Andrea...Rigby...again...you...smelly...little... prick....Do...you...under...stand?" It was hard to tell if Wooller was nodding or not, but he looked scared enough.

"Stop it," Wooller whined, putting his hand to the back of his head. "You've split my skull. Look, blood!"

He thrust his open palm under Graham's eyes, and there was clearly blood on it. Sharp felt a sudden lurch of fear in his stomach. He let go of Wooller and leaned against the doorway, pale and trembling. Wooller stared at him with his mouth open.

Quickly, Graham made the effort to pull himself together. He grabbed a glass from the draining-board and, without even bothering to see if it was clean or not, filled it with cold water from the tap and gulped it down.

Feeling a little better, he ran his hand through his hair and faced a confused Wooller, grasping the front of his pullover again. "I'm not going to tell you again," he said, injecting as much quiet menace into his tone as he could manage. "Do you understand me?"

Wooller swallowed and nodded. "Let me go! Let me go!"

"If you say one more word to Mrs Rigby," Graham went on, "even if you so much as look at her in a way she doesn't like, I'll be back to finish what I started. And don't think of talking to her husband, either. True, you might cause a bit of trouble if you do, but not half as much trouble as you'll be causing for yourself. Get it?"

Again Wooller's Adam's apple bobbed as he nodded. "Let me go! Please!"

Graham relaxed his grip a bit more, but didn't quite let go of Wooller's bunched-up pullover. "I want to hear you say you understand me, first," he said. "I want you to tell me you won't talk to anyone about this—not her husband, not the police, not anyone. Because if you do, Wooller, I swear it, I'll break every fucking bone in your stinking little body."

Wooller was shaking. "All right," he whimpered, trying to wriggle free. "All right, I'll say nothing, I'll leave her alone. I only wanted to be her friend, that's all I wanted."

Graham raised his fist, angered again by Wooller's pathetic lie, but he made the effort and restrained himself. He had almost gone too far, and he was certain now that Andrea and he would have no more trouble from Wooller.

IV

As soon as the back door cracked open, Trevor felt the thrill; it set his blood dancing and made the sweat prickle on his forehead and cheeks. The rough wool of the balaclava scratched at his face and made it itch like mad. The two of them entered the house cautiously, but all was as they had expected—dark and quiet. The narrow beams of their torches picked out dishes piled up for washing, a table littered with shadowy objects, a newspaper open at a half-finished crossword puzzle. Again, they were in a kitchen, but it seemed much less clean and tidy than the one they'd been in a few days ago.

The living-room, too, turned out to be in a bit of a mess: Sunday's paper lay scattered on the carpet, and Trevor's beam picked out a half-full coffee mug on the mantelpiece.

They'd been tipped by Lenny that the woman who lived there kept a lot of expensive jewellery, which he could easily fence in London, so they ignored the living-room and, keeping their torch beams pointed towards the floor, headed up the stairs. The first room they entered was empty except for a single bed—a guestroom, most likely—and two others were similarly ascetic. It felt eerie, as if the woman had once had family and now they were gone and the house was empty and bare. You could tell from the downstairs that she couldn't be bothered much any more; yet she was supposed to be well off.

Finally, after more false starts in the bathroom and airing-cupboard, they found what seemed to be her bedroom. At first they couldn't make it out, but by running the torches over a wider area they discovered that a large, four-poster bed stood at the centre of the room. Mick sat on the edge of the mattress and bounced up and down for a while before pronouncing it too lumpy. Then they began their search.

Again, there was an assortment of clothes, this time all female, and Trevor noticed that this woman's underwear was far more exotic than the other's. There were brassieres cut so low that they were practically non-existent; skimpy, see-through panties; a garter belt with roses embroidered on it; stockings with dark borders around the tops; and short, lacy nightdresses. The lingerie was all clean and it smelled of something faintly exotic: jasmine, Trevor thought it was. His mother had bought some jasmine tea once, many years ago, and the smell took him back and made him think of her. He remembered that none of them had liked the tea and his mother had laughed at their lack of adventurous spirit.

They found the jewellery in a lacquered box with a Chinese landscape painted on it. The box was locked but it broke open easily and they pocketed its contents. They poked around the room a bit longer, looking for cash, but found none. That made Trevor angry, because with cash he didn't have to rely on Lenny's spurious deals.

They set off back downstairs, and just as they were about to turn the final bend into the front hallway, the door opened and closed, the hall light came on and a woman began to take off her sleek fur coat.

Cautiously, Mick led the way down. The last stair creaked and the woman turned, but Mick got his hand over her mouth before she could scream. They dragged her into the living-room and switched on the standard-lamp. The curtains were already closed. Mick took the woman's head-scarf and fastened it tight, like a bit between her teeth; then he took the belt from her raincoat and tied her hands crudely behind her back.

"We need time to get away," he said to Trevor. "We've got to make sure she keeps quiet for long enough. Bring me that candlestick over there."

Trevor looked and saw an old brass candlestick with a heavy base. The woman whimpered behind her gag and struggled to free herself.

"No," he said.

"Come on," Mick urged him. "We've got to. We can't risk getting caught now."

Slowly, Trevor walked over to the mantelpiece, picked up the candlestick, felt its weight, then dropped it on the floor. "No," he said again. "You'd probably kill her. You don't know how little strength it takes."

"So what," Mick argued, stretching out his hand scornfully. "Give us it here."

"I've got a better idea," Trevor said.

"What?"

Trevor looked at the woman sprawled awkwardly on the sofa. She was about thirty-eight, forty maybe, but very well preserved. Her hair was blonde, but the dark roots showed, and perhaps she was wearing just a little too much mascara. But apart from that, she looked very tasty indeed to Trevor. Her breasts jutted behind the polo-necked sweater and her skirt had already slipped up high enough to show a spread of thigh. He got an eerie feeling that his moment had come at last.

"You must be mad," Mick gasped, realizing what Trevor meant. "We can't hang around here."

"Why not? We know she lives alone. She's here. So who else is going to come?"

Mick thought for a moment, licking his lips. "All right, then," he agreed, and began to move forward.

Trevor stood in front of him and nudged him gently out of the way. "Me first."

There was something determined in his tone, so Mick just shrugged and moved back. Trevor manoeuvred the woman awk-wardly onto the floor. She didn't struggle, but she seemed to have gone limp and heavy. He pulled the sweater up around her breasts but couldn't get it off while here hands were tied. There were some scissors by the stack of magazines on the coffee table, so he picked them up and carefully cut the material. Underneath, her bra was pink, and the hard nipples poked at its cups. Trevor grabbed the elastic in the middle and tried to tear it off, but it proved stronger than it looked. Again, he used the scissors. The whole thing was beginning to seem a lot harder than he'd imagined.

"For fuck's sake, hurry up," Mick urged him. "Get on with it!"

Trevor squeezed the woman's breasts. They were soft and slack and he didn't like the feel of them. Slowly, he cut off the rest of her clothes. Again, she didn't struggle; she just lay there like a sack of potatoes.

Finally, he pushed her legs apart, unbuckled his belt and unzipped his trousers. It was his first time, but it felt right; he knew what to do.

He tried to avoid looking her in the face. Because of the scarf between her teeth she seemed to be grinning maliciously, and when he caught her eyes he thought he saw mockery in them, not just fear. He'd soon teach her. When he started, he thought he heard her grunt with pain behind her gag as she whipped her head from side to side, and he could see her eyes were blurred with tears now.

The pressure was strong in Trevor and he could manage no more than three or four rough thrusts before it was all over. Exhausted even by such a meagre effort, he got to his knees and pulled up his pants. The woman just lay there. She wasn't crying now; her eyes were far away and the taut scarf still made her appear to grin.

"Your turn," he said, turning to Mick.

"Not on your bleeding Nelly! If you think I'm taking your sloppy seconds, you've got another bloody think coming, mate. Let's piss off out of here."

Before they left, Mick gave the woman a hard kick to the side of her head and told her there'd be more of that if she didn't keep her mouth shut. Trevor noticed a thin trickle of blood shining in her hair before he turned and followed Mick out through the kitchen.

TWELVE

I

After a dull, elementary talk by Fred Barton on the properties of the medium telephoto lens, the Tuesday evening Camera Club was devoted to mutual criticism of work produced at the session two weeks earlier when a nude model had been the subject. As expected, some ribald remarks came from less mature male amateurs, but on the whole the brief, informal session was productive.

Sandra looked over Norman's work and had to admit, if only to herself, that she liked it. It was far more experimental than anyone else's, she imagined, and she felt some sympathy because she, too, liked to take risks, though she rarely went as far as Norman. He had used a fast film and blown up the prints to give them a very coarse grain; consequently, the photographs did not look like shots of a naked woman; they looked more like moonscapes.

The usual crowd gathered at The Mile Post later. The pub was busier than usual; rock 'n' roll on the jukebox and bleeping video games made conversation difficult. There was also a group of local farmers celebrating something with a great deal of laughter and the occasional song, and some of the lads from the racing stables in Middleham were out enjoying a night on the town.

"Have you seen that new Minolta?" Norman asked, getting comfortable in his chair and arranging pipe and matches neatly in front of him on the varnished table.

"That's not a camera," Robin said. "It's a computer. All you have to do is programme it and it does everything for you, including focus."

"What do you think you're doing when you set your shutter speed and your aperture?" Norman asked. "You're programming your camera then, aren't you?"

"That's different."

"As far as I'm concerned," Sandra chipped in, "anything that makes the technical side easier and allows me to concentrate more on the photograph is fine by me."

Norman smiled indulgently. "Well put, Sandra. Although I would add that the 'technical side,' as you term it, is an integral part of the photograph."

"I know the selections are important," Sandra agreed, "and I'd always want a manual override—but the easier the better as far as I'm concerned."

"I've never found it particularly difficult to set the camera," Robin said. "Or to focus. I don't really see what all the fuss is about."

"Typical reactionary attitude," Norman sneered. "You can't ignore the new technology, lad. You might as well make good use of it."

"I've really nothing against it," Robin argued quietly. "I just don't think I need one, that's all. No more than I need an electric toothbrush."

"Oh, you'd be happy with a bloody pinhole camera, you would," Norman sighed.

"My excuse is that I can't afford one," Sandra said.

"I don't think any of us can," Harriet echoed. "It's a very expensive hobby, photography."

"True enough," Norman agreed. "I'd have to sell all the camera equipment I've already got. It might be worth it, though. I'll look into it a bit more closely. Another round?"

When Norman came back with the drinks, the conversation had shifted subtly to the evening's session. Sandra complimented him on his photos and he grudgingly admitted that hers, though they were in colour and had obviously been cropped, were fine compositions. He told her that she had done particularly interesting and unusual things with skin tone.

"Where are yours?" Norman asked Robin. "I don't think any of us had a look at them."

"They're not back yet. I took slides and I didn't finish the film. I only sent it off a couple of days ago."

"Slides!" exclaimed Norman. "What an odd thing to do."

"I used an Ektachrome 50," Robin argued. "It's very good for that kind of thing."

"But all the same," Norman repeated, "*slides* in a studio nude session? I'll bet you never even had a film in your camera, eh, Robin? I'll bet that's why you've got nothing to show us."

Robin ignored him and looked over to Sandra. "I talked to your husband," he said, "but I can't see how I was any help."

Sandra shrugged. "You never know. He's got to gather all the information he can. I should imagine it's like counting the grains of sand on a beach."

"I think I'd find that too frustrating."

Sandra laughed. "Oh, I'm sure Alan does, too. Especially when there's so many cases going at once and they keep him out till all hours. Still, that's not all there is to it."

"'A policeman's lot,'" quoted Norman "'is not a happy one.'"

"I wouldn't agree with that," Sandra said, smiling. "Alan's usually perfectly happy unless he's dealing with particularly unpleasant crimes, like the killing of a defenceless old woman."

"And a Peeping Tom," Norman added. "Let's not forget our Peeping Tom."

"No, let's not," Sandra said. "Anyway, Robin, you might have been helpful. Alan says it's often hard to know exactly where the solution comes from. Everything gets mixed in together."

"When are we going to see these slides, then?" Norman asked Robin impatiently.

"They should be back soon."

"I'll bet you don't even have a slide projector."

"So what? I could always borrow one."

"Not from me, you couldn't. I haven't got one either. I haven't even been able to show anyone last year's holiday pictures yet."

"Surely Robin must have one if he's been taking slides?" Harriet said.

"No, I don't," Robin mumbled apologetically. "I'm afraid I've never done transparencies before. I do have a small viewer, of course, but that's not much use."

"Well, I *do* have a projector and a screen," Sandra told them. "And if any of you want to borrow it, you're quite welcome. Just drop around sometime. You know where I live."

"Is that an invitation, Sandra?" Norman leered.

"Oh, shut up," she said, and pushed him playfully away.

"Don't you think there's something unnatural about taking pictures of nudes at the Camera Club?" Harriet asked suddenly. "I mean, we're all talking about it as if it's the most normal thing in the world."

"Why?" demanded Norman. "It's the only chance some of us get."

"What?" Sandra joked. "A gay, young blade like yourself, Norman. Surely they're just flocking to your studio, dying to take their clothes off for you?"

"Less of the 'gay,' if you please, love. And I don't have a studio. What about you, Robin?"

"What about me?"

"Do you agree with Harriet, that it's unnatural to photograph nudes in a studio?"

"I wouldn't say it's unnatural, no. I don't think my mother would approve, though," he added in an attempt at humour. "I sometimes have a devil of a job keeping things to myself."

At about ten o'clock, there was a general movement homewards, but Sandra managed to catch Harriet's eye and signal discreetly for her to stay. After the others had gone, Harriet moved her chair closer. "Another drink?" she asked.

"Please." Sandra said. She needed it. She also needed somebody to talk to, and the only person she could think of was Harriet. Even then, it would take another drink to make her open up.

The empty seats at the table were soon taken by a noisy but polite group of stable-lads. When she had adjusted to the new volume level, Harriet, who drove a mobile library around some of the more remote Dales villages, began to talk about work.

"Yesterday I got a puncture near the Butter Tubs Pass above Wensleydale," she said. "A car full of tourists came speeding round the corner, and I had to pull over quick. Some of those stones by the side of the road are very sharp, I can tell you. I was stuck there for ages till a kind young vet stopped to help me. When I got to Angram, old Mrs Wytherbottom played heck about having to wait so long for her new Agatha Christie." She paused. "Sandra, what's wrong? You haven't listened to a word I've said."

"What? Oh, sorry." Sandra gulped down the last of her vodka and slimline and took the plunge. "It happened to me, Harriet," she said quietly. "What we were talking about last week. It happened to me on Friday."

"Good Lord." Harriet whispered, putting her hand on Sandra's wrist. "What...how?"

"Just like everyone else. I was getting ready for bed and he was watching through the bottom of the curtains."

"Did you see him?"

"I saw him before I'd got too far, fortunately. But he was off like a shot. I didn't get a good look at him. The thing is, Harriet, this has got to be in strict confidence. Alan didn't report it because of the embarrassment it would cause us both. He feels bad enough about that, but if he thought anyone else knew..."

"I understand. Don't worry, Sandra, I won't tell a soul. Not even David."

"Thank you."

"How do you feel?"

"Now? Fine. It seems very distant already. It was a shock at first, and I certainly felt violated, but I wanted to tell you that I also felt some sort of pity for the man. It's odd, but when I could first think about it rationally, it just seemed so childish. That's the word that came to mind: childish. He needs help, not punishment. Maybe both, I don't know. It depends which gets the better of me, anger or pity. Every time I think about it they seem to be fighting in me."

"It was silly of me to say what I did last week," Harriet apologized. "About feeling sorry for him. I'd no idea...I mean, I've still no idea what it actually feels like. But they're closer than you think, aren't they, anger and pity?"

"Yes. Anyway, it's not as bad as you'd imagine," Sandra said, smiling. "You soon get over it. I doubt that it leaves any lasting scars on anyone, unlike most sex crimes." Even as she spoke the words, they sounded too glib to be true.

"I don't know. Has Alan got any leads yet?"

"Not much, no. A vague description. One of our neighbours saw a man hanging around the back alley a few days ago. He was dressed pretty much the same as the man I saw, but neither of us could give a clear description. Anyway, keep an eye on your neighbourhood, Harriet. It seems that he does a bit of research before he comes in to get his jollies."

"Yes, I read about that in the paper. Superintendent Gristhorpe gave a press release."

"Anyway," Sandra said, "there's a lot of women in Eastvale, so I would think the odds against you are pretty high."

Harriet smiled. "But why you?"

"What do you mean?"

"The odds against you must have been high, too."

"Alan thinks it's because of who I am. He says the man's getting bolder, more cocky, throwing down the gauntlet."

"A Peeping Tom with a sense of humour?"

"Why not? Plenty of psychos have one."

"You don't think he's looking for someone, do you?"

"Looking for someone? Who? What do you mean?"

"Someone in particular. You know, like Jack the Ripper always said that woman's name."

"Mary Kelly? That's just a rumour, though. Why would he be looking for someone in particular?"

"I don't know. It was just a thought. Somebody who reminds him of his first time, his first love or someone like that."

"You're quite the amateur psychologist, aren't you?" Sandra said, looking at Harriet through narrowed eyes.

"It's just something I thought of, that's all." Harriet shrugged.

"They've brought a professional psychologist in," Sandra said. "Woman called Fuller. Dr Jenny Fuller. According to Gristhorpe she's quite a looker, and Alan's been working late several evenings."

"Oh, Sandra," Harriet exclaimed. "You surely can't think Alan...?"

"Relax," Sandra said, laughing and touching Harriet's arm. "No, I don't think anything like that. I do think he fancies her, though."

"How do you know?"

"A woman can tell. Surely you could tell if David had his eyes on another woman?"

"Well, I suppose so. He is rather transparent."

"Exactly. I wouldn't use that word to describe Alan, but it's in what he doesn't say and how he reacts when the subject's brought up. He's been very cagey. He didn't even tell me it was an attractive woman he was working with."

"Does it worry you?"

"No. I trust him. And if he does yield to temptation, he wouldn't be the first."

"But what would you do?"

"Nothing."

"Would he tell you?"

"Yes. Eventually. Men like Alan usually do, you know. They think it's because they're being honest with you, but it's really because the guilt is too much of a burden; they can't bear it alone. I'd probably rather not know, but he wouldn't consider that."

"Oh, Sandra," Harriet snorted, "you're being a proper cynic. Don't you think you're being a bit hard on him?"

Sandra laughed. "I wouldn't be able to say it if I didn't love him, warts and all. And don't get upset. I don't think anything will come of it. If she's as beautiful as Gristhorpe says, Alan would hardly be normal if he didn't feel some attraction. He's a big boy. He can deal with it."

"You haven't met her, then?"

"No, he's not offered to introduce me."

"Maybe," Harriet suggested, leaning forward and lowering her voice, "you should get him to invite her for dinner? Or just suggest a drink together. See what he says."

Sandra beamed. "What a good idea! I'm sure it'd be a lot of fun. Yes, I think I'll get working on it. It'll be interesting to see how he reacts."

II

Police Constable Craig was one of the uniformed officers temporarily in plain clothes on the peeper case. It was his job to walk between as many pubs as possible within his designated area and to keep an eye open for any loiterers. The job was tiring and frustrating, as he was not allowed to enter any of the pubs; he simply had to walk the streets and pass each place more than once to see if anyone was hanging around for too long.

As he approached The Oak, near the end of his beat, for the second time that evening, he noticed the same man standing in the shadows of the bus shelter. From the few details that Craig could make out, the man was slim, of medium height and wearing a dark, belted raincoat and a flat cap. It wasn't a trilby, but there was no law against a man's owning more than one hat. Craig also knew that at least two buses must have stopped there since he had last walked by The Oak.

Following instructions, he went inside the noisy pub and sought out DC Richmond, who was by now sick to death of spending every evening—duty or no—in that loud, garish gin-palace. Richmond, hearing Craig's story, suggested that they call the station first, then check once more in about fifteen minutes. If the man was still there, they would approach him for questioning. Gratefully, Craig accepted a half of Guinness and the chance to sit down and take the weight off his feet.

Meanwhile, Mr Patel, who had become quite the sleuth since Banks's visit, glanced frequently out of his shop window, and wrote down, in a notebook bought especially for the purpose, that a man resembling the suspect he had already described to the police had been standing in the shelter for forty-eight minutes. He timed his entry "Tuesday, 9:56 P.M.," then picked up the phone and asked for Detective Chief Inspector Banks.

Banks was not, at first, happy to take the message. He was enjoying a pleasant evening with the children—no opera, no television—helping Brian construct a complicated extension of track for his electric train. Tracy was stretched out on her stomach, too, deciding where to place bridges, signal boxes and papier-mâché mountains. Everyone pulled a face when the phone rang, but Banks became excited when Sergeant Rowe passed on Mr Patel's information.

Back at The Oak, the fifteen minutes was up. Richmond had reported in, as arranged, and now it was time to approach the suspect and ask a few questions. As he and Craig headed for the pub's heavy smoked-glass and oak doors, Banks was just arriving at Mr Patel's shop, walking in as casually as any customer.

"Is that him?" he asked.

"I can't say for certain," Mr Patel answered, scratching his head. "But 'ee looks the same. 'Ee weren't wearing an 'at last time, though."

"How long did you say he's been there?"

Mr Patel looked first at his watch, then down at his notebook. "Sixty-three minutes," he answered, after a brief calculation.

"And how many buses have gone by?"

"Three. One to Ripon and two to York."

The bus shelter stood at the apex of a triangle, the base of which was formed by a line between Mr Patel's shop and The Oak itself. Banks was already at the door, keeping his eyes on the suspect across the road to his right, when Craig and Richmond, walking much too purposefully towards their man, were spotted, and the dark figure took off down the street.

But what could have been a complete disaster was suddenly transformed into a triumphant success. As the man sprinted by Mr Patel's shop with a good lead on his pursuers, Banks rushed out and performed the best rugby tackle he could remember making since he'd played scrum-half in a school game over twenty years ago.

The quartet returned to Eastvale station at ten-thirty, and the suspect, protesting loudly, was led into the interview room: a stark place with three stiff-backed chairs, pale green walls and a metal desk.

Richmond and Craig thought they were in for a telling-off, but Banks surprised them by thanking them for their help. They both knew that if the man had got away things would have been very different.

The suspect was Ronald Markham, age twenty-eight, a plumber in Eastvale, and apart from the headgear, his clothing matched all earlier descriptions of the peeper's. At first he was outraged at being attacked in such a violent manner, then he became sullen and sarcastic.

"What were you doing in the shelter?" Banks asked, with Richmond standing behind him instead of Hatchley, whom nobody had thought to disturb.

"Waiting for a bus," Markham snapped.

"Did you get that, Constable Richmond?"

"Yes sir. Suspect replied that he was 'waiting for a bus,'" Richmond quoted.

"Which bus?" Banks asked.

"Any bus."

"Where were you going?"

"Anywhere."

Banks walked over to Richmond and whispered in his ear. Then he turned to Markham, said "Won't be a minute, sir," and the two of them disappeared, leaving a uniformed constable to guard the room.

About forty-five minutes later, when they returned after a hastily grabbed pint and sandwich at the Queen's Arms, Markham was livid again.

"You can't treat me like this!" he protested. "I know my rights."

"What were you doing in the shelter?" Banks asked him calmly.

Markham didn't answer. He ran his thick fingers through his hair, turned his eyes up to the ceiling, then glared at Banks, who repeated his question: "What were you doing in the shelter?"

"Keeping an eye on my wife," Markham finally blurted out.

"Why do you think you need to do that?"

"Isn't it bloody obvious?" Markham replied scornfully. "Because I think she's having it off with someone else, that's why. She thinks I'm out of town on a job, but I followed her to The Oak."

"Did she enter alone or with a man?"

"Alone. But she was meeting him there, I know she was. I was waiting for them to come out."

"What were you going to do then?"

"Do?" Markham ran his hand through his thin, sandy hair again. "I don't know. Hadn't thought of it."

"Were you going to confront them?"

"I told you I don't know."

"Or were you just going to keep watching them, spying on them?"

"Maybe."

"Why would you do that?"

"To make sure, like, that they were having it off."

"So you're not sure?"

"I told you I'm not sure, no. That's what I was doing, trying to make sure."

"What would it take to convince you?" Banks asked.

"What do you mean?"

"What kind of evidence were you hoping to get?"

"I don't know. I wanted to see where they went, what they did."

"Did you hope to watch them having sex? Is that what you wanted to see?"

Markham snorted. "It's hardly what I *wanted* to see, but I expected it, yes."

"How were you going to watch them?"

"What do you mean?"

"The logistics. How were you going to spy on them? Use binoculars, climb a drainpipe, what? Were you going to take photographs, too?"

"I said before, I hadn't thought that far ahead. I was just going to follow them and see where they went. After that..." He shrugged. "Anyway, just what the hell are you getting at?"

"After that you were going to watch them and see what they did. Right?"

"Perhaps. Wouldn't you want to know, if it was your wife?"

"Have you done this kind of thing before?"

"What kind of thing?"

"Followed people and spied on them."

"Why would I?"

"I'm asking you."

"No, I haven't. And I don't see the point of all these questions. By now they're probably at it in some pokey bungalow."

"Bungalow? You know where he lives, then?"

"No. I don't even know who he is."

"But you said 'bungalow.' You know he lives in a bungalow?"

"No."

"Why did you say it, then?"

"For God's sake, what's it matter?" Markham cried, burying his long face in his hands. "It's over now, anyway."

"What's over?"

"My marriage. The cow!"

"Have you ever watched anybody getting undressed in a bungalow?" Banks persisted, though he was quickly becoming certain that it was all in vain now, that they had the wrong man.

"No," Markham answered, "of course I haven't." Then he laughed. "Bloody hell, you think I'm that Peeping Tom, don't you? You think I'm the bloody peeper!"

"Why did you run away when you saw my men approaching you?"

"I didn't know they were police, did I? They weren't wearing uniforms."

"But why run? They might simply have been walking to the bus stop, mightn't they?"

"It was just a feeling. The way they were walking. They looked like heavies to me, and I wasn't hanging around to get mugged."

"You thought they were going to mug you? Was that the reason?"

"Partly. It did cross my mind that they might be pals of the bloke my wife was meeting—that I'd been seen, like, and they wanted to warn me off. I don't know. All I can say is they didn't look like they were coming to wait for a bus."

It was almost midnight. Markham said that he was expected home late, at about one o'clock. He had arranged it that way so that he could give his wife enough time, enough rope to hang herself with. Banks suggested that to clear things up once and for all, they should return to Markham's house and wait for her.

The house, on Coleman Avenue about a mile northwest of the market square, was so spacious and well furnished that Banks found himself wondering if it was true that plumbers earned a fortune. The predominant colours were dark browns and greens, which, Banks thought, made the place seem a little too sombre for his taste.

At a quarter to one, the key turned in the door. Markham's wife had told him that she was visiting a friend and that if he did get home before her he shouldn't be surprised if she was a bit late. Curious about the light in the living-room, she peered around the door and walked in slowly when she saw her husband with a stranger.

Mrs Markham was a rather plain brunette in her late twenties, and Banks found it hard to imagine her as the type to have an affair. Still, it took all sorts, he reminded himself, and it never did to pigeon-hole people before you knew them.

After identifying himself, Banks asked Mrs Markham where she had spent the evening.

She sat down stiffly and started strangling one of her black leather gloves. "With a friend," she answered cautiously. "What's all this about?"

"Name?"

"Sheila Croft."

"Is she on the phone?"

"Yes."

"Would you call her, please?"

"Now? Why?"

"This is very important, Mrs Markham," Banks explained patiently. "Your husband might be in serious trouble, and I have to verify your story."

Mrs Markham bit her thin lower lip and glanced over at her husband.

There was fear in her eyes.

"The number?" Banks repeated.

"It's late, she'll be in bed now. Besides, we weren't at her house," Mrs Markham dithered.

"Where were you?"

"We went to a pub. The Oak."

"You weren't with no Sheila Croft, either, you bloody lying cow," Markham cut in. "I saw you go in there by yourself, all tarted up. And look at yourself now. Couldn't even be bothered to put a bit of make-up on again after."

Mrs Markham paled. "Call Sheila, then," she shouted. "Just you ask her. She was already there. I was late."

"Sheila would lie her pants off to protect you, and you bloody well know it. Who is he, you bitch?"

He got to his feet as if to strike her, and Banks stepped forward to push him back down.

"It's all right," Markham said bitterly. "I wouldn't hit her. She knows that. Who is he, you slut?"

At this point, Mrs Markham started weeping and complaining about being neglected. Banks, depressed by the entire scene and angry that it had not been the peeper they had caught, made his exit quietly.

III

A chill wind blew through Glue-Sniffers' Ginnel, where Mick and Trevor stood, jackets buttoned uptight, smoking and chatting.

"Did you like it, then, last night?" Mike asked.

"Not much," Trevor answered. "I suppose it was all right, but..."

"What? Too tight?"

"Yeah. Hurt a bit. Dry as a bone at first."

"Just wait till you get one that's willing. Slides in easy, then, it does. Plenty of 'em like it the hard way, though. You know, they like you to show 'em who's boss."

Trevor shrugged. "Where's the loot?"

"Got it hidden at my place. It's safe. Looks like we've struck the jackpot there, too, mate. Never seen any that sparkled so much."

"That depends on Lenny, doesn't it?"

"I told you, he's got the contacts. He'll get us the best he can. Probably a few G, there."

"Sure. And how much of that will we see?"

"Oh, don't go on about it, Trev," Mick grumbled, shifting from one foot to the other as if he had ants in his pants. "We'll get what's coming. And you did get a little bonus, didn't you?" he leered.

"What's Lenny doing?"

"Still in The Smoke setting up a business deal. Bit tight-lipped about it, right now."

"When's he coming back?"

"Don't know. Few days. A week."

"When are we going to get rid of the stuff?"

"What the bloody hell's wrong with you tonight, Trev? Nothing but fucking moan, moan, moan. You haven't spent all your readies yet, have you?"

"No. I just don't like the idea of that jewellery lying about, that's all."

"Don't worry. I told you it's safe. He'll be back soon."

"Heard from him, have you?"

"Got a letter from him this morning. Careful, our Lenny is. Thinks the blower might be tapped. He said he thought it'd be a good idea if we laid off on the jobs for a while. Just till things cool down, like."

"I've not noticed any heat."

"Bound to be going on, though, ain't it, behind the scenes. Stands to reason. There's been a lot of bother lately, and the rozzers must be getting their bleeding arses flayed. Mark my words, mate, they'll be working their balls off. Best lay off for a few weeks. We've got plenty to be going on with."

It wasn't the money that interested Trevor so much; it was the thrill of breaking in, the way it made his heart beat faster and louder in the darkness, pen-lights picking out odd details of paintings on walls or bottle-labels and family snapshots on tables. But he couldn't explain that to Mick.

"Well, what do you think?" Mick asked.

"I suppose he's right," Trevor answered, his mind wandering to the possibility of doing jobs alone. That would be much more exciting. The privacy, too, he could savour. Somehow, Mick just seemed too coarse and vulgar to appreciate the true joy and beauty of what they were doing.

"So we lie low, then?"

"All right."

"Till we hear from Lenny?"

"Yes."

A train rumbled over on the tracks above the ginnel. Mick looked at his watch and grinned. "Late."

"What is?"

"Ten-ten from 'Arrogate. Twenty minutes late. Typical bloody British Rail."

THIRTEEN

I

Banks spent most of the week in his office brooding on the three cases and smoking too much, but the figures refused to become clear; the shadowy man in the dark, belted raincoat seemed to float around in his mind with the two faceless youths, watching them watching the sailors on the deck of Alice Matlock's ship in a bottle, the *Miranda*. And somewhere among the crowd were all the people he had talked to in connection with the cases: Ethel Carstairs, the Sharps, "Boxer" Buxton the headmaster, Mr Price the form-master, Dorothy Wycombe, Robin Allott, Mr Patel, Alice Matlock herself, dead on the cold stone flags, and Jenny Fuller.

Jenny Fuller. Twice during the week he picked up the phone to call her, and twice he put it down without dialling. He had no excuse to see her—nothing new had happened—and he felt he had already misled her enough. When, on Wednesday evening, Sandra suggested that they invite Jenny to dinner, a silly argument followed, in which Banks protested that he hardly knew the woman and that their relationship was purely professional. His nose grew an inch or two, and Sandra backed down gracefully.

Richmond and Hatchley were in and out of his office with information, none of it very encouraging. Geoff Welling and Barry Scott appeared to be normal enough lads, and they had gone off on holiday to Italy the day before the Carol Ellis incident, so that let them out.

Sandra continued talking to the neighbours, but none of them had anything to add to Selena Harcourt's information.

The search continued for passers-by, shopkeepers and bus drivers

who might have been near The Oak the night Mr Patel saw the loiterer. Yes, one of the bus drivers remembered seeing him, but no, he
couldn't offer a description; the man had been standing in the shadows and the driver had been paying attention to the road. All the
shopkeepers had closed for the night and none of them lived, like Mr
Patel, above their premises. So far, no pedestrians had come forward,
despite the appeal in the *Yorkshire Post*.

Richmond had conducted a thorough search of Alice Matlock's
cottage, but no will turned up. Alice had nothing to her name but a
Post Office Savings Account, the balance of which stood at exactly
one hundred and five pounds, fifty-six pence on the day of her death.
She seemed to be one of that rare breed who do not live beyond their
means; all her life, she had made do with what she earned, whether it
was her nurse's salary or her pension. Ethel Carstairs said she had
never heard Alice talk of a will, and the whole motive of murder for
gain crumbled before it was fully constructed.

On Friday morning, Banks walked into the station, absorbed in
Monteverdi's *Orfeo*. Orpheus was pleading with Charon to allow him
to enter the underworld and see Eurydice.

> *Non viv'io, no, che poi de vita è priva*
> *Mia cara sposa, il cor non è più meco,*
> *E senza cor com'esser può ch'io viva?*

sang the man who could tame wild beasts with music: "I am no
longer alive, for since my dear wife is deprived of life, my heart
remains no longer with me, and without a heart, how can it be that
I am living?"

He didn't notice the woman waiting by the front desk to see him
until the desk-sergeant coughed and tapped him on the arm as he
drifted by, entranced. The embarrassed sergeant introduced them,
then went back to his duties as Banks, awkwardly removing his headphones, led the woman, Thelma Pitt, upstairs to his office.

She seemed very tense as she accepted the chair Banks drew out
for her. Though her hair was blonde, the dark roots were clearly visible, and they combined with the haggard cast of her still-attractive,
heart-shaped face and a skirt too short for someone of her age to give

the impression of a once gay and beautiful woman going downhill fast. Beside her right eye was a purplish-yellow bruise.

Banks took out a new file and wrote down, first, her personal details. He vaguely recognized her name, then remembered that she and her husband, a local farm labourer, had won over a quarter of a million pounds on the pools ten years ago. Banks had read all about them in the Sunday papers. They had been a young married couple at the time; the husband was twenty-six, Thelma twenty-five. For a while, their new jet-setting way of life had been a *cause célèbre* in Eastvale, until Thelma had walked out on her husband to become something of a local *femme fatale*. (Why, wondered Banks, were these delicate phrases always in French, and always untranslatable?) Thelma's legendary parties, which some said were thinly disguised orgies, involved a number of prominent Eastvalers, who were all eventually embarrassed one way or another. When the party was over, Thelma retreated into well-heeled obscurity. Her husband was later killed in an automobile accident in France.

It was a sad enough story in itself; now the woman sat before Banks looking ten years older than she was, hands clasped over her handbag on her lap, clearly with another tale of hard times to tell.

"I want to report a robbery," she said tightly, twisting a large ruby ring around the second finger of her right hand.

"Who was robbed?" Banks asked. "I assume it was..."

"Yes, it was me."

"When did it happen?"

"Monday evening."

"At your home?"

"Yes."

"What time?"

"It was just after ten. I got home early."

"Where had you been?"

"Where I usually go on Mondays, the Golf Club."

"Are you a player?"

"No," she smiled weakly, relaxing a little. "Just a drinker."

"You realize it's Friday now?" Banks prompted her, eager to set her at ease but puzzled about the circumstances. "You say the robbery took place on Monday .... It's a long time to wait before reporting it."

"I know," Thelma Pitt said, "and I'm sorry. But there's something else..."

Banks looked at her, his wide-open eyes asking the question.

"I was raped."

Banks put his pen down on the table. "Are you sure you wouldn't like to see a policewoman?" he asked.

"No, it doesn't matter." She leaned forward. "Inspector, I've lived with this night and day since Monday. I couldn't come in before because I was ashamed to. I felt dirty. I believed it was all my fault—a punishment for past sins, if you like. I'm a Catholic, though not a very good one. I haven't left the house since then. This morning I woke up angry, do you understand? I feel angry, and I want to do whatever I can to see that the criminals are caught. The robbery doesn't matter. The jewels were worth a great deal but not as much... not as much..." She gripped the sides of her chair until her knuckles turned white, then struggled for control of her emotions again.

Banks, who had been thinking that now the peeper had escalated to more serious crimes, was surprised by Thelma's description.

"Criminals?" he asked. "You mean there was more than one?"

"There were two of them. Kids, I think. They were wearing bala-clavas. Only one of them raped me. The other said he didn't fancy 'sloppy seconds.' That's the way he put it, Inspector, his exact words—'sloppy seconds.'" She pointed to her bruise. "He's the one that kicked me."

Banks didn't know what to say, and into the uneasy silence Thelma dropped what turned out to be the best lead of all.

"There's another thing," she said, looking away from him towards the wall as if she were examining the idyllic autumn scene on the cal-endar. "I've got VD."

II

Over the next half-hour, Banks listened to the details of Thelma Pitt's story as PC Susan Gay transcribed them.

Every Monday night Thelma went to the bar of the Eastvale Golf Club, where she kept up her association with some of the people she had got to know in earlier, better days. There was one man in particular, a Lewis Micklethwaite, with whom she had been going out for several weeks.

During a long weekend in London with a female friend a couple of weeks ago, Thelma had, while not entirely sober, allowed herself to be picked up by a younger man in a pub and had subsequently spent the night with him. She didn't remember much about the experience, but the following morning she felt terrible: physically and emotionally hungover. The young man lived in a small flat off the Brixton Road, and Thelma rushed outside as fast as she could and, unable to find a taxi, took the first bus into central London, returning to her friend at the hotel.

"To cut a long story short," she said, "I found out just over a week later that the bastard had kindly passed on his disease to me—gonorrhoea."

That was why she had left the Golf Club early. She didn't want to tell Lewis, nor did she want to infect him. They argued. He seemed unusually perturbed about her going, but she ran off anyway. And as a result of that, she had disturbed the burglars and got herself raped.

"Can you describe them at all?" Banks asked. "You said they were wearing balaclavas?"

"Yes."

"What colour?"

"Grey. Both grey."

"Any idea how old they were?"

"By the way they spoke and acted, I'd say they were both in their teens."

"How can you be sure?"

"The one who raped me was inexperienced. It was all over mercifully fast. I'd say it was his first time. A woman can tell these things, you know, Inspector."

"What about the other?"

"I think he was scared. He talked tough, but I don't think he dared do anything. He was smaller, more squat, and he had a very ugly voice. Raspy. And piggy eyes. He was edgy. I think he might have been on drugs. The one who raped me was leaner and taller. He didn't say an awful lot. I noticed nothing peculiar about his voice. His eyes were blue, and his breath didn't smell too good."

"Did they call each other by name?"

"No. They were careful not to do that."

"What about the rest of their clothing? Anything distinctive?"

Thelma Pitt shook her head. "Just what lots of kids wear these days. Bomber jackets, jeans..."

"There's nothing else you can remember?"

"Oh, I remember it all quite vividly, Inspector. I've replayed it over in my mind a hundred times since Monday. But that's all there is that's likely to help you. Unless it's of any use to know that the boy who raped me was wearing white Y-fronts. Marks and Sparks, I think," she added bitterly. Then she put her head in her hands and started to weep. Susan Gay comforted her, and after a few moments, Thelma Pitt again made the effort to control her feelings.

"I'm sorry," she apologized. "That was uncalled for."

Banks shrugged. "It must have been a terrifying experience," he said, feeling completely inadequate. "Would you recognize them again?"

"Yes, I think so. In the same circumstances. But that wouldn't help you because I can't identify their faces."

"That might not be necessary."

"I'd recognize the squat one's voice and eyes any time. As for the other... I do remember that he had a bit of decay between one of his front teeth and the one next to it, as if a filling had come out. But I couldn't give you a positive identification. I couldn't swear to anything in court."

She was remarkably calm as she relived it, Banks thought, trying to imagine the inner strength and courage it took to deal with such horror.

Finally, she described the jewellery that had been stolen, along with a valuable camera, then Banks let her leave, promising to get in touch as soon as anything happened. He also suggested, though it was much too late, that she see a doctor and have him look for and record any signs of assault for the purposes of evidence.

As soon as PC Gay had escorted Thelma Pitt from his office, Banks phoned Dr Glendenning. He was with a patient, so his receptionist said, but would call back in about ten minutes.

"What is it?" the old doctor asked brusquely about twenty minutes later.

"VD," Banks said. "Gonorrhoea, to be specific. What do you know about it?"

"Ah, gonorrhoea," Glendenning said, warming to the subject like a general admiring a brave opponent. "More commonly known as the clap, Cupid's revenge."

"What are the symptoms?"

"Discharge, a burning sensation while urinating. Inspector Banks, I hope you're not trying to tell me that you—"

"It's not me," Banks snapped, adding "you silly old sod" under his breath. "How soon do the symptoms appear?"

"It varies," Glendenning went on, unruffled. "Three to ten days is about usual."

"Treatment?"

"Penicillin. There have to be tests first, of course, just to make sure it isn't something else—particularly syphilis. The early symptoms can be similar."

"Where would a person find treatment?"

"Well, in the old days, of course, he'd go to his GP or perhaps to the infirmary. But nowadays, what with all the sexual promiscuity and what not, there are specialized VD clinics all over the place. Confidential treatment, naturally."

Banks had, indeed, heard of such places. "There's one here in Eastvale, right?" he asked. "Attached to the hospital?"

"Yes. And one in York."

"None nearer?"

"Not unless you count Darlington or Leeds."

"Thank you, doctor," Banks said hurriedly. "Thank you very much."

As soon as he'd hung up, he called in Hatchley and Richmond, and after explaining the situation, had them phone all the clinics within a fifty-mile radius and ask about a lean, tall teenager with decay between his front teeth, who would probably be very vague about where he had contracted the disease.

Fifteen minutes later, he was informed that nobody fitting the description had been into any of the clinics, which meant either that the suspect had not experienced the symptoms yet or that he was still worrying about what to do. Hatchley and Richmond had also requested that the staff of each clinic be on the lookout, and that they call their nearest police station if they became suspicious about anyone looking for treatment. After that, Hatchley phoned the local police in each area and asked them to detain the boy if he appeared at the clinic and to call Banks immediately.

Later, Banks talked to Jenny Fuller at her York University office and told her about Thelma Pitt. It wasn't part of the peeper case, but it was a sexual crime and he needed a woman's advice.

"Have you sent her for any help?" Jenny asked.

"I suggested she see a doctor. Mostly for our own official purposes, I have to admit."

"That won't do her a lot of good, Alan. There's a Rape Crisis Centre in York, a place where people can talk about their problems. I'm surprised you don't know about it. A lot of women find it hard to get on with their lives after an experience like that. Some never recover. Anyway, these people can help. They're not just doctors—a lot of them have been rape victims themselves. Just a minute and I'll get you the number."

Banks wrote down the telephone number and assured Jenny that he would pass it on to Thelma Pitt.

"Are we going to meet again soon?" she asked.

"Of course. I've got a lot on with this Thelma Pitt business at the moment, though, and there are no real developments on our case. I'll give you a call."

"The brush-off!" Jenny cried melodramatically.

"Don't be stupid," he laughed. "See you soon. And you never know," he added, "you might even get invited to dinner." Then he hung up before Jenny could respond.

The next job was to get Mr Lewis Micklethwaite in. Banks pulled the local directory out of his rattling desk drawer and reached for the phone again.

III

Micklethwaite was reluctant to drop in at Eastvale police station after work. He was also unwilling to have Banks call on him at home. In fact, Micklethwaite wanted to avoid all contact with the local constabulary, and when he finally did come to the office under threat of arrest, Banks immediately knew why.

"If it isn't my old pal Larry Moxton," Banks said, offering the man a cigarette.

"I don't know what you mean. My name's Micklethwaite."

But there was no mistaking him—the receding hairline, dark beady eyes, black beard, swarthy skin, fleshy lips—it was Moxton all right.

"Come on, Larry," Banks urged him. "You remember me, surely?"

"I've told you," Micklethwaite repeated, squirming in his chair. "I don't know what you're talking about."

Banks sighed. "Larry Moxton, ex-accountant. I put you away about ten years ago in London, remember, when you swindled that divorcée out of her savings? What was it—prime Florida real estate? Or was it gilt-edged securities?"

"It was a bloody frame-up, that's what it was," Moxton burst out. "It wasn't my fault my bloody partner took off with the funds."

Banks stroked his chin. "Bit of bad luck, that, Larry, I agree. We never did find him, did we? Probably sunning himself in Spain now. Still, that's the way it goes."

Moxton glared at him. "What do you want this time? I'm straight. Have been ever since I came out and moved up north. And the new name's legit, so don't waste your time on that."

It was hard to believe that such a surly, sneaky man had enough charm to cheat intelligent women out of their money, but that had been Moxton's specialty. For some reason, inexplicable to Banks, women found him hard to resist.

"Thelma Pitt, Larry. I want to know about Thelma Pitt."

"What about her?"

"You do know her, don't you?"

"So what if I do?"

"What are you after, Larry? A rich widow this time?"

"You've no right to make accusations like that. I've served my time—for a crime I didn't commit—and it's no bloody business of yours who I spend my time with."

"When was the last time you saw her?"

"Hey, what is this?" Moxton demanded, grasping the flimsy desk and half rising. "Nothing's happened to her, has it?"

"Never mind that. And sit down. When did you last see her?"

"I want to know. I've got a right to know."

"Sit down! You've got a right to know nothing, Larry. Now answer my questions. You wouldn't want me to lose my temper like last time, would you? When did you see her last?"

Moxton, like many others, had learned from experience that it was no use arguing with Banks, that he had the patience and persistence of a cat after a bird. He might not actually hit you, but you'd go away thinking it would have been easier if he had.

"Monday night," he answered sullenly. "I saw her on Monday night."

"Where?"

"Eastvale Golf Club."

"You a member, Larry?"

"'Course I am. I told you, I'm a respectable businessman. I *am* a CA, you know."

"You're an effing C, too, as far as I'm concerned, Larry. But that's beside the point, isn't it? How long have you been a member?"

"Two years."

"Two years." And to think that Ottershaw had told him it was an exclusive place—no riff-raff. "I don't know what the world's coming to, Larry, I really don't," Banks said.

Moxton glowered at him. "Get to the point, Inspector," he snapped, looking at his watch. "I've got things to do."

"I'll bet you have. All right, so you know Thelma Pitt. What's your relationship with her?"

"None of your business."

"Good friends, business partners, lovers?"

"So we go out together, have a bit of fun. What's it to you? What's happened to her?"

He did seem genuinely concerned about the woman's welfare, but Banks considered it unethical to tell him that Thelma Pitt had been robbed and raped. If she wanted him to know, she would tell him herself.

"What time did you leave her on Monday?" Banks pressed on.

"I didn't. She left me. It was earlier than usual—about a quarter to ten. I don't know why. She was upset. I suppose you could say we argued."

"Could I? What about?"

"None of your...Oh," he sighed and turned up his hands, "why not? She wanted to be alone, that's all. I wanted her to come with me as usual."

"Where did the two of you usually go?"

"To my place."

"Did you spend the night there?"

"Sometimes, yes."

"Why didn't you go there last Monday?"

"I told you. She wouldn't. Said she had a headache. You know women."

"But you pressed her to stay at the club?"

"Of course I did. I was enjoying her company."

"Even though she didn't feel very well?"

"It didn't look like anything to me. I think it was just an excuse. She seemed fine physically, just a bit upset about something."

"Any idea what?"

"No. She wasn't very communicative. She just stormed off."

"After you'd tried very hard to persuade her to stay and to accompany you to your house? Is that right?"

"What are you getting at?"

"Nothing. I'm just trying to establish the facts, that's all."

"Well, yes. Naturally, I wanted her to stay with me. I'm a man, like any other. I enjoy the company of attractive women."

"So Thelma Pitt isn't the only one?"

"We're not engaged to be married or anything, if that's what you're getting at. Come on, I've had enough of this pussyfooting around. What's it all about?"

"Know anyone else at the Golf Club?"

"One or two. It is a social place for professional men, you know."

"Maurice Ottershaw?"

A look of fear flashed in Moxton's eyes. It didn't last long, but Banks saw it.

"Maurice Ottershaw?" he repeated. "I know him. I mean, we've had a few drinks together. I wouldn't really say I know him. What is it you're getting at?"

"I'll tell you, Larry," Banks said, leaning forward on the desk and holding Moxton's eyes with his. "I think you've been fingering jobs for someone, that's what I think. You know when your rich friends at the club are likely to be away, and you tip someone the wink. But it went wrong with Thelma Pitt, didn't it? You couldn't keep her away from home long enough."

Moxton looked really frightened now. "What's happened to her? You've got to tell me. She isn't hurt, is she?"

"Why would she be?"

"After what you said...I thought..."

"Don't worry about it."

"You can't prove anything, you know."

"I know," Banks admitted. "But I also know you did it."

"Look, I wouldn't shit on my own doorstep, would I?"

"A creep like you would shit anywhere, Moxton. We're going to be watching you, keeping an eye on you. You won't be able to crap anywhere without being watched, understand?"

"That's intimidation, harassment!" Moxton yelled, jumping to his feet in exasperation.

"Oh, piss off," Banks said, and pointed to the door.

FOURTEEN

I

When Trevor awoke on Monday morning, he knew something was wrong.

"Trevor!" his father shouted as usual. "Breakfast's on the table! If you don't hurry up you'll be late for school."

At least he knew there would be no row over the table this morning. All day Sunday he had stayed in like a dutiful son; he'd helped his dad with the stock and had even done some homework. Such gestures as that could earn him a few days' peace, if not more.

Pity about the homework, he thought. It was a waste really because he wouldn't be there to hand it in. He was taking the afternoon off to go and discuss future plans with Mick. Just because Lenny had told them to lay off the break-ins for a while didn't mean they couldn't find some other ways of amusing themselves—perhaps out of town.

But something was wrong. He didn't feel right. He lay there with the sheets pulled up and looked at the glossy posters of pop stars on his walls, wondering if the stickiness he felt meant that he'd had a wet dream. Cautiously, he pushed the bedclothes aside and sat up on the edge of the bed. The front of his pyjamas was stained, and when he looked more closely he noticed a kind of yellowish discharge.

Alarmed, Trevor rushed to the bathroom and washed himself. When he stood to urinate, the fear really took hold of him. It hurt like hell. It felt as if he was pissing red-hot needles. He leaned against the wall in a cold sweat, pressing his forehead against the tiles. When he'd finished, the pain faded and all that remained was a lingering throb, the echo of an ache.

Trevor washed his face and stared at himself in the mirror. The dark patch between his teeth was spreading quickly, and he had two spots: one, still embryonic, wedged between the edge of his nostril and his upper lip; the other, yellow and juicy, exactly at the point where his chin curved under to become his throat. But they were the least of the worries. He was pale and his eyes were dull. He knew what he'd got; he'd got the clap. That flicking cunt had given him the clap.

With a great effort, Trevor pulled himself together. He finished washing, then returned to his bedroom to get dressed.

"Hurry up, our Trev!" his father called. "Your bacon and eggs are going cold!"

"Coming, dad," he yelled back. "Won't be a minute."

He pulled his white shirt and grey slacks on, picked out a sleeveless, V-neck pullover with a muted pattern of grey and mauve, and he was ready. They ate breakfast together quickly, Graham beaming at his son.

"It was a good day we had yesterday, wasn't it?" he asked.

"Yes," Trevor lied.

"Got a lot of work done."

"We did, didn't we?"

"And all your homework, too."

"That's right."

"Believe me, Trevor, it's worth it. You might not think so now, but you'll be grateful in the future, mark my words."

"I suppose so," Trevor mumbled. "Look at the time! I'll be late."

"Off you go, then," Graham said, ruffling Trevor's hair and smiling at him. "And don't forget to hand that homework in."

"Don't worry, I won't," Trevor said, forcing a grin and picking up his satchel.

"And you'd better get that tooth seen to, too, lad," Graham added, "or it'll only get worse. See if you can get an appointment with the school dentist."

"All right, dad," Trevor replied, and rushed off.

He had no intention of making any appointment with the school dentist, or with any other dentist, for that matter. It was Dr Himmler, as he called the school dentist, and his assistant Griselda who had put

Trevor off dentists in the first place. The man was grubby and his National Health glasses were stuck together across the bridge with Elastoplast. Griselda stood by, white-faced and red-lipped, like some mediaeval witch passing him the instruments of torture. He never gave anaesthetics for fillings; you simply had to grip the chair. For extractions he administered nitrous oxide, and Trevor would never forget that feeling of suffocation as the mask was finally pressed over his nose and mouth, like a polythene bag clinging to the pores, keeping all the air out. And afterwards, he would stand up groggily and stagger to the next room, where the previous patients were still standing around water fountains spitting or swilling the blood from their mouths.

Trevor set off in the right direction for school. He walked up through Leaview Estate, which was already busy with the postman, the milkman and wives seeing husbands off to work, then turned onto King Street with its cobbles and trendy tourist shoppes. The places all had looking-glass windows and black-leaded railings leading down to basements stuffed with mildewed books, spinning wheels, bobbins and other relics of the woollen industry, which were now sold as antiques.

The school was at the bottom of a narrow street to his left, and Trevor could see the white tips of the rugby posts and the dirty red-brick Victorian clocktower. Instead of turning down School Drive, though, he took the narrow, winding streets to the market square. On the eastern side of the square, between the National Westminster Bank and Jopling's Newsagent's, a short flight of worn stone steps led down to the El Toro Coffee Bar, a dim room with bullfight posters, castanets and maracas on the walls. Trevor slumped into the darkest corner, ordered an espresso coffee, and settled down to think.

He knew he had VD because he'd heard other kids talking and joking about it at school. Nobody ever thought it would happen to them, though. And because Trevor's intelligence was imaginative rather than scientific, his ideas about the consequences of the disease were far-fetched, to say the least. He pictured his penis turning black and rotten, the flesh coming away in great gobbets in his hands the next time he had to go to the toilet. He was convinced that it would drop off altogether within hours. There was treatment, he knew, though he had no idea what it was. But anything was better than dying that way; even the school dentist would be better than that.

He could not go to his GP, Dr Farmer, because his father would find out. He could bear the embarrassment, but not disclosure. Too many awkward questions would be asked. There were special clinics, or so he'd heard people say, and he figured that one of those was his best bet. There had been nothing in the papers about the woman he had raped, so Trevor assumed that Mick's boot had done the trick and she was keeping quiet for fear of worse reprisals. Still, the police didn't publicize everything they knew, so it would be best to avoid Eastvale, just in case. Trevor asked the owner for the phone directory and looked up hospitals and clinics. As he had guessed, there was a place in York. He scribbled down the address on a page torn out of a school exercise book and left the El Toro.

At the bus station, he put his satchel and school blazer in a locker, wearing only his duffle-coat over his shirt and pullover. That way he didn't look at all like a schoolboy. The next bus for York was due to leave in fifteen minutes. He bought a copy of *Melody Maker* at the newsstand and sat on the cracked green bench to wait.

II

All day Monday Banks seethed with impatience. He had made great efforts to put the Thelma Pitt business out of his mind over the weekend, mostly for the sake of his family. On Saturday, they had driven into York to do some shopping and on Sunday they had all gone on a vigorous walk from Bainbridge to Semerwater, in Wensleydale. It was a brisk day, sunny and cool, but they were all warm enough in their walking gear.

On Monday morning, though, Banks took off his Walkman, hardly having noticed which opera he'd been listening to, slammed it shut in the drawer and shouted for Hatchley.

"Sir?" the sergeant said, red-faced with the effort of running upstairs.

Banks looked at him sternly.

"You'd better do something about the shape you're in, Sergeant," he said first. "You'd not be much use in a chase, would you?"

"No, sir," Hatchley replied, gasping for breath.

"Anyway, that's not what I want to see you about. Anything from the clinics?"

"No, sir."

"Damn!" Banks thumped the desk.

"You did ask us to let you know, sir," Hatchley reminded him. "I'm sure you'd have heard if there'd been any news over the weekend."

Banks glared at him. "Of course," he said, scratching his head and sitting down.

"It can take up to ten days, sir."

"When would that take us to?"

"Wednesday or Thursday, sir."

"Thursday," Banks repeated, tapping a ruler against his thigh. "Anything could happen before then. What about Moxton?"

"Moxton, sir?"

"Micklethwaite, as he calls himself now."

"Oh, him. Nothing there either, I'm afraid."

Banks had ordered surveillance on Moxton, assuming that he might try to warn his partner, whoever that was.

"He didn't do much at all," Hatchley added, "though he did go and visit the woman."

"Thelma Pitt?"

"Yes, sir."

"And?"

"And nothing, sir. Stayed about fifteen minutes, then drove home. Seemed a bit pissed off, if you ask me. Slammed the car door. He stayed in all Saturday night, went for a walk on Sunday morning, washed his car, dropped in for a quick drink at that posh place, the Hope and Anchor, about nine o'clock, then went home and stayed there."

"Did he talk to anyone at the Hope and Anchor?"

"Only the landlord, sir."

"Anyone we know?"

"No, sir. Straight as a die. Never even sold short measure, far as we can tell."

Banks took a deep breath. "All right, Sergeant. Thank you," he said, softening his tone a little to mollify Hatchley. "Have some coffee sent up, will you?"

"Sir?"

Banks grinned. "I know it's awful muck, but I need it all the same."

"Will do," Hatchley said, lingering. "Er...Sir?..."

"What is it?"

"Have you got any idea who it was, sir? The rapist?"

"I'm not sure, Sergeant. It could be that Sharp kid and his mate or a pair very much like them. It's the same ones who robbed the old ladies and pissed on the Ottershaws' VCR—that I am sure about."

"And the Matlock killing?"

Banks shook his head. "I don't think so. That's something different. Another problem altogether."

"Why not bring the Sharp kid in for questioning?"

"Because I can't prove anything. Do you think I wouldn't have had him in before if I had something on him? Besides, I'm not certain yet that he is the one, I just got the feeling there was something wrong when I talked to him and his father."

"That bit about the bad tooth, sir. If he—"

Banks waved his hand as if to brush aside a fly. "By itself it's nothing. You know that as well as I do. On the other hand, if he's got the clap..."

"We could always bring him in, just to shake him up a bit."

"No good. His father would insist on being present. He'd probably send for a bloody solicitor, too, then they'd just clam up on us. If Sharp's our lad, we need evidence before we tackle him again or we'll lose him for good."

Hatchley scratched the seat of his pants. "What about the woman?" he asked.

"Thelma Pitt?"

"Yes."

"She said she couldn't positively identify them. We don't want to take any risks on this. When we get him, I want him to stay, not walk off on some technicality. Besides, I'd rather not put her through it until we've got a bit more to go on. If it's Sharp, we know he's got the clap. Sooner or later, he'll turn up at one of the clinics. Then we'll haul him in."

Hatchley nodded and went back downstairs.

When the coffee came, Banks realized all over again why he usually took his breaks in the Golden Grill. He sat with his chair turned to face the window, smoked and stared blankly over the market square, watching the first activities of the morning. Delivery vans double parked outside the shops; the minister, glancing at his watch, hurried into the church; a housewife in a paisley headscarf rattled the door of Bradwell's Grocery, which didn't appear to be open yet.

But all this was mere activity without meaning to Banks. He was close to solving the robberies and the rape of Thelma Pitt—he knew that, he could feel it in his bones—but there was nothing he could do to hurry things along. As so often in his job, he had to be patient; this time he literally had to let nature take its course.

Slowly, while he smoked yet another cigarette, the market square came to life. As the first tourists stepped into the Norman church, Bradwell's Grocery finally opened its doors and took delivery of boxes of fruit from an orange van with a sombrero painted on its side. The woman in the paisley headscarf was nowhere to be seen.

By mid-morning, Banks was sick of being cooped up in his office. He told Sergeant Rowe he was going out for half an hour or so, then went for a walk to burn off some of his impatience.

He hurried across the market square, fastening his overcoat as he went, then cut down the narrow backstreets and through the flower gardens to the riverside.

The slowly increasing cloud cover had not yet quite blotted out the sun, but it had drawn a thin veil over it that weakened the light and gave the whole landscape the look of a water-colour in pale greens, yellows, orange, brown and red. The scent of rain came on a chilling wind, which seemed to be blowing from the northwest, along the channel of Swainsdale itself. The breeze hurried the river over the terraced fulls and set up a constant skittering sound in the trees that lined the banks. Leaves were already falling and scraping along the ground. Most of them ended up in the water.

Across the Swain was another pathway, and behind that more trees and flowerbeds. The houses that Banks could just see through the waving branches were the ones fronting The Green, which separated them from the East Side Estate. Banks knew that Jenny's house was among them, but he couldn't tell which one it was from that distance and angle.

He pushed his hands deep into his overcoat pockets, hunched his shoulders and hurried on. The exercise was doing the trick, driving chaotic thoughts from his mind and helping him work up an appetite for lunch.

He doubled back around the castle to the market square. Hatchley and Richmond were lunching in the Queen's Arms when he got there, and Hatchley stopped in mid-sentence when he saw his boss enter. Banks remembered that he had been rude to the sergeant that morning and guessed that they were complaining about him. Taking a deep breath, he joined them at their table and set things right again by buying both his men a pint.

III

The York bus arrived at the station by the Roman wall at ten-thirty. Trevor walked along the wall, passed the railway station, then crossed the Ouse over Lendal Bridge by the ruins of St Mary's Abbey and the Yorkshire Museum. After that, he wandered in a daze around the busy city until he felt hungry. Just after opening time, he found a pub on Stonegate—with his height and out-of-school dress he certainly looked over eighteen—where he ate a steak-and-mushroom pie along with his pint of keg beer.

He lingered there for almost two hours, nursing his pint and reading every word (including the "Musicians Wanted" column) in his *Melody Maker*, before venturing out into the streets again. Everywhere he walked he seemed to stumble across pairs of American tourists, most of them complaining because they were inadequately dressed for the cool weather.

"Goddamn sun's out," he heard one fat man in thin cotton slacks and a blazer grumble. "You'd think there'd be some goddamn heat, for Christ's sake."

"Oh, Elmer," his wife said. "We've been in Yoorp for a month now. You oughtta know it never gets hot north of Athens."

Trevor sneered. Silly sods, he thought. Why even bother to come here and litter up the streets if they were too soft to take a bit of autumn chill. He imagined America as a vast continent baking in the sun—pavements you could fry eggs on; people stripped to the waist all the time having barbecues; enormous, uninhabitable stretches of desert and jungle.

About an hour later, he knew he was lost. He seemed to have wandered outside the city walls. This was no tourist area he was in; it was too working-class. The long straight rows of tiny back-to-backs built of dusty pink bricks seemed endless. Washing flapped on lines hung across the narrow streets. Trevor turned back, and at the end of the street saw the Minster's bright towers in the distance. He started walking in their direction.

He'd put it off for long enough, he decided. If he didn't want his penis to shrivel up and drop off, he'd better go for treatment, however frightening the prospect seemed.

In a newsagent's, he found time to look up the location of the clinic in a street guide before the suspicious owner told him to clear off if he wasn't going to buy anything.

"Bleeding Paki," Trevor muttered under his breath as he found himself being ushered out. But he'd got what he'd come for.

The clinic, not very far from the hub of the city, was a squat, modern building of windowless concrete with a flat, asphalt roof. Trevor presented himself at reception, where he was told to take a seat and wait until a doctor became available. There were two other people before him, a middle-aged man and a scruffy female student, and both of them looked embarrassed. As they waited, nobody spoke and they all avoided even accidental eye contact.

About an hour later, it was Trevor's turn. A bald, long-faced doctor led him into a small room and bid him sit in front of the desk. Trevor shifted anxiously, wishing to God the whole thing was over and done with. The place smelt of Dettol and carbolic; it reminded him of the dentist's.

"Right," the doctor said brightly, after scribbling a few notes on a form. "What can we do for you, young man?"

What a stupid question, Trevor thought. What the hell does he think I'm here for, to have my bunions seen to?

"I've got a problem," he mumbled, and gave the doctor the details.

"What's your name?" the doctor asked, after umming and ahing over Trevor's description of his symptoms.

"Peter Upshaw," Trevor answered smartly. It was something he'd had the foresight to work out in advance, a name he had picked out from the columns of *Melody Maker*.

"Address?"

"Forty-two Arrowsmith Drive."

The doctor glanced at him sharply: "Is that here, in York?"

"Yes."

"Whereabouts?" He scratched his shiny pate with his ballpoint pen. "I don't believe I know it."

"It's by the Minster," Trevor blurted out, reddening. He hadn't anticipated that the quack would be so inquisitive.

"The Minster? Ah, yes..." The doctor made an entry on the form. "All right, Peter," he said, putting down his pen. "We'll have some tests to do, of course, but first I have to ask you where you caught this disease, who you caught it from."

Trevor certainly hadn't bargained for this. He couldn't tell the truth, he couldn't name anyone he knew, and he certainly couldn't answer, "Nobody."

"A prostitute," he replied quickly. It was the first thing that came into his mind.

The doctor raised his thin eyebrows. "A prostitute? Where was this, Peter?"

"Here."

"In York?"

"Yes."

"When?"

"About a week ago."

"What was her name?"

"Jane."

"Where does she live?"

It was all going too fast for Trevor. He began to stumble over his answers. "I...I...don't know. I was with some other boys. We'd had a bit too much to drink, then we walked around and she just came up to us."

"In the street?"

"Yes."

"But you must have gone somewhere."

"No. I mean yes."

The doctor stared at him.

"In an alley," Trevor went on. "We went in an alley. There was nobody around. We stood up, leaning against a wall."

"What about your friends? Did they...er?"

"No," Trevor assured him hastily. He realized that he would be asked to name anybody else he implicated.

The doctor frowned. "Are you sure?"

"Yes. It was only me. It was my birthday."

"Ah," the doctor said, smiling benignly. "I understand. But you don't know where this woman lived?"

"No."

"Have you been with anyone else since it happened?"

"No."

"Very well, Peter. If you'll just walk down the corridor to the room at the end, you'll find a nurse there. She'll take a blood sample—just to make sure. After that, come back here and we'll get on with it."

The room was like the school chemistry laboratory, with glass-fronted cupboards full of labelled jars and long tables covered with retorts, bunsen burners, pipettes and racks of test tubes. It made Trevor nervous.

The nurse was quite pretty. "Relax," she said, rolling up his sleeve. "It won't hurt."

And it didn't. He couldn't feel the needle going in at all, but he turned his head away so he wouldn't see the blood running into the syringe. He felt a slight prick as it came out.

"There," the nurse said, smiling and wiping the spot with cotton-wool soaked in alcohol. "All done. You can go back to Doctor Willis now."

Trevor went back to the small examination-room, where Doctor Willis greeted him.

"I want you to sit back on that chair over there and relax, Peter," he said in a soft hypnotic voice. "This won't take very long. Just another little test."

Willis turned his back to Trevor and picked up something shiny from a white kidney-shaped tray.

"Just remove your trousers, Peter. Underpants, too. That's right," the doctor said, and came towards him. Willis held in his hand what looked like a sewing-needle. He seemed to be holding it by the point, though, and the angled eye was larger than normal.

Trevor tensed as Willis came closer. For a moment the doctor seemed to be wearing a dirty smock, and his National Health glasses were held together at the bridge by Elastoplast.

"Now, relax, Peter," he said, bending forward. "I'm just going to insert this gently inside..."

IV

The phone call came through at 4:17.

"Chief Inspector Banks?" It was an unfamiliar voice.

"Yes."

"This is Inspector MacLean here. York CID."

Banks tightened his grip on the receiver, his palms sweating, slippery against the black bakelite: "Yes, go on."

"It's about your request. The local clap-shop called us a few minutes ago. Seems they've got a kid down there. Looks about eighteen but could be younger and doesn't appear to know York very well. He was very vague about how he picked up the disease. Some claptrap—excuse the pun—about having a prossie in a back alley. Doctor got the distinct impression that he was making it up as he went along. Sound like your laddie?"

"It certainly does," Banks said, drumming on his desk with excitement. "Tell me more."

"Not a lot more to tell," MacLean went on in his deadpan voice. "Some decay between the front teeth, all right, but most kids have rotten teeth these days. I was over in the States two years ago on an exchange, and they think it's criminal there the way the British treat their teeth—or don't treat them, if you catch my drift. They say you can always spot a Brit by his teeth. You know—"

"Inspector..." Banks cut in.

"Sorry," MacLean said. "You must be eager to get your mitts on him."

"I am, rather. Where is he?"

"Still at the clap-shop. We're holding him there. Got a couple of uniforms on the job. We let him have his treatment, of course. You realize he'll need a few more shots yet? Do you want him delivered?"

"No, thanks. I'll pick him up myself."

"I'm glad you said that. We're a bit short of staff down here."

"What name did he give?"

"Upshaw. Peter Upshaw. Ring a bell?"

"No, but it'd be false, wouldn't it?" Banks took down the address of the clinic. "Be there in about an hour—and thank you, Inspector MacLean."

"You're welcome," MacLean said, and hung up.

"Sergeant Hatchley!" Banks bellowed, jumping up and flinging open his door.

For the second time that day, Hatchley arrived red-faced and breathless. But Banks made no comment on his physical condition. His dark eyes glittering with success, he clapped his hand gleefully on the sergeant's broad, well-padded shoulder and said, "Fancy a ride to York?"

V

Trevor, meanwhile, sat glumly in the examination room under the bored eyes of a fresh-faced constable no more than three or four years his senior. The other officer, of similar age and appearance (so much so that locals on their beat called them the Bobbie Twins) stood in the reception area waiting for the CID bigwig.

After the slight discomfort and great humiliation of his examination, Trevor had been told to await the test results. He felt edgy and afraid, but not of the police; there was room only for one worry at a time in his youthful mind. It was with great surprise, then, that he noted the arrival of Constable Parker, who preceded Dr Willis through the door.

"Sorry about this," Willis said embarrassedly, taking off his glasses and cleaning them on his smock. "A little misunderstanding, I'm sure. Soon have it straightened out, eh?" And under the policeman's eyes, he administered the first injection in Trevor's course of treatment.

After that, there was nothing to do but wait, and one worry very quickly replaced another in Trevor's mind.

It was closer to six o'clock when Banks and Hatchley arrived at the clinic. They hadn't reckoned on the rush-hour snarl-up in York's maze of one-way streets. Constable Spinks led them to the examination room, and Trevor sneered when he saw Banks walk in.

"Well, Trevor," Banks greeted him. "I see you've lost a filling since we last talked."

Trevor said nothing, but got sullenly to his feet and followed the two men out to their car. The drive back to Eastvale in the dark passed in silence.

The law stated that a juvenile could not be charged unless his parents were present, and as a charge was likely, Banks had to call Graham Sharp in as soon as the trio arrived back at the Eastvale station.

Nobody said a word to Trevor until his father arrived.

When Graham Sharp was shown into the already crowded office by PC Gay, Banks was just finishing his call to Sandra, letting her know that he would be late home again that evening.

Finally, with both Trevor and his father sitting opposite him at the desk and Sergeant Hatchley standing by the window with his notebook, gazing down on the quiet, darkening market square, Banks was ready to begin. He tidied the files on his desk, arranged the pencils in front of him, and caught Trevor's eye.

"What were you doing at that clinic?" he opened.

"What do you think?" Trevor mumbled scornfully.

"Well, you weren't having your filling replaced, that's for certain."

"What's all this?" Graham Sharp butted in. "What clinic? What are you talking about?"

"Mr Sharp," Banks said patiently, "according to the law, you have to be present if charges are likely to be laid, but I'm the one who's asking the questions, all right?"

"I've got a right to protect my son."

"Yes, you have. You're perfectly at liberty to advise him not to answer if you wish. But please bear in mind that he hasn't been charged with anything *yet*."

Graham Sharp settled back in his chair, looking angry and confused.

"Why didn't you go to the Eastvale Clinic?" Banks asked Trevor.

"Didn't know there was one."

"How did you find out about York?"

"A schoolmate told me."

"Who did you get the clap from?"

"Now, wait a minute!" Sharp interrupted again. "This is going too far. What clap? Who's got VD?"

"Your son has gonorrhoea, Mr Sharp. Haven't you, lad?"

Trevor said nothing.

"There's no point denying it," Banks pressed. "The doctor did the tests. We can easily call him and have him talk to your dad."

Trevor tamed away from his father and nodded. Graham Sharp put his head in his hands.

"Let's get back to my original question," Banks continued. "Where did you get this disease? You don't catch it from toilet seats, you know."

"It was like I told the doctor," Trevor answered.

"Ah yes," Banks said, speaking up so that Graham Sharp could hear him clearly. "You had a prostitute against a wall down a back alley in York. Is that right?"

Trevor nodded, pale.

"When was this?"

"About a week ago. Last Monday."

"You were in York last Monday?"

"Yes."

"What time did he get home, Mr Sharp?"

Sharp snapped to attention at the sound of his name. "What?"

"What time did your son get home last Monday night?" Banks repeated.

"About eleven. He always has to be in by eleven. It's his bedtime, see."

"Did you know where he was?"

"He said he was going to York, yes," Sharp said.

"Who did he go with?"

"I don't know. A friend. He didn't say."

"A friend?"

"I suppose so."

"Not friends?"

"For God's sake, I don't know."

"You see, the thing is, Mr Sharp, he told the doctor he went with a group of friends to celebrate his birthday, and that his friends got together and bought him, so to speak, a prostitute as a present. Was it your son's birthday last Monday, Mr Sharp?"

"Yes. Yes, it was, as a matter of fact."

"You realize," Banks said, "that we can always check the records?"

"Well, it wasn't officially his birthday, no. But it was his mother's birthday. He always used to celebrate his mother's birthday. He was very attached to her."

"Is that really what happened, Trevor?" Banks asked. "To celebrate your mother's birthday you had a prostitute up against a wall in a back alley in York? She said her name was Jane and you've no idea where she lives?"

Trevor nodded.

"Do you know, Trevor, that we can question every prostitute in York if we have to? It's not as big as Leeds or Bradford, and there aren't very many of them. The police know them all. They're on good terms—you know, you scratch my back, I'll scratch yours, that kind of thing? It wouldn't take us long to find out whether your story's true or not."

"All right," Trevor said defiantly. "Ask them. Bloody well ask them for all I care."

"Mind your language, Trevor," his father said.

Sergeant Hatchley, who had remained as impassive as a Buddha throughout the interrogation, suddenly moved away from the window and began pacing around the small office, making the floor creak. Trevor shot nervous glances at him and seemed to tense up when Hatchley walked behind him.

"Care to tell us the names of your friends, Trevor? Just so we can corroborate your story," Banks asked.

"No." Trevor glanced sideways at Hatchley, who leaned against the wall for a moment and cracked his knuckles before turning another page in his notebook.

"Where were you a week last Thursday evening?"

"He was at home with me," Graham Sharp answered quickly.

"I asked Trevor."

"Like he says." Trevor looked at his father.

"Doing what?"

"Watched a bit of telly, read a bit, did some homework."

"What about Tuesday, Wednesday, Friday, Saturday, Sunday?"

"Same thing."

"Don't have much of a social life, do you Trevor? When I was a lad I was all over the place. My mother and father couldn't keep track of me."

Trevor shrugged.

"Look," Graham Sharp cut in, eyeing Hatchley, who moved casually away from the wall and back over to the window, "this has gone far enough. What's it all about? What's my Trevor supposed to have done?"

"When?"

"What do you mean, 'when'?"

"I mean that we think Trevor's done a lot of things. I was asking you which night you meant."

"Don't be ridiculous. Trevor's a good kid. He's doing well at school and he'll be going on to university. He's going to make something out of his life."

Banks shook his head. "He's not doing so well at school, you know. I've checked."

Sharp's mouth dropped open, then he pulled himself together. "All right, so he's having one or two problems at the moment. We all go through difficult phases, Inspector, you must know that?"

"Yes, I know that," Banks replied evenly. "But I'm afraid that in your Trevor's case it's something more serious."

"What is it?" Sharp pleaded. "What on earth is he supposed to have done?"

Hatchley turned from the window and startled everybody with his gruff voice. He spoke, however, with a quiet intensity that enthralled his audience completely.

"Last Monday," he said, "two lads broke into a woman's house. They thought she was out and wouldn't be back till late. As it happened, she had a fight with her fancy man and came home early. She caught them at it, burgling her house. They tied her up, then one of them raped her and the other kicked her in the head. We think the crime was committed by the same two youths who also burgled a Mr Maurice Ottershaw's house, assaulted and robbed four old ladies and, possibly," he glanced at Banks, who nodded, "killed your neighbour, Alice Matlock."

"And you're saying my Trevor had something to do with this?" Sharp cried, getting to his feet. The veins on his temples stood out, throbbing wildly. "You must be insane!" He banged on the flimsy desk. "I want my solicitor here! I want him here now, before you say another word."

"You're perfectly at liberty to request that, of course, sir," Banks said mildly, giving Hatchley the signal to fade into the woodwork again. "But, I must repeat, your son hasn't been charged with anything yet. He's simply helping us with our enquiries."

The cliché seemed to calm Sharp down a little. He eased himself slowly back into his chair and brushed back the hair from his forehead. "I thought your man here just accused my son of rape, burglary, and murder," he snarled, glaring at Hatchley's back.

"Nothing of the sort," Banks assured him. "He simply gave details of the crimes we think your son might be able to help us with."

Though he no longer linked the robberies with the death of Alice Matlock, Banks knew how to exploit an unsolved killing in his favour. If Trevor thought he was going to get Alice's murder pinned on him, too, there was a slim chance he might confess to the other offences.

"What makes you think my Trevor knows anything about it?" Sharp asked.

"Because the woman who was raped had just discovered that she had contracted gonorrhoea," Banks said, directing his words at Trevor, who stared down at his knees. "And your son has just returned from a VD clinic in York, where he was diagnosed as having gonorrhoea. The symptoms show up, so I'm told, anywhere between three and ten days. I'd say that seven days fits into that time scale quite well, wouldn't you?"

"But surely," Sharp objected, "there are other people visiting these clinics? If Trevor really did go with a prostitute and catch VD from her as he says—and I believe him—then that's no crime. It's just youthful high spirits. I was a bit of a lad myself at his age."

"Are robbery, rape, assault and murder just youthful high spirits, too?" Banks asked sarcastically.

"Now, look here, you said you weren't accusing my son of anything."

"I'm not accusing him, I'm trying to get to the truth. I never said he wasn't a suspect, though. Are you sure he went to York last Monday?"

"That's where he said he was going."

"When did you lose that filling, Trevor?" Banks asked.

"Wednesday," Trevor replied. But not before his father had said, "Thursday."

"You see," Banks went on, "the woman who was raped said she remembered the kid's front teeth, that there was some decay between them, as if he had a missing filling. She said she'd recognize it again. She said she'd know his voice, too. And," here he directed his words at Trevor, "she'd know his technique. She said she could tell he was just an inexperienced kid because he shot his load almost as soon as he stuck it in."

Trevor flushed with anger and grasped the edge of the desk. Graham put a restraining hand on his shoulder.

"We'll bring her in, Trevor. She's not afraid to give evidence, you know, despite what your friend did to her. And we'll question all the prostitutes in York. We'll talk to the bus drivers and see if any of them remember you, and if you tell us you went by train we'll talk to the ticket collectors and train crews. We'll find out who else went to York that night and we'll ask if any of them saw you and your friends. Seeing as there were a few of you, I should imagine you were quite noisy—youthful high spirits and all that—and someone in whatever pub you were in is bound to remember. So why don't you make it easier for us, Trevor? Make it easier for everyone. It's up to you. We'll nail you in the end anyway."

"Come on, Trev," Hatchley piped up, putting a fatherly hand on the boy's shoulder. "Before it goes too far. It'll go easier on you this way."

Trevor shook his hand off.

"I refuse to believe this," said Sharp. "My son isn't capable of such actions. He can't be. I raised him myself after his mother left. Gave him everything he wanted. If he's done anything wrong—and I don't think he has—then he was led on. He was led on by that bloody Mick Webster. It's him you want, not my Trevor."

"Shut up, dad!" Trevor snapped. "For God's sake, shut up!" And he lapsed back into sullen silence.

Banks got to his feet and smiled down at Trevor, who caught his eye before turning away. Both of them knew, in that split second of eye contact, that Banks had won. He had nowhere near enough evidence yet to make a conviction, but if Mick Webster thought that Trevor had snitched on him...

"Where does he live, this Webster?" Banks asked Graham.

"On the East Side Estate. That first street, the one that faces The Green."

"I know it. Number?"

"I don't know, but it's the fifth house down after the tobacconist's. I've seen him coming and going a few times when I've been picking up stock."

"Got that?" Banks asked Hatchley, who nodded. "Take Richmond, and hurry up. Bring in Mick Webster."

FIFTEEN

I

After Alan's phone call, Sandra packed Brian off to the Lifeboys and Tracy to the Guides. They hadn't been interested in such organizations back in London, but since they'd started school in Eastvale and discovered that many of the other children were members, they decided it would be a good way to make friends. Tracy was still quite happy with it, but Brian was already chafing at the bit. He complained that he didn't like drill, and that he liked the leader, who spat as he shouted, even less. Sandra, having been a loner as a child, thought the whole network of Scouts, Cubs, Brownies and the rest rather silly, but she would never say anything about that in front of the children.

When they had finally gone, she took a deep breath and looked around the living-room, wondering what to do first. Though she managed to be a fairly efficient housewife, she wasn't an obsessive cleaner. Alan also helped out on the weekends, taking on jobs she didn't like, such as Hoovering the staircase and cleaning the bathroom.

It was seven o'clock. She didn't know when Alan would be back; he'd said he was questioning a suspect. Sandra was trying to decide between doing some dark-room work or settling down with the biography of Alfred Hitchcock she had taken out of Eastvale Library that morning, when there was a knock at the door.

Puzzled, she went to answer it, expecting perhaps Selena Harcourt wanting to borrow a cup of sugar. But it was Robin Allott from the Camera Club.

"You told us you were willing to lend out your slide projector, remember?" he said, standing in the doorway.

"Oh, of course, Robin," Sandra said. "I'm so sorry, it slipped my mind. I must have looked quite unwelcoming for a moment. Please come in."

"I hope I've not called at an inconvenient time."

"Not at all. I've just sent the children off and I was wondering what to do."

"Yes, I saw them," Robin said, smiling. "Lifeboys and Guides. It reminds me of my own childhood."

He wiped his feet carefully on the doormat and Sandra hung up his navy-blue raincoat in the hall closet, then directed him into the front room, which he admired politely. He unslung his old, heavy Pentax from his shoulder and put it on the table by the front window.

"Silly habit," he said. "But I always carry it with me. You never know."

Sandra laughed. "That's the sign of a true professional. Do sit down, Robin. Can I get you a drink?"

"Yes, please, if it's no trouble."

"None at all. Gin or scotch? I'm afraid that's all we've got."

"Quite all right. Scotch'll do fine."

"Water? Ice?"

"No, just as it comes, for me, please."

Sandra poured his drink, mixed herself a gin and slimline tonic, then sat in the armchair opposite him. He seemed more shy than he usually did in The Mile Post, as if he was embarrassed to be alone with her in the house, so Sandra broke the ice and asked him if he'd done anything interesting over the weekend.

Robin shook his head. "Not really. I did take a ride to the coast on Sunday, but it clouded over there, so I couldn't get any good shots."

"What about the evenings?" Sandra asked. "Don't you go to clubs or concerts?"

"No, I don't do much of that. Oh, I drop in at the local for the odd jar, but that's about all."

"That's not much of a social life, is it? What about girlfriends? Surely there must be someone?"

"Not really," Robin answered, looking down into his drink. "Since my divorce I've been, well, a bit of a hermit, really. It wouldn't feel right going out with anybody else so soon."

"It's not as if you're a widower, you know," Sandra argued. "When you get divorced it's all right to go out and have fun if you feel like it. Was it mutual?"

Robin nodded hastily, and Sandra sensed that he felt uncomfortable with the subject. "Anyway," she said, "you'll get over it. Don't worry. I'll just nip upstairs and fetch the projector."

"Would you like me to help?" Robin offered awkwardly. "I mean, it must be heavy."

"No, not at all," Sandra said, waving him back onto the sofa. "They're all made of light plastic these days."

Robin was gazing at the books on the shelves by the fireplace when Sandra came back down with the slide projector.

"Here it is," she said. "It's easy to work. Do you know how?"

"I'm not sure," Robin said. "Outside of cameras I'm not very mechanically minded. Look," he went on, "I've got those slides back, the ones I took at the Camera Club. Would you like to see them? You can show me how to set up the machine."

"Why not?"

Sandra set up the projector on the table at the far end of the room and fetched the screen from upstairs. She then drew the curtains and placed it in front of the window. Finally, she showed Robin how to switch on the power and fit the slides he gave her into the circular tray.

"It's automatic," she explained. "Once you've got it all set up you just press this button when you want to move on to the next slide. Or this one if you want to go back. And this is how you focus." She showed him the controls.

Robin nodded. "Excuse me," he said. "I think I would like some ice and water with my whisky after all."

Sandra moved forward to take his glass.

"No, it's all right," he said. "I can get it myself. You set up the show." And he went into the kitchen.

Sandra adjusted the height of the projector and turned off the light. Robin came back with his whisky as the first slide zoomed into focus.

It really was quite remarkable. The model was sitting with her

legs tucked under her, gazing away from the camera. The lines drew
the eye right into the composition and Robin had obviously used one
of the 81-series filters to bring out the warm flesh tones. What was
especially odd about the whole thing was that the model didn't seem
to be posing; she looked as if she were staring into space thinking of
a distant memory.

"It's excellent," Sandra remarked over the hum of the projector. "I
really didn't think a modelling session like that would work out well
on slides, but it's really amazing. Beautiful."

She heard the ice tinkling in Robin's glass. "Thank you," he said in
a far-off voice. "Yes, they did work out well. She's not as beautiful as
you, though."

Something in the way he said it sent a shiver of fear up Sandra's
spine, and she froze for a moment before turning slowly to look at
him. It was too dark to see anything except his silhouette, but in the
light that escaped from the edges of the lens, she could see the sharp
blade of one of her kitchen knives glinting.

Robin was on his feet, quite close to her. She could hear him
breathing quickly. She backed away and found herself between the
projector and the screen. The projection of the nude model distorted
as it wrapped around her figure like an avant-garde dress design, and
she froze again as a transformed Robin moved closer.

II

Mick gobbled up another mouthful of pills and went over to the window again. It was dark outside and the tall sodium lights glowed an
eerie red the way they always did before they turned jaundice yellow.

Still no sign. Mick started pacing the room again, one batch of
amphetamines wearing off and the new ones beginning to take effect.
Sweat prickled on his forehead and skull, itching between the spikes
of hair. His heart was pounding like a barrage of artillery, but he
didn't feel good. He was worried. Where the hell was Trevor? The
bastard was supposed to arrive two hours ago.

As the lights yellowed like old paper, Mick got more edgy and jittery. The room felt claustrophobic, too small to contain him. His

muscles were straining at his clothes and his brain felt like it was pushing at the inner edges of his skull. Something was going on. They were onto him. He looked out of the window again, careful not to be seen this time.

There was a man in a homburg walking his Jack Russell. He'd been walking that dog for hours up and down the street by the edge of The Green, under the lights, and Mick was sure he kept glancing covertly towards the house. A little further into The Green, where the lights of the posher houses at the other side seemed to twinkle between the leaves and branches that danced in the breeze, a young couple stood under a tree. The girl was leaning against the tree and the boy was talking to her, one arm outstretched, supporting his weight on the trunk above her head. Sure, they looked like lovers, Mick thought. That was the idea. But he wasn't fooled. He could see the way she kept looking sideways at him when she should have been paying closer attention to her man. He was probably speaking into a walkie-talkie or a microphone hidden in his lapel. They were communicating with the dog-walker. And they weren't the only ones. Deeper in the trees, what he had thought to be shadows and thick tree trunks turned into people, and if he listened closely enough he could hear them whispering to each other.

He put his hands over his ears and retreated into the room. He put a loud rock record on the stereo to shut out the noise of the whisperers, but it didn't work; they were in his head already, and even the music seemed part of a sinister plot. It was meant to put him off-guard, that was it. He snatched at the needle, scratching the record, and returned to the window. Vigilance, that was what was called for.

Nothing had changed. The man with the dog was walking back down the street. He stopped by a tree, holding the leash loosely and looking up at the sky as the dog cocked its leg. The couple on The Green were pretending to kiss now.

Perhaps there was time to get away, Mick thought, licking his lips and wiping his forehead with the back of his hand. He had to get himself ready. They probably didn't even know he was there yet. To escape, though, meant leaving the window for a few minutes, something he couldn't bear to do. But he had to. He couldn't let them catch him unprepared.

He dashed upstairs to Lenny's room first and pulled out the heavy gun from under the mattress; then he went into his own messy room and took all his cash out of its hiding place, a hollowed-out book called *The Practical Way to Keep Fit*. He had almost a hundred pounds. It should be enough.

Rushing back downstairs, he grabbed his parka from the hook in the hall, shoved the gun and money into its deep pockets and went back to watch from the window. Now he was ready. Now he could take on anybody. The familiar effect of the pills was returning. He felt the weight of the big gun in his pocket and waves of adrenalin surged through his veins, flooding him with a sense of power and well-being. But he had to do something; he had so much energy it was boiling over.

The man with the dog had gone and the young couple had moved to another tree. They thought they could fool him, but he wasn't that stupid. The Green was full of young couples now. They leaned against every tree, pretending to be kissing and feeling each other up. Mick felt a jolt of energy in his loins as he watched the erotic tableau of shadows.

When the police car finally came, he was ready. He saw its headlights approaching slowly, dispersing the watchers on The Green as its beams sought the right house, and he left softly by the back door. He had a plan. There was only one sensible thing he could do, and that was get out of Eastvale, disappear, go down to join Lenny in London for awhile. To get out of Eastvale, he had to cross The Green, then the river, and walk up around the castle to the bus station at the back of the market square. It was no good running east; in that direction there was nothing but fields and the long flat vale; he would be an easy target out in the open there.

Cautiously, he edged down the back alley to the end of the block, where a narrow snicket separated two terraces. As he crept out into the street again, he was about four houses north of the police. Now all he had to do was disappear quietly into the trees and he was home free.

He crossed the street without attracting any attention and stood on the verge of The Green. The police were still knocking at his door and trying to peer in through the windows, the fools. A few more paces and he would be among the shadows, the shadows that belonged to him again.

Suddenly, a voice called out behind him and for a moment he stopped dead in his tracks, feeling the adrenalin prickle inside him.

"Hey, you!" the voice called again. "Stop where you are! Police!"

For a second he thought it was all over, that they had him, but then he remembered he had an edge—the gun and the power he felt crackling inside him. The new plan came as a brainstorm, and he laughed out loud at the beauty of it as he ran across The Green with the police close behind, still shouting. He would never make it to the bus station, he knew that now, and even if he did they would be waiting for him, talking to each other on the airwaves. So he had to improvise, try something different.

The light was on. That was a good sign. Without hesitating, he leaped up the steps three at a time and ran his shoulder into the front door. It didn't give at once. The police were clearing the trees now, only about seventy-five yards away. Mick took a few paces back and crashed into the door again. This time it splintered open. The woman, alarmed by his first attempt, was peering, frightened, through a door in the hallway. Mick rushed in, grabbed her by her hair and dragged her to the front window. The police were halfway across the street by now. Taking out his gun, Mick smashed the window and held Jenny up by the hair.

"Stop!" he screamed at them. "Don't move another inch! I've got a gun and I've got the woman, and if you don't do what I say I'll fucking shoot the bitch."

III

Even Robin's voice was different. It had lost its timbre of shy cheerfulness and become forced and clipped.

Sandra edged backwards until she could feel the screen against her back. She was almost perfectly lined up with the projected model, whose image was wrapped around her body, the girl's face superimposed on her own.

"Robin," she said as calmly and quietly as she could manage, "you don't really want to do this, do you? Don't let things go too far."

"I have to," Robin said tersely. "It's already gone beyond."

"Beyond what?"

"Beyond where I thought I could go."

"You can still stop it."

"No."

"Yes, you can," Sandra insisted gently.

"No! Can't you see? I have to go further, always further, or it's no good, there's no point. When I watched you, Sandra, watched you undressing in your bedroom, it was the best, it was just like . . . I didn't think I could go any further than that. I didn't think I could ever go any further. Do you know what I mean? The ultimate."

Sandra nodded. The model's face remained still and detached, fixed on that far-off memory. Sandra felt as if she were tied to the screen by the projection. She wanted to tell Robin to turn it off but she didn't dare. The way he was talking, he was beyond reason. There was nothing she could do but keep asking him calmly to put the knife down and stop. But she knew he wouldn't. He'd gone too far now, and he could only go further. He'd made his greatest step and the rest would have to follow.

He was coming closer, the projected model bending around the knife blade, throwing its shadow onto Sandra's chest. She was backed up as far against the screen as she could get.

Robin stopped, still at an angle so as not to block the image projected on her. "Take your clothes off," he ordered, twitching the knife.

"No," Sandra replied. "You can't mean it. Put the knife away, Robin. It's not too late."

"Take your clothes off," he repeated. "I do mean it. Do as I say."

It was futile to protest any more. Sandra clenched her teeth, holding back the tears, and brought her trembling hands to the buttons on her shirt.

"Don't hurry," Robin said. "Take your time. Do it slow."

Each button seemed to take an eternity, but finally the shirt was undone. She dropped it on the floor and waited.

"Go on," he said. "The jeans."

Sandra was wearing tight Levis. She undid the top button and pulled down the zipper. It wasn't easy, but she managed to fold them over her hips and get out of each leg while still standing up.

She stood before Robin in her white bra and panties, shaking all

over. The image was still wrapped around her and now it seemed welcome, offering her a little covering, some protection. Robin pulled
the slide out of its slot, and the bright, piercing light of the lens
pinned Sandra to the screen. She put up a hand to shield her eyes.

Robin said nothing for a long time. He seemed to be just gazing
at her, a slender figure with long, blonde hair and shapely long legs.
He was awestruck. She could feel his eyes as they slid over her body,
probing every curve, every shadow. She noticed that the hand that
held the knife was trembling.

"Now the rest," he ordered in a voice that seemed caught deep in
his throat.

Sandra started to obey.

"Slower," Robin commanded her.

Finally, she stood naked in the harsh glare of the slide projector.
Now she made no pretence of not crying; her shoulders shook and
the tears flowed down her cheeks, fell onto her chest and trickled
across her breasts.

Suddenly, Robin gave a strangled cry, dropped the knife and
hurled himself down on his knees in front of her. The abruptness of
his action shocked Sandra out of her fear. He put his arms around her
hips and buried his face in her loins. She could hear him sobbing and
she could feel his warm tears. Quickly, she stretched out her left hand
to grab the camera that Robin had left on the table beside the screen.
Then, with both hands, she lifted it high in the air and brought it
down hard on the top of his head.

IV

It was quiet in Banks's office. He sat smoking a cigarette, feeling very
pleased with himself, waiting to hear from Hatchley and Richmond.
Opposite, Trevor sat sullen and withdrawn, while his father seemed
nervous, tapping on the edge of the desk and whistling between his
teeth.

There was a soft knock at the door and Sergeant Rowe's grey-
haired head popped around, indicating that he had something to say.

"Phone call," he said in the corridor, looking worried. "Your wife, sir. Said it was urgent. She sounded very upset." Banks had asked that all calls be intercepted while he was interrogating Trevor; he hadn't wanted to be interrupted.

Puzzled, and worried that something might have happened to Brian or Tracy, he told Rowe to keep an eye on the suspect for a few moments and ducked into the nearest empty room to take the call.

"Alan? Thank God," Sandra breathed. Rowe was right. Banks had never heard her sound like that before.

"What is it? What's wrong?"

"It was Robin, Alan. The peeper. He came here. He had a knife."

"What happened? Are you all right?"

"Yes, yes, I'm all right. A bit scared and shaky, but he didn't hurt me. Alan, I think I've killed him. I hit him with the camera. Too hard. I wasn't thinking. I was so frightened and angry."

"Stay there, Sandra," Banks told her. "Don't move. I'll be over in a few minutes. Understand?"

"Yes. Hurry, Alan. Please."

"I will."

Banks got Rowe out of his office again and told the sergeant that an emergency had arisen and he had to rush home.

"What about those two?" Rowe asked.

"I'll be back," Banks said, thinking quickly. "Have Sergeant Hatchley call me at home when they get back with Webster. And don't, under any circumstances, let the two kids see each other."

"Right, sir, got it," Rowe said. Banks could tell that he wanted to ask what was wrong or offer some sort of sympathy, but discretion got the better of him and he went back into Banks's office, shutting the door softly behind him.

Banks got as far as the front door before PC Craig, on temporary desk duty, shouted after him.

"Sir! Inspector Banks, sir!"

Banks turned. "What is it?" he snapped, still edging towards the door.

"A call, sir. Sergeant Hatchley. Says it's an emergency."

Banks was in two minds whether to take it or not, but his professional instinct made him reach for the phone. At least Sandra wasn't in immediate danger any longer. A minute or two more wouldn't hurt.

"What is it, Sergeant?"

"The kid, sir. Webster. He gave us the slip."

"Well, go after him."

"It's not as simple as that. We know where he is."

"Get to the bloody point, Sergeant," Banks growled. "I've got one bloody emergency on my hands already."

"He ran across The Green and broke into a woman's house, sir. He's got her held hostage there. He's got a gun."

Banks felt his stomach tighten. "Which house?"

"It's that doctor woman, sir. The one I saw coming out of the super's office."

"Christ," Banks gasped, rubbing his free hand over his eyes.

"But there's more, sir. He says he wants you there. He asked for you and said if you didn't get here in twenty minutes he'd kill the woman."

Banks had to think more quickly than he had ever done in his life. It was probably no more than a split second before he gave Hatchley his instructions, but in that period Banks felt as if he had been to hell and back. The two women flashed before his eyes. If he deserted Sandra when she needed him, he thought, things might never be right again; she would never fully trust him. If he didn't go to help Jenny, on the other hand, she would surely die. Banks reasoned that Sandra would, somehow, understand this if she knew, that his duty was to try to save a life rather than console his wife after she had already succeeded in freeing herself from a dangerous, terrifying situation. Though he was thinking specifically that it was Jenny in danger, that he couldn't let Jenny die, he knew he would also have to go even if it was a stranger Mick Webster had taken hostage. It was personal, yes, and this intensified his concern, but his job demanded that he do the same for anyone. Somebody, however, would have to go to Sandra. There was always the chance that the man would return to consciousness again. And if someone else dealt with it, then it would be official business. It was official anyway, he realized. It had gone too far to be covered up as easily as the peeper episode. No matter who went to Sandra now, all the details would have to come out.

"I'll be there, Sergeant," Banks said quickly. "Send DC Richmond over to my house. Got it? MY HOUSE. Immediately. I've not got time to explain, but it's urgent. Tell him to hurry and to explain to my wife about the situation here."

"Yes, sir," Hatchley said, sounding puzzled.

"And let the super know," Banks added. "We'll need him down there if there's any negotiating to be done."

"He's already on his way," Hatchley said, and hung up.

Not wasting another moment, Banks rushed through the desk area, picked up the keys to the same car he had driven to York, and, without signing for them, dashed out of the back into the yard where the vehicles were parked. In seven minutes, he was outside Jenny's house.

Hatchley and two uniformed men stood the low wall at the bottom of the garden, which sloped upwards quite steeply to the bay window. The light in the front room was on, and Banks could hear the strains of *Tosca* playing in the background.

"Any developments?" he asked Hatchley.

"No, sir," the sergeant replied. "Haven't seen hide nor hair of him since he told us to send for you. They're inside, though. I sent Bradley and Jennings round the back. Told them not to do nothing, just keep their eyes open."

Banks nodded. Hatchley had done well, considering that this was the first time he had had to deal with hostage taking. It was a difficult business, as Banks had found out for himself on one or two occasions down in London, but it was of chief importance to maintain as calm and reasonable an atmosphere as possible for negotiations.

Another car drew up by the kerb and Superintendent Gristhorpe got out. He looked like a bulky, absent-minded professor with his unkempt thatch of hair blowing in the breeze and his bushy eyebrows meeting in the middle of his frown.

Banks explained the situation to him as quickly as possible.

"Why does he want you here?" Gristhorpe asked.

"I don't know."

"Have you told him you've arrived?"

"Not yet."

"Better do it, Alan. He might be getting impatient."

"Is there a megaphone?" Banks asked.

Gristhorpe smiled wryly. "Now where the bloody hell would we get a megaphone, Alan?"

Banks acknowledged this fact, then simply spoke out loud towards the broken window.

"Mick! Mick Webster! I'm here. It's Inspector Banks."

There were sounds of scuffling inside, then Webster appeared at the window, gun pointed at the side of Jenny's head.

"What do you want?" Banks asked. "Why do you want me here?"

"I want you in here," Mick shouted back.

"Why do you want me? You've already got the girl."

"Just do as I say. Get in here. And no tricks."

"Mick, send the girl out. Send her out and then I'll come in."

"Nothing doing. Come in now or I'll blow her fucking head off."

"Come on, Mick, let's play fair. Let her go. We give a little and you give a little. Send her out and I'll come in."

"I told you, Banks. Either you come in now or she dies. I'll give you thirty seconds."

"Better do it, Alan," Gristhorpe said heavily. "He's not stable, you can't reason with him. Have you dealt with anything like this before?"

"Yes," Banks answered. "A couple of times. Usually with pros, though."

"But you know the ropes?"

Banks nodded.

"I'll try and keep him talking," Gristhorpe said, "keep negotiations open."

"Your time's running out, Banks," Mick yelled.

"All right," Banks said, climbing the steps, "I'm coming in, Mick." And as he walked, he thought of Sandra.

V

Mick Webster was in a dangerously unstable state. Banks could see that at once as he obeyed orders and emptied out his pockets. The boy was constantly edgy, always scratching, sweating, fidgeting, shifting from one foot to the other, and it didn't take Banks long to recognize the signs of an amphetamine user.

Jenny appeared to be calm enough. Her left cheek was inflamed, as if she had been hit, but she seemed to be trying to reassure him with the look in her eyes that all was well and that now he was here they had a chance to work together and get out alive. She was quick, Banks knew that, and he also felt that a certain intuitive bond had quickly been forged between them. If there was an opportunity, he thought, then they could probably do something about it between them. It was just a matter of waiting to see who took the initiative.

Mick's moods were shifting minute by minute. One moment he'd be joking, the next he'd become morose and say he had nothing to lose. And all that pacing and jittering was driving Banks crazy. *Tosca* still played in the background, well into the second act, and the cassette box lay on a pine table by the broken window.

"All right, Mick," Banks said quietly. "What is it you want?"

"What do you think?" Mick sneered. "I want out of here." He swaggered over to the window and shouted: "I want ten thousand quid and safe passage out of the country, or the girl and the cop die, got it?"

Outside in the cold evening, Gristhorpe whispered to Hatchley, "Not a snowball in hell's chance," and said back to Mick, "All right, we'll work on it. Stay in communication and we'll let you know."

"I don't want to talk to you fuckers," Mick yelled back. "I know you and all your games. Just get me what I asked for and fuck off out of the way." He kept the gun pointed at Jenny. "Hurry up, get back in those trees where I can't see you or I'll kill the girl now."

Reluctantly, Gristhorpe, Hatchley and the two uniformed men moved back across the road onto The Green.

"That's right," Mick shouted at them. "And fucking well stay there till you've got something to tell me."

Banks stood as close to Mick and Jenny as he dared. "Mick," he said, "they're not going to do it. You don't stand a chance."

"They'll do it," Mick said. "They don't want to see your brains splattered all over the garden. Or hers."

"They can't do it, Mick," Banks went on patiently. "They can't give in to demands like that. If they did, then every Tom, Dick and Harry would start taking hostages and asking for the world."

Mick laughed. "Maybe I'll start a trend then, eh? They'll do it, and you'd better hope they do, both of you."

The music went on quietly and the cool night air came in through the broken window. Outside, Banks could hear talking on a car radio. They would already have the street cordonned off, and should have evacuated the neighbours.

Mick licked his lips and looked from one to the other of them. "Well," he said, "what shall we do when the transport comes?" And his eyes stayed on Jenny, who stood by the tile fireplace. Banks stuck close to the table by the window.

"Don't make things worse, Mick," Banks said. "If you give up now, it'll be taken into consideration. Things wouldn't go too badly for you. But if you go any further..."

"You know as well as I do," Mick said, turning to Banks, "that I'm in about as deep as can be."

"That's not true, Mick. There's a way out of this."

"And what's going to happen to me then?"

"I can't make any promises, Mick. You know that. But it'll go in your favour."

"Yeah, it'll go in my fucking favour. I'll only get twenty years instead of twenty-five, is that what you're telling me?"

"You'll get a lot more if you hurt anyone, Mick. No one's been hurt yet. Remember that."

Mick turned to Jenny. "This is what we're gonna do," he said. "When they fix up my transport, you're coming with me and he's staying. He'll know if he lets his copper mates do anything to stop us, you'll be dead. They might not think I mean it, but he does."

"No," Jenny said.

"What do you mean, 'no,' you cunt? What the fuck do you think this is in my hand, a fucking cap-gun?"

Jenny shook her head. "I'm not going anywhere with you. I'm not going to let you lay one dirty finger on me."

Mick reddened and looked, to Banks, dangerously near the end of his tether. But Jenny was the psychologist, and she seemed to have taken the initiative; it was up to Banks to follow. While Mick glared at Jenny, Banks picked up the cassette box from the table and tossed it out through the broken window.

There was a sudden clattering sound on the path and Mick turned to aim the gun towards the noise. Banks was close enough to jump him when the gun was pointing out of the window. But before Banks could make his move, Mick actually fired into the garden. The gun made a dull explosion and they both heard Mick scream. Slowly, he turned back towards the room, his face white, mouth and eyes wide open with shock and pain. The blood from his hand dripped onto the clean pine table.

SIXTEEN

I

As soon as Hatchley and Gristhorpe heard the shot and the scream, they dashed out of the trees towards the house. Inside, Jenny rushed to help Banks, who had already ripped off Mick's shirt-sleeve to apply as a tourniquet.

"It's a mess," he said, tying the knot, then he caught Jenny's eye. "You did well," he told her. "But for a minute I thought you were going to push him too far."

"Me, too. The idea was just to confuse him, then attract his attention. The kid was so stoned he didn't know what was happening. I'm glad you caught the signal."

When Banks heard the others reach the steps, he walked over to the window to tell them it was all clear. Inside the house after that it was chaos—several people asking different questions at the same time, orders being given to uniformed men, phone calls being made for the ambulance and Scene-of-Crime Squad—and throughout it all, nobody thought to turn off the stereo; Tosca was still singing:

> Nell'ora del dolore
> Perché, perché, Signor,
> Perché me ne rimuneri così?

A still point for a moment at the centre of all the frenetic activity, Banks took in the familiar words: "In this, my hour of grief and tribulation, Why Heavenly Father, Why hast thou forsaken me?"

"Good work, Alan," Gristhorpe said, snapping Banks out of the music. "All right?"

"Fine."

"You look a bit pale."

"I always do when I've been in close contact with guns."

Gristhorpe looked down at Mick. "If all guns reacted the way that one did, Alan, it might be a better world. I'm not a religious man, as you know—too much of that pernicious Yorkshire Methodism in my background—but maybe sometimes God is there when we need him."

Banks looked over at Jenny, who was telling a constable what had happened. "*She* was certainly there."

He went on to explain about Sandra and asked permission to go home and skip the formalities until later.

"Of course," Gristhorpe said. "You should have told me earlier. Are you sure she sounded all right?"

"A bit shook up, but in control. Richmond's still with her."

"Off you go, then," Gristhorpe said, giving Banks a gentle push in the small of the back.

It was time to face Sandra.

As he walked to the door, he saw Jenny, neglected now, slumped on the sofa with her face in her hands. He looked around the room again—the cold night air coming in through the broken window, the blood on the table, the shards of glass on the floor.

"Jenny," he called softly, holding out his hand. "Come with me."

She did as she was asked, and on the way home Banks told her about Sandra's ordeal.

"Do you think it'll be all right?" she asked. "You know, me coming with you?"

"To tell you the truth, Jenny, I don't know what to expect. I couldn't leave you there, though. Don't worry, the superintendent will see that everything's taken care of."

Jenny shivered. "I don't think I could have stayed there. I'd have gone to a hotel. I still can. I shouldn't come with you."

"Don't be silly."

Banks drove on in silence.

Finally, they arrived at the house and hurried up the path. Sandra flung open the door. Banks winced as she ran towards him, but she threw her arms around him.

"Alan! Alan, thank God you're all right," she sobbed, burying her face in his shoulder.

He stroked her hair. "I'm all right, don't worry. Let's go inside. I could do with a drink."

Richmond stood up as they entered the living-room. The young DC stroked his moustache and cleared his throat. Banks suddenly remembered that it was Richmond he had seen that night in The Oak. Jenny had been with him then and they must have seemed very close. God only knew what he was thinking!

"There, I told you," Richmond said to Sandra. "I told you he'd be all right." He turned to Banks and gave him a nod, as if to signify that all was well. The two of them walked together to the door. "I've taken your wife's statement, sir. It's all very clear what happened. He's the peeper, no doubt about it."

"How is he?"

"Don't know yet, sir. It didn't look serious to me. They took him to the hospital about half an hour ago. Will that be all, sir?"

Banks could tell that Richmond was anxious to leave, that being involved with his inspector in such a personal way was exceedingly uncomfortable for him. "Yes," he said. "You can go now. And Detective Richmond..."

"Yes, sir?"

"Thanks."

Richmond blushed and muttered something about it being nothing before he took off at a fair pace down the path.

Banks closed the door and noticed Jenny and Sandra looking at each other. He knew that Sandra would be embarrassed at showing so much emotion in front of a stranger.

"I'm sorry," he apologized wearily, running his hand over his close-cropped hair. "I didn't introduce you, did I?"

After the introduction, Sandra offered Jenny a chair.

Banks went straight to the drinks cabinet.

"Something a bit stronger than tea, I think. Scotch all round?"

"Yes, please." The two women nodded.

It was hard to know what to do to break the ice, Banks realized as he poured them all generous measures of Macallan single malt. Jenny could hardly say to Sandra, "I heard you had a terrible ordeal tonight, dear?" nor could Sandra answer, "Oh yes, absolutely dreadful. I thought I was going to be raped, then murdered. You didn't have such an easy time, yourself, I hear?" So they sipped scotch and said nothing for a while and Banks smoked a much-needed cigarette.

"Look, if you'd rather I went," Jenny said, "I'm feeling much better now."

"Nonsense," Sandra told her. "You can't go back there. You're staying here, with us. I'll make up the spare bed. Oh, Alan, it's nearly time to pick the children up from the meetings. Shall I go?"

"No," Banks said, putting his hand on her shoulder. "You've had enough for tonight. Let me go. It's only down the road."

"You'll tell them?"

"I'll tell them that we had a break-in and you caught a burglar. You'll be a real heroine in their eyes then."

"It'll be in the papers, won't it, later?"

"Probably. We'll cross that bridge when we get there. Will you two be all right?"

"Of course we will," Sandra said, smiling at Jenny. "We're a couple of heroes, didn't you just say so?"

"I thought it was heroines?"

Sandra shook her head. "Somehow, 'heroines' doesn't have the right ring to it. I think heroines are always victims. They're pale and wan and they make a lot of noise. More scotch, Jenny?"

Banks walked to the car. On the way back from the church hall, he told Brian and Tracy that they had a guest for the evening and that they were to behave themselves and go to bed as soon as they'd had their cocoa. There seemed no point in even mentioning what had happened.

Back at the house, they interrupted Sandra and Jenny deep in conversation, and Brian and Tracy were bursting with comments about their evening. Brian announced that he was sick to death of the Lifeboys and he was never going again. Banks helped get them ready for bed, took them upstairs and tucked them in; then, yawning, he walked back downstairs.

"I have to go in," he said. "There's a few loose ends to tie up."

Sandra nodded. It was nothing new to her.

"I'll probably be late," he added, "so don't wait up."

It was confusing, saying goodbye to the two of them. He bent and kissed Sandra's cheek, then nodded at Jenny and hurried out. Even though he'd got his priorities sorted out, there was something disturbing about being with both women at once. It was extremely disconcerting, and the more Banks analyzed the feeling as he walked—Walkman-less, but grateful to be breathing the cool night air—the more he decided that it wasn't sexual. It had nothing at all to do with the beauty and desirability of both women, but everything to do with his sensing a strong bond between them that put him on the outside. They didn't even have to talk to make it clear. Banks had felt as if he were a clumsy, primitive beast in the presence of two alien creatures.

II

The station was humming with activity. Already, those on duty in plain clothes had been recalled from the pubs and were clustering around the duty roster trying to decide who should go home and who should stay. And downstairs, the phone kept ringing. Residents of the East Side Estate were still calling to report the gunshot.

Upstairs, things were quieter. The Sharps had been taken to an interview room, and Gristhorpe's door was open. As soon as Banks rounded the corner, the superintendent popped his head out and invited him in. One shaded table lamp provided the only illumination, and the bookcases and deep leather chairs gleamed in its dim light. The only thing Banks needed was another cigarette. As if reading his mind Gristhorpe took a Queen's Arms ashtray out of his bottom drawer and pushed it over to him.

"Just this once, Alan. I can see you need it. Though God knows why a person would crave something that's a proven carcinogen."

"There's none worse than ex-smokers," Banks joked. Everybody knew that Gristhorpe's anti-smoking campaign was of fairly recent origin.

"How are things, Alan?"

"Pretty good, considering. It's nice to be able to relax for a moment. I haven't really managed to bring my mind to bear on what happened yet."

"Plenty of time. Write it down in the morning. Sandra's well?"

"Yes. She's either tougher than I thought or she's a good actress."

"I think she's just got hidden depths, Alan. Strong reserves. You'd be surprised how many have. My wife, God bless her, was the mildest, gentlest woman on the face of the earth. Talk about frail—you'd think she'd faint at a cuss-word. But she was a nurse in the war, just like Alice Matlock, and she saw more than one member of her family from this world to the next. But she never once flinched or complained, even when the cancer got hold of her. 'Course, she was a Yorkshirewoman."

Banks smiled. "Of course."

"Many a copper would have run straight to his wife, Alan. You did the right thing. You weighed up both situations and decided where you could do the most good."

"It didn't seem as logical a process as that. When it comes down to it, there was only one place where I *had* to be."

"I know that, and so do you. But a lesser man might have let emotion confuse the issue."

"There were times when I thought I had. What's happened to Robin Allott?"

"Mild concussion. He'll be all right. Still at the hospital. If that camera had been out of its leather case, and if Sandra had hit him on the temple or the base of the skull, he might have been dead. It was an old one, metal body instead of that plastic they use nowadays. The young fellow was very lucky indeed."

"Sandra, too."

"No blame would have attached to her."

"But imagine how she'd feel, even so."

"Aye," Gristhorpe said, rubbing his prickly chin.

"Has he said anything?"

"Not a dicky bird, yet. Still too dazed. I don't think he'll hold back on us, though. Sandra made a very clear statement." His bushy brows knitted in a deep frown. "She went through a lot, you know."

"I know. At least I think I do. I don't know all the details yet."

One of the uniformed constables knocked softly at the half-open door before delivering a tray of coffee and biscuits.

"They're from downstairs, the biscuits, sir," he said. "We keep a few packets in, club together, like. Thought you might appreciate some."

"Thank you, Constable Craig," Gristhorpe said. "Much appreciated. You on late duty tonight?"

"Yes, sir. Me and Susan Gay."

There was something in the constable's clipped tone that prompted Gristhorpe to ask if anything was wrong.

"Well, sir," Craig said, "I don't mean to complain, but every time we're on duty together and something like this comes up—making coffee or delivering biscuits—she always manages to push me into doing it." His face reddened. "It's that blooming women's lib is what it is, sir."

Gristhorpe laughed. "It's what we call 'positive discrimination,' lad, and you'll just have to get used to it. Stick up for yourself. And I hope this coffee's a bit better than the usual muck we get around here."

"It should be, sir," Craig said proudly. "A satisfied customer presented us with one of those automatic drip-filter things earlier this evening, sir. I went across to that fancy tea and coffee shop in King Street and got some fresh-ground Colombian beans."

The superintendent turned his baby blue eyes on Craig. "Did you, now? Not only accepting gifts from the public but playing truant, eh?"

"Yes, sir. Sorry, sir," Craig replied, standing stiffly to attention.

"It's all right," Gristhorpe said. "Only joking, lad. Wherever it came from, it's most welcome. The chief inspector'll be able to drink it black. Off you go, lad."

The coffee was good, the best they'd tasted in a long time, and Banks had a fondness for McVities' Chocolate Digestives. Gristhorpe was on yet another diet, though, and refused to give in to his sweet tooth.

"How's Mick Webster?" Banks asked.

"He'll live. Lost a lot of blood, but that tourniquet of yours did the trick."

"His hand?"

"Lost two fingers, and the doc says he might lose another if surgery doesn't go well. Have you any idea where he got the gun from?"

"No. The first I heard of Webster was from Trevor Sharp earlier tonight. I think we should get a warrant and search his place."

"It's already being done. That's where Richmond and Hatchley are now. If I were you, Alan, I'd go home, take care of my wife and get some sleep."

"I want to talk to Sharp."

"It'll wait, Alan."

"No."

"I can do it."

"I started it, and I'd hate to have to begin all over again."

Gristhorpe tapped a pencil on his blotter. "You've got a point, I suppose. We don't want him fresh again after a night's sleep."

"Does he know about Webster?"

"No."

"Good."

"Sure you're up to it?"

"Yes. I wouldn't get any sleep for thinking about it anyway."

Gristhorpe pointed towards the corridor. "Interview room number three. I think Sergeant Rowe's still with them. He'll be worn out by now."

III

Banks took his second cup of black coffee into the small interview room.

Graham Sharp jumped to his feet. "You can't keep us here like this," he said. "We've been cooped up here for hours. It's not a police state yet, you know."

Banks sat down and spoke to Sergeant Rowe. "You can go now, Sergeant. Could you send someone in to take notes? Constable Craig will do."

He didn't speak until Craig arrived, then he lit a cigarette and took a long pull on his coffee.

"Right," he said, looking at Trevor. "We've got your mate Webster and he's told us all about your little capers."

"You're lying," Trevor said. "You must think I'm stupid to fall for that one."

"What one?"

"The one where the cops tell a suspect his accomplice has confessed and expect him to break down. I've seen it on telly."

"'Accomplice?' Accomplice in what?"

"It's just a word."

"Yes, I know. But words mean things. What's more, they imply things too. 'Accomplice' implies that you worked together in committing a crime."

"I told you, it's just a word."

"Stop beating around the bush," Graham Sharp said. "If we have to stay until you've finished, at least get on with it."

"It's true," Banks said to Trevor, and noticed that the boy had started to chew his bottom lip. "He told us all about the break-ins—first the old ladies, then the Ottershaws and Thelma Pitt. He told us how he tried to stop you from raping her but you were like a mad dog. Those were his words, 'mad dog.'"

"He's a liar," Trevor said.

"What do you mean, Trevor? That you weren't like a mad dog?"

"I didn't rape anybody."

"Why would he lie? We found Thelma Pitt's jewellery in his house, and some bits and pieces from the other robberies." Banks knew he was treading on very shaky ground by lying in the hope of getting a confession, but he kept his fingers crossed and trusted that Richmond and Hatchley would turn up something. "Why would he lie, Trevor? It's all up for him and he knows it."

"He's trying to put the blame on someone else, that's all."

"But there were two of you. We know that. A gangly one and a squat one. The gangly one had decay between his front teeth and caught the clap from Thelma Pitt. The squat one had piggy eyes and a raspy voice. You've got to admit that fits Mick to a tee. And your father told us about Mick, remember? He said Mick Webster was to blame if you'd done anything wrong. Now Mick says you're both to blame. What am I supposed to believe?"

"Believe what you want. I don't care."

"But you should, Trevor. Your father does. He cares enough to lie for you."

"Now just a minute—"

"Be quiet, Mr Sharp. You lied for your son and you know damn well you did. Well, Trevor?"

"Well what?"

"Why don't you admit it? That way we can say you helped us and it'll go easier for you in court. If we have to prove a case, we can, but it'll be more trouble for all of us."

"Admit what?"

"The truth."

"I've told you."

"Not the truth. Not like Mick did. He was on drugs, you know. Remember what he gets like? You can't trust him at all when he's on drugs."

"And you can't believe him, either."

"I do. A jury will. How about it, Trevor?"

"What?"

"Tell me what you did?"

"I didn't do nothing."

"Alice Matlock?"

"He never killed anyone," Graham Sharp protested.

"How do you know? He's lied to you about everything else."

Sharp looked at his son, who turned to face the wall. "He didn't. I just know. He couldn't. He's not capable of it."

"It didn't take much strength, you know," Banks said. "Probably an accident."

"You'll never prove it," Graham said.

Banks shrugged. "What do you think, Trevor?"

"Did Mick tell you that?"

"Tell me what?"

"That we killed the old bag down the street."

"What if he did?"

"Then you're lying," Trevor said, gripping the table edge and rising from his chair. "You're bloody lying. We didn't kill nobody. We didn't have nothing to do with Alice Matlock. If you say he told you that then you're a fucking liar."

"I'm right about the rest, though, aren't I?"

"You made it all up. You don't even have Mick. I'm not saying another word."

In the silence that followed, PC Craig answered the gentle tapping on the door and whispered to Banks, who left the room. In the corridor stood Hatchley and Richmond, both looking pleased as Punch.

"Don't just stand there like the cats that got the cream," Banks said. "What did you find?"

"We got back the Ottershaw and Pitt jewellery and one or two other trinkets."

"Prints?"

"Vic Manson says so. On the camera and a large brooch."

Banks breathed a sigh of relief.

"And," Hatchley added, "we've got a damn good idea who the fence is."

"Go on."

"There was a snapshot in one of the drawers, not a good one, a bit blurred, but as far as I could tell, it matched the sketch we got from Leeds," Hatchley explained. "And there was a letter from London, from a chap called Lenny. Apparently he's Webster's brother."

"Does he have a record?"

Hatchley shook his head. "Not up here. Not as far as we know. Spends most of his time down in The Smoke. I'll check with records."

"Do that. Have you got an address?"

"Yes."

"Excellent. Perhaps you'd better take your findings to Superintendent Gristhorpe. He'll get in touch with London CID and have Lenny Webster picked up. Then we'll see what we shall see." Banks yawned. "Sorry, lads. Afraid I'm tired. Go on up, the super's still in his office."

"Yes, sir," Richmond said, heading for the stairs. Hatchley hung back for a moment, shifting awkwardly.

"Something else, Sergeant?" Banks asked, his hand on the door handle.

"It's just what you did tonight, sir. I just wanted to say I admired you for it. It was a brave thing to do. I don't reckon I'm no softie myself, but I've never been stuck up with a gun. The very thought of it gives me the bloody collywobbles."

"Let's hope you never will be," Banks said. "It happens a lot less often up here than down south."

"I know," Hatchley agreed. "I never thought I'd see the day when I was glad we had a Southerner on the Eastvale force."

That final disclosure seemed too much for Hatchley's tight-lipped nature, and he rushed off, Banks thought, before he went too far and his boss could accuse him of sentimentality.

Smiling, Banks returned to the interview room. Graham Sharp was pale and Trevor wore his customary scowl. Though the father might never admit it, Banks knew that he now thought Trevor was guilty. The boy's reactions had convinced him just as they had confirmed beyond any doubt two things Banks already believed: that they had definitely not killed Alice Matlock, and that they had done everything else.

When Banks sat down and lit a cigarette, Trevor began to look apprehensive. Sipping tepid coffee, Banks let the silence stretch until both father and son were clearly as tense and anxious as he wanted them to be, then he turned to PC Craig and pointed at Trevor.

"Hold him, Constable. Suspicion of burglary, assault and rape will do for a start. I've had quite enough of his company for the time being. Get him fingerprinted immediately."

Graham Sharp tried to block his way as he left the room, but Banks pushed him gently aside: "The constable here will explain your son's rights," he said.

It was late, well after midnight, and the town outside was dark and quiet. Only the bell of the church clock broke the silence every fifteen minutes. Back in his office, Banks looked out through the slats of his venetian blinds. There wasn't a soul in sight; all the lights were out except for the old-style gas lamps around the market square and a shop window to the right, across Market Street, in which elegant mannequins modelled the kind of long, expensive dresses that Grace Kelly wore in *Rear Window*.

Banks lit another cigarette and drank some more hot coffee, then turned to the first buff folder on his desk. It was Sandra's statement. Not much of her personality came through in Richmond's precise, analytical prose, nor did any of her feelings. Banks could only imagine them, and he found himself doing so only too well. As he read of her being forced back towards the screen at knife-point and made to strip ("To what point?" an obviously embarrassed Richmond had asked) to her skin, tears burned his eyes and anger seethed in his veins. He closed the folder and slammed it with his fist.

At least from what Sandra had remembered of Robin Allott's words—and she had done well to remember so much—it sounded as if he was their man. It also sounded as if he had broken down at the end, that he couldn't go through with it. Banks recalled Jenny once saying that the man might have to keep going further and further to satisfy himself, but that he might also reach breaking point before doing any serious damage. Whether he had done any serious damage or not was a moot point.

It had been a long day. Banks yawned and felt his eyelids suddenly become heavy and scratchy. It was time to go home.

He pulled up his coat collar and stepped out into Market Street. The chill October air was invigorating, but Banks felt tired beyond revival. All the way home, something nagged at his mind, something about the Sharp interview. Trevor's reaction to the Alice Matlock business certainly confirmed his earlier suspicions, but that wasn't it, there was something else. It was no good trying to think, though, he decided. It would have to wait until tomorrow.

IV

Jenny and Sandra were still talking when Banks walked in the front door. They were drinking cocoa laced with scotch, and Sandra had lent Jenny one of her old dressing-gowns to wear.

"I thought you'd be in bed by now," Banks said, hanging up his overcoat.

"We didn't feel like sleeping," Sandra replied. "But now you mention it, I do feel tired."

"Me too," Jenny echoed.

"I've made up the bed," Sandra told her. "I hope it's comfortable enough for you."

"I could sleep on a slab of stone." Jenny smiled and stood up. "Goodnight, you two, and thanks very much."

She went upstairs and Banks flopped down on the sofa beside Sandra. Again he had noticed a strange atmosphere between them, as if they were in a world that excluded him, but he was too tired to delve into it. About ten minutes later, they followed Jenny up and slipped between the sheets.

"What were you talking about?" he asked as they snuggled close.

"Oh, this and that."

"Me?"

"A bit. Mostly what it felt like."

"What did it feel like?"

"You'll never know."

"You could try and describe it for me."

"I don't want to go through it all again tonight, Alan. Some other time."

"Maybe it felt something like being held up at gunpoint."

"Maybe it did. I'll tell you something, though. It's very odd. I was terrified and I hated him, but afterwards I felt sorry for him. He was like a little child when I hit him, Alan. He was down on his knees. He'd dropped his knife, and he was like a child. I couldn't handle the feelings at the time. I was scared, angry, hurt, and I hit him. I wanted to kill him, I really did. But it was pathetic. He was like a child crying out for his mother."

"You did the right thing," Banks said, holding her and feeling her warm tears on his shoulder.

"I know. But that's what I mean when I said you'd never understand. You never could. There are some things men could never grasp in a million years."

Banks felt shut out again, and it irked him that Sandra was probably right. He wanted to understand everything, and he had sympathy, feelings and imagination enough to do so, or so he had thought. Now Sandra was telling him that no matter how hard he tried, he could never fathom the bond that united her and Jenny and excluded him, simply because he was a man. They had both been victims, and he was a member of the sex that had the power to humiliate them. In a way, it didn't matter how gentle and understanding he was; he was guilty by association.

But perhaps, he thought, as he drifted into sleep, it was neither as important nor as devastating as it seemed at that moment. After all, he was tired out, and the evening's events had left their unassimilated residue in him, too. He was simply recognizing a chasm that had always existed, even before Sandra had been so abused. That unbridgeable gap had not interfered seriously with their happiness and closeness before, and it probably wouldn't do so in the future. The human spirit was a great deal more resilient than one imagined in one's darker moments. Still, the distance between them was more apparent now than ever, and it would have to be dealt with; he would have to make attempts to cross it.

He held Sandra tighter and told her he loved her, but she was already asleep. Sighing, he turned over and fell into his own dreamless darkness.

SEVENTEEN

I

When Banks met Robin Allott the next morning, he could see exactly what Sandra meant. He had expected to hate the man, but Robin, looking rather like a tonsured monk with the dressing fixed over the shaved centre of his skull, was pathetic. Banks found it easy to detach himself and deal with him as he would with any other criminal. Richmond sat in the corner taking notes.

"What did the hospital say?" he asked.

Allott shrugged and avoided looking Banks in the eye. "Not very much. They dressed the wound and sent me away with this." He held up a card which explained how to handle patients with head wounds. "I spent the rest of the night in your cells."

"Want to talk?"

Allott nodded. The first thing he did was apologize. Then he confessed to all the reported peeping incidents in addition to several more that had gone either unnoticed or unreported by the victims.

There was, however, another important matter to discuss. The timing of Allott's peeping on Carol Ellis coincided almost exactly with Alice Matlock's late evening visitor, who, if he wasn't her killer, was the last person to see her alive. Banks asked him if he had seen anyone as he ran along Cardigan Drive.

"Yes," Allott said eagerly. "I liked Alice. I've been wanting to tell you but I couldn't find a way without... It's been torturing me ever since. At first I thought he would have reported me. Then when he didn't... I'm so glad it's all over. I tried to suggest it might not have been kids, that it might have happened some other way, when you came to talk to me."

"I remember," Banks said. "But you didn't express the theory very forcefully."

"How could I? I was scared for myself."

"Who did you see?"

"It wasn't anyone I knew, but it was a man in his late thirties or early forties, I'd say. Medium height, slim. He had light brown hair combed back with a parting on the left."

"What was he wearing?"

"A beige overcoat, I think. I remember it was a chilly night. And gloves. Fawn gloves."

"Did you see where he came from?"

"No. He was by the end of Alice's house when I ran by on the other side of the street. You know, the end of the block that runs at right angles to Cardigan Drive. Gallows View."

"So he was actually on Cardigan Drive, walking by the end house of Gallows View."

"Yes. Just across the street from me."

"And you got a good look at him?"

"Good enough. There's a street-lamp only yards from the junction."

"Would you recognize him again?"

"Yes."

"Are you sure?"

"Definitely."

Jenny had asked if she could talk to Allott, and Banks had agreed, stipulating that he be present throughout the interview. When he had finished with his questions, he asked Richmond to call in at the interview room where she was waiting and send her along.

There was still something nagging at his mind. Though it often worked wonders on half-formed ideas, sleep had failed to solve the problem this time. It was like having the right word on the tip of his tongue but being unable to utter it.

Jenny seemed to be making a deliberate effort to hide her beauty by wearing some very unflattering horn-rimmed glasses and drab, baggy clothes that made her figure seem shapeless. She also wore her hair tied back in a severe bun.

Robin Allott looked up when she walked in stiffly with a file folder under her arm and a pencil behind her ear. She sat down opposite him, opened the folder, and only then, Banks noticed, did she look him in the eye.

"Would you like to tell me when you started watching women undress?" she asked first, in a business-like tone.

Now, Banks thought, it's my turn to watch the professional at work.

Allott looked away at the autumn scene on the calendar. "It was after my wife left me. I couldn't...she wasn't happy....She put up with me for a long time, but finally she couldn't stand it any longer. We hadn't had a proper life together, a real marriage. You know what I mean."

"Why was that?"

"I don't know. I didn't like to touch her. I couldn't be a man for her. I just wasn't interested. It wasn't her fault. She was a good woman, really. She put up with a great deal."

"What did she think?"

"She once told me she thought I was a latent homosexual, but I knew that was wrong. I never had any feelings like that for men. The whole idea repelled me. I never had any real feelings at all."

"What do you mean, you didn't have any real feelings?"

"You know, the things people are supposed to feel and do. Everything normal and carefree, like talking and kissing and loving. I felt like there was a big wall between me and the rest of the world, especially my wife."

"So she left you and then you started watching women get undressed. Why did you do that?"

"It was what I wanted to do. All I wanted to do, really. There was nothing else that gave me such a thrill. I know it was wrong but I couldn't...I tried to stop..."

"Can you think of any reason why you chose to do that particular thing? Why only that could satisfy you?"

Allott hesitated and bit his lip. "Yes," he said, after a few moments. "I did it before—a long time ago when I was a boy—and I couldn't get it out of my mind."

"What happened?"

He took a deep breath and his gaze turned inwards.

"We lived on a narrow street with a pub on the corner—The Barley Mow, it was called—and lots of times when I was supposed to be asleep in my room, I'd see this woman opposite walk back from the pub alone, go upstairs and undress for bed. She always left the curtains open, and I watched her.

"She was a beautiful woman and nobody in the neighbourhood really knew her. She never spoke to anyone and people tended to keep away from her, as if she was cold or above them somehow. People said she was foreign, a refugee from Eastern Europe, but nobody really knew. She was always alone. She was a mystery, but I could watch her unveil herself. At first it didn't feel like much, but I suppose it was just about that time of life when you change...and over a few weeks I had strange feelings watching her, feelings I'd never had before. They scared me, but they were exciting. I suppose I started to...to play with myself, unconsciously, and I remember thinking, 'What if she sees me, what will she do? I'll be in trouble then.' But in a way I wanted her to see me, too. I wanted her to know about me." He leaned forward on his chair and his liquid brown eyes began to shine as he talked.

"Did she ever see you?"

"No. One day she was just gone. Simple as that. I was devastated. I'd thought it would go on forever, that she was doing it just for me. When she left it felt as if my whole life had been smashed in pieces. Oh, I did all the usual things like the other boys, but it always felt like there was something missing—it was never as wonderful as the others made out it was, as I thought it should be. Even girls, real girls..."

"Why did you marry?"

"It was the normal thing to do. My mother helped me, arranged introductions, that kind of thing. It just didn't work, though. I was always thinking of this woman, even...I could only do it if I thought of her. When my wife left, something snapped in me. It was like a sort of fog came over my mind, but at the same time I felt free. I felt like I could do what I wanted, I didn't have to pretend any more. Oh, I could always be with other people easily enough—I had the Camera Club and all, but it was all inside, the mist. I felt I had to find her again, recapture what I'd lost."

"And did you?"

"No."

"What was she like?"

"Beautiful. Slender and beautiful. And she had black eyebrows and long, golden-blonde hair. That excited me, I don't know why. Maybe it was the contrast. Long, straight, blonde hair down over her shoulders. She looked like Sandra. That's why...I wouldn't have hurt her, never. And when it had gone so far, I just couldn't go through with it." He glanced over at Banks, who lit a cigarette and looked out of the window on the bustle of the market square.

"What did you have in mind?"

"Nothing clear. I wanted to touch her. Make love to her, I suppose. But I couldn't. Please believe me, I wouldn't have hurt her, honestly."

"But you did hurt her."

He hung his head. "I know. I'd like to tell her, say I'm sorry..."

"I don't think she wants to see you. You frightened her a great deal."

"I didn't mean to. It seemed like the only way."

"I'm not here to judge you," Jenny said.

"What's going to happen to me?"

"You need help. We'll try to help you."

"You?"

"Not me, but somebody qualified."

Robin gave a resigned nod. "I didn't mean to scare her. I would never have harmed a hair on her head, you've got to believe me. I thought it was the only way. I had to find out what it felt like to touch her, to have her in my power. But I couldn't do anything. I couldn't."

Jenny and Banks left him with a uniformed constable and walked out into the corridor. Jenny leaned against the institutional-green wall and took a deep breath, then she removed her glasses and loosened her hair.

"Well?" Banks asked.

"I think he's harmless," she said. "You heard him insist that he wouldn't have hurt Sandra. I believe him."

"But he did hurt her."

"I told him that, and I think he understood. He meant physically. What more can I say, Alan? He's suffering. Part of me hates him for what he did, but another part—the professional bit, I suppose—understands, in a way, that it's not his fault, that he needs help not punishment."

Banks nodded. "Coffee?"

"Oh, yes, please."

They walked across Market Street to the Golden Grill.

"You still seem a bit preoccupied, Alan," Jenny said, sipping her coffee. "Is there something else? I thought you'd caught enough criminals for one night."

"Lack of sleep, I suppose."

"That all?"

"Probably not. There's something bothering me, but I'm not quite sure what it is. You know we haven't got Alice Matlock's killer yet?"

"Yes."

"Allott gave us a description. It's definitely not the kids."

"So?"

"I feel that I ought to know who it is, and why. Like it's staring me in the face and I just can't bring it into focus."

"Is there some clue you can't think of?"

"No, it's nothing like that. It's a whole jumble of impressions. Not to worry, another night's sleep might do it. Maybe I'll even try an afternoon nap and hurry it along."

"So it's not all over?"

"Not yet."

"And our intrepid chief inspector won't rest until it is?"

Banks smiled. "Something like that. I'll tell you one thing, though. When I moved up to Yorkshire, I sure as hell expected a softer time of it than this."

II

Back at the station an excited Sergeant Hatchley came rushing to meet Banks.

"We've got him!"

"Who?"

"Lenny Webster. The fence. Mick's brother."

Banks grinned. "So London came through, then?"

"Didn't they just? Paid him a visit in the middle of the night at that address we got from the letter."

"Yes?"

"And sure enough, he was there. Babysitting an assortment of drugs—marijuana, cocaine, uppers, downers, even some heroin."

"Enough to put him away for a while?"

"Enough to put him away for a long while, sir."

"I'll bet he was intending to bring it all back up here to sell, am I right?"

"Exactly. And there's more."

"Go on."

"It seems that young Lenny's not as tough as he makes out, if you know what I mean. In fact, a little heavy leaning and he breaks down completely. First off, they've got the bloke who gave him the gun, and they found three more at his place—not duff ones, mind you. And next, Lenny sings all about his plans with Micklethwaite."

"Moxton."

"Pardon?"

"That's his real name. Moxton. Larry Moxton."

"Oh. Well, Webster knows him as Micklethwaite, and they were going to unload the stuff between them. Also, Micklethwaite put him onto the Ottershaw and Pitt jobs."

"Right, we'd better bring Larry in then, hadn't we?"

"Do you think we've got enough to nail him?"

"I think so, if we add it to what Thelma Pitt and Ottershaw have to tell us. What puzzles me is how a con-man like Larry could get mixed up with a low-life thug like Webster."

"That's explained in the telex," Hatchley said. "Apparently it's through the chap who was getting the drugs for them. He'd served time with Micklethwaite, and when he heard he was going to relocate up north he put him in touch with Lenny."

"Ah, the old-boy network. Right little den of thieves we've caught, haven't we?"

Hatchley beamed, his red balloon-face glowing with success.

"Aye, we have that, sir. Oh, I almost forgot. There's a woman waiting in your office for you."

"Not…"

"No, not that Wycombe woman. I've never seen this one before. Wouldn't say who she was. Wants to see you, though."

Curious, Banks poked his head around the office door. It was Mrs Allott, Robin's mother.

"What's all this nonsense about my son Robin?" she asked, puffing herself up.

Banks took a deep breath and sat down. It was the last thing he needed, another irate parent.

"Your son has been charged on several counts of voyeurism, Mrs Allott, and on one count of attempted rape. He threatened a woman at knife-point. That woman happened to be my wife."

Mrs Allott's tone altered not a jot. "Always look after your own, you coppers do. Well, you've got the wrong man this time. My Robin wouldn't hurt a fly."

"Perhaps not," Banks conceded, "but he's behaved very badly towards women."

"Who saw him, then? How many witnesses have you got?"

"We don't need witnesses, Mrs Allott. Your son gave us a full confession."

"Well, you must have sweated it out of him. You must have got the rubber hose-pipe out."

Banks got to his feet. "Mrs Allott, it's a cut and dried case. There's nothing more to be said about it. If you'll excuse me, I've got work to do."

"He was with me," she persisted. "All those times you say he was snooping on women he was with me. I've looked after him ever since that bitch of a wife ran off and left him, the no-good hussy. I warned him about her, I did. Told him she'd only bring trouble."

"Why don't you give a list of the dates and times your son was with you to the desk sergeant, then we'll see if we can match them with the incidents. I have to repeat, though, it's no use. Your son has already confessed."

"Under duress, I'm sure. He can't have done those things you say he did."

"I can assure you that he did do them."

"Then that wife of his drove him to it."

"Make up your mind, Mrs Allott. How could he be driven to do things you said he didn't do?"

"He was with me," she repeated firmly.

Banks couldn't be bothered to tell her that, in addition to her son's confession, he also had Sandra's statement. It was futile. Robin's innocence was fixed in her mind, and that was that. No amount of reason would change her opinion. She would even lie on the witness stand to save him.

"Look," Banks said in as kind a tone as he could manage, "I really do have a lot of work to do. If you'd care to give the dates to the sergeant at the front desk..."

"I'm not going to be soft-soaped like that. You're not going to fob me off with some menial. I demand my rights."

She was clinging as tight as a limpet and Banks was nearing the end of his tether. Brusquely, he picked up a clean sheet of paper and took out his pen.

"All right, then. The dates?"

"I can't remember the exact dates. What do you think I am, a computer? He's always at home. *You* know, you've seen him there. He helps me take care of his dad."

"I saw him there once, Mrs Allott. And he was expecting me. Are you telling me he's at home every night?"

"Yes."

"Including Tuesdays?"

She thought for a moment, a wary expression flickering over her pinched face. "Tuesdays. He goes to the Camera Club on Tuesdays. With his friends. Any of them will tell you what a good boy he is."

Banks could think of one who certainly wouldn't, but he said nothing. In fact, Mrs Allott's presence began to recede far into the distance as the subject of his recent brooding came slowly into focus. She had given him an idea. It still wasn't fully formed yet, and he wasn't sure what to do about it, but the lens was definitely closing in.

He forced his attention reluctantly back to the business in hand.

"So what you're telling me, Mrs Allott, is that every night of the week except Tuesdays, Robin was with you from the moment he left work till the moment he went again the next morning?"

"That's right."

"He never went out?"

"No."

"All right," Banks said, losing interest in her lies again as his idea came into sharper focus. "I'll get somebody to take your statement, Mrs Allott. You can go home now."

She got to her feet and flapped out of the office.

Almost as soon as she had slammed the door, Banks forgot her. He reached for a cigarette, asked Craig to send up some of the *special* new coffee, and slouched deep in his chair to think.

One hour, three cigarettes, and two cups of black coffee later, he knew what had been bothering him and what to do about it. He snatched up the phone and dialled the front desk.

"Put Sergeant Hatchley on," he snapped. He knew that Hatchley had a habit of chatting with Rowe.

"Sir?" Hatchley answered.

"Sergeant, I want you to go to Sharp's place and ask Graham Sharp to drop by and see me right away. Tell him it's to do with his son's statement and it's urgent. Got that?"

"Yes, sir."

"And don't take no for an answer, Sergeant. If he grumbles about locking up the shop and losing business, remind him what a difficult position young Trevor's in."

"Right," Hatchley answered, "I'm on my way, sir."

III

"Trevor Sharp's been bound over to the youth authorities," Richmond was saying. "Do you want me to get him over here?"

"No," Banks answered. "It doesn't matter. How's Webster?"

"The last I heard, sir, he's in fair shape. The surgeon managed to save that finger. Have you seen my report?"

"No, I haven't. It's been a busy morning. No time for reading. Give me a summary."

"It was just to tell you that Vic Manson got some good prints from the jewellery, sir. It seems the lads must have handled it at home after the burglaries, when they felt safe."

"And?"

"And both Sharp's and Webster's prints showed up, sir."

"We've got the buggers, then."

"Looks like it, sir. Webster's been doing a bit of talking, too. That shock to his system has shaken his ideas around no end. The doc won't let us talk to him for long yet, but he's already told us it was him and Sharp did the jobs."

"Good work," Banks said. "Could you bring in Allott for me, please?"

"The peeper, sir?"

"Yes. Robin Allott. Bring him up."

"Very well, sir. I'm afraid his mother's still downstairs on the bench. Refuses to leave until she sees the superintendent."

Banks scratched his chin. It was itchy because he hadn't shaved that morning. "I wouldn't wish her on him," he said. "Try and get rid of her. And whatever you do, make sure she doesn't see her son coming up."

"I'll do my best, sir."

A few moments later, Robin Allott was escorted into Banks's office and told to make himself comfortable. Allott still couldn't meet the inspector's eyes, and Banks almost felt like telling him to stop dwelling on it, that it was all over and done with. But he didn't. Why let the bastard off the hook after what he'd done to Sandra? If she hadn't already known Allott, Banks thought, there wouldn't have been any pity in her feelings towards him.

About fifteen minutes later, there was a knock at the door. Banks opened it to Sergeant Hatchley with an anxious Graham Sharp in tow.

"What is it, Inspector?" Sharp demanded angrily as he charged across the threshold. "Your sergeant told me it—"

And he froze. As the newcomer entered the room, Robin Allott had turned to see what the commotion was, and his jaw dropped in immediate recognition.

"That's him!" he said, pointing at Sharp. "That's the man I saw!"

Graham Sharp looked at him, then at Banks. His face drained of colour and he reached out to support himself on the edge of the flimsy desk. Banks gestured to a confused Hatchley to stay and to pull up a chair for him.

"Like to tell me about it, Mr Sharp?" he asked.

"What made you think of me?"

"Somebody else in your position."

"What do you mean?"

Banks looked at Robin, then back at Sharp. "His mother came in and swore blind he was with her when he had already admitted to being the peeper. I just got to thinking about the lengths some people would go to to protect their families. After a while, it all seemed to fit. Your son insisted that he and Webster had nothing to do with Alice Matlock's death and that was the only thing I believed from him. I'd already suspected that it was a different kind of crime. There was no senseless damage to Alice's sentimental possessions as there had been in the other cases, and she was the first victim to die.

"The problem then was who on earth would want to kill a harmless old woman, and why? Robin's mother gave me the answer. I remembered how protective you had been about Trevor, ready to perjure yourself and swear blind to false alibis. It didn't take much stretching of the imagination to figure out that you might go a lot further to protect your illusion of him. The simple fact is, Mr Sharp, that your son's a callous, vicious bastard, but to you he's a bright lad with a promising future. You would do anything to protect that future. Am I right?"

Sharp nodded.

"I don't know all the details," Banks went on, "but I think that Alice Matlock found out something about your son. Maybe she saw him leaving the scene of a break-in, saw him with some stolen goods or noticed him hiding his balaclava. She wasn't a very sociable person, but everybody knew about the other women who'd been robbed. Am I still right?"

Sharp sighed and accepted a cigarette with a trembling hand. He seemed on the verge of a nervous collapse.

"Are you all right?" Banks asked.

"Yes, Inspector. It's just the relief. You've no idea what a burden this has been for me. I don't think I could have stood it much longer, pushing it to the back of my mind, pretending it never really happened. It was an accident, you know."

"Do you mean you would have come forward eventually?"

"Possibly. I can't say. I know how far I'd go to protect my son, but not how far I'd go to save myself."

"Tell me about it."

"Yes. Alice Matlock told me that she had heard Trevor bragging about the robberies with another boy one evening when she was walking home from a friend's house. She came into my shop that Monday just before closing and told me about it. Said she was going to report him to the police the next day. She had no proof, no evidence, and at first it didn't bother me much because I thought nobody would take any notice of an old woman. But then I got to worrying about what damage it might do, what questions we might have to answer.

"I couldn't believe Trevor was guilty, even though I knew there was something wrong. Maybe I did know it, deep down. I can't say. But I wanted to protect him. Is that so unusual in a father? I thought that whatever it was it was just a phase he would pass through. I didn't want his life ruined because of a few foolish juvenile exploits."

"If you'd come forward with your suspicions a long time ago," Banks remarked, "you would have saved everybody, including your son, a lot of grief. Especially Thelma Pitt."

Sharp shook his head. "I still can't believe my Trevor did that."

"Take my word for it, Mr Sharp, he did. That's just the point."

Sharp flicked the ash off his cigarette and looked at the floor.

"What happened?" Banks asked.

"I went to talk to her that night. Just talk to her. I knocked on the door and she answered it. I'm not really sure that she recognized me. She seemed to think I was someone else. I told her what a good future Trevor had and what a crime it would be to spoil it for him. I was desperate, Inspector. I even pleaded with her, but it was no good."

"What did she say?"

"Nothing that made much sense to me. She said there was no point coming back and pretending to be him. I wasn't him. I was an evil imposter and she was going to the police. I couldn't talk any sense into her and when she started going on about calling the police I lost my temper and reached for her.

"I didn't intend to kill her, honestly. But she was so frail. I've got a terrible temper. Always have had. I couldn't help myself. She fell backwards. I tried to reach out, to stop her, but it all seemed to happen in slow motion, like one of them dreams when you can't run fast enough. I heard the sound, her skull cracking on the edge of the table. And the blood on the flags...I..." Sharp put his head in his hands and sobbed.

"What happened next?" Banks asked, after giving him a couple of minutes to pull himself together.

"I messed the place up a bit, as if I'd been a burglar, and I took some things—some money, a set of silver cutlery. You'll find it all buried on the edge of Gallows Field. I didn't touch a penny of the money, honest I didn't."

"You didn't think to call an ambulance?"

"I was scared. There would have been questions."

"We didn't find any fingerprints, Mr Sharp. Were you wearing gloves?"

"Yes."

"That would explain the muffled knocking," Hatchley interrupted, looking up from his note taking. "That Rigby woman said the knocking sounded muffled, distant, like it could have been a long way away."

Banks nodded. "Why were you wearing gloves, Mr Sharp?"

"It was a cold night. I've got bad circulation."

"But you didn't have very far to go."

"No, I suppose not."

"And you didn't take them off when you got inside."

"I never thought. Things just started happening too fast. Don't you believe me? Are you suggesting I intended to kill the woman?"

"That's for the court to decide," Banks said. "I'm just gathering the evidence. Did you see Mr Allott?"

"Yes, on my way in. He looked like he was running away from something himself. I didn't think he got a really good look at me. Still, I was a bit worried for a few days, but then I realized that, whoever he was, he hadn't come forward. Perhaps he hadn't heard of the old woman's death, or maybe he had his own secret to hide. I don't know."

"Did you have any idea why Alice Matlock didn't seem to recognize you but let you in anyway?"

Graham shrugged. "I can't say I gave it much thought. She was old. I suppose she did ramble a bit sometimes."

"Close," Banks said. "She probably couldn't even remember what day she overheard Webster and your son. You see, the irony of it is, Mr Sharp, that by the morning she would most likely have forgotten all about the incident anyway. And you were quite right to think that nobody would believe a woman who was beginning to live more in the past than the present. You killed her for nothing."

IV

There wasn't much left to do. Statements had to be written up and filed, charges laid, hearing dates fixed. But as far as Banks was concerned, the real job was finished. The rest was up to the courts and the twelve jurors "good and true."

He believed that Sharp had killed Alice Matlock by accident, that he was basically a good man driven too far. But so many criminals were good men gone wrong. It sometimes seemed a pity, or at least an inconvenience, that society seemed to have discarded the concept of evil, something which, in Banks's mind, would always separate Trevor Sharp from his father.

As he had no other pressing business, he decided to go home early and spend some time with Sandra. He would see Jenny again, too. No doubt Sandra would insist that she come over for dinner some evening. But not for a while. It was time to heal the wound and attempt to build more frail bridges between male and female; and the fewer confusing distractions, the easier that would be.

He would buy Sandra a small present, perhaps: that simple gold chain she had admired in H. Samuels' window the last time they were in Leeds; or the new lightweight camera-bag at Erricks' in Bradford. Or he could take her out for dinner and a show. Opera North were doing Gounod's *Faust* next month. But no, Sandra didn't like opera. Going to see a new film would be a better treat for her.

As he walked home in the steady drizzle, Banks began to feel some of the pleasurable release, the sense of lightness and freedom that was his usual reward at the end of a case.

Before leaving, he had slipped a cassette of highlights from *La Traviata*, usually reserved for the car, into his Walkman, and now he fumbled around in his pocket to switch it on. He walked down Market Street enjoying the cool needles of rain on his face and hummed along with the haunting prelude. Tourists heading for the car park, merchants closing up for the day, and disappointed shoppers rattling already-locked doors all seemed like actors in the opening scene of a grand opera. When the jaunty "Drinking Song" began, Banks started to sing along quietly, and his step lightened almost to a dance.

A DEDICATED MAN

For Jan

They were right, my dear, all those voices were right
And still are; this land is not the sweet home that it looks,
    Nor its peace the historical calm of a site
Where something was settled once and for all...

W.H. Auden
"In Praise of Limestone"

ONE

I

When the sun rose high enough to clear the slate roofs on the other side of the street, it crept through a chink in Sally Lumb's curtains and lit on a strand of gold-blonde hair that curled over her cheek. She was dreaming. Minotaurs, bank clerks, gazelles and trolls cavorted through the barns, maisonettes and gothic palaces of her sleep. But when she awoke a few hours later, all she was left with was the disturbing image of a cat picking its way along a high wall topped with broken glass. Dreams. Most of them she ignored. They had nothing to do with the other kind of dreams, the most important ones that she didn't have to fall asleep to find. In these dreams, she passed her exams and was accepted into the Marion Boyars Academy of Theatre Arts. There she studied acting, modelling and cosmetic technique, for Sally was realistic enough to know that if she lacked the dramatic talent of a Jessica Lange or a Kathleen Turner, she could at least belong to the fringes of the world of glamour.

When Sally finally stirred, the bar of sunlight had shifted to the floor beside her bed, striping the untidy pile of clothes she had dropped there the night before. She could hear plates and cutlery clatter in the kitchen downstairs, and the rich smell of roast beef wafted up to her room. She got up. It was good policy, she thought, to get downstairs as soon as possible and help with the vegetables before her mother's call—"It's on the table!"—came grating up to her. At least by showing a willingness to help, she could probably avoid too probing an investigation into her lateness last night.

Sally stared at herself in the full-length mirror of her old oak wardrobe. Even if there was still a little puppy fat around her hips and thighs, it would soon go away. On the whole, she decided, she had a good body. Her breasts were perfect. Most people, of course, complimented her on her long silky hair, but they hadn't seen her breasts. Kevin had. Just last night he had caressed them and told her they were perfect. Last night they had gone almost all the way, and Sally knew that the next time, soon, they would. She looked forward to it with a mixture of fear and desire that, according to what she had read in magazines and books, would soon fuse into ecstasy in the heat of passion and longing.

Sally touched her nipple with the tip of her forefinger and felt a tingle in her loins. The nipple hardened and she moved away from the mirror to get dressed, her face burning.

Kevin was good. He knew how to excite her; ever since summer began he had played carefully with the boundaries of her desire. He had pushed them back a little further each time, and soon the whole country would be his. He was young, like Sally, but still he seemed to know instinctively how to please her, just as she imagined an experienced older man would know. She even thought she loved Kevin a bit. But if someone else came along—somebody more mature, more wealthy, more sophisticated, someone who was at home in the exciting, fast-paced cities of the world—well, after all, Kevin was only a farm boy at heart.

Dressed in designer jeans and a plain white T-shirt, Sally drew back the curtains. When her eyes had adjusted to the glare, she looked out on a perfect Swainsdale morning. A few fluffy little clouds—one like a teddy bear, another like a crab—scudded across the piercing blue sky on a light breeze. She looked north up the broad slope of the valley side, its rich greens interrupted here and there by dark patches of heather and outcrops of limestone, to the long sheer wall of Crow Scar, and noticed something very odd. At first she couldn't make it out at all. Then she squinted, refocused and saw, spread out along the slope just above the old road, five or six blue dots that seemed to be moving in some kind of pattern. She put a finger to her lips, thought for a moment, and frowned.

II

Fifteen miles away in Eastvale, the dale's largest town, somebody else was anticipating a Sunday dinner of succulent roast beef and Yorkshire pudding. Detective Chief Inspector Alan Banks lay flat on his stomach in Brian's room watching an electric train whizz around bends, over bridges, through signals and under papier-mâché mountains. Brian himself was out riding his bike in the local park, but Banks had long since given up the pretence that he only played with the trains for his son's sake and finally admitted that he found the pastime even more relaxing than a hot bath.

He heard the phone ring out in the hall, and a few seconds later his daughter, Tracy, shouted through, "It's for you, Dad!"

As Banks rushed downstairs, the aroma from the kitchen made his mouth water. He thanked Tracy and picked up the receiver. It was Sergeant Rowe, desk-officer at Eastvale Regional Headquarters.

"Sorry to bother you, sir," Rowe began, "but we've just had a call from Constable Weaver over in Helmthorpe. Seems a local farmer's found a body in one of his fields this morning."

"Go on," Banks urged, snapping into professional gear.

"Chap said he was looking for a stray sheep, sir, when he found this body buried by a wall. Weaver says he shifted one or two stones and it's a dead 'un all right. Looks like someone bashed 'is 'ead in."

Banks felt the tightening in his stomach that always accompanied news of murder. He had transferred from London a year ago, sickened by the spiralling of senseless violence there, only to find in the Gallows View case that things could be just as bad, if not worse, up north. The business had left both him and Sandra emotionally exhausted, but since then things had settled down. There'd been nothing but a few burglaries and one case of fraud to occupy his attention, and he had really begun to believe that murders, Peeping Toms and vicious teenagers were the exception rather than the rule in Eastvale.

"Tell Constable Weaver to get back up there with as many local men as he can muster and rope off the area. I want them to start a systematic search, but I don't want anyone else closer to the body than ten yards. Got that?" The last thing he needed was half a dozen flat-foots trampling down the few square feet where clues were most likely to be found.

"Tell them to put everything they find into marked envelopes," he went on. "They should know the procedure, but it won't do any harm to remind them. And I mean everything. Used rubbers, the lot. Get in touch with Detective Sergeant Hatchley and Dr Glendenning. Tell them to get out there immediately. I'll want the photographer and the forensic team too. Okay?"

"Yes, sir," Sergeant Rowe replied. He knew that Jim Hatchley would be enjoying his usual Sunday lunch-time pint in The Oak and that it would give Banks a great deal of satisfaction to interrupt his pleasure.

"I suppose the super's been informed?"

"Yes, sir. It was him as said to tell you."

"It would be," Banks complained. "I don't suppose he wanted to miss *his* Sunday dinner." But he spoke with humour and affection. Superintendent Gristhorpe, of all his new colleagues, was the one who had given him the most support and encouragement during the difficult transition from city to country.

Banks hung up and slipped on his worn brown jacket with the elbow-patches. He was a small, dark man, in appearance rather like the old Celtic strain of Welshmen, and his physique certainly didn't give away his profession.

Sandra, Bank's wife, emerged from the kitchen as he was preparing to leave. "What is it?" she asked.

"Looks like a murder."

She wiped her hands on her blue checked pinafore. "So you won't be in for dinner?"

"Sorry, love. Doesn't look like it."

"And I don't suppose there's any point in keeping it warm?"

"Shouldn't think so. I'll grab a sandwich somewhere." He kissed her quickly on the lips. "Don't worry, I'll give you a call as soon as I know what's happening."

Banks drove his white Cortina west along the valley bottom by the riverside. He was entitled to a police car and driver, but he actually enjoyed driving and preferred his own company when travelling to and from a case. A generous mileage allowance more than compensated him for the cost.

With one eye on the road and one hand on the wheel, he flipped through an untidy pile of cassette tapes on the passenger seat, selected one and slipped it into the deck.

Though he swore that his passion for opera had not waned over the winter, he had to admit that he had been side-tracked into the world of English vocal and choral music. It was a change Sandra heartily approved of; she had never liked opera much in the first place, and Wagner had been the last straw for her. After she had finally gone so far as to attack one of his tapes with a magnet—the one with "Siegfried's Funeral March" on it, Banks remembered sadly—he had got the message. With Ian Partridge singing Dowland's "I Saw My Lady Weepe," he drove on.

Like the larger and more famous Yorkshire Dales, Swainsdale runs more or less from west to east, with a slight list towards the south, until the humble river loses itself in the Ouse. At its source near Swainshead, high in the Pennine fells, the River Swain is nothing more than a trickle of sparkling clear water, but in carving its way down towards the North Sea it has formed, with the help of glaciers and geological faults, a long and beautiful dale which broadens out as it approaches the Vale of York. The main town, Eastvale, dominated by its Norman castle, sits at the extreme eastern edge of the dale and looks out over the rich, fertile plain. On a clear day, the Hambleton Hills and the North York Moors are visible in the distance.

He saw Lyndgarth on the valley side to the north, near the dark ruins of Devraulx Abbey, and passed through peaceful Fortford, where the remains of a Roman fort were still under excavation on a hillock opposite the village green. Ahead, he could see the bright limestone curve of Crow Scar high up on his right, and, as he drew closer, he noticed the local police searching a field marked off by irregular dry-stone walls. The limestone shone bright in the sun, and the walls stood out against the grass like pearl necklaces on an emerald velvet cushion.

To get to the scene, Banks had to drive through Helmthorpe, the dale's central market village, turn right at the bridge onto Hill Road, and then turn right again onto a narrow road that meandered north-eastwards about halfway up the valley side. It was a miracle that the track had ever been tarmacked—probably a gesture towards increasing tourism, Ranks guessed. No good for tire-tracks, though, he thought gloomily.

Being more used to getting around in the city than in the countryside, he scraped his knee climbing the low wall and stumbled over the lumpy sods of grass in the field. Finally, out of breath, he got to where a uniformed man, presumably Constable Weaver, stood talking to a gnarled old farmer about fifty yards up the slope.

By the side of the north-south wall, loosely covered with earth and stones, lay the body. Enough of its covering had been removed to make it recognizable as a man. The head lay to one side, and, kneeling beside it, Banks could see that the hair at the back was matted with blood. A jolt of nausea shot through his stomach, but he quickly controlled it as he began to make mental notes about the scene. Standing up, he was struck by the contrast between the beautiful, serene day and the corpse at his feet.

"Anything been disturbed?" he asked Weaver, stepping carefully back over the rope.

"Not much, sir," the young constable replied. His face was white and the sour smell on his breath indicated that he had probably been sick over the wall. Natural enough, Banks thought. Probably the lad's first corpse.

"Mr Tavistock here,"—he gestured towards the whiskered farmer—"says he just moved those stones around the head to see what his dog was scratting at."

Banks looked at Tavistock, whose grim expression betrayed a man used to death. Ex-army, most likely, and old enough to have seen action in two world wars.

"I were lookin' fer one o'my sheep," Tavistock began in a slow, thick Yorkshire accent, "and I saw that there damage to t'wall. I thought there'd bin a c'lapse." He paused and rubbed his grizzly chin. "There shouldn't'a bin no c'lapse in a Bessthwaite wall. Bin there sin' eighteen thirty, that 'as. Anyroad, old Ben started scratting. At first I thought nowt on it, then..." He shrugged as if there was nothing more to be said.

"What did you do when you realized what it was?" Banks asked.

Tavistock scratched his turkey neck and spat on the grass. "Just 'ad a look, that's all. I thought it might'a bin a sheep somebody'd killed. That 'appens sometimes. Then I ran 'ome,"—he pointed to a farmhouse about half a mile away—"and I called young Weaver 'ere."

Banks was dubious about the "ran," but he was glad that Tavistock had acted quickly. He turned away and gave instructions to the photographer and the forensic team, then took off his jacket and leaned against the warm stone wall while the boffins did their work.

III

Sally slammed down her knife and fork and yelled at her father: "Just because I go for a walk with a boy it doesn't mean I'm a tramp or a trollop or any of those things!"

"Sally!" Mrs Lumb butted in. "Stop shouting at your father. That wasn't what he meant and you know it."

Sally continued to glare. "Well that's what it sounded like to me."

"He was only trying to warn you," her mother went on. "You have to be careful. Boys try to take advantage of you sometimes. Especially a good-looking girl like you." She said it with a mixture of pride and fear.

"You don't have to treat me like I'm a baby, you know," Sally said. "I'm sixteen now." She gave her mother a pitying glance, cast another baleful look at her father and went back to her roast beef.

"Aye," said Mr Lumb, "and you'll do as you're told till you're eighteen. That's the law."

To Sally, the man sitting opposite her was at the root of all her problems, and, of course, Charles Lumb fitted easily into the role his daughter had assigned him: that of an old-fashioned, narrow-minded yokel, whose chief argument against anything new and interesting was, "What was good enough for my father and his father before him is good enough for you, too, young lady." There was a strong conservative streak in him, only to be expected of someone whose family had lived in the area for more generations than could be remembered. A traditionalist, Charles Lumb often said that the dale as he had loved it was dying. He knew that the only chance for the

young was to get away, and that saddened him. Quite soon, he was
certain, even the inhabitants of the Dales villages would belong to
the National Trust, English Heritage or the Open Spaces Society.
Like creatures in a zoo, they would be paid to act out their quaint old
ways in a kind of living museum. The grandson of a cabinet-maker,
Lumb, who worked at the local dairy factory, found it hard to see
things otherwise. The old crafts were dying out because they were
uneconomical, and only tourists kept one cooper, one blacksmith and
one wheelwright in business.

But because Lumb was a Yorkshireman through and through, he
tended to bait and tease in a manner that could easily be taken too
seriously by an ambitious young girl like Sally. He delivered the most
outrageous statements and opinions about her interests and dreams in
such a deliberately deadpan voice that anyone could be excused for
not catching the gentle, mocking humour behind them. If he had
been less sarcastic and his daughter less self-centred, they might both
have realized that they loved each other very much.

The thing was, though, Charles Lumb would have liked to see
more evidence of common sense in his daughter. She was certainly a
bright girl, and it would be easy for her to get into university and
become a doctor or a lawyer. A damn sight easier, he reflected, than
it was in his day. But no, it had to be this bloody academy, and for all
he tried, he could see no value in learning how to paint faces and
show off swimsuits. If he had thought she had it in her to become a
great actress, then he might have been more supportive. But he didn't.
Maybe time would prove him wrong. He hoped so. At least seeing
her on the telly would be something.

Sally, after a few minutes' sulking, decided to change the topic of
conversation. "Have you seen those men on the hill?" she asked. "I
wonder what they're doing?"

"Looking for something, I shouldn't wonder," her father replied
drily, still not recovered from the argument.

Sally ignored him. "They look like policemen to me. You can see
the buttons on their uniforms shining. I'm going up there to have a
look after dinner. There's already quite a crowd along the road."

"Well, make sure you're back before midnight," her mother said. It
cleared the air a bit, and they enjoyed the rest of their meal in peace.

Sally walked up the hill road and turned right past the cottages. As she hurried on she danced and grabbed fistfuls of dry grass, which she flung up high in the air.

Several cars blocked the road by the field, and what had looked, from a distance, like a large crowd turned out to be nothing more than a dozen or so curious tourists with their cameras, rucksacks and hiking-boots. It was open country, almost moorland, Sally knew, despite the dry-stone walls that criss-crossed the landscape and gave it some semblance of order. They were old and only the farmers remembered who built them.

There was more activity in the field than she could recollect ever seeing in such an isolated place. Uniformed men crawled on all fours in the wild grass, and the area by the wall had been cordonned off with stakes and rope. Inside the charmed circle stood a man with a camera, another with a black bag and, seemingly presiding over the whole affair, a small wiry man with a brown jacket slung over his shoulder. Sally's eyesight was so keen that she could even see the small patches of sweat under his arms.

She asked the middle-aged walker standing next to her what was going on, and the man told her he thought there'd been a murder. Of course. It had to be. She'd seen similar things on the telly.

IV

Banks glanced back towards the road. He'd noticed a flashing movement, but it was only a girl's blonde hair catching the sun. Dr Glendenning, the tall, white-haired pathologist, had finished shaking limbs and inserting his thermometer in orifices; now he stood, cigarette dangling from the corner of his mouth, muttering about what a warm night it had been, as he made calculations in his little red notebook.

It was just as well, Banks thought as he looked over at the spectators, that two of the forensic team had first examined the roadside. They had found nothing—no skid marks or tire-tracks on the tarmac, no clear footprints on the grassy verge—but it looked as if someone or something had been dragged up the field from the road.

Glendenning confirmed that the victim had been killed elsewhere and merely dumped in an isolated spot. That would cause problems. If they had no idea where the man had been killed, they wouldn't know where to start looking for the killer.

The doctor rambled on, adjusting his column of figures, and Banks sniffed the air, feeling again that it was too fine a day and too beautiful a spot for such unpleasant business. Even the young photographer, Peter Darby, as he snapped the body from every conceivable angle, said that normally on such a day he would be out photographing Rawley Force at a slow shutter speed, or zooming in on petals with his macro lens, praying that a bee or a butterfly would remain still for as long as it took to focus and shoot. He had photographed corpses before, Banks knew, so he was used to the unpleasantness. All the same, it was worlds away from butterflies and waterfalls.

Glendenning looked up from his notebook and screwed up his eyes in the sunlight. A half-inch of ash floated to the ground, and Banks found himself wondering whether the doctor performed surgery with a cigarette in his mouth, letting ash fall around the incision. Smoking was strictly prohibited at the scene of a crime, of course, but nobody ever dared to mention this to Glendenning.

"It was a warm night," he explained to Banks, with a Scottish lilt to his nicotine-ravaged voice. "I can't give an accurate estimate of time of death. Most likely, though, it was after dark last night and before sunrise this morning."

Bloody wonderful! Banks thought. We don't know where he was killed but we know it was sometime during the night.

"Sorry," Glendenning added, catching Banks's expression.

"Not your fault. Anything else?"

"Blow to the back of the head, if I may translate the cumbersome medical jargon into layman's terms. Pretty powerful, too. Skull cracked like an egg."

"Any idea what weapon was used?"

"Proverbial blunt instrument. Sharp-edged, like a wrench or a hammer. I can't be more specific at this point, but I'd rule out a brick or a rock. It's too neat and I can't find any trace of particles. Full report after the autopsy, of course."

"Is that all?"

"Yes. You can have him taken to the mortuary now if you've finished with the pictures."

Banks nodded. He asked a uniformed constable to send for an ambulance, and Glendenning packed his bag.

"Weaver! Sergeant Hatchley! Come over here a minute," Banks called, and watched the two men walk over. "Any idea who the dead man was?" he asked Weaver.

"Yes, sir," the pale constable answered. "His name's Harry Steadman. Lives in the village."

"Married?"

"Yes, sir."

"Then we'd better get in touch with his wife. Sergeant, would you go over to Mr Tavistock's house and take an official statement?"

Hatchley nodded slowly.

"Is there a decent pub in Helmthorpe?" Banks asked Weaver.

"I usually drink at The Bridge, sir."

"Food?"

"Not bad."

"Right." Banks turned to Hatchley. "We'll go and see Mrs Steadman while you attend to Tavistock. Let's meet up in The Bridge for a bite to eat when we've done. All right?"

Hatchley agreed and lumbered off with Tavistock.

There was no chance of a roast beef dinner at home now. In fact, there would be few meals at home until the crime was solved. Banks knew from experience that once a murder investigation begins there is no stopping and little slowing down, even for family life. The crime invades mealtimes, ablutions and sleep; it dominates conversation and puts up an invisible barrier between the investigator and his family.

He looked down at the village spread out crookedly by a bend in the river, its grey slate roofs gleaming in the sun. The clock on the square church tower said twelve-thirty. Sighing, he nodded to Weaver, and the two of them set off towards the car.

They passed through the small crowd, ignoring the local reporter's tentative questions, and got into the Cortina. Banks cleared the cassettes from the passenger seat so that Weaver could sit beside him.

"Tell me what you know about Steadman," Banks said as he reversed into a gateway and turned around.

"Lived here about eighteen months," Weaver began. "Used to come regular for holidays and sort of fell in love with the place. He inherited a fortune from his father and set himself up here. Used to be a university professor in Leeds. Educated chap, but not stuck up. Early forties, bit over six-foot tall, sandy hair. Still quite young looking. They live in Gratly."

"I thought you said they lived in the village."

"Same thing, really, sir," Weaver explained. "You see, Gratly's just a little hamlet, a few old houses off the road. Doesn't even have a pub. But now the newer houses have spread up the hill, the two are as near as makes no difference. The locals like to keep the name, though. Sense of independence, I suppose."

Banks drove down the hill towards the bridge, Weaver pointed ahead over the river and up the opposite valley side: "That's Gratly, sir."

Banks saw the row of new houses, some still under construction; then there was a space of about a hundred yards before the crossroads lined with older cottages.

"I see what you mean," Banks said. At least the builders were doing a tasteful job, following the design of the originals and using the same local stone.

Weaver went on making conversation that was no doubt intended to help him forget the sight of his first corpse. "Just about all the new houses in Helmthorpe are at this side of the village. You'll get nothing new on the east side. Some bright sparks say it's because it was settled from the east. Vikings, Saxons, Romans and whatnot. Course, you won't find many traces of them now, but the place still seems to spread westwards." He thought about what he'd said for a moment and added with a smile, "Spreads slowly, that is, sir."

Much as Banks was interested in snippets of local history, he lost track of Weaver's words as he drove over the low stone bridge and crossed Helmthorpe High Street. He cursed to himself. It was early Sunday afternoon and, from what he could see around him, that meant car-washing time in the village. Men stood in driveways in front of garages with their sleeves rolled up and buckets of soapy water by their sides. Shiny car roofs gleamed and water dripped from doors and bumpers. Polished chrome shone. If Harry Steadman had been dumped from a local car, all traces of that grisly journey would have been obliterated by now in the most natural way: soaped and waxed over, vacuumed and swept out.

Steadman's house, last in a short block running left from the road, was larger than Banks had imagined. It was solidly built and looked weather-beaten enough to pass for a historic site. That meant it would sell for a historic price, too, he noted. A double-garage had been built on the eastern side, and the large garden, bordered by a low wall, consisted of a well-kept lawn with a colourful flowerbed at its centre and rose bushes against the house-front and the neighbour's fence. Leaving Weaver in the car, Banks walked down the crazy-paving and rang the doorbell.

The woman who answered, holding a cup of tea in her hand, looked puzzled to find a stranger standing before her. She was plain looking, with stringy, lifeless brown hair, and wore a pair of overlarge, unbecoming spectacles. She was dressed in a shapeless beige cardigan and baggy checked slacks. Banks thought she might be the cleaning lady, so he phrased his greeting as a question: "Mrs Steadman?"

"Yes," the woman answered hesitantly, peering at him through her glasses. He introduced himself and felt the familiar tightening in his stomach as he was ushered into the living-room. It was always like that. No amount of experience purged that gut-wrenching feeling of sympathy that accompanied the soothing, useless words, the empty gestures. For Banks there was always a shadow: it could be *my* wife, it could be someone telling me about *my* daughter. It was the same as that first glimpse of the murder victim. Death and its long aftermath had never become a matter of routine for him but remained always an abomination, a reminder one hardly needed of man's cruelty to his fellow man, his fallen nature.

Although the room was messy—a low table littered with magazines, knitting spread out on a chair, records out of their sleeves by the music centre—it was clean, and sunlight poured in over the red and yellow roses through spotless mullioned windows. Above the large stone fireplace hung a romantic painting of what Swainsdale must have looked like over a hundred years ago. It hadn't changed all that much, but somehow the colours seemed brighter and bolder in the picture, the contours more definite.

"What is it?" Mrs Steadman asked, pulling a chair forward for Banks. "Has there been an accident? Is something wrong?"

As he broke the news, Banks watched Mrs Steadman's expression change from disbelief to shock. Finally, she began to weep quietly. There was no sobbing; the tears simply ran down her pale cheeks and dripped onto the wrinkled cardigan as she stared blankly ahead. They could have been caused by an onion, Banks found himself thinking, disturbed by her absolute silence.

"Mrs Steadman?" he said gently, touching her sleeve. "I'm afraid there are a few questions I have to ask you right away."

She looked at him, nodded and dried her eyes with a screwed-up Kleenex: "Of course."

"Why didn't you report your husband missing, Mrs Steadman?"

"Missing?" She frowned at him. "Why should I?"

Banks was taken aback, but he pressed on gently. "I'm afraid you'll have to tell me that. He can't have come home last night. Weren't you worried? Didn't you wonder where he was?"

"Oh, I see what you mean," she said, dabbing at her damp, reddened cheeks with the crumpled tissue. "You weren't to know, were you? You see, I wasn't expecting him home last night. He went out just after seven o'clock. He said he was calling for a pint at The Bridge—he often went there—and then driving on to York. He had work to do there and he wanted to make an early start."

"Did he often do that?"

"Yes, quite often. Sometimes I went with him, but I was feeling a bit under the weather last night—summer cold, I think—and besides, I know they get much more done without me. Anyway, I watched television with Mrs Stanton next door and let him go. Harry stayed with his publisher. Well, more of a family friend really. Michael Ramsden."

"What kind of work did they do on a Sunday?"

"Oh, it wasn't what you or I would understand by *work*. They were writing a book. Harry mostly, but Michael was interested and helped him. A local-history book. That was Harry's field. They'd go off exploring ruins—Roman forts, old lead mines, anything."

"I see. And it was normal for him to go over the night before and stay with Mr Ramsden?"

"Yes. As I've said, they were more like friends than anything else. We've known the family for a long time. Harry was terrible at getting up in the morning, so if they wanted a full day, he'd go over the night before and Michael would be sure to get him up on time. They'd spend the evening going over notes and making plans. I'd no reason to report him missing. I thought he was in York." Her voice faltered and she started to cry again.

Banks waited and let her dry her eyes before asking his next question. "Wouldn't Mr Ramsden be worried if he didn't arrive? Didn't he call you to find out what had happened?"

"No." She paused, blew her nose and went on. "I told you it wasn't that kind of work. More like a hobby, really. Anyway, Michael doesn't have a telephone. He'd just assume that something had come up and Harry couldn't make it."

"Just one more thing, Mrs Steadman, then I won't bother you any further today. Could you tell me where your husband might have left his car?"

"In the big car park by the river," she replied. "The Bridge hasn't got a car park of its own so the customers use that one. You can't really leave cars in the street here; there's not enough room."

"Do you have a spare key?"

"I think he kept one around. I don't use it, myself. I have an old Fiesta. Just a moment." Mrs Steadman disappeared into the kitchen and returned a few moments later with the key. She also gave Banks the number of Steadman's beige Sierra.

"Could you tell me where Mr Ramsden lives, too? I'd like to let him know what's happened as soon as possible."

Mrs Steadman seemed a bit surprised, but she gave the information without question. "It's not so hard to find," she added. "There are no other houses within half a mile yet. Do you need me to...er..."

"To identify the body?"

Mrs Steadman nodded.

"Yes, I'm afraid we do. Tomorrow will do, though. Is there anyone you can get to stay with you for a while?"

She stared at him, her features ugly and swollen with crying; her eyes looked fishy behind the harsh magnification of the glasses. "Mrs Stanton, next door...if you would."

"Of course."

Banks went next door. Mrs Stanton, a long-nosed, alert-looking little woman, immediately grasped the situation. Banks sympathized with her shock. "I know," he said. "It must seem so abrupt. To think that you saw him only last night."

She nodded. "Aye. And to think what was happening while me and Emma were watching that silly old film. Still," she ended stoically, "who are we to question the ways of the Good Lord?" She told her husband, who sat slouched in an armchair reading his *News of the World*, to keep an eye on the roast, then went over to comfort her neighbour. Sure that he was leaving the widow in capable hands, Banks returned to his car and got in next to Weaver, who had regained his pinkish colour.

"I'm sorry, sir," he mumbled. "About being sick. I've—"

"Never seen a corpse before? I know. Never mind, Constable, there's a first time for everyone, more's the pity. Shall we go to The Bridge for a bite to eat?" Weaver nodded. "I'm starving, myself," Banks went on, starting the car, "and you look like you could do with a drop of brandy."

As he drove the short distance down to The Bridge on Helmthorpe High Street, Banks thought about his interview with Mrs Steadman. It had made him feel edgy and uneasy. At times, after the initial shock, her reaction had seemed more like relief than grief. Perhaps the marriage had been shaky, Banks found himself thinking, and Mrs Steadman had suddenly found herself both wealthy and free. Surely that would explain it?

TWO

I

Weaver pulled a face. "I don't like brandy, sir," he admitted sheepishly. "My mum always used to give me a drop for medicinal purposes whenever I got a cold as a lad. Never could stomach the stuff."

The two of them sat in a corner of The Bridge's quiet lounge. Banks nursed a pint of hand-drawn Theakston's bitter, and Weaver complained about his brandy.

"Did it do you any good?" Banks asked.

"I suppose so, sir. But it always reminds me of medicine, of being poorly, if you follow my drift."

Banks laughed and went to buy Weaver a pint to chase away the bad taste. They were waiting for Detective Sergeant Hatchley, who was still with Tavistock, no doubt enjoying a good cup of tea or something stronger and, perhaps, a plateful of roast beef.

"Tell me," Banks asked, "why is this place so empty? It's Sunday dinner-time and the village is crawling with tourists."

"That's right, sir," Weaver said. His boyish face had fully regained its natural pink flush. "But look around you."

Banks looked. They were in a small lounge with faded wallpaper and a cracked brown ceiling. A few water-colours of local scenes, reminiscent of the ones in old railway carriages, covered the most obvious damp spots on the walls. The tables were worn and scored from years of dominoes and shove ha'penny, and ringed by generations of overflowing beer glasses; around the edges were charred semi-circles where cigarettes had been left to burn out. A rack holding tongs and a bent poker stood by the small, tiled fireplace. True, it didn't look much.

"There are three pubs in Helmthorpe, sir," Weaver began, counting them off on his chubby red fingers. "That's if you don't count the Country Club, for the nobs. There's The Dog and Gun and The Hare and Hounds; they're for the tourists mostly. Real olde worlde country inns, if you get my meaning, sir—horse-brasses, copper bed-warmers, antique tables with knee-capper wrought-iron legs, you name it. They have big old fireplaces too, all done up with black lead. Now that every pub in Christendom seems to offer real ale, it's got trendy to advertise a real fire.

"The Dog and Gun's a kind of family place with tables out back by the river and a little enclosed area for the kiddies to play in, and The Hare and Hounds is more for the younger set. They have a disco there every Friday and Saturday in season and you get a lot of the campers going along. That's when we get most of our bother here—the odd fight, that kind of thing. Some nights during the week they have folk music, too. A bit more civilized, if you ask me."

Weaver sniffed and nodded towards the wall. "And then there's this place. It's fairly new by village standards—Victorian, I'd say at a pinch. And it's all that's left for the serious drinkers. The only people who drink here are the locals and a few visitors who know about the beer. It's a pretty well-guarded secret. Course, on weekends you do get a few hikers and whatnot in the public bar. They've all read their good beer guides these days, it seems. But they never cause much trouble; they're a quiet lot, really."

"Why did Steadman drink here, do you think?"

"Steadman?" Weaver seemed surprised to be so quickly jolted back to business. "Liked the beer, I suppose. And he was pally with a few of the regulars."

"But he had money, didn't he? A lot of money. He certainly didn't get that house on the cheap."

"Oh yes, he had money. Rumour has it he inherited over a quarter of a million from his father. His pals have money too, but they're not nobs. Much more down-to-earth."

Banks was still puzzled why someone so well-off would drink in such a dump, good beer or not. By all rights, Steadman ought to have been chugging champagne by the magnum to wash down his caviar. Those were London terms, though, he reminded himself: ostentatious display of wealth. Maybe people with over a quarter of a million who lived in Helmthorpe by choice were different. He doubted it. But Steadman certainly sounded unusual.

"Liked his drink, did he?"

"Never known him drink too much, sir. I think he just enjoyed the company here."

"Glad to get away from the wife?"

Weaver reddened. "I wouldn't know about that, sir. Never heard anything. But he was a funny sort of chap."

"In what way?"

"Well, sir, like I said, he used to be a professor at Leeds University. When he inherited the money, he just packed in his job, bought the old Ramsden house and moved up here."

"Ramsden house?" Banks cut in. "That wouldn't have anything to do with Michael Ramsden, would it?"

Weaver raised an eyebrow. "As a matter of fact, sir, yes," he answered. "It was his parents' house. Used to be a bed-and-breakfast place when Steadman and his wife started coming up here for their holidays ten years ago or more. Young Michael went to university and landed a good job with a publishing firm in London. Then, when old Mr Ramsden died, the mother couldn't afford to keep on the house, so she went off to live with her sister in Torquay. It all happened at just the right time for Steadman."

Banks looked at Weaver in astonished admiration. "How old are you?" he asked.

"Twenty-one, sir."

"How do you manage to know so much about things that happened before your time?"

"Family, sir. I was born and raised in the area. And Sergeant Mullins. He runs the show around here usually, but he's on holiday right now. There's not much escapes Sergeant Mullins."

Banks sat in silence for a moment and enjoyed his beer as he sifted over the information.

"What about Steadman's drinking companions?" he asked finally. "What kind of people are they?"

"He brought them all together, sir," Weaver answered. "Oh, they all knew each other well enough before he moved up here, like, but

Steadman was a friendly sort, interested in everything and everyone. When he wasn't busying himself with his books or poking around ruins and abandoned mines he was quite a socializer. There's Jack Barker, for one—you might have heard of him?"

Banks shook his head.

"Writer. Mystery stories." Weaver smiled. "Quite good really. Plenty of sex and violence." He blushed. "Nothing like the real thing, of course."

"Oh, I don't know," Banks said, smiling. "Go on."

"Well, sir, he's been here three or four years. Don't know where he started from. Then there's Doc Barnes, born and raised hereabouts, and Teddy Hackett, local entrepreneur. He owns the garage over there, and a couple of gift shops. That's all, really. They're all forty-ish. Well, Doc Barnes is a bit older and Barker's in his late thirties. An odd group, when you think about it. I've been in here a few times when they were together and from what I could hear they'd take the mickey out of Steadman a bit, him being an academic and all that. But not nasty like. All in good fun."

"No animosity? You're certain?"

"No, sir. Not so far as I could tell. I don't get in here as often as I'd like. Wife and kid, you see." He beamed.

"Work, too."

"Aye, that keeps me busy as well. But I seem to spend more time giving directions to bloody tourists and telling the time than dealing with local affairs. Whoever said 'If you want to know the way, ask a policeman' ought to be shot."

Banks laughed. "The locals are a fairly law-abiding lot, then?"

"On the whole, yes. We get a few drunks now and then. Especially at The Hare and Hounds disco, as I said. But that's mostly visitors. Then there's the odd domestic dispute. But most of our troubles come from tourists leaving their cars all over the place and making too much noise. It's a peaceful place, really, though there's some as would say it's boring."

At this point, Sergeant Hatchley walked in and joined them. He was a bulky, fair-haired and freckle-faced man in his early thirties, and he and Banks had developed a tolerable working relationship despite some early hostility—partly due to North-South rivalry, and partly to Hatchley's having hoped for the job Banks got.

Hatchley bought a round of drinks and they all ordered steak-and-kidney pies, which turned out to be very tasty. Not much kidney, as Weaver remarked. Banks complimented the landlord and was rewarded with an ambiguous "Aye."

"Anything new?" Banks asked the sergeant.

Hatchley lit a cigarette, lounged back in his chair, rubbed a hand like a hairy ham across his stubbly cheek and cleared his throat.

"Nowt much, by the look of things. Old Tavistock went looking for a stray sheep and dug up a fresh corpse. That's about the strength of it."

"Was it unusual for him to go poking around by that wall? Would other people be likely to go there?"

"If you're thinking that anyone could expect to dump a body there and leave it undiscovered for weeks, then you're barking up the wrong tree. Even if old Tavistock hadn't gone out looking for his bloody sheep, someone would've come along soon enough—hikers, courting couples."

Banks sipped some more beer. "So he wasn't dumped there for concealment, then?"

"Shouldn't think so, no. Probably put there just so we'd have to leg it halfway up to Crow bloody Scar."

Banks laughed. "More likely so we wouldn't know where he was killed."

"Aye."

"Why wasn't Steadman reported missing, sir?" Weaver cut in. He seemed anxious to restore to the chief inspector the respect that Hatchley appeared to be denying him.

Banks told him. Then he told Hatchley to get back to the Eastvale station, find out as much as he could about Steadman's background and collate any reports that came in.

"What about the press?" Hatchley asked. "They're all over the place now."

"You can tell them we've found a body."

"Shall I tell them who it is?"

Banks sighed and gave Hatchley a long-suffering look. "Don't be so bloody silly. Not until we've got a formal identification you can't, no."

"And what will you be doing, sir?"

"My job." Banks turned to Weaver. "You'd better get back to the station, lad. Who's in charge?"

Weaver blushed again, his pinkness deepening to crimson. "I am, sir. At least, I am at the moment. Sergeant Mullins is away for two weeks. Remember I told you about him, sir?"

"Yes, of course. How many men have you got?"

"There's only two of us, sir. It's a quiet place. I called some of the lads in from Lyndgarth and Fortford to help with the search. There's not more than half a dozen of us altogether."

"All right, then," Banks said, "it looks like you're in charge. Get a request for information printed up and distributed—shops, pubs, church notice-board. Then start a house-to-house enquiry up Hill Road. That body wasn't carried all the way up there, and somebody might just have seen or heard a car. At least it'll help us narrow down the time of death. All right?"

"Yes, sir."

"And don't worry. If you need any more men, let Eastvale station know and they'll see what they can do. I'm going to pay Michael Ramsden a visit myself, but if you ask for Sergeant Rowe, I'll make sure he has full instructions."

He turned to Hatchley again. "Before you go back, go and tell the men up in the field that they're temporarily transferred to Helmthorpe and they're to take their orders from Constable Weaver here. They'll probably understand the situation already, but make it official. And check the car park for a beige Sierra." He gave Hatchley the number of the car and handed him the keys. "It's Steadman's car," he added, "and while it doesn't look as if he got to use it last night, you never know. It might tell us something. Get forensic onto it right away."

"Yes, sir," Hatchley said through clenched teeth as he left. Banks could almost hear the "three bags full, sir" that the sergeant probably added when he got outside.

He grinned broadly at the nonplussed young constable and said, "Don't mind him, he's probably just got a hangover. Now, off you go, Weaver. Time to get to work."

Alone, he slipped his new pipe from his jacket pocket and stuffed it with shag. Drawing in the harsh tobacco, he coughed and shook his head. He still couldn't get used to the damn thing; maybe mild cigarettes would be better, after all.

II

Excited, Sally had watched Banks drive off towards the village and followed in the same direction. She stopped to pick a campion by the hedgerow and casually admired its pinkish-purple colour, the petals like a baby's splayed fingers. Then, thinking about what she had to tell her friends, she let it drop and hurried on her way.

She had actually seen the man, the policeman in charge, close up, and had had to stifle a giggle as he lost his footing climbing the low wall. It was obvious he wasn't used to bounding about the northern countryside; perhaps he'd been sent up by Scotland Yard. She found his gaunt, angled face under the short, neat black hair attractive, despite a nose that had clearly been broken and improperly reset. The sharp, restless eyes expressed energy and power, and the little white scar beside his right eye seemed, to Sally, a mark of exotic experience. She imagined he'd got into a fight to the death with a blood-crazed murderer. Even though he seemed too short for a policeman, his wiry body looked nimble and strong.

At the western edge of the village, near The Bridge, was a coffee-bar where Sally and her friends hung out. The coffee was weak, the Coke warm and the Greek owner surly, but the place boasted two video games, an up-to-date jukebox, and an ancient pinball machine. Of course, Sally would rather have expertly applied a little make-up and passed for eighteen in one of the pubs—especially The Hare and Hounds on disco night—but in such a small community everyone seemed to know a little about everyone else's business, and she was worried in case word got back to her father. She had been in pubs in Eastvale with Kevin, though even that was risky with the school so close by, and in Leeds and York, which were safer, and nobody had ever questioned her about her age.

The door rattled as she pushed it open and entered to the familiar bleeping of massacred aliens. Kathy Chalmers and Hazel Kirk were engrossed in the game, while Anne Downes looked on coolly. She was a bookish girl, plain and bespectacled, but she wanted to be liked, and if that meant hanging around with video-game players, then so be it. The others teased her a bit, but never maliciously, and she was blessed with a sharp, natural wit that helped her hold her own.

The other two were more like Sally, if not as pretty. They chewed gum, applied make-up (unlike Sally, they did this badly), and generally fussed about their hair and clothes. Kathy had even got away with a henna treatment. Her parents had been furious, but there was nothing much they could do after the fact. It was Hazel, the sultry, black-haired one, who spoke first.

"Look who's here," she announced. "And where have you been all weekend?" The glint in her eye implied that she knew very well where Sally had been and whom she had been with. Under normal circumstances Sally would have played along, hinting at pleasures she believed Hazel had only read about in books, but this time she ignored the innuendo and got herself a Coke from the unsmiling Greek. The espresso machine was hissing like an old steam engine and the aliens were still bleeping in their death-throes. Sally leaned against the column opposite Anne and waited impatiently for a silence into which she could drop her news.

When the game was over, Kathy reached for another coin, a manoeuvre that necessitated arching her back and stretching out her long legs so that she could thrust her hand deep enough into the pocket of her skin-tight Calvin Kleins. As she did this, Sally noticed the Greek ogling from behind his coffee machine. Choosing her moment for best dramatic effect, she finally spoke: "Guess what. There's been a murder. Here in the village. They dug up a body under Crow Scar. I've just come from there. I've *seen* it."

Anne's pale eyes widened behind her thick lenses. "A murder! Is that what those men are doing up there?"

"They're conducting a search of the scene," Sally announced, hoping she'd got the phrasing right. "The scene of the crime. And the forensic team was there too, taking blood samples and tissue. And the police photographer, and the Home Office pathologist. All of them."

Kathy slid back into her seat, forgetting the game. "A murder? In Helmthorpe?" She gasped in disbelief. "Who was it?"

Here Sally had to admit lack of information, which she disguised neatly by assuming that Kathy meant "who was the murderer?" "They don't know yet, you fool," she replied scornfully. "It's only just happened." Then she hurried on, keen not to lose their attention to further fleets of aliens. "I saw the superintendent close up. Quite a dish, actually. Not at all what you'd expect. And I could see the body. Well, some of it. It was buried by the wall up in Tavistock's field. Somebody had scraped away some of the loose soil and then covered it with stones. There was a hand and a leg sticking out."

Hazel Kirk tossed back a glossy raven's wing of hair. "Sally Lumb, you're a liar," she said. "You couldn't see that far. The police wouldn't have let anyone get that close."

"I did," Sally countered. "I could even see the wet patches under the superintendent's arms." She realized too late that this outburst clashed with her more romantic image of the "superintendent" and rushed on, hoping nobody would notice. Only Anne wrinkled her nose. "And old man Tavistock was there. I think he discovered the body. And all the policemen from miles around. Geoff Weaver was there."

"That pink-faced pansy," Kathy cut in.

"It wasn't so pink today, I can tell you. I think he'd been sick."

"Well wouldn't you be if you'd just found a dead body?" Anne asked, coming to the defence of young Weaver, on whom she had had a schoolgirl crush for nearly six months. "It was probably all decomposed and rotten."

Sally ignored her. "And there was another inspector, or whatever they call them. He wasn't in uniform anyway. Tall, strawy hair—a bit like your dad, Kathy."

"That'll be Jim Hatchley," Anne said. "Actually, he's only a sergeant. My father knows him. Remember when the social club was broken into last year? Well, they sent him from Eastvale. He even came to our house. My dad's treasurer, you know. Hatchley's a coarse pig. He's even got hairs up his nose and in his ears. And I'll bet that other chap was Chief Inspector Banks. He had his picture in the paper a while back. Don't you ever read the papers?"

Anne's stream of information and opinion silenced everyone for a moment. Then Sally, who read nothing but *Vogue* and *Cosmopolitan*, picked up the thread again. "They're here now. In the village. They drove down before I came."

"I'm surprised they didn't give you a lift," Hazel said, "seeing as how you're on such good terms."

"Shut up, Hazel Kirk!" Sally said indignantly. Hazel just smirked. "They're here. They'll be questioning everybody, you know. They'll probably want to talk to all of us."

"Why should they want to do that?" Kathy asked. "We don't know anything about it."

"It's just what they do, stupid," Sally retorted. "They do house-to-house searches and take statements from everyone. How do they know we don't know anything till they ask us?"

Sally's logic silenced Kathy and Hazel.

"We don't even know who the victim was yet," Anne chimed in. "Who do you think it was?"

"I'll bet it was that Johnnie Parrish," Kathy said. "He looks like a man with a past to me."

"Johnnie Parrish!" Sally sneered. "Why, he's about as interesting as a...a..."

"A dose of clap?" Anne suggested. They all laughed.

"Even that would be more interesting than Johnnie Parrish. I'll bet it was Major Cartwright. He's such a miserable, bad-tempered old bugger there must be lots of people want to kill him."

"His daughter, for one," Hazel said, and giggled.

"Why?" Sally asked. She didn't like to think she was excluded from what appeared to be common knowledge.

"Well, you know." Kathy stalled. "You know what people say."

"About what?"

"About Major Cartwright and his daughter. How he keeps such a tight rein on her since she came back to the village. Why she ran off in the first place. It's unnatural. That's what people say."

"Oh, is that all," Sally said, not quite sure she understood. "But she's got her own place, that cottage by the church."

"Maybe it was Alf Partridge," Hazel suggested. "Now there's a nasty piece of work. Be doing us all a favour if somebody did away with him."

"Wishful thinking," Kathy sighed. "Do you know, he chased me off his land the other day. I was only picking wild flowers for that school project. He had his shotgun with him, too."

"He sounds more like a murderer than a victim," Anne chipped in. "Who do you think did it?"

"Well, it might not be anyone from around here," Kathy answered. "I mean, we don't know, do we? It could have been a stranger."

"Of course it was someone from around here," Sally said, annoyed at the way her discovery seemed to have become common property. "You don't think somebody would drive a body all the way from Leeds or somewhere like that just to dump it under Crow Scar, do you?"

"They could have done." Kathy defended herself without much conviction.

"Well, I'm not going out after dark until he's been caught." Hazel hugged herself and shuddered. "It might be one of those sex murderers, another Ripper. It could even *be* Major Cartwright's daughter up there, for all we know. Or that Mrs Carey, the new barmaid at The Dog and Gun."

"I shouldn't worry," Kathy said. "Nobody would want to sex murder you." She spoke in the usual spirit of friendly banter, but somehow her joke flopped and the girls seemed distracted, each wrapped in her own thoughts. Kathy blushed. "Still," she said, "we'd better be careful."

"I'll bet it was Jack Barker that did it," Anne suggested.

"Who? That writer bloke?" Sally said.

"Yes. You know what kind of books he writes."

"I'll bet you haven't read any," Kathy taunted her.

"Yes, I have. I've read *The Butcher of Redondo Beach* and *The San Clemente Slasher*. They're lurid."

"I've read one, too," Hazel said. "I can't remember what it was called but it was about this man who went to his beach house somewhere in America and he found two people he'd never seen before chopped to pieces in his living-room. It was grisly. I only read it because he lives here."

"That's *The Butcher of Redondo Beach*," Anne informed her patiently. "That's what it's called."

Sally was bored by the direction the conversation was taking, and, besides, she thought Jack Barker looked far too handsome and debonair to be a murderer. He was a bit like one of those old film stars her mother was always going on about—Errol Flynn, Clark Gable or Douglas Fairbanks—the ones who all looked the same with their oily, slicked-down hair and little moustaches. He was the type, she thought, who might shoot his adulterous wife (if he had one) in a fit of passion, but he certainly wouldn't carry her body all the way up to Crow Scar afterwards, that was for sure. He was far too much of a gentleman to do that, whatever kind of books he wrote.

Sally finished her Coke and turned to leave, but before she did so she whispered, "The police will see me. I can tell you that for sure. I know something. I don't know who's dead or who the killer is yet, but I know something."

And with that, she exited quickly, leaving the others to gape after her and debate whether she was telling the truth or simply trying to draw even more attention to herself.

III

There are two routes to York from Helmthorpe. The first winds up through Gratly, continues diagonally across the dales, more or less as the crow flies, and eventually joins the main road a couple of miles outside the city; and the second, longer but quicker, involves taking the main road back to Eastvale, then driving south-east on the busy York Road. Because it was a beautiful day and he was in no real hurry, Banks took the first route on his visit to Ramsden.

He slipped the cassette back into the player and to the strains of "O, Sweet Woods" drove up the hill, turned left past the Steadman house and followed the road as it climbed the dale side slowly. He passed through the tiny hamlet of Mortsett and paused with his window down to look at an attractive cottage with a post-office sign above its door and a board advertising Wall's Ice Cream propped outside. Insects hovered and hummed in the still, warm air; it seemed unreal, an image of England from before the First World War.

Beyond Relton, at the junction with the Fortford road, he seemed to leave civilization behind. Soon, the greens of the hillside gave way to the darker hues of the heather-covered moors, which continued for about two miles before dropping slowly into the next dale. It was like a slow roller-coaster ride, and the only obstacles were the sheep that sometimes strayed onto the unfenced road, itself only a thin band hardly distinguishable from the landscape round it. Banks saw a few hikers, who stepped onto the rough grass when they heard his car, smiling and waving as he drove by.

The main road, busy with lorries and delivery vans, came as a shock. Following Mrs Steadman's directions, Banks found the turn-off, a narrow track with a lonely red phonebox on the corner, about a mile from York's boundary. He turned left and, after a quarter of a mile, came to the converted farmhouse. He pulled into the smooth dirt driveway and stopped outside the new-looking garage.

Ramsden answered the door shortly after the first ring and asked him who he was. When Banks showed some identification, he slipped off the chain and bid him enter.

"Can't be too careful," he apologized. "Especially in such an iso-lated place as this."

Ramsden was tall and pale, with the melancholic aspect of a Romantic poet. He had light-brown hair and, Banks soon noticed, a nervous habit of brushing back the stray forelock even when it hadn't slid down over his brow. The jeans and sweatshirt he wore seemed to hang on him as if they were a size too big.

"Please excuse the mess," he said as he led Banks into a cluttered living-room and installed him by the huge, empty fireplace. "As you can see, I'm decorating. Just finished the first coat." A clear polythene sheet covered half the floor, and on it stood a step-ladder, a gallon of pale blue paint, brushes, turps, tray and roller. "It's not about that woman, is it?" he asked.

"What woman?"

"An old lady not far from here was murdered by thugs a few months ago. I had a policeman around then."

"No, sir, it's not about the woman. That would have been York Region. I'm from Eastvale CID."

Ramsden frowned. "I'm afraid I don't understand, then. Pardon me, I don't mean to seem rude, but..."

"I'm sorry, sir," Banks apologized, accepting the whisky and soda

Ramsden had poured for him without asking. "This isn't easy for me. Would you care to sit down?"

Ramsden looked alarmed. "What is it?" he asked, fitting himself awkwardly into a small armchair.

"You were expecting Mr Steadman to visit you last night?"

"Harry? That's right. We had some notes to go over before today's field trip. Why? Has something happened?"

"Yes, I'm afraid it has," Banks said as gently as he could, aware of the muscles in his stomach clenching tightly. "Mr Steadman is dead."

Ramsden brushed back the phantom forelock. "I don't follow. Dead? But he was coming here."

"I know that, Mr Ramsden. That's why I wanted to tell you myself. Weren't you surprised when he didn't show up? Weren't you worried?"

Ramsden shook his head. "No, no, of course I wasn't. It wasn't the first time he hadn't come. But are you *sure*? About Harry, I mean. Can't there have been some mistake?"

"I'm afraid not."

"What on earth happened?"

"We're not certain about that yet, sir, but a farmer found his body this morning in a field under Crow Scar. It looks as if he was murdered."

"Murdered? Good God! Harry? I can't believe it."

"You know of no-one who'd have a reason?"

"Absolutely not. Nobody. Not Harry." He rubbed his face and stared at Banks. "I'm sorry Chief Inspector, I can't really think straight. I'm having trouble taking this all in. I've known Harry for a long time. A long time. This is such a shock."

"I realize it must be, sir," Banks persisted, "but if you could just spare the time to answer a couple of questions, I'll be on my way."

"Yes, of course." Ramsden got up and fixed a drink for himself.

"You said it had happened before, that he hadn't turned up?"

"Yes. It wasn't a formal arrangement. More casual, really."

"Why didn't he come?"

"Once when Emma wasn't too well he couldn't make it. And one time he had a stomach upset. Things like that. We were very close, Chief Inspector. There was always a bed made up for him, and he had a key in case I had to go out."

"Didn't it cross your mind to phone and ask what was wrong?"

"Not at all. I've already told you our arrangement was casual. Besides, I don't have a phone. I spend enough time on the blasted thing at work. The nearest public callbox is on the main road." He shook his head. "I just can't believe this is happening. It's like a bad dream. Harry, dead?"

"Did you go out last night?"

Ramsden looked at him blankly.

"You said Mr Steadman had a key in case you were out," Banks pressed on. "Were you out last night?"

"No, I wasn't. Actually, when Harry hadn't arrived by eleven o'clock, I was rather...I mean, don't get me wrong...a little relieved. You see, I'm working on a book of my own. A historical novel. And I was glad of the opportunity to get some writing done." He looked embarrassed about it.

"Didn't you like working with Mr Steadman?"

"Oh, of course I did. But it was his baby, really. I was just the editor, the research assistant."

"Where were you planning to go today?"

"We were going to visit an old lead mine in Swaledale. Quite a distance, really, so we wanted to get an early start. Emma!" he exclaimed suddenly. "Emma must be in a terrible state."

"She's upset, of course," Banks said. "Mrs Stanton, the neighbour, is looking after her."

"Should I go?"

"That's up to you, Mr Ramsden, but I'd say best leave her for today at least. She's in good hands."

Ramsden nodded. "Of course, of course..."

"What about you? Will you be all right?"

"Yes, I'll be fine. It's just the shock. I've known Harry for more than ten years."

"Would it be possible to talk to you again about this? Just to get some background, that kind of thing?"

"Yes, I suppose so. When?"

"The sooner the better, really. Tuesday morning, perhaps? We might know a bit more by then."

"I'll be at work. Fisher & Faulkner. We're not terrifically busy at the moment. If you really want to drop by..."

"Yes, that'll be fine."

Banks asked for directions to the publishers', then left Ramsden and returned to Eastvale by the quickest route. At the station, an invitation to call at Superintendent Gristhorpe's for tea awaited him. He phoned Sandra, who wasn't at all surprised at his absence, checked that no important news had come in while he had been at Ramsden's, and set off for Helmthorpe for the second time that day. It was only three o'clock, and, as he wasn't expected at Gristhorpe's until five, he would have plenty of time to see how the locals were coping.

The Helmthorpe Police Station was a converted cottage on a narrow cobbled road that forked from the eastern end of the High Street towards the river. There, Weaver, who was running off more copies of the request for information, told him that three constables were still making door-to-door enquiries along Hill Road and another had been dispatched to the campsite.

That was the biggest headache, Banks realized. They would have to try to find out who had been staying at the campsite on Saturday night. Most of the campers would have moved on by now, though, and it would be damn near impossible to get comprehensive or reliable information.

There was also the press to deal with. Besides Reg Summers of the local weekly, two other reporters were still hanging around outside the station, as Hatchley had warned, thrusting their notebooks at everyone who entered or left. Banks certainly liked to maintain good relations with the press, but at such an early stage in the investigation he could give them little of value. However, to gain and keep their goodwill—because he knew they would be useful eventually—he told them what he could in as pleasant a manner as possible.

At twenty to five, he left Weaver in charge and drove off to see Gristhorpe. On the way, he decided he would visit The Bridge that evening to see what he could get out of Steadman's cronies. More, he hoped, than he'd managed to pick up so far.

THREE

I

Banks pulled into the rutted drive at five to five and walked towards the squat stone house. Gristhorpe lived in an isolated farmhouse on the north daleside above the village of Lyndgarth, about halfway between Eastvale and Helmthorpe. It was no longer a functioning farm, though the superintendent still held onto a couple of acres, where he grew vegetables. Since his wife had died five years ago, he had stayed on there alone, and a woman from the village came up to "do" for him every morning.

The building was too austere for Banks, but he could see how it was ideally suited to the environment. In a part of the country that was wind-swept and lashed by rain much of the year, any human dwelling had to be built like a fortress to provide even the most basic domestic comforts. Inside, though, Gristhorpe's house was as warm and welcoming as the man himself.

Banks knocked at the heavy oak door, surprised at how the hollow sound echoed in the surrounding silence, but got no answer. On such a fine afternoon, he reasoned, he was more likely to find Gristhorpe in his garden, so he walked around to the back.

He found the superintendent crouching by a heap of stones, apparently in the process of extending his wall. The older man got to his feet, red-faced, at the sound of footsteps and asked, "Is it that time already?"

"It's almost five," Banks answered. "I'm a few minutes early."

"Mmm...I seem to lose all track of time up here. Anyway, sit down." He gestured towards the rough grass by the stones. The superintendent was in his shirt-sleeves, his ubiquitous Harris tweed jacket lying on the grass beside him. A gentle breeze ruffled his thick mop of silver hair. Below it, a red, pock-marked face, upper lip all but obscured by a bristly grey moustache, grinned down at Banks. The oddest thing about Gristhorpe's appearance—and it was a facet that disconcerted both colleagues and criminals alike—was his eyes. Deep set under bushy brows, they were those of a child: wide, blue, inno-cent. At odds with his six-foot-three wrestler's build, they had been known to draw out confessions from even the hardest of villains and had made many an underling, caught out in a manufactured statement or an over-enthusiastic interrogation, blush and hide in shame. When all was well, though, and the world seemed as fresh and clear as it did that day, Gristhorpe's eyes shone with a gentle love of life and a sense of compassion that would have given the Buddha himself a good run for his money.

Banks sat for a while and helped Gristhorpe work on the dry-stone wall. It was a project that the superintendent had started the previous summer, and it had no particular purpose. Banks had made one or two attempts at adding pieces of stone but had at first got them the wrong way around, so that the rain would have drained inwards and cracked the wall apart if a sudden frost came. Often, he had chosen pieces that simply would not fit. Lately, however, he had improved, and he found the occasional wall-building afternoons with Gristhorpe almost as relaxing and refreshing as playing with Brian's train set. A silent understanding had developed between them about what stone would do and who would fix it in place.

After about fifteen minutes, Banks broke the silence: "I suppose you know that somebody dismantled one of these walls last night to cover a body?"

"Aye," Gristhorpe said, "I've heard. Come on inside, Alan, and I'll make a pot of tea. If I'm not mistaken there are still a few of Mrs Hawkins's scones left, too." He rhymed "scones" with "on," not, like a southerner, with "own."

They settled into the deep, worn armchairs, and Banks cast his eyes over the bookcases that covered one entire wall from floor to ceiling. There were books on all kinds of subjects—local lore, geol-ogy, criminology, topography, history, botany, travel—and shelves of leather-bound classics ranging from Homer, Cervantes, Rabelais and Dante to Wordsworth, Dickens, James Joyce, W.B. Yeats and D.H. Lawrence. Jane Austen's *Pride and Prejudice* lay on the table; the position of the bookmark indicated that Gristhorpe had almost finished it. As always when he visited the superintendent, Banks mentally reminded himself that he should read more.

Gristhorpe's office in Eastvale was much the same: books everywhere, and not all of them relevant to police work. He came from old Dales farming stock, and his decision to join the police after university and army service had caused trouble. Nevertheless, he had persevered, and he had also helped out on the farm in his spare time. When Gristhorpe's father saw that his son's natural aptitude and capacity for hard work was getting him places, he stopped complaining and accepted the situation. Gristhorpe's father had been finally sad to see the farm dwindle to little more than a large back garden before he died, but his pride in his son's achievement and the status it gave him locally eased him, and his death was without acrimony.

Gristhorpe had told Banks all this during their frequent meetings, usually over a good single malt whisky after a wall-building session. The older man's candour, along with more practical advice, made Banks feel like an apprentice, or protege. Their relationship had developed this way since the Gallows View affair, Banks's dramatic introduction to northern police work. As he told what he knew about the Steadman murder, he was alert for any tips that might come his way.

"It's not going to be easy," Gristhorpe pronounced after a short silence. "And I won't say it is. For one thing, you've all those tourists and campers to consider. If Steadman had an enemy from the past, it would be an ideal way of doing the job. They never keep records at campsites as far as I know. All they care about is collecting the money." He nibbled at his scone and sipped strong black tea. "Still, the killer could be a lot closer to home. Doesn't look like you've got much physical evidence, though, does it? Somebody might have heard a car, but I doubt they'd have paid it much mind. I know that road. It swings northeast all the way over to Sattersdale. Still, I don't suppose I need tell you your job, Alan. First thing is to find out as much as you can about Steadman. Friends, enemies, past, the lot.

Nose about the village. Talk to people. Leave the donkey work to your men."

"I'm an outsider, though," Banks said. "I always will be as far as people around here are concerned. I look out of place and I sound out of place. Nobody's going to give much away to me."

"Rubbish, Alan. Look at it this way. You're a stranger in Helmthorpe, right?" Banks nodded. "People notice you. They'll soon get to know who you are. You don't look like a tourist, and no villager will mistake you for one. You're even a bit of a celebrity—at least for them as reads the papers around here. They'll be curious, interested in the new copper, and they'll want to find out what makes you tick. You'll be surprised what they'll tell you just to see how you react." He chuckled. "Before this is all over you'll feel like a bloody priest in his confessional."

Banks smiled. "I was brought up C. of E."

"Ah. We're all Methodists or Baptists hereabouts," Gristhorpe said. "But some of us are more lapsed than others, and most of the daftest sects—your Sandemanians, for example—have all but disappeared."

"I hope I won't have the same obligation to secrecy as a priest."

"Heavens, no!" Gristhorpe exclaimed. "I want to know everything you find out. You've no idea what an opportunity this is for me to catch up on Helmthorpe gossip. But seriously, Alan, do you see what I mean? Take Weaver. He's a pleasant enough lad. Trustworthy, competent, thorough. But as far as the villagers are concerned he's a fixture, boring as a rainy day—though I shouldn't make that comparison around these parts. See what I mean, though? Half the womenfolk in Helmthorpe probably changed his nappy when he was a nipper, and most of the menfolk'll have given him a clip around the ear once or twice. Nobody will tell Weaver anything. They won't confide in him. There's nothing in it for them. But you... You're the exotic newcomer, the father confessor."

"I hope you're right," Banks said, finishing his tea. "I was thinking of dropping in at The Bridge tonight. Weaver told me Steadman used to drink there regularly with a few friends."

Gristhorpe scratched his pitted red chin, and his bushy eyebrows merged in a furrow of concentration. "Good idea," he said. "Imagine it'll be a bit of a wake tonight. Good time to pick up stray words.

They'll all know who's been killed, of course, and probably how. Would that chap Barker be one of Steadman's cronies, by the way?"

"Yes. Jack Barker, the writer."

"Writer be damned!" Gristhorpe almost choked on a mouthful of scone. "Just because he makes money from the claptrap doesn't mean it's writing. Anyway, it's a good idea. You'll get something out of them, however useless it might seem at first. What time is it now?"

"Ten to six."

"Supper?"

"Yes, anytime you're ready." Banks had almost forgotten how hungry he was.

"It won't be owt special, you know," Gristhorpe called out as he went to the kitchen. "Just salad and left-over roast beef."

II

Sally and Kevin raced the last few yards and collapsed, panting, by Ross Ghyll. They were high up on Tetchley Fell, on the south side of the dale, having walked to the source of one of the numerous becks that meander their way down to the Swain.

When they had caught their breath, Kevin kissed her, thrusting his tongue deep into her mouth, and they lay down together on the pale, springy grass. He touched her breasts, felt the nipples harden through thin cotton, and slowly let his hand slide down between her legs. She was still wearing jeans, and the pressure of the thick seam against her sex made her tingle with excitement. But she broke free and sat up, distracted.

"I'm going to tell the police, Kevin," she said.

"B-but we—"

She laughed and hit him lightly on the arm. "Not about this, stupid. About last night."

"But then they'll know about us," he protested. "They'll be sure to tell."

"No they won't. Why should they? You can tell them things in confidence, you know, like Catholics and priests. Besides," she added, twirling a strand of hair between her slim fingers, "my mum and dad

know we were together. I told them we were at your house and we
forgot about the time."

"I just don't think we should get involved, that's all. It could be
dangerous, being a witness."

"Oh, don't be daft. I think it's rather exciting, myself."

"You would. What if the killer thinks we really saw something?"

"Nobody knew we were up there. Nobody saw us."

"How do you know?"

"It was dark, and we were too far away."

"He might see you going to the police station."

Sally laughed. "I'll wear a disguise, then. Now you're being really
silly. There's nothing to be afraid of."

Kevin fell silent. Once again he felt he'd been outwitted and out-
reasoned by a mere girl.

"I won't tell them who you are if it bothers you so much," Sally
went on, reassuring him. "I'll just say that I was with a friend I'd rather
not name. Talking."

"Talking!" Kevin laughed and reached for her. "Is that what we
were doing?"

Sally giggled. His hand was on her breast again, but she pushed
him away and stood up, brushing the grass from her jeans.

"Come on, Sally," he pleaded. "You know you want it as much as I
do."

"Do I, now?"

"Yes." He made a grab for her ankle but she stepped nimbly aside.

"Maybe," she said. "But not now. Especially with someone who's
ashamed to admit he was with me last night. Besides, I have to be
home for tea or my dad'll kill me." And she was off like the wind.
Sighing, Kevin got to his feet and plodded along behind her.

III

"When you hit someone over the head, Doc," Jack Barker asked,
"does the blood gush, pour or just flow?"

"That's a pretty tasteless question at a time like this, isn't it?" Barnes
said.

Barker reached for his pint. "It's for my book."

"In that case, I shouldn't think accuracy matters, then, does it? Use the most violent word you can think of. Your readers won't know any more than you do."

"You're wrong there, Doc. You should see some of the letters I get. There's plenty of ghouls among the reading public. Do you know how many of those little old ladies are hooked on gruesome forensic details?"

"No. And I don't want to, either. I see enough blood in my line of work as it is. And I still think you're showing poor taste talking like that before poor Harry's even in the ground."

It was early, and Barnes and Barker were the only members of the informal group sitting in the snug.

"Death comes to us all in the end, Doc," Barker replied. "You ought to know that. You've helped enough people shuffle off their mortal coils."

Barnes scowled at him. "How can you be so bloody flippant? For God's sake, have a bit of decency, Jack. Even you've got to admit that his death was an untimely one."

"It must have been timely enough for the killer."

"I don't understand you, Jack. Never in a million years..." Barnes sighed over his beer. "Still, I have to keep reminding myself you write about this kind of thing all the time."

"It's just shock," Barker said, reaching for a cigarette. "Believe it or not, I didn't personally witness every murder I've written about. And as you well know, I've never set foot on American soil either." He ran a hand across his slicked-back hair. "It's a bloody sad business, all right. I know we used to tease the poor bugger about his rusty nails and pigs of lead, but I'll miss him a lot."

Barnes acknowledged the eulogy with a curt nod.

"Have the police been talking to you yet?" Barker asked.

The doctor seemed surprised. "Me? Goodness, no. Why should they?"

"Oh, come off it, Doc. I know you're an eminent GP, pillar of the community and all that crap. But that kind of thing doesn't cut any ice with the CID, old man. And it doesn't alter the fact that you were here last night with the rest of us and you left quite a bit earlier than usual."

"You surely don't think the police would...?" he began. Then he relaxed and mumbled almost to himself, "Of course, they'll have to check every angle. Leave no stone unturned."

"Cut the clichés," Barker said. "They hurt."

Barnes snorted. "I can't see why; you write enough of them yourself."

"It's one thing giving the public what it wants, and the publishers what they pay for, but quite another to spout them out in intelligent company. Anyway, you look worried, Doc. What skeletons will they find in your cupboard?"

"Don't be ridiculous," Barnes said. "And I don't think you should joke about a matter as important as this. After all, poor Harry *is* dead. And you know damn well where I had to go last night. Mrs Gaskell is already a week overdue with her delivery, and, frankly, I'm getting a bit worried."

"I suppose she can give you an alibi, then?"

"Of course she can, should it ever come to that. Besides what possible motive could I have for harming Harry?"

"Oh, still waters run murky and deep," Barker replied, mimicking the doctor's own style of speech.

At that moment, Teddy Hackett arrived, looking every inch the flamboyant entrepreneur. He was a vain dresser, always wearing a shirt with a monogram or an alligator embroidered on its top pocket, a flashy gold medallion and expensive designer jeans. He tried to look younger than he was, but his dark hair was receding fast at the temples, and a flourishing beer belly hung over his belt, almost obscuring a hand-wrought silver buckle depicting a growling lion's head.

It was well known around the village that when Hackett wasn't making money or drinking with his cronies, he was living it up in nightclubs in Leeds, Darlington or Manchester, turning on the charm for any attractive young woman who came his way. He had certainly done well for himself—the garage, a couple of gift shops—and he kept a keen eye open for anything else that came on the market. He was the kind of businessman who, given free rein, would probably buy up the whole dale and turn it into a gigantic fun-fair.

"Bloody hell," he said, easing into his chair with a brimming pint grasped in his fist. "What a turn up for the book, hey?"

Barnes nodded and Barker stubbed out his cigarette.

"Got any details?" Hackett asked.

"No more than anyone else, I shouldn't think," Barker replied. "I bet the doc'll find out a thing or two after the autopsy."

Barnes reddened with anger. "That's enough, Jack," he snarled. "These things are confidential. It'll be done in Eastvale General by the pathologist, Glendenning. They're bloody lucky to have him up here. One of the best in the country, or so I've heard." He looked at his watch. "I wouldn't be surprised if he's at it already. Dead keen, they say." He faltered, catching the unintentional pun a moment after he'd let it out. "Anyway, you can be sure it'll go no further."

"Like young Joanie Lomax's recent dose of clap, eh?"

"You're going too far, Jack. I know you're upset like the rest of us. Why can't you just admit it instead of behaving like a bloody actress waiting for opening-night reviews?"

Barker shifted uncomfortably in his chair.

"Has anyone been questioned yet?" Hackett asked.

The other two shook their heads.

"It's just that I saw that detective fellow—I'm sure I recognize him from that photo in the local rag last autumn. He's at the bar right now."

They all looked out and saw Banks leaning against the bar, foot on the rail, apparently enjoying a quiet pint alone.

"That's him," Barker confirmed. "I saw him leaving Emma's this morning. What are you so nervous about, anyway, Teddy? You've got nothing to hide, have you?"

"Nothing, no. But we were all here last night with him, weren't we? I mean, they're sure to want to question us. Why haven't they done it yet?"

"You left just after Harry, as I remember," Barker said.

"Yes. It was Saturday night, wasn't it? Had to get up to Darly for Freddy's new club opening. Bloody good night it was, too. There were some real corkers around, Jack. Why don't you come along with me sometime? Handsome young bachelor like yourself ought to get around and about a bit more."

"Ah," Barker replied, shaking his head. "Better things to do with my time than chase scrubbers in a disco, mate. A writer's life..."

"Writer, my arse!" Hackett said. "I could turn out that junk in my coffee-break."

Barker raised an eyebrow and grinned. "Maybe so, Teddy, but you don't, do you? There's the difference. Besides, I hear you've had to hire a secretary with a B.A. in English to translate your business letters for you."

"My English would hardly be a handicap if I was in your line of work. Anyway, there's no room for fancy footwork in a business letter. You know that, Jack. Short and to the point."

"That's what the reviewers said about my last book," Barker sighed. "Well, perhaps not in so many words."

And even Doc Barnes had to laugh at that.

After that brief and traditional exchange the three of them fell silent, as if they knew that they had been talking and joking as usual just to fill the void of Harry's absence, to pretend for as long as possible that nothing had changed, that nothing so brutal and final as murder had touched the cosy little group.

Barker volunteered to buy another round and went to stand next to Banks at the bar. "Excuse me," he said, "but aren't you the policeman investigating Harry Steadman's death?" When Banks nodded, Barker stuck out his hand. "Jack Barker. I'm a friend of his."

Banks offered his condolences.

"Look," Barker went on, "we were wondering—I mean, we were all pals of Harry's and we spent a good deal of yesterday evening with him—would you care to join us in the snug? It'll be a sight more comfortable and convenient than hauling us all in to the station individually for questioning."

Banks laughed and accepted the offer. "I reserve the right to haul you in if I want to, though," he added, only half in jest.

Banks had been intending to drop in on them all along. He had been imitating the vampire, who will not enter his victim's room until invited, and was pleased that his little trick had worked. Perhaps there was something in Gristhorpe's advice after all. Curiosity had got the better of them.

Barker looked happy enough to be bringing him back in tow, but the other two appeared uneasy. Banks, however, was experienced enough not to read too much into their reaction. He knew what discomfort the arrival of the police always caused. Even the most innocent of men and women begin to worry about that forgotten parking ticket or the little income tax fiddle as soon as a copper comes in range.

A tense silence followed the introductions, and Banks wondered if they expected him to begin a formal interrogation, notebook in hand. Instead, he began to fill his pipe, glancing at them in turn as he did so. Barker looked suave in a forties film-star kind of way, and Barnes was a little balding grey man with glasses. He had that shabby look of a backstreet abortionist about him, Banks thought. Finally Hackett, the flashy one, started to chat nervously.

"We were just talking about Harry," he said. "Sad business. Can't think who'd want to do such a thing."

"Is that what you all think?" Banks asked, keeping his eyes on the pipe.

They all murmured their agreement. Hackett lit an American cigarette and went on: "It's like this. Harry might have been a bit of a dotty professor type, and I don't deny we teased him a bit, but it was all in good humour. He was a fine man, good tempered, even natured. He had a sharp mind—and a tongue to match when it came to it—but he was a good man, he never hurt a soul, and I can't think why anyone would want to kill him."

"Somebody obviously felt differently." Banks said. "I hear he inherited a lot of money."

"Over a quarter of a million. His father was an inventor. Patented some electronic device and opened a factory. Did very well. I suppose the wife'll get it now?"

"That's how it usually goes. What's your opinion of Mrs Steadman?"

"I can't say I really know her well," Hackett answered. "She only came down here occasionally. Seems a good woman. Harry never complained, anyway."

Barnes agreed.

"I'm afraid I can't add anything," Barker said. "I know her slightly better than the others—we were, after all, practically neighbours up in Gratly—but she seems unremarkable enough to me. Not much interested in Harry's work. Stays in the background mostly. But she's not stupid—and she knows how to cook a good dinner."

Banks noticed Barker look over his shoulder at the bar and turned to
see what the attraction was. He was just in time to see a young woman
with glossy black hair down to her waist. She wore a blue shawl over a
white silky blouse, and a long loose skirt that curved from her slim waist
over the graceful swell of her hips. He only glimpsed her face in profile
for a moment as she walked out. It looked good: angular, high cheekbones, straight nose, like a North American Indian. Half obscured by
her hair, a crescent of silver flashed where her jaw met her long neck.

"Who's that?" he asked Barker.

Barker smiled. "Oh, you noticed, I see. That's Olicana." He pronounced the foreign word slowly.

"Olicana?"

"Yes. At least that's what Harry used to call her. Apparently it's
what the Romans called Ilkley, the spirit of the place, the *genius loci*.
Her real name is Penny Cartwright. Not half as exotic, is it?"

"What happened last night?" Banks asked with an abruptness that
startled Barker. "Was it a normal evening's drinking as far as you were
all concerned?"

"Yes," Barker answered. "Harry was on his way to York and he
dropped in for a couple of swift halfs."

"He didn't drink any more than usual?"

"A little less, if anything. He was driving."

"Did he seem unusually excited or worried about anything?"

"No." Barker assumed the role of spokesman. "He was always
excited about his work—some rusty nail or broken cart-wheel."

"Rusty nail?"

"Yes. That's how we used to joke about it. It was his field of study.
Industrial Archaeology. His one great passion, really. That and the
Roman occupation."

"I see. I've been told that Mr Steadman was supposed to visit an
old lead mine in Swaledale today. Know anything about that?"

"I think he mentioned it, yes. We tried not to let him get away
with too much shop talk, though. I mean, it's not everyone's cup of
tea, is it, rusty nails?"

"What time did he leave here last night?"

Barker concentrated for a moment. "It'd be about a quarter to
nine," he answered finally, and the others nodded in agreement.

"When did you leave?"

Barker glanced at Barnes and Hackett before answering. "I left about ten-fifteen. I was alone by then and it was no fun."

Banks turned to the other two and they gave him their stories.

"So you see," Barker concluded, "any one of us could have done it. Our alibis are all weak."

"Just a minute!" Barnes cut in.

"Only joking, Doc. Sorry, it was in poor taste. But it is true, isn't it? Are we suspects, Inspector? It *is* Inspector, isn't it?"

"Chief Inspector," Banks answered. "And no, there aren't any suspects yet."

"I know what that means. When there are no suspects, everybody's a suspect."

"You write detective stories, don't you, Mr Barker?" Banks asked mildly. Barker flushed and the others laughed.

"Defective stories, I always call them," Hackett chipped in.

"Very droll," Barker growled. "There's hope for you yet."

"Tell me," Banks went on, pushing the pace now he'd got them going, "you're all well off. Why do you drink in a dump like this?" He looked around at the peeling wallpaper and the scored, stained tables.

"It's got character," Barker replied. "Seriously, Chief Inspector, we're not quite so well off as you think. Teddy here's been living on credit ever since he bought up Hebden's Gift Shop, and the doc's making as much as he can fiddle from the NHS." Barnes just glared, not even bothering to interrupt. "And I'm just dying for someone to buy the film rights to one of my books. Harry was loaded, true, but when it came, it came as a bit of a surprise to him, and he didn't know what to do with it. Apart from quitting his job and moving up here to devote himself to his studies, he didn't change his way of life much. He wasn't really interested in money for its own sake."

"You say it came as a surprise to him," Banks said. "I thought he inherited it from his father. Surely he must have known that he was in for a sizeable inheritance?"

"Well, yes he did. But he didn't expect as much as he got. I don't think he really paid much mind to it. Harry was a bit of an absent-minded prof. Took after his father. It seems that the old man had patents nobody knew about tucked away all over the place."

"Was Steadman mean, stingy?"

"Good heavens, no. He always paid for his round."

Hackett smiled tolerantly while Barnes sighed and excused Barker's flippancy. "What he's trying to say in his charming manner," the doctor explained, "is that none of us feel we belong to the country club set. We're comfortable here, and I'm not being facetious when I say it's a damn good pint."

Banks looked at him for a moment, then laughed. "Yes, it is, isn't it?" he agreed.

This was another thing Banks had picked up during his first year in the north—the passion a Yorkshireman has for his pint. The people in Swainsdale seemed to feel the same way about their beer as a man from, say, Burgundy, would feel about wine.

Banks got himself another drink and, by directing the conversation away from the murder, managed to get everyone talking more openly on general matters. They discussed ordinary things, it turned out, just like anyone else: politics, the economy, world affairs, sport, local gossip, books and television. They were three professionals, all more or less the same age, and all—except perhaps Barnes—just a little out of place in a small community that had its roots deep in agriculture and craftsmanship.

IV

Penny Cartwright locked and bolted the sturdy door behind her, drew the thick curtains tight and switched on the light. After she had put down her package and dropped her shawl over a chair, she went around the room lighting candles that stood, at various lengths, on saucers, in empty wine bottles, and even in candlesticks. When the room was flickering with tiny bright flames, which made the walls look like melting butter, she turned out the electric light, slipped a tape in the cassette player and flopped down on the sofa.

The room was now as private and cosy as a womb. It was the kind of place that looked bright and happy in sunlight, and warm and intimate by candle-light. There were a few things tacked to the walls: a postcard-size reproduction of Henri Matisse's "The Dance," which a friend had sent her from New York; a framed copy of Sutcliffe's photograph, "Gathering Driftwood"; and a glossy picture showing her singing at a concert she and the band had given years ago. Shadowed by candle-light, the alcoves at both sides of the fire-place overflowed with personal knick-knacks such as shells, pebbles, and the kind of silly keepsakes one buys in foreign lands—things that always seem to bring back the whole atmosphere of the place and details of the day on which they were bought: a plastic key-ring from Los Angeles; a miniature slide-viewer from Niagara Falls; a tiny porcelain jar emblazoned with her zodiac sign, Libra, from Amsterdam. Mixed in with these were earrings, which Penny collected, of all shapes, sizes and colours.

Penny took out papers and hash from a battered Old Holborn tin and rolled a small joint; then she unwrapped the half-bottle of Bell's. There seemed no point in getting a glass, so she drank straight from the bottle, and the whisky burned her tongue and throat as it sank to stir a warm glow deep inside her.

The tape played unaccompanied, traditional folk songs—a strong, clear woman's voice singing about men going off to war, lifeboat disasters, domestic tragedies and supernatural lovers of long ago. With part of her mind, Penny studied the vocal style critically; she admired the slight vibrato, but winced at the blurring on some of the high notes. As a professional, or an ex-professional, it was second nature to her to listen that way. Finally, she decided that she liked the woman's voice, flaws and all. It had enough warmth and emotional response to the lyrics to make up for the occasional lapses in technique.

One song, about a murder in Staffordshire over two hundred years ago, she knew well. She had sung it herself many times to appreciative audiences in pubs and concert halls. It had even been on the first record she had made with the band, and its modal structure had stood up well to the addition of electric guitars and percussion. But this time it sounded fresh. Though the song had nothing to do with the bad news she had heard that afternoon, murder was murder, whether it had been committed the previous night or two hundred years ago. Perhaps she would write a song herself. Others would sing it or listen to it in warm secure rooms hundreds of years in the future.

The whisky and hash were doing their work; Penny was drifting.

Suddenly, the memory of that summer so many years ago sprang clear as yesterday into her mind. There had been many good years, of course, many good times before the craziness of fame spoiled it all, but that summer ten years ago stood out more than the rest. As she relived it, she could smell the green warmth of the grass and catch the earth and animal scents on the feather-light breeze.

Then the general memory crystallized into one particular day. It was hot, so hot that Emma had refused to move out of the shade for fear of burning her sensitive skin. And Michael, who was sulking for some reason, had stayed home reading Chatterton's poems. So it was just Penny and Harry. They had walked all the way over to Wensleydale, Harry, tall and strong, leading the way, and Penny keeping up as best she could. That day, they had sat high on the valley side above Bainbridge, below Semerwater, where they ate salmon sandwiches and drank chilled orange juice from a flask as they basked in the heat and looked down on the tiny village with its neat central green and Roman hill-fort. They could see the white-washed front of the fifteenth-century Rose and Crown, and the River Bain danced and sparkled as it tripped down the falls to join the gleaming band of the Ure.

Then the scene dissolved, broke apart, and shifted back in time. So vividly had Harry recreated the past in her mind that she felt she had been there. The valley bottom was marshy and filled with impenetrable thickets. Nobody ventured there. The hillmen built circular huts in clearings they made high on the valley sides near the outcrops of limestone and grits, and it was there that they went about the business of hunting, raising oats, and breeding a few sheep and cattle. A Roman patrol marched along the road just below where they sat: strangers in a cold, alien landscape, but sure of themselves, their helmets shining, heavy cloaks pinned at the chest with enam-elled brooches.

The two scenes overlapped: ten years ago and seventeen hundred years ago. It had all been the same to Harry. She could sense the stub-born pride of the Brigantes and the confidence of the Roman con-querors. She could even, in a way, understand why Queen Cartimandua had sided with the invaders, who brought new, civilized ways to that barbaric outpost. The tension spread throughout the

Dales as Venutius, the Queen's ex-husband, and his rebellious fol-
lowers prepared for their last stand at Stanwick, north of Richmond.
Which they lost.

Harry brought it all alive for her, and if there had been, sometimes, an inexplicable awkwardness and uneasiness between them, it
had always disappeared when the past became more alive than the
present. How bloody innocent I was then, Penny thought, laughing
at herself, and all of sixteen, too. How long it took me to grow up,
and what a road it was.

Then she remembered the coins they had gone to see in the York
Museum—VOLISIOS, DUMNOVEROS and CARTIMANDUA, they were
marked—and the pigs of lead stamped IMP. CAES: DOMITIANO: AVG.
COS: VII, and, on the other side, BRIG. The Latin words had seemed
like magical incantations back then.

And so she drifted. The joint was long finished, the tape had
ended, the level in the whisky bottle had gone down and the memories came thick and fast. Then, as suddenly as they had started, they
ceased. All Penny was left with was blankness inside; there were
vague feelings but no words, no images. She worked at the bottle, lit
new cigarettes from the stubs of old ones, and at some point during
the evening the tears that at first just trickled down her cheeks turned
into deep, heart-racking sobs.

FOUR

I

Monday morning dawned on Helmthorpe as clear and warm as the five previous days. While this wasn't exactly unprecedented, it would have been enough to dominate most conversations had there not been a more sensational subject closer at hand.

In the post office, old, bent Mrs Heseltine, there to send her monthly letter to her son in Canada ("Doin' right well for 'imself... 'Ee's a full perfesser now!") was holding forth.

"Strangled by a madman," she repeated in a whisper. "And right 'ere in our village. I don't know what the world's coming to, I don't. We're none of us safe any more, and that's a fact. Best keep yer doors locked and not go out after dark."

"Rubbish!" Mrs Anstey said. "It was 'is wife as done it. Fer t'money, like. Stands to reason. Money's t'root of all evil, you mark my words. That's what my Albert used ter say."

"Aye," muttered Miss Sampson under her breath. "That's because 'ee never made any, the lazy sod."

Mrs Dent, having read every lurid novel in Helmthorpe Library and some especially imported from Eastvale and York, was more imaginative than the rest. She put forward the theory that it was the beginning of another series of Moors Murders.

"It's Brady and Hindley all over again," she said. "They'll be digging 'em up all over t'place. There was that Billy Maxton, disappeared wi'out a trace, and that there Mary Richards. You'll see. Digging 'em up all over t'place, they'll be."

"I thought they'd run off to Swansea together, Billy Maxton and

Mary Richards," chipped in Letitia Stanford, the spindly postmistress. "Anyway, they'll be questioning us all, no doubt about that. That little man from Eastvale, it'll be. I saw 'im poking about 'ere all day yesterday."

"Aye," added Mrs Heseltine. "I saw 'im, too. Looked too short for a copper."

"Ee's a southerner," said Mrs Anstey, as if that settled the matter of height once and for all.

At that moment, the loud bell jangled as Jack Barker walked in to send off a short story to one of the few magazines that helped him eke out a living. He beamed at the assembled ladies, who all stared back at him like frightened prunes, bid them good morning, conducted his business then left.

"Well," sighed Miss Sampson indignantly. "And 'im a friend of Mr Steadman's, too. I'd like to see what the poor man's enemies is doing."

"He's an odd one, all right," Letitia Stanford agreed. "Not the killing type, though."

"And how would you know?" asked Mrs Dent sharply.

"You should read some of 'is books. Fair make you blush, they would. And full of murder, too." She shook her head and clucked her tongue slowly at the sprightly figure disappearing down the street.

II

Sally Lumb sat in her best underwear before the dressing-table mirror. Her long honey-blonde hair was parted in the middle and brushed neatly over her white shoulders. A short, carefully maintained fringe covered just enough of her high forehead. As she studied her milky skin, she decided it was about time she did some sunbathing. Not too much, because she was so fair and it made her red and sore, but just an hour or so each day to give her skin a deep golden hue.

She had a good face, and she knew all her weak points. Her eyes were fine—big, blue and beguiling—and her nose was perfectly in proportion, with just a hint of a bob at its tip. If anything was wrong, it was her cheeks; they were a little too plump and her cheekbones weren't well enough defined. It was only puppy fat, though. Like that around her hips and thighs, it would disappear completely in time. Nevertheless, there were ways to play down its effect right now, so why wait? The same with her mouth. It was too full—voluptuous would be the kindest word—and that wasn't likely to change by itself.

Sally studied the array of tubes, palettes, brushes, sticks and bottles in front of her, then made her skilful choice of the correct shades and tints calculated to highlight the best and obscure the worst of her facial features. After all, Chief Inspector Banks was from London, so she'd heard, and he would naturally expect a woman always to look her best.

As she applied the cosmetics, she ran through the scene in her mind, imagining what she would say, and how he would jump up and dash off to make an arrest. Her name would be in all the papers; she would be famous. And what better start could an aspiring star wish for? The only thing better than that, she thought, carefully drawing her eyeliner, would be to catch the killer herself.

III

Banks sat in his office and gazed out over the market square with its ancient cross and uneven cobbles. The gold hands of the blue-faced clock on the church stood at ten-fifteen. A small group of tourists stood in front of the plain, sturdy building taking photographs, and shoppers in twos and threes ambled below along narrow Market Street. Banks could hear the occasional calls of greeting through his open window. He had been at the office for almost two hours, keen to read and digest all the information on the Steadman case as it came in.

After leaving Barker and company at The Bridge the previous evening, he had driven straight home, enjoyed a mug of hot chocolate and gone to bed. Consequently, on Monday morning he felt unusually fresh and wide awake, much to the surprise of Sandra and the children, who had been half asleep at the breakfast table as usual.

On his arrival at Eastvale station, he first found a message from Constable Weaver informing him that the house-to-house had produced negligible results. One person reported hearing a motorcycle at about eleven-thirty and two cars between midnight and twelve-forty-five (he had been eating Indian food in Harrogate and the resulting heartburn kept him awake later than usual). Everybody else was either away on holiday or fast asleep. One woman, who had spotted the request for information in the Helmthorpe parish church at evening service, had dropped by early to rant about the Devil, Hell's Angels, skinheads and the price of local produce. When the patient Weaver had tried to pin her down to specifics, so a laughing Sergeant Rowe reported to Banks, it turned out that she had spent all day Saturday, including the night, with her married daughter in Pocklington.

Banks fiddled with his pipe and frowned, annoyed at how little there was to go on. Every good policeman knew that the first twenty-four hours of an investigation were the most crucial ones. As time went on, the trail cooled. The press, of course, had been pestering him again on his way in, and he regretted that he had nothing to tell them. As a rule, for every piece of information he passed on to the papers, he had four more up his sleeve.

There was always a chance that visitors at the campsite might have seen something. Banks doubted it, though. Most of the ones questioned on Sunday afternoon and evening had either just arrived that day or had heard nothing at all. Many of Saturday's guests had left before the discovery of the body, according to the site manager, who explained that they had to be out by ten o'clock in the morning or pay an extra day's rent. Unfortunately, he kept no register of names and addresses, and he hadn't noticed anyone running around waving a blood-stained candlestick or hammer.

Banks had asked Sergeant Hatchley to check Dr Barnes's alibi and to issue an appeal for information in the *Yorkshire Post*, but his hopes were slim. One problem was that the campsite was on the northern bank of the River Swain, next to the cricket pitch, and the car park was on the south side, well set back from High Street and practically surrounded by trees and tall hedges. It was an ideal, secluded place for a murder after dark, except between eleven and half past, when the pubs were emptying. It was possible, according to Dr Glendenning's unchanged estimation of the time of death, that Steadman could have been killed between nine and ten o'clock, shortly after he left The Bridge. At that time it would have been just about dark enough, and the car park would have been quiet. Drinking hours being what they were, most people arrived between eight and nine and stayed until closing time.

So far, a thorough search had failed to find any traces of blood on the car park's pitted macadam surface. In fact, forensic had turned up little of interest at all. Glendenning, however, had proved as conscientious as usual. He had spent half the night on a thorough autopsy, and a clear, jargon-free report was waiting in Banks's in-tray at eight A.M.

The wound had been made by a metal object with at least one sharp edge, and was indeed the cause of death. Stomach contents revealed a low alcohol level, consistent with the evidence of The Bridge crowd, and the remains of an earlier dinner. The blow itself could have been inflicted by either a man or a woman, Glendenning had added, as the actual strength required to kill with such a weapon was minimal. Also, the killer was probably right-handed, so it would do Banks no good to follow the fictional detective's procedure of watching out for a left-handed suspect. It did, however, appear to rule out Emma Steadman, who was left-handed, but she had a solid alibi anyway.

Hypostasis indicated, as Banks had suspected, that Steadman had been killed elsewhere and his body driven to the field. Much of the lividity had formed on his right side, but he had been buried on his back.

There were no traces of blood in the car, but Vic Manson found plenty of prints. The trouble was that the few clear ones proved to be Steadman's. The prints on the steering wheel and the door handle were smudged, as they almost always were. When people drive, or open and close doors, their fingerprints slide against the smooth plastic or metal surface of the handle, and the result is a mess.

What fibres remained on the vinyl-covered seats were so common as to implicate half the dale, if taken seriously. They indicated nothing so unique as a personally imported Italian suit or a yak's wool sweater supplied by an exclusive local outfitter. Nor was there, on the tires, any trace of mud, soil or clay that could only be found in one specific place. There wasn't even, wedged in the tread, a chip of gravel from an easily identifiable driveway.

Banks had little faith in forensic evidence, anyway. Like most detectives, he had convicted criminals on fingerprints and blood groups, but he found that if the criminal had any brains at all, forensic evidence, though it might narrow the field of suspects, was useless until he had been caught by other means; then it might help to ensure a guilty verdict. It was surprising how many jury members still seemed to trust the experts, even though a skilled defence lawyer could easily discredit almost any scientist's testimony. Still, Banks supposed, if the public was willing to accept the "scientifically proven" superiority of certain toothpastes or breakfast cereals that advertisers claimed, then nothing was surprising.

Just after eleven o'clock, Sergeant Hatchley poked his head around the door. Although the station coffee had improved greatly since the introduction of an automatic filter system, the two men had established a tradition of walking across to the Golden Grill for their morning break.

They weaved through the groups of strolling tourists, called hellos to the few locals they recognized, and walked into the cafe. The only available table was at the back, by the washrooms. The petite waitress shrugged apologetically when she saw them take it.

"Usual?" she called out.

"Yes please, Gladys love," Hatchley boomed back.

The usual was coffee and toasted teacakes for both of them.

Hatchley put his buff folder on the red checked tablecloth and ran his hand through his hair. "Where the bloody hell's Richmond these days?" he asked, fishing for a cigarette.

"He's on a course. Didn't you know?"

"Course? What bloody course?"

"The super sent a memo round."

"Never read them."

"Maybe you should."

Hatchley scowled. "Anyway, what course is this?"

"Something to do with computers. It's down in Surrey."

"Jammy bastard. Probably at the seaside with his bucket and spade."

"Surrey doesn't have a coast."

"He'll find one. When's he due back?"

"Two weeks."

Hatchley cursed, but their order arrived before he could say anything else. He would have, Banks knew, two objections to Richmond's absence: in the first place, the sergeant had often said that he thought education was about as useful as a rubber with a hole in it; and secondly, even more serious, with Detective Constable Richmond away, Hatchley would have to do most of the legwork on the Steadman case himself.

"I checked on Doc Barnes's alibi this morning, like you asked," Hatchley said, reaching for his teacake.

"And?"

"It's true—he was there with that Mrs Gaskell, all right. Seems she's having a difficult pregnancy."

"What times?"

"Arrived about nine-thirty, according to the husband, and left at ten-fifteen."

"So he could still have easily killed Steadman first, and stuffed him in the boot of his car, or done it later."

"No motive," Hatchley said.

"Not that we know of yet. What's that?" Banks pointed at the folder.

"Gen on Steadman," Hatchley mumbled, his mouth half full of toasted teacake.

Banks browsed through the report as he ate. Steadman had been born in Coventry almost forty-three years ago, at a time when his father was busy setting up his electronics business. Educated at a local grammar school, he won a scholarship to Cambridge, where he got a first in History. After that, he did postgraduate work at Birmingham and Edinburgh, then landed a teaching job at Leeds University at the age of twenty-six. There he began to develop and pursue his interest in Industrial Archaeology, a new field then, and in Local History. In his first year of teaching, two important things happened. First, just before Christmas that year, his mother died, and second, at the end of the final term he married Emma Hartley, whom he had known for two years. Emma was the only daughter of a Norwich shopkeeper, and she had been working as a librarian in Edinburgh when Steadman was studying there. She was five years younger than her husband. They had no children.

The couple honeymooned in Gratly, staying at the house they now owned. Hatchley had put an asterisk by this piece of information, and when Banks turned to the note at the bottom of the page, it read: "Check with Ramsden. The house belonged to his parents." Banks knew this already, but he praised Hatchley's thoroughness; it was so unusual it deserved encouragement.

As Steadman's career continued to flourish—publications, praise, promotion—his father's health steadily declined. When the old man had finally died two years ago, the son inherited a considerable fortune. He first took his wife on a European tour, then, after seeing out the university year, he bought the house in Gratly, left his job and began to concentrate on his own interests.

"What do you make of it?" Banks asked Hatchley, who had finished eating and was now picking his teeth with his fingernails.

"Well, what would you do with all that money?" the sergeant said. "I'm damned if I'd buy a house around here and spend all my time poking about ruins."

"You think it was foolish of him?"

"Not much of a life, is it?"

"But it's what he wanted: independence to pursue his own studies."

Hatchley shrugged as if there were no answer to such a silly statement. "You asked what I'd do."

"But you didn't tell me."

Hatchley slurped down the last of his coffee; it was syrupy at the bottom with undissolved sugar. "I reckon I'd make a few choice investments, first. Just enough so I could live comfortable off the interest, like. Nothing risky. Then I'd take a few thousand and have a bloody good holiday."

"Where?"

"Everywhere. Fleshpots of the world."

Banks smiled. "And then?"

"Then I'd come back and live off the interest."

"But what would you do?"

"Do? Nowt much. Bit of this, bit of that. Might even go live in Spain or the south of France. Or maybe one of those tax havens like Bermuda."

"You'd leave your job then?"

Hatchley looked at Banks as if he was insane. "Leave my job? Course I'd leave my job. Wouldn't anyone?"

"I suppose so." But Banks wasn't sure what he would do himself. A holiday, yes. But afterwards? To him, Steadman had made an admirable choice; he had extricated himself from the pedestrian and stultifying elements of his work and turned to concentrate on its essence. Perhaps I'd set myself up like Sherlock Holmes—a Dalesman, himself—Banks thought, if I suddenly found myself with a private income. Take only the most interesting cases . . . wear a deer-stalker . . .

"Come on," he said, shaking off the fantasy. "It'll be a cold day in hell before you and I have to worry about problems like that."

When Banks got back to his office, he found Emma Steadman waiting for him. She had just been to identify her husband's body and was still distraught. There was little expression in her pale face, but the owlish eyes magnified by the lenses of her spectacles showed traces of recent tears. She sat upright in the hard chair, her hands clasped together on her lap.

"I won't keep you long," Banks said as he took his seat opposite her and started filling his pipe. "First, I'd like to know if your husband had any enemies. Is there anyone you can think of who might have wanted to do him harm?"

"No," she answered quickly. "Not that I can think of. Harold wasn't the kind of man who made enemies."

Banks decided not to point out the lack of reason in that statement; the bereaved relatives of murder victims frequently assumed that there could be no possible motive for the crime.

"Was there nobody he argued with, then? Even a slight disagreement? It could be important."

She shook her head, frowning. "No. I told you. He wasn't . . . Just a minute. There was something. I don't know how important it was though."

"Tell me."

"He did complain a bit about Teddy Hackett recently."

"Hackett? When was this?"

"About a week ago. They were friends really, I know, but they had some kind of ongoing feud about land. Oh, I suppose it was just silly.

Men often are, you know. Just like little boys. Anyway, I'm afraid I don't know all the details. You'll have to ask Mr Hackett."

"Do you have any idea at all what it was about?"

Mrs Steadman frowned again, this time in concentration. "I think it might have been something to do with Crabtree's Field. That's just a bit of overgrown land by the flyer. Harold was certain he'd located some Roman ruins there—he had some coins and bits of pottery he said were evidence—but Teddy Hackett was trying to buy the land."

"Why? What did he want with it?"

"Knowing Hackett, it would be some vulgar project for making money. I don't know exactly what he had in mind—a discotheque, perhaps, or a fairground, video arcade, supermarket . . ."

"Let me get this clear," Banks said, leaning forward. "What you're saying is that Hackett wanted some land for development and your husband was trying to get it preserved as a historic site? Is that right?"

"Yes. It wasn't the first time, either. Last year, Harold wanted to start a small local museum in a shopfront on High Street, but Hackett bought the place up quickly and turned it into a gift shop. They argued about that, too. Harold was too trusting, too . . . nice. He wasn't aggressive enough."

"There's no-one else you can think of? What about Dr Barnes? Did your husband ever say anything about him?"

"Like what?"

"Anything."

"No."

"Jack Barker?"

"No. He thought Barker was a bit of a cynic, a bit too flippant, but that's all."

"What about visitors to the house? Did you have many?"

"Just friends we entertained."

"Who?"

"Locals, mostly. We seem to have lost touch with the crowd from Leeds. Barker, Penny Cartwright, Hackett and Dr Barnes occasionally. Sometimes Michael Ramsden came over from York. Some of the teachers and kids from Eastvale Comprehensive—Harold gave guest lectures and took classes on field trips. That's all I can think of."

"There'll be a lot of money," Banks said casually.

"Pardon?"

"A lot of money. Your husband's. You'll inherit, I should imagine."

"Yes, I suppose so," she said. "I hadn't really thought...I don't know if Harold made a will."

"What will you do with it all?"

Mrs Steadman looked startled behind her glasses, and more than a little disapproving. "I've no idea. As I said, I haven't really given the matter much thought."

"What about your relationship with your husband? Were you on good terms? Was the marriage stable?"

Mrs Steadman froze. "What?"

"I have to ask."

"But I don't have to answer."

"That's true."

"I don't think I like what you're insinuating, Chief Inspector," she went on. "I think it's a very impertinent question. Especially at a time like this."

"I'm not insinuating anything, Mrs Steadman. Just doing my job, that's all." Banks held her cold gaze and remained silent.

"If that's all, then..." She stood up.

Banks followed her to the door and shut it quietly behind her before breathing a sigh of relief.

IV

After shocking the old ladies in the post office, Jack Barker set off down Helmthorpe High Street. It was only about ten-thirty, but already clusters of tourists sauntered along the pavements, cardigans draped over their shoulders to keep off the morning chill. They would stop now and then, holding onto impatient children, to glance at displays of local craftware in shop windows. Crow Scar loomed to the north, and the shadow of an occasional wispy cloud drifted across its limestone face.

Barker hesitated for a moment outside the tiny second-hand book-shop run by Mr Thadtwistle—at ninety-eight, the village's oldest inhabitant—then hurried on and turned into the narrow street of cottages opposite the church. At number sixteen he paused and knocked. Nothing happened. He knocked again. Then he heard stirrings inside and smoothed back his hair as he waited. The door opened a few inches.

"Oh, it's you," Penny Cartwright said, squinting at him closely.

"My God, you look awful," said Barker. "Old man not around, is he?"

Penny began to shake her head but immediately thought better of it.

"Can I come in?"

Silently, Penny stood aside and let him enter. "If you'll make me a strong cup of coffee."

"It's a deal. And I didn't mean what I said earlier. You look as lovely and fresh as a white rose in the morning dew."

Penny pulled a face and flopped down on the couch. Her long jet-coloured hair was uncombed and the whites around her blue eyes looked greyish and bloodshot. She had dark, puffy bags under her eyes, and her lips were cracked and dry. She held a bottle-green kimono-style dressing-gown closed at her throat. A red dragon reared and breathed fire on the back.

Barker busied himself in the small untidy kitchen and soon came out carrying two steaming mugs of coffee. He sat in the battered armchair at right angles to Penny. As she reached forward to pick up her mug from the low table, he could see her lightly freckled cleavage. The folds of her silky gown also revealed a long, delightful curve of thigh as she crossed her legs. She seemed entirely oblivious to the way she was making Jack Barker's pulse race.

"I suppose you've heard about Harry," he began, lighting a cigarette.

Penny reached out for one too. "Yes," she nodded, blowing out a lungful of smoke and coughing. "I've heard. These things'll ruin my voice." She glared at the cigarette.

"Have the police been to see you yet?"

"Why should they?"

"That Chief Inspector—Banks his name is—he was at The Bridge last night," Barker explained. "He talked to us for quite a while. Anyway, he saw you—at least he saw me glancing over at you and asked who you were."

"And you told him?"

"Yes."

"You told him I was a friend of Harry's?"

"Had to. He'd have found out sooner or later, wouldn't he? Then he'd have been suspicious about why I didn't tell him in the first place."

"So what? You've got nothing to hide, have you?"

Barker shrugged.

"Anyway," Penny went on, "you know how I feel about the police."

"He's not a bad sort. Quite friendly, really. But sharp as a knife. Doesn't miss a trick. He's the kind who'll spend a pleasant evening buying you drinks then ask you hard questions when you're sozzled."

"Sounds awful." Penny pulled a face and ground out her half-smoked cigarette in the glazed ashtray. "Still, they're all much the same."

"What will you tell him?"

She looked at him and frowned. "What is there to tell?"

"The old man?"

She shook her head.

"He's sharp," Barker repeated.

Penny smiled. "Well then, he'll be able to find out all he wants to know, won't he?"

Barker leaned forward and took her hand. "Penny..."

She shook him off gently. "No Jack, don't. Not now."

Barker slumped back in his chair.

"Oh come on, Jack," Penny chided him. "Don't behave like a sulky boy."

"I'm sorry."

Penny gathered her gown around her and stood up. "Think nothing of it. You'd better go, though, I'm a bit unsteady on my pins today."

Barker got to his feet. "Are you singing this week?"

"Friday. If my voice holds out. You'll be there?"

"Wouldn't miss it for the world, love," Barker answered. Then he left.

V

The police station didn't look at all like Sally expected. For one thing, the old Tudor-fronted building was modern inside, and the walls weren't papered with "wanted" posters. Instead, it was more like one of those pleasant open-plan offices with potted plants all over the place and nothing but screens separating the desks behind the reception area. It smelled of furniture polish and pine-scented air-freshener.

She told the polite young man at the front desk that she wanted to see Chief Inspector Banks, the man in charge of the Helmthorpe murder. No, she didn't want to tell the young man about it, she wanted the chief inspector. She had important information. Yes, she would wait.

Finally, her persistence paid off and she was shown upstairs to a network of corridors and office doors with things like "Interview Room" stencilled on them. There, she was given a seat and asked if she would mind waiting a few moments. No. She folded her hands in her lap and stared ahead at a door marked, disappointingly, "Stationery Supplies."

The minutes dragged on. She wished she had brought a copy of *Vogue* to flip through like at the dentist's. Suddenly, sounds of scuffling and cursing came from the stairwell and three men fell into the corridor only feet from where she was sitting. Two of them were obviously police, and they were struggling with a handcuffed third who wriggled like an eel. Finally, they dragged him to his feet again and hauled him off down the hall. He was squirming and swearing, and at one point he managed to twist free and run back down the hall towards her. Sally was terrified. At least half of her was. The other half was thinking how exciting, how much like "Hill Street Blues" it was. The policeman caught him again before he got too close and hustled him into a room. Sally's heart beat fast. She wanted to go home, but the chief inspector came out of his office and ushered her inside.

"I'm sorry about that," he apologized. "It doesn't happen often."

"Who is he?" Sally asked, wide-eyed and pale.

"A burglar. We think he broke into Merriweather's Stereo Emporium last week."

Sally found herself sitting before a flimsy metal desk littered with paperclips, pens and important-looking folders. The air was thick with pipe smoke, which reminded her of her father. She coughed, and Banks, taking the hint, went to open the window. Fragments of conversation drifted up on the warm air from Market Street.

Banks asked Sally what she wanted.

"It's private," she whispered, looking over her shoulder and leaning forward. She was unsettled by what she had just witnessed and found it much harder to get started than she had imagined. "I mean," she went on, "I want to tell you something but you have to promise not to tell anyone else."

"Anyone?" The smile disappeared from his lips but still lingered in his lively brown eyes. He reached for his pipe and sat down.

"Well," Sally said, turning up her nose at the smoke like she always did at home, "I suppose it's up to you, isn't it? I'll just tell you what I know, shall I?"

Banks nodded.

"It was last Saturday night. I was up below Crow Scar in that little shepherd's shelter—you know, the one that's almost collapsed." Banks knew it. The derelict hut had been searched after the discovery of Steadman's body. "Well, I heard a car. It stopped for about ten or fifteen minutes, then drove on."

"Did you see it?"

"No. I only heard it. I thought it was maybe a courting couple or something at first. But they'd stay longer than that, wouldn't they?"

Banks smiled. It was clear from the girl's desire for secrecy and her knowledge of the temporal requirements of courting exactly what she had been doing in the shepherd's shelter.

"Which direction did the car come from?" he asked.

"The village, I think. At least, it came from the west. I suppose it could have come from over the dale, up north, but there's nothing much on that road for miles except moorland."

"Where did it go?"

"Up along the road. I didn't hear it turn around and come back."

"The road that leads to Sattersdale, right?"

"Yes, but there's plenty of other little roads cross it. You could get almost anywhere from it."

"What time was this?"

"It was twelve-fourteen when it stopped."

"Twelve-fourteen? Not just after twelve, or nearly quarter past twelve? Most people aren't so accurate."

"It was a digi—" Sally stopped in her tracks. Banks was looking down at her wrist, on which she wore a small black watch with a pink plastic strap. It wasn't digital.

"Better tell the truth," he said. "And don't worry, your parents needn't know."

"I wasn't doing anything wrong," Sally blurted out, then she blushed and calmed down. "But thank you. I don't think they'd understand. Yes, I was with somebody. My boyfriend. We were just talking." This didn't sound convincing, but Banks didn't regard it as any of his business. "And then this car came," Sally continued. "We thought it was getting late anyway, so Kev—my boyfriend, looked at his watch—it's a digital one with a light in it—and it said twelve-fourteen. I knew I should have been home hours ago, but I thought I might as well be hung for a sheep as a lamb. We just stayed where we were, not paying it much mind really, then when we heard it go Kevin looked at his watch again and it said twelve twenty-nine. I remember because it was funny. Kevin said they hadn't much time to . . ."

Sally stopped and reddened. It had been all too easy, once she got going, to forget who she was talking to. Now, she realized, she had not only told this strange man with the pipe her boyfriend's name but had also given him the impression that she knew all about what men and women did together at night in cars on lonely hillsides.

But Banks didn't pursue her romantic activities. He was far more concerned about the accuracy of the information he was getting than about her love life. Besides, she looked at least nineteen—old enough to take care of herself, whatever her parents thought.

"I imagine Kevin, your boyfriend, could confirm these times?" he asked.

"Well . . . if he had to," she answered hesitantly. "I mean, I told him I wouldn't mention his name. We don't want any trouble. My mum and dad wouldn't like it, see. I told them we were at his house watching telly. They'd tell his mum and dad where we really were and they'd stop us seeing each other."

"How old are you, Sally?"

"Sixteen," she answered proudly.

"What do you want to do with your life?"

"I want to be an actress. At least, I want to be involved in pictures and theatre, that kind of thing. I've applied to the Marion Boyars Academy of Theatre Arts."

"I'm impressed," Banks told her. "I hope you get accepted." He noticed that she was already a dab hand at make-up. He had thought she was nineteen. Most girls of her age never seemed to know when enough was enough, but Sally obviously did. Her clothes sense was good too. She was dressed in white knee-socks and a cerulean skirt, gathered at the waist, that came to just above her dimpled knees. On top she wore a white cotton blouse and a red ribbon in her gold-blonde hair. She was a beautiful girl, and Banks wouldn't have been at all surprised to see her on stage or on television.

"Is it true you're from London?" Sally asked.

"Yes."

"Did Scotland Yard send you?"

"No. I moved here."

"But why on earth would you want to come up here?"

Banks shrugged. "I can think of plenty of reasons. Fresh air, beautiful countryside. And I had hoped for an easier job."

"But London," Sally went on excitedly. "That's where it all happens. I went there once on a day trip with the school. It was fabulous." Her wide eyes narrowed and she looked at him suspiciously. "I can't understand why anyone would want to leave it for this godforsaken dump."

Banks noted that in about twenty seconds Sally's opinion of him had undergone a radical reversal. At first she had been coquettish, flirtatious, but now she seemed disdainful, almost sorry for him, and much more brusque and businesslike in her manner. Again, he could hardly keep from smiling.

"Did you know Harold Steadman?"

"Is that who...the man?"

"Yes. Did you know him?"

"Yes, a bit. He often came to the school to give lectures on local history or geology. Boring stuff mostly about old ruins. And he took us on field trips sometimes to Fortford, or even as far as Malham or Keld."

"So the pupils knew him quite well?"

"As well as you can know a teacher." Sally thought for a moment. "But he wasn't really like a teacher. I mean, I know it was boring and all that, but he liked it. He was enthusiastic. And he even took us to his house for hot dogs and pop after some of the trips."

"Us?"

"Yes, the pupils who lived in Helmthorpe or Gratly. There were about seven of us usually. His wife made us all some food and we just sat and talked about where we'd been and what we'd found. He was a very nice man."

"What about his wife, did you know her?"

"Not really. She didn't stick around with us. She always had something else to do. I think she was just shy. But Mr Steadman wasn't. He'd talk to anybody."

"Was that the only time you saw him? At school, on trips?"

Sally's eyes narrowed again. "Well, apart from in the street or in shops, yes. Look, if you mean was he a dirty old man, the answer's no."

"That's not what I meant," Banks said. But he was glad that she had reacted as if it was.

He made her go through the story again while he took down all the particulars. She gave the information unwillingly this time, as if all she wanted was to get out of the place. When she finally left, Banks slouched back in his chair and grinned to think that all his appeal, all his glamour, had been lost in his move from London to Eastvale. Outside in the market square the clock chimed four.

FIVE

I

On Tuesday morning, having sent Sergeant Hatchley to Helmthorpe to check on Weaver's progress, search Harold Steadman's study and bring in Teddy Hackett for questioning, Banks set off for York to visit Michael Ramsden again.

He drove into the ancient Roman city at about eleven o'clock through small suburbs of red-brick boxes. After getting lost in the one-way system for half an hour, he found a parking space by the River Ouse and crossed the bridge to Fisher & Faulkner Ltd, a squat, ugly brick building by the waterside. The pavements were busy with tourists and businessmen, and the huge Minster seemed to dominate the city; its light stone glowed in the morning sun.

A smart male receptionist pointed him in the right direction, and on the third floor one of Ramsden's assistants called through to the boss.

Ramsden's office looked out over the river, down which a small tour boat was wending its way. The top deck was bright with people in summer holiday clothes, and camera lenses flashed in the sun. The boat left a long V of ripples, which rocked the rowboats in its wake.

The office itself was small and cluttered; beside the desk and filing cabinets stood untidy piles of manuscripts, some stacked on the floor, and two bookcases displaying a set of Fisher & Faulkner's titles. Even in a dark business suit, Ramsden still looked as if his clothes were too big for him; he had the distracted air of a professor of nuclear physics about to explain atomic fission to a layman while simultaneously working out complex formulae in his mind. He brushed back an invisible forelock and asked Banks to sit down.

"You were a close friend of Harold Steadman's," Banks began. "Could you tell me a little bit about him? His background, how you met, that kind of thing."

Ramsden leaned back in his swivel chair and crossed his long legs. "You know," he said, looking sideways towards the window, "I was always just a little bit in awe of Harry. Not just because he was nearly fifteen years my senior—that never really mattered—but because I don't think we ever really got over the student-professor relationship. When we met, he was a lecturer at Leeds and I was just about to begin my studies in London, so we weren't even at the same university. We weren't in the same field, either. But these ideas get fixed in one's mind nonetheless. I was eighteen and Harry was nearly thirty-three. He was a very intelligent, very dedicated man—exactly the kind of role model for someone like me at that time.

"Anyway, although I was, as I said, just about to go to university in London, I always came home at Christmas and in summer. I'd help around the house, do odd jobs, make bacon and eggs for the guests. And I loved being home, being in the Yorkshire countryside. It was best when Harry and Emma came to stay for their annual holidays. I'd walk for hours: sometimes alone, sometimes with Harold or Penny."

"Penny?" Banks cut in. "Would that be Penny Cartwright?"

"Yes, that's right. We were very close until I went off to London."

"Go on."

"We used to go out together, in a casual sort of way. It was all very innocent. She was sixteen and we'd known each other nearly all our lives. She'd even stayed with us for a while after her mother died."

"How old was she then?"

"Oh, about ten or eleven. It was tragic, really. Mrs Cartwright drowned in a spring flood. Terrible. Penny's father had a nervous breakdown, so she stayed with us while he recovered. It only seemed natural, later when...well, you know, we were a bit older.... Anyway, Harold was very knowledgeable and enthusiastic about the area. He took to Swainsdale immediately, and pretty soon he was teaching me more than I'd learned living there all my life. He was like that. I was impressed, of course, but as I was about to study English at university I was insufferably literary—always quoting Wordsworth and the like. I suppose you know he bought the house when mother couldn't afford to keep it on."

Banks nodded.

"Yes," Ramsden went on, "they came every year, Harry and Emma, and when father died they were in a position to help us out a great deal. It was good for Harry, too. His work at the university was too abstract, too theoretical. He published a book called *The Principles of Industrial Archaeology*, but what he really wanted was the opportunity to put those principles into practice. University life didn't give him time enough to do that. He fully intended to teach again, you know. But first he wanted to do some real pioneering work. When he inherited the money, all that became possible.

"When I graduated, I went to work for Fisher & Faulkner in London first. Then they opened the northern branch and offered me this job. I missed the north and I'd always hoped to be able to make a living up here someday. We published Harold's second book and he and I developed a good working relationship. The firm specializes in academic books, as you can see." He pointed towards the crowded shelves, and most of the titles Banks could make out had *principles* or *a study of* in them. "We do mostly literary criticism and local history," Ramsden went on. "Next Harry edited a book of local essays, and since that we've been working on an exhaustive industrial history of the dale from pre-Roman times to the present. Harry published occasional essays in scholarly journals, but this was to be his major work. Everybody was looking forward to it tremendously."

"What exactly is industrial archaeology?" Banks asked. "I've heard the term quite often lately, but I've only got a vague idea what it means."

"Your vague idea is probably as clear as anyone else's," Ramsden replied. "As yet, it's still an embryonic discipline. Basically, the term was first used to describe the study of machinery and methods of the Industrial Revolution, but it's been expanded a great deal to include other periods—Roman lead mines, for example. I suppose you could say it's the study of industrial artefacts and processes, but then you could argue for a month about how to define 'industrial.' To complicate matters even further, it's very hard to draw the line between the subject as a hobby and as an academic discipline. For instance, if someone happens to be interested in the history of steam trains, he can still make a contribution to the field, even though he actually works nine to five in a bank most days."

"I see," Banks said. "So it's a kind of hybrid area, an open field?"

"That's about it. Nobody's yet come up with a final definition, which is partly why it's so exciting."

"You don't think Mr Steadman's death could be in any way linked to his work, do you?"

Ramsden shook his head slowly. "I can't see it, no. Of course, there are feuds and races just like in any other discipline, but I can't see any of it going that far."

"Did he have rivals?"

"Professionally, yes. The universities are full of them."

"Could he have uncovered something that someone might wish to keep quiet?"

Ramsden thought for a moment, his sharp chin resting in his bony hand. "You mean the unsavoury past of a prominent family, that kind of thing?"

"Anything."

"It's an interesting theory. I can't say for certain one way or the other. If he had discovered something, he didn't tell me. It's possible, I suppose. But we're a long way from the Industrial Revolution. You'd have to dig back a very long way if you want to find a descendant of someone who made his fortune by exploiting child labour, for example, which wasn't entirely uncommon back then. I don't think there are many direct descendants of the Romans around who still have anything to hide."

Banks smiled. "Probably not. What about enemies, academic or otherwise?"

"Harry? Good Lord, I shouldn't think so. He wasn't the kind to make enemies."

Again, Banks refrained from stating the obvious. "Do you know anything about this business with Teddy Hackett?" he asked.

Ramsden glanced sharply at him. "You don't miss much, do you?" he said. "Yes, I know about it, for what it's worth. There's a field in Helmthorpe over the river near the cricket pitch—it's called Crabtree's Field because it used to belong to a farmer named Crabtree. He's long dead now, though. There's a small bridge, which connects the field with the campsite on the other side, and Hackett wants to provide more 'facilities' for the campers—by which he no doubt means junk food and video games. You must have noticed the increasing Americanization of the English countryside, Chief Inspector. McDonald's seem to be springing up everywhere now, even in places as small as Helmthorpe. Harold had good reason to suppose—and I've heard his evidence—that there was once a Roman camp there. It could be a very important discovery. He was trying to persuade the local authorities to protect it for excavations. Naturally, that caused a bit of friction between Harry and Teddy Hackett. But they remained friends. I don't think it was a serious quarrel."

"Not serious enough to lead to murder?"

"Not in my opinion, no." Ramsden turned sideways again and looked out over the river at the shining Minster towers. "They were quite close friends, though God knows why, seeing as their views on just about everything were always diametrically opposed. Harry enjoyed a good argument for its own sake—that was the academic in him—and Hackett is at least a fairly intelligent, if not a very tasteful, adversary. I'm afraid you'll have to ask Harry's friends in the village how serious the quarrel was. I didn't get over there often enough. I suppose you've met the good doctor and the resident scribbler?"

Banks nodded. "Do you know them?"

"A little. Not very well, though. As I said, I don't get to Helmthorpe as often as I'd like. Doc Barnes has been around as long as I can remember, of course. And I've had one or two beery evenings in The Bridge. Naturally, there was quite a bit of excitement when Jack Barker moved to Gratly three or four years back, but it soon settled down when he proved to be much like everyone else."

"Where did he come from? What made him choose Gratly?"

"Haven't a clue, I'm afraid. I have a vague notion he's from somewhere in Cheshire, but I couldn't swear to it. You'll have to ask him."

"Did he know Mr Steadman before he moved to Gratly?"

"Not as far as I know. Harry never mentioned him."

"Does your company publish his books?"

"Lord, no." Ramsden made curious snuffling noises through his nose, and Banks took the sound for laughter. "I told you what we specialize in. I believe Barker writes paperback originals."

"Did Mr Steadman ever say anything about Dr Barnes or Jack Barker?"

"He said a number of things, yes. What do you have in mind?"

"Anything odd. Did he ever tell you anything about them that you thought they might not want to be common knowledge?"

"Are you trying to suggest that Harry was a blackmailer?"

"Not at all. But if he did know something, they weren't to know what he'd do with the knowledge, were they? You say he was a decent, upright man—fair enough. If he knew of anything illegal or immoral anyone was involved in, what do you think he would have done?"

"I see what you mean." Ramsden tapped a yellow pencil on his bottom teeth. "He'd have done the right thing, of course. Gone to the authorities. But I still can't help you. He never indicated to me that either Barker or Barnes had ever been involved in anything untoward."

"What about Penny Cartwright?"

"What about her? Harry certainly never spoke ill of Penny."

"What about your relationship with her?"

Ramsden paused. "I'm not sure it's any of your business."

"Up to you," Banks said.

"It was all a long time ago. There was certainly nothing odd about it. I don't see how knowing can possibly help you."

Banks kept silent.

"Oh, what the hell, then," Ramsden said. "Why not? I told you— we were good friends, then we drifted apart. We were both in London at roughly the same time, but we moved in very different circles. She was a singer, so she hung around with musicians. She was always a bit of a rebel, too. You know, had to be different, embraced all the causes. She made a couple of records and even toured in Europe and America, I believe. It was traditional folk music they played—at first, anyway—but they jazzed it up with electronic instruments. Then she got tired of life in the fast lane and came home. Her father forgave her and she settled into her cottage. Apart from the old man getting a bit overprotective now and again, she more or less gets on with her own life. Still sings a bit around the local pubs, too."

"What's her father like?"

"The major? To do him justice, he never really recovered from his wife's death. He's a strange old bird. Lives right on High Street with his dog. Has a flat over old Thadtwistle's bookshop. There were rumours, you know, when Penny left. Look, I'm not sure I should be telling you this. It's just silly local gossip."

"I shouldn't worry about that, Mr Ramsden. I know a hawk from a handsaw."

Ramsden swallowed. His Adam's apple bobbed up and down. "People said they were a bit too close, father and daughter, living together after the mother died. They say the old man wanted her to take her mother's place in the bed and that's why she took off so young. Do you know what I'm saying? It's not entirely uncommon around these parts."

Banks nodded. "Do you believe it?"

"Not for a moment. You know how vindictive gossip can be."

"But what had they against the Cartwrights?"

Ramsden picked up his pencil again and started rolling it between his fingers. "People thought they were a bit stuck up, that's all. The major's always been stand-offish, and his wife wasn't from around these parts. People in the dale used to be a lot more parochial than they are now so many outsiders have moved in. Even now most of them think of Penny as some kind of scarlet woman."

"You were close to her. Did she say anything?"

"No, she didn't. And I think she would have done if anything unusual had been going on."

"Was she friendly with Mr Steadman?"

"Yes, they were very good friends. Penny knows a lot about folk traditions through her music, you see, and Harold was always willing to learn. She even taught him some guitar. Also, she was very disoriented for a while after she came back from her brush with fame and fortune, and I think Harry's support meant a lot. He thought the world of her. They both loved going for long walks, watching birds and wild flowers, talking about the past."

There was plenty to follow up in that, Banks thought. But he had no more questions to ask. He already had more than enough information to digest and analyse.

He thanked Ramsden, said goodbye and walked back over the sluggish Ouse to his car.

He stopped at the first likely looking village inn he saw and enjoyed a late, leisurely pub lunch of shepherd's pie and a refreshing pint of shandy made from Sam Smith's Old Brewery bitter. As he drove back to Eastvale listening to Purcell's airs, he began to go over the list of involved characters in his mind, trying to imagine motives and opportunities.

First there was Teddy Hackett. That field business might only be the tip of the iceberg, and if Steadman had been blocking similar projects, Hackett would have a good enough reason for wanting rid of him.

Then there was Jack Barker. No obvious motive there, but no alibi either, as Barker himself had admitted on Sunday evening. His glance at Penny Cartwright in The Bridge had spoken volumes, and if there was more to her relationship with Steadman than Ramsden had told him, then jealousy may have provided a very strong motive.

As for Dr Barnes, his alibi hadn't been nearly as solid as he had seemed to think, and though there was no motive apparent yet, Banks wasn't willing to consider him out of the running.

It seemed pointless to include Emma Steadman: for one thing, she was left-handed, and for another, she had been watching television with Mrs Stanton all evening. But there was the money. She did have a great deal to gain from her husband's death, especially if the two weren't seeing eye to eye any more. She could, possibly, have hired someone. It was unlikely, but he couldn't rule it out.

Ramsden seemed to have neither the motive nor the opportunity. In a way, Steadman was his bread and butter, an important client as well as an old friend. Perhaps he did envy Steadman, but that was no reason to kill him. Banks couldn't quite work Ramsden out. There was the business of the novel, for a start. He sensed that perhaps great things had been expected of Ramsden artistically but had never really materialized. Why? Indolence? Lack of talent? He seemed to have a rather *precious* personality, and Banks guessed that he had been pampered as a child, most likely by his mother, and led to believe that he was special and gifted. Now he was in his late twenties and the talent hadn't really made itself manifest.

Penny Cartwright remained a grey area. She might have had both motive and means, but they had yet to be discovered. Banks wanted very much to talk to her, and he decided to go to Helmthorpe that evening. He would have to see her father, too, at some point.

One problem was that there was so much time to account for. If Steadman had left The Bridge at about a quarter to nine and his body had been dumped at twelve-fourteen, where had he been and what had he been doing during those three and a half hours? Surely someone must have seen him?

Slowly, Banks's thoughts faded as the counter-tenor sang a mournful "Retir'd from any Mortal's Sight" and the poplars and privet hedges that lined the road gave way to the first houses of Eastvale.

II

"So you told him everything, then?"

"I didn't mean to, Kevin, honest—not your name and all. But it just slipped out."

Kevin leered and Sally's expression darkened. She elbowed him in the ribs. "You've got a filthy mind, you have. It was the time that did it. Twelve-fourteen. He could see I hadn't got a digital watch. Why do you have to wear that silly thing anyway?"

Kevin looked down at his watch, as if examining it for faults. "I don't know," he said.

"It beeps every hour," Sally went on, her voice softening. "No matter what you're doing."

Kevin leaned forward and kissed her. She squirmed beneath him and he slipped his hand under her blouse to hold her soft warm breast. Her body was pressed down hard against the ground, and the moist, sickly smell of the grass filled the air. Insects buzzed and whined all around. Finally, she broke away and gasped for breath. Kevin lay back with his hands behind his head and stared at the deep blue sky.

"What did you think of him, then, this hotshot from London?" he asked.

Sally snorted. "Some hotshot. Fancy leaving London to come up here. The bloke must be barmy."

Kevin turned to face her, leaning on one elbow and sticking a long stalk of grass between his teeth. "What did he say?"

"Didn't seem very interested, really. He just asked me a lot of daft questions. I don't know why I bothered. I won't be so fast to go out of my way and help the police next time, that's for sure."

"What do you mean, 'next time'?"

"I mean if I find out anything else."

"Why should that happen? It was only by chance we heard the car. We didn't even know what it was."

"But we do now. Aren't you curious? Don't you want to know who did it?"

Kevin shrugged. "I wouldn't want to get involved. Leave all that to the police. That's what they're paid for."

"Well, isn't that a typical small-minded attitude," Sally said scornfully.

"It's a sensible one, though."

"So? It's no fun being sensible all the time."

"What are you getting at?"

"Nothing. I just might do a bit of snooping on my own, that's all. I've lived here all my life. I ought to know what's going on in the village."

"What can you do that the police can't?"

"I don't know yet, but I bet I can do better than them. Wouldn't it be exciting if I solved the case for them?"

"Don't be an idiot, Sally. We've been through this before. You know what I think. It's dangerous."

"How?"

"What if the killer knew what you were doing? What if he thought you might be getting too close?"

Sally shivered. "I'll be careful, don't worry; Besides, you never get anywhere if you're frightened of a bit of danger."

Kevin gave up. Sally smoothed her skirt and lay on her back again. They were high on the southern slope of the dale, overlooking cross-shaped Gratly and Helmthorpe's checkerboard pattern of slate roofs. Sally plucked a buttercup and held it to her chin. Kevin took the flower from her hand and trailed it over her throat and collarbone. She shuddered. He kissed her again and put his other hand up her skirt to caress the tender flesh of her thighs just below her panties.

Suddenly Sally heard a sound: a snapping twig or a thwacking branch. She sat up quickly, leaving Kevin with his face in the grass.

"Someone's coming," she whispered.

A few moments later, a figure appeared from the small copse by the beck side. Sally put her hand over her eyes to shield them from the sun and saw who it was.

"Hello, Miss Cartwright," she called out.

Penny walked towards them, knelt on the grass and tossed back her hair. "Hello. It's a beautiful day, isn't it?"

"Yes," answered Sally. "We're just having a breather. We've been walking most of the afternoon."

"I used to walk around these parts a lot, too, when I was your age," Penny said quietly, almost to herself. "It seems like centuries ago now, but it was only ten years. You'll be surprised how quickly time passes. Enjoy it while you can."

Sally didn't know what to say; she felt embarrassed. After an uneasy silence, she said, "I'm sorry about your friend, Mr Steadman, really I am. He was a nice man."

Penny seemed to return from a great distance to focus on her. At first Sally thought the commiseration had gone unheard, but Penny smiled warmly and said, "Thank you. Yes, he was." Then she got to her feet and brushed the scraps of grass from her long skirt. "I must be off, anyway. Mustn't bore you young people with my memories."

In silence, Sally and Kevin watched her walk up the hillside with a strong, determined stride. She looked a lonely, wild figure, Sally thought, like Catherine in *Wuthering Heights*: a woman of the moors, spirit of the place. Then she felt Kevin's palm against her warm thigh again.

III

Further up the hillside, Penny paused as she stood on a stile and looked back on the dale she loved spread out below her. There was the church by her cottage, High Street and the whitewashed frontage of The Dog and Gun. On the other side of the river, past the cricket pitch and Crabtree's Field, the commons sloped up, rougher and rougher, to Crow Scar, which that day was almost too bright to look at.

But she couldn't gaze long without thinking of Harry, for he was the one who had shown her Swainsdale's secrets, given it depth and life beyond its superficial beauties. And now she fancied she could see the collapsed section of Tavistock's wall. The stones that had been used to cover Harry's body seemed darker than the rest.

Looking back the way she had come, Penny saw the two young lovers fuse in a tight embrace on the grass. She smiled sadly. When she'd first approached them, she had noticed how flustered and embarrassed they had looked.

Again she thought of Harry. Suddenly, the memory of a picnic they'd had ten years ago came into her mind. It must have been on the exact spot where Sally and Kevin were lying. She remembered the view of the village clearly, and they had been near a small copse, as Emma had sat in the shade, knitting. The more she concentrated on it, the more details came back. It was just around the time when she and Michael had started drifting apart. He had been reading Shelley's poetry. Penny could even remember the scuffed brown leather of the book's cover; it was a second-hand edition she'd bought him for his birthday. She and Harry had spread the red checked cloth on the grass and started to unload the hamper. Somehow, their hands had touched by accident. Penny remembered blushing, and Harry had busied himself looking for the corkscrew. It was for the Chablis. Yes, they had drunk Chablis, a good vintage, that day, and now, ten years later, she felt the crisp, flinty taste of the cool wine on her tongue again.

The picture faded as quickly as it had come. How innocent it had all been, how bloody innocent! Wiping the tears from her eyes with the back of her hand, she jumped down from the stile and strode sharply on.

IV

Hackett had already been waiting an hour when Banks got back from York, and he was not at all amused.

"Look here," he protested as Banks led him upstairs to the office, "you can't do this to me. You can't just drag me in like this without an explanation. I've got a business to run. I told you everything last night."

"You told me nothing last night." Banks took off his jacket and hung it at the back of the door. "Sit down," he said. "Make yourself at home."

The room was stuffy, so Banks reopened the window and the smells of Market Street wafted up: exhaust fumes, fresh-baked bread, something sweet and sickly from the chocolate shop. Hackett sat rigidly in his chair and lapsed into a tense, affronted silence.

"There's nothing to get excited about," Banks told him, taking out his pipe and fiddling with it over the wicker waste-basket.

"Then why did your sergeant kidnap me like that and rush me over here, eh? I want my lawyer."

"Oh, do relax, Mr Hackett! There's really no need for melodrama. You've been watching far too many American films on television. I've not brought you here to lay charges or anything like that. I'm sorry if Sergeant Hatchley seemed a little brusque—it's just his manner. I've got a few questions to ask you, that's all." He gave Hackett a sharp glance. "Just one or two little things we'd like to get cleared up."

"Why pick on me? What about Jack, or the doc?"

"Do you know of any reason they might have had for killing Mr Steadman?"

"Well, no. I didn't mean to imply that. It's just that..."

"Did he ever say anything about them to you, give you any reason to think one of them might want him out of the way?"

"No. That's not what I meant, anyway. I'm not trying to put the blame on someone else. I just want to know why you picked on me to haul in like this."

"Crabtree's Field." Banks picked up his pipe and reached for the matches.

Hackett sighed. "So that's it. Someone's been telling tales. I should have known you'd have found out before long."

Banks lit his pipe and gazed at the ceiling. Some old juices trickled down the stem and caught in his throat; he coughed and pulled a face.

Hackett looked at him angrily. "You don't give a damn, do you? Anyway, it's nobody's bloody business—"

"It's police business now, Mr Hackett," Banks interrupted. He put his pipe aside and drained the cold coffee left in his mug. "If it's all the same to you, the sooner we get it cleared up, the better."

Hackett shuffled in his chair and smoothed his droopy moustache. "It was nothing," he said. "Just a minor disagreement over an acre or two of land, that's all."

"Countries have been invaded for less," Banks remarked, and went on to give Hackett the details as he had heard them.

"Yes," Hackett agreed, "that's more or less it. But I wouldn't kill anyone for that, let alone a close friend like Harry. Even if he did want to wrap up the whole bloody dale and give it to the National Trust, I liked the man. I respected his principles, even though they weren't the same as mine."

"But you did argue about the field?" Banks persisted.

"We argued about it, yes. But it was half in fun. The others will tell you. Harry liked a good argument as well as the next man. It wasn't that important."

"Money is always important, Mr Hackett. How much did you expect to make from the land if you got it?"

"That's impossible to say. I wouldn't stand to make anything for ages, of course. I'd be out of pocket, in fact. There's the purchase price, construction, publicity... It could have been years before I started showing a profit."

"So you were only in it for the fun?"

"Not only that, no. I mean, I like business. It's a way of life that suits me. I like doing deals. I like building things up. But of course I wouldn't put out good money if I didn't think the eventual returns would be substantial."

"Can we agree," Banks asked, "that you did hope at some point to make a considerable amount from your investment?"

"Hell, yes. Eventually."

"And now?"

"What about now? I don't understand."

"Oh, come on Mr Hackett. Don't play the innocent. The pitch is clear now, isn't it? The field's yours."

Hackett laughed and relaxed in his chair. "That's just where you're wrong, I'm afraid. You see, I think Harry pulled it off. At least there's a freeze on the place right now. I suppose young Ramsden will carry on his master's work and wrap it up. A bloody Roman camp! I ask you! What's there but a few broken pots and stones? No wonder the bloody economy's in the state it's in. No room for initiative any more."

"Oh," said Banks, feigning surprise, "I thought our government wanted to encourage small businesses."

Hackett glared at him; whether for the slight about his fiscal proportions or for picking up a throwaway comment, Banks wasn't quite sure. "You know what I mean, Chief Inspector. We're hamstrung by these historical societies and tourist boards. They're all a load of bloody romantics as far as I can see. It's all a myth. The past wasn't like that; it wasn't neat and tidy like they all seem to think, for Christ's sake. Life was nasty, brutish and short, as the man said. Just because I never went to university, it doesn't make me an ignoramus, you know. I've read books, too. If you ask me, Harry walked around seeing the past through rose-coloured glasses. Penny Cartwright, too. In reality, life must have been bloody misery back then. Imagine them poor Roman sods freezing their balls off up north when they could have been lounging around in the sun on the seven hills drinking vino and rogering the local tarts. And as for the bloody Industrial Revolution, it was nothing but exploitation—hard, harsh work for most people. No, Chief Inspector, Harry hadn't a bloody clue about the past, for all his degrees."

"Maybe you should move somewhere else," Banks suggested. "I doubt they care much for local history in Wigan, for example, or Huddersfield."

"You'd be surprised," Hackett said. "It's all over the bloody place. They call it civic pride. They're even flogging Bradford as the 'gateway to Brontë country' now—and if they can get away with that they can do anything. Besides, I like it here. Don't think just because I'm a businessman I lack a finer appreciation of nature. I'm as much for the environment as the next man."

"What were you doing on Saturday night?" Banks asked, renewing the attack on his pipe with a cleaner.

Hackett scratched his receding hairline. "After I left The Bridge I went to a new club in Darlington. I drove up there, had a couple of drinks in a local, then went on to the club. I know the owner, like. We've done a bit of business together."

"So you left The Bridge at what time?"

"About half nine."

"And drove straight to Darlington?"

"Well, not exactly. I went home first to get changed."

"What time did you leave for Darlington?"

"About ten to ten."

"And arrived?"

"About half past, twenty to eleven."

"And you went to the club when?"

"Half eleven, quarter to twelve."

"What's it called?"

"The KitKat Klub. Only been open a few weeks. It's a sort of disco place, but not too loud. Caters for the more mature crowd."

"I suppose you knew people there, people who can corroborate your story?"

"I talked to a few people, yes. And there's Andy Shaw, the owner."

Banks took down the details, including the name of the pub, and noticed how anxious Hackett looked throughout the process.

"Anything else you can tell us, Mr Hackett?"

Hackett chewed on his lower lip and frowned. "No, nothing."

"Right then, off you go," Banks said. He stood up and walked over to open the door.

As soon as Hackett was out of the building, Banks called Sergeant Hatchley in and asked if he'd found anything in his search of Steadman's study.

"Nowt much of interest, no," Hatchley said. "A few manuscripts, letters to historical preservation societies—they're on my desk if you want to look at them."

"Later."

"And he had one of those fancy computers—a word processor. I suppose he had to spend his brass on something. Remember how much wheeling and dealing it took us to get central admin to let us have one downstairs?"

Banks nodded.

"And now they send bloody Richmond off t' seaside to learn how to use the bugger." Hatchley shook his head slowly and left the office.

V

It was about six-thirty, after what passed for rush-hour in that part of the country, when Banks pulled into Helmthorpe's main car park. He had attended the brief inquest, given the press a snippet or two of information and managed a quick dinner at home with Sandra and the kids.

Penny Cartwright was washing up the dinner dishes and enjoying the play of evening sunlight as it reflected from the shiny surfaces and skittered about the walls. When she heard a knock at the front door she quickly wiped her hands on her apron and went to answer it. She knew immediately that the dark-haired, wiry man standing there was the policeman Barker had told her about. She hadn't expected him to be so good looking, though, and immediately felt unattractive in her apron with her hair tied back in a long pony tail.

"You'd better come in," she said. "We wouldn't want to give the neighbours too much to talk about." She pointed him to a worn armchair and slipped into the kitchen, where she quickly divested herself of the stained apron, untied her hair and brushed it swiftly so that it fell around her face and spilled over her shoulders.

If Banks was struck by the abrupt, casual manner of his hostess, he was also struck by her beauty. She looked good in close-fitting jeans, and her striking hair framed a proud, high-cheekboned face without a trace of make-up. The combination of jet-black hair and sharp blue eyes added to the stunning effect.

Penny sat in a straight-backed chair by a writing-table and asked Banks what she could do for him.

He began casually, trying to establish a friendly tone: "Maybe nothing, Miss Cartwright. I'm just talking to Mr Steadman's friends, trying to get some idea of what he was like."

"Do you really need to know?" Penny asked. "I mean, do you care?"

"Perhaps not in the way that you do," Banks admitted. "After all, I didn't know him. But it might help me to find out who killed him. And I care about that. Obviously somebody did, but all I've heard so far is how wonderful he was—the kind of man who didn't have an enemy in the whole wide world."

"What makes you think you'll get anything different out of me?" Penny asked. Her lips curved slightly in a mocking smile.

"Just fishing."

"Well you won't catch anything, Inspector. Not from me. It's all absolutely true. I can't imagine for the life of me who'd want to do a thing like that to him."

Banks sighed. It was going to be a difficult evening. "Fortunately, Miss Cartwright," he said, "it's not your life we're concerned with, it's Mr Steadman's. And somebody brought that to an abrupt and cruel end. Do you know anything about his business affairs?"

"Do you mean that fuss over Crabtree's Field? Really, Inspector, does Teddy Hackett strike you as the murdering kind? He wouldn't have the guts to kill a worm if his life depended on it. He might be a ruthless businessman—though the competition around here isn't much cop, and, if you ask me, he's got by more on good luck than good management—but a killer? Hackett? Never."

"Stranger things have happened."

"Oh, I know: 'There are more things in heaven and earth, Horatio, than are dreamt of in your philosophy,'" she quoted.

"It might not be a serious possibility," Banks went on, "but it's the only one we've got so far."

"Typical bloody police, that is," Penny mocked. "Crucify the first poor bastard that comes out less than squeaky clean. Still," she added, "Hackett's no great loss to society. Not like Harry."

"How long had you known Mr Steadman?" Banks asked.

"Depends on what you mean by 'know.'" Penny lit a long, filter cigarette and went on. "I first met him years ago when I was a teenager and he and Emma came up to Gratly for their holidays. They'd been two or three times before I got to know them through Michael. That's Michael Ramsden. They stayed at his parents' bed-and-breakfast place, the house they live in now. I was about sixteen, and Michael and I were sweethearts at that time, so, naturally, I saw them quite often."

Banks nodded and sucked on his pipe. That archaic word, "sweet-hearts," sounded wonderfully erotic coming from Penny's lips. It seemed unselfconscious, at odds with her tight and aggressive manner.

"We went on walks together," she continued. "Harry knew a lot about the countryside and its history. That was his real love. And then...well. It was a beautiful summer, but it passed, as all summers do."

"Ah, yes: 'But where are the snows of yesteryear?'" Banks quoted back at her.

"It was summer; there wasn't much snow."

Again Banks noticed that tiny twitch of a smile at the corners of her pale lips. "That would be about ten years ago, wouldn't it?" he asked.

Penny nodded slowly. "Ten years, almost exactly. Yes. But things changed. Michael went to university. He was eighteen. I went away. Years passed. Harry came into some money and bought the house. I'd been back about eight months then—sort of return of the prodigal daughter. Black sheep. Most people had no time for me, but Harry always did."

"What do you mean they had no time for you? Where had you been? Why did you come back?"

"That's a long story, Inspector," Penny said. "And I'm not sure it comes under the heading of relevant information. Briefly, though, I spent about eight or nine years away, in the music business. Mostly I was homesick, despite all the fun and a moderate amount of acclaim. Finally, I got very cynical, and I decided it was time to come home. People weren't friendly because they can't accept anything modern around here and they no longer knew how to behave towards me. I'm sure they made up stories to suit their opinions. They didn't know who or what I was, so they made a lot of assumptions based on what they read in the Sunday papers about the music business—and I don't mean *The Sunday Times*, either. To them I became a degenerate, a scarlet woman. In fact, I always had been—they couldn't admit they'd ever been wrong about me. Does that answer your questions?"

She paused but didn't look at Banks for a response. "It was very hard for my father, but he took me back. Why don't I live with him?

Is that what you were going to ask next? For my sanity, Inspector, my mental health. He's just a bit too solicitous of my welfare, shall we say. And I think I'm a big girl now. It seemed best for both of us if I took this little cottage. Surely you can understand that?"

"Of course. There were rumours, too, weren't there?"

Penny laughed. "Oh, you know about that as well, do you? See what a nice close little community our village is? Well don't be embarrassed, Inspector, ask me. Go on, ask me."

Her bright blue eyes glittered with anger. Banks said nothing. Finally, Penny gave him a scornful look and turned away to pull another cigarette from her package.

"So only your father and Harold Steadman were kind to you?"

"Yes." Penny hesitated. "And Jack Barker, too. He'd been here a year or so by then, but he knew nothing of what happened. Not that it would have mattered to him. He's a friend, too."

"And now?"

"Oh, now?" Penny laughed. "People are beginning to say hello again."

"Do you still see Michael Ramsden?"

"Not much. Only when he calls in at The Bridge or drops by with Harry. Sometimes when you drift apart you never really drift back together."

"And you can't think of any reason why anyone would want to harm Mr Steadman?"

"None at all. I've told you." Penny's smooth brow creased in thought and she shook her head sadly. "He wasn't greedy or scheming. He never cheated or lied."

"What did his wife think of your relationship?"

"Emma? Nothing much, I should imagine. Probably glad to get him out of the way."

"Why do you say that? Were they unhappy together?"

Penny looked at him as if he'd just crawled out from under a stone and blew her smoke out angrily. "How should I know? Ask her."

"I'm asking *you*." Things were taking the kind of turn he had hoped to avoid, but with someone as anti-establishment as Penny Cartwright, he reflected, it was bound to happen. She had been toying with him all along. He pressed on: "Still no answer?"

"I told you, I don't know," she said. "For God's sake, what do you want me to say?"

"Was their marriage normal?"

"Normal! Ha! What the bloody hell does that mean? Yes, I suppose so. I've never been married, myself, so I'm hardly the best person to ask."

"Were they happy?"

"I should think so. As I said, I don't really know. It's not as if I was his confidante or his shoulder to cry on."

"Did he need one?"

Penny sighed and rested her head in her hands. "Look," she protested tiredly, "this is getting us nowhere. What do you want from me?"

Banks ignored her question and pressed on: "What were you to Mr Steadman?"

"Harry and I were friends. Just friends. I told you. We had interests in common."

"And his wife didn't object?"

"She never said anything to me. Why should she? Harry never said anything, either."

"You do know her, then?"

"Of course I bloody well know her. Harry and I weren't carrying on a clandestine relationship, like you seem to think. I went to their house for dinner plenty of times. She was always very kind and charming. She was a good cook, too."

"What did you talk about?"

"When Emma was around?"

"Yes."

"Nothing much. Just the usual stuff. She didn't really share Harry's passions. She likes music—mostly classical, though. Christ, what do you talk about when you go to someone's house for dinner?"

"Were you having an affair with Harold Steadman?"

At last, the inevitable question. And Banks felt a fool the moment it was out. If he had been expecting a burst of pent-up anger or a howl of derisive laughter in reply, he couldn't have been more surprised. His question seemed instead to deflate the interview of all its mounting tension, and Penny gazed at him steadily, a spark of amusement in her sapphire eyes, as if, in fact, she had goaded him into bluntness.

"No, Inspector," she said, "I was not having an affair with Harry Steadman, or with anyone else, for that matter. In fact, I'm not having an affair with Emma Steadman, or with my father, either. Everything is exactly as I've told you. I just didn't feel that way about Harry, nor he about me, as far as I could tell." Banks thought Steadman must have been mad. "He didn't excite me physically," she went on, lighting another cigarette and walking around the small room as she smoked it. "Only my mind, my imagination. And I liked him very much. I think he was a good man, a bright, sweet person. Perhaps I even loved him in a Platonic sort of way, but that's as far as it went." She tossed her hair back and sat down facing him, chin held high. Bright tears shone in her eyes but they never began to flow. "There you are, Inspector," she said with dignity. "I've bared my soul for you. Aren't you pleased?"

Banks was moved by the obvious intensity of her feeling, but he didn't want to let his disadvantage show.

"When did you last see him?" he asked.

Her eyes reflected a chain of options running through her mind. It was a phenomenon Banks had often observed in people who were trying to decide quickly whether to lie or tell the truth.

Penny opened her mouth, then closed it. She took a final drag on her cigarette, ground it out half smoked, and whispered, "Saturday. Saturday evening."

"What time?"

"About nine."

"After he'd left The Bridge?"

"Yes. He dropped by here."

"They why the hell didn't you tell me before? You knew damn well you were holding back important information."

Penny shrugged. "You didn't ask me. I didn't want to get involved."

"Didn't want to get involved?" Banks echoed scornfully. "You say you liked the man, that he helped you, and you couldn't be bothered to help us try and find his killer?"

Penny sighed and began to wind a strand of hair around her index finger. "Look, Inspector," she said, "I know it sounds shabby, but it's true. I don't see how his visit to me could help you in any way. And, dammit," she flashed, "I don't think I owe the police any bloody favours."

"That's not the point. I don't care about your personal feelings towards the police. What was important was the time. If nothing else, your information could help us pinpoint the time of the murder. When did he leave?"

"About ten."

"Did he say where he was going?"

"I assumed he was going to York. He'd mentioned it."

"But he didn't mention any other calls he wanted to make first, any errands to run?"

"No."

It was another hour accounted for, anyway. Banks had nothing more to say; his session with Penny had exhausted him. She seemed irritated and the tension grew between them again, as tangible as a tightening hacksaw blade. Finally, Penny broke it.

"Look," she began, "I'm sorry, I really am. I do care about Harry. The thing is that in my life involvement with the police has always meant trouble. I've never been involved in a murder investigation before, so I don't know what matters and what doesn't. When you're a musician, young, in with a certain crowd, you get a very warped view of authority—police, customs men, immigration officials, security guards—they all seem against you; they're all such a royal pain in the arse."

Banks couldn't help but grin. "Drugs?" he asked.

Penny nodded. "Not me. I was never into it. Not in a heavy way. But you know how it is in London. There's drugs all around you, whether you take them or not. Sure, I smoked a joint or two, maybe took some amphetamines to keep me awake on tour—but never the heavy stuff. Try and tell the drug squad that."

Banks wanted to argue, to defend the police, but he was too tired and he knew there would be no point anyway. Besides, he also knew that the police were just like everyone else; a lot were bastards and a few weren't. He had known a high-ranking officer in the drug squad who routinely planted illegal substances on people he wanted out of the way, and that was by no means rare or unusual behaviour. Also, he smelled something familiar in the air of Penny's cottage. He knew what it was, but he didn't care to pursue the matter any more than he wanted to tell her that his full title was Chief Inspector. People often got it wrong.

He stood up, and Penny walked to the door with him. He felt that she was seeking some kind words of reassurance from him, some forgiveness for acting in a way contrary to her feelings for Steadman. But he didn't know how to give it. At the door he said, "I hear you sing, Miss Cartwright?"

"Actually, it's Ms," Penny corrected him, a playful smile lighting her eyes. "Yes, I sing."

"Locally?"

"Sometimes. I'm at The Dog and Gun this Friday and Saturday. Competing with the disco in The Hare and Hounds."

"I'll see if I can drop by, then," Banks said. "If nothing turns up."

"Feel free." There was a trace of doubt in Penny's voice, as if she couldn't quite believe that a policeman would be interested in traditional folk music, or in any kind of music, for that matter.

Banks walked down the narrow cobbled street by the church wall, and as soon as he got to the corner he heard a hissing sound behind him and turned. An old woman stood at the door of the cottage next to Penny's and beckoned him over. When he got close enough she whispered, "You'll be that there p'liceman they're all talking about."

"Detective Chief Inspector Banks," he said, reaching for his card. "At your service."

"Nay, nay lad, there's no need for that. I believe thee," she said, waving it aside. "Been talking to 'er ladyship next door, I see." She jerked a shrivelled thumb in the direction of Penny's cottage. Puzzled, Banks nodded.

"Did she tell 'ee about Sat'day night?"

"What about Saturday night?"

"I thought she wouldn't," the old woman said triumphantly, crossing her arms with great satisfaction. "A proper ruckus there were. T'old major near flung 'im down t'garden path."

"Flung who?"

"Why, 'im as got 'isself murdered," she announced with obvious relish. "I don't 'old wi' married men sniffing around young lasses. And she's a flighty one, yon missy is, you mark my words. There again, though," she laughed, "t'major's mad as an 'atter 'imself."

"What are you talking about, Mrs...?"

"Miss," she said proudly. "Lived seventy-one years and never saw t'need for a 'usband yet. Miss Bamford it is, young man, and I'm talking about Sat'day night when Major Cartwright popped in on 'is daughter and caught 'er wi' that murdered chappie. 'Bout ten o'clock, it were. Now, don't ask me what they was doing, 'cos I couldn't say, but 'ee flew off t'handle, t'old man did. Told 'im not to come around no more."

"You mean the major physically threw Mr Steadman out of Penny Cartwright's house?" Banks asked, trying to get things straight. He was sure that something was bound to have got lost in translation.

"Well, not in so many words." Miss Bamford backed down; her chin retracted deep into the folds of her neck. "I couldn't see proper, like. Pushed 'im, though—and that chap so pale and weakly from shutting 'imsen up wi' books all day and night. I'll bet she didn't tell you about that, did she, yon Lady Muck?"

Banks had to admit that Penny had not told him about that. In fact, he had backed away from the whole issue of her father after she had challenged him to be direct.

"Did she go out afterwards?" he asked.

"'er Royal 'ighness? No. T'door banged about eleven, but that were t'major."

"Surely there's a back door, too?"

"Oh, aye," Miss Bamford answered. She hadn't missed his meaning.

Banks thanked her. With a smug smile on her wrinkled face, the old woman shut her door. After a quick and puzzled glance back at Penny's cottage, Banks walked towards his car and drove home.

SIX

I

"So according to your mate in Darlington—"

"Sergeant Balfour, sir. A good man."

"According to your Sergeant Balfour," Banks went on, "Hackett didn't arrive at the KitKat Klub until after one o'clock in the morning, and nobody in the pub he mentioned remembered seeing him?"

"That's right. The landlord said he often dropped by, but last week it was on Friday, not Saturday."

"So the bastard's been lying." Banks sighed. He was becoming more and more irritated with the inhabitants of Helmthorpe, and, as many London villains would testify, the more annoyed he got the harder it was all around. "I suppose we'd better have him in again. No, wait..." He glanced at his watch and stood up. "Better still, let's have a drive into Helmthorpe. There's a couple of things I want to do there."

Sandra was using the Cortina, so they signed out a car from the pool and Banks let Hatchley drive. The hedgerows by the river were dotted with clumps of white, yellow and purple wild flowers, none of which Banks could name. A few dark clouds skulked about the sky, but the sun pierced through here and there in bright lances of light that picked out green patches on the shadowed dalesides. The effect reminded Banks of some paintings he'd seen in a London gallery Sandra had dragged him to, but he couldn't remember the artist's name: Turner, Gainsborough, Constable? Sandra would know. He made a mental note to look into landscape painting a bit more closely.

"What do you think, then?" Hatchley asked. He drove with one hand and lit a cigarette from the glowing red circle of the dashboard lighter. "About Hackett, I mean."

"Could be our man. He's certainly hiding something."

"What about the others who were with Steadman that night?"

"We just don't know, do we? Any one of them could have done it. They've no real alibis—not even Barnes."

"But what motive could he have for killing Steadman? He's got a good reputation locally, always has had."

Banks fiddled with his pipe. "Could be blackmail. Maybe Barnes had something on Steadman, or vice versa. Maybe Steadman learned something that would ruin the doctor's reputation."

"It's possible, I suppose," Hatchley said. "But Steadman was rich; he didn't need to blackmail anyone, surely? And if he was paying Barnes it'd be daft to kill the goose that laid the golden egg, wouldn't it."

"Agreed. But it needn't have been money. Perhaps Steadman felt morally bound to tell what he knew. From all accounts, he was just the kind of person who would. I know it's all speculation at this point, but I still think we should look into the doctor's finances and background—and find out if Steadman made any large bank with- drawals recently."

"Won't do any harm, I suppose. Bloody hell!—" Hatchley swerved to avoid a wobbling cyclist and yelled out of the window, "Watch where you're going, bloody road hog!"

Banks tightened his safety belt; he remembered one of the reasons why he preferred driving his own car on the job.

They arrived safely and parked by the river, where Steadman had left his car, and walked up the alley to High Street. It was about mid- day; tourists thronged the small ice-cream shop, and the locals were out shopping or gossiping by cottage gates up the narrow, cobbled sidestreets. The two policemen were, by then, well known in the vil- lage, and voices lowered as they passed. Banks smiled to himself; he enjoyed the effect his presence had on people. In London, nobody but the criminals he'd put away more than once knew who he was.

They paused by a newsagent's, where racks of coloured postcards, maps and local guidebooks outside on the pavement flapped in the light breeze.

"Let's take Hackett together after lunch," Banks suggested.

"All right." Hatchley looked at his watch. "Want to eat now?"

"Not yet. Why don't you drop in on Weaver and see if anything's turned up? I want a word with Major Cartwright. Then we'll have a pie and a pint at The Bridge and work out how to tackle Hackett."

Hatchley agreed and walked off to the small local police station.

Nobody, Banks thought, could look more like a retired major than the man who opened the door next to Thadtwistle's bookshop. He was elderly but trim looking, with silver hair, a brick-red complexion and a grey handlebar moustache. After Banks had identified himself, the major grunted and led him up a narrow staircase. The flat turned out to be directly above the bookshop itself.

Banks followed him into a sitting-room dominated by a huge framed reproduction of a bare-breasted woman carrying a flag over a battlefield of dead and wounded soldiers; she was accompanied by a small boy with a gun in each hand.

"*Liberty Leading the People*," the major said, catching him staring at it. "Delacroix. That's what we were fighting for, isn't it?"

Luckily, Banks could recognize a rhetorical question when he heard one. He turned his attention to the terrier sniffing around his ankles and tried subtly shifting his feet to make it go away. Banks didn't like dogs—if anything, he was a cat man—but he liked it even less when their proud owners expected him to fuss over the damned animals as if they were new-born babies. Kicking out a bit harder, Banks finally persuaded the pooch to slink off to its basket, from where it gazed at him with an expression of resentment mingled with arrogance. The major was pouring drinks, so fortunately his back was turned.

Stale smoke made the warm room stuffy. Banks spotted an antique pipe-rack on the wall above the fireplace and, hoping to establish a rapport, he sat in a straight-backed chair and coaxed his own briar alight.

The major handed him a small whisky and soda, took a larger one for himself, and sat down in the scuffed leather armchair that had obviously been *his* since time immemorial.

Some military types, Banks found, regarded the police as fellow professionals, colleagues-in-arms almost, but others looked upon them as upstarts, petty dabblers who had not quite made the ranks.

Major Cartwright seemed to be of the latter type. He looked at Banks
with open hostility, the purple veins around his nose showing a clear
predilection for early morning snifters.

"What is it, then?" he asked, as if he had been interrupted in the
midst of planning a new assault on the Boers.

Banks explained about the murder, drawing only grunts and sharp
nods, and tried as delicately as he could to mention that the major
had probably been the last person, apart from the killer, to see
Steadman alive.

"When would that be?" Cartwright asked.

"Saturday night, about ten o'clock."

The major stared at him with icy blue eyes and sipped his whisky.
"Who told you that?"

"It doesn't matter who told me, Major. Is it true?"

"I suppose it was that busybody of a neighbour, eh? Silly old
biddy."

"Did you see him and did you have an argument?"

"You can't be suggesting—"

"I'm not suggesting anything. I'm just asking you a simple question."

The major swirled the whisky in his glass for a moment, then
answered, "All right, what if I did?"

"You tell me."

"Nothing to tell, really. Found him hanging about my daughter
again and told him to sling his hook."

"Why did you react so violently?"

"It's not right." Cartwright leaned forward in his chair. "A married
man, older than her. What would you do? It's not healthy." He
slumped back again.

"Did you assume they were having an affair?"

"Now hold on a minute, young man. Hold your horses. I never
said anything like that."

"Look," Banks pressed on, "I'm not making any accusations or
charges. I'm asking you what you thought. If you didn't think your
daughter was likely to be involved in anything unsavoury, then why
did you practically kick Steadman down the street?"

"She's exaggerating, the old bag." Cartwright sniffed. He tossed back the rest of his drink, then got up and picked an old briar from the rack and filled it with twist from a pouch. "We had words, yes, but I never laid a finger—or a toe—on him. Anyway, it's a matter of principle, isn't it? A married man. People talk."

Banks found it hard to see the link between principle and the fear of gossip, but he ignored the issue. "Is that why you objected to a harmless relationship that both parties seemed to enjoy?" he asked instead. "Did you behave the same way over all your daughter's friendships?"

"Dammit, the man was married," the major repeated.

"He was married ten years ago when they first met, but you didn't object then, did you?"

"That was all in the open. Always someone else around—young Michael. She was just a girl. Look, if they want to meet, they can do it openly, can't they? In a pub with other people there, for example. No reason to shut themselves up in private like that. They're a sharp tongued lot in this village, lad. You don't know the half of it."

"Were you worried that they'd talk like they did about you and your daughter? Is that what you wanted to protect her from?"

The major whitened and sagged in his chair. All of a sudden his belligerence seemed to desert him and he looked his age. He got up slowly and mixed himself another drink. "Heard about that, did you?"

Banks nodded.

"You weren't there," he said in a sad, bitter tone. "You can't know what it was like for the two of us after my wife died. I couldn't look after myself, had to go in hospital for a while, had to send Penny away to the Ramsdens. But she came back and cared for me. Selflessly, God bless her. She's an only child, you know. And then the vicious gossip started. It only takes one to start the rumour—just one rotten bastard—then it spreads like the plague until everyone's had enough of it and something better comes along. And it's just a game to them. They don't even care whether it's true or not; it just titillates their imaginations, that's all. I blame them for driving her away. They said it wasn't natural, the two of us together. After she left, I sold the house and moved here."

"I thought she left to start a career in music?"

"Oh, she'd have gone eventually. But she was too young. She

shouldn't have gone so soon, then things wouldn't have turned out the way they did for her."

"She seems well enough adjusted to me. Maybe a little sharp at the edges."

"You didn't know her before. Lost a lot of her spirit, joy. Too young to be a cynic. Anyway, she couldn't stand it here with people staring at her that way. Took a lot of courage for her to come back."

"So you forgave her?"

"Nothing to forgive, really. She thought she'd let me down, leaving me like that. There'd been rows, fights, yes. But I never stopped loving her. Steadman wasn't a bad sort, I know that. A bit wet, I always thought, but not a bad sort. I just wanted to spare her it all again. She's bitter enough already. But it's not the first time I've had words with him. Ask anyone. My argument with Steadman wasn't new."

"What happened on Saturday night?"

"Nothing, really. I told him not to call on her alone after dark again. I'd told him before. I suppose I just made things worse, drawing attention to it."

"What did you do afterwards?"

"When he'd gone?"

"Yes."

"I stayed and talked to Penny for an hour or so. She was a bit upset with me but we settled things amicably enough."

"Can you remember what time you left?"

"I can remember the church bells ringing eleven. It wasn't long after that."

"And Steadman left at ten?"

"That was when I arrived, yes."

"Did you notice anyone hanging around the area?"

"No. It was quiet. Always is up there. There were a few people on High Street, but nothing unusual."

"Did Steadman say where he was going? Did he give you any idea at all what he intended to do next?"

Major Cartwright shook his head. "No, he just took off. Sorry I can't be of more help to you, Inspector."

"Never mind. Thanks for your time, anyway, Major."

Cartwright turned and walked over to the cocktail cabinet, leaving Banks to make his own way back downstairs.

II

With her head propped up on cushions, Sally lay in the back garden, sunbathing in her pale blue bikini. It was a luxury she felt entitled to as she had made temporary peace with her parents by breaking a date with Kevin the previous evening in order to visit boring Aunt Madge in Skipton. There, she had sipped tea from tiny, fragile china cups with gilded rims and red roses painted on their sides, and had answered politely all the dull and predictable questions about her schoolwork. At least the television had been on—Aunt Madge never turned it off—so she had been able to half-watch an old Elizabeth Taylor film while pretending to pay attention to the conversation, which ranged from the shocking state of the neighbour's garden to news of a distant cousin's hysterectomy. The odd thing was that her parents hadn't seemed to enjoy the evening much either; her father hardly said a word. They all seemed relieved when the goodbyes had been said and they could troop out to the car.

With a sigh, Sally put down *Wuthering Heights* and rolled over on her stomach. Her skin was already glowing pleasantly, and even with the lotion she would have to be careful how long she spent outside.

She was puzzled and frustrated by the book. In the film—even the old black and white version with Laurence Olivier—Heathcliff had seemed so sexy and tragic. She remembered sharing tissues with her mother while they had watched it on television and her father had laughed at them. But the book was different. Not the story—that was basically the same—but the character of Heathcliff. True, he loved Catherine passionately, but in the book he was so much more cruel and violent. He seemed to want to destroy everyone around him. And worse, he was even more interested in getting his hands on the house and property. That was the real reason he married Isabella—though he did appear to be taking revenge for Edgar marrying Catherine—and an obsession with acquiring property was hardly romantic. He acted more like a demented (and much more handsome) Teddy Hackett than a true heroic figure.

She reached for her glass of Perrier. It was warm; the ice had all melted and the sparkle had vanished. Pulling a face, she rolled onto her back again and started thinking rather despondently about her sleuthing. There wasn't much to think about. She had no idea who the police suspected, what clues they had, what they knew about motives and opportunities. All she had to go on was what anyone in the village would know about Steadman: that he seemed fond of Penny Cartwright, much to her father's chagrin; that he worked a lot with Michael Ramsden; that he had been able to help the Ramsden family by buying the house when the father died; that he was generally well liked; that he drank in The Bridge with Jack Barker, Teddy Hackett and Dr Barnes. He just didn't seem the type to go around inflaming people's passions, like Heathcliff. But he must have done; somebody had killed him.

It had to be a man. Of that, Sally was sure. Steadman had been quite tall and must have weighed a bit; no woman could have manoeuvred his body over the wall and all that way up the field. But that still left too many suspects. If only she had had the foresight to watch from the shelter that night. Sally began to apply her imagination to the facts. Everyone knew that Michael Ramsden had once courted Penny Cartwright. What if he was still carrying a torch for her, like Heathcliff for Catherine, and was jealous of Steadman's attentions? But she remembered seeing Ramsden—and avoiding him—that evening she went drinking in Leeds with Kevin. He had been with a good-looking woman, and though Sally had only got a fleeting glance while pulling Kevin quickly back out through the door before they were seen, she knew it wasn't Penny. And he'd hardly be going out with someone else if he was still in love with her.

There was Jack Barker, too, of course. At first, she hadn't suspected him, but now she could see him acting in the heat of passion. She'd noticed how often he'd been walking out with Penny around the village lately and wondered if Barker might have seen Steadman as an obstacle. He wrote detective stories, after all, so he must know all about murder. Even though he was a gentleman, he would hardly stand there with the gun smoking in his hand and wait for the police to come. Surely he would try and get rid of the body so he could remain free and win Penny's love. She wondered if he had an alibi and if there was any way of finding out.

And then there was Hackett. No love interest there, of course, but she'd heard rumours of arguments over property. People certainly seemed to get all steamed up about such things in *Wuthering Heights*.

She reached out for her suntan lotion. One more coat, another hour or so, then she'd go in. As far as catching the murderer was concerned, all she could do was try to remember all she'd seen and heard in the village since the Steadmans came to Gratly eighteen months ago. Maybe there was something she'd overlooked: a word or gesture that had meant nothing or made no sense at the time but took on more significance in the light of the murder. She had a good visual memory—it probably came from watching so many films—so she could review facial expressions and body language. Maybe something would click if she worked at it.

The oil felt good as she massaged it slowly on her stomach and thighs, and she wished Kevin's hands were rubbing it on her flushed skin. A bee droned around the neck of the open bottle then floated away. Sally picked up her book again, leaving oily fingerprints on the pages.

III

The two men walked slowly along Helmthorpe High Street deep in conversation. Banks had one hand in his trouser pocket, and the other held the light sports jacket slung casually over his shoulder. The sleeves of his white shirt were rolled up above the elbows and he had loosened his tie enough to allow him to open his top button. Banks hated ties, and wearing them loosely was his way of compromising. He walked with his head bowed, listening to Hatchley, who towered beside him. The sergeant had both hands clasped behind his back and his head was tilted back on his thick neck as if he were examining the rooftops; a well-cultivated beer-belly hung over his tight belt. The weather was still undecided, and the sun popped in and out between quick-moving dark clouds that raced over on the wind and cast their shadows across the bright face of Crow Scar.

"Said he was in a bit of a state," Hatchley went on. "Shook up, like. Downed a quick double Scotch and went on his way."

The scrap of information Constable Weaver had been so eager to impart was that the barman of The Dog and Gun had told him Steadman had dropped in just after ten o'clock on Saturday night. He hadn't come forward earlier because he had been away fishing in Scotland and hadn't even heard about the murder.

"I can tell you the reason for that," Banks said, and proceeded to tell Hatchley about his interview with Major Cartwright. This took some of the wind out of the sergeant's sails, and he muttered a surly "no" when Banks asked him if there had been any other developments.

Hatchley began to smile again, however, as soon as he sniffed the beer fumes and tobacco smoke in The Bridge. They sat at the same scarred table as they had on their previous visit, and soon had two pints of Theakston's bitter before them and two steak-and-mushroom pies on order.

"Steadman could have gone back to the cottage, though, couldn't he?" Hatchley said. "Maybe he came to the boil when he thought about how he'd let the major walk all over him, so he went back to settle things. We can't rule him out yet, or the girl."

"No we can't. Steadman could have waited for the coast to clear and gone back to finish what he and Penny had started before they were interrupted. The major's certainly very protective towards her."

"From what I hear," Hatchley said with relish, "she always was a bit of a wild 'un. Running off to London, hanging around with those freaks and musicians. There were probably drugs involved, too, and I doubt she was very careful about who she hopped in and out of bed with. I think if she were a daughter of mine I'd keep her on a short leash after that."

"But the woman's twenty-six years old. Besides, Steadman was a safe enough companion, wasn't he?"

Hatchley shrugged. "As far as we know he was. But there could be more to it."

"Oh, there's more to it all right. There's always more to things like this. As far as Penny Cartwright's concerned, there are two points in her favour. First, the old woman didn't hear anyone else call at the cottage later, and she says Penny didn't go out either; and second, I doubt that she was strong enough to drag the body to its hiding place." Banks was about to add that he had also been convinced by Penny's genuine display of affection for Steadman, but he knew it wasn't the kind of evidence Sergeant Hatchley would appreciate. Besides, the spell of her presence had worn off, and he was beginning to wonder if she was not just a consummate actress. "Still," he went on, "she could have had help with the body; and there is a back door, so the old woman might not have heard if she was in the front room."

"Do you think the Cartwright girl really was having it off with Steadman, then?" Hatchley asked.

"I don't know. You can never tell about things like that. Sometimes couples can be having affairs for years and nobody knows."

"Why else would he be hanging around her?"

"There is such a thing as friendship, you know."

"In a pig's eye," Hatchley muttered.

The pies came and the two men ate silently until their plates were empty.

"Steadman had a lot of money," Banks said, reaching for his second pint. "And his wife stands to inherit. I'd say that was a pretty good motive, wouldn't you?"

"But we know she couldn't have done it," Hatchley objected. "I mean, why complicate something that's difficult enough already?"

"She could have hired someone."

"But Helmthorpe isn't New York or London."

"Doesn't matter. I once knew of a chap in Blackpool who had a price list—arms fifty quid, legs seventy-five, and so on. Mind you, his rates have probably gone up a bit with inflation now. It's naïve to think that kind of thing is restricted to the south, and you should bloody well know that as well as anyone. Are you telling me there's no-one in Eastvale would take a job like that? What about Eddie Cockley, for one? Or Jimmy Spinks? He'd slit his own mother's throat for the price of a pint."

"Aye," said Hatchley, "but how would a woman like Mrs Steadman get mixed up with the likes of Cockley and Spinks?"

"I admit it's unlikely, but hardly more than anything else in this bloody business. Put it this way. We don't know much about the

Steadman's marriage. It seemed ordinary enough on the surface, but what did she think about him and Penny Cartwright, for example? Maybe she was mad with jealousy. We just don't know. And even if we ask them, they'll lie. For some reason, they're all protecting one another."

"Perhaps they suspect each other."

"I wouldn't be surprised."

Hatchley guzzled his pint.

"You know what the trouble with this case is, Sergeant?" Banks went on. "Everyone except Major Cartwright seems to think the sun shone out of Steadman's arse."

Hatchley grinned. They drained their glasses and set off to see Hackett.

IV

Teddy Hackett sat in his office, part of an old mill that looked out on the River Swain behind the garage. The window was open and scents of flowers floated in with the sound of water rushing over pebbles. Occasionally, a bee strayed from the clematis that clung to the stone wall, buzzed into the room and, finding nothing of interest in human affairs, meandered out again.

Hackett was nervous and sweaty right from the start. He sat behind the defence of his cluttered desk, back to the window, and toyed with a letter-opener as Banks faced him from a chair. Hatchley leaned against the wall by the window. Banks filled his pipe, got it going, then brought up the subject of Hackett's false alibi.

"From what we've been able to discover, you arrived at the KitKat Klub alone after one o'clock, a little later than you said."

Hackett squirmed. "I'm not very good at times. Always late for appointments, that's me."

Banks smiled. "That's not a very good habit for a businessman, is it? Still, that's no concern of mine. What I want to know is what you were doing before then."

"I told you," Hackett said, slapping his palm with the letter-opener. "I went to a pub and had a couple of drinks."

"But closing time on Saturday is eleven o'clock, Mr Hackett. Even on the most liberal of premises you'd be out in the street by eleven-thirty. What did you do between eleven-thirty and one o'clock?"

Hackett shifted his weight from cheek to cheek and rubbed his chin. "Look, I don't want to get anyone into trouble. Know what I mean? But when you get pally with the bar staff you can sometimes get in an extra drink or two. Especially when the local copper's there, too." He winked. "I mean, if young Weaver ever wanted to—"

"I don't want to hear about Constable Weaver," Banks cut in. "I want to hear about you, and I'm getting impatient. What you're saying is that the publican broke the licensing laws by serving you after hours, as late as one o'clock. Is that what happened?"

"I wouldn't put it quite like that. It was more in the nature of a drink or two together. Privacy of his own home, like. There's no law says a man can't have a mate in for a drink whenever he wants, is there?"

"No, not at all," Banks answered. "Let's say you weren't breaking any laws, then. If you were so pally with the manager you'll remember the name of the pub, won't you?"

"I thought I told you already. Didn't I?"

Banks shook his head.

"I thought I did. I meant to. It was the Cock and Bull on Arthur Street, near the club." Hackett put down his letter-opener and lit a cigarette, taking deep, noisy drags.

"No, it wasn't," said Banks. "It wasn't the Cock and Bull on Arthur Street. The manager says he knows you, right enough, and that you'd been in on Friday, but not Saturday. Where were you, Mr Hackett?"

Hackett looked crestfallen. "He must have been mistaken. Got a bad memory, old Joey. I'm sure if you ask him again, jog his memory a bit, he'll remember. He'll tell you it's true. I was there."

"Come off it, man, tell us where you were!" Hatchley's loud voice boomed out from behind Hackett, unnerving him completely. During the preliminary part of the interrogation, the sergeant had remained so quiet that Hackett, must have forgotten he was in the room. Now he half-turned and looked terrified to find a new, more aggressive adversary towering over him. He got to his feet, but Hatchley still had the advantage of height.

"I don't know what you're getting at—"

"We're not getting at anything," Hatchley said. "We're telling you loud and clear. You never went to the Cock and Bull, did you? That was just a cock and bull story, wasn't it? You never went to any pub in Darlington. You waited for Steadman outside The Bridge, followed him to Penny Cartwright's, waited there, then followed him to The Dog and Gun and back to the car park. There, where it was dark and quiet, you hit him on the head and hid him in the boot of your car. Later, when the whole village was asleep, you dumped him in that field on your way over the dale to Darlington, didn't you? The timing's just right, Hackett, we've checked. What with all the lies you've told us and the traces we'll find in the boot of your car, we've got you by the short and curlies, mate."

Hackett turned to Banks for sympathy and support. "You can't let him bully me, accuse me like this," he spluttered. "It's not . . ."

"Not cricket?" said Banks. "But you must admit, Mr Hackett, it is a possibility, isn't it? A very strong possibility."

Hackett flopped back down into the chair behind his desk and Hatchley walked over to stand in front of him. "Look, sir," the sergeant began softly, "we know you didn't arrive at the club until after one o'clock, and that gives you plenty of time to dump Steadman's body and get there. Don't you think it would be easier all around if you told us what happened? Perhaps it was manslaughter? Perhaps you had an argument and came to blows, you didn't mean to kill him. Is that how it happened?"

Hackett stared at him, wary of his apparent friendliness. Banks got up and walked over to the window, through which he appeared to be gazing at the river.

"I walked around," Hackett said. "That's all. I set off for Darlington as soon as I'd left The Bridge and got changed, then I stopped on the way. It was a lovely evening. I didn't feel like a drink just then, so I went for a walk. I wanted to be alone."

"You and bloody Greta Garbo," Banks snarled from behind him, turning quickly from the window and knocking his pipe out in the thick glass ashtray. "I'm fast losing patience with you, sonny," he rushed on, raising his voice and glaring. It was a measure of Hackett's terror and confusion that he now looked to the huge Hatchley as a benign presence.

"But I—"

"Shut up," Banks ordered him. "I don't want to hear any more lies from you, Hackett. Get it? If I'm not satisfied your next story's true I'll have you in Eastvale nick before your feet touch the ground. Understand?"

Hatchley, enjoying himself tremendously, played the role of kindly uncle. "Best do as the chief inspector asks, sir," he advised the pale Hackett. "I'm sure it can't do any harm if you've nothing to hide."

Hackett stared at Hatchley for a good half-minute, then came that visible relaxation of tension, the moment that signalled the truth. Banks could feel it in his veins; he recognized it well from years of experience. Hackett was still so mixed up that he glowered at Hatchley and directed his statement towards Banks, who smiled and nodded at various points with benevolent understanding.

All in all, it was a great disappointment, but it did get one red herring out of the way. After leaving The Bridge, Hackett had gone home to shower and change, then he had driven to Darlington, where he first spent about two hours of uninhibited carnal bliss with a young married woman whose husband worked the night shift at the local colliery. After that, he had gone on to the KitKat Klub alone because he didn't want to be seen with her locally. People would talk. Banks finally extracted her name and address from him, along with pleas and warnings about not letting her muscle-bound husband find out.

"Please," he begged, "if you must talk to Betty, do it after ten at night. I'll get her to come in. That'll be even better, won't it?"

"If you don't mind, Mr Hackett," Banks replied, "we'll do it our way."

"Have a heart, Chief Inspector. Haven't you ever had a bit on the side?"

The muscles in Banks's jaw tightened. "No," he answered sharply. "And even if I had it wouldn't make a jot of difference to your situation." He put his hands on the desk and leaned forward so that his face was only inches from Hackett's. "What you don't seem to realize, Sonny Jim, is that this is a murder investigation. A friend of yours has been murdered, or don't you remember, and all you're concerned with is some bloody tart you've been poking in Darlington."

"She's not a tart. And there's no reason to ruin a perfectly good marriage, is there? That's what you'll be doing, you know."

"No. That's what you've done. It's what she's done, too. If I thought for a moment that you care more about the marriage than about your own skin, I might just consider doing things differently."

Banks nodded to Hatchley and the two of them left Hackett biting his fingernails and cursing the day he met nubile little Betty Fields in the Cock and Bull.

"Fancy a trip to Darlington, Sergeant?" Banks asked when they reached the High Street. "Best if you check it out yourself."

"Yes, sir," Hatchley replied, grinning.

"Right then. After ten o'clock tonight, if you can make it."

"What? But..."

"If you don't mind."

"It's not that I mind. I've got a couple of mates up there I've not seen in a while. But what about Hackett?"

"Simple really. Hackett's right—I don't see any point in putting unnecessary strain on a marriage, even one as flimsy as Betty Fields's. But he doesn't know that, does he? By the next time he hears from his young lady he'll be a gibbering wreck. Some of these miners are big chaps, so I've heard." He smiled as comprehension dawned on Hatchley. "You have to balance your cruelty with compassion, Sergeant. Come on, just one more visit to make, then home. And by the way..."

"Yes, sir?"

"That was a terrible pun back there. Cock and bull story."

"Oh. I thought it was quite good myself."

Taking advantage of the fine weather, Banks and Hatchley walked to Gratly. They took the shortcut through the cemetery and along a narrow path through a field. Lynchets led down to the beck like a broad flight of green velvet stairs. Sheep grazed under a clump of ash trees in the lush grass by the water.

This time, Banks was struck by the tranquillity and individuality of Gratly. At the centre of the hamlet was a low stone bridge under which a broad stream ran over several abrupt terraces and descended in a series of small waterfalls past a disused mill and down the valley side to the all-consuming Swain.

Gratly itself radiated like a cross from this central point, and gin-
nels and snickets here and there led to twisting backstreets and hidden outhouses. The houses were all old, built of local stone, but their
designs varied. Some, originally weavers' cottages, had many windows in their upper storeys, while others looked like old farmhouses
or labourers' quarters. The sun on the light stone and the steady
music of water as it trickled relaxed Banks, and he found himself
thinking that this was no day and no place for his kind of business.
The hamlet was silent and still; there were no signs of life at all.

Emma Steadman, wearing a brown apron over her shirt and slacks,
answered the door at the second ring and invited them inside, apol-
ogizing for the mess. She stopped at the entrance to the front room
and ushered the two men in, running a grimy hand over her moist
brow. Banks saw immediately what she meant. All Steadman's books
had been taken down from the shelves and stood in untidy, precari-
ously balanced piles on the floor.

The widow moved forlornly into the middle of the room and gestured around. "They're all his. I can't stand it, having them all over the
place. I don't know what to do with them." She seemed less frosty
than when they had parted on Monday afternoon, vulnerable among
the detritus of a shared life.

"There's a book dealer in Eastvale," Banks advised her. "I'm sure
he'll come out and appraise them if you give him a call. He'll give you
a fair price. Or what about Thadtwistle in Helmthorpe?"

"Yes, that's an idea. Thank you." Mrs Steadman sat down. "It'll
have to wait though, I'm afraid. I can't face that kind of thing yet. I
don't know what I'll do with all his things. I never realized he'd collected so much junk. I wish I could just get up and leave Gratly, go
live somewhere else."

"You'll not be staying here?" asked Hatchley.

She shook her head. "No, Sergeant, I don't think so. There's nothing for me here. It was Harold's work, really. His place."

"Where will you go?"

"I haven't really thought. A city, I suppose. Maybe London." She
looked at Banks.

"I shouldn't worry about it yet," he said. "You need a bit of time.
It'll all get taken care of."

Silence followed. Mrs Steadman offered to make a cup of tea, but Banks, much to Hatchley's distress, refused for them both. "No thanks. It's just a flying visit. We were in the area."

She raised her eyebrows, hinting that he should get to the point.

"It's about Penny Cartwright," Banks began, noting that her expression didn't alter a jot at the mention of the name. "I gather that she and your husband were rather close. Didn't that bother you at all?"

"What do you mean, 'bother me'?"

"Well," Banks went on cautiously, "she's an attractive woman. People talk. People have talked about her before. Weren't you worried that your husband might have been having an affair with her?"

It was immediately clear that the suggestion surprised rather than annoyed Emma Steadman, as if it were something she had never even thought of. "But they'd been friends for years," she answered. "Ever since she was a teenager, when we first came up here for our holidays. I don't—I mean, I never really thought of her as anything else, really. A teenager. More like a daughter than a rival."

Banks felt that it was short-sighted in the extreme to look upon a woman only twelve or thirteen years one's junior as a child, especially if that woman was over the age of sixteen. "It didn't bother you at all, then?" he went on. "It never caused any trouble, any jealousy?"

"Not on my part it didn't, no. As I said, Chief Inspector, she's been a friend of the family for years. I suppose you know that she and Michael Ramsden used to go out together ages ago? He brought her up here quite often—after all, it was his home then; we were only summer visitors. I think she had a lot in common with Harry. She looked up to him as a teacher, a man of knowledge. So did Michael, for that matter. I'm sorry, I'm afraid I can't really see what you're getting at."

"I simply wondered whether you suspected your husband of having an affair with Penny Cartwright."

"No, I didn't. First you cast doubts on my marriage, now you accuse my husband of adultery. What's going on? What is all this about?"

Banks held up his hand. "Wait a minute. I'm not making any accusations, I'm asking questions. It's my job."

"That's what you said last time," she said. "It didn't make me feel any better then, either. Don't you realize they're burying my husband tomorrow?"

"Yes I do, and I'm sorry. But if you want us to carry out a thorough investigation into his death, you've got to be prepared for some awkward questions. We don't find the truth by skating over the surface or by skirting difficult patches."

Mrs Steadman sighed. "I understand that. It's just . . . so soon."

"Did you see much of Penny after she left Helmthorpe?" Banks asked.

"Not much, no. Sometimes, if we were in the same place together—London, say—we'd have dinner together. But you could count the times on the fingers of one hand."

"What did she seem like during that period?"

"Like herself."

"She never seemed depressed, on drugs, strung out?"

"Not when we saw her."

"How well did your husband know Jack Barker?"

"Jack? I'd say they were fairly close. As close as Harry could be to someone who didn't share his enthusiasms."

"How long has Barker been living in Gratly?"

"I don't really know. Before us. Three or four years."

"How long had your husband known him?"

"They got to know each other over the past eighteen months. We'd met before, on our visits here, but it wasn't till we moved in that Harold really spent much time with the locals."

"Where did Barker come from?"

"He's from Cheadle, in Cheshire. But I think he lived in London for a while."

"And neither you nor your husband knew him when you first visited Gratly?"

"No. I don't think anyone in Helmthorpe or Gratly did. Why this fascination with the past, Chief Inspector?"

Banks frowned. "I'm not really sure, Mrs Steadman. I'm just trying to get a sense of the pattern of relationships: exits and entrances."

"And that's why you were asking me about Harry and Penny?"

"Partly, yes. Major Cartwright didn't seem too pleased about their friendship."

Mrs Steadman made a sound halfway between a sneeze and a guffaw. "The major! Everybody knows he's a crackpot. Mad as a March hare. She's all he's got, you know, and she did desert him for a long time."

"You know about the rumours?"

"Who doesn't? But I don't think you'll find anyone who takes them seriously these days."

"Forgiven and forgotten?"

"Something like that. People tire easily. Surely you don't think... the major?"

Banks didn't answer.

"You policemen have such wild imaginations," Emma Steadman went on. "What do you think happened? Do you think the major found out about this mythical affair and killed Harry to protect his daughter's virtue? Or do you think I did it in a jealous rage?"

"You couldn't have done it, could you? You were watching television with your neighbour at the time. We don't rely entirely on imagination, Mrs Steadman. I know it's a difficult period for you right now, and I apologize if I seem to be pestering you, but I'm simply trying to build up as complete a picture as I can of your husband and his circle. This is a difficult and vital time for us, too—memories fade and stories change with every hour that goes by. As yet, I don't know what's important and what isn't."

"I'm sorry for mocking you," Mrs Steadman apologized. "I know you have your job to do, but it is upsetting, you coming around talking about Harold having affairs and suggesting our marriage was in trouble. You must try and see it from my point of view. It's almost as if you're accusing me." She paused and smiled weakly. "He just wasn't that kind of man, and if you'd known him you'd see what I mean. If there's anything Harry was having an affair with, it was his work. In fact, sometimes I thought he was married to his work and having an affair with me."

She said this with good humour, not in bitterness, and Banks laughed politely. "I'm sure my wife thinks the same," he said, then called to Hatchley, who had turned to browse through the decimated bookshelves.

"I won't trouble you any further," Banks said at the door, "but there is one small piece of information you might be able to help me with."

"Yes?"

"Your husband taught at Leeds in the history department, am I right?"

She nodded. "Yes. That was his field."

"Who were his colleagues? Who did he spend most time with during your years there?"

She thought for a moment before replying. "We didn't socialize a great deal. Harry was too intent on making his career. But let me see...there was Tom Darnley, he was a fairly close friend, and Godfrey Talbot. I think he knew Harry at Cambridge, too. That's about all, except for Geoffrey Baynes, but he went off to teach in Winnipeg, in Canada, before Harry left. That's all I can think of."

"Thank you, Mrs Steadman," Banks said as the door closed slowly. "That'll do fine for a start. See you tomorrow."

They walked back the same way to the car, which was hot from standing in the sun most of the day, and drove back to Eastvale. Banks regretted not having the Cortina; the landscape inspired him to listen to music. Instead, Hatchley drove too fast and droned on about never having seen so many bloody books outside Gristhorpe's office. "Funny woman, that Mrs Steadman, don't you think?" he asked finally.

"Yes," Banks answered, staring at a pattern of six trees on a distant drumlin, all bent in the same direction. "She makes me uncomfortable, I've got to admit. I can't quite make her out."

SEVEN

I

Had an adventurous fell-walker found himself on top of Crow Scar at eleven o'clock that Thursday morning, he would have seen, to the south, what looked like two shiny black beetles followed by green and red aphids make their way slowly down Gratly Hill and turn right at the bottom into Helmthorpe village.

Pedestrians on High Street—locals and tourists alike—stopped as the funeral cortege crawled by. Some averted their gaze; others doffed their caps; and one or two, clearly visitors from afar, even crossed themselves.

Harold Steadman had been a believer because belief was, for him, inextricable from the men and the actions that had helped shape and mould the area he loved; therefore, the funeral was a traditional, if nowadays rare, graveside ceremony conducted by a visiting minister from Lyndgarth.

On the hottest day of the year thus far, the motley group stood uneasily around the grave as the Reverend Sidney Caxton recited the traditional words: "In the midst of life we are in death; of whom may we seek succour but Thee, O Lord.... Thou knowest, Lord, the secrets of our hearts; shut not Thy merciful ears to our prayer; but spare us, Lord most holy." He followed this, at Mrs Steadman's request, with the twenty-third Psalm: "The Lord is my shepherd; I shall not want. He maketh me to lie down in green pastures: he leadeth me beside still waters.... Yea, though I walk through the valley of the shadow of death, I will fear no evil: for Thou art with me; Thy rod and Thy staff they comfort me.... Surely goodness and mercy shall follow me all the days of my life: and I will dwell in the house of the Lord forever." It was a sombre pastoral and an eerily appropriate farewell for a man like Harold Steadman.

To Sally Lumb, representing Eastvale Comprehensive School along with Hazel, Kathy, Anne and Mr Buxton, the headmaster, it was a gloomy and uncomfortable affair indeed. For one thing, in the tasteful navy blue outfit her mother had made her wear, she was far too hot; her blouse was absolutely stuck to her back, and the beads of sweat that occasionally ran down her spine tickled like spiders.

Reverend Caxton took a handful of earth and cast it down on the coffin: "For as much as it hath pleased Almighty God of His great mercy to receive unto Himself the soul of our dear brother here departed; we therefore commit his body to the ground..."

To pass the time, Sally studied the others covertly. Penny Cartwright was the most striking. Dressed in black from head to foot, her pale face in stark contrast, she wore just enough make-up to hide the bags under her eyes from all but the most discerning of onlookers, and to highlight her tragic, romantic cheekbones. She really did look extraordinarily beautiful, Sally thought, but in an intense, frightening and overwhelming way. On the other hand, Emma Steadman, in a conservative, unfashionable, charcoal-grey suit, didn't look much. She could have done herself up a bit, at least for the funeral, Sally thought, mentally adding a touch of blush, eyeliner and a slash of lipstick. Immediately, though, she felt ashamed of herself for thinking such worldly thoughts at a time like this; after all, Mrs Steadman had always been nice to her.

"Earth to earth, ashes to ashes, dust to dust; in sure and certain hope of the Resurrection to eternal life, through our Lord Jesus Christ, who shall change our mortal body..."

Between the two grieving women stood Michael Ramsden, who looked, to Sally, rather like one of those doomed, tubercular young men in the black and white Gothic films her mother liked to watch on Channel Four. At Penny's other side was Jack Barker in a dark suit with a black armband. He really did look dashing and dangerous— that Errol Flynn moustache, the glint in his eyes—and Sally lost herself for a few moments in a swashbuckling fantasy.

The policeman, Banks, didn't detain her for long. True, he was handsome in a lean and bony kind of way, and the scar was mysterious, but she had seen his true colours and found them lacking. He was soft; he had lived in London, had adventure all around him, countless opportunities for heroism, and he had given it all up to retire to this godforsaken part of the county. Old before his time, obviously. Dr Barnes looked as grey and insignificant as ever, and Teddy Hackett wore an ostentatious gold medallion which glinted in the sun against the background of his black shirt whenever he shifted from foot to foot.

"...that it may be like unto His glorious body, according to the mighty working whereby He is able to subdue all things to Himself."

When Sally turned her attention back to the ceremony, it was all over. Slowly, as if reluctant to leave the deceased once and for all, the mourners edged away. Penny and Emma had their handkerchiefs out, and each hung onto the arm of the nearest man. In Penny's case, that was Jack Barker, and Sally noticed what an attractive couple they made. The others left in groups of two or three, and the policeman sidled away alone. Harold Steadman, lowered to rest, had become a part, in death, of the dale he had loved so much in life.

II

At one o'clock, after having spent an hour discussing their lack of progress with Constable Weaver in the Helmthorpe station, Banks sat alone at a white table in the back garden of The Dog and Gun sipping a pint of shandy. The tables around him were all full. Tourists chatted about their holidays, the weather, their jobs (or lack of them), and children buzzed around unhindered like the wasps that flitted from glass-rims to the remains of gateaux and sticky buns left on paper plates.

Banks didn't mind the squealing and the chatter; he was always able to shut out distracting background noise when he wanted to. He sat in his shirt-sleeves and fiddled with his pipe, dark suit jacket slung over the back of a chair. The pipe was a blasted nuisance. It kept going out or getting clogged up, and the bitter juices trickled down the stem onto his tongue. It suited him, though; it was a gesture towards establishing the kind of identity and image he wanted to develop and project.

A wasp droned onto his sleeve. He brushed it away. Across the dazzling river with its overgrown banks, the local club was playing cricket on a field of freshly mown grass. The slow pace of the game made it look like a Renaissance pavane. The harmony of white against green, the sharp crack of willow against leather, and the occasional smatterings of applause seemed to blend with the scent of the grass and enhance the sensation of peace. He rarely went to matches these days—and if he did, he got bored after a few overs—but he remembered the famous England cricketers of his school days: Ted Dexter, "Fiery" Fred Trueman, Ken Barrington, Colin Cowdrey; and the classroom games he had played with dice and paper, running his own county championships and Test Match series. The clichés about cricket were true, he reflected; there was something about the game that was essentially English—it made one feel that God was in his heaven and all was well with the Empire.

Far from it, though, he realized with a jolt. Beyond the pitch, the valley side sloped up gently at first, veined with dry-stone walls, then steepened and peaked into the long, sheer curve of limestone, Crow Scar, above which Banks actually fancied he could see crows wheeling. And about halfway between the pitch and the scar, as far as the eye's imperfect perspective could make out, was the spot where Steadman's body had been found.

Banks didn't like funerals, and in a way it seemed a pointless convention to attend the funerals of people he had never known. Not once had he caught a murderer that way: no graveside confessions, no mysterious stranger lurking behind the yew trees. Still, he did it, and when he probed his motives he found that it was because of a strange and unique bond he felt with the dead man, perhaps more intimate even than if he had known him. In a sense, Banks saw himself as the victim's appointed avenger, and, in an odd way, he worked together with the dead man to redress the balance of nature; they were co-workers of light against darkness. In this case, Steadman was his guide from the spirit-world: a silent and shapeless guide, perhaps, but present nonetheless.

Banks looked back at the game just in time to see the batsman swipe a badly paced off-spinner towards the boundary. The bowler found his length in the next two deliveries, though, and play slowed down as the batsman was forced to switch to defensive tactics. Banks, aided by the warm air, drifted back into reverie about his first year and a half in Yorkshire.

The landscape, it went without saying, he found beautiful. It was wild and rough, unlike the southern downs, but its scale inspired awe. And the people. Whatever he had heard about the stubborn intractability of the Yorkshire character, the gruffness, the slowness in taking to strangers, was all true to some extent, but like all generalizations it didn't do justice to the full reality. He had grown to appreciate the stoic humour, the quick wit and instinctive good sense, the friendliness beneath the crusty surface.

Banks also liked the feeling of being an outsider. Not a stranger, as he had been among the anonymous, international crowds of London, but an outsider. He knew he always would be, no matter how deep he put his roots.

Knocking out his pipe in exasperation, he tried to bring his mind to bear on the case again. It had the same sordid elements as any murder, but in such an environment it seemed even more of a blasphemy. The whole way of life in the small dale—the people, their priorities, beliefs and concerns—was different from that in London, or even in Eastvale. Gristhorpe had said that being an outsider would give him an advantage, a fresh perspective, but Banks wasn't too sure; he seemed to be getting nowhere fast.

He turned as a long shadow brushed across the white table and saw Michael Ramsden disappearing into the pub.

"Mr Ramsden!" he called after him. "A word, if you've got a moment to spare."

Ramsden turned. "Chief Inspector Banks. I didn't see you there."

Banks thought he was lying, but it meant nothing. As a policeman, he was used to being avoided. Ramsden perched at the very edge of the chair, indicating through his body language that he had no intention of staying for more than a minute or two.

"I thought you'd be at the funeral lunch," Banks said.

"I was. You know what those things are like: all that false humour and *bonhomie* to cover up what's really happened. And someone inevitably drinks too much and gets silly." He shrugged. "I left. Was there something you wanted to ask me?"

"Yes. Are you certain you didn't go out on Saturday night?"

"Of course I'm certain. I've already told you."

"I know, but I want to make absolutely sure. Not even for half hour or so?"

"You've seen where I live. Where would I go?"

Banks smiled. "A walk? A run? I've heard that writers get blocked sometimes."

Ramsden laughed. "That's true enough. But no, not me, not on Saturday, anyway. I was in all evening. Besides, Harry had a key; he would have let himself in and waited."

"Had he done that before?"

"Once, yes, when I had to work late at the office."

"He wouldn't, say, visit another friend in the area and come back later?"

"I don't think Harry really knew anyone else in the York area. Not well enough to drop in on, at least. Why do you want to know all this, if you don't mind me asking?"

"We need to know where Mr Steadman was between ten-fifteen and the time of death. But there's something else," Banks went on quickly, sensing Ramsden's restlessness. "I'd like to talk to you a bit more about the past—your relationship with Penny Cartwright."

Ramsden sighed and made himself more comfortable. A white-coated waiter passed by. "Drink?" Banks asked.

"Might as well, if you intend to keep me here a while. But it's all so long ago—I don't see how you expect me to remember. And I can't imagine what any of it has to do with Harry's death."

Banks ordered two pints of lager. "Just bear with me, that's all. Ten years ago," he went on, "was a very important time in your life. It was summer, and you were eighteen, all set for university, courting the prettiest girl in Swainsdale. Harold and Emma Steadman came to stay at your parents' guest house for a month, as usual. By all accounts that was a memorable summer—long walks, expeditions to local sites of interest. Surely you remember?"

Ramsden smiled. "Yes, of course I do, now you put it like that. I just hadn't realized it was so long ago," he said wistfully.

"Time does seem to pass quickly," Banks agreed. "Especially when you lose your sense of continuity, then look back. Anyway, it came to an end. Things changed. What happened between you and Penny?"

Ramsden sipped his lager and brushed away a troublesome wasp. "I've told you before. Like most teenage lovers, we just drifted apart."

"Did you ever regret it?"

"What?"

"The turn of events. Perhaps you could have been happily married to Penny now, and none of this would ever have happened."

"None of what? I fail to see the connection."

"Everything: Penny's adventures in the music business; your bachelorhood."

Ramsden laughed. "You make it sound like a disease, Chief Inspector. I may be a bachelor, but that doesn't mean I live a celibate life. I have lovers, a social life. I enjoy myself. As for Penny...well, it's her life. Who's to say things haven't turned out for the best for her, too?"

Banks tried to coax his pipe alight. A baby in a high chair two tables away started to cry. Its cheeks were smeared with strawberry jam. "Perhaps if Steadman hadn't come along, though, and spirited her away...?"

"What are you suggesting? That Harry and Penny were involved?"

"Well, he was older, more mature. You have to admit, it's a possibility. She certainly spent a lot of time with him. Isn't that why you split up? Didn't you argue about Steadman?"

Ramsden was at the edge of his seat again. "No, we didn't," he said angrily. "Look, I don't know who's been telling you all this, but it's lies."

"Did you split up because Penny wouldn't give you what you wanted? Maybe she was giving it to Steadman?"

This time Ramsden seemed on the point of getting up and hitting Banks, but he took a deep breath, scratched the back of his ear and smiled. "You know, you really are irritating," he said. "I should imagine people tell you things just to make you go away."

"Sometimes," Banks admitted. "Go on."

"Maybe there's some truth in the first part of your question. A man can only wait so long, as you probably know yourself. I was definitely ready, and Penny was a very beautiful girl. It's only natural, isn't it? We were both a bit naïve, scared of sex, but it didn't help that she kept saying no."

Banks laughed. "It certainly wouldn't," he said knowingly. "I dare say I'd have been climbing the walls myself. But why do you think she kept saying no? Was it something to do with Steadman? Or did she have another boyfriend?"

Ramsden thought, frowning, before he answered: "No, there wasn't another boyfriend, I'm sure of that. I think it was just a matter of morality. Penny was brought up to be a nice girl, and nice girls don't. As for Harry, I don't think he did what you're suggesting. I'm sure I'd have known, somehow. I suppose at times I was a bit peeved about how close they were. Not that I thought there was anything going on, mind, but they did spend a lot of time together, time she could have spent with me. Harry was so much more sure of himself than I was. I was shy and clumsy. So yes, I might have been a bit envious, but I didn't feel the kind of jealousy you have in mind."

"Oh? What kind of jealousy do I have in mind?"

"You know. The kind that eats away at you and ends in murder," he answered, deepening his voice for dramatic effect.

Banks laughed. Ramsden had nearly finished his drink and looked anxious to leave, but there were a couple more areas Banks wanted to probe. "What about her father, the major? Do you think he had anything to do with you two drifting apart?"

"I don't think so, no. As far as I know, he approved of me. He's a bit cracked, but he never really gave us any trouble."

"Did you ever get together with Penny again later? You were both in London at times, weren't you?"

"I suppose so. But I never saw her. Once it was over, that was it."

"What did you do while she was off with Steadman?"

"It wasn't the way you make it sound, Chief Inspector. Often we all went together; sometimes I just didn't want to go with them. I read a lot. I'd just discovered the pleasures of literature. My sixth-form English teacher, Mr Nixon, was a brilliant, inspiring man, and he managed to undo, in one year, all the damage that the others had done. For the first time, I could enjoy Shakespeare, Eliot, Lawrence, Keats, and the rest with a joy I'd not known before. What I'm saying is that I was a very romantic and introspective young man; I was happy enough to sit by a 'babbling brook' and read Wordsworth."

"When you weren't trying to get Penny into bed," said Banks, who had once, on Gristhorpe's recommendation, tried Wordsworth and found him an insufferable bore.

Ramsden blushed. "Yes, well...I was a normal adolescent; I don't deny that." He looked at his watch. "Look, I don't mean to seem rude, but I do have to get back to the office. Tell me, before I go, why this fascination with past events?"

"I'm not really sure," Banks said, reaching for his glass. "I'm just fol-lowing my instincts."

"And what do your instincts tell you?"

"That Harold Steadman's death wasn't a spur-of-the-moment affair; it was premeditated, and it probably had its roots in the past. You see, you were all together ten years ago—you, Penny Cartwright, her father, the Steadmans—and now you're all back in more or less the same place. Eighteen months after Steadman comes to live in Gratly, he's dead. Doesn't that strike you as odd?"

Ramsden brushed back his forelock, which this time actually had slipped over his eyes, then he drained his glass and stood up. "Put that way, I suppose it does," he said. "But I think your instinct is wrong. Things aren't the same as they were before. For one thing, there are other people around now, too. If you think Harry's death had any-thing to do with Penny, I suggest you follow your instinct to Jack Barker. He's been hanging around with her a lot lately, so I hear. Now, good day, Chief Inspector, and thanks for the drink."

Banks watched Ramsden thread his way between the white tables and turned his attention back to the cricket game just in time to see a wicket fall dramatically. The bails flew high in the air and the bowler threw up his arms and yelled, "Owzat!"

Banks thought about his talk with Ramsden and wondered if there was anything in what he'd said about Barker. "Men have died from time to time, and worms have eaten them, but not for love." So his daughter Tracy, playing the fair Rosalind, had said in *As You Like It*, which had been Eastvale Comprehensive's school play that term. But it wasn't true; many had killed and many had died for love. And Penny Cartwright was certainly the kind of woman to stir up such strong feelings.

Suddenly, the air roared and screamed as two F-111s from a nearby U.S. airbase shot overhead. They flew so low that Banks could almost see the pilots' faces. It was a common enough occurrence in the Dales; jet-bombers frequently ripped through the peaceful land-scape and shattered the idyll as they broke the sound barrier. On the hillside below Crow Scar, scared sheep huddled together and ran for the cover of a dry-stone wall. People at the table put their hands over their ears and screwed up their faces.

The planes broke the spell for Banks. There was paperwork to be done that afternoon. Grabbing his jacket, he drained his glass and left the cricketers to finish their game.

III

Dinner in the Banks household that evening was a lively affair. It seemed like ages since the family had all sat down together and enjoyed one of Sandra's delicious concoctions: chicken in tarragon and white-wine sauce. She had a wonderful knack of making the most inexpensive cuts of meat taste like gourmet creations. This skill, Banks thought, was characteristic of someone with inborn good taste and a poor, working-class background. All it took, said Sandra, clearly delighted with the compliments, was the right cooking method and a little care with the sauce.

Most of the conversation was taken up by the children's accounts of their day trip to York.

"The Minster was smashing," enthused Tracy, the bright four-teen-year-old with a passion for history. "Do you know, Daddy, there's more stained glass in there than in any other cathedral in Europe?"

Banks expressed interest and surprise. Architecture had not, so far, been one of his interests, but it was becoming more and more appealing. At the moment he was still reading up on the geology of the Dales.

"And the Five Sisters are simply stunning," Tracy went on.

"Five Sisters?" Banks asked. "In a minster?"

"Oh, Daddy," Tracy laughed. "You don't know anything, do you?

The Five Sisters are lancet windows in the north transept. They're made of grisaille glass. Thirteenth century, I think. And the Rose Window—"

"It was boring," cut in Brian, who all the while had been feeling left out. "Just a lot of old statues of dead kings and stuff. Junk, it was. Boring."

"You're just a philistine," Tracy retorted, pronouncing the word with both difficulty and authority. "I'll bet you didn't even notice that monument of Archbishop Scrope."

"Scrope? Who's he?" Banks asked. While sympathizing with Brian, he didn't feel justified in cheating Tracy out of her excitement. She was at an age now when one of her great thrills was to educate her parents, whom she thought dreadfully ignorant of the past that surrounded them. Very soon, Banks mused sadly, all that would be forgotten, at least for a few years, and life would be all clothes, pop music, make-up, hairstyles and boys.

"He was a rebel," Tracy informed him. "Henry the Fourth had him executed in 1405."

"Oh shut up with all them dates, clever-clogs," Brian burst out. "You think you know it all." And before Tracy could respond, he turned to his father and launched into his own account.

"We went on a boat down the river, Dad, and she felt seasick." He cast a look of pitying contempt at his sister. "And we passed this big chocolate factory. Me and some of the boys wanted to go on a tour but the teacher wouldn't let us. She just wanted to show us history and stuff and all those silly old narrow streets."

"The Shambles," Tracy interrupted. "And Stonegate and Petergate. Anyway, the chocolates would only have made you sick."

"It didn't need chocolates to make *you* sick, did it?" Brian taunted her.

"That's enough, Brian!" Sandra cut in. "Stop it, both of you!"

As so it went on; Brian sulked and Tracy scowled at him until they both went upstairs to watch television while Sandra cleared the table and Banks helped her with the dishes. Finally, still arguing, they were packed off to bed, and Banks suggested a nightcap.

"I've got a new job," Sandra said, pouring the scotch. "Well, not really new, just different."

Banks asked what it was. Sandra worked as a dentist's receptionist three mornings a week in Eastvale.

"Dr Maxwell's going on holiday, shutting up shop for three weeks, and Peggy Matthews—that's Dr Smedley's receptionist—is off at the same time, too."

"Not together, I hope?"

Sandra laughed. "No. Fine bedfellows they'd make, I'm sure. Maxwell's going to the Greek Islands and Peggy's off to Weymouth. Anyway, apparently Smedley asked if he could borrow me while the boss was away. Maxwell asked me and I said yes. It's all right, isn't it? I didn't think we had any plans."

"Yes, it's fine, if you want to. I can't really plan anything until this Steadman business is settled."

"Good. Smedley's a real perfectionist, so I hear. Especially when it comes to fitting caps and crowns, matching the colours and all that. They say he's one of the best in Yorkshire."

"You might get to meet the local gentry, then. Who knows?"

Sandra laughed. "Well, Peggy did say that Mrs Steadman goes there. She's having some root-canal work done. She's a bit of a local celebrity now."

"It's amazing, isn't it?" Banks said. "The husband gets murdered and people suddenly line up to look at the wife as if she were bloody royalty."

"It's only natural, though. We all have some morbid curiosity."

"Not me. Look," Banks said, "we haven't been out for a long time, and there's supposed to be a good folk singer on in Helmthorpe tomorrow. Do you fancy going?"

"Changing the subject, eh? Helmthorpe? Isn't that where the Steadmans live?"

"Yes."

"This isn't work, is it, Alan? It's not connected to the case?"

"Cross my heart. We'll just go and listen to some good folk music like we've done plenty of times before. Ask Harriet and David along, too."

"If they can get a sitter. It's such short notice. What about Jenny Fuller? Think she might like to come?"

"She's in France," Banks said. "Don't you remember? That wine-tasting tour. Took off as soon as term ended."

"Lucky her. All right, then, I'll call Harriet. As long as you promise it's nothing to do with work! I don't much fancy sitting there like a spare part while you grill some suspect."

"Scout's honour. And I'm not sure I like what you're implying. I don't grill people."

Sandra smiled. Banks moved closer and put his arm around her. "You know—" he began.

"Ssshhh . . ." Sandra put her finger to his lips. "Let's go to bed."

"What's wrong with the sofa?" Banks asked, and pulled her gently towards him.

IV

Sally Lumb was finding it difficult to get to sleep. She had put aside *Wuthering Heights* because her eyes were getting tired, but sleep just would not come.

First she thought of Kevin. She would have to give in soon or he'd be off after someone more experienced. He was right on the edge and she couldn't tease him for much longer. She didn't want to, anyway. The last time they'd been together, the day they saw Penny Cartwright, she had let him put himself close to her sex; she had felt his heat and hardness right at her very entrance and it made her tremble and go all wet, just like it said in the books. It had been cruel to stop him then, she knew, but they had no protection; she didn't want to get pregnant. There were ways around that, though. Next time . . .

Turning over and praying for sleep to come, she started thinking about the implications of what she had remembered that afternoon. Not the car on Saturday night—that was nothing—but something she hadn't fully perceived at the time that now had more sinister, far-reaching possibilities. It was her first real clue, and she had to decide what to do about it. She wouldn't go to the police, that was for certain—a proper fool she'd make of herself if she was wrong! Besides, she was already determined to solve the affair herself. Perhaps she might even become a heroine.

And the police were fools anyway; she could easily one-up them. That man from London had treated her like a silly child. And what had he done that was so wonderful? Given up an exciting metropolitan life for the boredom of Swainsdale, that's what he'd done. Lord, the man could have been working for Scotland Yard!

And so, as her mind tossed and turned towards sleep, the first step became clear. If she was right, then someone was in danger; a warning had to be given. She would arrange a secret meeting, and maybe after that, if her suspicions were proved correct, she could go about setting a trap. That thought worried her, as she really would be making herself vulnerable. But she could always rope Kevin in; he was a big, strong lad, and he'd do anything for her.

As Sally finally drifted into the dream-world that usually puzzled and irritated her, she could see the lights of London strung out before her like a diamond necklace. Why stop there? the dream insisted. And the images progressed, built up from magazine photographs and television programmes: *Vogue* models sashayed down the Champs Elysées, famous actresses stepped out of limousines under the neons of Sunset Strip and all the well-known television personalities she had ever seen chatted over cocktails at a party in Manhattan . . . But soon it all faded, and what she remembered in the morning was a rather absurd image of being in Leeds, a place she had visited several times on shopping expeditions with her mother. In the dream it felt like a foreign city. There were uniformed policemen all over the place, and Sally had to push her bicycle because she didn't have a licence—at least, not one that was valid in Leeds. She was there, she vaguely remembered, because she was searching for a bird, a white one that had flown from her garden, a vast dark expanse like a tilled field after rain. She didn't know if the bird had been her pet, her responsibility, or just a wild creature she had taken a fancy to, but it was important, and she was there in an alien familiar city pushing her bicycle among the policemen looking for it . . .

V

Banks slipped Finzi's choral setting of "Intimations of Immortality" into the car stereo as he turned off the A1 at the Wetherby roundabout and took the A58 to Leeds. It was eleven-thirty on Friday morning, just five days after the discovery of Steadman's body. Hatchley, under the weather on Thursday morning after his visit to Darlington, had checked Hackett's alibi thoroughly and found that it held. Barnes, too, was out of the running; though he was unmarried and had no-one to confirm that he went straight home after visiting Mrs Gaskell, his finances were in order and there had never been even the slightest hint of malpractice or wrong-doing of any kind during his twenty years as a doctor in Helmthorpe.

In his office earlier that morning, Banks had completed the mass of paperwork he had started the day before: transcripts of interviews, maps and timetables of people's movements, lists of unasked or unanswered questions. He had gone over the forensic evidence again, but found nothing new. Constable Weaver and his reinforcements were still asking questions around the village, the campsite and outlying farms, but the likelihood of their turning up new evidence after so long was fast diminishing.

The hushed choir entered, repeating the opening theme—"There was a time when meadow, grove, and stream . . ."—over the baritone's solo line, and Banks forgot his frequently distasteful job for a few moments. Finzi's music made Wordsworth's poem bearable.

The drive, which he took slowly, turned out to be quite pleasant once he'd left the Great North Road and its never-ending stream of lorries. It was the quickest way, the same route as he had taken on his last trip to Leeds to interview a pawnbroker in connection with a series of robberies. But that had been a grey, rainy day in late October. Now it was summer and he drove through the kind of peaceful, green countryside one so often finds close to large English cities.

Banks puffed at his pipe as Finzi played on, not bothering to relight it after the second time it went out, and soon found himself in the Seacroft area. He had to concentrate hard on directions; the tower blocks all looked much the same, and there were few landmarks to go by. He came out finally through an underpass near the city centre and parked close to the Town Hall. From there, he could see the high white tower of the library building, something Gristhorpe had told him about that morning in his potted history of the city and its architecture.

Banks had no fixed ideas about how to approach the professors; he intended to play it by ear. He had called earlier and arranged to have lunch with Darnley and Talbot in a pub near the university. Though term was officially over, they still travelled to their offices almost every day to carry on with their research or simply to get out from under their wives' feet. Darnley, to whom Banks had spoken, seemed quite excited by the prospect of a chat with the police, or so he had said in a rather detached way, as if he were discussing the mating habits of lemurs.

Banks still had an hour to kill, so he decided to take Gristhorpe's advice and take a look at the Town Hall. It was an impressive Victorian edifice, complete with fluted columns, huge domed roof, clock and a pair of lions guarding the entrance by the broad flight of stone steps. The stone, sandstone by the look of it, seemed light and clean. Gristhorpe had told him that it had been sandblasted a few years ago, as few such structures had withstood a hundred years or more of industry without turning black.

Banks admired the bulk of the place and the bold, classical lines of its design. He felt he could grasp, just by looking, some of the civic pride that had gone into its construction. Queen Victoria herself had attended the grand opening. She must have spent a lot of time opening buildings, Banks reflected.

He ventured inside past the statues of Victoria and Albert in the foyer and into the main hall, which appeared to have been recently restored. Enormous pillars of what looked like marble streaked with pink, green and blue were spaced along the walls, and the ceiling was divided into brightly coloured square panels, gilded around their edges. Mottoes and proverbs beloved of the pious Victorians adorned the high places: EXCEPT THE LORD BUILD THE HOUSE, THEY LABOUR IN VAIN THAT BUILD IT; EXCEPT THE LORD KEEP THE CITY, THE WATCHMAN WATCHETH BUT IN VAIN; WEAVE THE TRUTH WITH TRUST; and LABOUR OMNIA VINCIT. Behind the orchestra stood a majestic pipe-organ.

Banks glanced at his watch and walked out slowly; his footsteps echoed in the silence. Yes, it was impressive, and he could begin to see what Steadman found so fascinating about northern history.

But he also remembered Hackett's outburst about false, romanticized views of the past. The wealthy city officials and merchants had gone to great trouble to make sure that Queen Victoria's route avoided the more squalid areas of the city: row upon row of over-crowded back-to-backs with leaky roofs and damp walls, where the nameless masses lived. It was from their labours and in their name, the name of civic pride, that such glories as the Town Hall were built, yet they were condemned to live in squalor, and then accused of becoming animals. There had even been one man, a chemist, according to Gristhorpe, who had perfumed the air outside his shop as the royal progress passed. It all depended on what side you were on, Banks thought, on what your perspective was.

He consulted his pocket map and walked up between the Town Hall and the library, carried on along Caverley Street past the Civic Hall, a white building with twin pointed towers and colourful gardens, past the General Infirmary and Leeds Polytechnic and into the outer reaches of the university campus. Finally, he came to a quadrangle surrounded by modern, office-style buildings. It was a long way from the dreaming spires of Oxford and Cambridge, but Leeds was supposed to be a redbrick university, even if there were no red bricks in sight.

He found Darnley's office in the History Department with the help of an angular, bespectacled secretary. After a quick, firm handshake, Darnley was ready to take off for a pub lunch.

"Talbot's going to meet us there," he explained. "He's got a session with one of his doctoral students right now."

He led Banks across a dirt path behind the building and onto a narrow, cobbled street. The pub was actually part of a hotel, and it stood back from the road at the end of a short driveway. As it was such a warm, sunny day, they sat at one of the outside tables.

Darnley was a tall man: about forty, well built and in good shape. He had a trace of a northern accent and did not seem at all the absent-minded professor type that Banks had expected. His short brown hair was neatly combed, and although his suit seemed half a size too big, it was of good quality. It had probably been a perfect fit when he bought it, Banks guessed, but like many men of his age fearing heart attacks and other plagues of the sedentary life, he had begun to exercise.

The two men sipped draught Guinness, squinting in the bright sun, and Banks laid his pipe, tobacco and lighter on the table.

"Aha, a pipe-smoker, I see," Darnley noted. "Touch of the Maigret, eh? Thought of taking it up myself, but it's too much trouble. Wasted years trying to stop smoking, cutting down, switching to milder brands, and in the end I found the only way to bloody well stop was cold turkey."

"It can't have been as easy as you make it sound," Banks said, stuffing his pipe with rubbed flake and tamping it gently.

"No, no it wasn't." Darnley laughed. "I had a few relapses. But I've been playing a lot of squash and tennis lately and running a few miles each day. You'd be surprised how that kind of thing puts you off smoking. You'd never believe it, but a year or so ago I was over-weight, drinking too much—ugh!"

"Doctor's orders?"

"Told me point blank. 'Go on like you are doing, old chap, and I'll give you another ten years at most.' It was a toss-up which would go first—heart, liver or lungs. Anyway, he said if I shaped up the sky's the limit. Well, not in so many words, but I got the point." He watched Banks light his pipe. "Still," he said, "I suppose you need props in your business. False sense of security and all that."

Banks smiled and admitted it helped. He liked the look of curiosity and intelligence in Darnley's eyes.

"I hope you don't think you need it with me? I mean, I'm not a suspect, am I?" He was smiling, but the tension showed in the tight set of his lips.

"Not yet," Banks replied, returning his gaze.

"Touché. You mean if I start to put myself forward as one, all offers are welcome?"

"I shouldn't worry about it," Banks assured him. He was still trying to work out the best approach to this edgy, intelligent man whose quick, playful exterior no doubt masked a mind like a steel trap and covered up a complex, perhaps even devious personality.

He decided to play along a little longer, certain that the arrival of Talbot would alter the light-hearted mood. "You might as well tell me where you were last Saturday night, though," he asked.

Darnley looked at him, bright eyes twinkling, but hard. "Do you know, Chief Inspector, I have no alibi at all for last weekend. I had a lot of work to do so I stayed in all Saturday evening marking examination papers and reading a new account of the Peterloo massacre. Of course, my wife was at home too, but I don't suppose she counts, does she?"

Banks laughed. "I wouldn't know till I asked her, would I?"

"You're a canny man, as the Scots say. No, I don't suppose you would."

"Why weren't you at the funeral yesterday?"

"Wasn't invited, was I? Neither of us. Actually, I didn't even know about it. I only knew about Harry because I read it in the *Yorkshire Evening Post*."

"You'd lost touch?"

"Sort of, yes."

After a little more banter and a good draught of stout, Darnley seemed to relax more. Trying to establish the conversation as one between professionals, Banks asked the professor about his job: "I suppose you need props, too? It can't be easy standing up there alone in front of a hundred or so students and just talking for an hour."

"Put like that, it does sound rather awful," Darnley conceded. "You get used to it, of course, but you're right, there's always a bit of stage-fright till you get going. I've always got my notes to fall back on, though. No teacher worth his salt dries up in front of a class. You can always waffle and students would never know the difference. Sometimes I think I could tell them that Adolf Hitler was one of the heroes of twentieth-century politics and they'd just write it down without question. But props...yes...one tends to find a position one is comfortable in. Funny thing, that. Some people pace back and forth, some hunch over the lectern, and others sit on the edge of a desk and fold their arms. One chap I knew always used to play with his keys while he was lecturing. Trouble was, they were in his trouser pocket and the students all thought he was playing with himself."

They both laughed. "What about Harry Steadman?" Banks asked casually.

Darnley squinted. "Harry was good," he answered. "It's true we've been out of touch and I've not seen much of him since he left, but we were quite close at one time, and I was sorry to hear about his death. I'd say we were colleagues rather than friends, if there's a difference. He was exceptionally bright—but I suppose you know that already.

Ambitious, yes, but only in his field. He genuinely believed in what he was doing—teaching, research, breaking new ground. He thought it all had some real value for society. And, believe me, that's rare these days. There's so much cynicism around in education, especially as the government doesn't seem to set much store in us any more."

Banks nodded. "It's the same with crime. You're fighting a losing battle, or so it seems most of the time, and that's no good for anyone's professional pride."

"But at least the government believes in your value: pay rises, recruitment, modern equipment."

"True," Banks agreed. "But it's all long overdue." He didn't want to get sidetracked into an argument, especially as he had many objections to the way the government seemed to look upon the police as a private army of well paid bully-boys to pit against people with genuine grievances and a constitutional right to air them. A copper with humanist, socialist leanings would be a bit hard for Darnley to take, he thought. Besides, he was a detective—CID, a paid thinker— and he didn't have to go on "crowd control" bashing the bonces of the proletariat.

"I'm envious," Darnley said. "That's all. I just wish we could get a larger slice of the cake, too. Academics are very big on pride as well, believe me. Harry was a good lecturer and he always managed to stimulate enthusiasm among his students. That's hard to do these days when you're in competition with television, video games and God knows what. Stop me if I'm beginning to sound too much like a good reference for him, but it's true. Most of all, he loved research, real field work, and that's why he left. When he found himself with enough money to do as he pleased, that's exactly what he did. Some chaps might have packed it all in and buggered off to the south of France for a life of idleness, sin and luxury, but not Harry. He was a dedicated man."

At this point they were joined by a smaller, pudgy man, bald except for a few wisps of grey hair above his ears. He had a deeply ingrained frown in his broad brow and a tiny, pursed mouth that gave him, overall, a surly and miserly look. His cultured voice was surprisingly soft, and Banks wondered how he managed to get across to a large room full of students. He proved rather taciturn, and after they had ordered roast-beef sandwiches and another round of stout, he simply sat and listened as Banks and Darnley went on talking.

"I think I've got a fairly clear picture of Mr Steadman's professional life now," Banks said. "It's something everyone seems to agree on—bright, dedicated, obsessed even."

At this Talbot tut-tutted, and when he spoke his voice was redolent of Cambridge quadrangles, effete dons and afternoon glasses of Amontillado. "Surely, er, Chief Inspector, an obsession is something we might define as intrinsically *unhealthy*, wouldn't you say? I don't mean to nit-pick over semantics, of course, but one must admit that the term has definite connotations of mental imbalance. Harold Steadman was most certainly not unbalanced; therefore, he was not obsessed." And all the time he talked he frowned, as if the usage really upset him.

"Sorry, Professor Talbot," Banks apologized. "I didn't mean to imply anything as drastic as that. No, I realize that there's a difference between dedication and obsession. What I'd like to know is whether he found time for other pursuits. Social life, for example. Did he mix, go to parties, drink?"

Talbot returned in moody silence to his drink, perhaps to contemplate the exact OED definition of "obsessed" as if such eccentricities as "social life" were best left to the lower classes.

"Do you know, Godfrey," Darnley said cheerfully, oblivious to his colleague's disdain, "the chief inspector might not be far wrong." He turned to Banks and winked. "Yes, Harry liked a few drinks now and then, and he went to the occasional faculty party. But he was never really at ease socially—especially when he was out of his element, so to speak, when there was nobody to talk to about his field. He didn't care much for sports, never watched television, and he certainly wasn't a woman-chaser."

"Do you mean he was uncomfortable in the presence of non-academics?"

"Oh no, not that at all. I didn't mean to give you that impression. Harry certainly wasn't an academic snob. As a matter of fact, he invited me up to Gratly once, shortly after he'd moved, and we spent a very pleasant evening in a dingy local with a thriller writer and some other chaps. No, Harry would talk to anybody. That was one of his beefs against academic life, the rampant intellectual snobbery. What I mean is that his heart was in his work, and his work was basically to do with people, so he enjoyed their company. There's a strong human element in his field, you know. It's not all abstract. He was interested in ordinary people, their background and ways of life. I suppose you know that his main fields were Industrial Archaeology and the Roman occupation? But he also loved folk music, local lore, things like that. He was fascinated by the history of trade unions, the early working-class radicals. So you could say that Harry was quite at home with the common man, he'd just no time for petty chit-chat like you so often get at parties. He always tended to edge conversations in the direction of his interests."

Talbot nodded in grudging agreement and lit a cigarette. "Let me put it this way, Chief Inspector Banks," he said in a tone of professor to lowly student. "If you were to—if you were able to—sit right down now and talk to Harold Steadman, he would probably begin by asking you about your job, how you feel about it, just to get things going. He would discover where you come from and find out about your family background. Then, depending on how interesting he found all that, he would either question you further—say, if your father had been a union man or a farm-labourer in the Dales—or he would proceed to tell you about the history of your area, how it fits in with the rest of the country, what the Romans did there, and so on. People usually enjoyed his company. He could sense when he was becoming a bore and would usually stop and listen politely for a while. Of course," Talbot added, with a deft flick of ash, "if he found you boring, then you wouldn't get much out of him. Am I right, Darnley?"

Darnley nodded.

"What about Mrs Steadman?" Banks asked. "Did you see much of her when she was in Leeds?" He addressed the question to Talbot, who seemed to have become quite garrulous, but it was Darnley who answered.

"At first we did, yes. Quite a pretty little thing, really. Naturally, they were in a new environment and wanted to meet people and settle in. But like many faculty wives, she soon withdrew. It's common enough, believe me. My wife, for example, wouldn't be seen dead at an academic gathering these days. It bores them, you see. And they let themselves go over the years. You know, not bothering much about their appearance any more."

Banks couldn't be sure whether the professor was talking about his own wife or about Emma Steadman.

The conversation moved on to generalities again, with Darnley doing most of the entertaining, and Banks soon realized he wasn't going to learn anything more of value.

When he left, he carried away with him the image of a young couple—perhaps not unlike Sandra and himself in the old days—newly married, the husband beginning what was likely to be a distinguished academic career. There were long summer holidays in Gratly at the Ramsden house; there was the young ambitious Michael courting Penny, the flower of the dale; it was pure peace and innocence with nothing but a bright future ahead for them all.

For Steadman, things seemed to get better and better; for Emma, there was a withdrawal from the dull academic life into domestic boredom; for Penny, a wild exciting fling in the fast lane that left her isolated and cynical, cut off from her roots; and for Ramsden, a steady advance up the publishing ladder and a return to his beloved north. It all sounded so idyllic, but one of them was dead. What had gone wrong, and why?

An hour later he was no closer to the solution, but his spirit felt lighter, despite the clouds, as he drove into the Dales countryside and sang along with Britten's versions of old English folk songs.

VI

They were sipping Coke and talking about boys under the scornful, lascivious eyes of the old Greek. Hazel Kirk had had her first date with Terry Preston, son of the local grocer, the previous night, and she was titillating her friends with an account of her attempt to keep his wandering hands from her most private parts. Once in a while she would blush while describing the indefinable feelings she had when she failed in her task.

But Sally Lumb, usually so interested—not to mention

condescending—during such discussions, seemed preoccupied. The others noticed, but Hazel, for one, was not going to be done out of her moments of glory simply because madam was sulking.

Anne Downes, perhaps more sensitive to mood, and certainly less interested in boys and their inexplicable desires, waited patiently until Kathy Chalmers had stopped giggling and tried to change the subject.

"They haven't caught him yet, you know," she announced, adjusting her glasses on the bridge of her nose.

"Who?" Hazel asked abruptly, annoyed at being dragged away from other, more important thoughts.

"The killer, of course. Who else? The man who killed Mr Steadman."

"How do you know it was a man?" Hazel asked. It was a question she'd heard on countless television programmes.

"Stands to reason, doesn't it," Anne snorted. "It'd have to be a pretty strong woman to slug him and carry him all the way up that field below Crow Scar."

"Mrs Butterworth could have done it," Kathy chipped in. They all giggled. Mrs Butterworth was the butcher's wife, an enormous red-faced woman who towered above her meek, hunched husband.

"Don't be silly," Anne said, allowing herself a smile. "Why should she do it? Besides, the effort would probably give her a heart attack."

"Jimmy Collins told me that the police have been talking to Penny Cartwright and the major," Kathy said. "He said the old man didn't give them much time."

"How would Jimmy Collins know?" Anne asked.

"He was in the shop downstairs. 'Where there's a will, there's a way,' my mother always says. I think Penny did it. I think her and Mr Steadman were having a torrid love affair and when she wanted him to leave his wife and marry her he wouldn't do it so she killed him."

"Don't be so stupid," Anne said. "If it was really like that she'd have killed Mrs Steadman, not him."

That silenced Kathy, but Hazel picked up the thread. "Well if that wasn't why," she said, "there could have been plenty of other reasons. Everybody knows she went away for ages and took drugs and was pro—prom—"

"Promiscuous?" suggested Anne.

"Yes, promiscuous, clever-clogs that's what I said. Maybe she had his baby or he knew something about her past. They've known each other a long time, you know."

The others were silent, taking it all in. "You might be right about the last bit," Anne allowed, "but she wouldn't kill him just because she had his baby, would she? I think it was Jack Barker."

"Why would he do it?" Kathy asked.

"Maybe he was just doing research for his next book," Hazel joked.

"And maybe he's in love with Penny Cartwright and wanted to get Mr Steadman out of the way so he could have her all to himself," Anne said. "And there's another thing—I heard the police gave Teddy Hackett a nasty time the other day."

"He certainly looked a little pale when I saw him," Hazel added.

"My dad heard them arguing a couple of weeks ago—Hackett and Mr Steadman," Anne said.

"But they can't think he did it," Hazel reasoned, "or they'd have arrested him in custody by now. I bet he's got a skin-tight alibi."

"It's 'watertight,' you fool," Anne laughed. "And he can't be 'arrested in custody,' only 'in custody.'"

"All right, Miss Know-it-all. So what?"

"I wonder who she was," Kathy said, "Teddy Hackett's alibi."

And they all laughed. To them, Hackett, with his droopy moustache, receding hairline, gold medallions and beer belly hanging over his fancy belt buckle, was a figure of ridicule, the male equivalent of mutton dressed up as lamb.

"What do you think, Sally?" Anne asked. "I must say, you're very quiet today."

"I've got a few ideas of my own," Sally replied slowly and quietly. "But I've got to check them out."

And with that, she walked out leaving them all gaping again, not knowing whether to believe her or not.

EIGHT

I

By seven-thirty, the lounge bar of The Dog and Gun was almost full. It was a long, narrow room with only one vaguely demarcated aisle down the centre. The audience was clustered around small tables, and a white-jacketed waiter had been employed so that people wouldn't have to move about to get drinks. He moved awkwardly among the crowd, a tray full of black and amber drinks tottering menacingly at shoulder height. The jukebox had been unplugged for the evening, and piped folk music played softly enough to make conversation easy. Dim wall-lights gave the room a dark orange glow, and at the bar the brass rail, polished hand-pumps and coloured bottles by the mirrors gleamed. At the far end of the room was a low, wooden platform, too makeshift to be dignified with the name of a stage, and on it stood a couple of microphones on crossbeam stands, two large speakers, three stools and an amplifier with its red light on.

Banks and Sandra sat with Harriet and David about halfway down the room on the right-hand side. Harriet, pixyish in looks, animated and intelligent in character, drove a mobile library around the more remote Dales villages. Her husband, David, was an assistant bank manager in Eastvale, and if truth be told, Banks found him a bit of a bore.

David had clearly said something that required more than a mere nod in response, but Banks had been watching a fresh-faced young camper, probably under eighteen, who was already displaying the effects of too much alcohol in his desire to show off to his girlfriend.

"Pardon?" Banks said, cupping his hand to his ear.

"I said, I suppose you know all about computers yourself, being on the force," David repeated. "I'm afraid I've been boring you."

"Not at all," lied Banks. He tamped down the tobacco in his pipe and lit it in defiance of Sandra's sharply aimed frown. "No, not at all. But yes, I know a little bit about computer languages." That old-fashioned phrase, "on the force," made him smile. It was an odd way of looking at his job, he thought. On what force? The forces of law and order, no doubt. "May the force be with you." The force of good against evil? It was a stiff, dry phrase that hardly did the job justice.

While telling David what little he did know about the subject, Banks noticed Penny Cartwright come in with Jack Barker. The two of them made their way to the front, where chairs had been saved for them. Shortly afterwards, a nervous, spotty young man took the stage, tapped the microphones, said "testing" in each one three or four times, then welcomed everyone to folk night at The Dog and Gun. One by one, the conversations all died down until all that could be heard was the barman ringing up sales and the steady humming of the amplifier. The microphone shrieked when the young man got too close, and he backed off quickly, pulling a face. Banks couldn't catch the names of all the scheduled performers, but he gathered that Penny was set to sing two forty-minute sets, the first starting at eight-thirty and the second at about ten-fifteen.

After more notices and introductions, a duo clambered onto the stage. The boy had only a guitar, but the girl spread several ancient and obscure stringed instruments on the floor around her. First they launched into a Bob Dylan song, and what they lacked in talent, Banks thought, they made up in enthusiasm. After the applause, the young man made jokes about the notes he had missed and apologized for the rawness of his technique. It worked: after that, the audience wanted him to succeed and most people were willing to overlook the rough edges.

The girl said nothing, but concentrated on tuning what looked to Banks like a mandolin. She played extremely well on the next number, a medley of old English dances. On the whole, the audience was respectful and attentive, but there were occasional, unavoidable interruptions as the waiter passed by and more drinks were ordered. Someone told the inebriated young camper to shut up, too.

Banks and David seemed to have settled into buying rounds, the two men drinking pints of bitter and the women lager and lime. Banks had to watch his intake because he didn't want to appear even slightly intoxicated in the village where he was conducting a murder investigation. Two pints in an hour and a half wasn't at all bad, he told himself, but it was only just after eight o'clock. He was aware that he tended to speed up towards closing-time.

The first intermission came and people started making their ways to the toilets and the bar. As he walked down the narrow aisle, Jack Barker noticed Banks's party and came over.

"Good evening," he said, extending his hand. "What a surprise to find you here. I'd no idea you were a folkie." There was just enough of a twinkle in his eye to make the irony apparent. "Mind if I join you for a moment?" He grabbed a nearby chair and pulled it up before Banks could object. "Is it just Miss Cartwright you've come to hear?"

"Actually, it's Ms Cartwright," Banks corrected him. "And yes, I've heard she's very good." His tone was brusque; he wished Barker would go away.

"You're in for a real treat, Chief Inspector, a real treat. People come from miles away to hear Penny Cartwright, you know. She's got a solid reputation in these parts, especially since she gave up fame and fortune to return to her roots. People appreciate that."

From what Banks had heard, appreciation wasn't quite the word for the gossip that surrounded Penny's return to her roots, but he kept quiet. Barker obviously wanted to show off, and, short of being rude, there was no way to stop him. Sandra returned from the Ladies and looked at Barker curiously. There was no escape, Banks realized, cursing himself; he would have to introduce them.

Barker favoured the women with what Banks suspected was a well-practised Clark Gable smile.

"Delighted," he said theatrically, taking Sandra's hand. "I never imagined a policeman's wife could be so charming and so beautiful." Banks was irritated; David simply looked on, a vacant grin on his face.

It was not only Barker's charm and social finesse that annoyed Banks. It was all very well socializing in the community, but to be seen with his wife openly fraternizing with a suspect jarred against his deepest instincts as a detective. It made him feel conspicuous, for one thing, and that was a feeling he disliked. Gristhorpe's advice— get in there and let them talk to you—was all very well, but a line had to be drawn. He was off duty, and the whole thing was just too pally for his taste. He sat sucking on his dead pipe, glowering and contributing monosyllables only when necessary.

"How do you manage to fit in here?" Sandra asked after Barker had told her his occupation. "Aren't writers usually regarded with a good deal of suspicion?"

Barker nodded. "True. They didn't like me being here at first," he replied. "Not one bit. You're right—people don't trust writers in small communities, and they've good reason not to. Some communities have had bad experiences with chaps who live among them, fit in, then go and write devastating critiques, hardly even bothering to disguise names and identities. It's like the way some Indians see photographers—people who steal their souls. Quite right, too, in my opinion. The kind of writers they have in mind are unscrupulous. They give us all a bad name."

"But don't you think writers have to be a little ruthless?" Harriet asked. "Especially if they're to tell the truth."

"Perhaps. But the ones I'm talking about accept your hospitality, then strip you naked on the page. Some writers even worm their way into people's confidence and set up situations, manipulate events just to see how their 'characters' will react. I knew one chap, for example, who used to throw regular parties. This was in London. Real lavish dos, they were, no expense spared—champers, single malt Scotch, beluga caviar, quail—more than anyone could hope to devour in an evening. When everyone got sozzled and started arguing, crying, or pawing other people's partners, there he was, sober as a judge, sitting in a corner making mental notes. It took people a long time to figure out what was going on—after all, they were having a good time—but sure enough, they'd appear, thinly disguised, in stories published in magazines, and their friends and colleagues would recognize them. A couple of marriages broke up, reputations were destroyed. All in the name of 'art.' After a while, attendance dropped dramatically."

"What happened to him?" Harriet asked, sitting at the edge of her chair.

Barker shrugged. "Moved on, I suppose. I've no idea where he is now. Pastures new. He still publishes regularly."

"And is that what you do, Mr Barker?" Sandra asked. "Move in on people and steal their souls."

Barker laughed. "Please, call me Jack," he said, and Banks felt his upper lip begin to curl. "No, that's not what I do at all. At first, everyone was suspicious of me, but then they always are like that with incomers, as they call us. After a while, out of curiosity I suppose, someone read a couple of my books, then someone else, and their comments got around. As soon as everyone realized I wrote hardboiled private-eye stories set in southern California in the thirties, they decided I wasn't a threat. Believe it or not, I even have a few fans here."

"I know," Harriet said. "I've carried enough of your books around in the mobile library."

Barker honoured her with a smile. "As soon as they get to know you're harmless," he went on, "you're as close to being accepted as you'll ever be. It was the same with Harry."

"What about Harry?" Banks asked, trying to sound casual but failing miserably. Sandra frowned at him for being a killjoy.

"All I meant," Barker explained, "is that Harry was a writer too, in his way, but nobody ever worried about him because he wrote about the Romans and old lead mines. I mean, only people like Penny and Michael Ramsden were interested. That stuff's as dry as dust to most people." He looked back at the ladies and smiled again, clearly hoping to get off on another track.

"Do you know Ramsden well?" Banks asked, unmoved by Barker's discomfort and Sandra's piercing glances. Harriet and Sandra began to chat between themselves, and David looked on, lost.

"I've met him," Barker replied curtly.

"What do you think of him?"

"Pleasant enough fellow," he said, looking to the women for support in his levity. "But you can hardly expect a writer to say nice things about an editor, can you? I spend two days working on a fine descriptive paragraph, and my editor wants it cut out because it slows the action."

"Ramsden's not your publisher, though, is he?" Banks persisted.

"Good Lord, no. He only deals with academic stuff."

"Did you know about Ramsden and Penny Cartwright?"

"That was years ago. What on earth are you getting at?"

"Just trying to sort out the tangle of relationships," Banks answered, smiling. "That's all."

"Look, they're starting again," Barker said, rising. "Please excuse me." He gave a brief bow to Harriet and Sandra, then made his way back to the front. It was almost eight-thirty. As the lights dimmed, Banks saw him talking to Penny and glancing back over his shoulder. The last thing he noticed before it got too dim was Barker whispering in Penny's ear and Penny looking behind her and laughing.

As the master of ceremonies began his rambling and incoherent introduction, Sandra leaned over to Banks. "You were a bit sharp with him, weren't you?" she said. "Was it really necessary? You did promise we were having a social evening."

Banks muttered a sullen apology and busied himself with his pipe. It wasn't a new situation, the job interfering with personal life, but it never ceased to cause friction. Perhaps Sandra had expected the move to change all that. A new life—what rubbish, Banks thought. Different landscapes, same old people with the same old failings. He gestured to the waiter to bring another round. Bugger it, let someone else drive home. It was a social occasion, after all, he reminded himself ironically.

Penny Cartwright took the stage to much applause and several loud whistles from the back of the room. Banks was still furious with Barker for being so damn charming and witty, and with Sandra for encouraging him and with himself for spoiling it. He attacked the fresh pint of bitter with angry gusto and glared at his pipe as if that meagre engine were at the root of all his troubles. It had gone out yet again and he was sick to death of tamping, emptying, cleaning, scraping and relighting it.

Penny began with an unaccompanied ballad called "Still Growing." It was a sad tale about an arranged marriage between a woman and a boy on the edge of manhood. The husband died young and the widow lamented, "O once I had a sweetheart, but now I have none. / Death has put an end to his growing." The story was simply and economically told, and Banks found himself entering into the music as he had with opera, his recent irritation wrapped up and put away in a dim corner of his mind. Her voice had both passion and control—it was that of a survivor singing about the lost and the less fortunate with honest sympathy. She was an alto, pitched lower than Banks had expected, husky on the low notes but pure and clear in the higher range.

Banks clapped loudly when she finished, and Sandra turned to him with raised eyebrows and a smile of appreciation. Other songs in the same traditional folk vein followed, and sometimes Penny accompanied herself on guitar while another young woman playing the flute or the fiddle joined her. Mixed in with the stories of demon lovers and forbidden affairs were light-hearted jigs and reels and sensational broadside ballads, like "The Murder of Maria Marten."

Despite his enjoyment of the music, Banks found his mind wandering back to Barker's reaction at the mention of Michael Ramsden. There had seemed to be a dislike beyond the general lack of love between writers and publishers. Ramsden had been a close friend of Steadman's and had known Penny Cartwright since childhood. Did they still see each other, despite what they said? Was Barker simply jealous? And if he was jealous of Ramsden, wasn't he also likely to have felt the same way about Steadman?

Banks looked at Penny and noticed Barker's finely chiselled, handsome profile in silhouette. He was in love with her, of course. Ramsden had been right to suggest that possibility. And who could blame him? Her beauty was radiant; her talent was moving. But she and Ramsden had parted. Of course, it had happened years ago, before she had fully blossomed, and it could only have been puppy love. Still, such events endure in small communities. Perhaps to some of the more shrewish local gossips Penny would always be known as a wayward lass who lost that nice Michael Ramsden who had gone on and done so well for himself. And what did Ramsden really feel about their parting?

Banks laid his pipe to rest in the ashtray and Penny announced "Little Musgrave and Lady Barnard," the last song of the set.

II

At about nine o'clock, Sally Lumb left the house on Hill Road. Because it was Friday, her mother was at bingo in Eastvale with Mrs Crawford, and her father was down in the public bar of The Bridge playing in a local darts match. They wouldn't be back till about eleven o'clock, which gave her plenty of time. There would be no awkward questions to answer.

Despite the gathering clouds, it was a warm evening: a bit too hot and sticky, if anything. Sally knew from experience that such signs meant a storm was on its way. She walked down the hill and turned left, by The Bridge, onto High Street. It was a quiet time in Helmthorpe; most people were either in the pubs or sat glued to the idiot-box in their living-rooms. There'd be nothing much stirring until closing-time unless a party of campers got too rowdy at The Hare and Hounds disco and Big Cyril had to chuck them out.

She walked on down the street and paused outside The Dog and Gun. The front door was open and she could hear singing from inside. Penny Cartwright, by the sound of it. Sally had heard her before but hadn't known she was singing in the village that evening. She looked at her watch. Plenty of time. The words of the song drifted out on the humid air:

> "A grave, a grave," Lord Barnard cried,
>   "To put these lovers in;
> But bury my lady on the top
>   For she was of noble kin."

With the familiar tune in her mind, Sally walked on, pausing for a moment to listen to the broad beck flowing under the bridge at the eastern end of High Street. She quickened her pace and, leaving the road, struck out up the long, wild southern slope of the dale, past where she and Kevin had seen Penny the other day. She had an appointment to keep, a warning to give. Everything would be sorted out soon.

III

During the intermission, Penny Cartwright walked by Banks on her way out of the pub and flashed him a cool smile of acknowledgement. Barker, following closely behind her, nodded and bowed to Harriet and Sandra.

"She's so talented and beautiful," Sandra said after they'd gone. "Surely she can't be one of your suspects?"

Banks just told her that Penny had been a friend of the victim, and Sandra left it at that. The four chatted about the music, which they had all enjoyed, ordered more drinks, suffered through a mercifully short set of contemporary "protest" folk music, and awaited Penny's second set. She came back at ten-fifteen and walked straight to the stage.

This time there was a new, slightly distant quality in her performance. She was still involved in what she did, but it didn't have the same emotional cutting edge. Banks listened to the ballads and was struck by the parallel that he was dealing with exactly the same kinds of feelings and events that the old songs were forged from. And he wondered how The Ballad of Harry Steadman would end. Nobody would be "hung high," of course, not these days. But who would the killer turn out to be? What was his motive, and what would be Banks's own part in the song? All of a sudden, it seemed as if he was in another century, and that this beautiful young woman in the spotlight, life's disappointments and cruelties showing just enough in her voice to intensify her beauty, was singing a tragic ballad about the murder of Harry Steadman.

The sharp change to a brisk, sing-along tune snapped him out of his reverie, and he finished off his drink, noting that he immediately felt impatient for another. He was drunk, or at least tipsy, and it wasn't far off closing-time. If Barker was in love with the girl, and if there had been anything between her and Steadman...if Ramsden still...if Mrs Steadman knew...if Steadman and his wife hadn't been quite as close as everyone made out...The random thoughts curled like pipe smoke and evaporated in the air.

When the set ended to loud and prolonged applause, Banks

caught the passing waiter and ordered another pint for himself and a half for David. Sandra looked at him with a hint of reprimand in her eyes, but he just shrugged and grinned foolishly. He had never had a problem with alcohol, but he knew he could sometimes be quite adolescent in his unthinking consumption of numerous pints. He could tell that Sandra was worried he might make an idiot of himself, but he knew he could handle his drink. He hadn't had all that much, anyway. There might even be room for another one if he had time.

IV

There was going to be a storm, Sally was sure of it. She sat on the low pack-horse bridge dangling her legs over the warm stone as she watched the sun go down. When it had disappeared behind the hills, leaving a halo of dark red-gold, it seemed to shine upwards from the depths of the earth and pick out the relief of the heavy grey clouds that massed high above. Insects buzzed on the still, humid air.

It was an isolated spot, ideal for such business, barely even suitable for cars. During her walk, Sally had enjoyed the peace and the strange tremors of excitement that the anticipation of a storm seemed to impart to the landscape. The colours were richer, the wild flowers and rough grass more vibrant, and the clouds' shadows seemed palpable masses on the distant valley side.

But now she was nervous, and she didn't know why. It was the coming storm, she told herself, the electricity in the air, the isolation, the gathering darkness. Soon the wind would shake the rough moorland grass and rain would lash the dale. It was the perfect place for a secret meeting; she understood that. If they were seen together, word might get back to the chief inspector and awkward questions would be asked. She wanted to handle this herself, perhaps save a life and catch a killer. Nonetheless, she knew deep down that her shivers were not entirely due to the weather.

Idly, she cast a loose stone from the bridge into the shallow, slow-moving beck. After the rain, she thought, it would be swift, sparkling and ringing with fresh water cascading down the valley side and right under Helmthorpe High Street.

She looked at her watch. Twenty to ten. Tired of waiting, she wished it was all over. The aftermath of sunset was quickly vanishing as the clouds thickened overhead. A curlew called plaintively in the distance. The place began to feel like a wilderness in a Gothic romance. It was creepy, even though she'd been there often enough. A flock of rooks spun across the sky like oily rags. Sally became aware of a new sound throbbing through the silence. A car. She pricked up her ears, cast another stone in the beck and stood to face the track. Yes, she could see the headlights as they dipped and flashed on the winding road. It wouldn't be long now.

V

The storm finally broke at about five A.M. Sharp cracks of thunder woke Banks from a vaguely unpleasant dream. He had a dry mouth and a thick head. So much for control. But at least he hadn't made fool of himself; that he remembered.

Careful not to disturb Sandra, he walked over to the window and looked out on the back garden just in time to see a jagged bolt of lightning streak from north to south across the sky. The first few drops of rain, fat and heavy, came slowly. They burst at intervals on the window-pane and smacked against the slates of the sloping tool-shed roof; then they came more quickly and slapped against the leaves of the trees that lined the back alley beyond the garden gate. Soon the rain was coursing down the window and over the slates into the gutter before it gurgled down the drainpipe.

Banks made his way to the bathroom, took two Panadol tablets and went back to bed. Sandra hadn't woken and the children remained silent. He remembered when Tracy had been afraid of storms and had always run to her parents' bed, where she nestled between them and felt safe. But now she knew what caused the electrical activity—knew more about it than Banks did—the fear had gone. Brian had never really cared either way, except that an evening thunderstorm meant the television had to be unplugged sometimes in the middle of his favourite programme. It was something Banks's father had always done, and Banks followed suit without really knowing why.

The steady rhythm of the rain and the sudden release from tension that the start of a storm brings helped Banks to drift uneasily off to sleep again. Only seconds later, it seemed, the alarm clock rang and it was time to get ready for work.

When Banks arrived at the station, he was surprised to find an unusual flurry of activity. Superintendent Gristhorpe was waiting for him.

"What's going on?" Banks asked, hanging his wet mackintosh in the small closet.

"A young girl's been reported missing," Gristhorpe told him, bushy eyebrows knitted together in a frown.

"From Eastvale?"

"Get yourself some coffee, lad. Then we'll talk about it."

Banks took his mug to the small lunch-room and poured himself a cup of fresh black coffee. Back in the office, he sat behind his desk and sipped the hot drink, waiting for Gristhorpe to begin. He knew there was never any point in hurrying the superintendent.

"Helmthorpe," Gristhorpe said finally. "Local bobby down there, Constable Weaver, got woken up by worried parents just after the storm broke. Seems their young lass hadn't come home, and they were worried. The mother said she sometimes stayed out late—she was at that age, sixteen or so—so they hadn't worried too much earlier. But when the storm woke them and she still wasn't back... Apparently she's not done anything like that before."

"What's the girl's name?"

"Sally Lumb." The words sounded flat and final in Gristhorpe's Yorkshire accent.

Banks rubbed his face and drank some more coffee. "I was talking to her just the other day," he said at last. "In here. She came to see me."

Gristhorpe nodded. "I know. I saw the report. That's why I wanted to talk to you."

"Attractive young girl," Banks said, almost to himself. "Looked older than she was. Sixteen. Interested in acting. She wanted to get away to the big city." And all of a sudden, he thought of Penny

Cartwright, who had been to so many big cities, only to return to Helmthorpe.

"We're covering that angle, Alan. You know as well as I do how most of these cases turn out. In all likelihood she's run off to Manchester or London. Her mother told Weaver there'd been a few rows at home lately. Seems the lass didn't get on too well with her father. She probably just took off somewhere."

Banks nodded. "Most likely."

"But you don't believe it?"

"I didn't say that, sir."

"No, but you sounded like it."

"Shock, I suppose. There could have been an accident. She goes off with her boyfriend. You know, they find isolated places where they can kiss and cuddle. That area's full of old lead mines and gullies."

"Aye, it's possible. For the moment we'll just have to assume it's either that or she's run off. We've wired her description to all the big cities. I just hope to God we've not got a sex killer on our hands." He paused and looked through the window, where the steady downpour had almost emptied Market Street and the square. Only a few shoppers soldiered on under umbrellas. "Trouble is," he went on, "we can't organize search parties in this kind of weather. Too bloody dangerous by far up on the moors and valley sides."

"What do you think's happened?" Banks asked.

"Me?" Gristhorpe shook his head. "I don't know, Alan. Like I told you, I've been reading through that interview report again and I can't really see as she gave us any valuable information. She just helped us pinpoint the time the body was dumped, that's all. She didn't actually see anything."

"You mean she wasn't a danger to anyone—to our killer?"

"Aye. Naturally, you make connections when something like this happens. You'd be a poor copper if you didn't. But you can't let it get in the way. As it stands now, we've still got a murder to solve and we've got a missing girl to cope with, too."

"But you do think there might be a connection?"

"I hope not. I bloody hope not. It's bad enough knowing there's someone who killed once out there, but a hell of a lot worse thinking they'd go as far as to kill a kid too."

"We can't be sure she's dead yet, sir."

Gristhorpe looked at Banks steadily for a few moments, then turned back to the window. "No," he said. "Was there anything else? Anything else to link her to the Steadman case?"

"Not that I know of. The only time I saw her was when she came to tell me about hearing the car. I got the impression that she went away distinctly dischuffed with me for giving up the bright lights. We had Willy Fisher in at the time, too. He put up a bit of a struggle with two uniformed lads, and I think that unnerved her a bit."

"What are you getting at, Alan?"

"I don't know, really. But maybe if she did figure anything out, she might not have come to me with it."

"You can't blame yourself for that," Gristhorpe said, rising wearily to leave. "Let's hope she's run off somewhere. The link's got to be pursued, though. Were you thinking of going to Helmthorpe today?"

"No. It's so bloody miserable outside I thought I'd go over the paperwork again. Why?"

"The paperwork can wait. I'd feel easier if you did go."

"Of course. What do you want me to do?"

"Have a word with the boyfriend, for a start. Find out if he saw her last night, or if not, why not. And Weaver tells me she hung around the coffee-bar with three other girls. You might have a chat with them. Weaver will give you the names and details. Be as casual as you can. If she knew anything, or had any theories, she's far more likely to have told her friends than her parents. No need to trouble them." Banks was relieved. Twice before, he had had to spend time with the parents of missing children, and he could think of no worse task.

"I'll take care of the rest," Gristhorpe added. "We'll be getting search parties organized as soon as this rain slacks off a bit."

"Should I leave now?" Banks asked.

"No hurry. In fact, it might be better if you held off till mid-morning. I don't know a lot about teenage lasses, but I shouldn't imagine they'll be up and about right now. It might be best if you can find them in the coffee-bar. It'll be a more comfortable environment for the kind of chat you want, and you'll get them all together."

Banks nodded. "You'll keep me up to date, sir?"

"Yes, of course. Just check in with Weaver. I'll send Sergeant Hatchley on later, too. He's busy getting the girl's description around the country right now."

"Just a small point," Banks said, "but it might be a good idea if you had someone get in touch with theatre companies, drama schools, that kind of place. If she has run off, the odds are she's headed for the stage."

"Aye," Gristhorpe said, "I'll do that." Then, looking tired and worried, he left the office.

Outside, it was still pouring bucketsful onto Market Street and looked as if it would never stop. Banks stared down at the shifting pattern of umbrellas as pedestrians dodged one another crossing the square on the way to work. He scratched his chin and found a rough patch the electric razor had missed. Gristhorpe was right; they had to think in terms of a connection with the Steadman business. It had to be pursued quickly, as well, and the irony was that they had to hope they were wrong.

Banks looked over Sally Lumb's interview transcript and tried to visualize her as she had sat before him. Was there something she hadn't told him? As he read the printed words he had written up from his notes, he tried to picture her face, remembering pauses, changes in expression. No. If there was anything else, it must have occurred to her after the interview, and she might then have gone to the wrong person with her information or ideas. Banks tried to stop himself from imagining her battered body stuffed down a disused mine-shaft, but the images were hard to dismiss. Sally may have been eager to move away to the big city, but she had struck him as a sensible girl, even calculating—the kind who would make a clean and open move when the right time came. According to her mother, nothing spectacularly dramatic had happened at home to make her run. Rows were common enough, surely, and, if anything, the parents seemed too liberal. Banks remembered the curfews (broken, many of them) of his own adolescence as he tried to coax his pipe alight. The blasted thing remained as reluctant as ever. In a sudden flash of anger and frustration, he threw it across the room and the stem snapped in two.

VI

As Banks approached Helmthorpe later that Saturday morning, the coloured tents across the river strained at their ropes in the wind and rain like the sails of hidden boats, and the dark water danced wildly with ripples. In such weather, the houses themselves looked like dull outcrops of the stone they were built from, and the valley sides were shrouded in a haze of vapour. A few locals and unfortunate holiday-makers tramped the streets.

Banks pulled into the small parking space next to the police station, and the first person he saw inside was PC Weaver. The constable looked pale, and there were dark smudges under his eyes.

"We can't even organize a search," he said, pointing out of the window. "Our men would get bogged down on the moors, and the visibility's hopeless."

"I know," Banks said. "Any luck?"

Weaver shook his head. "Her parents last saw her just before they went out for the evening at about seven-thirty. Before that, her friends saw her in the coffee-bar earlier in the afternoon. We've not had time to ask much yet, though, sir. I've still got some lads out there. There'll likely be more information coming in before long."

Banks nodded. "And she didn't say to anyone where she was going?"

"No, sir. Her mother thought she might have met her boyfriend somewhere."

"Did she?"

"He says not sir," Weaver pointed towards a bedraggled young man in a wet, clinging T-shirt and soggy jeans, hair plastered down by the rain. "That's him there, sir. He's pretty upset, and I see no reason not to believe him."

"Have you questioned him?"

"Just talked to him, really, sir. Not questioned him proper. I mean, I thought I'd leave that . . ."

"That's fine, Constable," Banks said, smiling his approval. "You did right."

He walked over to Kevin, who was staring fixedly at a "Crime

Doesn't Pay" poster and chewing his fingernails. Banks introduced himself and sat down on the bench.

"How long have you known Sally?" he asked.

Kevin rubbed his eyes. "Years, I suppose. We only started going together this summer."

"How do you feel about Swainsdale?"

"What?"

"How do you feel about living in the Dales, your home? Sally doesn't like it much, does she? Wasn't she always talking about going away?"

"Oh aye, she talked," Kevin said scornfully. "She's full of big talk, is Sally. Got a lot of grand ideas."

"Don't you think she might have run off to London or somewhere, then?"

Kevin shook his head. "No. I can't see her taking off like that. That's why I'm worried. She'd've told me."

"Perhaps she's running from you, too."

"Don't be daft. We've just started going together. We're in love." He bent forward and put his head in his hands. "I love her. We're going to get married, start a little farm...I know Sally, and she just wouldn't run off without telling me. She wouldn't."

Banks held himself back from agreeing. Whatever Kevin believed, there was still hope. He couldn't picture Sally Lumb settling down to domestic rural life in the Dales, though. Kevin had a lot to learn about women and about dreams, but he seemed a decent and honest enough boy on the surface. Banks was inclined to agree with Weaver and see no harm in him, but he had to press on with the questioning.

"Did you talk to Sally yesterday?" he asked.

Kevin shook his head.

"You didn't see her at all yesterday evening?"

"No. I was playing cricket with some mates over in Aykbridge."

"Did Sally know about that? Didn't she expect to see you?"

"Aye, she knew. You can't see each other every night, can you?" he burst out. "You'd soon get sick of each other, then, wouldn't you? You've got to do other things sometimes, don't you?"

He was blaming himself and Banks helped him fight back the guilt. He wanted to ask him about the night he and Sally had heard the car; he wanted to know if she had said anything more about it, or if either of them had noticed something they hadn't mentioned. But if he did that, he realized, he would be putting ideas into Kevin's mind, making him think that Sally's disappearance was somehow related to Steadman's murder. He would have to do that eventually, but it could wait. If there was anything, Kevin would probably blurt it out himself in his attempt to help find Sally.

It was almost noon. If the girls were going to meet up as usual in the coffee-bar, they'd probably be there by now, Weaver told him. Banks dashed out to the car. In good weather, he would have walked the short distance, but after only a moment's exposure to the heavy rain, droplets were running down his neck from his sodden collar.

The three girls sat in silence, toying with straws angled in their Coke cans. Banks told them who he was and pulled up a chair to the stained, cracked Formica table. The video games and pinball machine were silent.

"Do you think Sally's the kind of girl to run away without telling anyone?" he asked first.

They all shook their heads slowly. The plain-looking girl with thick glasses, who had introduced herself as Anne Downes, answered: "She's full of ideas, is Sally. But that's all they are. She's nowhere to run to. She doesn't know anyone outside Swainsdale."

"Was she doing well at school?"

"Well enough," replied Kathy Chalmers, the one with the henna hair. "She's clever. Not a swot, like. She could always get away without studying much and get good marks. She's bound to pass all her exams."

"A sensible girl, you'd say?"

"As sensible as any of us teenagers," Anne Downes answered, and the irony wasn't lost on Banks. "It depends on your point of view."

Kathy gave a short giggle and blushed. "I'm sorry," she apologized, putting her hand over her mouth. "But her parents might not have thought she was sensible. You know parents."

Being one himself, Banks did. "But she's not the kind of girl to ..." He paused, searching for words to avoid the phrase "get into trouble," with all its connotations. "She doesn't cause trouble, make a nuisance of herself?"

Kathy shook her head. "No. Not at all. She's well behaved enough. Gets on well with most of the teachers. She's just full of ideas, like Anne said. A big dreamer. She wouldn't do anything to hurt anybody."

Banks wondered if the girls connected Sally's disappearance with the Steadman business; her visit to the Eastvale station was exactly the kind of thing she'd tell them about, and he wanted to know if she had made any remarks. Again, the problem was to avoid alerting and alarming them.

"I suppose you know she came to see me a few days ago?" he began casually. "And I agree, she struck me as being exactly like you all say—bright, full of plans, well behaved. I didn't really get to hear much about any of her ideas, though."

Kathy Chalmers blushed again. The other girl, Hazel Kirk, who had so far sat silently throughout the conversation, began to seem ill at ease. Again it was Anne Downes who answered with a forthrightness completely in harmony with her precocious intelligence.

"Take this murder business," she began. "I suppose that's what she went to see you about?"

Banks nodded.

"Well, she found it all rather glamorous, exciting, as if it was something she was watching on telly. I don't mean to say she wasn't sorry about poor Mr Steadman, we all were, it's just that she didn't see it from that point of view. To Sally it was an adventure. Do you know what I mean? It was all a bit of a game with her as the heroine."

This was exactly what Banks wanted. He nodded in appreciation of Anne's observation. "Did she talk about it much?" he asked.

"Only in a mysterious kind of way," Anne answered.

"As if she knew something nobody else did?"

"Yes. Exactly like that. I think it made her feel important, that she'd noticed something and been to see you. She thought you were rather dishy at first." Anne said this with a perfectly straight face, as if she didn't quite know what the word meant. "Then she seemed disappointed with your response. I don't know what it was, she didn't say, but she got even more mysterious as the week went on."

"Did she say anything specific?"

"Oh, she tried to convince us that she was hot on the trail," Anne said, adjusting her glasses. "That she had an idea who dunnit. But that's all. Just hints. She didn't do anything about it, as far as I know."

Banks was dreading the moment, which surely couldn't be far off, when Anne would realize the significance of his line of questioning. But, luckily, it didn't come. He thanked the girls for their time and, as he left, noted again how distracted Hazel Kirk seemed to be. Instead of questioning her there and then, he decided to leave it for a while and see what developed.

NINE

I

It was time to concentrate on the Steadman case again. However disturbing her disappearance was, Banks thought, Sally Lumb might turn up in Birmingham or Bristol any moment. But Steadman was dead and his killer was still free.

He told Weaver where he was going and drove up the hill to Gratly, turning right after the small, low bridge in the centre of the hamlet and pulling up outside Jack Barker's converted farmhouse by the side of the broad beck. The water was already running faster and louder over the series of terraced falls. In a day or two, when the rain percolated down from the moorlands and higher slopes, the stream would turn into a deafening torrent.

Banks realized as he rang the doorbell that he had not visited Barker at home before, and he wondered what the house would reveal of the man.

"Oh, it's you, Chief Inspector," a puzzled-looking Barker said, after keeping Banks waiting at the door for an unusually long time. "Come in. Excuse my surprise, but I don't get very many visitors."

Banks took off his wet mac and shoes in the hall and followed Barker inside. Although it wasn't cold, the rain had certainly put a damp chill in the stone, and Banks decided to keep his jacket on.

"Do you mind if we talk in the study?" Barker asked. "It's warmer up there. I've just been working, and that's where the coffee-pot is. You look as if you could use some."

"Good idea," Banks replied, following his host through a sparsely furnished living-room and up a very narrow flight of stone stairs into a cosy room that looked out on the fell-sides at the back of the house. Two walls were lined with books, and by a third, where the door was, stood a filing cabinet and a small desk stacked with papers. Barker's work-table, on which an electronic typewriter hummed, stood directly by the window. Through the streaming rain, the sharply rising slope outside had the look of an Impressionist painting. At the centre of the room was a low coffee-table. The red light of the automatic drip-filter machine was on, and the Pyrex pot was half full of rich dark coffee. By the table, there were two small but comfortable armchairs. The two men sat down with their coffee—both took black, no sugar.

"I'm sorry to disturb you at work," Banks said, sipping the refreshing liquid.

"Think nothing of it. It's an occupational hazard."

Banks raised an eyebrow.

"What I mean is," Barker explained, "that if you work at home, you're at home, aren't you? Fair game for any salesman and bill-collector. Somehow, the old Puritan work ethic won't allow most people to accept that writing books in the comfort of one's own home is really work, if you see what I mean. I can't think why, mind you. It was common enough for weavers and loom operators to work at home before the Industrial Revolution. These days, work has to be something we hate, something we do in a noisy, dirty factory or an antiseptic, fluorescent office. No offence."

But Banks could tell by the sparkle in his eyes that Barker was baiting him gently. "None taken," he replied. "As a matter of fact, I'd be happier to spend a bit more time in my office and less of it tramping about the Dales in this weather."

Barker smiled and reached for a cigarette from the pack on the table. "Anyway," he said, "I don't seem to get many visitors, except salesman. I take the phone off the hook, too. Work was going well. I'd just got to a good part, and it's always been my practice to stop for a while when things get good. That way I feel excited about going back to work later."

"That's an interesting work-habit," Banks remarked, trying to ignore the craving he felt when Barker lit his cigarette and inhaled deeply.

"Sorry," Barker said, offering him a cigarette as if he had read his mind.

Banks shook his head. "Trying to stop."

"Of course. You're a pipe man, aren't you? Please feel free. Pipe smoke doesn't bother me at all."

"It broke."

After the two of them had laughed at the absurdity of the broken pipe, Banks gave in. "Perhaps I will have a cigarette," he said. As he reached for one, he noticed Barker tense up to face the inevitable questions. The cigarette tasted good. Every bit as good as he remembered. He didn't cough or feel dizzy. In fact, he felt no indication that he had ever given up cigarettes in the first place; it was like a reunion with a long lost friend.

"So, what can I do for you this time?" Barker asked, putting unnecessary emphasis on the last two words.

"I suppose you've heard about the girl from the village, Sally Lumb?" he asked.

"No. What about her?"

"You mean you don't know? I'd have thought in a community this size the news would spread fast. People certainly knew about Harold Steadman soon enough."

"I haven't been out since I walked Penny home after the folk club last night."

"The girl's missing," Banks told him. "She didn't go home last night."

"Good Lord!" Barker said, looking towards the window. "If she's wandered off and got lost in this weather... What do you think?"

"It's too early to know yet. She could have got lost, yes. But she grew up around here and she seemed like a sensible girl."

"Run away?"

"Another possibility. We're checking on it."

"But you don't think so?"

"We just don't know."

"Have you got search parties out?"

"We can't in this weather."

"But still... Something's got to be done."

"We're doing all we can," Banks assured him. "Did you know her?"

Barker narrowed his eyes. "I wouldn't say I really knew her, no. I've seen her around, of course, to say hello to. And she once came to me about a school project. Pretty girl."

"Very," Banks agreed.

"I don't suppose that's what you came to talk to me about, though, is it?"

"No." Banks stubbed out his cigarette. "I wanted to ask you about Penny Cartwright."

"What about her?"

"Are you in love with her?"

Barker laughed, but Banks could see the strain in his eyes. "What a question. I don't know whether to tell you it's none of your business or applaud your insight."

"You are, then?"

"I'll admit I'm rather smitten with Penny, yes. What red-blooded young bachelor wouldn't be? But I don't see what my feelings for her have to do with anything else."

"Was she having an affair with Harold Steadman, do you think?"

Barker gazed at Banks for a few moments. "Not that I know," he answered slowly. "But how would I know?"

"You knew the two of them quite well."

"True. But a man's private life . . . and a woman's . . . ? If they wanted to conceal something like that from the world, it wouldn't have been very difficult, would it? Even here, it could be done. Look, if you want my answer to your question, you'll have to understand that it's just an opinion, like yours. Certainly neither of them confided in me, or anything like that. And I'd say no, they weren't having an affair. As you guessed, I am very fond of Penny, and given that, I'd naturally be interested in her relationships. As far as I can make out, though, their friendship was based on mutual respect and admiration, not sexual desire."

This was almost exactly what Banks had heard from Penny herself and from Emma Steadman. Indeed, the only person who seemed to think differently about Penny and Harold Steadman was the major, and he was very much a victim of his own obsessions. But what if he was right?

"You seemed rather sharp last night when I mentioned Michael

Ramsden," Banks said, changing tack. "Do you have any particular reason to dislike him?"

"I don't dislike him. I hardly even know him. He's been in The Bridge a few times with Harry, and he always seemed pleasant enough. I will admit that I found something a little sly about him, a bit off-putting, but that's a minor personal reaction—it's neither here nor there."

"I suppose you knew about his relationship with Penny?"

"Yes, and I'm quite willing to confess to a touch of instinctive lover's jealousy. Come to that, I may have been envious of her relationship with Harry, too. It seemed so close and easy. But I've no claim on Penny's emotions, sad to say. And as far as Ramsden was concerned, that was years ago. They can't have been more than kids."

"Where were you then?"

"What? On the night of the twelfth of February, nineteen sixty-three, between the hours of—"

"You know what I mean."

"Ten years ago?"

"Yes."

"I lived in London then, in a poky little bedsit in Notting Hill writing real novels that nobody wanted to buy. Penny wasn't around when I first came to Gratly—we didn't meet till she came back here—but I did see her play once down south."

"Why do you think Ramsden and Penny split up?"

"How should I know? It's not a question I've concerned myself with. Why does any young couple split up? I suppose they felt themselves moving in different directions. Christ, they were only kids."

"That was when Michael lived at home with his parents, wasn't it? In the same house Steadman and his wife used to visit on holidays?"

"Yes," Barker answered. "Ten years ago. It was just before Ramsden went off to university. Penny was just discovering her talent then. Harry told me he used to teach her folk-songs he'd collected."

"And the kids just drifted apart?"

"Well, Michael went to university, and Penny went all over the place with the group. That kind of folk-music was still popular then. It still is, actually. I mean, there's always a sizeable audience for it."

"How was Penny discovered?"

"The usual way, as far as I know. An agent for a record company was scouting the provinces for new folk-talent. He offered her a chance to make a demo and off she went. The rest is history, as they say."

"Has she talked to you about the past much, the time she spent away?"

"Not a great deal, no." Barker seemed interested in the conversation now, despite himself. He poured more coffee and Banks cadged another cigarette. "I'm sure you know, Chief Inspector," he went on, "that we all have phases of our lives we're not particularly proud of. Often circumstances give us the opportunity to behave in a careless, irresponsible way, and most of us take it. It pains me to admit that I was once a very young 'Teddy boy,' and I even ripped a few seats in the local flea-pit." He grinned. "You won't arrest me, will you?"

"I think the statute of limitations has run out on seat-ripping," Banks answered, smiling. "It would be rather difficult to prove, too."

"You do make me feel old," Barker sighed. "But do you see what I mean? Penny was not only young and inexperienced, she was also, for the first time in her life, fairly well off, popular, in with the 'in crowd.' I don't doubt that she tried drugs and that sex was a fairly casual matter. 'Make Love, Not War,' as they used to say. But the important thing is that she grew up, left all that behind and pulled her life together. Plenty of people don't survive the modern music world, you know. Penny did. What I'd like to know is why on earth you seem so obsessed with the events of ten years ago."

"I don't know," Banks answered, scratching the scar at the side of his eye. "Everybody speaks so highly of Steadman. He didn't seem to have an enemy in the world. Yet somebody murdered him. Don't you find that strange? He wasn't robbed, and his body was taken up to the hillside below Crow Scar. We don't know where he was killed. I suppose what I'm saying, Mr Barker, is that if the answer isn't in the present, which it doesn't seem to be, then it must be in the past, however unlikely that may seem to you."

"And has this background information given you any clues?"

"None at all. Not yet. But there's one more thing that's been on my mind. Could Harold Steadman have been a homosexual?"

Barker almost choked on his coffee. "That takes the biscuit," he spluttered, wiping at the spilt liquid on his lap. "Where on earth did you get a wild idea like that?"

Banks saw no reason to tell him that he had got the idea from Sergeant Hatchley, who had said in the Queen's Arms, in his usual manner, "About this Steadman business, those weekend trips to Ramsden's place. Do you think he was queer?"

Banks admitted that it was an angle he had not considered; he had taken Steadman's dedication to work at face value and presumed that the overnight visits took place for the reasons Ramsden and Mrs Steadman had given him.

"Even assuming you're right," Banks had said, "it doesn't really help us much, does it? His wife can't have killed him out of disgust—she has an alibi. And Ramsden would hardly have killed his lover, even if he could have."

"There's blackmail, though," Hatchley had suggested. "Steadman was a rich man."

"Yes. It's a possibility. Who do you think was blackmailing him?"

"Could have been anyone he knew. Barker. The girl. Barnes. One of his old mates from Leeds."

"We'll check it out, then," Banks had said. "Ask around about Ramsden, and I'll ask some more questions in Helmthorpe. I wouldn't hold out too much hope, though. It doesn't feel right to me."

How did you ask someone if a friend was homosexual, he wondered? Just come right out with it? How would they know? Penny would certainly assume Ramsden was normal if he had been ten years ago, and there was still a chance that she knew more about Steadman's sexual habits than she let on.

So now he sat in Barker's study waiting for him to get over the shock and attempt an answer. When it came, it was disappointing. Barker simply denied the possibility and would only admit, when pushed, that anything, however outlandish, *could* be possible, but that didn't mean it *was*.

"Look," Barker said, leaning forward, "I realize that I must be a suspect in this business. I've no alibi and I seem unable to convince you that I really had nothing against Harry—I'm not gay, either, just for the record—but I assure you that I did not kill him, and I'm perfectly willing to help in any way I can. I just don't know how I can help, and, if you don't mind my saying so, some of the directions you're pursuing seem to me to be quite silly."

"I can understand that," Banks said, "but it's for me to decide what's relevant and what isn't."

"You pick up bits and pieces from everyone and put them together. Yes, I suppose that's true. None of us gets to touch any more than a small area of the elephant, do we? But you get to see the whole beast."

Banks smiled at the analogy. "Eventually, yes," he said. "I hope so. What are you working on, or don't you like to discuss work in progress?"

"I don't mind. As a matter of fact, you've just given me an idea. All that about putting the pieces together. I think I can use it. It's another in the Kenny Gibson series. Have you read any?"

Banks shook his head.

"Of course not," Barker said. "I ought to know by now that few real policemen read detective novels. Anyway, Kenny Gibson is a private eye in the Los Angeles area. Period stuff, the thirties. I get most of my background information from Raymond Chandler and the old *Black Mask* magazines—but don't tell anyone! This time he's working for a rich society woman whose husband has disappeared. The plot's taken care of; it's the characters and atmosphere that are really hard to do."

"Sex and violence?"

"Enough to sell a few thousand copies."

"Just out of interest," Banks asked as he got up to leave, "do you have it all planned out in advance—the plot, the solution?"

"Good Lord, no," Barker answered, following him down the stairs. "The plot takes care of itself as I go along. At least I hope it does. If it's going well, there are fewer and fewer options at each turn until it's perfectly clear who the criminal is. I'm never really sure where I'm going from one day to the next. It'd be boring any other way, don't you think?"

"Perhaps," Banks answered, putting on his shoes and mac. "In writing, yes. In fiction. But in real life, I'm not so sure. It'd be a damn sight easier if I knew who the criminal was without having to write the whole book and make all the mistakes along the way. Anyway, good-bye, and thanks for your time."

"My pleasure," said Barker.

And Banks ducked quickly through the rain to his car.

II

On High Street, Banks glimpsed Penny Cartwright nipping into The Bridge. Consulting his watch and his stomach, he decided it was well past lunch-time, and he could do with a pie and a pint if the landlord had any food left.

Penny was at the bar shaking her umbrella when she glanced over her shoulder and saw Banks enter.

"Can't a lady indulge her alcoholic cravings without the police turning up?" she asked sharply.

"Of course," Banks replied. "As a matter of fact, I'd be honoured if you'd join me for a late lunch."

Penny looked at him through narrowed eyes. "Business or pleasure, Inspector?"

"Just a chat."

"For 'chat' read 'interrogation,' I'll bet. Go on, then. I must be a fool. You're buying."

They were lucky enough to get two steak-and-mushroom pies, and Penny asked for a double Scotch. Carrying the drinks, Banks followed her into the lounge.

"Why don't they do something with this place?" he asked, looking around and turning his nose up.

"Why should they? I wouldn't have taken you for one of these horse-brass and bedpan types." Penny stood her umbrella by the fireplace and sat down, shaking her hair.

Banks laughed. "I always thought they were bedwarmers. And no, I'm not, not at all. Give me spittoons and sawdust any day. I was simply thinking that the owner would see renovations as a way to do more business in the long run."

"Oh, Inspector Banks! I can see you're not a true Yorkshireman yet. We don't care about a speck or two of dirt in these parts. It's the company and the ale that count—and this is one place the locals can count on for both."

Banks grinned and accepted the criticism with a humble sigh.

"So what is it you want to know this time?" Penny asked, lighting a cigarette and leaning back in her chair.

"I enjoyed your performance last night. I liked the songs, and you've got a beautiful voice."

Did she blush just a little? Banks couldn't be sure, the lighting in the room was so dim. But she faltered over accepting the compliment and was clearly embarrassed.

The pies arrived and they each took a few bites in silence before Banks opened the conversation again.

"I'm stuck. I'm not getting anywhere. And now there's a girl gone missing."

Penny frowned. "Yes, I've heard."

"Do you know her? What do you think might have happened?"

"I know Sally a little, yes. She always wanted to know about the big, wide world out there. I think she was secretly a bit disappointed with me for leaving it behind and coming home. But she struck me as a sensible girl. I can't really picture her running off like that. And she was born and raised in these parts, like me. She knows the country-side around here like the back of her hand, so she wasn't likely to get lost either."

"Which leaves?"

"I don't like to think about it. You hear of young girls going miss-ing so often in the cities. But here..." Penny shuddered. "I suppose it could mean we've got a maniac in our midst. What are the police doing, apart from buying me lunch?"

It was the second time Banks had been asked that, and he found it just as depressing to have so little to say in reply again. But Penny understood about the weather; she knew how dangerous it made Swainsdale, and she showed a surprising amount of sympathy for Banks's obvious frustration.

They sat in silence again and returned to their food. When they had finished, Banks put his knife and fork down and faced Penny.

"Tell me about your father," he said.

"You sound like a bloody psychiatrist. What about him?"

"You must know better than anyone else what a hothead he is?"

"I probably gave him reason enough."

"You mean the city, the wild life?"

She nodded. "But honestly, you make it sound much worse than it was. What would you do in that position? Everything was new. I had money, people I thought were my friends. It was exciting then, people were trying new things just for the hell of it. My father didn't speak to me for a long time after I left. I couldn't explain; it was just too claustrophobic at home. But when I came back he was kind to me and helped me to get set up in the cottage. He takes it upon himself to act as my protector, I know. And, yes, he has a temper. But he's harmless. You can't seriously suspect him of harming Harry, can you?"

Banks shook his head. "Not any more, no. I think it was too well planned to be his kind of crime. I just wanted to know how you saw things. Tell me more about Michael Ramsden."

Flustered, Penny reached for another cigarette. "What about him?"

"You used to go out with him, didn't you? Can I have one of those?"

"Sure." Penny gave him a Silk Cut. "You know I used to go out with him. So what? It was years ago. Another lifetime."

"Were you in love?"

"In love? Inspector, it's easy to be in love when you're sixteen, especially when everybody wants you to be. Michael was the bright boy of the village, and I was the talented lass. It was one match my father didn't oppose, and he's always held it against me that we didn't marry."

"Did you think of marrying?"

"We were talking about getting engaged, like kids do. That's as far as it went. Look, I was young and innocent. Michael was just a boy. That's all there is to it." Penny shifted in her seat and pushed her hair back over her shoulders.

"Was it a sexual relationship?"

"None of your bloody business."

"Did he ditch you?"

"We just drifted apart."

"Is that all?"

"It's all you're getting." Penny stood up to leave, but Banks reached out and grabbed her arm. She stared at him angrily, and he let go as if he had received an electric shock. She rubbed the muscle.

"I'm sorry," he said. "Please sit down again. I haven't finished yet. Look, you might think I'm just prying into your personal life for the fun of it, but I'm not. I don't give a damn who you've slept with and who you haven't slept with, what drugs you've taken and what you haven't taken, unless it relates to Harold Steadman's murder. Is that clear? I don't even care how much hash you smoke now."

Penny eyed Banks shrewdly. Finally, she nodded.

"So why did you split up?" Banks asked.

"Buy me another drink and I'll tell you."

"Same again?" Banks got up to go to the bar.

Penny nodded. "I can't promise it'll be interesting, though," she called after him.

"There was nothing mature about our relationship," she said as Banks sat down with a pint and a double Scotch. "Neither of us really knew anything different until something else came along."

"Another man?"

"No. Not until later. Much later."

"You mean university for Michael and a singing career for you?"

"Yes, partly. But it wasn't as simple as that."

"What do you mean?"

Penny frowned as if she had just thought of something, or tried to grasp the shadow of a memory. "I don't know. We just drifted apart, that's all there is to it. It was summer, ten years ago. Every bit as hot as this one was. I told you it wasn't exciting."

"But there must have been a reason."

"Why do you want to know?"

"Because I think the answer to Steadman's death lies in the past, and I want to know as much about it as possible."

"Why do you think that?"

"I'm asking the questions. Did he dump you because you wouldn't have sex with him?"

Penny blew out a stream of smoke. "All right, so I wouldn't let him fuck me. Is that what you want to hear?" The word was clearly meant to shock Banks.

"You tell me."

"Oh, this is bloody insufferable. Here." She tossed him another cigarette. "Maybe sex was part of it. He was certainly getting persistent. Perhaps I should have let him. I don't know . . . I'm sure I was ready. But then he seemed different. He got more withdrawn and distant. Things just felt strange. I was changing, too. I was singing in the village pubs and Michael was studying to go to university. Harry and Emma were up for quite a while, and it was hot, very hot. Emma would hardly go outside because her skin burned so easily. Harry and I spent quite a bit of time at the Roman site near Fortford. It was just being excavated then. We went for walks as well, long walks in the sun."

"Did Michael go with you?"

"Sometimes. But he wasn't very interested in that kind of thing then. He'd just discovered the joys of English Literature. It was all Shelley, Keats, Wordsworth and D.H. Lawrence for him. He spent most of the time with his nose stuck in a book of poems, whether he was with us or not. That's when he wasn't trying to stick his hands up my skirt."

"Must have been Lawrence's influence."

Penny's lips twitched in a brief smile. She put her hand to her forehead and swept back her hair. "Maybe."

"And Mrs Steadman?"

"As I said, she didn't like the sun. Sometimes she'd come if we went in the car and sit under a makeshift parasol by the side of the road while we had a picnic like characters from a Jane Austen novel. But she wasn't really interested in the Romans or folk traditions, either. Maybe it wasn't the best of marriages, I don't know. Lord knows, they didn't have much in common. But they put up with it, and I don't think they treated each other unkindly. Harry shouldn't have married, really. He was far too dedicated to his work. Mostly I just remember him and me tramping over the moors and naming wild flowers."

Steadman must have been in his early thirties then, Banks calculated, and Penny was sixteen. That wasn't such an age difference to make attraction impossible. Quite the contrary: he was exactly the age a girl of sixteen might be attracted to, and Steadman had certainly been handsome, in a scholarly kind of way, right up to the end.

"Didn't you have a crush on Harry?" he asked. "Surely it would have been perfectly natural?"

"Perhaps. But the main thing—the thing you don't seem able to understand—is that Harry really wasn't like that. He wasn't sexy, I suppose. More like an uncle. I know it must be hard for you to believe, but it's true."

If I don't believe it, Banks thought, it's not for want of people trying to convince me. "Don't you think Michael might have seen the relationship differently?" he suggested. "As a threat, perhaps. An older, more experienced man. Might that not have been why he seemed strange?"

"I can't say I ever thought of it that way," Penny answered.

Banks wasn't sure whether he believed her or not; she lied and evaded issues so often he was becoming more and more convinced that she was an actress as well as a singer.

"It's possible, though, isn't it?"

She nodded. "I guess so. But he never said anything to me. You'd think he would have, wouldn't you?"

"You didn't argue? Michael never said anything about you going off with Harry? He didn't always insist on accompanying you?"

Penny shook her head at each question.

"He was very shy and awkward," she said. "It was very difficult for him to express himself emotionally. If he did think anything, he kept it to himself and suffered in silence."

Banks sipped his pint of Theakston's, brooding on how best to put his next question. Penny offered him another Silk Cut.

"If I read you right, Inspector," she said, "you seem to be implying that Michael Ramsden might have killed Harry."

"Am I?"

"Come on! Why all the questions about him being jealous?"

Banks said nothing.

"They became great friends, you know," Penny went on. "When Michael graduated and got interested in local history, he helped Harry a lot. He even persuaded his firm to publish Harry's books. It was more than just a publisher-author relationship."

"That's what I was wondering," Banks cut in, seizing his opportunity. "Is there any possibility of a homosexual relationship between them? I know it sounds odd, but think about it."

Unlike Barker, Penny took the question seriously before concluding that she doubted it very much. "This had better not be a trick," she said. "I hope you're not trying to trap me into admitting intimate knowledge of Harry's sexual preferences."

Banks laughed. "I'm not half as devious as you make out."

Her eyes narrowed sharply. "I'll bet. Anyway," she went on, "I really can't help you. You'd think you'd know all about a friend you've known for years, but it's just not so. Harry could have been gay, for all I know. Michael, on the other hand, seemed very much like a normal adolescent, but there's no reason why he couldn't have been bi. Who can tell these days?"

And she was right. Banks had known a sergeant on the Metropolitan force for six years—a married man with two children—before finding out at the inquest into his suicide that he had been homosexual.

"You still seem to be saying Michael did it," she said. "In fact, you're hounding all of us—his friends. Why? Why pick on us? What about his enemies? Couldn't it have been somebody just passing through who killed Harry?"

Banks shook his head. "Contrary to popular belief," he said, "very few murders happen that way. I think the myth of the wandering vagrant killer was invented by the aristocracy to keep suspicion away from their own doorsteps. Most often, people are killed by family or friends, and motives are usually money, sex, revenge or the need to cover up damaging facts. In Harold Steadman's case, we found no evidence of robbery and we've had no luck so far in digging up an enemy from his past. Believe me, Ms Cartwright, we dig deep. We've been checking alibis of anyone outside his immediate circle who might have had even the remotest reason for killing him. Really, not many people walk around the country bashing others on the head for no reason. So far, statistics and evidence point to someone closer to home. According to his friends, though, he was too damn perfect to have an enemy, so where am I supposed to look? Obviously Mr Steadman was a far more complicated man than most people have admitted, and his network of relationships wasn't a simple one, either. His murder wasn't a spur of the moment job, or at least the killer was frightened or cold-blooded enough to throw us off the scent by moving the body."

"And you're not going to stop pestering us until you know who it is?"

"No."

"Are you close?"

"I can't see it if I am, but detection doesn't work like that, anyway. It's not a matter of getting closer like a zoom lens, but of getting enough bits and pieces to transform chaos into a recognizable pattern."

"And you never know when you have enough?"

"Yes. But you can't predict when that moment will come. It could be in the next ten seconds or the next ten years. You don't know what the pattern will look like when it's there, so you might not even recognize it at first. But soon enough, you'll know you've got a design and not just a filing cabinet full of odds and sods."

"What about money as a motive?" Penny asked. "Harry was very well off."

"He didn't leave a will, which was foolish of him. Naturally, it all goes to Mrs Steadman. It would have been more convenient for us if he'd left it all to the National Trust and we could have pulled in the first nutty conservationist we could find, but life isn't as easy as fiction. Motive and opportunity just don't seem to go together in this case."

"Well, that's your problem, isn't it?"

"Yes. Have I explained why I'm pestering you so much now?"

"Very clearly, thank you," Penny said, giving him a mock bow.

"You don't see Michael much these days?"

"No, not often. Occasionally in The Bridge. He was always especially awkward with me after we split up, though. You're not suggesting that Michael is still in love with me, are you? Let me get this right. He thought Harry and I were having an affair all those years ago and backed off. But all the time he's been holding a grudge. He worked his way into Harry's confidence over the years just looking for an opportunity to do away with him, and finally took his revenge. Am I right?"

Banks laughed, but it sounded hollow. Perhaps Ramsden did have sufficient motive, but he would have been hard pushed to make an opportunity. First of all, he would hardly come to Helmthorpe and hang around in the car park all evening waiting, even if he was certain

Steadman would be going there. And if Steadman had gone to York, how did his car get back to Helmthorpe? Ramsden could hardly have driven two cars, and he would have needed his own to get home. There were certainly no buses at that time of night, and he would not have risked arranging for a taxi.

"It's ludicrous," Penny said, as if she had been listening in on Banks's thoughts. "I see what you mean when you say you're stuck." She finished her drink, put down the glass, and stood up to leave.

Banks stayed on, drinking rather gloomily and craving another cigarette, when Hatchley walked in. The sergeant brought two pints over and wedged himself into the chair Penny had just left.

"Any developments?" Banks asked.

"Weaver's men have talked to someone who saw Sally Lumb in the public callbox on Hill Road at four o'clock Friday afternoon," Hatchley reported. "And someone else thinks he saw her walking along Helmthorpe High Street at about nine o'clock."

"What direction?"

"East."

"She could have been going anywhere."

"Except west," Hatchley said. "By the way, I've been in touch with a mate of mine in York. Keeps tabs on all the queers and perverts down there, and there's nothing on Ramsden at all. Not a dicky bird."

"I didn't think there would be," Banks said glumly. "We're barking up the wrong tree, Sergeant."

"That's as maybe, but who's going to lead us to the right 'un?"

Banks watched the rain stream down the dirty windowpane and sighed. "Do you think the two are linked?" he asked "Steadman and the Lumb girl?"

Hatchley wiped his lips with the back of his hand and burped. "Bit of a coincidence, isn't it? The girl has the only piece of real information we get about the dumping of Steadman's body, and she goes missing."

"But she'd already told us what she knew."

"Did the killer know that?" Hatchley asked.

"It doesn't matter, does it? He didn't even know anybody had heard him burying Steadman below Crow Scar, unless..."

"Unless the girl let him know."

"Right. Either intentionally or otherwise. But that still assumes she knew more than she told us, that she knew who it was."

"Not if it was unintentional," Hatchley pointed out. "A girl like that tells all her friends, maybe hints that she knows more than she does. This is a small place, remember. It's not like London. It's easy to be overheard here, and word travels quickly."

"The coffee-bar," Banks muttered.

"Come again?"

"The coffee-bar. The place she hung around with her friends. Come on, we'd better question those girls again. If they know what Sally knew, they could be in danger as well. I didn't want them to think that Sally had been killed, or that her disappearance had anything to do with Steadman, but there's no time for soft-stepping any more."

Hatchley gulped down the rest of his pint, then dragged himself to his feet and plodded along behind.

TEN

I

Anne Downes was both nervous and excited to find herself in the police station. Not that it was much of a place, but it was alive with important activity: people coming and going, phones ringing, the ancient telex machine clattering. The two other girls paid less attention to their surroundings and seemed more preoccupied with their internal sense of unease. Hazel was the worst, biting her nails and shifting position as if she had St Vitus's dance; Kathy pretended to lounge coolly, casually uninterested in the whole affair, but she was biting her lower lip so hard it turned red.

The policewoman had been friendly enough when she'd picked them up at the coffee-bar and driven them the short distance to the station, and the small, attractive chief inspector had smiled and said he wouldn't keep them long. But they all knew there was something going on.

Anne was the first to be called into the tiny interview room. Its walls were bare and the mere two chairs and a table made the place seem over-furnished. It was the kind of room that made you claustrophobic.

Banks sat opposite Anne, and a policewoman with a notebook in her hand stood in the corner by a narrow, barred window.

"I'd just like to ask you a few questions, Anne," Banks began.

She looked at him quizzically from behind the thick lenses and nodded.

"First of all, I suppose you know why I want to see you again?"

"Yes," Anne replied. "You think Sally's been murdered because of something she knew."

Banks, taken aback by her directness, asked what her opinion was.

"I'd say it's possible, yes," Anne answered, her young brow furrowed in thought. "I've already told you that I don't believe she's run away or got lost, and that doesn't leave much more to choose from, does it, especially with this other business going on?"

She'd make a good detective, Banks thought—quick, perceptive, logical. "Have you got any other ideas?" he asked.

"Maybe I was wrong," Anne said, her voice beginning to shake.

"Wrong about what?"

"When I said Sally was all talk, all big ideas. Maybe she really did know something. Maybe she thought she'd make a name for herself by following it up."

"Why should she do that?"

Anne adjusted her glasses and shook her head. The thick lenses magnified the tears forming in her eyes. "I don't know," she answered.

"Did she tell you anything at all that indicated she knew who the person was? Think about it. Anything."

Anne thought, and the tears held off. "No," she said finally. "She just hinted that she knew things, that she'd solved some kind of mystery. I mean, yes, she did sort of say that she knew who it was, but she didn't give us any names or anything. She said she had to make sure, she didn't want to cause any trouble."

"Do Sally's parents have a telephone?"

"Yes. They've had one for ages. Why?"

"Can you think of any reason why Sally would use a public phonebox on Friday afternoon?"

"No."

"Not even if she wanted to call Kevin or some other boyfriend? I know that parents aren't always understanding."

"There was only Kevin, and Sally's mum and dad knew about him. They weren't a hundred percent keen, but he's a nice enough boy, so they didn't make a fuss about it."

"Did Sally say where she was going on Friday evening?"

"No. I'd no idea she was going anywhere."

"Thank you very much, Anne," Banks said.

The policewoman showed her out and brought Kathy Chalmers in next. Kathy was upset by then, but there were no tears, and although she seemed to realize dimly what it was all about, she had nothing to add.

The last girl, Hazel Kirk, was another matter. She knew as well as the others what was going on, but she pretended ignorance. She said she couldn't even remember whether Sally had said anything about knowing who the killer was. The more Banks questioned her, the more fidgety and edgy she became. Finally, she burst into tears and told Banks to leave her alone. He nodded to the policewoman, who moved forward to speak to her, and left the room.

Sergeant Hatchley was sitting on the edge of Weaver's desk looking over reports from provincial police and railway authorities. He glanced up as Banks approached: "Any luck?"

Banks shook his head. "The first one's the most intelligent, but even she couldn't tell us much. What she did say confirms our suspicions, though. If Sally thought she knew who the killer was and arranged for a meeting, then we can be pretty sure what's happened to her. It must have been someone she knew, someone she wasn't afraid of. There's got to be a motive, dammit, and it's got to be right before our eyes." He banged his fist on the desk, surprising Hatchley with the sudden burst of violence. It reminded the sergeant that his boss came from a tough patch. He wasn't a plodder; he was used to action.

"Got a cigarette?" Banks asked.

"Thought you'd stopped and taken up pipe-puffing," Hatchley said, handing over his packet of Senior Service.

"Not any more. I never could stand the blasted thing."

Hatchley smiled and gave him a light. "Then I suggest, sir," he said, "that you start buying your own."

The door of the interview room opened and a pacified Hazel Kirk came out to rejoin her waiting friends, who had all been whispering, wondering what was going on. The policewoman, looking concerned, stood in the doorway and beckoned Banks over.

"What is it?" he asked, closing the door behind him.

"The girl, sir," the PC began. "Why she was upset. It might mean something."

"Well? Go on."

"Sorry, sir. She got upset because Sally had told her she thought she knew who the killer was, and when she got home, Hazel told her parents." She paused, and Banks drew on his cigarette waiting for her to continue. "They just laughed and said Sally Lumb always did have an over-active imagination, but the girl's father had had a bit of a run in with Steadman a few weeks ago, and Hazel thought..."

"Yes, I can imagine what she thought," Banks said. For all his virtues, Steadman had certainly been a thorn in the side of some locals. "What was it this time?" he asked. "Arguments over land or charges of moral laxity?"

"Sir?"

"Sorry, it doesn't matter," Banks said. "Go on. What's the background?"

"She didn't say, sir. Wouldn't. I'm brought in from Wensleydale. Constable Weaver might know something."

"Yes, of course. Thank you very much, Constable...?"

"Smithies, sir."

"Thank you very much Constable Smithies. You did a good job calming her down and getting her to open up like that," Banks said, then left her blushing in the interview room.

Weaver was on the phone when Banks reached the desk, but he cut the conversation short.

"The weather people from Reckston Moor, sir," he explained. "They say it'd be madness to send out search parties on the moors for at least twenty-four hours."

"Bloody northern weather," Banks cursed. Hatchley, eavesdropping, grinned and winked at Weaver, who ignored him.

"They don't expect the rain to let up for a while, and the land's boggy. Visibility is as bad as you can get up the valley sides. It's all moorland above there, sir, both ways, miles of it."

"Yes, I know," Banks said. "And there's nothing we can do about it, is there? Just make sure everything's set to go the minute the situation improves. Have you arranged for helicopters?"

"Yes, sir. Superintendent Gristhorpe's handling it. But they can't go out in this weather."

"No, of course not. Look, you know that girl who was in here a few minutes ago?"

Weaver nodded. "Hazel Kirk. Yes."

"Know anything about her father?"

"Robert Kirk. Family's been here for generations. Came from Scotland originally."

"What does he do?"

"He works at Noble's in Eastvale. You know, the big shoe shop in that new shopping centre near the bus—station."

"I know it. Anything else."

"He's very active in the local church, sir," Weaver went on. "One or two people think he's a bit of a religious nutter, if you know what I mean. Touch of the fire and brimstone. Strong Presbyterian streak— his ancestors brought it with them from Scotland, if you ask me. Anyway, he's always writing letters to the papers about too much sex on television. His latest fad is a campaign to ban rock videos and bring censorship into the music business. There's not much support for that 'round here, though, sir. Nobody really cares one way or another."

"What's your opinion of him?"

"Nutty but harmless."

"Certain?"

Weaver nodded. "Never been in trouble with us, sir. And he is very religious, like. Wouldn't harm a fly."

"Religious people are often the most violent. Aren't the Iranians religious? Anyway, have a chat with him, would you, and ask him what he argued with Harold Steadman about."

"There wasn't any argument, sir," Weaver replied. "Kirk complained to the headmaster of Eastvale Comprehensive about letting someone with such lax moral standards as Harold Steadman mix with teenage girls."

"What?"

"It's true, sir," Weaver went on, grinning. "He'd seen Steadman with Penny Cartwright now and then, and to Kirk she was nothing less than the Whore of Babylon. Remember, he was around when Penny left Helmthorpe in the first place—all those rumours of incest, then the Sodom and Gomorrah of the music business. Steadman would sometimes give Hazel and the other girls a ride home from school, and he'd take them on field trips and invite them to his house. Kirk complained. Nobody took him seriously, of course. I even overheard Steadman and his mates having a good chuckle over the business in The Bridge one night."

"Why didn't you tell me this before?" Banks asked. There was something in the icy quietness of his tone that sent danger signals to Weaver.

"I—it didn't seem important, sir."

"Didn't seem important?" Banks repeated. "We're investigating a murder, laddie. Do you realize that? Everything's important. Even if it's not important it's important if it has anything to do with the victim and his circle. Do you understand?"

"Yes, sir," Weaver said shakily. "Will that be all, sir?"

"Is that all?"

"Sir?"

"Is there anything else you ought to tell me?"

"No, sir. I don't think so, sir."

"Then that's all. Come on, Sergeant Hatchley, let's get back to civilization."

"Bit rough on him, weren't you, sir?" said Hatchley as they turned up their collars and walked to their cars.

"It won't kill him."

"Think there's owt in it, this Kirk business?"

"No. No more than there was in the major. Unless Kirk's a serious nutter, and Weaver assures me he isn't. Like nearly everything else in this case, there's just too much damn gossip. That's why it's hard to tell the lies from the truth. Kirk, Major Cartwright, nothing but gossip. Better run a check on his background, though, just to make sure. I suppose he thinks Steadman was trying to corrupt his angelic young Hazel."

"I wouldn't blame him," Hatchley said. "The jeans these kids wear nowadays... You'd need a bloody shoehorn to get into them."

Banks laughed. "Enough lewd thoughts about teenagers, Sergeant."

"Aye," Hatchley said. "It's a bloody good job we can't be arrested for what we think. Look, sir, there's a tobacconist's. And it's open."

II

It was late Sunday afternoon before the rain stopped completely, but the first search parties set out at mid-morning. By then it was only drizzling; the clouds had thinned, promising a fine day, and visibility was good. Plenty of locals had been willing to go out on Saturday, despite the weather conditions, but they had been warned against doing so.

The Sunday search was co-ordinated by Superintendent Gristhorpe, who had marked out areas on ordnance survey maps and designated these to each small party. He directed operations from the communications room in Eastvale Regional Headquarters, and as the reports came in, he shaded the ground that had been covered.

Meanwhile, enquiries continued in the major cities. In addition to their regular duties, police on car and foot patrols in Newcastle, Leeds, London, Liverpool, Manchester, Birmingham and other large cities were also keeping an eye out for the young blonde girl. Theatres, drama companies and acting schools were all checked carefully, and though numerous sightings were called in and followed up, they all proved to be false. Closer to home, Robert Kirk was investigated, questioned and let go. For one thing, he couldn't drive, and certainly nobody had carried Harold Steadman all the way from Helmthorpe to Crow Scar.

Sally's father, enraged with grief after receiving a letter from the Marion Boyars Academy of Theatre Arts saying they would be pleased to accept Sally as a student, had begun his search alone on Saturday in the rain. As the day drew on, the weather so affected his rheumatism and his spirits that he was confined to bed by Dr Barnes the following day. Charles Lumb knew that Sally hadn't run away, despite their differences; for him, anxiety and anger gave way to resignation. Even if the searchers did find her, what state would she be in after three or more nights out in the wilds?

On Sunday, the first area searched was the wide stretch of moorland to the north of Helmthorpe, above Crow Scar. Gristhorpe, in making his decision, realized he might have been influenced by the fact that Steadman's body had been found on the northern slopes, but he reasoned that the area was, after all, the wildest spread of countryside— seven miles of rough, high moors before the next dale—and had the greatest number of hiding places: old mines, steep quarries, pot-holes.

The only result of Sunday's effort was an accident in which a police constable drafted in from Askrigg fell down a twenty-foot bell-pit.

Fortunately, his fall was broken by accumulated water and mud, but it took over two hours of valuable time to rig up ropes and pull him out. Up on the moorland, two small parties got so bogged down in mud that they were unable to continue, and progress everywhere was slow.

By Monday, the sun was out to stay and conditions had improved. Gristhorpe, who had been up since five in the morning, sat red-eyed in the communications room logging check-in calls from search parties, and the map before him soon began to look like a chess-board. This was one task he refused to delegate.

At about three o'clock, the superintendent took Sergeant Rowe's advice and dropped by Banks's office to suggest a walk.

They walked into Market Street, which was crowded with tourists from the nearby cities who, seeing an end to the rain, had decided on an afternoon out. It was also market day, and the cobbled square in front of the church was thronged with colourful stalls selling everything from Marks and Spencer's rejects to dinner sets and toilet-bowl brushes. There were stalls of second-hand paperbacks, yards of plain and patterned material—cotton, linen, muslin, rayon, denim, cheese-cloth—spilling over almost to the ground, and stalls piled with dish-ware and cutlery. Skilled vendors drew crowds by shouting out the virtues of their wares as they juggled plates and saucers. The people milled around to listen, take photographs and, occasionally, to buy things. In the narrow, twisting sidestreets around the central market square—old alleys where the sun never penetrated and you could shake hands across second-storey bay windows—the small souvenir and local delicacy shops with magnifying-glass windows did good business. Everything, from toffee and tea to spoons and fluffy toys, was labelled "Yorkshire," no matter where it had actually been made.

Gristhorpe directed Banks to a small tea-shop and the two of them settled down to tea and gateaux.

Gristhorpe ran his hand through his thick, messy mop of grey hair and smiled weakly. "Had to get out for a bit," he said, spooning sugar into his mug. "It gets so damn stuffy in that little room."

"You look all in," Banks said, lighting a Benson and Hedges Special Mild. "Perhaps you should go home and get some sleep."

Gristhorpe grunted and waved away the smoke. "Thought you'd given that filthy habit up," he grumbled. "Anyway, I suppose I am tired. I'm not as young as I used to be. But it's not just tiredness, Alan. Have you ever taken part in an operation like this before?"

"Not a search in open country, no. I've looked for missing teens in Soho, but nothing like this, in these conditions. Do you think there's any hope?"

Gristhorpe shook his head slowly. "No. I think the girl's been killed. Stupid bloody kid. Why couldn't she have come to us?"

Banks had no answer. "Have you been involved in this kind of search before?" he asked.

"More than twenty years ago, now," Gristhorpe said, adding an extra spoonful of sugar to his tea. "And this makes it feel like only yesterday."

"Who was it?"

"Young girl called Lesley Ann Downey. Only ten. And a lad called John Kilbride, twelve. You'll have heard about all that, though: Brady and Hindley, the 'Moors Murders'?"

"You were in on that?"

"Manchester brought some of us in for the search. It's not that far away, you know. Still, that was different."

"Sir?"

"Brady and Hindley were involved in Naziism, torture, fetishism, you name it. This time it's more calculated, if we're right. I don't know which is worse."

"The result's the same."

"Aye." Gristhorpe gulped some tea and nibbled at his gateau. "Getting anywhere?"

Banks shook his head. "Nothing new. Hackett's in the clear now. Barnes, too, by the looks of it. We're stuck."

"It's always like that when the trail goes cold. You know that as well as I do, Alan. If the answer isn't staring you in the face within twenty-four hours, the whole thing goes stale. When you get stuck you just have to push a bit harder, that's all. Sometimes you get lucky."

"I've been thinking about the time of Sally Lumb's disappearance," Banks said, trying to waft his smoke away from Gristhorpe. "She was last seen on Helmthorpe High Street walking east around nine o'clock on Friday evening."

"Well?"

"I was in Helmthorpe at that time, in The Dog and Gun with Sandra and a couple of friends. We went to listen to Penny Cartwright sing. Jack Barker was there, too."

"So that lets them off the hook."

"No, sir. That's just it. She finished her first set just after nine, then she and Barker disappeared from the pub for about an hour."

"Right after Sally had been seen in the village?"

"Yes."

"Better follow it up, then. What do you think?"

"I've talked to them both a couple of times. They're difficult, sharp. If I were easily swayed by sentiment, I'd say no, not a chance. Penny Cartwright seems sincere, and Barker's a clever bugger but likeable enough when you take the time to chat with him. He swears blind he'd nothing to do with Steadman's death. But I've met some damn good liars in my time. He's got no alibi and he might have been jealous about Steadman and the Cartwright woman."

Gristhorpe ate the final few crumbs of gateau and suggested they carry on walking. They headed east and looped down by the river near the terraced gardens.

"The Swain's filling up," Gristhorpe said. "I hope we don't have a bloody flood to contend with, too."

"Does that happen often?"

"Often enough. Usually at spring thaw after a particularly snowy winter. But if you get enough water channelled down from the Dales, it might break the banks here."

They turned up a dank, waterside alley, where moss and lichen grew on the rough stone, skirted the base of Castle Hill, and arrived back at the market square. Gristhorpe headed straight for the communications room and Banks accompanied him. There was nothing new.

III

Even Purcell's "Hail Bright Cecilia" failed to cheer Banks up as he drove into Helmthorpe that evening. When he walked along High Street past the gift shop with its revolving racks of postcards and the small newsagent's with the evening papers outside fluttering in the light breeze, he could sense the mood of the village. Nothing was obvious; people went about their business as usual, shutting up shop for the day and coming home from work, but it felt like a place that had drawn in on itself. Even the air, despite the wind, seemed tight and grim. The small noises—footsteps, doors opening, distant telephones ringing—sounded eerie and isolated against the backdrop of the silent, green valley sides and massive brow of Crow Scar, bright in the evening sun.

Push, Gristhorpe had said, so push he would. Push hard enough, in the right places, and something would give. Push those closest to Steadman—Penny, Ramsden, Emma, Barker—for if none of them had actually done it, Banks was sure that one of them knew who had. He would probably have to revisit Darnley and Talbot again, too. There was something that one of them had said—a chance remark, a throwaway line—that Banks felt was important, but he couldn't remember what it was. It would return to him in time, he knew, but he couldn't afford to sit and wait; he had to push.

Would Sally Lumb have confronted any of them with her evidence? he asked himself as he took the shortcut through the cemetery and turned right along the pathway to Gratly. It didn't seem likely; she wasn't a fool. But she had phoned someone, and had used a public callbox for privacy. It must, then, have been someone she knew, someone she had no reason to fear.

The sheep on his right fled and stood facing the dry-stone wall, their backs to him; the ones on his left scampered down the grassy terraces to the stream and stood bleating under the willows. Funny creatures, Banks thought. If they're frightened, they simply run a short distance and turn their backs. It might be effective against people who wished them no harm, but he doubted if it would deter a hungry wolf.

Emma Steadman was watching television, but she turned the sound down after Banks had followed her into the living-room. The place was much barer now that most of the books and records were gone; it was more of an empty shell than a home.

Banks waited until Emma had made some tea, then sat opposite her at the low table.

"I've been meaning to ask you a few things for a while now," he said. "Mostly to do with the past."

"The past?"

"Yes. Those wonderful summers you used to have up here when the Ramsden family ran the guest house."

"What about them? You don't mind, do you?" she asked, picking up some knitting. "It helps me relax, takes my mind off things. Sorry, go ahead."

"Not at all. It's just that the impression I got was of your husband running around the Dales with Penny Cartwright while Michael Ramsden buried his head in his books."

Emma smiled but said nothing.

"And you never thought anything of it."

"Perhaps if you'd known my husband, Chief Inspector, you wouldn't think anything of it, either."

"But something's missing."

"What?"

"You. What were you doing?"

Emma sighed and put her knitting down on her lap. "Contrary to what you seem to believe, I'm not simply a passive housewife. I did have, and still do have, interests of my own. Back in Leeds, I was involved in amateur dramatics for a while. On holidays in Gratly I used to knit and read. I even tried my hand at writing a few short stories—unsuccessfully, I'm afraid—but I can't prove it, I threw them away. I also went for walks."

"Alone?"

"Yes, alone. Is that so strange?"

Banks shrugged.

"What you seem to forget is that we were only up here for a month or so at a time. During that period I spent a lot more time with my husband than you think. I did accompany them sometimes, especially if they went by car. But I'm very susceptible to the sun, so I never ventured far on sunny days unless I could find some shade. I still fail to see why you find all this so fascinating."

"Sometimes present events have their roots in the past. Did you enjoy your visits?"

"They made a nice break. Leeds isn't the cleanest city in the world, I enjoyed the fresh air, the landscape."

"One more thing. I've been given to believe that your husband was universally liked. Even Teddy Hackett, who had good reason to disagree with him, thought of him as a friend. Since I've been looking into his death, though, I've found at least two people who didn't feel the same way—Major Cartwright and Robert Kirk. We might regard them as cranks, but I'm beginning to wonder if there's anyone else. Someone I don't know about. You were a close group, all those years ago, and your husband was still close to Michael Ramsden and Penny Cartwright when he died. Was there anybody else around? Anybody who might have held a grudge?"

Emma Steadman pursed her lips and shook her head slowly.

"Think about it."

"I am. Of course there were other people around, but I can't imagine any of them had a reason to harm Harold."

"The point is, Mrs Steadman, that somebody did. And if none of you can help me find out who it was, I don't know who can. Is there any reason why he was killed at this particular time rather than, say a year ago, or five years ago?"

"I've no idea."

"You must know something about his affairs. Was he planning to do anything with his money? Write a will, leave it to the National Trust or something? Was there any other land he was after, anyone else's toes he was treading on?"

"No. No to all those questions. And I think I would have known, yes."

"Well, that doesn't leave much, does it?"

"You think one of us did it, don't you?"

Banks kept silent.

"Do you think I did it? For his money?"

"You couldn't have, could you?"

"Maybe you think Mrs Stanton was lying to give me an alibi?"

"No."

"Then why keep bothering me? I only buried my husband a few days ago."

As Banks could think of no answer to that question, he sighed and got up to leave. Before Emma closed the door on him, he turned and spoke again: "Just consider what I said, will you? Try to remember any enemies your husband might have made, however insignificant they might have seemed at the time. Think about it. I'll be back."

Penny Cartwright was listening to music, and when she grudgingly let Banks in, flashing him a "you again" look, she didn't bother to turn it down.

"I won't keep you," Banks said, sitting on a hard-backed chair by the window and lighting a cigarette. "It's just about the other night."

"What night? There's been a lot lately," Penny said, pouring herself a drink.

"Friday night."

"What about it?"

"You were singing at The Dog and Gun, remember?"

Penny scowled at him. "Of course I remember. You were there, too. What is this?"

"Just refreshing your memory. Between sets you went off with Jack Barker. You were gone for about an hour. Where were you?"

"What's that got to do with anything?"

"Look, it's about time you got this right. I ask the questions. You answer. Understand?"

"Oh, poor Inspector Banks," Penny cooed. "Have I been undermining your authority?" Her eyes challenged him. "What was the question again?"

"Friday night, between sets. Where were you?"

"We went for a walk."

"Where?"

"Oh, hither and thither."

"Can you be more specific?"

"Not really. I go for a lot of walks. There's a lot of places to walk around Helmthorpe. That's why so many tourists come here in summer."

"Stop the games and tell me where you went."

"Or else?"

After a thirty second staring match, Penny looked away and reached for a cigarette.

"All right," she said. "We came here."

"What for?"

"What do you think?"

"Sex?"

"That's not the kind of question a lady answers. And it's nothing to do with your investigation."

Banks leaned forward and spoke quietly. "Would it interest you to know that I've got a damn good idea why you came here? And I've got some colleagues back in Eastvale who'd be more than happy to come out here and prove it for me. Help me and you help yourself."

"I'm not admitting anything."

"Where were you at four o'clock on Friday afternoon?"

"I was here practising. Why?"

"Anybody with you?"

"No. There usually isn't when I practise."

"Did you receive any telephone calls?"

Penny looked confused. "Telephone calls? No. What are you getting at?"

"And you refuse to tell me where you went and what you did during the interval on Friday evening?"

"It's none of your business," she said suspiciously. "Wait a minute. Sally. Sally Lumb. She disappeared on Friday, didn't she? Christ, you bastard!" She glared at Banks. Angry tears made her eyes glitter. "Are you implying that I had something to do with that?"

"Where were you?"

"If you already know, why do you want me to tell you?"

"I need to hear it from you."

Penny sagged in her chair and looked away. "All right. So we came back here and smoked a couple of joints. Big deal. Is that what you wanted to hear? What are you going to do now, bring in the dogs and tear the place apart?"

Banks stood up to leave. "I'm not going to do anything. I remembered the difference between the last set and the first, how you seemed more remote, detached. If it's any consolation to you," he said, opening the door, "I believe you, and I'm glad I was right."

But Penny didn't move or say anything to make his exit easier.

IV

Later, as Penny lay in bed that night unable to sleep, the images came again, just as they had been coming ever since Harold Steadman's death: those summers so long ago—innocent, idyllic. Or so they had seemed.

It was a time she had had neither reason nor inclination to think about over the past ten years—the kind of period, like an idealized childhood, that one looks back on when one gets older and life loses its edge. Life had been too busy, too exciting, and when she finally had crashed, she had been as far in her mind from idyllic summers as ever a person could be. It had seemed, then, that her earlier life had been lived by somebody else. Next she had come back home to Helmthorpe, where they were all together again. Now Harold was dead and that wretched detective was probing, asking questions, churning up memories like tides stir sand.

So she re-examined it. She re-ran the walks to Wensleydale along the Pennine Way and the drives to Richmond or the Lake District in Harold's old Morris 1100 like old movies, and she spotted things she had never noticed at the time—little things, vague and unclear, but certainly disturbing. And the more she thought about old times, the less she liked what she was thinking.

She turned over again and tried to cast the images from her mind. They were like dreams, she told herself. She had taken the truth, in all its purity, and warped it in her imagination. That must be what had happened. The problem was that now these dreams seemed so real. She couldn't shake them, and she wouldn't rest until she knew what was fantasy and what was reality. How could the past, something that had really happened, become so altered, so unclear? And as she finally drifted towards sleep, she began to wonder what she should do about it.

ELEVEN

I

The numerous becks that ran down the slopes of Swainsdale to the river were flowing copiously, bringing rainwater from the higher land. A fine mist, like baby's hair, rose from the valley sides as the sun warmed the waterlogged earth. The colours were newly rinsed, too; fresh, vibrant greens sloped up from the road, and bright skull-caps of purple heather, softened by the thin veil of mist, fringed the peaks.

Penny, walking with Jack Barker along High Street, was the first to notice a small crowd gathered on the bridge, under which a combination of becks, grown almost to the strength of a river themselves, cascaded from the southern heights down to the Swain.

A woman in a sleeveless yellow dress was pointing up the valley side, and the others followed her gaze, leaning over the low, stone parapet. Penny and Barker soon reached the spot and stopped casually to see what the excitement was. They had an uninterrupted view up the dale-side along the beck's course, onto which backed several gardens full of bright flowers. Some distance away, they could see what looked like a child's rag doll tumbling recklessly down the fast, swollen stream. It was hypnotic, Penny thought, to watch the thing turn cartwheels and flail, snag on the rocks and break free as the water pushed and dragged it.

Then the woman in the yellow dress put her hand over her mouth and gasped. The others, including Penny, whose long-distance eyesight had never been really good, leaned further over and screwed up their eyes to peer more closely. It was only after the shock-wave had rippled through the crowd that Penny realized what was happening.

It was not a rag doll that came head over heels down the stream, but a body. Tufts of clothing still clung to the torn flesh. It looked raw, like a side of beef in a butcher's window; patches of skin had been ripped clean off, hair torn away from the scalp, and splintered bones stuck through at elbows and shins.

There was no face to recognize, but Penny knew, as did all the other locals on the bridge, that it was the body of Sally Lumb come back to the village where she was born.

Penny wrenched her eyes away while Barker and the others still stared in disbelief. Somebody mentioned an ambulance, somebody else the police, and the group split up in chaos.

Penny and Barker walked in a daze until they got to The Hare and Hounds, then they went inside and ordered double Scotches.

"Seen a ghost?" the barman asked.

"Something like that," Barker said, and gave a garbled version of what had happened. Soon, customers went streaming out to look, leaving drinks on tables, cardigans and handbags on chairs.

The barman gave them each another double Scotch on the house and rushed off to see the spectacle himself. The pub was empty; anybody could have walked in and robbed the place blind, but nobody did. Penny downed the fiery whisky; she was aware of her hand gripping Barker's so tight that the nails must have dug into his flesh.

II

"It's a bugger, Alan," Gristhorpe said, rubbing his eyes, which had lost much of their child-like innocence through lack of sleep. He looked tired, pale and hurt, as if the whole affair, done right on his doorstep, was a personal affront. "A bugger..."

They were in the Queen's Arms opposite the station, and it was almost afternoon closing time. Only a few dedicated drinkers and tourists in need of a late sandwich and shandy sat scattered around the lounge.

"We've got nothing so far," the superintendent went on, sniffing as Banks lit a cigarette. "The body was so bloody waterlogged and badly battered Glendenning couldn't give us any idea of what killed her. For all he can say, she might have fallen in and hit her head, or just drowned. A full autopsy's going to take time, and even then they can't promise owt."

"What's Glendenning doing now?"

"You know him, Alan—couldn't wait to get at it. Stomach contents, organs, tissue samples. God knows, they've got to keep looking. It could even be poison."

"What do you think?" Banks asked, sipping his pint of Theakston's bitter.

Gristhorpe shook his head. "I don't know. They've got their jobs to do. Does it matter what killed her at this point? If we're right, and it's what we think it is, there was probably just a blow to the head, like Steadman. Glendenning might not even be able to verify that."

"I just wish we knew a bit more about why it happened," Banks said. "Certainly I think there's a connection to the Steadman case— has to be—I just don't know what it is. The girl knew something and instead of coming to me she confronted the killer. I suppose she wasn't sure and simply wanted to find out for herself. Add it all up and we've still got nothing. So she knew something. What? She phoned someone. Who? Why? They met. Where?"

"We might be able to answer that last one soon," Gristhorpe said. "I've got men following the becks all the way up the hillside looking for physical evidence. There'll be some kind of grisly map of her progress."

III

"That's scotched work for today," Jack Barker punned weakly as he accepted his third refill from Penny. It was over two hours since they had seen the wreckage of Sally Lumb tumble down the valley side. Penny had stopped after her second drink, but Barker was still at it.

"Maybe you shouldn't," Penny warned him.

"It's already too late. Thanks for your concern, though."

When Penny looked down at Barker, she felt the stirring of something like love. Whatever it was, the feeling disoriented her and she was angry with herself for not knowing what to do. Though it had felt good at first when they had come back to the cottage and he had held her, she hated the feeling of weakness that came with it. She knew that her feelings for him were not Platonic, but instead of reaching out, she drew in and strengthened her shell.

Barker seemed to sense something of her chaotic emotions, she thought, when he reached out again for her hand, which she allowed him to hold lightly.

"I suppose I always did have a weak stomach," he said. "Pathetic, really, isn't it? Here I am writing about blood and guts for a living and as soon as I see..." His words trailed off and he started to shake. He put his glass on the table, spilling some Scotch as he did so. Then Penny sat beside him and held him. It seemed ages to her before either of them moved, and each would have said the other broke away first.

"You should get some sleep, Jack," Penny said softly.

"What the hell's going on, Penny?" he asked. "What's happening to this place?"

"I don't know," Penny answered, stroking his hair. "At least, I..."

"What?"

"Nothing," she said. "Or maybe nothing, I don't know. But it's got to stop."

IV

"Under a pack-horse bridge," Banks said. "That's what the super told me. On the south slope."

"What does that mean?" Sandra asked. They were having an early evening drink in the Queen's Arms. Sandra had just finished shopping, and Banks had suggested that, as they had seen so little of one another the past few days, they meet for a chat. Brian and Tracy were old enough to manage on their own for an hour or two.

"It means he was wrong about where to look first, and he's kicking himself for that."

"But he couldn't have known," Sandra said. "It made perfect sense to look on the north side first."

"That's what everyone says, but you know what he's like."

"Yes. Just like you. Stubborn. Takes it all on himself."

"He'll get over it," Banks said. "Anyway, they found clothes fibres on the stones under this bridge. She must have been hidden there and covered with stones. Then when the heavy rains came, some of the stones were washed aside and she was carried down the valley. They've not found any traces above the bridge, and it looked like an ideal place—isolated but accessible by car, just."

"Does it help, finding the body?"

"Not really. Not the state it's in. And too much time has gone by. We'll ask around of course—anybody heading that way, or back—but we can't expect too much. Whoever we're dealing with is smart, and he's not likely to make silly mistakes."

"This probably had to be done in a hurry, though," Sandra reminded him. "There wouldn't have been much time for planning."

"Still, it's not going to be easy."

"Is it ever?"

Banks shrugged and lit a cigarette.

"By the way," Sandra said, "I haven't had chance to say so before now, but I'm glad you got rid of that bloody pipe."

"It didn't suit me."

"No."

"Too *Country Life*?"

Sandra laughed. "Yes, I'd say so. You'd not fool many, though. Least of all yourself."

"There's not many would say they're glad to see a person smoke, either," Banks said, holding out the pack while Sandra, an occasional smoker, helped herself. "But I do intend to cut down and stick to these mild things."

"Promises!"

"The girl, you know," Banks said after a brief pause. "She was a virgin as far as forensic could make out. Hadn't been shot, stabbed, poisoned or sexually assaulted. Virgin."

"I wonder if that's a good thing," Sandra asked.

"What? That she hadn't been assaulted?"

"No. That she died a virgin."

"It won't make any difference to her now, poor beggar," said Banks. "And I doubt it's the kind of thing they inscribe on tombstones. But at least we can be sure she wasn't tormented or tortured. She probably died very quickly, without even knowing what was happening."

"Are you going to get the killer soon, Alan?" Sandra asked, swirling the smooth fragments of ice in the bottom of her glass. "And don't treat me like a reporter. Be honest."

"I'd like to say yes, but we've got so damn little to go on. We can trace the girl's movements until about nine o'clock Friday evening, and that's it."

"While we were at the folk club?"

"Yes."

Sandra shivered. "We were so close."

"Does that make a difference?"

"It's just a funny feeling, that's all. What about the writer and the singer?"

"She could be protecting him, or they could be working together. It's hard to know what to believe when things are clouded by so much gossip. The others all go back so far, too. Years. Lord knows what complex webs of feelings they've set up between one another over the years. It seems to me that in a place like Helmthorpe, emotions go deeper and last longer than in a big city."

"Nonsense. Think about all those feuds and gang rivalries in London."

"That's business, in a way. I mean the ordinary things between people."

"Who had the best motive?" Sandra asked.

"The one with the least opportunity." Banks smiled at the irony. "That's if you call a lot of money a good motive. There could also be all kinds of jealousies involved. That's why I can't leave Barker and Penny Cartwright out of it altogether."

"The wife inherits?"

"Yes."

"She came in for some bridge-work yesterday."

"What did you think of her?"

"I didn't see much of her, really. Only when she came to the window to confirm her appointment. She seemed like quite an attractive woman."

"She didn't look much to me."

"That's typical of a man," Sandra said. "All you can see is the surface."

"But you must admit she's let herself go."

"It looks like it, yes," Sandra said slowly. "But I don't think so. It's all there. She's in good shape under all those awful clothes. Her bone structure's good, too. Of course, if you'd known her before or not seen her for a long time, she'd definitely look as if she'd gone downhill, I suppose."

"A pretty young thing."

"Pardon?"

"Oh, nothing," Banks said. "Just remembering something. Go on."

"All I'm saying is the potential's there for her to be an attractive woman. She can't be much older than me."

"Late thirties."

"Well, then. She must only look plain because she wants to, because it doesn't matter to her. Not all women are obsessed with their looks, you know. Perhaps there are other things more important to her."

"Perhaps. What you're saying," Banks went on slowly, "is that with the right hair-style, good clothes and a little makeup . . ."

"She could be quite a stunner, yes."

V

Penny was at the stove roasting spices for a curry when Barker made his way down the narrow stairs.

"So, the sleeper awakes," she greeted him.

"What time is it?"

"Seven o'clock."

"At night?"

"Yes. It's still the same day. Hungry? I shouldn't think so, with a hangover like you must have. Anyway, I'm making a curry. Take it or leave it."

"Your generosity and grace overwhelm me," Barker said. "As a matter of fact, I don't feel too bad. I've just got a hell of a headache."

"Aspirin's in the bathroom cabinet."

"What happened?" Barker asked.

"You mean you don't remember?"

"Not after the third drink. Or was it the fourth?" He rubbed his eyes with his knuckles.

"You really don't remember?" Penny repeated, sounding shocked. "Well that's a fine compliment, isn't it?"

"You mean...?"

Penny laughed. "Don't be a fool, Jack. I'm only kidding. You got tired and I helped you upstairs to sleep it off. That's all."

"All?"

"Yes. You don't think I'd fall into bed with you the way you were earlier, do you?"

"I'll get some aspirin," Jack said, and made his painful way back upstairs to the bathroom.

"We'll let that simmer for a while," Penny said when he came back, "and have a sit down. Drink?"

"My God, no!" Barker groaned. "But on the other hand...hair of the dog and all that. Not whisky, though."

"Beer do?"

"Yes."

"Sam Smith's?"

"Fine."

"Good. It's all I've got. Chilled too."

Penny brought the beer and Barker sat on the sofa drinking out of the bottle.

"What you said, Penny," he began, "about not, you know, sleeping with me in a state like that..."

"I doubt you'd have been able to get it up, would you?" she mocked, a mischievous smile crinkling the corners of her mouth.

"I might be a bit slow," Barker replied, "but are you implying that if I'd been sober...I mean, you might actually...you know?"

Penny put her finger to his lips and stopped him. "That's for me to know and you to find out," she said.

"Dammit, Penny," he said, "you can't just ignore me half the time and then tease me the rest. It's not fair. I'm upset enough as it is about the girl floating down and all that."

"I'm sorry, Jack. It just doesn't come out right. I stop one game and start another, don't I?"

"That's how it seems. Why don't you give me a straight answer?"

"What's the question?"

"I've already asked you."

"Oh, that. I'm glad you were drunk, Jack, because, no, I don't think I would have. Is that straight enough?"

"It seems to be," Barker said, disappointment clear in his tone.

Penny went on quickly. "It's not as straight as you think. What I mean is I'm glad I wasn't forced into making a decision there and then. I'm weak, I might have said yes and regretted it. It would have been so easy, then, so natural to make love after being confronted with death. But I wouldn't have been able to get Sally out of my mind, that awful torn body . . ."

"I understand that. But why would you regret it?"

Penny shrugged. "Lots of reason. So much has happened. It's too quick, too soon. It would be easy to jump into bed with you. You're an attractive man. But I want more than that, Jack. I don't just want to be like one of the bimbos you sleep with when you're down in London publicizing your books."

"I don't, and you never could be."

"Whatever. I've had enough disappointments in my life. I want some stability. I know it sounds conventional and corny, but I want to settle down, and I think I might be better off doing it by myself. I'm not one of these women who depends on a man."

"It's just as well. I'm hardly dependable." Barker lit a cigarette and coughed. "Look," he said, "I don't care whether this is the right place and time or what it is, but I love you, Penny. That's what I'm trying to get at. Not whether you'll sleep with me or not. There, I've said it. Maybe I've made a fool of myself."

Penny looked at him carefully for a long time, then she said, "I don't know if I can handle being in love."

"Try it," Barker said, leaning forward and stroking her hair. "You never know, you might like it."

Penny looked away. Barker moved closer and took her in his arms. She tensed up a bit, but didn't break the embrace.

Finally, she disengaged herself and looked at him seriously. "Don't expect too much of me," she said. "I'm used to fending for myself and I like it."

"You and I," Jack said, "we've been living alone so long it's frightening to think about change. So let's just take it easy, slowly."

A bell rang in the kitchen.

"That's telling me the curry's ready." Penny got up.

Barker followed her into the kitchen and leaned in the narrow doorway as she stirred the pungent sauce. "Do you know," he said, "it took that bloody policeman, as you call him, to make me realize that I was jealous of you and Harry. I wondered, why the hell should you give so much of yourself to him and so little to me?"

"That's not fair, Jack." Penny's face darkened as she turned to him. "Don't talk like that. You sound just like Banks."

"I'm sorry," Barker apologized. "I didn't mean anything by it."

"Forget it."

"The past won't go away, Penny," Barker said. "There's a lot of things need explaining."

"Like what?" Penny asked suspiciously, taking the pot off the ring.

"You know more about it than I do."

"More about what?"

"Everything that's happened. Come on, Penny, don't tell me you haven't got any ideas. You know more about this business than you're letting on."

"Why should you think that?"

"I don't really know," Barker answered. "It's just that you've been awfully mysterious and touchy about it these past few days."

Penny turned back to the curry in silence.

"Well?" Barker asked.

"Well what?"

"Do you?"

"Do I what?"

"Oh come on. You know what I mean. Do you know something I don't?"

"How do I know what you know?"

"I don't know anything. Do you?"

"Of course not," Penny said, pouring the curry into dishes. "It's your imagination, Jack. You writers! Don't you think if I knew something I'd tell you?"

"As a matter of fact, I don't. Sally Lumb didn't tell anyone either. Or she told the wrong person."

"And you think it was me?"

"Don't be ridiculous."

"Go on, you might as well say it," Penny shouted, brandishing the spoon like a club. "Just like Banks. Go on!"

"I don't know what you're talking about."

"Friday evening, when she disappeared."

"But we were in The Dog and Gun."

"Not all the time."

"So? You came home for a rest and I went for a walk. So what?"

"You don't know?"

"Know what?"

"Banks hasn't been to pester you?"

"About what?"

"That's when Sally was last seen. While we were away. Somebody saw her in High Street about nine o'clock."

"So Banks thinks...?"

Penny shrugged. "He asked me. You?"

"No. I've not seen him for a few days."

"You will. He's getting very pushy."

"I suppose he must be desperate. Surely you don't think I was implying you had anything to do with it?"

"Well weren't you?"

"I'd hardly declare my undying love to someone I thought was a murderess, would I?"

Penny smiled.

"And what about you?" he went on. "Do you believe me?"

"About what?"

"That I just went for a walk."

"Well, yes. Of course I do. I don't even remember how all this started."

"I was simply asking you if you knew anything you hadn't told me. That's all."

"And I thought I'd answered that," Penny said, her dark eyes narrowing. "I've been no more mysterious about it than you have."

"Oh come off it, Penny. You can't get out of it that easily. You've been around here much longer than I have. You're bound to know more about what goes on than I do."

"You seem to be treating me like a criminal, Jack. Is this your idea of love? If this is what it comes down to, just how bloody jealous were you?"

"Forget it," Barker sighed. "Just forget I opened my mouth."

"I'd like to, Jack, I really would."

They eyed each other warily, then Penny broke off to carry the bowls through to the dining table. She pushed one towards Barker, who sat down to eat.

"You've put me in a right mood for a romantic candlelight dinner, you have," she complained. "I'm not even hungry now."

"Try some," Barker said, offering her a spoonful. "It's very good."

"I've lost my appetite." Penny reached for a cigarette, then changed her mind and picked up her light jacket. "I'm going out."

"But you can't," Barker protested. "We've got a lot to talk about. What about the candles? You've made dinner."

"Eat it yourself," Penny told him, opening the door. "Eat the bloody candles, too, for all I care."

Barker half rose from the table. "But where are you going?"

"To see a man about a dog," she said, and slammed the door behind her.

VI

Though the sun still lingered low on the horizon, it was dark on Market Street in the shadow of the buildings on the western side, and the cobbled square was deserted. Banks hadn't even bothered to turn on his office light after returning to go over his notes. Sandra had gone home to assure Brian and Tracy that they weren't becoming latchkey children. The door was closed and the dark room was full of smoke. Occasionally, he heard footsteps in the corridor outside, but nobody seemed to know he was there.

As was his habit when a case felt near to its end, he sat by the window smoking and rearranged the details in his mind four or five times. After about an hour, things still looked the same. The pattern, the picture, was complete, and however unbelievable it was, it had to be right. Eliminate the impossible and whatever is left, however improbable, must be the truth. Or so Sherlock Holmes had said.

It was time for action.

Banks played no music as he drove towards the purplish-red sunset west along Swainsdale; his mind was far too active to take in anything more. Finally, he swung up the hill to Gratly, turned sharp left after the bridge and pulled up outside the Steadman house. There were no lights on. Banks cursed and walked down the path to Mrs Stanton's.

"Oh, hello Inspector," she greeted him. "I didn't expect to see you again. Please come in."

"Thank you very much," Banks said, "but I don't think I will. I'm a bit pushed for time. If you could just answer a couple of quick questions?"

Mrs Stanton frowned and nodded.

"First of all, have you any idea where Mrs Steadman is?"

"No, I don't. I think I heard her car about an hour or so ago, but I've no idea where she was going."

"Did you see her?"

"No, I wasn't looking. Even if I was it wouldn't matter, though. They've got a door from the kitchen goes straight into the garage. Money," she said. "They've even got those automatic doors. Just press a button."

"Which direction did she drive off in?"

"Well, she didn't come past here."

"So she went east?"

"Aye."

"Do you remember that Saturday you spent watching television with her?" Mrs Stanton nodded slowly. "Do you know if she went out again after she got home?"

Mrs Stanton shook her head. "I certainly didn't hear her, and I was up for more than an hour puttering around."

"Last Friday night, did she go out at all?"

"Couldn't tell you, Inspector. That was my bingo night."

"Your husband?"

"Pub. As usual."

"This was a regular Friday night arrangement?"

"Ha! For him it's a reg'lar every night arrangement."

"And you?"

"Aye, I go to bingo every Friday. So does half of Swainsdale."

"Mrs Steadman?"

"Never. Not her. Not that she's a snob, mind. What pleases some folks leaves others cold. Each to his own is what I say."

"Thank you very much, Mrs Stanton," Banks said, leaving her mystified as he got back into the Cortina and set off towards Helmthorpe.

He parked illegally in High Street by the church, right at the bottom of Penny's street. There was a light on in her front room. Banks walked quickly up the path and knocked.

He was surprised when Jack Barker answered the door.

"Come in, Chief Inspector," Barker said. "Penny's not here, I'm afraid. Or have you come to ask me where I was on Friday evening?"

Banks ignored the taunt; he had no time for games. "Has she said anything odd lately about the Steadman business?" he asked.

Puzzled, Barker shook his head. "No. Why?"

"Because I got the impression she was holding something back. Something she might not have been sure about herself. I was hoping I could persuade her to tell me what it was."

Barker lit a cigarette. "As a matter of fact," he said. "Penny has been a bit strange the few times I've seen her lately. Secretive and touchy. She hasn't said anything, though."

Banks sat down and began tapping the frayed arm of the chair. "You two," he said, looking around the room. "Are you ... er ...?"

"Playing house? Not really. No such luck. I was here for dinner. We just had a bit of a row about the very thing you just mentioned, actually. She took off and I'm waiting for her to come back."

"Oh?"

"I suggested she knew more than she was letting on, and she accused me of treating her like a criminal, just like you did."

"That's what she thinks?"

"Well you have been giving her a rough time, you can't deny it."

Banks looked at his watch. "Is she coming back soon?"

"I've no idea."

"No idea? Where is she?"

"I told you," Barker said. "We had a row and she stormed out."

"Where to?"

"I don't know."

"Did she say anything?"

"She said she was going to see a man about a dog."

"A lot of help that is."

"Just what I thought."

"And you'd been on at her about knowing something?"

"Yes."

"Did she take the car?"

"Yes."

"Right." Banks got to his feet. "Come on."

Without thinking, Barker jumped up and obeyed the command. Banks only gave him time to blow out the candles and lock the door.

"Look, what's going on?" Barker asked as they shot into the darkening dale. "You're driving like a bloody lunatic. Is something wrong? Is Penny in danger?"

"Why should she be?"

"For Christ's sake, I don't know. But you're behaving damned oddly, if you ask me. What the hell's happening?"

Banks didn't reply. He focused all his concentration on driving, and the silence intensified as darkness grew. On the northern outskirts of Eastvale, he turned onto York Road.

"Where are we going?" Barker asked a few minutes later.

"Almost there," Banks replied. "And I want you to do exactly as I say. Remember that. I've only brought you with me because I know you're fond of Penny and you happened to be in her house. I'd no time to waste, and you might be some use, but do as I say." He broke off to overtake a lorry.

Barker gripped the dashboard. "So you've not brought me along for the pleasure of my company?"

"Give me a break."

"Seriously, Chief Inspector, is she in danger?"

"I don't know. I don't know what we're going to find. Don't worry, though, it won't be long now," he said, and the tires squealed as he turned sharp left. About a quarter of a mile along the bumpy minor road, Banks pulled into a driveway and Barker pointed and said, "That's her car. That's Penny's car."

A face peered through a chink in the curtains as they jumped out of the Cortina and hurried towards the door.

"No time for pleasantries," Banks said after trying the handle to no avail. He stood back and gave a hard kick, which splintered the wood around the lock and sent the door flying open. With Barker close behind, he rushed into the living-room and quickly took in the strange tableau.

There were three people. Michael Ramsden stood facing Banks, white-faced and slack-jawed. Penny lay inert on the couch. And the woman stood with her back to them all.

In a split second, it came to life. Barker gasped and ran over to Penny, and Ramsden started to shake.

"My God," he groaned, "I knew this would happen. I knew it."

"Shut up!" the woman said, and turned to face Banks.

She wore a clinging red dress that accentuated her curves; her hair was drawn back into a tight V on her forehead; and carefully applied blush highlighted the cheekbones of her heart-shaped face. But the most striking thing about her was her eyes. Before, Banks had only seen them watery and distorted through thick lenses, but now she was wearing contacts, they were the chilly green of moss on stones, and the power that shone through them was hard and piercing. It was Emma Steadman, transformed almost beyond recognition.

Ramsden collapsed into the armchair, head in hands, whimpering, while Emma continued to glare at Banks.

"You bastard," she said, and spat at him. "You ruined it all." Then she lapsed into a silence he never heard her break.

TWELVE

I

But Ramsden talked as willingly as a sinner in the confessional, and what he said over the first two hours following his arrest gave the police enough evidence to charge both of them. Banks was astonished at Ramsden's compulsion to unburden himself, and realized only then what terrible pressure the man must have been under, what inner control he must have exerted.

As for Penny, she said she had been doing a great deal of thinking over the last few days. Steadman's death, Banks's questions and Sally's disappearance had all forced her to look more deeply into a past she had ignored for so long, and especially into the events of a summer ten years ago.

At first, she remembered nothing. She hadn't lied; everything had seemed innocent to her. But then, she said, the more she found herself dwelling on the memory, the more little things seemed to take on greater significance than they had done at the time. At first, she thought she'd got things out of all proportion: glances exchanged between Emma Steadman and Michael Ramsden—had they really happened or were they just her imagination? Ramsden's insistent overtures, then his increasing lack of interest—again, had it really happened that way? Was there, perhaps, a simple explanation? All these things had inflamed her curiosity.

Finally, after the argument with Jack Barker, she knew it wouldn't all just go away. She had to do something or her doubts about the past would poison any chance of a future. So she went to visit Ramsden to find out if there was any truth in her suspicions.

Yes, she knew what had happened to Sally Lumb, and she also knew the police linked the girl's death to Steadman's, but she honestly didn't believe she had anything to fear from Michael Ramsden. After all, they'd known each other off and on since childhood.

She questioned Ramsden and, finding his responses nervous and evasive, pushed even harder. They drank tea and ate biscuits, and Ramsden tried to convince her that there was nothing in her fears. Eventually she found difficulty focusing; the room darkened and she felt as if she were looking at it through the wrong end of a telescope. Then Penny fell asleep. When she awoke she was in Barker's arms and it was all over.

Banks told her that Ramsden had sworn he wouldn't have hurt her. True, he had drugged her with some prescription Nembutal and driven to the public telephone on the main road to send for Emma, but only because he was confused and he didn't know what to do. When Emma had insisted that they would have to kill Penny because she knew too much, Ramsden claimed that he had tried to stand up to her. She had called him weak and said she would do what was necessary if he wasn't man enough. She said it would be easy to arrange an accident. According to Ramsden, they were still arguing when Banks and Barker arrived.

Penny listened to all this at about one o'clock in the morning over a pot of fresh coffee in Banks's smoky office. All she could say when he had finished was, "I was right, wasn't I? He wouldn't have hurt me."

Banks shook his head. "He would," he insisted, "if Emma Steadman told him to."

II

It was a couple of days before all the loose ends were tied up. Hatchley made notes and wrote up the statements, complaining all the while about DC Richmond sunning himself in Surrey, and Gristhorpe went over the details. Emma Steadman said nothing; she didn't even bother to deny Ramsden's accusations. To Banks, she was a woman who had risked everything and lost. There was no room for regret or recrimination now it was all over.

Later in the week, Banks took Sandra over to Helmthorpe, where they heard Penny sing at a special memorial concert for Sally Lumb. Afterwards, as it was a warm night and the show ended early, they went with Penny and Jack Barker for a drink in the beer garden of The Dog and Gun. Crow Scar gathered the failing light and gleamed as the hills around it fell into shadow. It looked like a pale curtain hanging in the sky.

Sandra and the others pressed Banks for an explanation of the Steadman business, and though he felt very uncomfortable in the role they forced on him, he did feel he owed Barker and Penny something, at least; nor had he had much time to talk to Sandra since the arrests, and she had helped him arrive at the correct pattern.

"When did it start?" Sandra asked first.

"About ten years back," Banks told her. "That makes Penny here sixteen, Michael Ramsden eighteen, Steadman about thirty-three and his wife just twenty-eight. Harold Steadman had a promising career as a university professor. If he wasn't exactly rich then, he was certainly comfortably off, and he did have the inheritance to look forward to. Emma, too, must have been quite pleased with life in those days, but I imagine she quickly got bored. She was beginning to fade into the background like so many faculty wives. When I talked to Talbot and Darnley, two of Steadman's colleagues at Leeds University, one of them remembered Emma as a 'pretty young thing' at first, then she just seemed to disappear into the woodwork. I dare say she'd have liked to go abroad for her holidays more often. But no, Steadman had discovered Helmthorpe—Gratly, rather—and that satisfied all his requirements of a busman's holiday, so that was that. For Emma, life seemed to be passing by too quickly and too dully, and she felt too young to give it all up.

"That summer was beautiful, just like this one." Banks paused to look around at the other drinkers with their jackets and cardigans hung on the backs of chairs. "How often can you do this in England?" he asked, sipping chilled lager. "Especially in Yorkshire. Anyway, Penny and Michael were the pride of the village—two bright kids with their whole lives ahead of them. Michael was a lean, serious, romantic young fellow, and if he imagined he was losing Penny to an older, wiser man, then he still had a steady diet of Keats and Shelley to keep him nicely melancholy. Penny here simply enjoyed Steadman's company, as she's told me often enough. They had a lot in common, and there were no amorous inclinations on either side. Or if there were, they were well repressed."

He glanced at Penny, who looked down into her beer.

"So," Banks went on after a deep breath, "one sunny day Penny's out with Steadman looking at the Roman excavations in Fortford, say, and Michael's languishing in the garden reading 'Ode to a Nightingale' or something. His parents are out shopping in Leeds or York and won't be back till it's time to prepare the evening meal. Emma Steadman is moping around the place staying out of the sun, and probably feeling bored and neglected. I'm making this up, by the way. Ramsden didn't give me a blow by blow account. Anyway, Emma seduces young Michael. Not so difficult when you consider his age and his obsession with sex. Surely it's every schoolboy's fantasy—the experienced older woman. To Emma, he must have seemed like a younger, more vital version of her husband. Perhaps he wrote poetry for her. He was certainly gawky and shy, and she gave him his first sexual experience.

"Most people probably thought of Emma Steadman as a married woman going quickly to seed, but Michael made her feel wanted, and then she began to see definite advantages in not being thought particularly attractive. That way, nobody would think of her as the type to be having an affair."

Banks stopped to drink some more lager, pleased to see that he hadn't lost his audience. "The affair went on over the years," he continued. "There were gaps and breaks, of course, but Ramsden told us they often got together in London when Emma went down for a weekend's 'shopping,' or when she went to 'Norwich' to 'visit her family.' I don't think her husband paid her a great deal of attention—he was far too busy poring over ruins.

"Anyway, Emma developed a powerful hold over Michael. As his first lover, she had a natural advantage. She taught him all he knew. And he was still shy in company and found it hard to meet girls his own age. But why bother? Emma was there and she gave him all he needed, far more than the inexperienced girls of his own age group could have given him. And, in turn, he made her feel young, sexy and powerful. They fed off each other, I suppose.

"Over the years, Emma developed two distinct personalities. Now I'm not suggesting for a moment that she's mentally ill—there's nothing at all clinically wrong with her—all her actions were deliberate, willed, calculated. But she had one face for the world and another for Ramsden. If you think about it, it wasn't that difficult for her to change her appearance. She only had to do it to please Ramsden, and he was strongly under her influence anyway. Visiting him in London would have been no problem, of course. But even after she moved to Gratly and he moved to York, it was simple enough. She could easily do herself up a bit in the car on the way to see him—a little make-up, a hairbrush. She could even change her clothes after she arrived, if she wanted. With Harold gone, it was even easier. Her neighbour told me there's a door from the kitchen right into the garage, and it's a lonely road over the moors to Ramsden's place. But it wasn't just looks, it was attitude, too. With Ramsden, she felt her sexual power, something that was more or less turned off the rest of the time.

"As time went by, everything she expected to happen happened. Steadman threw himself more and more into his work, and she found herself, except for Ramsden, increasingly isolated. Why did she stay with her husband? I'm only guessing here, but I can think of two good reasons. First of all, security, and secondly, the promise of the inheritance, the possibility that things might improve when they became rich. And what happens? The money comes through, all right, but nothing changes. In fact, things get worse. And here I can sympathize with her, to some extent. She's a woman with dreams—travel, excitement, wealth, a social life—but all that happens is her husband buys the Ramsden house and she ends up even more bored and cut off while he spends the money on historical research. A dedicated man. Even though I can't condone what she did to him, I can understand why she was driven to it. Steadman wasn't exactly sensitive to her needs—emotional or material. He was selfish and mean. There they were, rich as bloody Croesus, and he spends his time drinking in The Bridge and his money on his work. I'm sure Emma Steadman would have preferred the Country Club. In fact, she was little more than a prisoner, and the only person her husband was really close to was Penny again."

"That's not quite true," Penny said. "He was close to Michael. He liked him."

"Yes," Banks agreed. "But that was much more of a working relationship. Michael was of use to him. I think they were colleagues, or partners, rather than friends. Don't forget, Michael killed him."

"She made him."

"Yes, but he did it."

A waiter came out and they ordered another round.

"Go on," Penny urged him after the drinks arrived.

"Michael Ramsden is ambitious, but he's weak. He's not good with people. He shared Steadman's interests, yes, but he wasn't obsessed— a word that offended one of Steadman's colleagues, but apt, I think. Also, Ramsden resented Harold Steadman, and this really had nothing to do with you, Penny, even if he did feel jealous all those years ago. No, he resented Steadman in the way many of us come to detest people we first set up as examples, models, call them what you will. He hated always playing second fiddle—the publisher, the assistant—never the creative one, the leader, although he was busy working on a novel himself. Emma must have played on this, I think, dwelling on her husband's bad points when she was with Ramsden, playing on Michael's growing resentment for his mentor. Soon he began to recognize Steadman's meanness and his lack of consideration for anybody with interests other than his own. I think, too, that he was always, deep down, irritated at the way Harold could communicate so easily with Penny, how fond they were of one another. Anyway, this animosity grew and grew over the years, fuelled by sexual desire for Emma, and finally there came a chance to get rich, to take it all.

"Emma Steadman used Ramsden, manipulated him, without a doubt. But that doesn't absolve him from blame. Slowly, she introduced the idea of murder to him, helped him over his initial resistance and nervousness. She did this partly by playing on his existing feelings about her husband, and partly through sex. Denial, satisfaction. More denial, greater satisfaction than he'd ever had before. That's what he told me, anyway. He's not a fool; he knew what was happening and he went along with it. Together, they killed Harold Steadman.

"Naturally, as Emma stood to inherit, she'd be the first suspect, so she had to be sure of an airtight alibi, which she had. Also, Ramsden seemed to have neither motive nor opportunity, no matter how I went at him, until the connection with Emma finally came into focus. There were also a number of other possibilities I had to pursue."

Both Barker and Penny looked at him reprovingly as he said this.

"Yes," he went on, acknowledging them. "You two. Hackett, for a while. Barnes. Even the major and Robert Kirk, fleetingly. Believe me, I blame myself for not arriving at the answer before Sally Lumb had to die, too, but I couldn't see the truth for the gossip, or the past for the present."

"Why did Sally have to die?" Barker asked. "Surely she couldn't have been a threat? What could she have known?"

"Sally was older than her years in many ways," Banks replied. "She misread the situation. But I'll get back to her a bit later. On the Saturday that Steadman was killed, Ramsden drove close to Gratly. He parked his car in one of those derelict old barns on the minor road just east of the Steadman house, the one Emma always used to get to York. Remember, Ramsden had been brought up in Gratly; he knew every twist and dip in the dale."

"But how did he get back?" Penny asked. "It's an impossibly long walk, and the only bus to Eastvale goes early in the morning."

"Easy," Banks answered. "He wouldn't have taken the bus any-way—too many people might have noticed him. Emma Steadman drove him back. She picked him up on the road at a pre-arranged time—a fairly isolated spot, so there'd be no chance of their being seen. Then she dropped him off at the end of his lane and went shopping in York. We've checked on that now, and her neighbour remembers it because Emma brought back some material she'd asked for. There was nothing unusual in all that. Emma Steadman often spent afternoons shopping in York. After all, she was a lady of leisure. They just had to be careful not to be seen. And even if they had been, Ramsden looked enough like Steadman from a distance through a car window, so nobody would have thought twice about seeing them."

"What about that night?" Penny asked. "After Harry had the row with my father?"

"That's another thing hindsight tells me I should have known," Banks answered. "There was only one place Steadman would have gone after recovering from the barney, and that's exactly where he intended to go in the first place, to Ramsden's. Remember, he was a dedicated man, and you, Penny, were the only person he allowed to make emotional inroads into his valuable time. So he did exactly what he intended; he drove to York. And Ramsden killed him.

"It was all planned in advance, perhaps even rehearsed. Ramsden already had plastic sheeting on the floor because he was painting his living-room. He hit Steadman from behind with a hammer, wrapped his body in the sheet, bundled it in the boot of Steadman's own car, drove it up near Crow Scar and buried it. He couldn't bury him in the plastic because that might have given too much away, but he told us where he buried it and we've dug it up."

Penny put her head in her hands and Barker put his arms around her.

"I'm sorry, Penny," Banks said. "I know it sounds brutal, but it was."

Penny nodded and took a sip of her drink, then she reached for a cigarette. "I know," she said. "It's not your fault. I'm sorry to be such a cry-baby. It's just the shock. Please go on."

"It was well after midnight and the village was deserted. He put Steadman's car back in the car park, cut through the graveyard and over the beck, then drove his own car home to York. All he had to worry about was getting stopped on the way, but the road he chose made that most unlikely. As I said, the whole thing was carefully planned to throw all suspicion away from Ramsden and Emma Steadman, who had the best motive. It even helped them that Steadman's car was a beige Sierra. They're quite common around here. I looked in the car park myself yesterday and saw three of them. And there are others that look much the same, especially in dim light—Allegros, for example. Of course, there were minor risks, but there was a hell of a lot at stake. It was worth it."

"What about Sally, then?" Sandra asked. "How does she fit into it?"

"She wasn't part of the plan at all," Banks said. "She was just one of the innocent bystanders whose memory got jogged too much for her own good. Like Penny here."

"There but for the grace of God," Penny muttered.

"Too true," Banks agreed. "Whatever you believe, Emma would have convinced Ramsden it was necessary to get rid of you. She'd probably have had to do it herself, but he wouldn't have stopped her. He was too far gone."

"You said he seemed almost glad when you arrived," Penny said.

"Yes in a way. It was the end; he was free. I really think he was relieved. Anyway, according to Ramsden, Sally said she saw him and Emma together in Leeds. They were very careful. They'd never think of going out in York or Eastvale, but Leeds seemed safe enough. None of Steadman's old colleagues would have recognized Emma, and she knew the kind of places they went to, the places to avoid. Sally was there with her boyfriend. I've talked to him again and he said they did go to Leeds once when he borrowed a friend's car, and Sally pulled him out of one pub—Whitelock's—pretty sharpish when she spotted someone she knew. But she didn't realize who it was at the time. She was more concerned with Ramsden not seeing her than about who he was with. I suspect she and Kevin went to quite a few pubs. Sally certainly looked old enough to pass for eighteen, but she was underage, so she couldn't afford to get caught.

"Now, most people would have just thought that Michael Ramsden had got himself a good-looking girlfriend, and I'm sure that's what Sally believed until events in Helmthorpe made her start re-examining little things like that. She was perceptive and imaginative. But it wasn't until I'd managed to link Emma and Ramsden that I knew how Sally fitted in at all. One thing I noticed when I saw her was that she seemed very skilled with make-up for a girl of her age, and she was interested in acting, the theatre. She had seen Ramsden in Leeds with an attractive woman, forgotten about it, then seen the image again when her mind was on the Steadman business—maybe at the funeral, when she had plenty of time to examine what everyone was wearing and how they looked. I was there, too, and I noticed how she seemed to be scrutinizing us all, though it didn't mean anything to me at the time. However it happened, she remembered, and she became convinced it was Emma, carefully made up, that she had seen with Ramsden. So Sally phoned her.

"That was where she went wrong. Emma Steadman told Ramsden

later that Sally had gone on about *Wuthering Heights* on the phone, and about how she thought Ramsden had killed Harold Steadman so he could marry Emma just to get his hands on the house and money. Sally was convinced that Ramsden would murder Emma, too, after he had married her. She seemed to think the Ramsdens had gone down in the world and that Michael must resent Steadman tremendously for buying the house from his family and taking over. She suggested a secret meeting to discuss things and see if they could find a way to deal with the situation. She thought that, together, they could solve the case and make the police look silly. Emma was terrified of anything that could link her with Ramsden, so she killed the girl."

"Emma killed Sally Lumb?" Penny repeated numbly.

"Yes. Up by the pack-horse bridge on Friday night. She hid the body under the bridge—the water was low then—and piled stones on it."

"But why on earth did Sally meet her like that?" Barker asked. "She must have known it might be dangerous."

"Not at all. As far as Sally was concerned, she was simply warning Emma, saving her life. Besides, even if she did have second thoughts, ask Penny. She was about to do much the same thing, and she never seriously considered that Ramsden would harm her."

"But that was different," Penny argued. "I'd known Michael all my life. I knew he wouldn't hurt me, even if what I thought was true."

"Somebody would have hurt you," Banks replied. "You wouldn't find much comfort in being right about Ramsden while Emma was killing you. It wouldn't matter to you who did it then, would it?"

"Only to the police, I suppose."

"You're wrong about that," Banks said, leaning forward and looking straight into her eyes. "It matters to everyone except the corpse. Murder is the one crime that can't be put right. It upsets the balance. The dead can't be restored like stolen property; death doesn't heal like physical or emotional scars left by assault or rape. It's final. The end. Sally Lumb made a mistake and she died for it."

"She was reading the wrong book," Barker said. "And misreading it, at that. She should have been reading *Madame Bovary*. That's about a woman who considers murdering her husband."

Banks hadn't read *Madame Bovary* but made a mental note to do so as soon as possible. When the waiter reappeared, Banks and Penny were the only ones to order more drinks.

Banks lit another cigarette. "Ramsden got really scared after Emma killed Sally," he said. "But life went on and no thunderbolts from heaven struck him down. Then Penny started to figure things out. You know the rest."

Penny shivered and draped her shawl over her shoulders.

"Emma Steadman was far more powerful than any of us had imagined," Banks said. "She also had a solid alibi for her husband's murder. There was no way she could have done that, and though I flirted with the idea that she might have paid someone, it didn't seem likely. Sergeant Hatchley was right—she wouldn't have known how to contact a hired killer. Besides, if she had, it would have meant someone else to fear, someone who knew about her and what she'd done. Ramsden was ideal; Emma could control him, and he stood to gain, too. Sally knew that Mrs Steadman couldn't have carried the body up Tavistock's field—another reason not to fear her—but she didn't know that Ramsden seemed to have a perfect alibi. I certainly didn't tell her, and I don't think anyone else did.

"I was thinking about all the wrong combinations," he said to Penny. "You and Steadman, you and Ramsden, you and Barker here. For a while I even considered maybe Ramsden and Steadman were homosexually involved. Like everyone else, I was taken in by Emma Steadman's outer drabness. I just couldn't picture her as a woman of passion and power. I didn't even try. But she had the most dangerous combination of all—a passionate and calculating nature."

"What did make you think of her?" asked Barker. "I'd never have got it in a million years."

"That's because you only write books," Banks joked, "while I do the real work."

"*Touché.* But really? I'm curious."

"Tell me, didn't you ever notice anything odd about Emma Steadman?"

Barker thought for a while. "No," he answered. "I can't say I did. I didn't really see a lot of her. When I did I always felt a bit uneasy."

"Why?"

"I don't know. There are some women just make you feel like that."

"You didn't tell me that when I asked you about her."

"Never really thought of it till you mentioned it just now," Barker said. "Besides, what difference would it have made?"

"None I suppose," Banks admitted. "It's just that I felt uneasy with her, too. Claustrophobic, even. It was a kind of gut reaction, and I ought to know better than that."

"But what did it mean?" Barker asked.

"This is all hindsight," Banks said, "so it did me no good until it was too late, but I think I was responding to her sexual power unconsciously, and I was put off by her appearance. I couldn't accept being attracted to her, so I felt dislike, revulsion. It might sound silly, but I couldn't see beneath the surface. Still, that was the last thing I realized. First of all, there was something Darnley had said in Leeds that I couldn't for the life of me remember. It was just the kind of casual, throwaway remark anyone might overlook."

"What was it?" Penny asked.

"He said that Emma had been a pretty little thing at first in Leeds. Of course, that meant nothing at the time. Then Sally disappeared. I thought she must be connected in some way to the Steadman business, but I couldn't figure out how. I knew about her theatrical interests, but there was no way of getting from that to seeing Michael Ramsden as Steadman's killer. Besides, I was still too busy looking in every direction but the right one. I was blinded by Emma's alibi, too.

"Finally, Sandra said she'd seen Emma and noticed that she was still in good shape. That was when the bits and pieces seemed to fit together: a pretty young thing, Sally's skill at make-up—which is just altering appearances, when you get right down to it—and Emma Steadman as the outline, still, of an attractive woman. And she did tell me she'd been involved in amateur dramatics. When I thought about what others had told me about Emma, I realized that nobody had ever mentioned her being attractive. Penny wouldn't, of course—like her husband, I don't think you ever really noticed Emma—and Jack here hadn't known her that far back. Ramsden never said that she was attractive, either, and that, finally, seemed odd. Then I got to thinking about Ramsden alone with her at the house that summer, about how he suddenly seemed to drift away from Penny. I'd always seen him as a kind of pale loiterer, but it took me a long time to see Emma

Steadman as a *belle dame*. My view of the past was wrong, just like
Teddy Hackett said Steadman's was, and everyone else seemed to
look back on that summer through rose-coloured glasses. If truth be
told, it was a period of desire, greed, deception, adultery—hardly an
idyll at all. Even Sally got it wrong.

"When I asked my questions, I never had Ramsden and Emma in
mind, but it was easy enough to review what I'd learned in the light
of a new perspective. Once I'd got that far, it seemed possible. Two
people working together could have handled the Steadman killing,
while both seeming to have solid alibis. Sally could have posed a
threat to Emma if she had seen her, transformed from the drab housewife into the sexy siren, with Michael Ramsden. All I had to do then
was go and push even harder. At least I knew I was going in the right
direction. But events turned out differently."

"You were certainly fixed in your ideas about me and Harry,"
Penny said.

"Yes," Banks agreed. "Maybe Ramsden and Emma was a combination I shouldn't have overlooked. But it's easy to say that now it's over.
Whenever I thought of that summer I knew there was something
missing, so I assumed that people had been lying to me, hiding something. They hadn't. As far as you knew, it had all happened the way
you told me. Almost all, anyway."

"Don't blame yourself," Sandra said to him, winking at Penny.
"After all, you're only a man."

"I'll drink to that," Penny said, raising her glass and nudging Jack
Barker.

While Banks joined in the toast and the chit-chat that followed,
he thought deep, guilty thoughts about Sally Lumb, who had seen
beneath the surface, only to find yet another romantic illusion. Above
them, as all traces of the sun disappeared, Crow Scar began to gleam
like bone in the light of the rising moon.

A NECESSARY END

For Martin, Chris, Steve
and Paul—old friends
who all contributed.

Author's Note

Though most of this story takes place in the fictional region of Swainsdale and its main town, Eastvale, some scenes are set in real places, such as Hebden Bridge and Scarborough. Whatever the setting, all characters in the story are purely imaginary and bear no resemblance to anyone living or dead.

ONE

I

The demonstrators huddled in the March drizzle outside Eastvale Community Centre. Some of them held home-made placards aloft, but the anti-nuclear slogans had run in the rain like the red lettering at the beginning of horror movies. It was hard to make out exactly what they said any more. By eight-thirty, everyone was thoroughly soaked and fed up. No television cameras recorded the scene, and not one reporter mingled with the crowd. Protests were *passé*, and the media were only interested in what was going on inside. Besides, it was cold, wet and dark out there.

Despite all the frustration, the demonstrators had been patient so far. Their wet hair lay plastered to their skulls and water dribbled down their necks, but still they had held up their illegible placards and shifted from foot to foot for over an hour. Now, however, many of them were beginning to feel claustrophobic. North Market Street was narrow and only dimly lit by old-fashioned gaslamps. The protestors were hemmed in on all sides by police, who had edged so close that there was nowhere left to spread out. An extra line of police stood guard at the top of the steps by the heavy oak doors, and opposite the hall more officers blocked the snickets that led to the winding back streets and the open fields beyond Cardigan Drive.

Finally, just to get breathing space, some people at the edges began pushing. The police shoved back hard. The agitation rippled its way to the solidly packed heart of the crowd, and suppressed tempers rose. When someone brought a placard down on a copper's head, the other demonstrators cheered. Someone else threw a bottle. It smashed harmlessly, high against the wall. Then a few people began to wave their fists in the air and the crowd started chanting, "WE WANT IN! LET US IN!" Isolated scuffles broke out. They were still struggling for more ground, and the police pushed back to contain them. It was like sitting on the lid of a boiling pot; something had to give.

Later, nobody could say exactly how it happened, or who started it, but most of the protestors questioned claimed that a policeman yelled, "Let's clobber the buggers!" and that the line advanced down the steps, truncheons out. Then all hell broke loose.

II

It was too hot inside the Community Centre. Detective Chief Inspector Alan Banks fidgeted with his tie. He hated ties, and when he had to wear one he usually kept the top button of his shirt undone to alleviate the choking feeling. But this time he toyed with the loose knot out of boredom, as well as discomfort. He wished he was at home with his arm around Sandra and a tumbler of good single-malt Scotch in his hand.

But home had been a cold and lonely place these past two days because Sandra and the children were away. Her father had suffered a mild stroke, and she had taken off down to Croyden to help her mother cope. Banks wished she were back. They had married young, and he found that the single life, after almost twenty years of (mostly) happy marriage, had little to recommend it.

But the main cause of Banks's ill humour droned on and on, bringing to the crowded Eastvale Community Centre a particularly nasal brand of Home Counties monetarism. It was the Honourable Honoria Winstanley, MP, come to pour oil on the troubled waters of North-South relations. Eastvale had been blessed with her presence because, though not large, it was the biggest and most important town in that part of the country between York and Darlington. It was also enjoying a period of unprecedented and inexplicable growth, thus marking itself out as a shining example of popular capitalism at work. Banks was present as a gesture of courtesy, sandwiched between two taciturn Special Branch agents. Superintendent

Gristhorpe had no doubt assigned him, Banks thought, because he had no desire to listen to the Hon Honoria himself. If pushed, Banks described himself as a moderate socialist, but politics bored him and politicians usually made him angry.

Occasionally, he glanced left or right and noticed the restless eyes of the official bodyguards, who seemed to be expecting terrorist action at any moment. For want of their real names, he had christened them Chas and Dave. Chas was the bulky one with the rheumy eyes and bloated red nose, and Dave was blessed with the lean and hungry look of a Tory cabinet minister. If a member of the audience shifted in his or her seat, raised a fist to muffle a cough or reached for a handkerchief, either Chas or Dave would slip his hand under his jacket towards his shoulder-holster.

It was all very silly, Banks thought. The only reason anyone might want to kill Honoria Winstanley would be for inflicting a dull speech on the audience. As motives for murder went, that came a long way down the list—though any sane judge would certainly pronounce it justifiable homicide.

Ms Winstanley paused and took a sip of water while the audience applauded. "And I say to you all," she continued in all-out rhetorical flight, "that in the fullness of time, when the results of our policies have come to fruition and every vestige of socialism has been stamped out, all divisions will be healed, and the north, that revered cradle of the Industrial Revolution, will indeed prosper every bit as much as the rest of our glorious nation. Once again this will be a *united* kingdom, united under the banner of enterprise, incentive and hard work. You can already see it happening around you here in Eastvale."

Banks covered his mouth with his hand and yawned. He looked to his left and noticed that Chas had become so enrapt by Honoria that he had momentarily forgotten to keep an eye open for the IRA, the PLO, the Bader Meinhoff group and the Red Brigade.

The speech was going down well, Banks thought, considering that members of the same government had recently told the north to stop whining about unemployment and had added that most of its problems were caused by poor taste in food. Still, with an audience made up almost entirely of members of the local Conservative Association— small businessmen, farmers and landowners, for the most part—such whole-hearted enthusiasm was only to be expected. The people in the hall had plenty of money, and no doubt they ate well, too.

It was getting even hotter and stuffier, but the Hon Honoria showed no signs of flagging. Indeed, she was off on a laudatory digression about share-owning, making it sound as if every Englishman could become a millionaire overnight if the government continued to sell off nationalized industries and services to the private sector.

Banks needed a cigarette. He'd been trying to give up again lately, but without success. With so little happening at the station and Sandra and the children away, he had actually increased his intake. The only progress he had made was in switching from Benson and Hedges Special Mild to Silk Cut. He'd heard somewhere that breaking brand loyalty was the first step towards stopping entirely. Unfortunately, he was beginning to like the new brand more than the old.

He shifted in his seat when Honoria moved on to the necessity of maintaining, even expanding, the American military presence in Britain, and Chas gave him a challenging glance. He began to wonder if perhaps this latest digression was a roundabout way of approaching the issue the many people present wanted to hear about.

There had been rumours about a nuclear-power station across the North York Moors on the coast, only about forty miles from Eastvale. With Sellafield to the west, that was one too many, even for some of the more right-wing locals. After all, radioactivity could be quite nasty when you depended on the land for your prosperity. They all remembered Chernobyl, with its tales of contaminated milk and meat.

And as if the peaceful use of nuclear power weren't bad enough, there was also talk of a new American air-force base in the area. People were already fed up with low-flying jets breaking the sound barrier day in, day out. Even if the sheep did seem to have got used to them, they were bad for the tourist business. But it looked as if Honoria was going to skirt the issue in true politician's fashion and dazzle everyone with visions of a new Golden Age. Maybe the matter would come up in question time.

Honoria's speech ended after a soaring paean to education reform, law and order, the importance of military strength, and private ownership of council housing. She had made no reference at all to the nuclear-power station or to the proposed air base. There was a five-second pause before the audience realized it was all over and began to clap. In that pause, Banks thought he heard signs of a ruckus outside. Chas and Dave seemed to have the same notion too; their eyes darted to the doors and their hands slid towards their left armpits.

III

Outside, police and demonstrators punched and kicked each other wildly. Parts of the dense crowd had broken up into small skirmishes, but a heaving, struggling central mass remained. Everyone seemed oblivious to all but his or her personal battle. There were no individuals, just fists, wooden sticks, boots and uniforms. Occasionally, when a truncheon connected, someone would scream in agony, fall to his knees and put his hands to the flow of blood in stunned disbelief. The police got as good as they gave, too; boots connected with groins, fists with heads. Helmets flew off and demonstrators picked them up to swing them by the straps and use as weapons. The fallen on both sides were trampled by the rest; there was no room to avoid them, no time for compassion.

One young constable, beset by two men and a woman, covered his face and flailed blindly with his truncheon; a girl, blood flowing down the side of her neck, kicked a policeman, who lay in the rain curled up in the foetal position. Four people, locked together, toppled over and crashed through the window of Winston's Tobacco Shop, scattering the fine display of Havana cigars, bowls of aromatic pipe tobacco and exotic Turkish and American cigarette packets onto the wet pavement.

Eastvale Regional Police Headquarters was only a hundred yards or so down the street, fronting the market square. When he heard the noise, Sergeant Rowe dashed outside and sized up the situation quickly. He then sent out two squad cars to block off the narrow street at both ends, and a Black Maria to put the prisoners in. He also phoned the hospital for ambulances.

When the demonstrators heard the sirens, most of them were aware enough to know they were trapped. Scuffles ceased and the scared protestors broke for freedom. Some managed to slip by before the car doors opened, and two people shoved aside the driver of one car and

ran to freedom across the market square. A few others hurled themselves at the policemen who were still trying to block off the snickets,
knocked them out of the way, and took off into the safety and obscurity of the back alleys. One muscular protestor forced his way up the
steps towards the Community Centre doors with two policemen hanging onto the scruff of his neck trying to drag him back.

IV

Loud and prolonged applause drowned out all other sounds, and the
Special Branch men relaxed their grips on their guns. The Hon
Honoria beamed at the audience and raised her clasped hands above
her head in triumph.

Banks still felt uneasy. He was sure he'd heard sounds of an argument or a fight outside. He knew that a small demonstration had
been planned, and wondered if it had turned violent. Still, there was
nothing he could do. At all costs, the show must go on, and he didn't
want to create a stir by getting up and leaving early.

At least the speech was over. If question time didn't go on too long
he'd be able to get outside and smoke a cigarette in half an hour or so.
An hour might see him at home with that Scotch, and Sandra on the
other end of the telephone line. He was hungry, too. In Sandra's
absence, he had decided to have a go at *haute cuisine*, and though it
hadn't worked out too well so far—the curry had lacked spiciness,
and he'd overcooked the fish casserole—he was making progress.
Surely a Spanish omelette could present no real problems?

The applause died down and the chairman announced question
time. As the first person stood up and began to ask about the proposed site of the nuclear-power station, the doors burst open and a
hefty, bedraggled young man lurched in with two policemen in tow.
A truncheon cracked down, and the three fell onto the back row. The
young man yelped out in pain. Women screamed and reached for
their fur coats as the flimsy chairs toppled and splintered under the
weight of the three men.

Chas and Dave didn't waste a second. They rushed to Honoria,
shielding her from the audience, and with Banks in front, they left

through the back door. Beyond the cluttered store-rooms, an exit opened onto a complex of back streets, and Banks led them down a narrow alley where the shops on York Road dumped their rubbish. In no time at all the four of them had crossed the road and entered the old Riverview Hotel, where the Hon Honoria was booked to stay the night. For the first time that evening, she was quiet. Banks noticed in the muted light of the hotel lobby how pale she had turned.

Only when they got to the room, a suite with a superb view over the terraced river-gardens, did Chas and Dave relax. Honoria sighed and sank into the sofa, and Dave locked the door and put the chain on while Chas headed over to the cocktail cabinet.

"Pour me a gin-and-tonic, will you, dear?" said Honoria in a shaky voice.

"What the hell was all that about?" Chas asked, also pouring out two stiff shots of Scotch.

"I don't know," Banks said. "There was a small demonstration out-side. I suppose it could have—"

"Some bloody security you've got here," said Dave, taking his drink and passing the gin-and-tonic to Honoria.

She gulped it down and put her hand to her brow. "My God," she said, "I thought there was nobody but farmers and horse-trainers liv-ing up here. Look at me, I'm shaking like a bloody leaf."

"Look," Banks said, hovering at the door, "I'd better go and see what's happening." It was obvious he wasn't going to get a drink, and he was damned if he was going to stand in as a whipping boy for the security organizers. "Will you be all right?"

"A damn sight safer than we were back there," Dave said. Then his tone softened a little and he came to the door with Banks. "Yes, go on. It's your problem now, mate." He smiled and lowered his voice, twitching his head in Honoria's direction. "Ours is her."

In the rush, Banks had left his raincoat in the Community Centre, and his cigarettes were in the right-hand pocket. He noticed Chas lighting up as he left, but hadn't the audacity to ask for one. Things were bad enough already. Flipping up his jacket collar against the rain, he ran down to the market square, turned right in front of the church and stopped dead.

The wounded lay groaning or unconscious in the drizzle, and

police still scuffled with the ones they'd caught, trying to force them into the backs of the cars or into the Black Maria. Some demonstrators, held by their hair, wriggled and kicked as they went, receiving sharp blows from the truncheons for their efforts. Others went peacefully. They were frightened and tired now; most of the fight had gone out of them.

Banks stood rooted to the spot and watched the scene. Radios crackled; blue lights spun; the injured cried in pain and shock while ambulance attendants rushed around with stretchers. It defied belief. A full-blown riot in Eastvale, admittedly on a small scale, was near unthinkable. Banks had got used to the rising crime rate, which affected even places as small as Eastvale, with just over fourteen thousand people, but riots were surely reserved for Birmingham, Liverpool, Leeds, Manchester, Bristol or London. It couldn't happen here, he had always thought as he shook his head over news of Brixton, Toxteth and Tottenham. But now it had, and the moaning casualties, police and demonstrators alike, were witness to that hard truth.

The street was blocked off at the market square to the south and near the Town Hall, at the junction with Elmet Street, to the north. The gaslamps and illuminated window displays in the twee tourist shops full of Yorkshire woollen wear, walking gear and local produce shone on the chaotic scene. A boy, no more than fifteen or sixteen, cried out as two policemen dragged him by his hair along the glistening cobbles; a torn placard that had once defiantly read NO NUKES flapped in the March wind as the thin rain tapped a faint tattoo against it; one policeman, helmet gone and hair in disarray, bent to help up another, whose moustache was matted with blood and whose nose lay at an odd angle to his face.

In the revolving blue lights, the aftermath of the battle took on a slow-motion, surrealistic quality to Banks. Elongated shadows played across walls. In the street, odd objects caught the light for a second, then seemed to vanish: an upturned helmet, an empty beer bottle, a key-ring, a half-eaten apple browning at the edges, a long white scarf twisted like a snake.

Several policemen had come out of the station to help, and Banks recognized Sergeant Rowe standing behind a squad car by the corner.

"What happened?" he asked.

Rowe shook his head. "Demo turned nasty, sir. We don't know how or why yet."

"How many were there?"

"About a hundred." He waved his hand at the scene. "But we didn't expect anything like this."

"Got a cigarette, Sergeant?"

Rowe gave him a Senior Service. It tasted strong after Silk Cut, but he drew the smoke deep into his lungs nonetheless.

"How many hurt?"

"Don't know yet, sir."

"Any of ours?"

"Aye, a few, I reckon. We had about thirty or so on crowd-control duty, but most of them were drafted in from York and Scarborough on overtime. Craig was there, and young Tolliver. I haven't seen either of them yet. It'll be busy in the station tonight. Looks like we've nicked about half of them."

Two ambulance attendants trotted by with a stretcher between them. On it lay a middle-aged woman, her left eye clouded with blood. She turned her head painfully and spat at Sergeant Rowe as they passed.

"Bloody hell!" Rowe said. "That was Mrs Campbell. She takes Sunday School at Cardigan Drive Congregationalist."

"War makes animals of us all, Sergeant," Banks said, wishing he could remember where he'd heard that, and turned away. "I'd better get to the station. Does the super know?"

"It's his day off, sir." Rowe still seemed stunned.

"I'd better call him. Hatchley and Richmond, too."

"DC Richmond's over there, sir." Rowe pointed to a tall, slim man standing near the Black Maria.

Banks walked over and touched Richmond's arm.

The young detective constable flinched. "Oh, it's you, sir. Sorry, this has got me all tense."

"How long have you been here, Phil?"

"I came out when Sergeant Rowe told us what was happening."

"You didn't see it start, then?"

"No, sir. It was all over in fifteen minutes."

"Come on. We'd better get inside and help with the processing."

Chaos reigned inside the station. Every square inch of available space was taken up by arrested demonstrators, some of them bleeding from minor cuts, and most of them complaining loudly about police brutality. As Banks and Richmond shouldered their way towards the stairs, a familiar voice called out after them.

"Craig!" Banks said, when the young constable caught up with them. "What happened?"

"Not much, sir," PC Craig shouted over the noise. His right eye was dark and puffed up, and blood oozed from a split lip. "I got off lucky."

"You should be at the hospital."

"It's nothing, sir, really. They took Susan Gay off in an ambulance."

"What was she doing out there?"

"They needed help, sir. The men on crowd control. We just went out. We never knew it would be like this...."

"Is she hurt badly?"

"They think it's just concussion, sir. She got knocked down, and some bastard kicked her in the head. The hospital just phoned. A Dr Partridge wants to talk to you."

A scuffle broke out behind them and someone went flying into the small of Richmond's back. He fell forward and knocked Banks and Craig against the wall.

Banks got up and regained his balance. "Can't anyone keep these bloody people quiet!" he shouted to the station in general. Then he turned to Craig again. "I'll talk to the doctor. But give the super a call, if you're up to it. Tell him what's happened and ask him to come in. Sergeant Hatchley, too. Then get to the hospital. You might as well have someone look at your eye while you pay a sick call on Susan."

"Yes, sir." Craig elbowed his way back through the crowd, and Banks and Richmond made their way upstairs to the CID offices.

First Banks reached into his desk drawer, where he kept a spare packet of cigarettes, then he dialled Eastvale General Infirmary.

Reception paged the doctor, who picked up the phone about a minute later.

"Are there any serious injuries?" Banks asked.

"Most of them are just cuts and bruises. A few minor head wounds. On the whole, I'd say it looks worse than it is. But that's not—"

"What about PC Gay?"

"Who?"

"Susan Gay. The policewoman."

"Oh, yes. She's all right. She's got concussion. We'll keep her in overnight for observation, then after a few days' rest she'll be right as rain. Look, I understand your concern, Chief Inspector, but that's not what I wanted to talk to you about."

"What is it, then?" For a moment, Banks felt an icy prickle of irrational fear. Sandra? The children? The results of his last chest X-ray?

"There's been a death."

"At the demonstration?"

"Yes."

"Go on."

"Well, it's more of a murder, I suppose."

"Suppose?"

"I mean that's what it looks like. I'm not a pathologist. I'm not qualified—"

"Who's the victim?"

"It's a policeman. PC Edwin Gill."

Banks frowned. "I've not heard the name. Where's he from?"

"One of the others said he was drafted in from Scarborough."

"How did he die?"

"Well, that's the thing. You'd expect a fractured skull or some wound consistent with what went on."

"But?"

"He was stabbed. He was still alive when he was brought in. I'm afraid we didn't . . . There was no obvious wound at first. We thought he'd just been knocked out like the others. He died before we could do anything. Internal bleeding."

Banks put his hand over the receiver and turned his eyes up to the ceiling. "Shit!"

"Hello, Chief Inspector? Are you still there?"

"Yes. Sorry, doc. Thanks for calling so quickly. I'll send down some more police guards. Nobody's to leave, no matter how minor their injuries. Is there anyone from Eastvale station there? Anyone conscious, that is."

"Just a minute."

Dr Partridge came back with PC Tolliver, who had accompanied Susan Gay in the ambulance.

"Listen carefully, lad," Banks said. "We've got a bloody crisis on our hands back here, so you'll have to handle the hospital end yourself."

"Yes, sir."

"There'll be more men down there as soon as I can round some up, but until then do the best you can. I don't want anyone from tonight's fracas to leave there, do you understand?"

"Yes, sir."

"And that includes our men, too. I realize some of them might be anxious to get home after they've had their cuts dressed, but I need statements, and I need them while things are fresh in their minds. Okay?"

"Yes, sir. There's two or three more blokes here without serious injuries. We'll see to it."

"Good. You know about PC Gill?"

"Yes, sir. The doctor told me. I didn't know him."

"You'd better get someone to identify the body formally. Did he have a family?"

"Don't know, sir."

"Find out. If he did, you know what to do."

"Yes, sir."

"And get Dr Glendenning down there. We need him to examine the body. We've got to move quickly on this, before things get cold."

"I understand, sir."

"Good. Off you go."

Banks hung up and turned to Richmond, who stood in the doorway nervously smoothing his moustache. "Go downstairs, would you, Phil, and tell whoever's in charge to get things quietened down and make sure no one sneaks out. Then call York and ask if they can spare a few more men for the night. If they can't, try Darlington. And you'd better get someone to rope off the street from the market square to the Town Hall, too."

"What's up?" Richmond asked.

Banks sighed and ran a hand through his close-cropped hair. "It looks like we've got a murder on our hands and a hundred or more bloody suspects."

TWO

I

The wind chimes tinkled and rain hissed on the rough moorland grass. Mara Delacey had just put the children to bed and read them Beatrix Potter's *Tale of Squirrel Nutkin*. Now it was time for her to relax, to enjoy the stillness and isolation, the play of silence and natural sound. It reminded her of the old days when she used to meditate on her mantra.

As usual, it had been a tiring day: washing to do, meals to cook, children to take care of. But it had also been satisfying. She had managed to fit in a couple of hours throwing pots in the back of Elspeth's craft shop in Relton. If it was her lot in life to be an earth mother, she thought with a smile, better to be one here, away from the rigid rules and self-righteous spirituality of the ashram, where she hadn't even been able to sneak a cigarette after dinner. She was glad she'd left all that rubbish behind.

Now she could enjoy some time to herself without feeling she ought to be out chasing after converts or singing the praises of the guru—not that many did now he was serving his stretch in jail for fraud and tax evasion. The devotees had scattered: some, lost and lonely, had gone to look for new leaders; others, like Mara, had moved on to something else.

She had met Seth Cotton a year after he had bought the place near Relton, which he had christened Maggie's Farm. As soon as he showed it to her, she knew it had to be her home. It was a typical eighteenth-century Dales farmhouse set in a couple of acres of land on the moors above the dale. The walls were built of limestone, with gritstone corners and a flagstone roof. Recessed windows looked north over the dale, and the heavy door-head, supported on stacked quoins, bore the initials T.J.H.—standing for the original owner—and the date 1765. The only addition apart from Seth's workshop, a shed at the far end of the back garden, was a limestone porch with a slate roof. Beyond the back-garden fence, about fifty yards east of the main house, stood an old barn, which Seth had been busy renovating when she met him. He had split it into an upper studio-apartment, where Rick Trelawney, an artist, lived with his son, and a one-bedroom flat on the ground floor, occupied by Zoe Hardacre and her daughter. Paul, their most recent tenant, had a room in the main house.

Although the barn was more modern inside, Mara preferred the farmhouse. Its front door led directly into the spacious living-room, a clean and tidy place furnished with a collection of odds and sods: an imitation Persian carpet, a reupholstered fifties sofa, and a large table and four chairs made of white pine by Seth himself. Large beanbag cushions lay scattered against the walls for comfort.

On the wall opposite the stone fireplace hung a huge tapestry of a Chinese scene. It showed enormous mountains, their snow-streaked peaks sharp as needles above the pine forests. In the middle-distance, a straggling line of tiny human figures moved up a winding path. Mara looked at it a lot. There was no overhead light in the room. She kept the shaded lamps dim and supplemented them with fat red candles because she liked the shadows the flames cast on the tapestry and the whitewashed stone walls. Her favourite place to curl up was near the window in an old rocking chair Seth had restored. There, she could hear the wind chimes clearly as she sipped wine and read.

In her early days, she had devoured Kerouac, Burroughs, Ginsberg, Carlos Castaneda and the rest, but at thirty-eight she found their works embarrassingly adolescent, and her tastes had reverted to the classics she remembered from her university days. There was something about those long Victorian novels that suited a place as isolated and slow-moving as Maggie's Farm.

Now she decided to settle down and lose herself in *The Mill on the Floss*. A hand-rolled Old Holborn and a glass of Barsac would also go down nicely. And maybe some music. She walked to the stereo, selected Holst's *The Planets*, the side with "Saturn," "Uranus" and

"Neptune," then nestled in the chair to read by candlelight. The others were all at the demo, and they'd be sure to stop off for a pint or two at the Black Sheep in Relton on the way back. The kids were sleeping in the spare room upstairs, so she wouldn't have to keep nipping out to the barn to check on them. It was half-past nine now. She could probably count on at least a couple of hours to herself.

But she couldn't seem to concentrate. The hissing outside stopped. It was replaced by the steady dripping of rain from the eaves-troughs, the porch and the trees that protected Maggie's Farm from the harsh west winds. The chimes began to sound like warning bells. There was something in the air. If Zoe were home, she'd no doubt have plenty to say about psychic forces—probably the moon.

Shrugging off her feeling of unease, Mara returned to her reading: "And this is Dorlcote Mill. I must stand a minute or two here on the bridge and look at it, though the clouds are threatening, and it is far on in the afternoon...." It was no good; she couldn't get into it. George Eliot's spell just wasn't working tonight. Mara put down the book and concentrated on the music.

As the ethereal choir entered towards the end of "Neptune," the front door rattled open and Paul rushed in. His combat jacket was dark with rain and his tight jeans stuck to his stick-insect legs.

Mara frowned. "You're back early," she said. "Where are the others?"

"I don't know." Paul was out of breath and his voice sounded shaky. He took off his jacket and hung it on the hook at the back of the door. "I ran back by myself over the moors."

"But that's more than four miles. What's wrong, Paul? Why didn't you wait for Seth and the others? You could have come back in the van."

"There was some trouble," Paul said. "Things got nasty." He took a cigarette from his pack of Player's and lit it, cupping it in his hands the way soldiers do in old war films. His hands were trembling. Mara noticed again how short and stubby his fingers were, nails bitten to the quick. She rolled another cigarette. Paul started to pace the room.

"What's that?" Mara asked, pointing in alarm to the fleshy spot at the base of his left thumb. "It looks like blood. You've hurt yourself."

"It's nothing."

Mara reached out, but he pulled his hand away.

"At least let me put something on it."

"I told you, it's nothing. I'll see to it later. Don't you want to hear what happened?"

Mara knew better than to persist. "Sit down, then," she said. "You're driving me crazy pacing around like that."

Paul flopped onto the cushions by the wall, taking care to keep his bloodied hand out of sight.

"Well?" Mara said.

"The police set on us, that's what. Fucking bastards."

"Why?"

"They just laid into us, that's all. Don't ask me why. I don't know how cops think. Can I have some wine?"

Mara poured him a glass of Barsac. He took a sip and pulled a face.

"Sorry," she said. "I forgot you don't like the sweet stuff. There's some beer in the fridge."

"Great." Paul hauled himself up and went through to the kitchen. When he came back he was carrying a can of Carlsberg lager and he'd stuck an Elastoplast on his hand.

"What happened to the others?" Mara asked.

"I don't know. A lot of people got arrested. The police just charged into the crowd and dragged them off left, right and centre. There'll be plenty in hospital, too."

"Weren't you all together?"

"We were at first, right up at the front, but we got separated when the fighting broke out. I managed to sneak by some cops and slip down the alley, then I ran all the way through the back streets and over the moor. I'm bloody knackered." His Liverpudlian accent grew thicker as he became more excited.

"So people did get away?"

"Some, yes. But I don't know how many. I didn't hang around to wait for the others. It was every man for himself, Mara. The last I saw of Rick he was trying to make his way to the market square. I couldn't see Zoe. You know how small she is. It was a bleeding massacre. They'd everything short of water cannons and rubber bullets. I've seen some bother in my time, but I never expected anything like this, not in Eastvale."

"What about Seth?"

"Sorry, Mara. I've no idea what became of him. Don't worry, though, they'll be all right."

"Yes." Mara turned and looked out of the window. She could see her own reflection against the dark glass streaked with rain. It looked like a candle flame was burning from her right shoulder.

"Maybe they got away," Paul added. "They might be on their way back right now."

Mara nodded. "Maybe."

But she knew there'd be trouble. The police would soon be round, bullying and searching, just like when Seth's old friend Liz Dale ran away from the nut-house and hid out with them for a few days. They'd been looking for heroin then—Liz had a history of drug abuse—but as far as Mara remembered they'd just made a bloody mess of everything in the place. She resented that kind of intrusion into her world and didn't look forward to another one.

She reached for the wine bottle, but before she started pouring, the front door burst open again.

II

When Banks went downstairs, things were considerably quieter than they had been earlier. Richmond had helped the uniformed men to usher all the prisoners down to the cellar until they could be questioned, charged and released. Eastvale station didn't have many cells, but there was plenty of unused storage space down there.

Sergeant Hatchley had also arrived. Straw-haired, head and shoulders above the others, he looked like a rugby prop-forward gone to seed. He leaned on the reception desk looking bewildered and put out as Richmond explained what had happened.

Banks walked up to them. "Super here yet?"

"On his way, sir," Richmond answered.

"Can you get everyone together while we're waiting?" Banks asked. "There's a few things I want to tell them right now."

Richmond went into the open-plan office area, the domain of the uniformed police at Eastvale, and rounded up everyone he could. The men and women sat on desks or leaned against partitions and waited for instructions. Some of them still showed signs of the recent battle: a bruised cheekbone, torn uniform, black eye, cauliflower ear.

"Does anyone know exactly how many we've got in custody?" Banks asked first.

"Thirty-six, sir." It was a constable with a split lip and the top button torn off his jacket who answered. "And I've heard there's ten more at the hospital."

"Any serious injuries?"

"No, sir. Except, well, Constable Gill."

"Yes. So if there were about a hundred at the demo, there's almost a fifty-fifty chance we've already caught our killer. First, I want everyone searched, fingerprinted and examined for Gill's bloodstains. Constable Reynolds, will you act as liaison with the hospital?"

"Yes, sir."

"The same procedure applies there. Ask the doctor to check the ten patients for blood. Next we've got to find the murder weapon. All we know so far is that PC Gill was stabbed. We don't know what kind of knife was used, so anything with a blade is suspicious, from a kitchen knife to a stiletto. There's some extra men on the way from York, but I want a couple of you to start searching the street thoroughly right away, and that includes having a good look down the grates, too. Clear so far?"

Some muttered, "Yes, sir." Others nodded.

"Right. Now we get to the hard work. We'll need a list of names: everyone we've got and anyone else we can get them to name. Remember, about sixty people got away, and we have to know who they were. If any of you recall seeing a familiar face we don't have here or at the hospital, make a note of it. I don't suppose the people we question will want to give their friends away, but lean on them a bit, do what you can. Be on the look-out for any slips. Use whatever cunning you have. We also want to know who the organizers were and what action groups were represented.

"I want statements from everyone, even if they've nothing to say. We're going to have to divide up the interrogations, so just do the best you can. Stick to the murder; ask about anyone with a knife. Find out if we've got any recorded troublemakers in the cells; look up their files and see what you come up with. If you think someone's lying or being evasive, push them as far as you can, then make a note of your reservations on the statement. I realize we're going to be swamped with paperwork, but there's no avoiding it. Any questions?"

Nobody said a word.

"Fine. One last thing: we want statements from all witnesses, too, not just the demonstrators. There must have been some people watching from those flats overlooking the street. Do the rounds. Find out if anyone saw anything. And rack your own brains. You know there'll be some kind of official enquiry into why all this happened in the first place, so all of you who were there might as well make a statement now, while the events are fresh in your minds. I want all statements typed and on Superintendent Gristhorpe's desk first thing in the morning."

Banks looked at his watch. "It's nine-thirty now. We'd better get cracking. Anything I've overlooked?"

Several officers shook their heads; others stood silent. Finally a policewoman put her hand up. "What are we to do with the prisoners, sir, after we've got all the statements?"

"Follow normal procedure," Banks said. "Just charge them and let them go unless you've got any reason to think they're involved in PC Gill's death. They'll appear before the magistrate as soon as possible. Is that all?" He paused, but nobody said anything. "Right. Off you go then. I want to know about any leads as soon as they come up. With a bit of luck we could get this wrapped up by morning. And would someone take some of the prisoners upstairs? There'll be three of us interviewing up there when the super arrives." He turned to Richmond. "We'll want you on the computer, Phil. There'll be a lot of records to check."

"The super's here now, sir." PC Telford pointed to the door, which was out of Banks's line of vision.

Superintendent Gristhorpe, a bulky man in his late fifties with bushy grey hair and eyebrows, a red pock-marked face and a bristly moustache, walked over to where the three CID men were standing by the stairs. His eyes, usually as guileless as a baby's, were clouded with concern, but his presence still brought an aura of calm and unhurried common sense.

"You've heard?" Banks asked.

"Aye," said Gristhorpe. "Not all the details, but enough. Let's go upstairs and you can tell me about it over a cup of coffee." He put his hand on Banks's arm gently.

Banks turned to Sergeant Hatchley. "You might as well get started on the interviews," he said. "We'll help you out in a minute when I've filled the super in." Then the four CID men trudged upstairs and PC Telford ushered a brace of wet, frightened demonstrators up after them.

III

"Zoe! Thank God you're all right!"

Paul and Mara stared at the slight figure in the glistening red anorak. Her ginger hair was stuck to her skull, and the dark roots showed. Rain dripped onto the straw mat just inside the doorway. She slipped off her jacket, hung it next to Paul's and walked over to hug them both.

"You've told her what happened?" she asked Paul.

"Yes."

Zoe looked at Mara. "How was Luna?"

"No trouble. She fell asleep when Squirrel Nutkin started tickling Mr Brown with a nettle."

Zoe's face twitched in a brief smile. She went over to the bookcase. "I threw an I Ching this morning," she said, "and it came up 'Conflict.' I should have known what would happen." She opened the book and read from the text: "'Conflict. You are being sincere and are being obstructed. A cautious halt halfway brings good fortune. Going through to the end brings misfortune. It furthers one to see the great man. It does not further one to cross the great water.'"

"You can't take it so literally," Mara said. "That's the problem. It didn't tell you what would happen, or how." Though she was certainly interested in the I Ching and tarot cards, herself, Mara often thought that Zoe went too far.

"It's clear enough to me. I should have known something like this would happen: 'Going through to the end brings misfortune.' You can't get any more specific than that."

"What if you *had* known?" Paul said. "You couldn't call it off, could you? You'd still have gone. Things would still have worked out the same."

"Yes," Zoe muttered, "but I should have been prepared."

"How?" asked Mara. "Do you mean you should have gone armed or something?"

Zoe sighed. "I don't know. I just should have been prepared."

"It's easy to say that now," Paul said. "The truth is nobody had the slightest idea the demo would turn nasty, and there wasn't a damn thing they could do about it when it did. There were a lot of people involved, Zoe, and if they'd've all done the I Ching this morning they'd've all got different answers. It's a load of cobblers, if you ask me."

"Sit down," said Mara. "Have a glass of wine. Did you see what happened to the others?"

"I'm not sure." Zoe sat cross-legged on the carpet and accepted Paul's glass. "I think Rick got arrested. I saw him struggling with some police at the edge of the crowd."

"And Seth?"

"I don't know. I couldn't see." Zoe smiled sadly. "Most people were bigger than me. All I could see was shoulders and necks. That's how I managed to get away, because I'm so little. That and the rain. One cop grabbed my anorak, but his hand slipped off because it was wet. I'm a Pisces, a slippery fish." She paused to sip her Barsac. "What'll happen to them, Mara, the ones who got caught?"

Mara shrugged. "I should imagine they'll be charged and let go. That's what usually happens. Then the magistrate decides what to fine them or whether to send them to jail. Mostly they just get fined or let off with a caution."

Mara wished she felt as confident as she sounded. Her uneasiness had nothing to do with the message Zoe had got from the I Ching, but the words of the oracle somehow emphasized it and gave her disquietude a deeper dimension of credibility: "Going through to the end brings misfortune. It furthers one to see the great man." Who was the great man?

"Shouldn't we do something?" Paul asked.

"Like what?"

"Go down there, down to the police station and find out what's happened. Try and get them out."

Mara shook her head. "If we do that, it's more likely they'll take us in for obstructing justice or something."

"I just feel so bloody powerless, so useless, not being able to do a damn thing." Paul's fists clenched, and Mara could read the words jaggedly tattooed just below his knuckles. Instead of the more common combination, LOVE on one hand and HATE on the other, his read HATE on both hands. Seeing the capitalized word so ineptly tattooed there reminded Mara how hard and violent Paul's past had been and how far he had come since they'd found him sleeping in the open, early the past winter on their way to a craft fair in Wensleydale.

"If we had a phone we could at least call the hospital," Zoe said. "Maybe one of us should walk down to Relton and do it anyway."

"I'll go," Mara said. "You two have had enough for one night. Besides, the exercise will do me good."

She got to her feet before either of the others could offer to go instead. It was only a mile down to Relton, a village high on the southern slope of Swainsdale, and the walk should be a pleasant one. Mara looked out of the window. It was drizzling lightly again. She took her yellow cyclist's cape and matching rainhat out of the cupboard and opened the door. As she left, Paul was on his way to the fridge for another beer, and Zoe was reaching for her tarot cards.

Zoe worried Mara sometimes. Not that she wasn't a good mother, but she did seem too offhand. True, she had asked about Luna, but she hadn't wanted to go and look in on her. Instead she had turned immediately to her occult aids. Mara doted on both children: Luna, aged four, and Julian, five. Even Paul, just out of his teens, seemed more like a son than anything else at times. She knew she felt especially close to them because she had no children of her own. Many of her old schoolfriends would probably have kids Paul's age. What an irony, she thought, heading for the track—a barren earth mother!

The rain was hardly worth covering up for, but it gave an edge to the chill already present in the March air, and Mara was glad for the sweater she wore under her cape. The straight narrow track she followed was part of an old Roman road that ran diagonally across the moors above the dale right down to Fortford. Just wide enough for the van, it was dry-walled on both sides and covered with gravel and small chips of stone that crunched and crackled underfoot. Mara could see the lights of Relton at the bottom of the slope. Behind her the candle glowed in the window, and Maggie's Farm looked like an ark adrift on a dark sea.

She shoved her hands through the slits in her cape, deep into the pockets of her cords, and marched the way she imagined an ancient Roman would have done. Beyond the clouds, she could make out the pearly sheen of a half moon.

The great silence all around magnified the little sounds—the clatter of small stones, the rhythmic crunch of gravel, the swishing of her cords against the cape—and Mara felt the strain on her weak left knee that she always got going downhill. She raised her head and let the thin, cool rain fall on her closed eyelids and breathed in the wet-dog smell of the air. When she opened her eyes, she saw the black bulk of distant fells against a dark grey sky.

At the end of the track, Mara walked into Relton. The change from gravel to the smooth tarmac of Mortsett Lane felt strange at first. The village shops were all closed. Television sets flickered behind drawn curtains.

Just to be sure, Mara first popped her head inside the Black Sheep, but neither Seth nor Rick was there. A log fire crackled in the corner of the cosy public bar, but the place was half-empty. The landlord, Larry Grafton, smiled and said hello. Like many of the locals, he had come to accept the incomers from Maggie's Farm. At least, he had once told Mara, they weren't like those London yuppies who seemed to be buying up all the vacant property in the Dales these days.

"Can I get you anything?" Grafton called out.

"No. No, thanks," Mara said. "I was looking for Seth. You haven't seen him, have you?"

Two old men looked up from their game of dominoes, and a trio of young farm labourers paused in their argument over subsidies and glanced at Mara with faintly curious expressions on their faces.

"No, lass," Grafton said. "They've not been in since lunchtime. Said they were off to that there demonstration in Eastvale."

Mara nodded. "That's right. There's been some trouble and they haven't come back yet. I was just wondering—"

"Is it right, then?" one of the farm labourers asked. "Tommy Exton dropped in half an hour sin' and said there'd been some fighting in Market Street."

Mara told him what little she knew, and he shook his head. "It don't pay to get involved in things like that. Best left well alone," he said, and returned to his pint.

Mara left the Black Sheep and headed for the public telephone-box on Mortsett Lane. Why they didn't have a phone installed at the farm she didn't know. Seth had once said he wouldn't have one of the things in the house, but he never explained why. Every time he needed to make a few calls he went down to the village, and he never once complained. At least in the country you could usually be sure the telephones hadn't been vandalized.

The receptionist at Eastvale General Infirmary answered and asked her what she wanted. Mara explained that she was interested in news of a friend of hers who hadn't come home from the demonstration. The receptionist said, "Just a minute," and the phone hiccupped and burped a few times. Finally a man's voice came on.

"Can I help you, miss?"

"Yes. I'd like to know if you have a patient called Seth Cotton and one called Rick Trelawney."

"Who is this calling?"

"I . . . I'd rather not say," Mara answered, suddenly afraid that if she gave her name she would be inviting trouble.

"Are you a relation?"

"I'm a friend. A very close friend."

"I see. Well, unless you identify yourself, miss, I'm afraid I can't give out any information."

"Look," Mara said, getting angry, "this is ridiculous. It's not as if I'm asking you to break the Official Secrets Act or anything. I just want to know if my friends are there and, if so, how badly they're injured. Who are you, anyway?"

"Constable Parker, miss. If you've any complaints you'd better take them up with Chief Inspector Banks at Eastvale CID Headquarters."

"Chief Inspector Banks? CID?" Mara repeated slowly. She remembered the name. He was the one who had visited the farm before, when Liz was there. "Why? I don't understand. What's going on? I only want to know if my friends are hurt."

"Sorry, miss. Orders. Tell me your name and I'll see what I can do."

Mara hung up. Something was very wrong. She'd done enough damage already by mentioning Seth and Rick. The police would surely take special note of their names and push them even harder than the rest. There was nothing to do but wait and worry. Frowning, she opened the door and walked back into the rain.

IV

"Feel like a broke-down engine, ain't got no drivin' wheel," sang Blind Willie McTell.

"I know exactly what you mean, mate," Banks mumbled to himself as he poured a shot of Laphroaig single-malt, an indulgence he could scarcely afford. It was almost two in the morning and the interrogations had produced no results so far. Tired, Banks had left the others to it and come home for a few hours' sleep. He felt he deserved it. *They* hadn't had to spend the morning in court, the afternoon on a wild-goose chase after a stolen tractor, and the evening listening to the Hon Honoria, who would no doubt by now be sleeping the sleep of the truly virtuous before heading back, with great relief, down south in the morning.

Banks put his feet up, lit a cigarette and warmed the glass in his palm. Suddenly the doorbell rang. He jumped to his feet and cursed as he spilled a little valuable Scotch on his shirt front. Rubbing it with the heel of his hand, he walked into the hall and opened the door a few inches on the chain.

It was Jenny Fuller, the psychologist he had met and worked with on his first case in Eastvale. More than that, he had to admit, there had been a mutual attraction between them. Nothing had come of it, of course, and Jenny had even become good friends with Sandra. The three of them had often been out together. But the attraction remained, unresolved. Things like that didn't seem to go away as easily as they arrived.

"Jenny?" He slipped off the chain and opened the door wider.

"I know. It's two o'clock in the morning and you're wondering what I'm doing at your door."

"Something like that. I assume it's not just my irresistible charm?"

Jenny smiled. The laugh lines around her green eyes crinkled. But the smile was forced and short-lived.

"What is it?" Banks asked.

"Dennis Osmond."

"Who?"

"A friend. He's in trouble."

"Boy-friend?"

"Yes, boy-friend." Jenny blushed. "Or would you prefer beau? Lover? Significant other? Look, can I come in? It's cold and raining out here."

Banks moved aside. "Yes, of course. I'm sorry. Have a drink?"

"I will, if you don't mind." Jenny walked into the front room, took off her green silk scarf and shook her red hair. The muted trumpet wailed and Sara Martin sang "Death Sting Me Blues."

"What happened to opera?" Jenny asked.

Banks poured her a shot of Laphroaig. "There's a lot of music in the world," he said. "I want to listen to as much as I can before I shuffle off this mortal coil."

"Does that include heavy metal and middle-of-the-road?"

Banks scowled. "Dennis Osmond. What about him?"

"Ooh, touchy, aren't we?" Jenny raised her eyes to the ceiling and lowered her voice. "By the way, I hope I haven't disturbed Sandra or the children?"

Banks explained their absence. "It was all a bit sudden," he added, to fill the silence that followed, which seemed somehow more weighty than it should. Jenny expressed her sympathy and shifted in her seat. She took a deep breath. "Dennis was arrested during that demonstration tonight. He managed to get in a phone call to me from the police station. He's not come back yet. I've just been there and the man on the desk told me you'd left. They wouldn't tell me anything about the prisoners at all. What's going on?"

"Where hasn't he come back to?"

"My place."

"Do you live together?"

Jenny's eyes hardened and drilled into him like emerald laser beams. "That's none of your damn business." She drank some more Scotch. "As a matter of fact, no, we don't. He was going to come round and tell me about the demonstration. It should have been all over hours ago."

"You weren't there yourself?"

"Are you interrogating me?"

"No. Just asking."

"I believe in the cause—I mean, I'm against nuclear power and American missile bases—but I don't see any point standing in the rain in front of Eastvale Community Centre."

"I see." Banks smiled. "It *was* a nasty night, wasn't it?"

"And there's no need to be such a cynic. I had work to do."

"It was a pretty bad night inside, too."

Jenny raised her eyebrows. "The Hon Hon?"

"Indeed."

"You were there?"

"I had that dubious honour, yes. Duty."

"You poor man. It might have been worth a black eye to get out of that."

"I take it you haven't heard the news, then?"

"What news?"

"A policeman was killed at that peaceful little demonstration tonight. Not a local chap, but one of us, nonetheless."

"Is that why Dennis is still at the station?"

"We're still questioning people, yes. It's serious, Jenny. I haven't seen Dennis Osmond, never even heard of him. But they won't let him go till they've got his statement, and we're not giving out any information to members of the public yet. It doesn't mean he's under suspicion or anything, just that he hasn't been questioned yet."

"And then?"

"They'll let him go. If all's well you'll still have some of the night left together."

Jenny lowered her head for a moment, then glared at him again. "You're being a bastard, you know," she said. "I don't like being teased that way."

"What do you want me to do?" Banks asked. "Why did you come?"

"I . . . I just wanted to find out what happened."

"Are you sure you're not trying to get him special treatment?"

Jenny sighed. "Alan, we're friends, aren't we?"

Banks nodded.

"Well," she went on, "I know you can't help being a policeman, but if you don't know where your job ends and your friendships begin . . . Need I go on?"

Banks rubbed his bristly chin. "No. I'm sorry. It's been a rough night. But you still haven't answered my question."

"I'd just hoped to get some idea of what might have happened to him, that's all. I got the impression that if I'd lingered a moment longer down at the station they'd have had me in for questioning, too. I didn't know about the death. I suppose that changes things?"

"Of course it does. It means we've got a cop killer on the loose. I'm sure it's nothing to do with your Dennis, but he'll have to answer the same questions as the rest. I can't say exactly how long he'll be. At least you know he's not in hospital. Plenty of people are."

"I can't believe it, Alan. I can understand tempers getting frayed, fists flying, but not a killing. What happened?"

"He was stabbed. It was deliberate; there's no getting around that."

Jenny shook her head.

"Sorry I can't be any more help," Banks said. "What was Dennis's involvement with the demo?"

"He was one of the organizers, along with the Students Union and those people from Maggie's Farm."

"That place up near Relton?"

"That's it. The local women's group was involved, too."

"WEEF? Dorothy Wycombe?"

Jenny nodded. Banks had come up against the Women of Eastvale for Emancipation and Freedom before—Dorothy Wycombe in particular—and it gave him a sinking feeling to realize that he might have to deal with them again.

"I still can't believe it," Jenny went on. "Dennis told me time and time again that the last thing they wanted was a violent confrontation."

"I don't suppose anybody wanted it, but these things have a way of getting out of hand. Look, why don't you go home? I'm sure he'll be back soon. He won't be mistreated. We don't suddenly turn into vicious goons when things like this happen."

"*You* might not," said Jenny. "But I've heard how you close ranks."

"Don't worry."

Jenny finished her drink. "All right. I can see you're trying to get rid of me."

"Not at all. Have another Scotch if you want."

Jenny hesitated. "No," she said finally. "I was only teasing. You're right. It's late. I'd better get back home." She picked up her scarf. "It was good, though. The scotch. So rich you could chew it."

Banks walked her to the door. "If there are any problems," he said, "let me know. And I could do with your help, too. You seem to know a bit about what went on behind the scenes."

Jenny nodded and fastened her scarf.

"Maybe you could come to dinner?" Banks suggested on impulse. "Try my gourmet cooking?"

Jenny smiled and shook her head. "I don't think so."

"Why not? It's not that bad. At least—"

"It's just...it wouldn't seem right with Sandra away, that's all. The neighbours..."

"Okay. We'll go out. How does the Royal Oak in Lyndgarth suit you?"

"It'll do fine," Jenny said. "Give me a call."

"I will."

She pecked him on the cheek and he watched her walk down the path and get into her Metro. They waved to each other as she set off, then he closed his door on the wet, chilly night. He picked up the Scotch bottle and pulled the cork, thought for a moment, pushed it back and went upstairs to bed.

THREE

I

COP KILLED IN DALES DEATH-DEMO, screamed the tabloid headlines the next morning. As he glanced at them over coffee and a cigarette in his office, Banks wondered why the reporter hadn't gone the whole hog and spelled cop with a "k."

He put the paper aside and walked over to the window. The market square looked dreary and desolate in the grey March light, and Banks fancied he could detect a shell-shocked atmosphere hovering around the place. Shoppers shuffled along with their heads hung low and glanced covertly at the site of the demonstration as they passed, as if they expected to see armed guards wearing gas masks, and tear-gas drifting in the air. North Market Street was still roped off. The four officers sent from York had arrived at about four in the morning to help the local men search the area, but they had found no murder weapon. Now, they were trying again in what daylight there was.

Banks looked at the calendar on his wall. It was March 17, St Patrick's Day. The illustration showed the ruins of St Mary's Abbey in York. Judging by the sunshine and the happy tourists, it had probably been taken in July. On the real March 17, his small space-heater coughed and hiccupped as it struggled to take the chill out of the air.

He turned back to the newspapers. The accounts varied a great deal. According to the left-wing press, the police had brutally attacked a peaceful crowd without provocation; the right-wing papers, however, maintained that a mob of unruly demonstrators had provoked the police into retaliation by throwing bottles and stones. In the more moderate newspapers, nobody seemed to know exactly what had happened, but the whole affair was said to be extremely unfortunate and regrettable.

At eight-thirty, Superintendent Gristhorpe, who had been up most of the night interviewing demonstrators and supervising the search, called Banks in. Banks stubbed out his cigarette—the super didn't approve of smoking—and wandered into the book-lined office. The shaded table-lamp on Gristhorpe's huge teak desk cast its warm glow on a foot-thick pile of statements.

"I've been talking to the Assistant Chief Constable," Gristhorpe said. "He's been on the phone to London and they're sending a man up this morning. I'm to cover the preliminary inquiry into the demo for the Police Complaints Authority." He rubbed his eyes. "Of course, someone'll no doubt accuse me of being biased and scrap the whole thing, but they want to be seen to be acting quickly."

"This man they're sending," Banks asked, "what's he going to do?"

"Handle the murder investigation. You'll be working with him, along with Hatchley and Richmond."

"Do you know who he is?"

Gristhorpe searched for the scrap of paper on his desk. "Yes . . . let me see. . . . It's a Superintendent Burgess. He's attached to a squad dealing with politically sensitive crimes. Not exactly Special Branch, but not quite your regular CID, either. I'm not even sure we're allowed to know *what* he is. Some sort of political trouble-shooter, I suppose."

"Is that Superintendent Richard Burgess?" Banks asked.

"Yes. Why? Know him?"

"Bloody hell."

"Alan, you've gone pale. What's up?"

"Yes, I know him," Banks said. "Not well, but I worked with him a couple of times in London. He's about my age, but he's always been a step ahead."

"Ambitious?"

"Very. But it's not his ambition I mind so much," Banks went on. "He's slightly to the right of . . . Well, you name him and Burgess is to the right."

"Is he good, though?"

"He gets results."

"Isn't that what we need?"

"I suppose so. But he's a real bastard to work with."

"How?"

"Oh, he plays his cards close to his chest. Doesn't let the right hand know what the left hand's doing. He takes short cuts. People get hurt."

"You make him sound like he doesn't even have a left hand," Gristhorpe said.

Banks smiled. "We used to call him Dirty Dick Burgess."

"Why?"

"You'll find out. It's nothing to do with his sexual activities, I can tell you that. Though he did have a reputation as a fairly active stud-about-town."

"Anyway," Gristhorpe said, "he should be here around midday. He's taking the early Intercity to York. There's too long a wait between connections, so I'm sending Craig to meet him at the station there."

"Lucky Craig."

Gristhorpe frowned. Banks noticed the bags under his eyes. "Yes, well, make the best of it, Alan. If Superintendent Burgess steps out of line, I won't be far away. It's still our patch. By the way, Honoria Winstanley called before she left—at least one of her escorts did. Said all's well, apologized for his brusqueness last night and thanked you for handling things so smoothly."

"Wonders never cease."

"I've booked Burgess into the Castle Hotel on York Road. It's not quite as fancy or expensive as the Riverview, but then Burgess isn't an MP, is he?"

Banks nodded. "What about office space?"

"We're putting him in an interview room for the time being. At least there's a desk and a chair."

"He'll probably complain. People like Burgess get finicky about offices and titles."

"Let him," Gristhorpe said, gesturing around the room. "He's not getting this place."

"Any news from the hospital?"

"Nothing serious. Most of the injured have been sent home. Susan Gay's on sick-leave for the rest of the week."

"When you were going through the statements," Banks asked, "did you come across anything on a chap called Dennis Osmond?"

"The name rings a bell. Let me have a look." Gristhorpe leafed through the pile. "Yes, I thought so. Interviewed him myself. One of the last. Why?"

Banks explained about Jenny's visit.

"I took his statement and sent him home." Gristhorpe read through the sheet. "That's him. Belligerent young devil. Threatened to bring charges against the police, start an enquiry of his own. Hadn't seen anything, though. Or at least he didn't admit to it. According to records he's a CND member, active in the local anti-nuclear group. Amnesty International, too—and you know what Mrs Thatcher thinks of *them* these days. He's got connections with various other groups as well, including the International Socialists. I should imagine Superintendent Burgess will certainly want to talk to him."

"Hmmm." Banks wondered how Jenny would take that. Knowing both her and Burgess as he did, he could guarantee sparks would fly. "Did anything turn up in the statements?"

"Nobody witnessed the stabbing. Three people said they thought they glimpsed a knife on the road during the scuffles. It must have got kicked about quite a bit. Nothing I've heard so far brings order out of chaos. The poor lighting didn't help, either. You know how badly that street is lit. Dorothy Wycombe's been pestering us about it for weeks. I keep putting her onto the council, but to no avail. She says it's an invitation to rape, especially with all those unlit side alleys, but the council says the gaslamps are good for the tourist business. Anyway, PC Gill was found just at the bottom of the Community Centre steps, for what that's worth. Maybe if we can find out the names of the people on the front line we'll get somewhere."

Banks went on to tell Gristhorpe what he'd discovered from Jenny about the other organizers.

"The Church for Peace group was involved, too," Gristhorpe added. "Did I hear you mention Maggie's Farm, that place near Relton?"

Banks nodded.

"Didn't we have some trouble with them a year or so ago?"

"Yes," Banks said. "But it was a storm in a teacup. They seemed a harmless enough bunch to me."

"What was it? A drug raid?"

"That's right. Nothing turned up, though. They must have had the foresight to hide it, if they had anything. We were acting on a tip from some hospital social workers. I think they were over-reacting."

"Anyway," Gristhorpe said, "that's about it. The rest of the people we picked up were just private citizens who were there because they feel strongly about nuclear power, or about government policy in general."

"So what do we do now?"

"You'd better look over these statements," Gristhorpe said, shoving the tower of paper towards Banks, "and wait for the great man. Sergeant Hatchley's still questioning those people in the flats overlooking the Street. Not that there's much chance of anything there. They can't have seen more than a sea of heads. If only the bloody TV cameras had been there we'd have had it on video. Those buggers in the media are never around when you need them."

"Like policemen," Banks said with a grin.

The phone rang. Gristhorpe picked it up, listened to the message and turned back to Banks. "Sergeant Rowe says Dr Glendenning's on his way up. He's finished his preliminary examination. I think you'd better stay for this."

Banks smiled. "It's a rare honour indeed, the good doctor setting foot in here. I didn't know he paid house-calls."

"I heard that," said a gruff voice with a distinct Edinburgh accent behind him. "I hope it wasn't meant to be sarcastic."

The tall, white-haired doctor looked down sternly at Banks, blue eyes twinkling. His moustache was stained yellow with nicotine, and a cigarette hung from the corner of his mouth. He was wheezing after climbing the stairs.

"There's no smoking in here," Gristhorpe said. "You ought to know better; you're a doctor."

Glendenning grunted. "Then I'll go elsewhere."

"Come to my office," Banks said. "I could do with a fag myself."

"Fine, laddie. Lead the way."

"Bloody traitor." Gristhorpe sighed and followed them.

After they'd got coffee and an extra chair, the doctor began. "To put it in layman's terms," he said, "PC Gill was stabbed. The knife entered under the rib-cage and did enough damage to cause death from internal bleeding. The blade was at least five inches long, and it looks like it went in to the hilt. It was a single-edged blade with a very sharp point. Judging by the wound, I'd say it was some kind of flick-knife."

"Flick-knife?" echoed Banks.

"Aye, laddie. You know what a flick-knife is, don't you? They come in all shapes and sizes. Illegal here, of course, but easy enough to pick up on the continent. The cutting edge was extremely sharp, as was the point."

"What about blood?" Gristhorpe asked. "Nobody conveniently covered in Gill's type, I suppose?"

Dr Glendenning lit another Senior Service and shook his head. "No. I've checked the tests. And I'd have been very surprised if there had been," he said. "What most people don't realize is that unless you open a major vein or artery—the carotid or the jugular, for example—there's often very little external bleeding with knife wounds. I'd say in this case that there was hardly any, and what there was would've been mostly absorbed by the man's clothing. The slit closes behind the blade, you see—especially a thin one—and most of the bleeding is internal."

"Can you tell if it was a professional job?" Gristhorpe asked.

"I wouldn't care to speculate. It could have been, but it could just as easily have been a lucky strike. It was a right-handed up-thrust wound. With a blow like that on a dark night, I doubt that anybody would have noticed, unless they saw the blade flash, and there's not enough light for that on North Market Street. It would have looked more like a punch to the solar plexus than anything else, and from what I hear, there was plenty of that going on. Now if he'd raised his hand above his head and thrust downwards..."

"People aren't usually so obliging," Banks said.

"If we take into account the kind of knife used," Gristhorpe speculated, "it could easily have been a spontaneous act. Pros don't usually use flick-knives—they're street weapons."

"Aye, well," said Glendenning, standing to leave, "that's for you fellows to work out. I'll let you know if I find anything more at the post-mortem."

"Who identified the body?" Banks asked him.

"Sister. Pretty upset about it, too. A couple of your lads did the paperwork. Luckily, Gill didn't have a wife and kids." A quarter inch of ash fell onto the linoleum. Glendenning shook his head slowly. "Nasty business all round. Be seeing you."

When the doctor had left, Gristhorpe stood up and flapped his hand theatrically in front of his face. "Filthy bloody habit. I'm off back to my office where the air's clean. Does this Burgess fellow smoke, too?"

Banks smiled. "Cigars, if I remember right."

Gristhorpe swore.

II

Over the valley from Maggie's Farm, mist clung to the hillsides and limestone scars, draining them of all colour. Soon after breakfast, Seth disappeared into his workshop to finish restoring Jack Lippett's Welsh dresser; Rick did some shopping in Helmthorpe, then went to his studio in the converted barn to daub away at his latest painting; Zoe busied herself in her flat with Elsie Goodbody's natal chart and Paul went for a long walk on the moors.

In the living-room, Mara kept an eye on Luna and Julian while she mended the tears in Seth's jacket. The children were playing with Lego bricks and she often glanced over, awed by the look of pure concentration on their faces as they built. Occasionally, an argument would break out, and Julian would complain that the slightly younger Luna wasn't doing things right. Then Luna would accuse him of being bossy. Mara would step in and give them her advice, healing the rift temporarily.

There was nothing to worry about really, Mara told herself as she sewed, but after what Seth and Rick had said about the dead police-man, she knew they could expect to come under close scrutiny. After all, they were different. While not political in the sense of belonging to any party, they certainly believed in protection of the environ-ment. They had even allowed their house to be used as a base for planning the demo. It would only be a matter of time before the knock at the door. There was something else bothering Mara, too, hovering at the back of her mind, but she couldn't quite figure out what it was.

Seth and Rick had been tired and hungry when they got back just after two in the morning. Seth had been charged with threatening behaviour and Rick with obstructing a police officer. They hadn't much to add to what Mara had heard earlier except for the news of PC Gill's murder, which had soon spread around the police station.

In bed, Mara had tried to cheer Seth up, but he had been difficult to reach. Finally, he said he was tired and went to sleep. Mara had stayed awake listening to the rain for a long time and thinking just how often Seth seemed remote. She'd been living with him for two years now, but she hardly felt she knew him. She didn't even know if he really was asleep now or just pretending. He was a man of deep silences, as if he were carrying a great weight of sadness within him. Mara knew that his wife, Alison, had died tragically just before he bought the farm, but really she knew nothing else of his past.

How different from Rick he was, she thought. Rick had tragedy in his life, too—he was involved in a nasty custody suit with his ex-wife over Julian—but he was open and he let his feelings show, whereas Seth never said much. But Seth was strong, Mara thought—the kind of person everyone else looked up to as being really in command. And he loved her. She knew she had been foolish to feel such jealousy when Liz Dale had run away from the psychiatric hospital and come to stay. But Liz had been a close friend of Alison's and had known Seth for years; she was a part of his life that was shut off from Mara, and that hurt. Night after night Mara had lain awake listening to their muffled voices downstairs until the small hours, gripping the pillow tightly. It had been a difficult time, what with Liz, the plague of social workers and the police raid, but she could look back and laugh at the memory of her jealousy now.

As she sat and sewed, watching the children, Mara felt lucky to be alive. Most of the time these days she was happy; she wouldn't change things for the world. It had been a good life so far, though a confusing one at times. After her student days, she had thrown herself into life—travel, communal living, love affairs, drugs—all without a care in the world.

Then she had spent four years with the Resplendent Light Organization, culminating in nine long months in one of their ashrams, where all earnings were turned over to the group and freedom was severely limited. There were no movies, no evenings in the pub, no frivolous, chatty gatherings around the fire; there was very little laughter. Mara had soon come to feel trapped, and the whole episode had left her with a bitter taste in her mouth. She felt she had been cheated into wasting her time. There had been no love there, no special person to share life with. But that was all over now. She had Seth—a solid dependable man, however distant he could be—Paul, Zoe, Rick and, most important of all, the children. After wandering and searching for so long, she seemed at last to have found the stability she needed. She had come home.

Sometimes, though, she wondered what things would be like if her life had been more normal. She'd heard of business executives dropping out in the sixties: they took off their suits and ties, dropped LSD and headed for Woodstock. But sometimes Mara dreamed of dropping in. She had a good brain; she had got a first in English Literature at the University of Essex. At moments, she could see herself all crisp and efficient in a business suit, perhaps working in advertising, or standing in front of a blackboard reading Keats or Coleridge to a class of spellbound children.

But the fantasies never lasted long. She was thirty-eight years old, and jobs were hard to come by even for the qualified and experienced. All those opportunities had passed her by. She knew also that she would no more be able to work in the everyday world, with its furious pace, its petty demands and its money-grubbing mentality, than she would be able to join the armed forces. Her years on the fringes of society had distanced her from life inside the system. She didn't even know what people talked about at work these days. The new BMW? Holidays in the Caribbean? All she knew was what she read in the papers, where it seemed that people no longer lived their lives but had "life-styles" instead.

The closest she came to a normal middle-class existence was working in Elspeth's craft shop in Relton three days a week in exchange for the use of the pottery wheel and kiln in the back. But Elspeth was hardly an ordinary person; she was a kindly old silver-haired lesbian who had been living in Relton with her companion, Dottie, for over thirty years. She affected the tweedy look of a country matron, but the twinkle in her eyes told a different story. Mara loved both of them very much, but Dottie was rarely to be seen these days. She was ill—dying of cancer, Mara suspected—and Elspeth bore the burden with her typical gruff stoicism.

At twelve o'clock, Rick knocked and came in through the back door, interrupting Mara's wandering thoughts. He looked every inch the artist: beard, paint-stained smock and jeans, beer belly. His whole appearance cried out that he believed in himself and didn't give a damn what other people thought about him.

"All quiet on the western front?" he asked.

Mara nodded. She'd been half listening for the sound of a police car above the wind chimes. "They'll be here, though."

"It'll probably take them a while," Rick said. "There were a lot of others involved. We might not be as important as we think we are."

He picked up Julian and whirled him around in the air. The child squealed with delight and wriggled as Rick rubbed his beard against his face. Zoe tapped at the door and came in from the barn to join them.

"Stop it, Daddy!" Julian screamed. "It tickles. Stop it!"

Rick put him down and mussed his hair. "What are you two building?" he asked.

"A space station," answered Luna seriously.

Mara looked at the jumble of Lego and smiled to herself. It didn't look like much of anything to her, but it was remarkable what children could do with their imaginations.

Rick laughed and turned to Zoe. "All right, kiddo?" he asked, slipping his arm around her thin shoulder. "What do the stars have to say today?"

Zoe smiled. She obviously adored Rick, Mara thought; otherwise she would never put up with being teased and treated like a youngster at the age of thirty-two. Could there be any chance of them getting together? she wondered. It would be good for the children.

"Elsie Goodbody's wasted as a housewife," said Zoe. "By the looks of her chart she should be in politics."

"She's in domestic politics," Rick said, "and that's even worse. Anyone for the pub?"

They usually all walked down to the Black Sheep on Saturday and Sunday lunchtimes. The landlord was good about the children as long as they kept quiet, and Zoe took along colouring books to occupy them. Mara fetched Seth from his workshop, Julian got up on his father's shoulders, and Luna held Zoe's hand as they walked out to the track.

"Just a minute, I'll catch you up," Mara said, dashing back into the house. She wanted to leave a note for Paul to tell him where they were: a formality, really, an affectionate gesture. But as she wrote and her mind turned back to him, she suddenly realized what had been nagging her all morning.

Last night, Paul's hand had been bleeding and he had put an Elastoplast on it. This morning, when he came down, the plaster had slipped off, probably when he was washing, and the base of his thumb was as smooth as ever. There was no sign of a cut at all.

Mara's heart beat fast as she hurried to catch up with the others.

III

"Detective Superintendent Burgess, sir," PC Craig said, then left.

The man who stood before them in Gristhorpe's office looked little different from the Burgess that Banks remembered. He wore a scuffed black leather sports jacket over an open-necked white shirt, and close-fitting navy-blue cords. The handsome face with its square determined jaw hadn't changed much, even if his slightly crooked teeth were a little more tobacco-stained. The pouches under his cynical grey eyes still suited him. His dark hair, short and combed back, was touched with grey at the temples, and by the look of it he still used Brylcreem. He was about six feet tall, well-built but filling out a bit, and looked as if he still played squash twice a week. The most striking thing about his appearance was his deep tan.

"Barbados," he said, catching their surprise. "I'd recommend it highly, especially at this time of year. Just got back when this business came up."

Gristhorpe introduced himself, then Burgess looked over at Banks and narrowed his eyes. "Banks, isn't it? I heard you'd been transferred. Looking a bit pasty-faced, aren't you? Not feeding you well up here?"

Banks forced a smile. It was typical of Burgess to make the transfer sound like a punishment and a demotion. "We don't get much sun," he said.

Burgess looked towards the window. "So I see. If it's any consolation, it was pissing down in London when I left." He clapped his hands together sharply. "Where's the boozer, then? I'm starving. Didn't dare risk British Rail food. I could do with a pint, as well."

Gristhorpe excused himself, claiming a meeting with the Assistant Chief Commissioner, and Banks led Burgess over to the Queen's Arms.

"Not a bad-looking place," Burgess said, glancing around and taking in the spacious lounge with its dimpled copper-topped tables with black wrought-iron legs, and deep armchairs by the blazing fire. Then his eyes rested on the barmaid. "Yes. Not bad at all. Let's sit at the bar."

Some of the locals paused in their conversations to stare at them. They knew Banks already, and Burgess's accent still bore traces of his East End background. As right-wing as he was, he didn't come from the privileged school of Tories, Banks remembered. His father had been a barrow-boy, and Burgess had fought his way up from the bottom. Banks also knew that he felt little solidarity with those of his class who hadn't managed to do likewise. To the locals, he was obviously the London big-wig they'd been expecting after the previous night's events.

Banks and Burgess perched on the high stools. "What'll you have?" Burgess asked, taking a shiny black leather wallet from his inside pocket. "I'm buying."

"Thanks very much. I'll have a pint of Theakston's bitter."

"Food?"

"The hot-pot is usually good."

"I think I'll stick to plaice and chips," Burgess said. He ordered the food and drinks from the barmaid. "And a pint of Double Diamond for me, please, love." He lit a Tom Thumb cigar and poked it at Banks's glass. "Can't stand that real ale stuff," he said, rubbing his stomach and grimacing. "Always gives me the runs. Ah, thank you, love. What's your name?"

"Glenys," the barmaid said. She gave him a coy smile with his change and turned to serve another customer.

"Nice," Burgess said. "Not exactly your buxon-barmaid type, but nice nonetheless. Lovely bum. A flyer says I'll bonk her before this business is over."

Banks wished he would try. The muscular man drying glasses at the far end of the bar was Glenys's husband, Cyril. "You're on," he said, shaking hands. Though how Burgess would prove it if he won, Banks had no idea. Perhaps he'd persuade Glenys to part with a pair of panties as a trophy? The most likely outcome, though, would be a black eye for Burgess and a flyer in Banks's pocket.

"So, I hear you had a riot on your hands last night."

"Not quite a riot," Banks said, "but bad enough."

"It shouldn't have been allowed."

"Sure. It's easy to say that from hindsight, but we'd no reason to expect trouble. A lot of people around here have sympathy with the cause and they don't usually kill policemen."

Burgess's eyes narrowed. "Including you? Sympathy with the cause?"

Banks shrugged. "Nobody wants any more air-base activity in the Dales, and I'm no great fan of nuclear power."

"A bloody Bolshy on the force, eh? No wonder they sent you up here. Like getting sent to Siberia, I'll bet?" He chuckled at his own joke, then sank about half a pint in one gulp. "What have you got so far, then?"

Banks told him about the statements they'd taken and the main groups involved in organizing the protest, including the people at Maggie's Farm. As he listened, Burgess sucked on his lower lip and tapped his cigar on the side of the blue ashtray. Every time Glenys walked by, his restless eyes followed her.

"Seventy-one names," he commented when Banks had finished. "And you think there were over a hundred there. That's not a lot, is it?"

"It is in a murder investigation."

"Hmmm. Got anyone marked out for it?"

"Pardon?"

"Local trouble-maker, shit-stirrer. Let's be honest about this, Banks. It doesn't look like we'll get any physical evidence unless someone finds the knife. The odds are that whoever did it was one of the ones who got away. You might not even have his name on your list. I was just wondering who's your most likely suspect."

"We don't have any suspects yet."

"Oh, come on! No one with a record of political violence?"

"Only the local Conservative member."

"Very good," Burgess said, grinning. "Very good. It seems to me," he went on, "that there are two possibilities. One: it happened in the heat of the moment; someone lost his temper and lashed out with a knife. Or, two: it was a planned deliberate act to kill a copper, an act of terrorism calculated to cause chaos, to disrupt society."

"What about the knife?" Banks said. "The killer couldn't be sure of getting away, and we've found no traces of it in the area. I'd say that points more towards your first theory. Someone lost his temper and didn't stop to think of the consequences, then just got lucky."

Burgess finished his pint. "Not necessarily," he said. "They're kamikaze merchants, these bloody terrorists. They don't care if they get caught or not. Like you said, whoever it was just got lucky this time."

"It's possible, I suppose."

"But unlikely?"

"In Eastvale, yes. I told you, most of the people involved were fairly harmless; even the groups they belonged to have never been violent before."

"But you don't have everyone's name."

"No."

"Then that's something to work on. Sweat the ones you've got and get a full list."

"DC Richmond's working on it," Banks said, though he could hardly see Philip Richmond sweating anyone.

"Good." Burgess gestured to the barmaid. "Another two pints, Gladys, love," he called out.

"It's Glenys," she said, then she blushed and lowered her head to keep an eye on the pint she was pulling.

"Sorry, love, I'm still train-lagged. Have one for yourself, too, Glenys."

"Thank you very much." Glenys smiled shyly at him and took the money for a gin and tonic. "I'll have it later when we're not so busy, if you don't mind."

"As you will." Burgess treated her to a broad smile and winked. "Where were we?" he asked, returning to Banks.

"Names."

"Yes. You must have a list of local reds and what not? You know the kind I mean—anarchists, skinheads, bum-punchers, women's libbers, uppity niggers."

"Of course. We keep it on the back of a postage stamp."

"You mentioned three organizations earlier. What's WEEF?"

"Women of Eastvale for Emancipation and Freedom."

"Oh, very impressive. Touch of the Greenham Common women, eh?"

"Not really. They mostly stick to local issues like poor streetlighting and sexual discrimination in jobs."

"Still," Burgess said, "it's a start. Get your man—Richmond, is it?— to liaise with Special Branch on this. They've got extensive files on Bolshies everywhere. He can do it through the computer, if you've got one up here."

"We've got one."

"Good. Tell him to see me about access." Their food arrived, and Burgess poured salt and vinegar on his fish and chips. "We can set them against each other, for openers," he said. "Simple divide-and-conquer tactics. We tell those WEEF people that the Students Union has fingered them for the murder, and vice versa. That way if anyone does know anything they'll likely tell us out of anger at being dropped right in it. We need results, and we need them quick. This business can give us a chance to look good for once. We're always looking like the bad guys these days—especially since that bloody miners' strike. We need some good press for a change, and here's our chance. A copper's been killed—that gets us plenty of public sympathy for a start. If we can come up with some pinko terrorist we've got it made."

"I don't think setting the groups against each other will get us anywhere," Banks said. "They're just not that aggressive."

"Don't be so bloody negative, man. Remember, *somebody* knows who did it, even if it's only the killer. I'll get myself acclimatized this afternoon, and tomorrow—" Burgess clapped his hands and showered his plate with ash "—we'll swoop into action." He had a nasty habit of sitting or standing motionless for ages, then making a sudden jerky movement. Banks remembered how disconcerting it was from their previous meetings.

"Action?"

"Raids, visits, call them what you will. We're looking for documents, letters, anything that might give us a clue to what happened. Any trouble getting warrants up here?"

Banks shook his head.

Burgess speared a chip. "Nothing like a Sunday morning for a nice little raid, I always say. People have funny ideas about Sundays, you know. Especially churchy types. They're all comfortable and complacent after a nice little natter with the Almighty, and then they get pissed off as hell if something interrupts their routine. Best day for raids and interrogations, believe me. Just wait till they get their feet up with the Sunday papers. You mentioned some drop-outs at a farm earlier, didn't you?"

"They're not drop-outs," Banks said. "They just try to be self-sufficient, keep to themselves. They call the place Maggie's Farm," he added. "It's the title of an old Bob Dylan song. I suppose it's a joke about Thatcher, too."

Burgess grinned. "At least they've got a sense of humour. They'll bloody need it before we're through. We'll pay them a visit, keep them on their toes. Bound to be drugs around, if nothing else. How about dividing up the raids? Any suggestions?"

Banks had no desire to tangle with Dorothy Wycombe again, and sending Sergeant Hatchley to WEEF headquarters would be like sending a bull into a china shop, as would sending Burgess up to Maggie's Farm. On the other hand, he thought, meeting Ms Wycombe might do Dirty Dick some good.

"I'll take the farm," he said. "Let Hatchley do the church group, Richmond the students, and you can handle WEEF. We can take a couple of uniformed men to do the searches while we ask the questions."

Burgess's eyes narrowed suspiciously, then he smiled and said, "Right, we're on."

He knows I'm setting him up, Banks thought, but he's willing to go along anyway. Cocky bastard.

Burgess washed down the last of his plaice and chips. "I'd like to stay for another," he said, "and feast my eyes more on the lovely

Glenys, but duty calls. Let's hope we'll have plenty of reason to celebrate tomorrow lunch-time. Why don't you catch up on a bit of
paperwork this afternoon? There's not a lot we can do yet. And
maybe this evening you can show me some of these quaint village
pubs I've read about in the tourist brochures?"

The prospect of a pub crawl with Dirty Dick Burgess, following
hot on the heels of an evening with the Hon Honoria Winstanley,
appealed to Banks about as much as a slap in the face with a wet fish,
but he agreed politely. It was a job, after all, and Burgess was his senior officer. They'd be working together for a few days, probably, and
it would do no harm to get on as good terms as possible. Make the
best of it, Gristhorpe had said. And Banks did have a vague recollec-
tion that Burgess wasn't such bad company after a few jars.

Burgess slid off his chair and strode towards the door. "Bye,
Glenys, love," he called out over his shoulder as he left. Banks noticed
Cyril scowl and tighten his grip on the pump he was pulling.

Banks pushed his empty plate aside and lit a Silk Cut. He felt
exhausted. Just listening to Burgess reminded him of everything he
had hated about his days on the Met. But Burgess was right, of course:
they were looking into a political murder, and the first logical step
was to check out local activist groups.

It was the obvious relish with which the superintendent contemplated the task that irked Banks and reminded him so much of his
London days. And he remembered Burgess's interrogation technique,
probably learned from the Spanish Inquisition. There were hard
times ahead for a few innocent people who simply happened to
believe in nuclear disarmament and the future of the human race.
Burgess was like a pit-bull terrier; he wouldn't let go until he got what
he wanted.

Oh, for a nice English village murder, Banks wished, just like the
ones in books: a closed group of five or six suspects, a dodgy will, and
no hurry to solve the puzzle. No such luck. He drained his pint,
stubbed out the cigarette and went back across the street to read
more statements.

IV

Mara sipped at her half of mild without really tasting it. She couldn't seem to relax and enjoy the company as usual. Seth sat at the bar chatting with Larry Grafton about some old furniture the landlord had inherited from his great-grandmother, and Rick and Zoe were arguing about astrology. By the window, the children sat colouring quietly.

What did it mean? Mara wondered. When she had tackled Paul about the blood on his hand the previous evening, he had gone into the kitchen and put on a plaster without showing her the cut. Now, it turned out, there was no cut. So whose blood had it been?

Of course, she told herself, anything could have happened. He could have accidentally brushed against somebody who had been hurt in the demo, or even tried to help someone. But he had clearly run all the way home; when he had arrived he had been upset and out of breath. And if the explanation was an innocent one, why had he lied? Because that's what it came down to in the end. Instead of telling the simple truth, he had let her go on believing he was hurt, albeit not badly, and she couldn't come up with a convincing reason why he had done that.

"You're quiet today," Seth said, walking over with more drinks.

It's easy for you, she felt like saying. You can cover up your feelings and talk about hammers and planes and chisels and bevels and chamfering as if nothing has happened, but I don't have any small talk. Instead, she said, "It's nothing. I'm just a bit tired after last night, I suppose."

Seth took her hand. "Didn't you sleep well?"

No, Mara almost said, No I didn't bloody sleep well. I was waiting for you to share your feelings with me, but you never did. You never do. You can talk about work to any Tom, Dick and Harry, but not about anything else, not about anything important. But she didn't say any of that. She squeezed his hand, kissed him lightly and said she was all right. She knew she was just irritable, worried about Paul, and the mood would soon pass. No point starting a row.

Rick, his conversation with Zoe finished, turned to the others.

Mara noticed streaks of orange and white paint in his beard. "They were all talking about the Eastvale demo," he said. "Plenty of tongues started clucking in the grocer's when I walked in."

"What did they think about it?" Mara asked.

Rick snorted. "They don't think. They're just like the sheep they raise. They're too frightened to come out with an opinion about anything for fear it'll be the wrong one. Oh, they worry about nuclear fall-out. Who doesn't? But that's about all they do, worry and whine. When push comes to shove they'll just put up with it like everything else and bury their heads in the ground. The wives are even worse. All they can do if anything upsets the nice, neat, comfortable little lives they've made for themselves is say tut-tut-tut, isn't it a shame."

The door creaked open and Paul walked in.

Mara watched the emaciated figure, fists bunched in his pockets, walk over to them. With his hollow, bony face, tattooed fingers, and the scars, needle-tracks and self-inflicted cigarette burns that Mara knew stretched all the way up his arms, Paul seemed a frightening figure. The only thing that softened his appearance was his hair-style. His blond hair was short at the back and sides but long on top, and the fringe kept slipping down over his eyes. He'd brush it back impatiently and scowl but never mention having it cut.

Mara couldn't help thinking about his background. Right from childhood, Paul's life had been rough and hard. He never said much about his real parents, but he'd told Mara about the emotionally cold foster home where he had been expected to show undying gratitude for every little thing they did for him. Finally, he had run away and lived a punk life on the streets, done whatever he'd had to to survive. It had been a life of hard drugs and violence and, eventually, jail. When they had met him, he had been lost and looking for some kind of anchor in life. She wondered just how much he really had changed since he'd been with them.

Remembering the blood on his hand, the way he had lied, and the murdered policeman, she began to feel frightened. What would he do if she were to question him? Was she living with a killer? And if she was, what should she do about it?

As the conversation went on around her, Mara began to feel herself drifting off on a chaotic spate of her own thoughts. She could hear the sounds the others were making, but not the words, the meaning. She thought of confiding in Seth, but what if he took some kind of action? He might be hard on Paul, even drive him away. He could be very stern and inflexible at times. She didn't want her new family to split apart, imperfect as she knew it was. It was all she had in the world.

No, she decided, she wouldn't tell anyone. Not yet. She wouldn't make Paul feel as if they were ganging up on him. The whole thing was probably ridiculous anyway. She was imagining things, filling her head with stupid fears. Paul would never hurt her, she told herself, never in a million years.

FOUR

I

Sunday morning dawned clear and cold. A brisk March wind blew, restoring the sun and the delicate colours of early spring to the lower hillsides. Women hung on to their hats and men clutched the lapels of their best suits as they struggled to church along Mortsett Lane in Relton. The police car, a white Fiesta Popular, with the official red and blue stripes on its sides, turned and made its way up the bumpy Roman road to Maggie's Farm. PC McDonald drove, with Craig silent beside him and Banks cramped in the back.

The view across the dale was superb. Banks could see Fortford on the valley bottom and Devraulx Abbey below Lyndgarth on the opposite slope. Behind them all, the northern daleside rose, baring along its snowy heights scars of exposed limestone that looked like rows of teeth gleaming in the light.

Banks felt refreshed after an evening at home reading *Madame Bovary*, followed by a good night's sleep. Luckily, Dirty Dick had phoned to cancel their pub crawl, claiming tiredness. Banks suspected he had decided to drop in at the Queen's Arms—just around the corner from his hotel—to work on Glenys, but Burgess looked relatively unscathed the next morning. He seemed tired, though, and his grey eyes were dull, like champagne that had lost its fizz. Banks wondered how he was getting on with Dorothy Wycombe.

As the car pulled onto the gravel outside the farmhouse, someone glanced through the window. When Banks got out, he could hear the wind chimes jingling like a piece of experimental music, harmonizing strangely with the wind that whistled around his ears. He had for-gotten how high on the moorland Maggie's Farm was.

His knock was answered by a tall, slender woman in her mid- to late-thirties wearing jeans and a rust-coloured jumper. Banks thought he remembered her from his previous visit. Her wavy chestnut hair tumbled over her shoulders, framing a pale, heart-shaped face, free of make-up. Perhaps her chin was a little too pointed and her nose a bit too long, but the whole effect was pleasing. Her clear brown eyes looked both innocent and knowing at once.

Banks presented his warrant and the woman moved aside wearily. They knew we were coming sometime, he thought; they've just been waiting to get it over with.

"They'd better not damage anything," she said, nodding towards McDonald and Craig.

"Don't worry, they won't. You won't even know they've been here." Mara sniffed. "I'll get the others."

The two uniformed men started their search, and Banks sat in the rocking chair by the window. Turning his head sideways, he scanned the titles in the pine bookcase beside him. They were mostly nov-els—Hardy, the Brontës, John Cowper Powys, Fay Weldon, Graham Greene—mixed in with a few more esoteric works, such as an intro-duction to Jung's psychology and a survey of the occult. On the lower shelves rested a number of older, well-thumbed paperbacks—*The Teachings of Don Juan, Naked Lunch, Lord of the Rings*. In addition, there were the obligatory political texts: Marcuse, Fanon, Marx and Engels.

On the floor beside Banks lay a copy of George Eliot's *The Mill on the Floss*. He picked it up. The bookmark stood at the second page; that was about as far as he'd ever got with George Eliot himself.

Mara came back from the barn with the others, three of them vaguely familiar to Banks from eighteen months ago: Zoe Hardacre, a slight, freckle-faced woman with frizzy ginger hair and dark roots; Rick Trelawney, a big bear of a man in a baggy paint-smeared T-shirt and torn jeans; and Seth Cotton, in from his workshop, wearing a sand-coloured lab coat, tall and thin with mournful brown eyes and neatly trimmed dark hair and beard framing a dark-complexioned face. Finally came a skinny, hostile-looking youth Banks hadn't seen before.

"Who are you?" he asked.

"Paul's not been here long," Mara said quickly.

"What's your last name?"

Paul said nothing.

"He doesn't have to say," Mara argued. "He's done nothing."

Seth shook his head. "Might as well tell him," he said to Paul. "He'll find out anyway."

"He's right, you know," Banks said.

"It's Boyd, Paul Boyd."

"Ever been in trouble, Paul?"

Paul smiled. It was either that or a scowl, Banks couldn't decide. "So what if I have? I'm not on probation or parole. I don't have to register at the local nick everywhere I go, do I?" He fished for a cigarette in a grubby ten-pack of Player's. Banks noticed that his stubby fingers were trembling slightly.

"Just like to know who we've got living among us," Banks said pleasantly. He didn't need to pursue the matter. If Boyd had a record, the Police National Computer would provide all the information he wanted.

"So what's all this in aid of?" Rick said, leaning against the mantelpiece. "As if I need ask."

"You know what happened on Friday night. You were arrested for obstructing a police officer." Rick laughed. Banks ignored him and went on. "You also know that a policeman was killed at that demonstration."

"Are you saying you think one of us did it?"

Banks shook his head. "Come on," he said, "you know the rules as well as I do. A situation like this comes up, we check out all political groups."

"We're not political," Mara said.

Banks looked around the room. "Don't be so naïve. Everything you have here, everything you say and do, makes a political statement. It doesn't matter whether or not any of you belong to an official party. You know that as well as I do. Besides, we've got to act on tips we get."

"What tip?" Rick asked. "Who's been talking?"

"Never mind that. We just heard you were involved, that's all." Burgess's trick seemed at least worth a try.

"So we were there," Rick said, "Seth and me. You already know that. We gave statements. We told you all we knew. Why come back pestering us now? What are you looking for?"

"Anything we can find."

"Look," Rick went on, "I still don't see why you're persecuting us. I can't imagine who's been telling you things or what they've been saying, but you're misinformed. Just because we employed our right to demonstrate for a cause we happen to believe in, it doesn't give you the right to come around with these Gestapo tactics and harass us."

"The Gestapo didn't need a search warrant."

Rick sneered and scratched his straggly beard. "With a JP like the one you've got in your pocket, I'd hardly consider that a valid argument."

"Besides," Banks went on, "we're not persecuting you or harassing you. Believe me, if we were, you'd know it. Do any of you remember anything else about Friday night?"

Seth and Rick shook their heads. Banks looked around at the others. "Come on, I'm assuming you were all there. Don't worry, I can't prove it. I'm not going to arrest you if you admit it. It's just that one of you might have seen something important. This is a murder investigation."

Still silence. Banks sighed. "Fine. Don't blame me if things do get rough. We've got a man up from London. A specialist. Dirty Dick, his friends call him. He's a hell of a lot nastier than I am."

"Is that some kind of threat?" Mara asked.

Banks shook his head. "I'm just letting you know your options, that's all."

"How can we tell you we saw something if we didn't?" Paul said angrily. "You say you know we were there. Okay. Maybe we were. I'm not saying we were, but maybe. That doesn't mean we saw anything or did anything wrong. It's like Rick says, we had a right to be there. It's not a fucking police state yet." He turned away sullenly and drew on his cigarette.

"Nobody's denying your right to be there," Banks said. "I just want to know if you saw anything that could help us solve this murder."

Silence.

"Does anyone here own a flick-knife?"

Rick said no and the others shook their heads.

"Ever seen one around? Know anyone who does have one?"

Again nothing. Banks thought he saw an expression of surprise flit across Mara's face, but it could have been a trick of the light.

In the following silence, Craig and McDonald came downstairs, shook their heads and went to search the outbuildings. Two small children walked in from the kitchen and hurried over to Mara, each taking a hand. Banks smiled at them, but they just stared at him, sucking their thumbs.

He tried to imagine Brian and Tracy, his own children, growing up under such conditions, isolated from other children. For one thing, there didn't seem to be a television in the place. Banks disapproved of TV in general, and he always tried to make sure that Brian and Tracy didn't watch too much, but if children saw none at all, they would have nothing to talk to their pals about. There had to be a compromise somewhere; you couldn't just ignore the blasted idiot-box in this day and age, much as you might wish you could.

On the other hand, these children certainly showed no signs of neglect, and there was no reason to assume that Rick and the rest weren't good parents. Seth Cotton, Banks knew, had a reputation as a fine carpenter, and Mara's pottery sold well locally. Sandra even had a piece, a shapely vase glazed in a mixture of shades: green, ultramarine and the like. He didn't know much about Rick Trelawney's paintings, but if the local landscape propped up by the fireplace was his, then he was good, too. No, he had no call to impose his own limited perspective on them. If the children grew up into creative, free-thinking adults, their minds unpolluted by TV and mass culture, what could be so wrong about that?

Apart from the sounds of the wind chimes, they sat in silence until Rick finally spoke. "Do you know," he said to Banks, "how many children come down with leukaemia and rare forms of cancer in areas around Sellafield and other nuclear-power stations? Do you have any idea?"

"Look," said Banks. "I'm not here to attack your views. You're entitled to them. I might even agree. The thing is, what happened on Friday night goes beyond all that. I'm not here to argue politics or philosophy; I'm investigating a murder. Why can't you get that into your heads?"

"Maybe they can't be as neatly separated as you think," Rick argued. "Politics, philosophy, murder—they're all connected. Look at Latin America, Israel, Nicaragua, South Africa. Besides, the police started it. They kept us penned in like animals, then they charged with their truncheons out, just like some Chilean goon squad. If some of them got hurt, too, they bloody well deserved it."

"One of them got killed. Is that all right?"

Rick turned away in disgust. "I never said I was a pacifist," he muttered, looking at Seth. "There'll be a local police inquiry," he went on, "and the whole thing'll be rigged. You can't expect us to believe there's going to be any objectivity about all this. When it comes to the crunch you bastards always stick together."

"Believe what you like," Banks said.

Craig and McDonald came back in through the kitchen. They'd found nothing. It was eleven o'clock. At twelve Banks was to meet Burgess, Hatchley and Richmond in the Queen's Arms to compare notes. There was nothing to be gained by staying to discuss nuclear ethics with Rick, so he stood up and walked over to the door.

As he held his jacket closed and pushed against the wind to the car, he felt someone staring at his back through the window. He knew he had sensed fear in the house. Not just fear of a police raid they'd been expecting, but something different. All was not as harmonious as it should have been. He filed away his uneasiness to be mulled over later along with the thousand other things—concrete or nebulous—that lodged themselves in his mind during an investigation.

II

"Nothing," Burgess growled, grinding out his cigar viciously in the ashtray at the centre of the copper-topped table. "Absolutely bugger all. And that woman's crazy. I'll swear I thought she was going to bite me."

For the first time ever, Banks felt a sudden rush of affection for Dorothy Wycombe.

All in all, though, the morning had been disappointing for every-one. Not surprisingly, the searches had produced no murder weapon or documents attesting to the terrorist plot that Burgess suspected; none of the witnesses had changed their statements and the reaction to Burgess's divide-and-conquer tactic had been negligible.

Sergeant Hatchley reported that the Church for Peace group seemed stunned by the murder and had even offered prayers for PC Gill in their service that morning. The Students Union, according to DC Richmond, who had visited the leaders—Tim Fenton and Abha Sutton—at their flat, thought it typical of the others to blame them for what happened, but insisted that assassination was not part of their programme for a peaceful revolution. While Burgess thought Dorothy Wycombe quite capable of murder—especially of a member of the male species—she had stuck to her guns and ridiculed any such suggestion.

"So it's back to square one," Hatchley said. "A hundred suspects and not one scrap of evidence."

"I did find out from one of the lads on duty," said Richmond, "that Dorothy Wycombe, Dennis Osmond and some of the people from Maggie's Farm were close to the front at one time. But he said every-thing went haywire when the fighting started. He also said he noticed a punkish-looking kid with them."

"That'd be Paul Boyd," Banks said. "He seems to live up at the farm, too. Run him through the computer, will you, Phil, and see what comes up. I wouldn't be surprised if he's done time. While you're at it, find out what you can about the lot of them up there. I've got a funny feeling that something's not quite right about that place."

He glanced at Burgess, who seemed to be staring abstractedly over at Glenys. Her husband was nowhere in sight.

"Maybe we should have a look into Gill's background," Banks suggested.

Burgess turned. "Why?"

"Someone might have had a reason for wanting him dead. We'll get nowhere on means and opportunity unless the knife turns up, but if we could find a motive—"

Burgess shook his head. "Not in a crime like this. Whether it was planned or spur-of-the-moment, the victim was random. It could have happened to any of the coppers on duty that night. It was just poor Gill's bad luck, that's all."

"But still," Banks insisted, "it's something we can do. Maybe the demo was just used as a cover."

"No. It'll look bad, for a start. What if the papers find out we're investigating one of our own? We've got enough trouble already with an enquiry into the whole bloody mess. That'd give the press enough ammo to take a few cheap shots at us without us making things easier for them. Jesus, there's enough weirdos and commies to investigate already without bringing a good copper into it. What about this Osmond character? Anyone talked to him yet?"

"No," said Banks. "Not since Friday night."

"Right, this is what we'll do. Get another round in, Constable, would you?" Burgess handed Richmond a flyer.

Richmond nodded and went to the bar. Burgess had switched from Double Diamond to double Scotch, claiming it was easier on his stomach, but Banks thought he was just trying to impress Glenys with his largesse. And now he was showing her he was too important to leave the conference and that he had the power to order others to do things for him. Good tactics, but would they work on her?

"You and I, Banks," he said, "will pay this Osmond fellow a visit this afternoon. DC Richmond can check up on those drop-outs you went to see and feed a few more names into the PNC. Sergeant Hatchley here can start making files on the leaders of the various groups involved. We want every statement cross-checked with the others for inaccuracies, and all further statements checked against the originals. Someone's going to slip up at some point, and we're going to catch the bugger at it. Bottoms up." He drank his Scotch and turned to wink at Glenys. "By the way," he said to Banks, "that bloody office you gave me isn't big enough to swing a dead cat in. Any chance of another?"

Banks shook his head. "Sorry, we're pushed for space. It's either that or the cells."

"What about yours?"

"Too small for two."

"I was meaning for one. Me."

"Forget it. I've got all my files and records in there. Besides, it's cold and the blind doesn't work."

"Hmmm. Still..."

"You could do most of the paperwork in your hotel room," Banks suggested. "It's close enough, big enough and there's a phone." And you'll be out of my way, too, he thought.

Burgess nodded slowly. "All right. It'll do for now. Come on!" He jumped into action and clapped Banks on the back. "Let's see if anything's turned up at the station first, then we'll set off and have a chat with Mr Dennis Osmond, CND."

Nothing had turned up, and as soon as Richmond had located Paul Boyd's record and Banks had had a quick look at it, the pair set off for Osmond's flat in Banks's white Cortina.

"Tell me about this Boyd character," Burgess asked as Banks drove.

"Nasty piece of work." Banks slipped a Billie Holiday cassette in the stereo and turned the volume down low. "He started as a juvenile—gang fights, assault, that kind of thing—skipping school and hanging around the streets with the rest of the dead-beats. He's been nicked four times, and he drew eighteen months on the last one. First it was drunk and disorderly, underage, then assaulting a police officer trying to disperse a bunch of punks frightening shoppers in Liverpool city centre. After that it was a drugs charge, possession of a small amount of amphetamines. Then he got nicked breaking into a chemist's to steal pills. He's been clean for just over a year now."

Burgess rubbed his chin. "Everything short of soccer hooliganism, eh? Maybe he's not the sporting type. Assaulting a police officer, you say?"

"Yes. Him and a couple of others. They didn't do any real damage, so they got off lightly."

"That's the bloody trouble," Burgess said. "Most of them do. Any political connections?"

"None that we know of so far. Richmond hasn't been onto the Branch yet, so we haven't been able to check on his friends and acquaintances."

"Anything else?"

"Not really. Most of his probation officers and social workers seemed to give up on him."

"My heart bleeds for the poor bastard. It looks like we've got a likely candidate. This Osmond is a social worker, isn't he?"

"Yes."

"Maybe he'll know something about the kid. Let's remember to ask him. Where's Boyd from?"

"Liverpool."

"Any IRA connections?"

"Not as far as we know."

"Still..."

Dennis Osmond lived in a one-bedroom flat in north-east Eastvale. It had originally been council-owned, but the tenants had seized their chance and bought their units cheaply when the government started selling them off.

A shirtless Osmond answered the door and led Banks and Burgess inside. He was tall and slim with a hairy chest and a small tattoo of a butterfly on his upper right arm. He wore a gold crucifix on a chain around his neck. With his shaggy dark hair and Mediterranean good looks, he looked the kind of man who would be attractive to women. He moved slowly and calmly, and didn't seem at all surprised by their arrival.

The flat had a spacious living-room with a large plate-glass window that overlooked the fertile plain to the east of Swainsdale: a checkerboard of ploughed fields, bordered by hedgerows, rich brown, ready for spring. The furniture was modern—tubes and cushions—and a large framed painting hung on the wall over the fake fireplace. Banks had to look very closely to make sure the canvas wasn't blank; it was scored with faint red and black lines.

"Who is it?" A woman's voice came from behind them. Banks turned and saw Jenny Fuller poking her head around a door. From what he could tell, she was wearing a loose dressing-gown, and her hair was in disarray. His eyes caught hers and he felt his stomach tense up and his chest tighten. Meeting her in a situation like this was something he hadn't expected. He was surprised how hard it hit.

"Police," Osmond said. But Jenny had already turned back and shut the door behind her.

Burgess, who had watched all this, made no comment. "Can we sit down?" he asked.

"Go ahead." Osmond gestured to the armchairs and pulled a black T-shirt over his head while they made themselves as comfortable as possible. The decal on the front showed the CND symbol—a circle with a wide-spread, inverted Y inside it, each branch touching the circumference—with NO NUKES written in a crescent under it.

Banks fumbled for a cigarette and looked around for an ashtray.

"I'd rather you didn't," Osmond said. "Second-hand smoke can kill, you know." He paused and looked Banks over. "So you're Chief Inspector Banks, are you? I've heard a lot about you."

"Hope it was good," Banks said, with more equilibrium than he felt. What had Jenny been telling him? "It'll save us time getting acquainted, won't it?"

"And you're the whiz-kid they sent up from London," Osmond said to Burgess.

"My, my. How word travels." Dirty Dick smiled. He had the kind of smile that made most people feel nervous, but it seemed to have no effect on Osmond. As Banks settled into the chair, he could picture Jenny dressing in the other room. It was probably the bedroom, he thought gloomily, and the double bed would be rumpled and stained, the *Sunday Times* review section spread out over the creased sheets. He took out his notebook and settled down as best he could for the interrogation.

"What do you want?" Osmond asked, perching at the edge of the sofa and leaning forward.

"I hear you were one of the organizers of Friday's demonstration," Burgess opened.

"So what if I was?"

"And you're a member of the Campaign for Nuclear Disarmament and the International Socialists, if I'm not mistaken."

"I'm in Amnesty International, as well, in case you don't have that in your file. And as far as I'm aware it's not a crime yet."

"Don't be so touchy."

"Look, can you get to the point? I haven't got all day."

"Oh yes, you have," Burgess said. "And you've got all night, too, if I want it like that."

"You've no right—"

"I've every right. One of your lot—maybe even you—killed a good, honest copper on Friday night, and we don't like that; we don't like it at all. I'm sorry if we're keeping you from your fancy woman, but that's the way it is. Whose idea was it?"

Osmond frowned. "Whose idea was what? And I don't like you calling Jenny names like that."

"You don't?" Burgess narrowed his eyes. "There'll be a lot worse names than that flying around, sonny, if you don't start to co-operate. Whose idea was the demonstration?"

"I don't know. It just sort of came together."

Burgess sighed. "'It just sort of came together,'" he repeated mockingly, looking at Banks. "Now what's that supposed to mean? Men and women come together, if they're lucky, but not political demonstrations—they're planned. What are you trying to tell me?"

"Exactly what I said. There are plenty of people around here opposed to nuclear arms, you know."

"Are you telling me that you all just happened to meet outside the Community Centre that night? Is that what you're trying to say? 'Hello, Fred, fancy meeting you here. Let's have a demo.' Is that what you're saying?"

Osmond shrugged.

"Well, balls is what I say, Osmond. Balls to that. This was an organized demonstration, and that means somebody organized it. That somebody might have also arranged for a little killing to spice things up a bit. Now, so far the only somebody we know about for sure is you. Maybe you did it all by yourself, but I'm betting you had some help. Whose tune do you dance to, Mr Osmond? Moscow's? Peking's? Or is it Belfast?"

Osmond laughed. "You've got your politics a bit mixed up, haven't you? A socialist is hardly the same as a Maoist. Besides, the Chairman's out of favour these days. And as for the IRA, you can't seriously believe—"

"I seriously believe a lot of things that might surprise you," Burgess cut in. "And you can spare me the fucking lecture. Who gave you your orders?"

"You're wrong," Osmond said. "It wasn't like that at all. And even if there was somebody else involved, do you think I'm going to tell you who it was?"

"Yes, I do," Burgess said. "There's nothing more certain. The only question is when you're going to tell me, and where."

"Look," Banks said, "we'll find out anyway. There's no need to take it on yourself to carry the burden and get done for withholding information in a murder investigation. If you didn't do it and you don't think your mates did, either, then you've nothing to worry about, have you?" Banks found it easy to play the nice guy to Burgess's heavy, even though he felt a strong, instinctive dislike for Osmond. When he questioned suspects with Sergeant Hatchley, the two of them switched roles. But Burgess only had one method of approach: head on.

"Listen to him," Burgess said. "He's right."

"Why don't you find out from someone else, then?" Osmond said to Banks. "I'm damned if I'm telling you anything."

"Do you own a flick-knife?" Burgess asked.

"No."

"Have you ever owned one?"

"No."

"Know anybody who does?"

Osmond shook his head.

"Did you know PC Gill?" Banks asked. "Had you any contact with him before last Friday?"

Osmond looked puzzled by the question, and when he finally answered no, it didn't ring true. Or maybe he was just thrown off balance. Burgess didn't seem to notice anything, but Banks made a mental note to check into the possibility that Osmond and Gill had somehow come into contact.

The bedroom door opened and Jenny walked out. She'd brushed her hair and put on a pair of jeans and an oversized plaid shirt. Banks bet it belonged to Osmond and tried not to think about what had been going on earlier in the bedroom.

"Hello, love," Burgess said, patting an empty chair beside him. "Come to join us? What's your name?"

"In the first place," Jenny said stiffly, "I'm not 'love,' and in the second, I don't see as my name's any of your damn business. I wasn't even there on Friday."

"As you like," Burgess said. "Just trying to be friendly."

Jenny glanced at Banks as if to ask, "Who is this bastard?" and Burgess caught the exchange.

"Do you two know each other?" he asked.

Banks cursed inwardly and felt himself turning red. There was no way out. "This is Dr Fuller," he said. "She helped us on a case here a year or so back."

Burgess beamed at Jenny. "I see. Well, maybe you can help us again, Dr Fuller. Your boy-friend here doesn't want to talk to us, but if you've helped the police before—"

"Leave her alone," Osmond said. "She had nothing to do with it." Banks had felt the same thing—he didn't want Burgess getting his claws into Jenny—and he resented Osmond for being able to defend her.

"Very prickly today, aren't we?" Burgess said. "All right, sonny, we'll get back to you, if that's the way you want it." But he kept looking at Jenny, and Banks knew he was filing her away for future use. Banks now found it hard to look her in the eye himself. He was only a chief inspector and Burgess was a superintendent. When things were going his way, Burgess wouldn't pull rank, but if Banks let any of his special feeling for Jenny show, or tried in any way to protect her, then Burgess would certainly want to humiliate him. Besides, she had her knight in shining armour in the form of Osmond. Let him take the flack.

"What were you charged with on Friday?" Burgess asked.

"You know damn well what I was charged with. It was a trumped-up charge."

"But what was it? Tell me. Say it. Just to humour me." Burgess reached into his pocket and took out his tin of Tom Thumbs. Holding Osmond's eyes with his own all the time, he slowly took out a cigar and lit it.

"I said I don't want you smoking in here," Osmond protested on cue. "It's my home and—"

"Shut up," Burgess said, just loudly enough to stop him in his tracks. "What was the charge?"

"Breach of the peace," Osmond mumbled. "But I told you, it was trumped up. If anyone broke the peace, it was the police."

"Ever heard of a lad by the name of Paul Boyd?" Banks asked.

"No." It was a foolish lie. Osmond had answered before he'd had time to register the question. Banks would have known he was lying even if he hadn't already learned, via Jenny, that Osmond was acquainted with the people at Maggie's Farm.

"Look," Osmond went on, "I'm starting an inquiry of my own into what happened on Friday. I'll be taking statements, and believe me, I'll make sure your behaviour here today goes into the final report."

"Bully for you," said Burgess. Then he shook his head slowly. "You don't get it, do you, sonny? You might be able to pull those outraged-citizen tactics with the locals, but they won't wash with me. Do you know why not?"

Osmond scowled and kept silent.

"I said, do you know why not?"

"All right, no, I don't bloody well know why not!"

"Because I don't give a flying fuck for you or for others like you," Burgess said, stabbing the air with his cigar. "As far as I'm concerned, you're shit, and we'd all be a hell of a lot better off without you. And the people I work with, they feel the same way. It doesn't matter if Chief Inspector Banks here has the hots for your Dr Fuller and wants to go easy on her. It doesn't matter that he's got a social conscience and respects people's rights, either. I don't, and my bosses don't. We don't piss around, we get things done, and you'd do well to remember that, both of you."

Jenny was flushed and speechless with rage; Banks himself felt pale and impotent. He should have known that nothing would slip by Burgess.

"I can't tell you anything," Osmond repeated wearily. "Why can't you believe me? I don't know who killed that policeman. I didn't see it, I didn't do it, and I don't know who did."

A long silence followed. At least it seemed long to Banks, who was aware only of the pounding of his heart. Finally Burgess stood up and walked over to the window, where he stubbed out his cigar on the white sill. Then he turned and smiled. Osmond gripped the tubular arms of his chair tightly.

"Okay," Burgess said, turning to Banks. "We'll be off, then, for the moment. Sorry to spoil your afternoon in bed. You can get back to it now, if you like." He looked at Jenny and licked his lips. "That's a fetching shirt you've got on, love," he said to her. "But you didn't need to leave it half-unbuttoned just for me. I've got plenty of imagination."

Back in the car, Banks was fuming. "You were way out of line in there," he said. "There was no reason to insult Jenny, and there was especially no need to bring me into it the way you did. What the hell were you trying to achieve?"

"Just trying to stir them up a bit, that's all."

"So how does making me out to be a bloody lecher stir them up?"

"You're not thinking clearly, Banks. We make Osmond jealous, maybe he lets his guard down." Burgess grinned. "Anyway, there's nothing in it, is there, you and her?"

"Of course there isn't."

"Methinks this fellow doth protest too much."

"Fuck off."

"Oh, come on," Burgess said calmly. "Don't take it so seriously. You use what you need to get results. Christ, I don't blame you. I wouldn't mind tumbling her, myself. Lovely pair of tits under that shirt. Did you see?"

Banks took a deep breath and reached for a cigarette. There was no point, he realized, in going on. Burgess was an unstoppable force. However angry and disoriented Banks felt, it would do no good to let more of it show. Instead, he put his emotions in check, something he knew he should have done right from the start. But the feelings still rankled as they knotted up below the surface. He was mad at Burgess, he was mad at Osmond, he was mad at Jenny and he was mad, most of all, at himself.

Starting the car with a lurch, he shoved the cassette back in and turned up the volume. Billie Holiday sang "God Bless the Child," and Burgess whistled blithely along as they sped through the bright, blustery March day back to the market square.

III

They were all a bit drunk, and that was unusual at Maggie's Farm. Mara certainly hadn't been so tipsy for a long time. Rick was sketching them as they sat around the living-room. Paul drank lager from the can, and even Zoe had turned giggly on white wine. But Seth was the worst. His speech was slurred, his eyes were watery, and his co-ordination was askew. He was also getting maudlin about the sixties, something he never did when he was sober. Mara had seen him drunk only once before, the time he had let slip about the death of his wife. Mostly, he was well-guarded and got on with life without moaning.

Things had begun well enough. After the police visit, they had all walked down to the Black Sheep for a drink. Perhaps the feeling of relief, of celebration, had encouraged them to drink more than usual, and they had splurged on a few cans of Carlsberg Special Brew, some white wine and a bottle of Scotch to take home. Most of the afternoon Seth and Mara had lounged about over the papers or dozed by the fire, while Paul messed about in the shed, Rick painted in his studio, and Zoe amused the children. Early in the evening they all got together, and the whisky and wine started making the rounds.

Seth stumbled over to the stereo and sought out a scratchy old Grateful Dead record from his collection. "Those were the days," he said. "All gone now. All people care about today is money. Bloody yuppies."

Rick looked up from his sketch-pad and laughed. "When was it ever any different?"

"Isle of Wight, Knebworth..." Seth went on, listing the rock festivals he'd been to. "People really shared back then...."

Mara listened to him ramble. They had been under a lot of stress since the demo, she thought, and this was clearly Seth's way of getting it out of his system. It was easy to fall under the spell of nostalgia. She remembered the sixties, too—or more accurately the late sixties, when the hippie era had really got going in England. Things *had* seemed better back then. Simpler. More clear-cut. There was us and them, and you knew *them* by the shortness of their hair.

"....Santana, Janis, Hendrix, the Doors. Jesus, even the Hare Krishnas were fun back then. Now they all wear bloody business suits and wigs. I remember one time—"

"It's all crap!" Paul shouted, banging his empty can on the floor. "It was never like that. It's just a load of cobblers you're talking, Seth."

"How would you know?" Seth sat up and balanced unsteadily on his elbow. "You weren't there, were you? You were nought but a twinkle in your old man's eye."

"My mum and dad were hippies," Paul said scornfully. "Fucking flower children. She OD'd, and he was too bloody stoned to take care of me, so he gave me away."

Mara was stunned. Paul had never spoken about his true parents before, only about the way he had been badly treated in his foster home. If it was true, she thought, did he really see Seth and her in the same light? They were about the right age. Did he hate them, too?

But she couldn't believe that. There was another side to the coin. Maybe Paul was looking for what he had lost, and he had found at least some of it at Maggie's Farm. They didn't take drugs and, while she and Seth might have grown up in the sixties and tried to cling onto some of its ideals, they neither looked nor acted like hippies any longer.

"We're not like that," she protested, looking over at Zoe for support. "You know it, Paul. We care about you. We'd never desert you. It was fun back then for a lot of people. Seth's only reminiscing about his youth."

"I know," Paul said grudgingly. "I can't say I had one worth reminiscing about, myself. Anyway, I'm only saying, Mara, that's all. It wasn't all peace and love like Seth tells it. He's full of shit."

"You're right about that, mate," Rick agreed, putting down his sketch-pad and pouring another shot of Scotch. "I never did have much time for hippies myself. Nothing but a moaning, whining bunch of little kids, if you ask me. Seth's just pissed, that's all. Look at him now, anyway—he's a bloody landowner, a landlord even. Pretty soon it'll be baggy tweeds and out shooting pheasant every afternoon. Sir Seth Cotton, Squire of Maggie's Farm."

But Seth had slumped back against a beanbag and seemed to have lost all interest in the conversation. His eyes were closed, and Mara guessed that he was either asleep or absorbed in the soaring Jerry Garcia guitar solo.

"Where's your father now?" Mara asked Paul.

"I don't fucking know. Don't fucking care, either." Paul ripped open another can of lager.

"But didn't he ever get in touch?"

"Why should he? I told you, he was too zonked out to notice me even when I was there."

"It's still no reason to say everyone was like that," Mara said. "All Seth was saying was that the spirit of love was strong back then. All that talk about the Age of Aquarius meant something."

"Yeah, and what's happened to it now? Two thousand years of this crap I can do without, thanks very much. Let's just forget the fucking past and get on with life." With that, Paul got up and left the room.

Jerry Garcia played on. Seth stirred, opened one bloodshot eye, then closed it again.

Mara poured herself and Zoe some more white wine, then her mind wandered back to Paul. As if she weren't confused enough already, the hostility he'd shown tonight and the new information about his feelings for his parents muddied the waters even more. She was scared of approaching him about the blood on his hand, and she was beginning to feel frightened to go on living in the same house as someone she suspected of murder. But she hated herself for feeling that way about him, for not being able to trust him completely and believe in him.

What she needed was somebody to talk to, somebody she could trust from outside the house. She felt like a woman with a breast lump who was afraid to go to the doctor and find out if it really was cancer.

And what made it worse was that she'd noticed the knife was missing: the flick-knife Seth said he had bought in France years ago. Everybody else must have noticed, too, but no one had mentioned it. The knife had been lying on the mantelpiece for anyone to use ever since she'd been at Maggie's Farm, and now it was gone.

IV

Banks ate the fish and chips he had bought on the way home, then went into the living-room. Screw gourmet cooking, he thought. If that irritating neighbour, Selena Harcourt, didn't turn up with some sticky dessert to feed him up "while the little woman's away," he'd have the evening to relax instead of mixing up sauces that never turned out anyway.

He had calmed down soon after leaving Burgess at the station. The bastard had been right. What had happened at Osmond's, he realized, had not been particularly serious, but his shock at finding Jenny there had made him exaggerate things. His reaction had been extreme, and for a few moments, he'd lost his detachment. That was all. It had happened before and it would happen again. Not the end of the world.

He poured a drink, put his feet up and turned on the television. There was a special about the Peak District on Yorkshire TV. Half-watching, he flipped through Tracy's latest copy of *History Today* and read an interesting article on Sir Titus Salt, who had built a Utopian community called Saltaire, near Bradford, for the workers in his textile mills. It would be a good place to visit with Sandra and the kids, he thought. Sandra could take photographs; Tracy would be fascinated; and surely even Brian would find something of interest. The problem was that Sir Titus had been a firm teetotaller. There were no pubs in Saltaire. Obviously one man's Utopia is another man's Hell.

The article made him think of Maggie's Farm. He liked the place and respected Seth and Mara. They had shown antagonism towards him, but that was only to be expected. In his job, he was used to much worse. He didn't take it personally. Being a policeman was like being a vicar in some ways; people could never be really comfortable with you, even when you dropped into the local for a pint.

The TV programme finished, and he decided there was no point putting off the inevitable. Picking up the phone, he dialled Jenny's number. He was in luck; she answered on the third ring.

"Jenny? It's Alan."

There was a pause at the other end. "I'm not sure I want to talk to you," she said finally.

"Could you be persuaded to?"

"Try."

"I just wanted to apologize for this afternoon. I hadn't expected to see you there."

Only the slight crackle of the line filled the silence. "It surprised me, too," Jenny said. "You keep some pretty bad company."

I could say the same for you, too, Banks thought. "Yes," he said, "I know."

"I do think you should keep him on a leash in future. You could maybe try a muzzle on him as well." She was obviously warming to him again, he could tell.

"Love to. But he's the boss. How did Osmond take it?" The name almost stuck in his throat.

"He was pissed off, all right. But it didn't last. Dennis is resilient. He's used to police harassment."

There was silence again, more awkward this time.

"Well," Banks said, "I just wanted to say I was sorry."

"Yes. You've said that already. It wasn't your fault. I'm not used to seeing you in a supporting role. You're not at your best like that, you know."

"What did you expect me to do? Jump up and hit him?"

"No, I didn't mean anything like that. But when he said what he did about us I could see you were ready to."

"Was it so obvious?"

"It was to me."

"I blew up at him in the car."

"I thought you would. What did he say?"

"Just laughed it off."

"Charming. I could have killed him when he said that about my shirt being undone."

"It was, though."

"I dressed in a hurry. I wanted to know what was going on."

"I know. I'm not trying to make out you did it on purpose or anything. It's just that, well, with a bloke like him around you've got to be extra careful."

"Now I know. Though I hope I won't have the pleasure again."

"He doesn't give up easily," Banks said gloomily.

"Nor do I. Where are you? What are you doing?"

"At home. Relaxing."

"Me, too. Is Sandra back?"

"No." The silence crackled again. Banks cleared his throat. "Look," he said, "when I mentioned dinner the other day, before all this, I meant it. How about tomorrow?"

"Can't tomorrow. I've got an evening class to teach."

"Tuesday?"

Jenny paused. "I suppose I can break my date," she said. "It had better be worth it, though."

"The Royal Oak is always worth it. My treat. I need to talk to you."

"Business?"

"I'm hoping you can help me get a handle on some of those

Maggie's Farm people. Seth and Mara are about my age. It's funny how we all grew up in the sixties and turned out so different."

"Not really. Everybody's different."

"I liked the music. I just never felt I fit in with the longhaired crowd. Mind you, I did try pot once or twice."

"Alan! You didn't?"

"I did."

"And here's me thinking you're so strait-laced. What happened?"

"Nothing, the first time."

"And the second?"

"I fell asleep."

Jenny laughed.

"Still," Banks mused, "Burgess is about my age, too."

"He was probably sitting around in jackboots and a leather overcoat pulling the wings off flies."

"Probably. Anyway, dinner. Eight o'clock all right?"

"Fine."

"I'll pick you up."

Jenny said good night and hung up. Still friends. Banks breathed a sigh of relief.

He went back to his armchair and his drink, but he suddenly felt the need to call Sandra.

"How's your father?" he asked.

Sandra laughed. "Cantankerous as ever. But mother's coping better than I'd hoped." The line was poor and her voice sounded far-away.

"How much longer will you be down there?"

"A few more days should do it. Why? Are you missing us?"

"More than you know."

"Hang on a minute. We had a day in London yesterday and Tracy wants to tell you about it."

Banks talked to his daughter for a while about St Paul's and the Tower of London, then Brian cut in and told him how great the record shops were down there. There was exactly the guitar he'd been looking for.... Finally, Sandra came back on again.

"Anything happening up there?"

"You could say that." Banks told her about the demo and the killing.

Sandra whistled. "I'm glad I'm out of it. I can imagine how frantic things are."

"Thanks for the support."

"You know what I mean."

"Remember Dick Burgess? Used to be a chief inspector at the Yard?"

"Was he the one who pawed the hostess and threw up in the geraniums at Lottie's party?"

"That's the one. He's up here, in charge."

"God help you. Now I'm really glad I'm down here. He had his eyes on me, too, you know, if not his hands."

"I'd like to say it was good taste, but don't flatter yourself, love. He's like that with everyone in a skirt."

Sandra laughed. "Better go now. Brian and Tracy are at it again."

"Give them my love. Take care. See you soon."

After he'd hung up, Banks felt so depressed that he almost regretted phoning in the first place. Why, he wondered, does a phone call to a distant loved one only intensify the emptiness and loneliness you were feeling before you called?

At a loose end, he turned off the television in the middle of a pop-music special that Brian would have loved and put on the blues tape an old colleague had sent him from London. The Reverend Robert Wilkins sang "Prodigal Son" in his eerie voice, unusually thin and high-pitched for a bluesman. Banks slouched in the armchair by the gas fire and sipped his drink. He often did his best thinking while drinking Scotch and listening to music, and it was time to put some of his thoughts about Gill's murder in order.

A number of things bothered him. There were demonstrations all the time, much bigger than the one in Eastvale, and while opposing sides sometimes came to blows, policemen didn't usually get stabbed. Call it statistics, probability or just a hunch, but he didn't believe in Burgess's view of the affair.

And that was a problem, because it didn't leave much else to choose from. He still had uneasy feelings about some of the Maggie's Farm crowd. Paul Boyd was a dangerous character if ever he'd met one, and Mara had seemed extremely keen to come to his defence. Seth and Zoe had been especially quiet, but Rick Trelawney had

expressed more violent views than Banks had expected. He didn't
know what it added up to, but he felt that somebody knew something, or thought they did, and didn't want to communicate their
suspicions to the police. It was a stupid way to behave, but people did
it all the time. Banks just hoped that none of them got hurt.

As for Dennis Osmond, putting personal antipathy aside, Banks
had caught him on two lies. Osmond had said he didn't know Paul
Boyd, when he clearly did, and Banks had also suspected him of lying
when he denied knowing PC Gill. It was easy enough to see why he
might have lied: nobody wants to admit a connection with a murdered man or a convicted criminal if he doesn't have to. But Banks
had to determine if there was anything more sinister to it than that.
How could Osmond have known PC Gill? Maybe they'd been to
school together. Or perhaps Gill had had occasion to arrest Osmond
at some previous anti-nuclear protest. If so, it should be on the files.
Richmond would have the gen from Special Branch in the morning.

Nothing so far seemed much like a motive for murder, though. If
he was really cautious, he might be able to get something out of
Jenny on Tuesday. She didn't usually resent his trying to question
her, but she was bound to be especially sensitive where Osmond was
concerned.

Perhaps he had reacted unprofessionally on finding Jenny in
Osmond's bedroom and to Burgess's approach to interrogation. But,
he reminded himself, Dirty Dick had made him look a proper wally,
and what was more, he had insulted Jenny. Sometimes Banks thought
that Burgess's technique was to badger everyone involved in a case
until someone was driven to try to throttle him. At least then he
could lay a charge of attempted murder.

Halfway through his third Laphroaig and the second side of the
tape, Banks decided that there was only one way to get back at the
bastard, and that was to solve the case himself, in his own way.
Burgess wasn't the only one who could play his cards close to his
chest. Let him concentrate on the reds under the bed. Banks would
do a bit of discreet digging and see if he could come up with anyone
who had a motive for wanting PC Edwin Gill, and not just any copper, dead.

But if Gill the person rather than Gill the policeman was the victim, it raised a number of problems. For a start, how could the killer know that Gill was going to be at the demo? Also, how could he be sure that things would turn violent enough to mask a kill? Most puzzling of all was how could he have been certain of an escape? But at least these were concrete questions, a starting point. The more Banks thought about it, the more the thick of a political demonstration seemed the ideal cover for murder.

FIVE

I

The funeral procession wound its way from Gordon Street, where Edwin Gill had lived, along Manor Road to the cemetery. Somehow, Banks thought, the funeral of a fellow officer was always more solemn and grim than any other. Every policeman there knew that it could just as easily have been him in the coffin; every copper's wife lived with the fear that her husband, too, might end up stabbed, beaten or, these days, shot; and the public at large felt the tremor and momentary weakness in the order of things.

For the second time in less than a week, Banks found himself uncomfortable in a suit and tie. He listened to the vicar's eulogy, the obligatory verses from the *Book of Common Prayer*, and stared at the bristly necks in front of him. At the front, Gill's immediate family—mother, two sisters, uncles and aunts, nephews and nieces—snuffled and slipped each other wads of Kleenex.

When it was over, everyone filed out and waited for the cars to take them to the funeral lunch. The oaks and beeches lining the cemetery drive shook in the brisk wind. One moment the sun popped out from behind the clouds, and the next, a five-minute shower took everyone by surprise. It was that kind of day: chameleon, unpredictable.

Banks stood with DC Richmond by the unmarked black police Rover—his own white Cortina was hardly the thing for a funeral—and waited for someone to lead the way. He wore a light grey raincoat over his navy-blue suit, but his head was bare. With his close-cropped black hair, scar beside the right eye, and lean, angular features, he thought he must look a suspicious figure as he held his raincoat collar tight around his throat to keep out the cold wind. Richmond, rangy and athletic, wearing a camel-hair overcoat and trilby, stood beside him.

It was early Tuesday afternoon. Banks had spent the morning reading over the records Richmond had managed to gather on Osmond and the Maggie's Farm crowd. There wasn't much. Seth Cotton had once been arrested for carrying an offensive weapon (a bicycle chain) at a mods-and-rockers debacle in Brighton in the early sixties. After that, he had one marijuana bust to his credit—only a quid deal, nothing serious—for which he had been fined.

Rick Trelawney had been in trouble only once, in St Ives, Cornwall. A tourist had taken exception to his drunken pronouncements on the perfidy of collecting art, and a rowdy argument turned into a punch-up. It had taken three men to drag Rick off, and the tourist had ended up with a broken jaw and one permanently deaf ear.

The only other skeleton in Rick's cupboard was the wife from whom he had recently separated. She was an alcoholic, which made it easy enough for Rick to get custody of Julian. But she was now staying with her sister in London while undergoing treatment, and there was a legal battle brewing. Things had got so bad at one point that Rick had applied for a court order to prevent her from coming near their son.

There was nothing on Zoe, but Richmond had checked the birth registry and discovered that the father of her child, Luna, was one Lyle Greenberg, an American student who had since returned to his home in Eau Claire, Wisconsin.

On Mara there was even less. Immigration identified her as Moira Delacey, originally from Dublin. With her parents, she had come to England at the age of six, and they had settled in Manchester. No known Republican connections.

Most interesting and disturbing of all was Dennis Osmond's criminal record. In addition to arrests for his part in anti-government demonstrations—with charges ranging from breach of the peace to theft of a police officer's helmet—he had also been accused of assault by a live-in girl-friend called Ellen Ventner four years ago. At the woman's insistence, the charges had later been dropped, but Ventner's injuries—two broken ribs, a broken nose, three teeth knocked out and concussion—had been clearly documented by the hospital, and Osmond came out of the affair looking far from clean. Banks wasn't sure whether to bring up the subject when he met Jenny for dinner that evening. He wondered if she already knew. If she didn't she might not take kindly to his interference. Somehow, he doubted that Osmond had told her.

They were still waiting for the information from Special Branch, who had files on Osmond, Tim Fenton, the student leader, and five others known to have been at the demo. Apparently, the Branch needed Burgess's personal access code, password, voice-print and genetic fingerprint, or some equally ludicrous sequence of identification. Banks didn't expect much from them, anyway. In his own experience, Special Branch kept files on everyone who had ever bought a copy of *Socialist Weekly*.

Today, while Banks and Richmond were attending Gill's funeral, Burgess was taking Sergeant Hatchley to do the rounds again. They intended to revisit Osmond, Dorothy Wycombe, Tim Fenton and Maggie's Farm. Banks wanted to talk to the students himself, so he decided to call on them when he got back that evening—if Burgess hadn't alienated them beyond all communication by then.

Burgess had been practically salivating at the prospect of more interrogations, and even Hatchley had seemed more excited about work than usual. Perhaps it was the chance to work with a superstar that thrilled him, Banks thought. The sergeant had always found "The Sweeney" much more interesting than the real thing. Or maybe he was going to suck up to Dirty Dick in the hope of being chosen for some special Scotland Yard squad. And the devil of it was, perhaps he would be, too.

Banks had mixed feelings about that possibility. He had got used to Sergeant Hatchley sooner than he'd expected to, and they had worked quite well together. But Banks had no real feeling for him. He couldn't even bring himself to call Hatchley by his first name, Jim.

In Banks's mind, Hatchley was a sergeant and always would be. He didn't have that extra keen edge needed to make inspector. Phil Richmond did, but unfortunately there wasn't anywhere for him to move up to locally unless Hatchley was promoted, too.

Superintendent Gristhorpe wouldn't have that, and Banks didn't blame him. If Burgess liked Hatchley enough to suggest a job in London, that would solve all their problems. Richmond had already passed his sergeant's exams—the first stage on the long road to promotion—and perhaps PC Susan Gay, who had shown remarkable aptitude for detective work, could be transferred in from the uniformed branch as a new detective constable. PC Craig would be opposed, of course. He still called policewomen "wopsies," even though the gender-specific designation, WPC, had been dropped in favour of the neutral PC as far back as 1975. But that was Craig's problem; Hatchley was everyone's cross to bear.

Finally, the glossy black cars set off. Banks and Richmond followed them through the dull, deserted streets of Scarborough to the reception. There was nowhere quite as gloomy as a coastal resort in the off-season. If it hadn't been for the vague whiff of sea and fish in the air, nobody would have guessed they were at the seaside.

"Fancy a walk on the prom after lunch?" Banks asked.

Richmond sniffed. "Hardly the weather for that, is it?"

"Bracing, I'd say."

"Maybe I'll wait for you in a nice cosy pub, if you don't mind, sir."

Banks smiled. "And put your notes in order?" He knew how fussy Richmond was about notes and reports.

"I'll have to, won't I? It'll not stick in my memory that long."

On the way to Scarborough, Banks had put forward his theory about Gill's murder not being quite what it seemed. While Richmond had expressed reservations, he had agreed that it was at least worth pursuing. They had decided to chat up Gill's colleagues at the reception and see what they could pick up about the man. Burgess, of course, was to know nothing about this.

Richmond had argued that even if there was something odd about Gill, none of his mates would say so at his funeral. Banks disagreed. He thought funerals worked wonders on the conscience. The phoney platitudes often stuck in people's craws and made them want to tell someone the truth. After all, it wasn't as if they were trying to prove corruption or anything like that against Gill; they just wanted to know what kind of man he was and whether he might have made enemies.

The procession pulled into the car park of the Crown and Anchor, where a buffet had been arranged in the banquet room, and the guests hurried through a heavy shower to the front doors.

II

"Bloody hell! What stone did you crawl out from under?" Burgess said when Paul Boyd walked into the front room to see what was going on.

Paul scowled. "Piss off."

Burgess strode forward and clipped him around the ear. Paul flinched and stumbled back. "Less of your cheek, sonny," Burgess said. "Show a bit of respect for your elders and betters."

"Why should I? You didn't show any fucking respect for me, did you?"

"Respect? For you?" Burgess narrowed his eyes. "What makes you think you deserve any respect? You're an ugly little pillock with a record as long as my arm. And that includes assaulting a police officer. And while we're at it, mind your tongue. There's ladies present. At least, I think there are."

Mara felt cold as Burgess ran his eyes up and down her body.

Burgess turned back to Paul, who stood in the doorway holding his hand to his ear. "Come on, who put you up to it?"

"Up to what?"

"Killing a police officer."

"I never. I wasn't even there."

"It's true, he wasn't," Mara burst out. "He was here with me all evening. Somebody had to stay home and look after the children."

She had held her tongue so far, trying to figure Burgess out. He didn't seem as mild-mannered as Banks, and she was afraid of attracting his attention. Even as she spoke, her stomach muscles tensed.

Burgess looked at her again and shook his head. His eyes were as sharp as chipped slate. "Very touching, love. Very touching. Didn't your mother and father teach you not to tell lies? He was spotted in the crowd. We know he was there."

"You must have been mistaken."

Burgess glanced at Paul, then looked at Mara again. "Mistaken!

How could anyone mistake this piece of garbage for someone else? You need your mouth washing out with soap and water, you do, love."

"And don't call me love."

Burgess threw up his arms in mock despair. "What's wrong with you lot? I thought everyone called each other love up north. Anyway, I can't for the life of me see why you're defending him. He's got a limited vocabulary, and with a body like that, I doubt if he's much good in bed."

"Bastard," Mara said between clenched teeth. There was going to be no reasoning with this one, that was certain. Best just stick it out.

"That's right, love," Burgess said. "Get it off your chest. You'll feel all the better for it." He eyed her chest, as if to prove his point, and turned to Paul again. "What did you do with the knife?"

"What knife?"

"The one you used to stab PC Gill. The flick-knife. Just your kind of weapon, I'd say."

"I didn't stab anyone."

"Oh, come on! What did you do with it?"

"I didn't have no fucking knife."

Burgess wagged a finger at him. "I warned you, watch your tongue. Are you getting all this, Sergeant Hatchley? The kid's denying everything."

"Yes, sir." Hatchley was sitting on the beanbag cushions, looking, Mara thought, rather like a beached whale.

"All we need is the knife," Burgess said. "Once we trace it back to you, you'll be in the nick before your feet can touch the ground. With your record, you won't have a chance. We've already placed you at the scene."

"There were about a hundred other people there, too," Paul said.

"Count them, did you? I thought you said you weren't there."

"I wasn't."

"Then how did you know?"

"Read it in the papers."

"Read? You? I doubt you'd get past the comics."

"Very funny," Paul said. "But you can't prove nothing."

"You might just be right about that," Burgess said. "But remember, if I can't prove nothing, it means I *can* prove something. And when I do...when I do..." He left the threat hanging and turned to the room at large. They were all gathered in the house except Rick, who had taken the children to town for new clothes. "The rest of you are just as guilty," he went on. "When we build a case against dick-head here, you'll all get done for withholding information and for being accessories. So if any of you know anything, you'd best tell us now. Think about it."

"We don't know anything," Seth said quietly.

"Well, there we are then." Burgess sighed and ran his free hand through his hair. "Stalemate."

"And don't think we won't complain about the way you've treated us and how you hit Paul," Mara said.

"Do it, love. See if I care. Want me to tell you what'll happen? If you're lucky, it'll get passed down the line back to my boss at the Yard. And do you know what? He's an even bigger bastard than I am. No, your best bet's to come clean, tell the truth."

"I told you," Paul said. "I don't know anything about it."

"All right." Burgess dropped his cigar stub into a teacup balanced on the arm of a chair. The hot ash sizzled as it hit the dregs. "But don't say I didn't warn you. Come on, Sergeant. We'll leave these people to think about it a bit more. Maybe one of them'll come to his senses and get in touch with us."

Hatchley struggled to his feet and joined Burgess by the door. "We'll be back, don't worry," Burgess said. As they walked out of the small porch, he reached up, slapped the wind chimes and snarled, "Bloody tuneless racket."

III

Banks waited, glass of sherry in hand, until the crowd around the buffet had dwindled before he collected his own paper plateful of cold cuts and salad.

"Ee, it's a bit of all right, this, i'n't it," a grey-haired woman in a powder-blue crepe dress was saying to her friend.

"Aye," the other said. "Better'n old Ida Latham's do. Nobbut them little sarnies wi' t'crusts cut off. No bigger'n a postage stamp they weren't. Cucumber, too. It allus gives me gas, cucumber does."

"Chief Inspector Banks?"

The man who suddenly materialized beside Banks was about six-two with a shiny bald head, fuzzy white hair above the ears, and a grey RAF moustache. He wore a black armband over his dark grey suit, and a black tie. Even the rims of his glasses were black. Banks nodded.

"Thought it must be you," the man went on. "You don't look like a relation, and I've never seen you around here before. Superintendent Gristhorpe sent word you were coming." He stretched out his hand. "Detective Chief Inspector Blake, Scarborough CID." Banks managed to balance his sherry glass on his plate and shake hands.

"Pleased to meet you," he said. "Shame it has to be at something like this."

They walked over to a quieter and less crowded part of the hall. Banks put down his plate on a table—after all, he couldn't eat while talking—and took out a cigarette.

"How's the investigation going?" Blake asked.

"Nothing yet. Too many suspects. Anything could have happened in a situation like that." He looked around the hall. "Lot of people here. PC Gill must have been a popular bloke."

"Hmmm. Didn't know him well, myself. It's a big station."

"Keen, though," Banks said. "Volunteering for overtime on a Friday night. Most of our lads would've rather been at the pub."

"It's more likely he needed the money. You know how half the bloody country lives on overtime. Has to, the wages we get paid."

"True. Fond of money, was he?"

Chief Inspector Blake frowned. "Are you digging?"

"We don't know anything about Gill," Banks admitted. "He wasn't one of ours. Every little bit helps. I'm sure you know that."

"Yes. But this is hardly a normal case, is it?"

"Still..."

"As I said, I didn't really know him. I hear you've got a whiz-kid from the Yard in charge."

Banks stubbed out his cigarette and picked up his plate. He knew he wasn't going to get anything out of Blake, so he ate his lunch while exchanging small talk. From the corner of his eye, he noticed Richmond talking to one of the uniformed pallbearers, probably one of the locals who had been bussed in with Gill to the demo. They had all given statements, of course, but none had seen Gill get stabbed. He hoped that Richmond was doing better than he was.

Chief Inspector Blake drifted away after about five minutes, and Banks took the opportunity to refill his sherry glass. At the bar, he found himself standing next to another pallbearer.

Banks introduced himself. "Sad occasion," he said.

"Aye," PC Childers replied. He was young, perhaps in his early twenties. Banks felt irritated by his habit of looking in another direction while speaking.

"Popular bloke, PC Gill, by the look of it," Banks said.

"Oh, aye. A right card, old Eddie was."

"That right? Keen on his work?"

"You could say that. Certain parts of it, anyway."

"I'll bet the overtime came in handy."

"It's always good to have a bit extra," Childers said slowly. Banks could tell he was holding back; whether out of friendship, a sense of occasion, or out of simple duty, he couldn't be sure. But something was wrong. Childers was getting edgier, staring at the far wall. Finally, he excused himself abruptly and went to talk to his sergeant.

Banks was beginning to feel his mission had been wasted. He was also aware that very soon he would become an unwelcome guest if Childers and Blake mentioned his probings to others. Christ, he thought, they were a bloody sensitive lot here. It made him wonder if they'd got something to hide.

Back at the table for a helping of trifle, Banks manoeuvred himself next to a third pallbearer, a moon-faced lad with bright blue eyes and fine, thinning hair the colour of wheat. Taking a deep breath, he smiled and introduced himself.

"I know who you are, sir," the PC said. "Ernie Childers told me. I'm PC Grant, Tony Grant. Ernie warned me. Said you were asking questions about Eddie Gill."

"Just routine," Banks said. "Like we do in all murder investigations."

Grant glanced over his shoulder. "Look, sir," he said, "I can't talk to you here."

"Where, then?" Banks felt his heart speed up.

"Do you know the Angel's Trumpet?"

Banks shook his head. "Don't know the place well. Only been here once before."

"It'll take too long to explain," Grant said. They finished helping themselves to dessert and turned around just in time to spot one of Grant's colleagues walking towards them.

"Marine Drive, then, just round from the fun-fair," Banks said quickly out of the corner of his mouth. It was the only place he could think of offhand. "About an hour."

"Fine," Grant said as a uniformed sergeant joined them.

"Good of you to come, Chief Inspector," the sergeant said, holding out his hand. "We appreciate it."

Grant had merged back into the crowd, and as Banks exchanged trivialities with the sergeant, his mind was on the meeting ahead, and the nervous, covert way in which it had been arranged.

IV

"He made me feel dirty," Mara said to Seth. "The way he looked at me."

"Don't let it get to you. That's just his technique. He's trying to goad you into saying something you'll regret."

"But what about Paul? You saw the way he was picking on him. What can we do?"

Paul had taken off as soon as Burgess and Hatchley left. He had said he was feeling claustrophobic and needed a walk on the moors to calm down after the onslaught. He hadn't objected to Zoe's company, so Seth and Mara were left alone.

"What is there to do?" Seth said.

"But you saw the way that bastard went at him. I wouldn't put it past him to frame Paul if it came down to it. He *has* got a record."

"They'd still need evidence."

"He could plant it."

"He couldn't just plant any old knife. It'd have to be the one that fitted the wound. They have scientists working for them. You can't put things across on that lot so easily, you know."

"I suppose not." Mara bit her lip and decided to take the plunge.

"Seth? Have you noticed that the knife's missing? That old flick-knife from the mantelpiece."

Seth looked at her in silence for a while. His brown eyes were sad, and the bags under them indicated lack of sleep. "Yes," he said, "I have. But I didn't say anything. I didn't want to cause any alarm. It'll probably turn up."

"But what if... what if that was the knife?"

"Oh come on, Mara, surely you can't believe that. There are plenty of flick-knives in the country. Why should it be that one? Somebody's probably borrowed it. It'll turn up."

"Yes. But what if? I mean, Paul could have taken it, couldn't he?"

Seth drummed his fingers on the chair arm. "You know how many people were around on Friday afternoon," he said. "Any one of them could have taken it. When did you last notice it, for example?"

"I don't remember."

"See? And it still doesn't mean it was the knife that was used. Someone might just have borrowed it and forgot to say anything."

"I suppose so." But Mara wasn't convinced. It seemed too much of a coincidence that a flick-knife had been used to kill the policeman and the flick-knife from the mantelpiece was missing. She thought Seth was grasping for straws in trying to explain it away as he was, but she wanted to believe him.

"There you are, then," he said. "Why assume it's Paul just because he has a violent past? He's changed. You're thinking like the police."

Mara wanted to, but she couldn't bring herself to tell Seth about the blood. Somehow, along with everything else, that information seemed so final, so damning.

She had decided to get in touch with that friend of Dennis Osmond's, Jenny. Mara liked her, though she wasn't too sure about Osmond himself. And Jenny was a professional psychologist. Mara could put her a theoretical case, using Paul's background, and ask if such a person was likely to be dangerous. She could say it was a part of some research she was doing for a story or something. Jenny would believe her.

"Maybe he should go away," Seth said after a while.

"Paul? But why?"

"It might be best for him. For all of us. Till it's over. You can see how all this is getting to him."

"It's getting to all of us," Mara said. "You, too."

"Yes, but—"

"Where would he go? You know he hasn't got anybody else to turn to." Despite her fears, Mara couldn't help but want to protect Paul. She didn't understand her feelings, but as much as she suspected him, she couldn't just give up and send him away.

Seth stared at the floor.

"It could look bad, too," Mara argued. "The police would think he was running away because he was guilty."

"Let him stay, then. Just make up your mind."

"Don't you care about him?"

"Of course I care about him. That's why I suggested he get away. Come on, Mara, which way do you want it? If I suggest he goes, I'm being cruel, and if he stays he might have to put up with a hell of a lot more from that fascist bastard we had around this afternoon. What do you want? Do you think he can take it? Look how he reacted to today's little chat. That was a picnic compared to what'll happen if they decide to take him in for questioning. And we can't protect him. Well? How much do you think he can take?"

"I don't know." Things had suddenly got even more complicated for Mara. "I want what's best for Paul."

"Let's ask him, then. We can't make his decisions for him."

"No! We've got to stand by him. If we approach him, he might think we believe he's guilty and want him out of the way."

"But we'd have to approach him to ask if he'd like to go away for a while, until things settle down."

"So we do nothing. If he wants to stay, he stays, and we stand by him, whatever. If he goes, then it's his decision. We don't force him out. He's not stupid, Seth, I'm sure he knows he's in for a lot of police harassment. The last thing he needs is to feel that we're against him, too."

"Okay." Seth nodded and stood up. "We'll leave it at that. I've got to go and do some work on that old sideboard now. I'm already late. You all right?"

Mara looked up at him and smiled. "I'll manage."

"Good." He bent and kissed her, then went out back to his workshop.

But Mara wasn't all right. Left to herself, she began to imagine all kinds of terrible things. The world of Maggie's Farm had seemed at first to offer the stability, love and freedom she had always been searching for, but now it had broken adrift. The feeling was like that she remembered having during a mild earthquake in California, when she'd travelled around the States, with Matthew, eons ago. Suddenly, the floor of the room, the house's foundations, the solid earth on which they were built, had seemed no more stable than water. A ripple had passed fleetingly under her, and what she had always thought durable turned out to be flimsy, untrustworthy and transient. The quake had only lasted for ten seconds and hadn't registered above five on the Richter scale, but the impression had remained with her ever since. Now it was coming back stronger than ever.

On the mantelpiece, among the clutter of sea shells, pebbles, fossils and feathers, she could see the faint outline of dust around where the knife had been. As she wiped the surface clean, she thanked her lucky stars that the police had been looking for material things, not absences.

V

Banks drove along Foreshore Road and Sandside by the Old Harbour. The amusement arcades and gift shops were all closed. In season, crowds of holiday-makers always gathered around the racks of cheeky postcards, teenagers queued for the Ghost Train and children dragged their parents to the booths that sold candyfloss and Scarborough rock. But now the prom was deserted. Even on the seaward side, there were no stalls selling cockles, winkles and boiled shrimp. A thick, high cloud-cover had set in, and the sea sloshed at the barnacle-crusted harbour walls like molten metal. Fishing boats rocked at their moorings, and stacks of lobster-pots teetered on the quayside. Towering over the scene, high on its promontory, the ruined castle looked like something out of a black-and-white horror film.

Banks dropped Richmond off at a pub near the West Pier and carried on along Marine Drive, parking just beyond the closed fun-fair.

He buttoned up his raincoat tight and walked along the road that curved around the headland between the high cliff and the sea. Signs on the hillside warned of falling rocks. Waves hit the sea-wall and threw up spray onto the road.

Tony Grant was already there, leaning on the railing and staring out to the point where sea and sky merged in a uniform grey. He wore a navy duffle coat with the hood down, and his baby-fine hair fluttered in the wind. A solitary oil tanker was moving slowly across the horizon.

"I like it best like this," he said as Banks joined him. "If you don't mind getting a bit wet."

They both looked out over the ruffled water. Salt spray filled the air and Banks felt the ozone freshen his lungs as he breathed deep. He shivered and asked, "What is it you want to tell me?"

Grant hesitated. "Look, sir," he said after staring at the oil tanker for half a minute, "I don't want you to get me wrong. I'm not a grass or anything. I've not been long on the force, and mostly I like it. I didn't think I would, not at first, but I do now. I want to make a career out of it." He looked at Banks intensely. "I'd like to join the CID. I'm not stupid, I've got brains. I've been to university, and I could maybe have got into teaching—that's what I thought I wanted to do—but, well, you know the job situation. Seems all that's going these days is the police force. So I joined. Anyway, as I said, I like it. It's challenging."

Banks took out a cigarette and cupped his hand around his blue Bic lighter. It took him four attempts to get a flame going long enough. He wished Grant would get to the point, but he knew he had to be patient and listen. The kid was about to go against his peers and squeal on a colleague. Listening to the justification, as he had listened to so many before, was the price Banks had to pay.

"It's just that," Grant went on, "well...it's not as clean as I expected."

Naïve bugger, Banks thought. "It's like anything else," he said, encouraging the lad. "There's a lot of bastards out there, whatever you do. Maybe our line of work attracts more than the usual quota of bullies, lazy sods, sadists and the like. But that doesn't mean we're all like that." Banks sucked on his cigarette. It tasted different, mixed with the sea air. A wave broke below them and the spray wet their feet.

"I know what you're saying," Grant said, "and I think you're right. I just wanted you to know what side I'm on. I don't believe that the end justifies the means. With me they're innocent until proven guilty, as the saying goes. I treat people with respect, no matter what colour they are or how they dress or wear their hair. I'm not saying I approve of some of the types we get, but I'm not a thug."

"And Gill was?"

"Yes." A big wave started to peak as it approached the wall, and they both stepped back quickly to avoid the spray. Even so, they couldn't dodge a mild soaking, and Banks's cigarette got soggy. He threw it away.

"Was this common knowledge?"

"Oh, aye. He made no bones about it. See, with Gill it wasn't just the overtime, the money. He liked it well enough, but he liked the job more, if you see what I mean."

"I think I do. Go on."

"He was handy with his truncheon, Gill was. And he enjoyed it. Every time we got requests for manpower at demos, pickets, and the like, he'd be first to sign up. Got a real taste for it during the miners' strike, when they bussed police in from all over the place. He was the kind of bloke who'd wave a roll of flyers at the striking miners to taunt them before he clobbered them. He trained with the Tactical Aid Group."

The TAG, Banks knew, was a kind of force within a force. Its members trained together in a military fashion and learned how to use guns, rubber bullets and tear-gas. When their training was over, they went back to normal duties and remained on call for special sit-uations—like demos and picket lines. The official term for them had been changed to PSU—Police Support Unit—as the TAGs got a lot of bad publicity and sounded too obviously martial. But it was about as effective as changing the name of Windscale to Sellafield; a nuclear-power station by another name....

"Is that how he behaved in Eastvale?" Banks asked.

"I wouldn't swear to it, but I'm pretty sure it was Gill who led the charge. See, things were getting a bit hairy. We were all hemmed in so tight. Gill was at the top of the steps with a few others, just looking down at people pushing and shoving—not that you could see much, it was so bloody dark with those old-fashioned street-lamps. Anyway, one of the demonstrators chucked a bottle, and someone up there, behind me, yelled, 'Let's clobber the bastards.' I think I recognized Gill's voice. Then they charged down and... well, you know what happened. It needn't have—that's what I'm saying. Sure, there was a bit of aggro going on, but we could have sat on it if someone had given the order to loosen up a bit, give people room to breathe. Instead, Gill led a fucking truncheon charge. I know we coppers are all supposed to stick together, but..." Grant looked out to sea and shivered.

"There's a time to stick together," Banks said, "and this isn't it. Gill got himself killed, remember that."

"But I couldn't swear to anything. I mean, officially...."

"Don't worry. This is off the record." At least it is for now, he told himself. If anything came of their discussion, young Grant might find himself with a few serious decisions to make. "How did the others feel about Gill?" he asked.

"Oh, most of them thought it was all a bit of a joke, a lark. I mean, there'd be Gill going on about clobbering queers and commies. I don't think they really took him seriously."

"But it wasn't just talk? You say he liked smashing skulls."

"Yes. He was a right bastard."

"Surely they knew it?"

"Yes, but..."

"Did they approve?"

"Well, no, I wouldn't say that. Some, maybe...but I didn't, for one."

"But nobody warned him, told him to knock it off?"

Grant pulled up his collar. "No."

"Were they scared of him?"

"Some of the lads were, yes. He was a bit of a hard case."

"What about you?"

"Me? Well, I wouldn't have taken him up on anything, that's for sure. I'm scarcely above regulation height, myself, and Gill was a big bugger."

A seagull screeched by them, a flash of white against the grey, and began circling over the water for fish. The tanker had moved far over to the right of the horizon. Banks felt the chill getting to him. He put his hands deep in his pockets and tensed up against the cold, wet wind.

"Did any of the others actually like him?" he asked. "Did he have any real mates at the station?"

"I wouldn't say so, no. He wasn't a very likeable bloke. Too big-headed, too full of himself. I mean, you couldn't have a conversation with him; you just had to listen. He had views on everything, but he was thick. I mean, he never really thought anything out. It was all down to Pakis and Rastas and students and skinheads and unemployed yobbos with him."

"So he wasn't popular around the station?"

"Not really, no. But you know what it's like. A few of the lads get together in the squad room—especially if they've had TAG training—and you get all that macho, tough-guy talk, just like American cop shows. He was good at that, Gill was, telling stories about fights and taking risks."

"Are there any more like him in your station?"

"Not as bad, no. There's a few that don't mind a good punch-up now and then, and some blokes like to pull kids in on a sus just to liven up a boring night. But nobody went as far as Gill."

"Did he have any friends outside the station?"

"I don't know who he went about with off duty."

"Did he have a girl-friend?"

"I don't know. He never mentioned anyone."

"So he didn't brag about having women like he did about thumping people?"

"No. I never heard him. Whenever he did talk about women it was always like they were whores and bitches. He was a foul-mouthed bastard. He'd hit them, too, at demos. It was all the same to him."

"Do you think he could have been the type to mess around with someone else's girl-friend or wife?"

Grant shook his head. "Not that I know of."

The seagull flew up towards the cliffs behind them, a fish flapping in its beak. The sea had settled to a rhythmic slapping against the stone wall, hardly sending up any spray at all. Banks risked another cigarette.

"Did Gill have any enemies that you know of?"

"He must have made plenty over the years, given his attitude towards the public," Grant said. "But I couldn't name any."

"Anyone on the force?"

"Eh?"

"You said nobody at the station really liked him. Had anyone got a good reason to dislike him? Did he owe money, cheat people, gamble? Any financial problems?"

"I don't think so. He just got people's backs up, that's all. He talked about betting on the horses, yes, but I don't think he did it that much. It was just the macho sort of thing that went with his image. He never tried to borrow any money off me, if that's what you mean. And I don't think he was on the take. At least he was honest on that score."

Banks turned his back to the choppy water and looked up towards the sombre bulk of the ruined castle. He couldn't see much from that angle; the steep cliff, where sea-birds made their nests, was mottled with grass, moss and bare stone. "Is there anything else you can tell me?" he asked.

"I don't think so. I just wanted you to know that all that crap at the funeral was exactly that. Crap. Gill was a vicious bastard. I'm not saying he deserved what happened to him, nobody deserves that, but those who live by the sword. . . ."

"Did you have any particular reason to dislike Gill?"

Grant seemed startled by the question. "Me? What do you mean?"

"What I say. Did he ever do you any harm personally?"

"No. Look, if you're questioning my motives, sir, believe me, it's exactly like I told you. I heard you were asking questions about Gill, and I thought someone should tell you the truth, that's all. I'm not the kind to go around speaking ill of the dead just because they're not here to defend themselves."

Banks smiled. "Don't mind me, I'm just an old cynic. It's a long time since I've come across a young idealist like you on the force." Banks thought of Superintendent Gristhorpe, who had managed to hang on to a certain amount of idealism over the years. But he was one of the old guard; it was a rare quality in youth these days, Banks had found—especially in those who joined the police. Even Richmond could hardly be called an idealist. Keen, yes, but as practical as the day was long.

Grant managed a thin smile. "It's nice of you to say that, but it's not exactly true. After all," he said, "I laid into them with the rest last Friday, didn't I? And do you know what?" His voice caught in his throat and he couldn't look Banks in the eye. "After a while, I even started to enjoy myself."

So, Banks thought, maybe Grant had told all because he felt ashamed of himself for acting like Gill and enjoying the battle. Getting caught up in the thrill of action was hardly unusual; the release of adrenalin often produced a sense of exhilaration in men who would normally run a mile from a violent confrontation. But it obviously bothered Grant. Perhaps this was his way of exorcising what he saw as Gill's demon inside him. Whatever his reasons, he'd given Banks plenty to think about.

"It happens," Banks said, by way of comfort. "Don't let it worry you. Look, would you do me a favour?" They turned and started walking back to their cars.

Grant shrugged. "Depends."

"I'd like to know a bit more about Gill's overtime activities—like where he's been and when. There should be a record. It'd also be useful if I could find out about any official complaints against him, and anything at all about his private life."

Grant frowned and pushed at his left cheek with his tongue as if he had a canker. "I don't know," he said finally, fiddling in his duffle-coat pocket for his car keys. "I wouldn't want to get caught. They'd make my life a bloody misery here if they knew I'd even talked to you like this. Can't you just request his record?"

Banks shook his head. "My boss doesn't want us to be seen investigating Gill. He says it'll look bad. But if we're not seen. . . . Send it to my home address, just to be on the safe side." Banks scribbled his address on a card and handed it over.

Grant got into his car and opened the window. "I can't promise anything," he said slowly, "but I'll have a go." He licked his lips. "If anything important comes out of all this. . ." He paused.

Banks bent down, his hand resting on the wet car roof.

"Well," Grant went on, "I don't want you to think I'm after anything, but you will remember I said I wanted to join the CID, won't you?" And he smiled a big, broad, innocent, open smile.

Bloody hell, there were no flies on this kid. Banks couldn't make him out. At first he'd taken such a moral line that Banks suspected chapel had figured strongly somewhere in his background. But despite all his idealism and respect for the law, he might well be another Dirty Dick in the making. On the other hand, that damn smiling moon-face looked so bloody cherubic. . . .

"Yes," Banks said, smiling back. "Don't worry, I won't forget you."

SIX

I

In the cross-streets between York Road and Market Street, near where Banks lived, developers had converted terraces of tall Victorian family houses into student flats. In one of these, in a two-room attic unit, Tim Fenton and Abha Sutton lived.

If Tim and Abha made an unlikely-looking couple, they made an even more unlikely pair of revolutionaries. Tim had all the blond good looks of an American "preppie," with dress sense to match. Abha, half-Indian, had golden skin, beetle-black hair, and a pearl stud through her left nostril. She was studying graphic design; Tim was in the social sciences. They embraced Marxism as the solution to the world's inequalities, but were always quick to point out that they regarded Soviet Communism as an extreme perversion of the prophet's truth. Both were generally well-mannered, and not at all the type to call police pigs.

They sat on a beat-up sofa under a Che Guevara poster while Banks made himself comfortable on a second-hand office swivel chair at the desk. The cursor blinked on the screen of an Amstrad PC, and stacks of paper and books overflowed from the table to the floor and onto any spare chairs.

After getting back from Scarborough, Banks had just had time to drop in at the station and see what Special Branch had turned up. As usual, their files were as thin as Kojak's hair, and gathered on premises as flimsy as a stripper's G-string. Tim Fenton was listed because he had attended a seminar in Slough sponsored by *Marxism Today*, and some of the speakers there were suspected of working for the Soviets. Dennis Osmond had attracted the Branch's attention by writing a

series of violently anti-government articles for various socialist journals during the miners' strike, and by organizing a number of political demonstrations—especially against American military presence in
Europe. As Banks had suspected, their crimes against the realm hardly
provided grounds for exile or execution.

Tim and Abha were, predictably, hostile and frightened after
Burgess's visit. Banks had previously been on good terms with the two
after successfully investigating a series of burglaries in student resi-
dences the previous November. Even Marxists, it appeared, valued
their stereos and television sets. But now they were cautious and
guarded. It took a lot of small talk to get them to relax and open up.
When Banks finally got around to the subject of the demo, they
seemed to have stopped confusing him with Burgess.

"Did you see anything?" Banks asked first.

"No, we couldn't," Tim answered. "We were right in the thick of
the crowd. One of the cops shouted something and that was that.
When things went haywire we were too busy trying to protect ourselves to see what was happening to anyone else."

"You were involved in organizing the demo, right?"

"Yes. But that doesn't mean—"

Banks held up his hand. "I know," he said. "And that's not what I'm
implying. Did you get the impression that anyone involved—anyone
at all—might have had more on his mind than just protesting
Honoria Winstanley's visit?"

They both shook their heads. "When we got together up at the
farm," Abha explained, "everyone was just so excited that we could
organize a demo in a place as conservative as Eastvale. I know there
weren't many people there, but it seemed like a lot to us."

"The farm?"

"Yes. Maggie's Farm. Do you know it?"

Banks nodded.

"They invited us up to make posters and stuff," Tim said. "Friday
afternoon. They're really great up there; they've really got it together.
I mean, Seth and Mara, they're like the old independent craftsmen,
doing their own thing, making it outside the system. And Rick's a
pretty sharp Marxist."

"I thought he was an artist."

"He is," Tim said, looking offended. "But he tries not to paint anything commercial. He's against art as a saleable commodity."

So that pretty water-colour Banks had noticed propped by the fireplace at Maggie's Farm couldn't have been one of Rick's.

"What about Paul Boyd?"

"We don't know him well," Abha said. "And he didn't say much. One of the oppressed, I suppose."

"You could say that. And Zoe?"

"Oh, she's all right," Tim said. "She goes in for all that bourgeois spiritual crap—bit of a navel-gazer—but she's okay underneath it all."

"Do you know anything about their backgrounds, where they come from?"

They shook their heads. "No," Tim said finally. "I mean, we just talk about the way things are now, how to change them, that kind of thing. And a bit of political theory. Rick's pissed off about his divorce and all that, but that's about as far as the personal stuff goes."

"And you know nothing else about them?"

"No."

"Who else was there?"

"Just us and Dennis."

"Osmond?"

"That's right."

"Does either of you recall seeing a flick-knife that day, or hearing anyone mention one?"

"No. That's what the other bloke went on about," Tim said, getting edgy. "Bloody Burgess. He went on and on about a flick-knife."

"He almost came right out and accused us of killing that policeman, too," Abha said.

"That's just his style. I wouldn't worry about it. Did anyone at the meeting mention PC Gill by name?"

"Not that I heard," Tim said.

"Nor me," said Abha.

"Have you ever heard anyone talk about him? Dennis Osmond, for example? Or Rick?"

"No. The only thing we knew about him," Abha said, "was that he'd trained with the TAG groups and he liked to work on crowd control. You know—demos, pickets and such."

The chair creaked as Banks swivelled sharply. "How did you know that?"

"Word gets around," Abha said. "We keep—"

Tim nudged her in the ribs and she shut up.

"What she means," he said, "is that if you're politically involved up here, you soon get to know the ones to watch out for. You lot keep tabs on us, don't you? I'm pretty sure Special Branch has a file on me, anyway."

"Fair enough," Banks said, smiling to himself at the absurdity of it all. Games. Just little boys' games. "Was this fairly common knowledge? Could anyone have known to expect Gill at the demo that night?"

"Anyone involved in organizing it, sure," Tim said. "And anyone who'd been to demos in Yorkshire before. There aren't many like him, thank God. He did have a bit of a reputation."

"Did you *know* he was going to be on duty?"

"Not for certain, no. I mean, he could have had flu or broke his leg."

"But short of that?"

"Short of that he was rarely known to miss. Look, I don't know what all this is in aid of," Tim said, "but I think you should know we're still going to do our own investigation."

"Into the murder?"

Tim gave him a puzzled glance. "No. Into the police brutality. We're all getting together again up at the farm in a few days to compare notes."

"Well, if you find anything out about PC Gill's death, let me know."

Banks looked at his watch and stood up. It was time he went and got ready for his evening out with Jenny. After he'd said goodbye and walked back down the gloomy staircase to the street, he reflected how odd it was that wherever he went, all roads seemed to lead to Maggie's Farm. More than that, almost anyone involved could have known that Gill was likely to be there that night. If Gill cracked heads in Yorkshire for a hobby, then the odds were that one or two people might hold a strong grudge against him. He wished Tony Grant would hurry up and send the information from Scarborough.

II

Mara put on her army-surplus greatcoat and set off down the track for Relton. It was dark now and the stars were glittering flecks of ice in the clear sky. Distant hills and scars showed only as muted silhouettes, black against black. The crescent moon was up, hanging lopsided like a backdrop to a music-hall number. Mara almost expected a man with a top hat, cape and cane to start dancing across it way up in the sky. The gravel crackled under her feet, and the wind whistled through gaps in the lichen-covered dry-stone wall. In the distance, the lights of cottages and villages down in the dale twinkled like stars.

She would talk to Jenny, she decided, thrusting her hands deeper into her pockets and hunching up against the chill. Jenny knew Chief Inspector Banks, too. Though she distrusted all policemen, even Mara had to admit that he was a hell of a lot better than Burgess. Perhaps she might also be able to find out what the police really thought, and if they were going to leave Paul alone from now on.

Mara's mind strayed back to the I Ching, which she had consulted before setting off. What the hell was it all about? It was supposed to be an oracle, to offer words of wisdom when you really needed them, but Mara wasn't convinced. One problem was that it always answered questions obliquely. You couldn't ask, "Did Paul kill that policeman?" and get a simple yes or no. This time, the oracle had read: "The woman holds the basket, but there are no fruits in it. The man stabs the sheep, but no blood flows. Nothing that acts to further." Did that mean Paul hadn't killed anyone, that the blood on his hand had come from somewhere else? And what about the empty basket? Did that have something to do with Mara's barren womb? If there was any practical advice at all, it was to do nothing, yet here she was, walking down the track on her way to call Jenny. All the book had done was put her fears into words and images.

At the end of the track, Mara walked along Mortsett Lane, past the closed shops and the cottages with their television screens flickering behind curtains. In the dimly lit phone booth, she rang Jenny's number. She heard a click followed by a strange, disembodied voice that she finally recognized as Jenny's. The voice explained that its owner was out, but that a message could be left after the tone. Mara, who had never dealt with an answering machine before, waited nervously, worried that she might miss her cue. But it soon came, the unmistakable high-pitched bleep. Mara spoke quickly and loudly, as people do to foreigners, feeling self-conscious about her voice: "This is Mara, Jenny. I hope I've got this thing right. Please, will you meet me tomorrow lunch-time in the Black Sheep in Relton? It's important. I'll be there at one. I hope you can come." She paused for a moment and listened to the silence, feeling that she should add something, but she could think of nothing more to say.

Mara put the phone back gently. It had been rather like sending a telegram, something she had done once before. The feeling that every word cost money was very inhibiting, and so, in a different way, was the sense of a tape winding around the capstan past the recording head as she talked.

Anyway, it was done. Leaving the booth, she hurried towards the Black Sheep, feeling lighter in spirit now that she had at least taken a practical step to deal with her fears.

III

Banks and Jenny sat in the bar over aperitifs while they studied the menu. The Royal Oak was a cosy place with muted lights, mullioned windows and gleaming copper-ware in little nooks and crannies. Fastened horizontally between the dark beams on the ceiling was a collection of walking-sticks of all lengths and materials: knobbly ash-plants, coshers, sword-sticks and smooth canes, many with ornate brass handles. On a long shelf above the bar stood a row of toby jugs with such faces as Charles II, Shakespeare and Beethoven; some, however, depicted contemporaries, like Margaret Thatcher and Paul McCartney.

Jenny sipped a vodka-and-tonic, Banks a dry sherry, as they tried to decide what to order. Finally, after much self-recrimination about the damage it would do to her figure, Jenny settled for *steak au poivre* with a wine-and-cream sauce. Banks chose roast leg of lamb. Much as he liked to watch the little blighters frolic around the dale every spring, he enjoyed eating them almost as much. They'd only grow up into sheep anyway, he reasoned.

They followed the waitress into the dining-room, pleased to find only one other table occupied, and that by a subdued couple already on dessert. Mozart's Clarinet Quintet played quietly in the background. Banks watched Jenny walk ahead of him. She was wearing a loose top, cut square across the collarbone, which looked as if it had been tie-dyed in various shades of blue and red. Her pleated skirt was plain rust-red, the colour of her tumbling, wavy hair, and came to midway down her calves. The tights she wore had some kind of pattern on them, which looked to Banks like a row of bruises up the sides of her legs. Being a gentleman, though, he had complimented her on her appearance.

The waitress lit the candle, took their orders and moved off soundlessly, leaving them with the wine list to study. Banks lit a cigarette and smiled at Jenny.

Despite the claims of *Playboy*, the Miss Universe contest and other promoters of the feminine image to men, Banks had often found that it was the most insignificant detail that made a woman physically attractive to him: a well-placed mole, a certain curve of the lips or turn of the ankle; or a mannerism, such as the way she picked up a glass, tilted her head before smiling, or fiddled with a necklace while speaking.

In the case of Sandra, his wife, it was the dark eyebrows and the contrast they made with her naturally ash-blonde hair. With Jenny, it was her eyes, or rather the delta of lines that crinkled their outer edges, especially when she smiled. They were like a map whose contours revealed a sense of humour and a curious mixture of toughness and vulnerability that Banks, himself, felt able to identify with. Her beautiful red hair and green eyes, her shapeliness, her long legs and full lips were all very well, but they were just icing on the cake. It was the lines around the eyes that did it.

"What are you thinking?" Jenny asked, looking up from the list.

Banks gave her the gist of it.

"Well," she said, after a fit of laughter, "I'll take that as a compliment, though there are many women who wouldn't. What shall we have?"

"They've got a nice Seguret 1980 here, if I remember rightly. And not too expensive, either. That's if you like Rhône."

"Fine by me."

When the waitress returned with their smoked salmon and melon appetizers, Banks ordered the wine.

"So what's all this decadence in aid of?" asked Jenny, her eyes twinkling in the candle flame. "Are you planning to seduce me, or are you just softening me up for questioning?"

"What if I said I was planning to seduce you?"

"I'd say you were going about it the right way." She smiled and looked around the room. "Candlelight, romantic music, nice atmosphere, good food."

The wine arrived, shortly followed by their main courses, and soon they were enjoying the meal to the accompaniment of the Flute Quartets.

Over dinner, Jenny complained about her day. There had been too many classes to teach, and she was tired of the undergraduates' simplistic assumptions about psychology. Sometimes, she confessed, she was even sick of psychology itself and wished she'd studied English literature or history instead.

Banks told her about the funeral, careful to leave out his meeting with Tony Grant. It would be useful to have something in reserve later, if he could steer her around to talking about Osmond. He also mentioned his visit to Tim and Abha and how Burgess's approach had soured the pitch.

"Your Dirty Dick is a real jerk," Jenny said, employing an Americanism the man himself would have been proud of. "Dare I ask about dessert?" she asked, pushing her empty plate aside.

"It's *your* figure."

"In that case, I think I'll have chocolate mousse. Absolutely no calories at all. And coffee and cognac."

When the waitress came by, Banks ordered Jenny's dessert and liqueur along with a wedge of Stilton and a glass of Sauternes for himself. "You didn't really answer my question, you know," he said.

"What question's that?"

"The one about seducing you."

"Oh, yes. But I did. I said you were going about it the right way."

"But you didn't say whether I'd get anywhere or not."

Jenny's eyes crinkled. "Alan! Are you feeling the itch because Sandra's away?"

Banks felt foolish for bringing the subject up in the first place. Flirting with Jenny might be fun, but it also had a serious edge that neither really wanted to get too close to. If it hadn't been for that damned incident at Osmond's flat, he thought, he'd never have been so silly as to start playing games like this. But when he had seen Jenny look around Osmond's bedroom door like that—the robe slipping off her shoulder, the tousled hair, the relaxed, unfocused look that follows love-making—it hadn't only made him jealous, it had also inflamed old desires. He had felt that nobody else should enjoy what he couldn't enjoy himself. And he couldn't; of that there was no doubt. So he played his games and ended up embarrassing both of them.

He lit a cigarette to hide behind and poured the last of the Seguret. "Change the subject?"

Jenny nodded. "A good idea."

The dessert arrived at the same time as a noisy party of businessmen. Fortunately, the waitress seated them at the far end of the room.

"This is delicious," Jenny said, spooning up the chocolate mousse. "I suppose you're going to question me now? I've got a feeling that seduction would probably have been a lot more fun."

"Don't tempt me," Banks said. "But you're right. I would like your help on a couple of things."

"Here we go. Can I just finish my sweet first?"

"Sure."

When the dishes were empty, Jenny sipped some cognac. "All right," she said, saluting and sitting up to attention. "I'm all ears."

"Were you there?" Banks asked.

"Where?"

"At the demo. You came to see me at two in the morning. You said you'd been waiting at your house for your boy-friend—"

"Dennis!"

"Yes, all right. Dennis." Banks wondered why he hated the sound of the name so much. "But you could have been at the demo, too."

"You mean I could have been lying?"

"That's not what I'm getting at. You might have just failed to mention it."

"Surely you don't think I'm a suspect now? Being seduced by Quasimodo would be more fun than this."

Banks laughed. "That's not my point. Think about it. If you were there with Osmond right up until the time he got arrested, then you'd be a witness that he didn't stab PC Gill."

"I see. So Dennis is a prime suspect as far as you're concerned?"

"He is as far as Burgess is concerned. And that's what counts."

Banks wondered if he, too, wanted Osmond to be guilty. Part of him, he had to admit, did. He was also wondering whether or not to tell Jenny about the assault charges. It would be a mean thing to do right now, he decided, because he couldn't trust his motives. Would he be telling her for her own good, or out of the jealousy he felt, out of a desire to hurt her relationship with Osmond?

"I see what you mean," Jenny said finally. "No, I wasn't at the demo. I don't know what happened. Dennis has talked to me about it, of course—and, by the way, he's going ahead with his own inquiry into the thing, you know, along with Tim and Abha. And Burgess is going to come off pretty badly. Apparently he was around again today with Hatchley."

Banks knew that. He also knew that the dirty duo had got no more out of anyone than they had the first time around. They'd probably be drowning their sorrows in the Queens Arms by now, and with a bit of luck Dirty Dick would push it too far with Glenys and her Cyril would thump him.

"Back to the demo," Banks said. "What exactly has Dennis said?"

"He doesn't know what happened to that policeman. Do you think I'd be sitting here talking to you, answering your questions, if I wasn't trying to convince you that he had nothing to do with it?"

"So he saw nothing?"

"No. He said he heard somebody shout—he didn't catch the words—and after that it was chaos."

That seemed to square with what Tony Grant and Tim and Abha had said about the riot's origin. Banks took a sip of Sauternes and watched it make legs down the inside of his glass.

"Did he ever mention PC Gill to you?"

Jenny shrugged. "He may have done. I didn't have much to do with the demo, as I said."

"Did you ever hear the name?"

"I don't know." Jenny was getting prickly. "I can't say I pay much attention to Dennis's political concerns. And if you're going to take a cheap shot at that, forget it. Unless you want a lap full of hot coffee."

Banks decided it was best to veer away from the subject of Osmond. "You know the people at Maggie's Farm, don't you?" he asked.

"Yes. Dennis got friendly with Seth and Mara. We've been up a few times. I like them, especially Mara."

"What's the set-up there?"

Jenny swirled the cognac and took another sip. "Seth bought the place about three years ago," she said. "Apparently, it was in a bit of a state, which was why he got it quite cheaply. He fixed it up, reno-vated the old barn and rented it out. After Mara, Rick came next, I think, with Julian. He was having some problems with his wife."

"Yes, I've heard about his wife," Banks said. "Do you know any-thing else about her?"

"No. Except according to Rick her name must be Bitch."

"What about Zoe?"

"I'm not sure how she met up with them. She came later. As far as I know she's from the east coast. She seems like a bit of a space cadet, but I suspect she's quite shrewd, really. You'd be surprised how many people are into that New Age stuff these days. Looking for some-thing, I suppose...reassurance...I don't know. Anyway, she makes a good living from it. She does the weekly horoscope in the *Gazette*, too, and takes a little booth on the coast on summer weekends for doing tarot readings and what not. You know, Madame Zoe, Gypsy Fortune Teller..."

"The east coast? Could it be Scarborough?"

Jenny shook her head. "Whitby, I think."

"Still," Banks muttered, "it's not far away."

"What isn't?"

The waitress brought coffee, and Banks lit another cigarette, care-ful to keep the smoke away from Jenny.

"Tell me about Mara."

"I like Mara a lot. She's bright, and she's had an interesting life. She was in some religious organization before she came to the farm, but she got disillusioned. She seems to want to settle down a bit now. For some reason, we get along quite well. Seth, as I say, I don't know much about. He grew up in the sixties and he hasn't sold out—I mean he hasn't become a stockbroker or an accountant, at least. His main interest is his carpentry. There's also something about a woman in his past."

"What woman?"

"Oh, it was just something Mara said. Apparently Seth doesn't like to talk about it. He had a lover who died. Maybe they were even married, I don't know. That was just before he bought the farm."

"What was her name?"

"Alison, I think."

"How did she die?"

"Some kind of accident."

"What kind?"

"That's all I know, really. I'm not being evasive. Mara said it's all she knows, too. Seth only told her because he got drunk once. Apparently he's not much of a drinker."

"And that's all you know?"

"Yes. It was some kind of motor accident. She got knocked down or something."

"Where was he living then?"

"Hebden Bridge, I think. Why does it matter?"

"It probably doesn't. I just like to know as much as I can about who I'm dealing with. They were involved in the demo, and every time I question someone, Maggie's Farm comes up."

It would be easy enough to check the Hebden Bridge accident records, though where Gill might come into it, Banks had no idea. Perhaps he had been on traffic duty at the time? He would hardly have been involved in a religious organization either, unless he felt a close friend or relation had been brainwashed by such a group.

"What about Paul Boyd?" he asked.

Jenny paused. "He's quite new up there. I can't say I know him well. To tell you the truth—and to speak quite unprofessionally—he gives me the creeps. But Mara's very attached to him, like he's a younger brother, or a son, even. There's about seventeen years between them. He's another generation, really—punk, post-sixties. Mara thinks he just needs tender loving care, something he's never had much of, apparently."

"What do you think of Paul professionally?"

"It's hard to answer that. As I said, I haven't really talked to him that much. He seems angry, antisocial. Maybe life at the farm will give him some sense of belonging. If you think about it, what reason does he have to love the world? No adult has ever given him a break, nor has society. He feels worthless and rejected, so he makes himself look like a reject; he holds it to him and shouts it out, as people do. And that," Jenny said with a mock bow, "is Dr Fuller's humble opinion."

Banks nodded. "It makes sense."

"But it doesn't make him a killer."

"No." He couldn't think of any more questions without returning to the dangerous territory of Dennis Osmond, and things had gone so well for the past half hour or so that he didn't want to risk ending the evening on a sour note. Jenny was bound to be guarded if he really started pushing about Osmond again.

Banks picked up the bill, which Jenny insisted on sharing, and they left. The drive home went smoothly, but Banks felt guilty because he was sure he was a bit over the limit, and if anyone ought to know better about drunken driving, it was a policeman. Not that he felt drunk. After all, he hadn't had much to drink, really. He was perfectly in control. But that's what they all said when the crystals changed colour. Jenny told him not to be silly, he was quite all right. When he dropped her off, there was no invitation to come in for a coffee, and he was glad of that.

Luckily, he thought as he tried to fall asleep, Jenny hadn't pushed him about his own theories. If she had, he would have told her—and trusted her to make sure it got no further—about his little chat with Tony Grant on Marine Drive, the implications of which put a different light on things.

On the one hand, what Grant had told him made the possibility of a personal motive for killing Gill much more likely. He didn't know who might have had such a motive yet, but according to what Tim and Abha had said, almost any of the demonstrators—especially the organizers or people close to them—would have known to expect Gill at the demo. And if Gill was there, wasn't it a safe bet that violence would follow?

On the other hand, Banks found himself thinking that if Gill had enemies within the force, perhaps a fellow policeman, not a demonstrator, might have taken the opportunity to get rid of him: someone whose wife or girl-friend Gill had fooled around with, for example; or a partner in crime, if he had been on the take. Tony Grant hadn't thought so, but he was only a naïve rookie, after all.

It wasn't an idea Banks would expect Burgess to entertain for a moment; for one thing, it would blow all political considerations off the scene. But another policeman would have expected Gill to cause trouble, could have arranged to be on overtime with him and could have been sure of getting away. None of which could be said for any of the demonstrators. Nobody searched the police; nobody checked their uniforms for Gill's blood.

Maybe it was the kind of far-fetched theory one usually got on the edge of sleep and would seem utterly absurd in the morning light. But Banks couldn't quite rule it out. He'd known men on the Metropolitan force more than capable of murdering fellow officers, and in many cases, the loss would hardly have diminished the quality of the human gene pool. The only way to find out about that angle, though, was to press Tony Grant even further into service. If there was anything in it, the fewer people who knew about Banks's line of investigation, the better. It could be dangerous.

And so, the Sauternes still warm in his veins and a stretch of cold empty bed beside him, Banks fell asleep thinking of the victim, convinced that someone not too far away had had a very good reason for wanting PC Edwin Gill dead.

SEVEN

I

Banks turned up the track to Gristhorpe's old farmhouse above Lyndgarth, wondering what the superintendent was doing at home on a Wednesday morning. The message, placed on his desk by Sergeant Rowe, had offered no explanation, just an invitation to visit.

Pulling up in front of the squat, solid house, he stubbed out his cigarette and ejected the Lightning Hopkins cassette he'd been listening to. Breathing in the fresh, cold air, he looked down over Swainsdale and was struck by the way Relton and Maggie's Farm, directly opposite on the south side of the dale, formed almost a mirror image of Lyndgarth and Gristhorpe's house. Like the latter, Maggie's Farm stood higher up the hillside than the village it was close to—so high it was on the verge of the moorland that spread for miles on the heights between dales.

Looking down the slope from the farmhouse, Banks could see the grey-brown ruins of Devraulx Abbey, just west of Lyndgarth. On the valley bottom, Fortford marked the western boundary of the river-meadows. Swainsdale was at its broadest there, where the River Swain meandered through the flats until it veered south-east to Eastvale and finally joined the Ouse outside York.

In summer, the lush green meadows were speckled with golden buttercups. Bluebells, forget-me-nots and wild garlic grew by the riverside under the shade of ash and willow. The Leas, as they were called locally, were a favourite spot for family picnics. Artists set up their easels there, too, and fishermen spent idle afternoons on the riverbank and waded in the shallows at dusk. Now, although the promise of spring showed in the grass and clung like a green haze around the branches of the trees, the meadows seemed a haunted and desolate spot. The snaking river sparkled between the trees, and a brisk wind chased clouds over from the west. Shadows flitted across the steep green slopes with a speed that was almost dizzying to watch.

Gristhorpe answered the door and led Banks into the living room, where a peat fire burned in the hearth, then disappeared into the kitchen. Banks took off his sheepskin-lined car-coat and rubbed his hands by the flames. Outside the back window, a pile of stones stood by the unfinished dry-stone wall that the superintendent worked on in his spare time. It fenced in nothing and went nowhere, but Banks had enjoyed many hours placing stones there with Gristhorpe in companionable silence. Today, though, it was too cold for such outdoors activity.

Carrying a tray of tea and scones, Gristhorpe returned and sat down in his favourite armchair to pour. After small talk about the wall and the possibility of yet more snow, the superintendent told Banks his news: the enquiry into the demo had been suspended.

"I'm on ice, as our American cousins would put it," he said. "The Assistant Chief Commissioner's been talking to the PCA about getting an outsider to finish the report. Maybe someone from Avon and Somerset division."

"Because we're too biased?"

"Aye, partly. I expected it. They only set me on it in the first place to make it look like we were acting quickly."

"Did you find anything out?"

"It looks like some of our lads over-reacted."

Banks told him what he'd heard from Jenny and Tim and Abha.

Gristhorpe nodded. "The ACC doesn't like it. If you ask me, I don't think there'll be an official inquiry. It'll be postponed till it's no longer an issue. What he's hoping is that Superintendent Burgess will come up with the killer fast. That'll satisfy everyone, and people will just forget about the rest."

"Where does that leave you?"

"I'm taking a few days' leave, on the ACC's advice. Unless anything else comes up—something unconnected to Gill's death—then that's how I'll stay. He's right, of course. I'd only get in the way. Burgess is in charge of that investigation, and it wouldn't do to have the two of us treading on each other's toes. But don't let the bugger near my office with those foul cigars of his! How are you getting on with him?"

"All right, I suppose. He's got plenty of go, and he's certainly not stupid. Trouble is, he's got a bee in his bonnet about terrorists and lefties in general."

"And you see things differently?"

"Yes." Banks told him about the meeting with Tony Grant and the possibilities it had opened up for him. "And," he added, "you'd think Special Branch would have known if there'd been some kind of terrorist action planned, wouldn't you?"

Gristhorpe digested the information and mulled it over for a few moments, then turned his light-blue eyes on Banks and rubbed his chin. "I'll not deny you might be right," he said, "but for Christ's sake keep your feet on the ground. Don't go off half-cocked on this or you could bring down a lot of trouble on yourself—and on me. I appreciate you want to follow your own nose—you'd be a poor copper if you didn't—and maybe you'd like to show Dirty Dick a thing or two. But be careful. Just because Gill turned out to be a bastard, it doesn't follow that's why he was killed. Burgess could be right."

"I know that. It's just a theory. But thanks for the warning."

Gristhorpe smiled. "Think nothing of it. But keep it under your hat. If Burgess finds out you've been pursuing a private investigation, he'll have your guts for garters. And it won't be just him. The ACC'll have your balls for billiards."

"I don't know as I've got enough body parts to go around," Banks said, grinning.

"And this conversation hasn't taken place. I know nothing about what you're up to, agreed?"

"Agreed."

"But keep me posted. God, how I hate bloody politics."

Banks knew that the superintendent came from a background of Yorkshire radicals—Chartists, the anti-Corn Laws crowd—and there was even a Luddite lurking in the family tree. But Gristhorpe himself was conservative with a small "c." He was, however, concerned with the preservation of human rights that had been fought for and won over the centuries. That was how he saw his job—as a defender of the people, not an attacker. Banks agreed, and that was one reason they got along so well.

Banks finished his tea and looked at his watch. "Talking of Dirty Dick, I'd better be off. He's called a conference in the Queen's Arms for one o'clock."

"Seems like he's taken up residence there."

"You're not far wrong." Banks explained about Glenys and put on his car-coat. "Besides that," he added, "he drinks like a bloody fish."

"So it's not only Glenys and her charms?"

"No."

"Ever seen him pissed?"

"Not yet."

"Well, watch him. Drinking's an occupational hazard with us, but it can get beyond a joke. The last thing you need is a piss-artist to rely on in a tight spot."

"I don't think there's anything to worry about," Banks said, walking to the car. "He's always been a boozer. And he's usually sharp as a whippet. Anyway, what can I do if I think he is overdoing it? I can just see his face if I suggest a visit to AA."

Gristhorpe stood by the car. Banks rolled the window down, slipped Lightning Hopkins back in the slot, and lit a cigarette.

The superintendent shook his head. "It's about time you stopped that filthy habit, too," he said. "And as for that racket you call music..."

Banks smiled and turned the key in the ignition. "Do you know something?" he said. "I do believe you're becoming an insufferable old fogey. I know you're tone-deaf and wouldn't know Mozart from the Beatles, but don't forget, it wasn't that long ago you gave up smoking yourself. Have you no bad habits left?"

Gristhorpe laughed. "I gave them all up years ago. Are you suggesting I should take some up again?"

"Wouldn't be a bad idea."

"Where do you suggest I start?"

Banks rolled up the window before he said, "Try sheep-shagging." But judging by the raised eyebrows and the startled smile, Gristhorpe could obviously read lips. Grinning, Banks set off down the track, the still, deserted river-meadows spread out below him, and headed for the Eastvale road.

II

Jenny was already five minutes late. Mara nursed her half of mild and rolled a cigarette. It was Wednesday lunch-time, and the Black Sheep was almost empty. Apart from the landlord reading his *Sun*, and two old men playing dominoes, she was the only other customer in the cosy lounge.

Now that the time was close, she was beginning to feel nervous and foolish. After all, she didn't know Jenny *that* well, and her story did sound a bit thin. She couldn't put the real problem into words. How could she say that she suspected Paul had killed the policeman and that she was even beginning to be afraid living in the same house, but despite it all she wouldn't give him away and still wanted to keep him there? It sounded insane without the feelings that went with it. And to tell Jenny that she just wanted information for a story she was writing hardly ranked as the important reason for the meeting she had claimed on the telephone. Perhaps Jenny wasn't going to come. Maybe Mara hadn't responded to the answering machine properly and she hadn't even got the message.

All she could hear was the sound of asthmatic breathing from one of the old men, the occasional rustling of the newspaper, and the click of dominoes as they were laid on the hard surface. She swirled the beer in the bottom of her half-pint glass and peered at her watch again. Quarter past one.

"Another drink, love?" Larry Grafton called out.

Mara flashed a smile and shook her head. Why was it that she didn't mind so much being called "love" by the locals, but when Burgess had said it, her every nerve had bristled with resentment? It must be something in the tone, she decided. The old Yorkshiremen who used the word were probably as chauvinistic as the rest—in fact, sex roles in Dales family life were as traditional as anywhere in England—but when the men called women "love," it carried at least overtones of affection. With Burgess, though, the word was a weapon, a way of demeaning the woman, of dominating her.

Jenny arrived and interrupted her train of thought.

"Sorry I'm late," she said breathlessly. "Class went on longer than I expected."

"It's all right," Mara said. "I haven't been here long. Drink?"

"Let me get them."

Jenny went to the bar, and Mara watched her, a little intimidated, as usual, by her poise. Jenny always seemed to wear the right, expensive-looking clothes. Today it was a waist-length fur jacket (fake, of course—Jenny wouldn't be caught dead wearing real animal fur), a green silk blouse, close-fitting rust cords, and well-polished knee-length boots. Not that Mara would want to dress like that—it wouldn't suit her personality—but she did feel shabby in her moth-eaten sweater and muddy wellingtons. Her jeans hadn't been artificially aged like the ones teenagers wore, either; they had earned each stain and every faded patch.

"Quiet, isn't it?" Jenny said, setting the drinks down. "You looked thoughtful when I came in. What was it?"

Mara told her her feelings about being called "love."

"I know what you mean. I could have throttled Burgess when he did it to me." She laughed. "Dorothy Wycombe once chucked her drink at a stable-lad for calling her 'love.'"

"Dorothy doesn't have much to do with us," Mara said. "I think we're too traditional for her tastes."

Jenny laughed. "You should count yourself lucky, then." She took off her fur jacket and made herself comfortable. "I heard she made mincemeat of Burgess. She gave Alan a hard time once, too. He gives her a wide berth now."

"Alan? Is that the policeman you know? Chief Inspector Banks?"

Jenny nodded. "He's all right. Why? Is that what you wanted to talk about?"

"What do you mean?"

"Don't be so cagey. I know you've come in for a lot of police attention since the demo. I just wondered if that was what was on your mind. Your message wasn't exactly specific, you know."

Mara smiled. "I'm not used to answering machines, that's all. Sorry."

"No need. You just came across as frightfully worried and serious. Are you?"

A domino clicked loudly on the board, obviously a winning move. "Not as much as I probably sounded, no," Mara said. "But it is about the demo. Partly, anyway." She had decided that, as Jenny had mentioned Banks, she might as well begin by seeing if she could find anything out about the investigation, what the police were thinking.

"Go ahead, then."

Mara took a deep breath and told Jenny about recent events at the farm, especially Burgess's visit.

"You ought to complain," Jenny advised her.

Mara sniffed. "Complain? Who to? He told us what would happen if we did. Apparently his boss is a bigger bastard than he is."

"Try complaining locally. Superintendent Gristhorpe isn't bad."

Mara shook her head. "You don't understand. The police would never listen to a complaint from people like us."

"Don't be too sure about that, Mara. Alan wants to understand. It's only the truth he's after."

"Yes, but...I can't really explain. What do they really think about us, Jenny? Do they believe that one of us killed that policeman?"

"I don't know. Really I don't. They're interested in you, yes. I'd be a liar if I denied that. But as far as actually suspecting anyone...I don't think so. Not yet."

"Then why do they keep pestering us? When's it going to stop?"

"When they find out who the killer is. It's not just you, it's everyone involved. They've been at Dennis, too, and Dorothy Wycombe and the students. You'll just have to put up with it for the time being."

"I suppose so." The old men shuffled dominoes for another game, and a lump of coal shifted in the fire, sending out a shower of sparks and a puff of smoke. Flames rose up again, licking at the black chimneyback. "Look," Mara went on, "do you mind if I ask you a professional question, something about psychology? It's for a story I'm working on."

"I didn't know you wrote."

"Oh, it's just for my own pleasure really. I mean, I haven't tried to get anything published yet." Even as she spoke, Mara knew that her excuse didn't ring true.

"Okay," Jenny said. "Let me get another round in first."

"Oh no, it's my turn." Mara went to the bar and bought another half for herself and a vodka-and-tonic for Jenny. If only she could get away with some of her fears about Paul allayed—without giving them away, of course—then she knew she would feel a lot better.

"What is it?" Jenny asked when they'd settled down with their drinks again.

"It's just something I'd like to know, a term I've heard that puzzles me. What's a sociopath?"

"A sociopath? Good Lord, this is like an exam question. Let me think for a bit. I'll have to give you a watered-down answer, I'm afraid. I don't have the textbook with me."

"That's all right."

"Well...I suppose basically it's someone who's constantly at war with society. A rebel without a cause, if you like."

"Why, though? I mean, what makes people like that?"

"It's far from cut and dried," Jenny said, "but the thinking is that it has a lot to do with family background. Usually people we call sociopaths suffered abuse, cruelty and rejection from their parents, or at least from one parent, from an early age. They respond by rejecting society and becoming cruel themselves."

"What are the signs?"

"Antisocial acts: stealing, doing reckless things, cruelty to animals. It's hard to say."

"What kind of people are they?"

"They don't feel anything about what they do. They can always justify acts of cruelty—even murder—to themselves. They don't really see that they've done anything wrong."

"Can anyone help them?"

"Sometimes. The trouble is, they're detached, cut off from the rest of us through what's happened to them. They rarely have any friends and they don't feel any sense of loyalty."

"Isn't it possible to help them, then?"

"They find it very hard to give love and to trust people, or to respond to such feelings in others. If you don't give your love, then you save yourself from feeling bad if it's rejected. That's the real problem: they need someone to trust them and have some feeling for them, but those are the things they find it hardest to accept."

"So it's hopeless."

"Often it's too late," Jenny said. "If they're treated early, they can be helped, but sometimes by the time they reach their teens the pattern is so deeply ingrained it's almost irreversible. But it's never hopeless." She leaned forward and put her hand on Mara's. "It's Paul you're asking about, isn't it?"

Mara withdrew sharply. "What makes you say that?"

"Your expression, the tone of your voice. This isn't just for some story you're writing. It's for real, isn't it?"

"What if it is?"

"I can't tell you if Paul's a sociopath or not, Mara. I don't know enough about him. He seems to be responding to life at the farm."

"Oh, he is," Mara said. "Responding, I mean. He's got a lot more outgoing and cheerful since he's been with us. Until these past few days."

"Well, it's bound to get to him, all the police attention. But it doesn't mean anything. You don't think he might have killed the policeman, do you?"

"You mustn't tell anyone we've been talking like this," Mara said quickly. "Especially not Inspector Banks. All they need is an excuse to bring Paul in, then I'm sure that Burgess could force him to confess."

"They won't do that," Jenny said. "You don't have any concrete reason for thinking Paul might be guilty, do you?"

"No." Mara wasn't sure she sounded convincing. Things had gone too far for her, but it seemed impossible to steer back to neutral ground. "I'm just worried about him, that's all," she went on. "He's had a hard life. His parents rejected him and his foster parents were cold towards him."

"Well that doesn't mean a lot," Jenny said. "If that's all you're worried about, I shouldn't bother yourself. Plenty of people come from broken homes and survive. It takes very special circumstances to create a sociopath. Not every ache and pain means you've got cancer, you know."

Mara nodded. "I'm sorry I tried to con you," she said. "It wasn't fair of me. But I feel better now. Let's just forget all about it, shall we?"

"Okay, if you want. But be careful, Mara. I'm not saying Paul isn't dangerous, just that I don't know. If you do have any real suspicions..."

But Mara didn't hear any more. The door opened and a strange-looking man walked in. It wasn't his odd appearance that bothered her, though; it was the knife that he carried carefully in his hand. Pale and trembling, she got to her feet. "I've got to go now," she said. "Something's come up.... I'm sorry." And she was off like a shot, leaving Jenny to sit and gape behind her.

III

"Bollocks!" said Burgess. "They're shit-disturbers. You ought to know that by now. Why do you think they're interested in a nuclear-free Britain? Because they love peace? Dream on, Constable."

"I don't know," Richmond said, stroking his moustache. "They're just students, they don't know—"

"Just students, my arse! Who is it tries to bring down governments in places like Korea and South Africa? Bloody students, that's who. Just students! Grow up. Look at the chaos students created in America over the Vietnam war—they almost won it for the commies single-handed."

"What I was saying, sir," Richmond went on, "is that none of them are known to be militant. They just sit around and talk politics, that's all."

"But Special Branch has a file on Tim Fenton."

"I know, sir. But he's not actually *done* anything."

"Not until now, perhaps."

"But what could he gain from killing PC Gill, sir?"

"Anarchy, that's what."

"With all due respect," Banks cut in, "that's hardly consistent. The students support disarmament, yes, but Marxists aren't anarchists. They believe in the class—"

"I know what bloody Marxists believe in," Burgess said. "They'll believe in anything if it furthers their cause."

Banks gave up. "Better have another try, Phil," he said. "See if you can tie any of them into more extreme groups, or to any previous acts of political violence. I doubt you'll come up with anything Special Branch doesn't know about already, but give it a try."

"Yes, sir."

"I need another drink," Burgess said.

Sergeant Hatchley volunteered to go for a round. The Queen's Arms was busy. Wednesday was farmers' market day in Eastvale, and the whole town bustled with buyers and sellers. Glenys was too busy to exchange glances with Burgess even if she wanted to.

Burgess turned to Banks. "And I'm still not happy about Osmond. He's on file, too, and I got the distinct impression he's been lying every time I've talked to him."

Banks agreed.

"We'll have another go at him," said Burgess. "You can come with me again. Who knows, that bird of his might be there. If I put a bit of pressure on her, he might appeal to you for help and let something slip."

Banks reached for a cigarette to mask his anger. The last thing he felt like was facing Osmond and Jenny together again. But in a way Burgess was right. They were looking for a cop killer, and they needed results. As each day went by, the media outcry became more strident.

When PC Craig came in and walked over to their table, he seemed unsure whom to address. After looking first to Banks and then to Burgess, like a spectator following the ball at Wimbledon, he settled on Banks.

"We've just had a call, sir, from Relton. There's a bloke in the pub there says he's found a knife. I just thought... you know... it might be the one we're looking for."

"What are we waiting for?" Burgess jumped to his feet so quickly he knocked the table and spilt the rest of his beer. He pointed at Hatchley and Richmond. "You two get back to the station and wait till you hear from us."

They picked up Banks's white Cortina from the lot behind the police station. Market Street and the square were so busy that Banks took the back streets to the main Swainsdale road.

Automatically, he reached forward and slipped a cassette into the player. "Do you mind?" he asked Burgess, turning the volume down. "Hello Central" came on.

"No. That's Lightning Hopkins, isn't it? I quite like blues myself. I enjoyed that Billie Holiday the other day, too." He leaned back in the seat and lit a cigar from the dashboard lighter. "My father bunked with a squadron of Yanks in the last war. Got quite interested in jazz and blues. Of course, you couldn't get much of the real stuff over here at that time, but after the war he kept in touch and the Yanks used to send him seventy-eights. I grew up on that kind of music and it just seemed to stick."

Banks drove fast but kept an eye open for walkers on the verges. Even in March, the backpack brigade often took to the hills. As they approached Fortford, Burgess looked out at the river-meadows. "Very nice," he said. "Wouldn't be a bad place to retire to if it wasn't for the bloody weather."

They turned sharp left in Fortford, followed the unfenced minor road up the daleside to Relton and parked outside the pub. Banks had been to the Black Sheep before; it was famous in the dale because the landlord brewed his own beer on the premises, and you couldn't get it anywhere else. Black Sheep bitter had won prizes in national competitions.

If beer wasn't the first thing on Banks's mind when they entered, he certainly couldn't refuse the landlord's offer of a pint. Burgess declined the local brew and asked for a pint of Watney's.

Banks knew there were shepherds in the area, but they were an elusive breed, and he'd never seen one before. Farmers who tended their own sheep were common enough, but on the south Swainsdale commons, they banded together to hire three shepherds. Most of the sheep were heughed; they grew up on the farms and never strayed far. But not all of them; winter was a hard time, and many animals got buried under drifts. The shepherds know the moors, every gully and sink-hole, better than anyone else, and to them, sheep are as different from one another as people.

Jack Crocker's face had as many lines as a tough teacher gives out in a week, and its texture looked as hard as tanned leather. He had a misshapen blob of a nose, and his eyes were so deeply hooded they looked as if they had been perpetually screwed up against the wind. His cloth cap and old, flapping greatcoat set the final touches. His crook, a long hazel shaft with a metal hook, leaned against the wall.

"Christ," Banks heard Burgess mutter behind him. "A bloody shepherd!"

"I don't mind if I do," Crocker said, accepting a drink. "I were just fetching some ewes in for lambing, like, and I kicked that there knife." He placed the knife on the table. It was a flick-knife with a five-inch blade and a worn bone handle. "I didn't touch it, tha knows," he went on, putting a surprisingly smooth and slender forefinger to the side of his nose. "I've seen telly."

"How did you pick it up?" Burgess asked. Banks noticed that his tone was respectful, not hectoring as usual. Maybe he had a soft spot for shepherds.

"Like this." Crocker held the ends of the handle between thumb and second finger. He really did have beautiful hands, Banks noticed, the kind you'd picture on a concert pianist.

Burgess nodded and took a sip of his Watney's. "Good. You did the right thing, Mr Crocker." Banks took an envelope from his pocket, dropped the knife in, and sealed it.

"Is it t'right one, then? T'one as killed that bobby?"

"We can't say yet," Banks told him. "We'll have to get some tests done. But if it is, you've done us a great service."

"'T'weren't owt. It's not as if I were looking fer it." Crocker looked away, embarrassed, and raised his pint to his lips. Banks offered him a cigarette.

"Nay, lad," he said. "In my job you need all t'breath you can muster."

"Where did you find the knife?" Burgess asked.

"Up on t'moor, Eastvale way."

"Can you show us?"

"Aye." Crocker's face creased into a sly smile. "It's a bit on a hike, though. And tha can't take thy car."

Burgess looked at Banks. "Well," he said, "it's your part of the country. You're the nature-boy. Why don't you go up the moor with Mr Crocker here, and I'll phone the station to send a car for me?"

Yes, Banks thought, and you'll have another pint of Watney's while you're warming your hands in front of the fire.

Banks nodded. "I'd get that knife straight to the lab if I were you," he said. "If you send it through normal channels they'll take days to get the tests done. Ask for Vic Manson. If he's got a spare moment he'll dust it for prints and persuade one of the lads to try for blood-typing. It's been exposed to the elements a bit, but we might still get something from it."

"Sounds good," Burgess said. "Where is this lab?"

"Just outside Wetherby. You can ask the driver to take you straight there."

Burgess went over to the phone while Banks and Crocker drank off their pints of Black Sheep bitter and set off.

They climbed a stile at the eastern end of Mortsett Lane and set off over open moorland. The tussocks of moor grass, interspersed with patches of heather and sphagnum, made walking difficult for Banks. Crocker, always ahead, seemed to float over the top of it like a hovercraft. The higher they climbed, the harsher and stronger the wind became.

Banks wasn't dressed for the moors, either, and his shoes were soon mud-caked and worse. At least he was wearing his warm sheep-skin-lined coat. Though the slope wasn't steep, it was unrelenting, and he soon got out of breath. Despite the cold wind against his face, he was sweating.

At last, the ground flattened out into high moorland. Crocker stopped and waited with a smile for Banks to catch up.

"By heck, lad, what'd tha do if tha 'ad to chase after a villain?"

"Luckily, it doesn't happen often," Banks wheezed.

"Aye. Well, this is where I found it. Just down there in t'grass." He pointed with his crook. Banks bent and poked around among the sods. There was nothing to indicate the knife had been there.

"It looks like someone just threw it there," he said.

Crocker nodded. "It would've been easy enough to hide," he said. "Plenty of rocks to stuff it under. He could've even buried it if he'd wanted."

"But he didn't. So whoever it was must have panicked, perhaps, and just tossed it away."

"Tha should know."

Banks looked around. The spot was about two miles from Eastvale; the jagged castle battlements were just visible in the distance, down in the hollow where the town lay. In the opposite direction, also about two miles away, he could see the house and outbuildings of Maggie's Farm.

It looked like the knife had been thrown away on the wild moorland about halfway or more on a direct line between Eastvale and the farm. If someone from the farm had escaped arrest or injury at the demo, it would have been a natural direction in which to run home. That meant Paul or Zoe, as Rick and Seth had been arrested and searched. It could even have been the woman, Mara, who might have been lying about staying home all evening.

On the other hand, anyone could have come up there in the past few days and thrown the knife away. That seemed much less likely, though, as it was a poor method of disposal, more spontaneous than planned. Certainly it seemed to make mincemeat of one of Banks's theories—that a fellow policeman might have committed the murder. Again, the finger seemed to be pointing at Maggie's Farm.

Banks pulled the sheepskin collar tight around his neck and screwed up his eyes to keep the tears from forming. No wonder Crocker's eyes were hooded almost shut. There was nothing more to be done up here, he decided, but he would have to mark the spot in some way.

"Could you find this place again?" he asked.

"'Course," the shepherd answered.

Banks couldn't see how; there was nothing to distinguish it from any other spot of moorland. Still, it was Crocker's job to be familiar with every square inch of his territory.

He nodded. "Right. We may have to get a few men up here to make a more thorough search. Where can I get in touch with you?"

"I live in Mortsett." Crocker gave him the address.

"Are you coming back down?"

"Nay. More ewes to fetch in. It's lambing season, tha knows."

"Yes, well, thanks again for your time."

Crocker nodded curtly and set off further up the slope, walking just as quickly and effortlessly as if he were on the flat. At least, Banks thought, turning around, it would be easier going down. But before he had even completed the thought, he caught his foot in a patch of heather and fell face forward. He cursed, brushed himself off and carried on. Fortunately, Crocker had been going the other way and hadn't seen his little accident, otherwise it would have been the talk of the dale by evening.

He got back over the stile without further incident and nipped into the Black Sheep for another quick pint and a warm-up. There was nothing he could do now but wait for Burgess to finish at the lab. Even then, there might be no results. But a nice set of sweaty fingerprints on a smooth surface could survive the most terrible weather conditions, and Banks thought he had glimpsed flecks of dried blood in the joint between blade and handle.

EIGHT

I

A sudden, heavy shower drove the merchants from the market square. It was almost time to pack up and leave anyway; market days in winter and early spring were often cold and miserable affairs. But the rain stopped as quickly as it started, and in no time the sun was out again. Wet cobblestones reflected the muted bronze light, which slid into the small puddles and danced as the wind ruffled them.

The gold hands on the blue face of the church clock stood at four-twenty. Burgess hadn't returned from the lab yet. Banks sat waiting by his window, the awkward venetian blind drawn up, and looked down on the scene as he smoked and drank black coffee. People crossed the square and splashed through the puddles that had gathered where cobbles had been worn or broken away. Everyone wore grey plastic macs or brightly coloured slickers, as if they didn't trust the sun to stay out, and many carried umbrellas. It would soon be dark. Already the sun cast the long shadow of the Tudor-fronted police headquarters over the square.

At a quarter to five, Banks heard a flurry of activity outside his office, and Burgess bounded in carrying a buff folder.

"They came through," he said. "Took them long enough, but they did it—a clear set of prints and a match with Gill's blood type. No doubt about it, that was the knife. I've already got DC Richmond running a check on the prints. If they're on record we're in business."

He lit a Tom Thumb and smoked, tapping it frequently on the edge of the ashtray whether or not a column of ash had built up. Banks went back to the window. The shadow had lengthened; across the square, secretaries and clerks on their way home dropped in at Joplin's newsagent's for their evening papers, and young couples walked hand in hand into the El Toro coffee bar to tell one another about the ups and downs of their day at the office.

When Richmond knocked and entered, Burgess jumped to his feet. "Well?"

Richmond stroked his moustache. He could barely keep the grin of triumph from his face. "It's Boyd," he said, holding out the charts. "Paul Boyd. Eighteen points of comparison. Enough to stand up in court."

Burgess clapped his hands. "Right! Just as I thought. Let's go. You might as well come along, Constable. Where's Sergeant Hatchley?"

"I don't know, sir. I think he's still checking some of the witness reports."

"Never mind. Three's enough. Let's bring Boyd in for a chat."

They piled into Banks's Cortina and headed for Maggie's Farm. Banks played no music this time; the three of them sat in tense silence as the river-meadows rolled by, eerie in the misty twilight. Gravel popped under the wheels as they approached the farm, and the front curtain twitched when they drew up outside the building.

Mara Delacey opened the door before Burgess had finished knocking. "What do you want this time?" she asked angrily, but stood aside to let them in. They followed her through to the kitchen, where the others sat at the table eating dinner. Mara went back to her half-finished meal. Julian and Luna shifted closer to her.

"How convenient," Burgess said, leaning against the humming refrigerator. "You're all here together, except one. We're looking for Paul Boyd. Is he around?"

Seth shook his head. "No. I've no idea where he is."

"When did you last see him?"

"Last night, I suppose. I've been out most of the day. He wasn't here when I came back."

Burgess looked at Mara. Nobody said anything. "One of you must know where he is. What's it to be—now or down at the station?"

Still silence.

Burgess walked forward to pat Julian on the head, but the boy pulled a face and buried his head in Rick's side. "It'd be a shame,"

Burgess said, "if things got so that you couldn't look after the kids here and they had to be taken away."

"You'd never dare!" Mara said, her face flushed. "Even you can't be as much of a bastard as that."

Burgess raised his left eyebrow. "Can't I, love? Are you sure you want to find out? Where's Boyd?"

Rick got to his feet. He was as tall as Burgess and a good thirty pounds heavier. "Pick on someone your own size," he said. "If you start messing with my kid's life, you'll bloody well have me to answer to."

Burgess sneered and turned away. "I'm quaking in my boots. Where's Boyd?"

"We don't know," Seth said quietly. "He wasn't a prisoner here, you know. He pays his board, he's free to do what he wants and to come and go as he pleases."

"Not any more he isn't," Burgess said. "Maybe you'd better get Gypsy Rose Lee here to ask the stars where he is, because if we don't find him soon it's going to be very hard on you lot." He turned to Banks and Richmond. "Let's have a look around. Where's his room?"

"First on the left at the top of the stairs," Seth said. "But you're wasting your time. He's not there."

The three policemen climbed the narrow staircase. Richmond checked the other rooms while Banks and Burgess went into Paul's. There was only room for a single mattress on the floor and a small dresser at the far end, where a narrow window looked towards Eastvale. Sheets and blankets lay rumpled and creased on the unmade bed; dirty socks and underwear had been left in a pile on the floor. A stale smell of dead skin and unwashed clothes hung in the air. A couple of jackets, including a parka, hung in the tiny cupboard, and a pair of scuffed loafers lay on the floor. There was nothing much in the dresser drawers besides some clean underwear, T-shirts and a couple of moth-eaten pullovers. A grubby paperback copy of H.P. Lovecraft's *The Shadow over Innsmouth* lay open, face down on the pillow. On the cover was a picture of a semi-transparent, frog-faced monster dressed in what looked like an evening suit. Out of habit, Banks picked the book up and flipped through the pages to see if Boyd had written anything interesting in the margins or on the blank pages at the back. He found nothing. Richmond came in and joined them.

"There's nothing here," Burgess said. "It doesn't look like he's scarpered, though, unless he had a lot more clothes than this. I'd have taken a parka and a couple of sweaters if I'd been him. What was the weather like on the night Gill was stabbed?"

"Cool and wet," Banks answered.

"Parka weather?"

"I'd say so, yes."

Burgess took the coat from the closet and examined it. He pulled the inside of each pocket out in turn, and when he got to the right one, he pointed out a faint discoloured patch to Banks. "Your men must have missed this the other day. Could be blood. He must have put the knife back in his pocket after he killed Gill. Hang on to this, Richmond. We'll get it to the lab. Why don't you two go have a look in the outbuildings? You never know, he might be hiding in the woodpile. I'll poke around a bit more up here."

Downstairs, Banks and Richmond went back into the kitchen and got Mara to accompany them with the keys. They left by the back door and found themselves in a large rectangular garden with a low fence. Most of the place was given over to rows of vegetables—dark empty furrows at that time of year—but there was also a small square sand-box, on which a plastic lorry with big red wheels and a yellow bucket and spade lay abandoned. At the far end of the garden stood a brick building with an asphalt roof, just a little larger than a garage, and to their left was a gate that led to the barn.

"We'll have a look over there first," Banks said to Mara, who fiddled with the key-ring as she followed them to the converted barn. It wasn't a big place, nowhere the size of many that had been converted into bunk barns for tourists, but it followed the traditional Dales design, on the outside at least, in that it was built of stone.

Mara opened the door to the downstairs unit first, Zoe's flat. Banks was surprised at the transformation from humble barn into comfortable living-quarters; Seth had done a really good job. The woodwork was mostly unpainted, and if it looked a little makeshift, it was certainly sturdy and attractive in its simplicity. Not only, he gathered, did each unit have its own entrance, but there were cooking and bathing facilities, too, as well as a large, sparsely furnished living-room, one master bedroom, and a smaller one for Luna. But there was no sign of Paul Boyd.

The places were perfectly self-contained, Banks noticed, and if Rick and Zoe hadn't become friendly with Seth and Mara, they could easily have led quite separate lives there. Noting Mara's reaction to Burgess's threat, and remembering what Jenny had said at dinner, Banks guessed that Mara's fondness for the children was one unifying factor—anyone would be glad of a built-in baby-sitter—and perhaps another was their shared politics.

Upstairs, the layout was different. Both bedrooms were quite small, and most of the space was taken up by Rick's studio, which was much less tidy than Zoe's large work-table downstairs, with books and charts spread out on its surface. Seth had added three skylights along the length of the roof to provide plenty of light, and canvases, palettes and odd tubes of paint littered the place. From what Banks could see, Rick Trelawney's paintings were, as Tim Fenton had said, unmarketable, being mostly haphazard splashes of colour, or collages of found objects. Sandra knew quite a bit about art, and Banks had learned from her that many paintings he wouldn't even store in the attic were regarded by experts as works of genius. But these were different, even he could tell; they made Jackson Pollock's angry explosions look as comprehensible as Constable's landscapes.

As he poked around among the stuff, though, Banks discovered a stack of small water-colour landscapes covered with an old sack. They resembled the one he'd noticed in the front room on his last visit, and he realized that they were, after all, Rick's work. So that was how he made his money! Selling pretty local scenes to tourists and little old ladies to support his revolutionary art.

Mara, who all the time had remained quiet, watching them with her arms folded, locked up as they left and led the way back to the house.

"You two go ahead," Banks said when he had closed the gate behind them. "I'm off to take a peek in the shed. It's not locked, is it?"

Mara shook her head and went back into the house with Richmond.

Banks opened the door. The shed was dark inside and smelled of wood shavings, sawdust, oiled metal, linseed oil and varnish. He tugged the chain dangling in front of him, and a naked bulb lit up, revealing Seth's workshop. Planks, boards and pieces of furniture at

various stages of incompletion leaned against the walls. Spider webs
hung in the dark corners. Seth had a lathe and a full set of well-kept
tools—planes, saws, hammers, bevels—and boxes of nails and screws
rested on makeshift wooden shelves around the walls. There was no
room for anyone to hide.

At the far end of the workshop, an old Remington office typewriter sat on a desk beside an open filing cabinet. Inside, Banks found
only correspondence connected with Seth's carpentry business: esti-
mates, invoices, receipts, orders. Close by was a small bookcase.
Most of the books were about antique furniture and cabinet-making
techniques, but there were a couple of old paperback novels and two
books on the human brain, one of which was called *The Tip of the
Iceberg*. Maybe, Banks thought, Seth harboured a secret ambition to
become a brain surgeon. Already a carpenter, he probably had a better start than most.

He walked back to the door and was about to turn off the light
when he noticed a tattered notebook on a ledge by the door. It was
full of measurements, addresses and phone numbers—obviously
Seth's workbook. When he flipped through it, he noticed that one
leaf had been torn out roughly. The following page still showed the
faint impression of heavily scored numbers. Banks took a sheet from
his own notebook, placed it on top and rubbed over it with a pencil.
He could just make out the number in relief: 1139. It was hard to tell
if it was in the same handwriting as the rest because the numbers were
so much larger and more exaggerated.

Picking up the workbook, he turned to leave and almost bumped
into Seth standing in the doorway.

"What are you doing?"

"This book," Banks said. "What do you use it for?"

"Work notes. When I need to order new materials, make measurements, note customers' addresses. That kind of thing."

"There's a page missing." Banks showed him. "What does that
mean—1139?"

"Surely you can't expect me to remember that," Seth said. "It must
have been a long time ago. It was probably some measurement or
other."

"Why did you tear it out?"

Seth looked at him, deep-set brown eyes wary and resentful. "I don't know. Maybe it wasn't important. Maybe I'd written something on the back that I had to take with me somewhere. It's just an old notebook."

"But there's only one page missing. Doesn't that strike you as odd?"

"I've already said it doesn't."

"Did you tear out the page to give to Paul Boyd? Is it a number for him to call? Part of an address?"

"No. I've told you, I don't remember why I tore it out. It obviously wasn't very important."

"I'll have to take this notebook away with me."

"Why?"

"There are names and addresses in it. We'll have to check and see if Boyd's gone to any of them. As I understand it, he did spend quite a bit of time working with you in here."

"But it's *my* notebook. Why would he be at any of those places? They're just people who live in the dale, people I've done work for. I don't want the police bothering them. It could lose me business."

"We still have to check."

Seth swore under his breath. "Please yourself. You'd better give me a receipt, though."

Banks wrote him one, then pulled the chain to turn off the light. They walked back to the house in silence.

Seth sat down again to finish his meal and Mara followed Banks towards the front of the room. They could hear Burgess and Richmond still poking about upstairs.

"Mr Banks?" Mara said quietly, standing close to him near the window.

Banks lit a cigarette. "Yes?"

"What he said about the children...It's not true, is it? Surely he can't..."

Banks sat in the rocking chair and Mara pulled up a small three-legged stool opposite him. One of Zoe's tarot decks, open at "The Moon," lay on the table beside him. The moon seemed to be shedding drops of blood onto a path that led off into the distance, between two towers. In the foreground, a crab was crawling up onto land from a pool, and a dog and a wolf stood howling at the moon. It was a disturbing and hypnotic design. Banks shivered, as if someone had just walked over his grave, and turned his attention to Mara.

"They're not your children, are they?" he said.

"You know they're not. But I love them as if they were. Jenny Fuller told me she knows you. She said you're not as bad as the rest. Tell me they can't make us give the children up."

Banks smiled to himself. Not as bad as the rest, eh? He'd have to remember to tease Jenny about that backhanded compliment.

He turned to face Mara. "Superintendent Burgess will do whatever he has to to get to the bottom of things. I don't think it'll come to taking the children away, but bear in mind that he doesn't make idle threats. If you know anything, you should tell us."

Mara sucked on her bottom lip. She looked close to tears. "I don't know where Paul is," she said finally. "You can't really think he did it?"

"We've got some evidence that points that way. Have you ever seen him with a flick-knife?"

"No."

Banks thought she was lying, but he knew it was no good pushing her. She might offer him a titbit of information in the hope that it would ease the pressure, but she wasn't going to tell the full truth.

"He's gone," she said finally. "I know that. But I don't know where."

"How do you know he's gone?"

Mara hesitated, and her voice sounded too casual to be telling the truth. Before starting, she tucked her long chestnut hair behind her ears. It made her face look thinner and more haggard. "He's been upset these past few days, especially after your Superintendent Burgess came and bullied him. He thought you'd end up framing him because he's been in jail and because he . . . he looks different. He didn't want to bring trouble down on the rest of us, so he left."

Banks turned over the next tarot card: "The Star." A beautiful naked woman was pouring water from two vases into a pool on the ground. Behind her, trees and shrubs were blossoming, and in the sky one large, bright central star was surrounded by seven smaller ones. For some reason, the woman reminded him of Sandra, which was odd because there was no strong physical resemblance.

"How do you know why he went?" Banks asked. "Did he leave a note?"

"No, he just told me. He said last night he was thinking of leaving. He didn't say when."

"Or where?"

"No."

"Did he say anything about PC Gill's murder?"

"No, nothing. He didn't say he was running away because he was guilty, if that's what you mean."

"And you didn't think to let us know he was running off, even though there's a chance he might be a killer?"

"He's no killer." Mara spoke too quickly. "I'd no reason to think so, anyway. If he wanted to go he was quite free as far as we were concerned."

"What did he take with him?"

"What do you mean?"

Banks glanced towards the window. "It's brass-monkey weather out there; rains a lot, too. What was he wearing? Was he carrying a suitcase or a rucksack?"

Mara shook her head. "I don't know. I didn't see him go."

"Did you see him this morning?"

"Yes."

"What time?"

"About eleven or half-past. He always sleeps late."

"What time did he leave? Approximately."

"I don't know. I was out at lunch-time. I left at twenty to one and got back at about two. He'd gone by then."

"Was anyone else in the house during that time?"

"No. Seth was out in the van. He took Zoe with him because she had to deliver some charts. And Rick took the children into Eastvale."

"And you don't know what Boyd was wearing or what he took with him?"

"No. I told you, I didn't see him go."

"Come upstairs."

"What?"

Banks headed towards the staircase. "Come upstairs with me. Now."

Mara followed him up to Paul's room. Banks opened the cupboard and the dresser drawers. "What's missing?"

Mara put her hand to her forehead. Burgess and Richmond looked in at the doorway and carried on downstairs.

"I . . . I don't know," Mara said. "I don't know what clothes he had."

"Who does the washing around here?"

"Well, I do. Mostly. Zoe does some, too."

"So you must know what clothes Boyd had. What's missing?"

"He didn't have much."

"He must have had another overcoat. He's left his parka."

"No, he didn't. He had an anorak, though. A blue anorak."

Banks wrote it down. "What else?"

"Jeans, I suppose. He never wore much else."

"Footwear."

Mara looked in the closet and saw the scuffed loafers. "Just a pair of old slip-ons. Hush Puppies, I think."

"Colour?"

"Black."

"And that's it?"

"As far as I know."

Banks closed his notebook and smiled at Mara. "Look, try not to worry about the children too much. As soon as Superintendent Burgess catches Paul Boyd, he'll forget all about the threats he made. If we catch him soon, that is."

"I really *don't* know where he's gone."

"Okay. But if you come up with any ideas. . . . Think about it."

"People like Burgess shouldn't be allowed to run free," Mara said. She folded her arms tightly and stared at the floor.

"Oh? What do you suggest we should do with him? Lock him up?"

She looked at Banks. Her jaw was clenched tight and her eyes burned with tears.

"Or should we have him put down?"

Mara brushed past him and hurried down the stairs. Banks followed slowly. Burgess and Richmond stood in the front room ready to leave.

"Come on, let's go," Burgess said. "There's nothing more here." Then he turned to Seth, who stood in the kitchen doorway. "If I find out you've been helping Boyd in any way, believe me, I'll be back.

And you lot'll be in more trouble than you ever dared imagine. Give my love to the kids."

II

Mara watched the car disappear down the track. She felt reassured by Banks, but wondered just how much he could do if Burgess had made his mind up about something. If the children were taken away, she thought, she could well be driven to murder the superintendent with her bare hands.

She became aware of the others behind her in the room. She hadn't told them anything about what had happened with Paul, and none of them knew yet that he had run off for good. For one thing, she'd hardly had time to say anything. They had all drifted back close to meal-time anyway, when she was busy in the kitchen; then the police had arrived.

"What's going on, Mara?" Seth asked, coming up to her and resting his hand on her shoulder. "Do you know?"

Mara nodded. She was trying to keep the tears from her eyes.

"Come on." Seth took her hand and led her to a chair. "Tell us."

Seeing them all watching her, expectant, Mara regained her control. She reached for her tin of Old Holborn and rolled a cigarette.

"He's gone, that's all there is to it," she said, and told them about seeing old Crocker carrying the knife into the Black Sheep. "I ran back here to warn him. I didn't want the police to get him, and I thought if they'd got the knife they might find his fingerprints or something. He's been in jail, so they must be on record."

"But what made you think of Paul?" Zoe asked. "That knife was just lying around on the mantelpiece as usual, I suppose. Nobody ever paid it any mind. Any of the people here on Friday afternoon could have taken it."

Mara drew on her cigarette and finally told them about the blood she'd seen on Paul's hand when he got back from the demo. The hand that turned out to be unmarked the following morning.

"Why didn't you tell us?" Seth asked. "I don't suppose you approached Paul about it, either. There might have been a simple explanation."

"I know that," Mara said. "Don't you think I've been over it time and again in my mind? I was frightened of him. I mean, if he had done it.... But I wanted to stand by him. If I'd told you all, you might have asked him to leave or something."

"How did he react when you came and told him the knife had been found?" Rick asked.

"He went pale. He couldn't look me in the eye. He looked like a frightened animal."

"So you gave him money and clothes?"

"Yes. I gave him your red anorak, Zoe. I'm sorry."

"It's all right," Zoe said. "I'd have done the same."

"And I told the police he was probably wearing a blue one. He took his blue one with him, but he wasn't wearing it."

"Where's he heading?" asked Rick.

"I don't know. I didn't want him to tell me. He's a survivor; he can live out on the streets. I gave him some money, some I'd saved from working at the shop and selling my pottery. He'll have enough to get wherever he wants."

Later that evening, when the others had drifted off back to the barn and Seth had settled down with a book, Mara began to think about the few months that Paul had been around, and how alive he had made her feel. At first, he had been sullen and unresponsive, and there had come a point when Seth had considered asking him to leave. But Paul hadn't been long out of jail then; he wasn't used to dealing with people. Time and care had worked wonders. Soon, he was taking long walks alone on the moors, and the claustrophobia that had so often made his nights unbearable in jail became easier to control. Nobody forced him to, but he really took to working with Seth.

When she thought about his progress and what it had all come to, Mara couldn't help but feel sad. It would all be for nothing if he got caught and sent to prison again. When she pictured him cold and alone in the strange and frightening world beyond Swainsdale, it made her want to cry. But she told herself again that he was strong, resourceful, a survivor. It wouldn't feel the same to him as it would to her. Besides, imagined horrors were always far worse than the reality.

"I hope Paul makes it far away," Seth said in the silence that followed their love-making that night. "I hope they never catch him."

"How will we know where he is, what's happening to him?" Mara asked.

"He'll let us know one way or another. Don't you worry about it." He put his arm around her and she rested her head against his chest. "You did the right thing."

But she couldn't help but worry. She didn't think they'd hear from Paul again, not after all that had happened. She didn't know what else she could have done, but she wasn't sure she had done the right thing. As she tried to sleep, she remembered the expression on his face just before he left. There had been gratitude, yes, for the warning, the money and the clothes, but there had also been resentment and disappointment. He'd looked as if he was being sent into exile. She didn't know if he'd expected her to ask him to stay no matter what— she certainly hadn't told him he *had* to go away—but there had been a hint of accusation in his actions, as if to say, "You think I did it, don't you? You don't want me here causing trouble. You didn't trust me in the first place. I'm an outcast, and I always will be." She hadn't told Seth and the others about that.

III

Banks waited his turn at the busy bar of the Queen's Arms while Burgess sat at a round table by the Market Street entrance. It was eight-thirty. Hatchley had just left to keep a date with Carol Ellis, and Richmond had gone to a do at the Rugby Club.

Dirty Dick was clearly pleased with himself. He leaned back in his chair and positively beamed goodwill at everyone who looked his way. Nobody gave him much more than a scowl in return, though.

"'Ey, Mr Banks," said Cyril. "A minute, if you've got one."

"'Course. For you, Cyril, anything. And you might as well pull me a pint of bitter and a pint of Double Diamond while you're talking."

"It's about that there mate of yours." Cyril nodded his head aggressively in the direction of Burgess.

"He's not really a mate," Banks said. "More like a boss."

"Aye. Well, anyways, tell him to stop pestering my Glenys. She's got too much work to do without passing the time of day with the likes of him." Cyril leaned forward and lowered his voice. The muscles bulged above his rolled-up shirt sleeves. "And you can tell him I don't care if he is a copper—no disrespect, Mr Banks. If he doesn't keep out of my way I'll give him a bloody knuckle sandwich, so help me I will."

Glenys, who seemed to have grasped the tenor of the conversation, blushed and busied herself pulling a pint at the other end of the bar.

"I'd be delighted to pass on your message," Banks said, paying for the drinks.

"Don't forget his lordship's Double Diamond," Cyril said, his voice edged with contempt.

"You can wipe that bloody grin off your face," Burgess said after Banks had passed on Cyril's warning. "You're a long way from collecting that flyer yet. She fancies me, does young Glenys, there's no doubt about it. And there's nothing like a bit of danger, a touch of risk, to get the old hormones flowing. Look at her." True enough, Glenys was flashing Burgess a flush-cheeked smile while Cyril was looking the other way. "If we could only get that oaf out of the way.... Anyway, it's her night off next Monday. She usually goes to the pictures with her mates."

"I'd be careful if I were you," Banks said.

"Yes, but you're not me, are you?" He gulped down about half of his pint. "Ah, that's good. So, we've got the bastard. Or will have soon."

Banks nodded. That, he assumed, was why they were celebrating. Burgess was on his fourth pint already and Banks on his third.

They had done everything they could. Boyd had certainly done a bunk, though Banks had no idea how he knew about the discovery of the knife. It was likely he had headed for Eastvale and taken a bus. The number forty-three ran along Cardigan Drive, on the town's western edge. He would simply have had to walk across the moors and up Gallows View to get there. Also, buses to York and Ripon passed along the same road. Somebody must have seen him. Banks had circulated his description to the bus companies and sent out his mug-shot to police around the country, paying particular attention to Leeds, Liverpool and London. As Burgess said, it was simply a matter of time before he was caught.

"Where did you get that bloody scar?" Burgess asked.

"This?" Banks fingered the white crescent by his right eye. "Got it in Heidelberg. It's a duelling scar."

"Ha bloody ha! You're a funny man, aren't you? Have you heard the one about the—" Burgess stopped and looked up at the person standing over them. "Well, well," he said, scraping his chair aside to make room. "If it isn't—"

"Dr Fuller," Jenny said. She glanced at Banks and pulled up a chair next to his.

"Of course. How could I forget? Drink, love?"

Jenny smiled sweetly. "Yes, please. I'll have a half of lager."

"Oh, come on, have a pint," Burgess insisted.

"All right. A pint."

"Good." Burgess rubbed his hands together and set off for the bar. His thigh caught the edge of the table as he stood up. Beer rippled in the glasses but didn't spill.

Jenny pulled a face at Banks. "What's with him?"

Banks grinned. "Celebrating."

"So I see." She leaned closer. "Look, I've got something to ask you—"

Banks put a finger to his lips. "Not now," he said. "He's getting served. He'll be back soon." True enough, in no time Burgess was on his way back, trying to carry three pints in his hands and slopping beer over the rims onto his shoes.

"What are you celebrating, anyway?" Jenny asked after Burgess had managed to set the drinks on the table without spilling much.

Banks told her about Paul Boyd.

"That's a shame."

"A shame! You said he gave you the creeps."

"He does. I'm just thinking of the others, that's all. It'll be a hell of a blow for Seth and Mara. They've done so much for him. Especially Mara." Jenny seemed unusually distracted at the thought of Mara Delacey, and Banks wondered why.

"You know," Burgess said, "I'm a bit sorry it turned out to be Boyd myself."

Jenny looked surprised: "You are? Why?"

"Well..." He moved closer. "I was hoping it might be that

boy-friend of yours. Then we could get him locked up for a good long while, and you and me could...you know."

To Banks's surprise, Jenny laughed. "You've got some imagination, I'll say that for you, Superintendent Burgess."

"Call me Dick. Most of my friends do."

Jenny stifled a laugh. "I really don't think I could do that. Honest."

"Aren't you relieved it's all over?" Banks asked her. "I'll bet Osmond is."

"Of course. Especially if it means we won't have to put up with any more visits from him." She nodded at Burgess.

"I could still visit," Dirty Dick said, and winked.

"Oh, put another record on. So where do you think Paul is?" she asked Banks.

"We've no idea. He took off early this afternoon, before we got a positive identification. Could be anywhere."

"But you're confident you'll get him?"

"I think so."

Jenny turned to Burgess. "So your job's over, then? I don't suppose you'll want to stick around this god-forsaken place much longer, will you?"

"Oh, I don't know." Burgess lit a cigar and leered at her. "It has its compensations."

Jenny coughed and waved the smoke away.

"Seriously," he went on, "I'll stay around till he's brought in. There's a lot I want to ask him."

"But that could take days, weeks."

Burgess shrugged. "It's the taxpayers' money, love. Your round again, Banks."

"Nothing for me this time," Jenny said. "I'll have to be off soon." She still had over half her drink left.

Feeling a little light-headed, Banks went to the bar.

"'Ave you told him?" Cyril asked.

"Yes."

"Good. I just hope he knows what's best for him. Look at the bugger, he can't keep his hands off them."

Banks looked around. Dirty Dick seemed to have edged closer to Jenny, and his elbow rested on the back of her chair. She was behaving very calmly, Banks thought. It wasn't like her to take such sexist patronizing so well. Maybe she fancies him, he thought suddenly. If Glenys does, then maybe Jenny does, too. Perhaps he really does have the magic touch with women. At least he's available. And he's handsome enough, too. That casual look—the worn leather jacket, openneck shirt—it suits him, as do the touches of grey hair at his temples.

Banks brushed the idea aside. It was ridiculous. Jenny was an intelligent, tasteful woman. A woman like her could never fall for Dirty Dick's brazen charm. But women were a mysterious lot, Banks thought glumly, carrying the drinks back. They were always falling for worthless men. He clearly recalled the beautiful Anita Howarth, object of his adolescent lust back in the third form. She had been quite oblivious to Banks's lean good looks and taken up with that spotty, good-for-nothing Steve Naylor. And Naylor hadn't seemed to give a damn about her. He gave the impression he would rather be playing cricket or rugby than go anywhere with Anita. But that just made her more crazy about him. And Banks had had to spend all his time fending off unwelcome advances from Cheryl Wagstaff, the one with the yellow buck teeth.

"I was just offering to show this lovely young lady the sights of London," Burgess said.

"I'm sure she's seen them before," Banks replied stiffly.

"Not the way I'd show her." Burgess moved his arm so that his hand rested on Jenny's shoulder.

Banks was wondering if he should act gallantly this time and defend Jenny's honour. After all, they were sort of off duty. But he remembered she was quite good at taking care of herself. Her face took on an ominously sweet expression.

"Please take your hand off my shoulder, Superintendent," she said.

"Oh, come on, love," Burgess said. "Don't be so shy. And call me Dick."

"Please?"

"Give me a chance. We've hardly even got—"

Burgess stopped abruptly when Jenny calmly and slowly picked up her glass and poured the rest of her chilled lager on his lap.

"I told you I only wanted a half," she said, then picked up her coat and left.

Burgess rushed for the gents. Luckily, Jenny had acted so naturally, and everyone around them had been so engrossed in conversation, that the event had gone largely unnoticed. Cyril had seen it, though, and his face was red with laughter.

Banks caught up with Jenny outside. She was leaning against the ancient, pitted market cross in the centre of the square with her hand over her mouth. "My God," she said, letting the laughter out and patting her chest, "I haven't had as much fun in years. That man's a positive throwback. I'm surprised you seem to be enjoying his company so much."

"He's not so bad," Banks said. "Especially after a few jars."

"Yes, you'd need to be at least half-pissed. And you'd need to be a man, too. You're all locker-room adolescents when it comes down to it."

"He's got quite a reputation as a womanizer."

"They must be desperate down south, then."

Banks's faith in women was partially restored.

It was cold outside in the deserted square. The cobbles, still wet with rain, glistened in the dim gaslight. The church bells rang half-past nine. Banks turned up his jacket collar and held the lapels close together. "What was it you wanted to ask me?"

"It's nothing. It doesn't matter now."

"Come on, Jenny, you're hiding something. You're not good at it. Is it to do with Paul Boyd?"

"Indirectly. But I told you, it doesn't matter."

"Do you know why he ran away?"

"Of course not."

"Look, I know you're a friend of Mara's. Is this to do with her? It could be important."

"All right," Jenny said, holding up her hand. "Give it a rest. I'll tell you everything you want to know. You're getting almost as bad as your mate in there. Mara just wondered how the investigation was going, that's all. They're all a bit tense up at the farm, and they wanted to know if they could expect any more visits from God's gift to women. Will you believe me now that it doesn't matter?"

"When did you talk to her?"

"This lunchtime in the Black Sheep."

"She must have seen the knife," Banks said, almost to himself.

"What?"

"The shepherd, Jack Crocker. He found the knife. She must have seen it, recognized it as Boyd's, and dashed off to warn him. That's why he took off just in time."

"Oh, Alan, surely not?"

"I thought she was lying when I talked to her earlier. Didn't you notice any of this?"

"She did take off in rather a hurry, but I'd no idea why. I left just after. You're not going to arrest her, are you?"

Banks shook his head. "It makes her an accessory," he said, "but I doubt we'd be able to prove it. And when Burgess gets Boyd, I don't think he'll spare another thought for Mara and the rest. It was just a bloody stupid thing to do."

"Was it? Would you split on a friend, just like that? What would you do if someone accused Richmond of murder, or me?"

"That's not the point. Of course I'd do what I could to clear you. But she should have let us know. Boyd could be dangerous."

"She cares about Paul. She's hardly likely to hand him over to you just like that."

"I wonder if she's told him where to run and hide as well."

Jenny shivered. "It's cold standing about here," she said. "I should go before Dirty Dick comes out and beats me up. That's just about his level. And you'd better get back or he'll think you've deserted him. Give him my love." She kissed Banks quickly on the cheek and hurried to her car. He stood in the cold for a moment thinking about Mara and what Jenny had said, then rushed back into the Queen's Arms to see what had become of the soused superintendent.

"She's certainly got spirit, I'll say that," Burgess said, not at all upset by the incident. "Another pint?"

"I shouldn't really."

"Oh, come on Banks. Don't be a party pooper." Without waiting for a reply, Burgess went to the bar.

Banks felt that he'd had enough already, and soon he would be past the point of no return. Still, he thought, after a couple more pints he wouldn't give a damn anyway. He sensed that Burgess was lonely and in need of company in his moment of triumph, and he didn't feel he could simply desert the bastard. Besides, he had only an empty house to go home to. He could leave the Cortina in the police car-park and walk home later, no matter how much he'd drunk. It was only a mile and a bit.

And so they drank on, and on. Burgess was easy enough to talk to, Banks found, once you got used to his cocky manner and stayed off politics and police work. He had a broad repertoire of jokes, an extensive knowledge of jazz and a store of tales about cock-ups on the job. On the Met, as Banks remembered, there were so many dif-ferent departments and squads running their own operations that it wasn't unusual for the Sweeney to charge in and spoil a fraud-squad stake-out.

An hour and two pints later, as Burgess reached the end of a tale about a hapless drug-squad DC shooting himself in the foot, Banks suggested it was time to go.

"I suppose so," Burgess said regretfully, finishing his drink and get-ting to his feet.

He certainly didn't seem drunk. His speech was normal and his eyes looked clear. But when they got outside, he had difficulty walk-ing on the pavement. To keep himself steady, he put his arm around Banks's shoulder and the two of them weaved across the market square. Thank God the hotel's just around the corner, Banks thought.

"That's my only trouble, you know," Burgess said. "Mind clear as a bell, memory intact, but every time I go over the limit my motor con-trol goes haywire. Know what my mates call me down at the Yard?"

"No."

"Bambi." He laughed. "Bloody Bambi. You know, that little what-sit in the cartoon—the way the damn thing walks. It's not my sweet and gentle nature they're referring to." He put his hand to his groin. "Bloody hell, I still feel like I've pissed myself. That damn woman!" And he laughed.

Banks declined an invitation to go up to Burgess's room and split a bottle of Scotch. No matter how sorry he felt for the lonely bugger, he wasn't that much of a masochist. Grudgingly, Burgess let him go. "I'll drink it myself, then," were his final words, delivered at full vol-ume in front of an embarrassed desk clerk in the hotel lobby.

As he set off home, Banks wished he'd brought his Walkman. He could be listening to Blind Willie McTell or Bukka White as he walked. He was steady on his feet, though, and arrived at the front door of the empty house in about twenty minutes. He was tired and he certainly didn't want another drink, so he decided to go straight to bed. As usual, though, when things were bothering him he couldn't get to sleep immediately. And there were plenty of things about the Gill case that still puzzled him.

Motive was a problem, unless Burgess was right and Boyd had simply lashed out indiscriminately. In this case, it seemed that knowing *who* didn't explain *why*. Boyd wasn't political as far as anyone knew, and even street punks like him weren't in the habit of stabbing policemen at anti-nuclear demos. If someone had a private reason for wanting to do away with Gill, then there was plenty to consider in the personal lives of the other suspects: Osmond's assault charges, Trelawney's custody battle, Seth's wife's accident, Mara's religious organization, and even Zoe's seaside fortune-telling. It was hard to imagine a connection at this point, but stranger things had happened. Tony Grant's report might prove useful, if it ever arrived.

Banks was also curious about the prints on the knife. Usually when a knife is thrust into a body, the fingers holding the handle slip and any impression is blurred. Boyd's prints had been perfectly clear, just as if he had carefully applied each one. It could have happened if he'd folded up the knife and carried it in his hand before throwing it away, or if he'd just picked it up after someone else had used it. There were other prints under his, but they were too blurred to read. They could be his, too, of course, but there was no way of knowing.

Boyd had certainly carried the knife in his pocket. The stains inside the parka matched PC Gill's blood type. But if he had used it, why had he been foolish enough to pick it up after dropping it? He must have let it fall at some point, because several people had seen it being kicked around by the crowd. And if he had just left it there, it was very unlikely that it could have been traced to the farm.

But if Boyd hadn't done it, why had he picked up a knife that wasn't his? To protect someone? And who would he be more likely to protect than the people at Maggie's Farm? Or had there been someone else he knew and cared about who had access to the knife? There were a lot more questions to be asked yet, Banks thought, and Burgess was being very premature in celebrating his victory tonight.

Then there was the matter of the number torn out of Seth Cotton's notebook. Banks didn't know what it meant, but there was something familiar about it, something damn familiar. Boyd was close to Seth and spent plenty of time helping him in the workshop. Could the number be something to do with him? Could it help tell them where he'd gone?

It could be a phone number, of course. There were still plenty of four-digit numbers in the Swainsdale area. On impulse, Banks got out of bed and went downstairs. It was after eleven, but he decided to try anyway. He dialled 1139 and heard a phone ring at the other end. It went on for a long time. He was just about to give up when a woman answered, "Hello. Rossghyll Guest House, bed and breakfast." The voice was polite but strained.

Banks introduced himself and some of the woman's politeness faded when it became clear that he wasn't a potential customer. "Do you know what time it is?" she said. "Couldn't this have waited till morning? Do you know what time I have to get up?"

"It's important." Banks gave a description of Paul Boyd and asked if she'd seen him.

"I wouldn't have that kind of person staying here," the woman answered angrily. "What kind of place do you think this is? This is a decent house." And with that she hung up on him.

Banks trudged back up to bed. He'd have to send a man over, of course, just to be sure, but it didn't seem a likely bet. And if it was a phone number outside the local area, it could be almost anywhere. With the dialling code missing, there was no way of telling.

Banks lay awake a while longer, then he finally drifted off to sleep and dreamed of Burgess humble in defeat.

NINE

I

The overcast sky seemed to press on Banks's nagging headache when he set off for Maggie's Farm at eleven-thirty the next morning. Burgess had called in earlier to say he was going over some paper-work in his hotel room and didn't want to be disturbed unless Paul Boyd turned up. That suited Banks fine; he wanted a word with Mara Delacey, and the less Dirty Dick knew about it, the better.

He pulled up outside the farmhouse and knocked. He wasn't sur-prised when Mara opened the door and moaned, "Not again!"

Reluctantly she let him in. There was no one else in the place. The others were probably working.

Banks wanted to get Mara away from the house, on neutral ground. Perhaps then, he thought, he could get her to open up a bit more.

"I'd just like to talk to you, that's all," he said. "It's not an interro-gation, nothing official."

She looked puzzled. "Go on."

Banks tapped his watch. "It's nearly lunch-time and I haven't eaten yet," he said casually. "Do you fancy a trip down to the Black Sheep?"

"What for? Is this some subtle way of getting me to accompany you to the station?"

"No tricks. Honest. What I've got to say might even be of advan-tage to you."

She still regarded him, suspiciously, but the bait was too good to refuse. "All right." She reached for an anorak to put over her sweater and jeans. "I'm going into the shop this afternoon anyway." She pulled back her thick chestnut hair and tied it in a pony-tail.

In the car, Mara leaned forward to examine the tapes Banks kept in the storage rack Brian had bought him for his birthday the previous May—his thirty-eighth. There, mixed in with Zemlinsky's *Birthday of the Infanta*, Mozart's *Magic Flute*, Dowland's *Lachrimae* and Purcell's airs, were Lightning Hopkins, Billie Holiday, Muddy Waters, Robert Wilkins and a number of blues-anthology tapes.

Picking up the Billie Holiday, Mara managed a thin smile. "A policeman who likes blues can't be all bad," she said.

Banks laughed. "I like most music," he said, "except for country-and-western and middle-of-the-road crooning—you know, Frank Sinatra, Engelbert Humperdinck and that lot."

"Even rock?"

"Even rock. Some, anyway. I must admit I'm still stuck in the sixties as far as that's concerned. I lost interest after the Beatles split up. I even know where the name of your house comes from."

Banks was pleased to be chatting so easily with Mara. It was the first time his interest in music had helped create the kind of rapport he wanted with a witness. So often people regarded it as an eccentricity, but now it was actually helping with an important investigation. A common interest in jazz and blues had also helped him to relax with Burgess a little. Still, he thought, Mara probably wouldn't stay so convivial when she followed the drift of the questions he had to ask her.

They found a quiet corner in the pub by the tiled fireplace. In a glass case on the wall beside them was a collection of butterflies pinned to a board. Banks bought Mara a half of mild and got a pint of Black Sheep bitter for himself. Maybe the hair of the dog would do the trick and get rid of his headache. He ordered a ploughman's lunch; Mara asked for lasagne.

"Ploughman's lunches were invented for tourists in the seventies," Mara said.

"Not authentic?"

"Not a bit."

"Oh well. I can think of worse inventions."

"I suppose you want to get down to business, don't you?" Mara said. "Did Jenny Fuller tell you about our meeting?"

"No, but I figured it out. I think she's worried about you."

"She needn't be. I'm all right."

"Are you? I thought you'd be worried sick about Paul Boyd."

"What if I am?"

"Do you think he's guilty?"

Mara paused and sipped some beer. She swept a stray wisp of hair from her cheek before answering. "Maybe I did at first, a bit," she said. "At least, I was worried. I mean, we don't know a lot about him. I suppose I looked at him differently. But not now, no. And I don't care what evidence you've got against him."

"What made you change your mind?"

"A feeling, that's all. Nothing concrete, nothing you'd understand."

Banks leaned forward. "Believe it or not, Mara, policemen have feelings like that, too. We call them hunches, or we put them down to our nose, our instinct for truth. You may be right about Boyd. I'm not saying you are, but there's a chance. Things aren't quite as cut and dried as they appear. In some ways Paul is too obvious."

"Isn't that what appeals to you? How easy it is to blame him?"

"Not to me, no."

"But...I mean...I thought you were sure, that you had evidence?"

"The knife?"

"Yes."

"You recognized it, didn't you, when Jack Crocker brought it in here yesterday lunch-time?"

Mara said nothing. Before Banks could speak again, the food arrived and they both tucked in.

"Look," said Banks, after polishing off the best part of a chunk of Wensleydale and a pickled onion, "let's assume that Boyd's innocent, just for the sake of argument." Mara looked at him, but her expression was hard to fathom. Suspicion? Hope? Either reaction would be perfectly natural. "If he is," Banks went on, "then it raises more questions than it answers. It's easier for everyone if Boyd turns out to be guilty—everyone but him, that is—but the easiest way isn't necessarily the true one. Do you know what I mean?"

Mara nodded and her lips curved just a little at the edges. "Sounds like the Eightfold Path," she said.

"The what?"

"The Eightfold Path. It's the Buddhist way to enlightenment."

Banks speared another pickled onion. "Well, I don't know much about enlightenment," he said, "but we could do with a bit more light on the case." He went on to tell her about the blood and prints on the knife. "That much we know," he said. "That's the evidence, the facts, if you like. Boyd was there, and we can prove that he handled the murder weapon. Superintendent Burgess thinks it's enough to convict him, but I'm not so sure myself. Given the political aspect, though, he might just be right. Finding Boyd guilty will make us look good and it'll discredit everyone who seems a bit different."

"Isn't that what you want?"

"I wish you'd stop making assumptions like that. You sound like a stoned hippie at a rock festival. Maybe you'd like to call me a pig, too, and get it over with? Either that or grow up."

Mara said nothing, but Banks saw the faint flush suffuse her face.

"I want the truth," Banks went on. "I'm not out to get any group or person, just a killer. If we assume that Boyd didn't do it, then why are his prints on the knife, and why was it found on the moors about halfway between Eastvale and Maggie's Farm?"

Mara pushed her half-eaten lasagne aside and rolled a cigarette. "I'm no detective," she said, "but maybe he picked it up and threw it away on his way home, when he realized what it was."

"But why? Would you have done something as stupid as that? Bent down at a demonstration to pick up a blood-stained knife? Think about it. Boyd had no guarantee of getting away. What if he'd been caught on the spot with the knife on him?"

"He'd probably have had time to drop it if he saw the cops closing in on him."

"Yes, but it would still have his prints on it. I doubt if he'd have been calm enough to wipe it before they grabbed him. Even if he had, there would probably have been some of Gill's blood on him."

"This is all very well," Mara said, "but I don't know what you're getting at."

"I'll tell you in a moment." Banks went to the bar and bought two more drinks. The place had filled up a bit since they'd come in, and there were even two well-wrapped hikers resting their feet by the fire.

Banks sat down and drank some beer. The hair of the dog was

working nicely. "It all comes back to the knife," he said. "You recognized it; Paul Boyd must have done, too. It comes from the farm, doesn't it?"

Mara turned aside and studied the butterflies.

"You're not helping anyone by holding back, you know. I only want you to confirm what we already know."

Mara stubbed out her cigarette: "All right, so it comes from the house. What of it? If you know already, why bother to ask?"

"Because Paul might have been protecting someone, mightn't he? If he found the knife and took it away, he must have thought it was evidence pointing to someone he knew, someone at the farm. Unless you think he's just plain stupid."

"You mean one of us?"

"Yes. Who would he be most likely to protect?"

"I don't know. There were a few people up at the farm that afternoon."

"Yes, I know who was there. Could anyone have taken the knife?"

Mara shrugged. "It was on the mantelpiece, in plain view of everyone."

"Whose knife is it?"

"I don't know. It's always been there."

"Never mind, then. Let's just call it a communal flick-knife. Do you think Paul would have picked it up to protect Dennis Osmond? Or Tim and Abha?"

Mara twirled a loose strand of hair. "I don't know," she said. "He didn't know them very well."

"What part did he play that afternoon? Was he around?"

"Most of the time, yes, but he didn't say much. Paul has an inferiority complex when it comes to students and political talk. He doesn't know about Karl Marx and the rest, and he doesn't have enough confidence in his own ideas to feel he can contribute."

"So he was there but he wasn't very involved?"

"That's right. He agreed with everything in principle. I mean, he wasn't at the demo just to...just to..."

"Cause trouble?"

"No. He was there to demonstrate. He's never had a job, you know. He's got nothing to thank Thatcher's government for."

"You say the knife was usually kept on the mantelpiece. Did you see anyone pick it up that afternoon, just to fidget with, perhaps?"

"No."

"When did you notice it was missing?"

"What?"

"You must have noticed it was gone. Was it before you saw Jack Crocker walk in here with it yesterday?"

"I ... I ..."

Banks waved his hand. "Forget it. I think I get the gist. You had noticed it was missing, and for some reason you thought Paul might have taken it with him last Friday."

"No!"

"Then why did you run off and warn him?"

"Because I thought you'd pick on him if the knife had been found here. Jack Crocker works these moors. I knew when I saw him he couldn't have found it far away."

"Plausible," Banks said. "But I'm not convinced. You weren't at the demo, were you?"

"No. It's not that I don't believe in the cause, but somebody had to stay home and look after the children."

"You didn't put them to bed early and sneak out?"

"Are you accusing me?"

"I'm asking you."

"Well, I don't know how you'd expect me to do that. The others had taken the van and it's a good four miles' walk across the moor to Eastvale."

"So that leaves Paul, Zoe, Seth and Rick. Seth and Rick were arrested, but if Paul had picked up the knife at the demo, either one of them could have stabbed Gill, too."

"I don't believe it."

"Did Osmond or any of the others dislike you enough to want to put the blame on one of you?"

"I don't think so. Nobody had reason to hate us that much."

"If you really hadn't noticed the knife for some time, someone else could have taken it earlier, couldn't they? Did you have any visitors during the week?"

"I ... I don't remember."

"Do you keep the place securely locked up?"

"You must be joking. We've nothing worth stealing."

"Think about it. You see my problem, don't you? How it becomes more complicated if we leave Boyd out of it. And if someone did take the knife, there's premeditation involved. Do you know of anyone with a reason to murder PC Gill?"

"No."

"Was he mentioned that afternoon up at the farm?"

"Not that I heard. But I was in and out. You know, making tea, clearing up."

Banks drank some more Black Sheep bitter. "Does the number 1139 mean anything to you?"

Mara frowned. The lines curved down from each side of her forehead and converged at the bridge of her nose. "No," she said. "At least I don't think so. Why? Where did you find it?"

"It's not part of an address or a telephone number, for example?"

"I've told you, no. Not that I know of. It sounds vaguely familiar, but I can't place it."

"Have you ever heard of the Rossghyll Guest House?"

"Yes, it's up the dale. Why?"

Banks watched her expression closely and saw no sign that the place meant anything to her. "Never mind. Let me know if anything comes to you. It might be important."

Mara finished her drink and shifted in her chair. "Is there anything else?"

"Just one thing. It looks bad for Paul, running off like this. I know I can't ask you to turn him in, even if you do know where he is. But it really would be best for him if he gave himself up. Is there any chance of that?"

"It's unlikely. He's scared of the police, especially that bastard of a superintendent you've got." She shook her head. "I don't think he'll turn himself in."

"If you hear from him, tell him what I said. Tell him I promise he'll get a fair deal."

Mara nodded slowly. "I don't think it'll do much good, though," she said. "He won't believe me. He doesn't trust us now any more than he trusts you."

"Why not?"

"He knows I suspected him, just for a while. Paul's had so little love in his life he finds it hard enough to trust people in the first place. If they let him down, even in the slightest, then that's it."

"Still," Banks said, "if you get the chance, put in a word."

"I'll tell him. But I don't think any of us are likely to hear from Paul again. Can I go now?"

"Wait a moment and I'll give you a lift." Banks still had half a pint left and made to finish it off.

Mara stood up. "No, I'll walk. The shop's not far, and I could do with some fresh air."

"Are you sure?"

"Yes."

After she'd gone, Banks relaxed and savoured the rest of his beer. The meeting had gone better than he'd expected, and he had actually learned something about the knife. Mara had been evasive, mostly to avoid incriminating herself, but that was only to be expected. He didn't blame her for it.

Banks decided to keep his knowledge from Burgess for a while. He didn't want Dirty Dick to go charging in like a bloody elephant and frighten everyone into their corners as usual. Banks had managed to overcome some of Mara's general resentment for the police—whether through Jenny's influence, his taste in music, or sheer charm, he wasn't sure—but if Burgess turned up again, Mara's hatred for him would surely rub off on Banks as well.

By the time he set off back to Eastvale, his head had stopped aching and he felt able to tolerate some music. But he couldn't shake off the feeling that he was missing something obvious. He had the strange sensation that two insignificant things either he or Mara had said should be joined into one truth. If they made contact, a little bulb would light up and he would be that much closer to solving the case. Billie Holiday sang on regardless:

> Sad am I, glad am I
> For today I'm dreaming of
> Yesterdays.

II

Mara walked along the street, head down, thinking about her talk with Banks. Like all policemen, he asked nothing but bloody awkward questions. And Mara was sick of awkward questions. Why couldn't things just get back to normal so she could get on with her life?

"Hello, love," Elspeth greeted her as she walked into the shop.

"Hello. How's Dottie?"

"She won't eat. How she can expect to get better when she refuses to eat, I just don't know."

They both knew that Dottie wasn't going to get better, but nobody said so.

"What's wrong with you?" Elspeth asked. "You've got a face as long as next week."

Mara told her about Paul.

"I don't want to say I told you so," Elspeth said, smoothing her dark tweed skirt, "but I thought that lad was trouble from the start. You're best rid of him, all of you."

"I suppose you're right." Mara didn't agree, but there was no point arguing Paul's case against Elspeth. She hadn't expected any sympathy.

"Go in the back and get the wheel spinning, love," Elspeth said. "It'll do you a power of good."

The front part of the shop was cluttered with goods for tourists. There were locally knit sweaters on shelves on the walls, tables of pottery—some of which Mara had made—and trays of trinkets, such as key-rings bearing the Dales National Park emblem—the black face of a Swaledale sheep. As if that weren't enough, the rest of the space was taken up by fancy notepaper, glass paperweights, fluffy animals and fridge-door magnets shaped like strawberries or Humpty Dumpty.

In the back, though, the set-up was very different. First, there was a small pottery workshop, complete with wheel and dishes of brown and black metallic oxide glaze, and beyond that a drying room and a small electric kiln. The workshop was dusty and messy, crusted with bits of old clay, and it suited a part of Mara's personality. Mostly she preferred cleanliness and tidiness, but there was something special, she found, about creating beautiful objects in a chaotic environment.

She put on her apron, took a lump of clay from the bin and weighed off enough for a small vase. The clay was too wet, so she wedged it on a flat concrete tray, which absorbed the excess moisture. As she wedged—pushing hard with the heels of her hands, then pulling the clay forward with her fingers to get all the air out—she couldn't seem to lose herself in the task as usual, but kept on thinking about her conversation with Banks.

Frowning, she cut the lump in half with a cheese-wire to check for air bubbles, then slammed the pieces together much harder than usual. A fleck of clay spun off and hit her forehead, just above her right eye. She put the clay down and took a few deep breaths, trying to bring her mind to bear only on what she was doing.

No good. It was Banks's fault, of course. He had introduced her to speculations that caused nothing but distress. True, she didn't want Paul to be guilty, but if, as Banks had said, that meant someone else she knew had killed the policeman, that only made things worse.

Sighing, she started the wheel with the foot pedal and slammed the clay as close to the centre as she could. Then she drenched both it and her hands with water from a bowl by her side. As the wheel spun, clayey water flew off and splashed her apron.

She couldn't believe that any of her friends had stabbed Gill. Much better if Osmond or one of the students had done it for political reasons. Tim and Abha seemed nice enough, if a bit naïve and gushing, but Mara had never trusted Osmond; he had always seemed somehow too oily and opinionated for her taste.

But what about Rick? He had strong political views, more so than Seth or Zoe. He'd often said someone should assassinate Margaret Thatcher, and Seth had argued that someone just as bad would take her place. But it was only a policeman who'd been killed, not a politician. Despite what Rick said about the police being mere instruments of the state, paid enforcers, she couldn't believe that would make him actually kill one of them.

She leaned forward, elbows in, and pushed hard to centre the clay. At last, she managed it, and, allowing herself a smile of satisfaction, stuck her thumb in the top and pushed down about an inch. She then filled the hole with water and began to drive deeper to where she wanted the bottom of the vase to be.

Holding the inside with one finger, she slowed the wheel and began to make a ridge from the outside bottom, raising the clay to the height she wanted. It took several times to get there, pulling just a little further each time, watching the groove flow up the outside of the clay and disappear.

She was determined not to let Banks get to her. There was no way she was going to start suspecting Rick the way she had Paul. She had good reason for worrying about him, she told herself: his violent past; the blood he had lied about. And the knife had his fingerprints on it. She had no reason at all for suspecting anyone else. If only Paul could get far away and never be seen again. That would be best—if the police continued to believe he had done it but were never able to find him.

She could hear Elspeth out front trying to sell a sweater to a customer. "Traditional Dales pattern...local wool, of course...hand-knit, naturally...."

Almost there. But her hands weren't steady, and when she'd lost her concentration she had increased the pressure with her right foot, speeding up the wheel. Suddenly the clay began to spin wildly off centre—insane shapes, like Salvador Dali paintings or plastic melting in a fire—and then it collapsed in on itself on the wheel-head. And that was that. Mara took the cheese-wire and sliced off the mess. There was enough left for an egg-cup maybe, but she couldn't face starting again. That damn Banks had ruined her day.

In disgust, she tore off her wet apron and cleaned the rest of the clay from the wheel. Putting on her anorak again, she walked through to the front.

"Sorry, Elspeth," she said, "I just can't seem to concentrate today. Maybe I'll go for a walk."

Elspeth frowned. "Are you sure you're all right?"

"Yes. Don't worry, I'll be fine. Give my love to Dottie."

"Will do."

As she left the shop, the bell clanged loudly behind her.

Instead of heading back home, she climbed the stile at the end of

Mortsett Lane and struck out for the moors. As she walked, she ran over the events of last Friday afternoon up at the farm.

Most of the time she'd been in the kitchen preparing a stew for dinner—something to fortify them all against the cold and rain—and making pots of tea. The children had been a nuisance, too, she remembered. Over-excited because there were so many adults around, they'd kept coming in and tugging at her apron strings, pestering her. She hadn't been paying much attention to what the others were saying or doing in the front room even when she was there, and she hadn't noticed anybody pick up anything from the mantelpiece.

The only thing that struck a chord was that number Banks had mentioned: 1139, was it? She thought that she had heard it mentioned recently. Half heard it, really, because she had been thinking about something else at the time. The ashram, that was it. She had been remembering how, after the evening meal of brown rice and vegetables (every day!), they had all sat cross-legged in the meditation room, with its shrine to the guru and the smell of sandalwood incense heavy in the air. They had talked about how their lives had been empty until they had found the True Path. How they had been searching in all the wrong places for all the wrong things. And they had sung songs together, holding hands. "Amazing Grace" had been a particular favourite. Somehow, the gathering at the farm that afternoon had made her think of those days, though it was different in almost every way.

That was what she had been thinking about when the number had been mentioned. And she had been in the kitchen, too, because she clearly recalled the earthy feel of the potatoes she'd been peeling. Wasn't it odd how the mind worked? All the components of the experience were there, clear as day, but she couldn't remember who had mentioned the number, or in what context. And people had been in and out of the kitchen all afternoon.

Worrying about Paul again, wondering where he was, she lowered her head against the wind and marched on through the rough grass and heather.

III

There was little else to do but wait for Boyd to turn up. Whatever his suspicions, Banks had nothing concrete to go on, and he wasn't likely to have until he'd questioned Boyd. Dirty Dick was still sleeping last night's beer and Scotch off in his hotel room and Richmond was running around putting together as much information as he could get on the suspects. Criminal records weren't enough; they tended to leave out the all-too-important human factor, the snippet that gives a clue to motivation and makes the pattern clear.

Mostly Banks smoked too much and stared gloomily out of his window onto the grey market square. At four o'clock, he heard a knock on his door and called, "Come in."

PC Craig stood there looking as pleased as Punch. "We've got a line on Boyd, sir," he said, ushering in a stout middle-aged woman with curlers in her hair.

Banks pulled out a chair for her.

"This is Mrs Evans," Craig said. "I went knocking on doors on Cardigan Road to find out if anyone had seen Boyd, and Mrs Evans here said she had. She kindly offered to come in with me and talk to you, sir."

"Good work," Banks said. Craig smiled and left.

Banks asked Mrs Evans what she'd seen.

"It was about three o'clock yesterday afternoon," she began. "I know the time because I'd just got back from Tesco's with the shopping and I were struggling to get off t'bus."

"Which bus was that?"

"A forty-four. Two forty-six from t'bus station."

Banks knew the route. The bus took the long way around Cardigan Road for the benefit of local passengers, then carried on to York.

"And you saw Paul Boyd?"

"I saw a lad what looked like that photo." PC Craig had taken a prison photograph of Boyd to show from door to door. "His hair's different now, but I know it was him. I've seen him before."

"Where?"

"Around town. More often than not coming out of t'dole office. I always hold my handbag tighter when I see him. I know it's not fair to judge a book by its cover, but he looks like a bad sort to me."

"Where did you see him this time?"

"He was running up Gallows View from t'fields."

"From Relton way?"

"Aye, as t'crow flies."

"And where did he go?"

"Go? He didn't go anywhere. He were running for t'bus. Just caught it an' all. Nearly knocked me over, and me carrying two heavy shopping bags."

"What was he wearing? Do you remember?"

"Aye, that I do. A red anorak. I noticed because it looked too small for him. A bit short in t'sleeves and tight around t'armpits."

Why, Banks asked himself, wasn't he surprised that Mara had lied about Boyd's clothes?

"Was he carrying anything?"

"One of those airline bags—British Airways, I think."

"Do you remember anything else?"

"Just that he seemed in such a hurry and looked worried. I mean, as a rule, like I said, it'd be me who'd be frightened of him, but this time he looked like he were scared out of his wits."

Banks went over to the door and called Craig back. "Thanks, Mrs Evans," he said. "We appreciate your coming in like this. PC Craig here will drive you home." Mrs Evans nodded gravely and Craig escorted her out.

As soon as he was alone, Banks checked the bus timetable and found that the two forty-six from Eastvale was indeed the milk run to York; it didn't get there until 4:09. Next he phoned the York railway station and, after speaking to a succession of surly clerks, finally got put through to a pleasant woman in charge of information. From her, he discovered that Boyd could have taken a train almost anywhere between four-fifteen and five o'clock: Leeds, London, Newcastle, Liverpool, Edinburgh, plus points in between and anywhere else that connections might take him. It didn't seem much of a help, but he called Sergeant Hatchley in and put him on tracking down the train-catering crews and ticket collectors. It would mean a trip to York, and it might take a long time, but at least it was action. Of course, Hatchley pulled a long face—it seemed he had plans for the evening—but Banks ignored him. It wasn't as if Hatchley had any other work to do. Why wag your own tail when you've got a dog?

At home that evening, Banks ate a tin of Irish stew and pottered restlessly about the house waiting to hear from Hatchley. At nine o'clock, unable to concentrate on reading and almost wishing he'd gone to York himself, he turned on the TV and watched a beautiful blonde policewoman and her loud-mouthed American partner dash around spraying London with lead. It was background noise, something to fill the emptiness of the house. Finally, he could stand his own company no longer and phoned Sandra.

This time he felt even more lonely after he hung up, but the feeling didn't last as long. Twenty minutes later Hatchley phoned from York. He had managed to get the addresses of most of the ticket collectors and catering staff on the trains out of York, but none of them lived locally. All in all, the first lead seemed to be petering out. That happened sometimes. Banks told Hatchley to go over to York CID headquarters and phone as many of the crew members as he could get through to, and to call back if he came up with anything. He didn't. At eleven-thirty Banks went to bed. Maybe tomorrow morning, after Boyd's photograph appeared in all the national dailies, they would get the break they needed.

TEN

I

The big break came early Friday morning. The Rossghyll Guest House proved to be a dead end, and all the train crews out of York had been too busy to remember anyone, but an Edinburgh barber phoned to say he recognized Paul Boyd's photograph in the morning paper. Though Banks found the man's accent difficult to understand, he managed to learn what Paul's new haircut looked like. Even more important, he discovered that Paul had ditched his red anorak for a new grey duffle coat.

As soon as he hung up, Banks checked the map. Paul had headed north rather than to London or Liverpool. That had been a clever move; it had gained him time. But now that his photograph was on the front page of all the tabloid dailies, his time was running out. In addition to getting the photo in the papers as soon as possible, Banks and his men had also circulated Boyd's description to police in all major cities, ports and airports. It was routine, the best they could do with limited knowledge, but now there was somewhere concrete to start.

Assuming that Paul would ultimately want to leave the country, Banks took out his AA road map and ran his finger up the outline of the Scottish coast looking for ways out. He could find only two ferry routes north of Edinburgh on the east coast. The first, from Aberdeen to Lerwick, on the Shetlands, could take Boyd eventually to Bergen and Torshavn, in Norway, or to Seydhisfjordhur, in Iceland. But looking at the fine print, Banks saw that those ferries ran only in summer—and as the grey sky and drizzle outside testified, it certainly wasn't summer.

Another ferry ran from Scrabster, further north, to Stromness, on mainland Orkney, but that hardly seemed like a place to run and hide. Boyd would stand out there like an Eskimo in the tropics.

Turning to the west coast, Banks saw dozens of broken red lines leading to such places as Brodick, on the Isle of Arran; Port Ellen, on Islay; and Stornaway, on Lewis, in the Outer Hebrides. The whole map was a maze of small islands and ferry routes. But, Banks reasoned, none of those isolated places would suit Boyd. He would be trapped, as well as conspicuous, on any of Scotland's islands, especially at this time of year.

The only trip that made any sense in the area was Stranraer to Lame. Then Boyd would be in Northern Ireland. From there, he didn't need a passport to cross the border to the Republic. Boyd was from Liverpool, Banks remembered, and probably had Irish friends.

So the first call he made, after giving Richmond and Hatchley the task of informing the other Scottish ferry ports just in case, was to the police at Stranraer. He was told that there had been no sailings the previous day because of a bad storm at sea, but this morning was calm. There were sailings at 1130, 1530, 1900 and 0300, all with easy connections from Edinburgh or Glasgow. Banks gave Boyd's description and asked that the men there keep a special watch for him, especially at ferry boardings. Next he issued the new description to police in Edinburgh, Glasgow, Inverness, Aberdeen and Dundee, and passed a list of smaller places to PCs Craig and Tolliver downstairs. Then he phoned Burgess, who had been keeping a low profile in his hotel room since their drunken night, and gave him the news.

Banks knew from experience that leads like this could bring results in a matter of minutes or days. He was impatient to have Boyd in and get the truth out of him, as much to test his own theories as anything else, but he'd get nowhere pacing the room. Instead, he sent for some coffee and went over the files Richmond had put together.

Information is a policeman's life-blood. It comes in from many sources: interviews, gossip, criminal records, informers, employers, newspaper reporters, and registries of births, marriages and deaths. It has to be collated, filed and cross-referenced in the hope that one day it will prove useful. DC Richmond was the best ferret they had at Eastvale, in addition to being practically invisible on surveillance and handy in a chase. Sergeant Hatchley, though tough, tenacious and good at interrogation, was too lazy and desultory to tie everything together. He overlooked minor details and took the easy way out. Put more simply, Richmond enjoyed gathering and collating data, whereas Hatchley didn't. It made all the difference.

Banks spread out the sheets in front of him. He already knew a bit about Seth Cotton, but he had to be thorough in his revision. In the end, though, the only extra knowledge he gleaned was that Cotton had been born in Dewsbury and that in the mid-seventies he had settled in Hebden Bridge and led a quiet life, as far as the local police were concerned. Richmond had picked up the accident report on Alison Cotton, which didn't say very much. Banks made a note to look into it further.

There was nothing new on Rick Trelawney, either, apart from the name and address of his wife's sister in London. It might be worth a call to get more details on the divorce.

Zoe Hardacre was a local girl. Or near enough. As Jenny had said, she hailed from Whitby on the east coast, not far from Gill's home town, Scarborough. After school she had tried secretarial work, but drifted away. Employers had complained that she couldn't seem to keep her mind on the important tasks they gave her, and that she always seemed to be in another world. That other world was the one of the occult: astrology, palmistry and tarot card readings. She had studied the subjects thoroughly enough to be regarded as something of an expert by those who knew about such things. Now that the occult seemed to have come into fashion among the New Age yuppie crowd, she made a living of sorts producing detailed natal charts and giving tarot readings. Everyone seemed to agree that Zoe was harmless, a true flower child, though too young to have been part of the halcyon days of the sixties. She seemed about as political as a flower, too: she supported human rights, and she wanted the bomb banned, but that was as far as it went.

As far as Banks could make out, she had never come into contact with PC Gill. Banks imagined him bursting into her booth at Whitby, truncheon raised, and arresting her for charlatanism; or perhaps she had read his palm and told him he was a repressed homosexual. The absurdity of Banks's theories served only as a measure of his frustration over motive. The connection between one of the suspects and Gill's murder was there somewhere, but Banks didn't have enough data yet to see it. He felt as if he were trying to do a join-the-dots drawing with too few dots.

While Banks was almost convinced that Mara Delacey had been at the farm looking after the children at the time PC Gill was stabbed, he glanced over her file anyway. She had started out as a bright girl, a promising student, gaining a good degree in English, but she had fallen in with the hippie crowd when LSD, acid rock, bandanas and bright caftans were all the rage. The police knew she took drugs, but never suspected her of dealing in them. Despite one or two raids on places where she happened to be living, they had never even been able to find her in possession.

Like Zoe, Mara had done occasional stints of secretarial work, most often as a temp, and she had never really put her university education to practical use. She'd spent some time in the USA in the late seventies, mostly in California. Back in England, she had drifted for a while, then become involved with a guru and ended up living in one of his ashrams in Muswell Hill for a couple of years. After that, the farm. There was nothing to tie Mara to PC Gill, unless he had crossed her path during the two years she had been in Swainsdale.

Banks walked over to the window to rest his eyes and lit a cigarette. Outside, two elderly tourists, guidebooks in hand, paused to admire the Norman tower, then walked into the church.

Nothing in what Banks had read seemed to get him any further. If Gill did have a connection with someone at the farm, it was well buried and he'd have to dig deep for it. Sighing, he sat down again and flipped open the next folder.

Tim Fenton had been born in Ripon and was now in his second year at Eastvale College of Further Education. With Abha Sutton, he ran the Students Union there. It was a small one, and usually stuck to in-college issues, but students were upset about government health and education policies—especially as far as they were likely to affect grants—and took every opportunity to demonstrate their displeasure. Tim, whose father was an accountant, was only nineteen and had no blots on his copy-book except for attending the seminar that got him into Special Branch's files.

Abha Sutton was born in Bradford of an Indian mother and a Yorkshire father. Again, her upbringing had been solidly middle-class, and like Tim, as Richmond had tried to tell Burgess, she had no history of violence or involvement in extremist politics. She had been living with Tim for six months now, and together they had started the college Marxist Society. It had very few members, though; many of the college students were local farmers' sons studying agriculture. Still, the Social Sciences department and the Arts faculty were expanding, and they had managed to recruit a few new members among the literary crowd.

Banks read even more closely when he got to Dennis Osmond's file. Osmond was thirty-five, born in Newcastle-on-Tyne. His father had worked in the shipyards there, but unemployment had forced the family to move when Osmond was ten. Mr Osmond had found a job at the chocolate factory, where he'd been known as a strong union man, and he had been involved in the acrimonious and sometimes violent negotiations that marked its last days. Osmond himself, though given at first to more intellectual pursuits, had followed his father politically.

A radical throughout university, he had dropped out in his third year, claiming that the education he was being given was no more than an indoctrination in bourgeois values, and had taken up social work in Eastvale, where he'd been working now for twelve years. During that period, he had become one of the town's chief spokes-men, along with Dorothy Wycombe, for the oppressed, neglected and unjustly treated. He had also beat up Ellen Ventner, a woman he had lived with. Some of his cronies were the kind of people that Burgess would want shot on sight—shop stewards, feminists, poets, anarchists and intellectuals.

Whatever good Osmond had done around the place, Banks still couldn't help disliking the man and seeing him, somehow, as a sham. He couldn't understand Jenny's attraction to him, unless it was purely physical. And Jenny, of course, still didn't know that Osmond had once assaulted a woman.

It was after one o'clock, time for a pie and a pint in the Queen's Arms. But no sooner had Banks settled down in his favourite armchair by the fire to read the *Guardian* than PC Craig came rushing into the pub.

"They've got him, sir," he said breathlessly. "Boyd. Caught him trying to get on the half-past eleven ferry to Larne."

Banks looked at his watch. "It's taken them long enough to get
onto us. Are they holding him?"

"No, sir. They're bringing him down. Said they should be here late
this afternoon."

"No hurry, then, is there?" Banks lit a cigarette and rustled his
paper. "Looks like it's all over."

But it didn't feel as if it was all over; it felt more like it was just
beginning.

II

Burgess paced the office like an expectant father, puffing on his cigar
and glancing at his watch every ten seconds.

"Where the bloody hell are they?" he asked for what seemed to
Banks like the hundredth time that afternoon.

"They'll be here soon. It's a long drive and the roads can be nasty
in this weather."

"They ought to be here by now."

The two of them were in Banks's office waiting for Paul Boyd.
Scenting the kill, Burgess didn't seem able to relax, but Banks felt
unusually calm. Along Market Street the shopkeepers were shutting
up for the day, and it was already growing dark. In the office, the
heater coughed and the fluorescent light hummed.

Banks stubbed out his cigarette and said, "I'm off for some coffee.
Want some?"

"I'm jittery enough as it is. Oh, what the hell. Why not? Black,
three sugars."

In the corridor, Banks bumped into Sergeant Hatchley on his way
downstairs. "Anything?" he asked.

"No," said Hatchley. "Still waiting to hear. I'm on my way to check
with Sergeant Rowe if there's been any messages."

Banks took the two mugs of coffee back to his office and smiled
when Burgess jumped at the sound of the door opening. "It's all right,"
he said. "Don't get excited. It's only me."

"Do you think the silly buggers have got lost?" Burgess asked, scowling. "Or broken down?"

"I'm sure they know their way around just as well as anyone else."

"You can never be sure with bloody Jocks," Burgess complained. Eastvale was the farthest north he had ever been, and he had already made it quite clear that he didn't care to venture any farther. "If they've let that bastard escape—"

But he was interrupted by the phone. It was Sergeant Rowe. Boyd had arrived.

"Tell them to bring him up here." Burgess took out another Tom Thumb. He lit it, brushed some ash off his shirt and picked up his coffee.

A few moments later there was a knock at the door, and two uniformed men entered with Paul Boyd between them. He looked pale and distant—as well he might, Banks thought.

"Sorry, sir," said the driver. "We had a delay setting off. Had to wait till the doc had finished."

"Doctor?" Burgess said. "Why, what's wrong? Young dick-head here didn't hurt anyone, did he?"

"Him? No." The constable gave Paul a contemptuous glance. "Fainted when they caught him, that's all, then came round screaming about walls closing in. Had to get the doc to give him a sedative."

"Walls closing in, eh?" Burgess said. "Interesting. Sounds like a touch of claustrophobia to me. Never mind. Sit him down, and you two can bugger off now."

"See the desk sergeant about expenses and accommodation," Banks said to the two Scotsmen. "I don't suppose you'll be wanting to set off back tonight?"

The driver smiled. "No, sir. Thanks very much, sir."

"Thank you," Banks said. "There's a good pub across the road. The Queen's Arms. You can't miss it."

"Yes, sir."

Burgess could hardly wait to close the door behind them. Paul sat facing Banks in a tubular metal chair with a wooden seat and back. Burgess, preferring a free rein and the advantage of height, chose to lean against the wall or stride around as he talked.

"Get the sergeant in, will you?" he asked Banks. "With his notebook."

Banks sent for Hatchley, who arrived red-faced and out of breath a minute later. "Those bloody stairs again," he grumbled. "They'll be the death of me."

Burgess pointed to a chair in the corner and Hatchley sat down obediently. He found a clean page in his notebook and took out his pencil.

"Right," said Burgess, clapping his hands. "Let's get cracking."

Paul looked over at him, hatred and fear burning in his eyes.

If Burgess had one professional fault, Banks thought, it was as an interrogator. He couldn't seem to take any part but that of his own pushy, aggressive self. It wouldn't prove half as effective with Boyd as the Mutt & Jeff routine Banks and Hatchley had worked out, but it would have to do. Banks knew he would be forced into the role of the nice guy, the father confessor, for the duration.

"Why don't you just tell us about it?" Burgess began. "That way we won't have to resort to the Chinese water torture, will we?"

"There's nothing to tell." Boyd glanced nervously at the window. The slats of the venetian blind were up, letting in grey light from the street below.

"Why did you kill him?"

"I didn't kill anyone."

"Did you just lose your temper, is that it? Or did someone pay you? Come on, we know you did it."

"I told you, I didn't kill anyone."

"Then how come that knife with PC Gill's blood on it also happens to have your dabs all over it too? Are you trying to tell me you never touched it?"

"I didn't say that."

"What are you trying to say?"

Paul licked his lips. "Can I have a cigarette?"

"No, you bloody can't," Burgess growled. "Not until you've told us what happened."

"I didn't do anything, honestly. I've never killed anyone."

"So why did you run?"

"I was frightened."

"What of?"

"Frightened you'd fit me up for it anyway. You know I've done time."

"Is that how you think we operate, Paul?" Banks asked gently. "Is that really what you think? You're wrong, you know. If you just tell us the truth you've nothing to fear."

Burgess ignored him. "How did your prints get on the knife?"

"I must have handled it, I suppose."

"That's better. Now when did you handle it, and why?"

Paul shrugged. "Could've been anytime."

"Anytime?" Burgess shook his head with exaggerated slowness. "No it couldn't, sonny. No it couldn't. Want to know why? Your prints were right on top, numero uno, clear as day. You were the last person to handle that knife before we found it. How do you explain that?"

"All right, so I handled it after it'd been used. That still doesn't mean I killed anyone."

"It does unless you've got a better explanation. And I haven't heard one yet."

"How did you know we'd found the knife?" Banks asked.

"I saw that shepherd find it on the moor, so I took off."

He was lying, Banks thought. Mara had told him. But he let it go for the moment.

Paul fell silent. The floor creaked as Burgess paced the office. Banks lit a Silk Cut, his last, and leaned back in his chair. "Look, Paul," he said, "consider the facts. One: we found PC Gill's blood on the knife, and the doc tells us the blade fits the wound. Two: we found your prints on the handle. Three: we know you were at the demo—you were seen. Four: as soon as things start adding up, you bugger off to Scotland. Now you tell me what to make of it all. What would you think if you were me?"

Paul still said nothing.

"I'm getting fed up of this," Burgess snarled. "Let's just lock the bastard up now. He's in on a warrant. We've got enough evidence. We don't need a confession. Hell, we don't even need a motive."

"No!" Paul yelled.

"No what? You don't want us to lock you up? Dark down there, isn't it? Even a normal person feels the walls closing in on him down there, in the dark."

Paul was pale and sweating now, and his mouth was clamped so tight that the muscles in his jaw quivered.

"Come on," Banks said. "Why don't you just tell us. Save us all a lot of trouble. You say you've done nothing. If that's so, you've nothing to be worried about. Why hold back?"

"Stop mollycoddling him," Burgess said. "He's not going to talk, you know that as well as I do. He's guilty as sin, and he knows it." He turned to Hatchley. "Sergeant, send for a couple of men to take dickhead here down to the cells."

"No!" Paul leaned forward and gripped the edge of the desk until his knuckles turned white.

Burgess gestured to Hatchley to sit down again. The command was a bit premature, as the sergeant moved slowly and hadn't even got as far as putting his notebook away.

"Let me make it easy for you, Paul," Banks said. "I'll tell you what I think happened and you tell me if it's true. All right?"

Paul took a deep breath and nodded.

"You took the knife from the farm. It was usually just lying around the place. It didn't belong to anyone in particular. Mara used it occasionally to cut twine and wool; maybe Seth used it sometimes to whittle a piece of wood. But that day, you picked it up, carried it to the demo with you, and killed PC Gill. Then you folded the blade over again, made your way to the edge of the crowd, and escaped down an alley. You ran to the edge of town, then across the moors back to the farm—almost four miles. About halfway there, you realized what you'd done, panicked, and chucked the knife away. Am I right. Paul?"

"I didn't kill anyone," Paul repeated.

"But am I right about the rest?"

Silence.

"It's beginning to look like the thumbscrews for you, sonny." Burgess leaned forward, his face only inches from Paul's. "I'm getting bored. I'm sick of the bloody north and this miserable bloody weather. I want to get back home to London, the civilized world. Understand? And you're standing in my way. I don't like people who stand in my way, and if they do it for long enough, they get knocked down. Savvy?"

Paul turned to Banks. "You're right about everything else," he said. "But I didn't take the knife. I didn't kill the copper."

"Police officer to you, dick-head," Burgess snapped.

"How did you end up with it?" Banks asked.

"I got knocked down," Paul said. "At the demo. And I curled up, like, with my hands behind my neck and my knees up in my chest, in the . . . the . . . what do you call it?"

"Foetal position?"

"Yes, the foetal position. There were people all around me, it was bloody awful. I kept getting booted. Then this knife got kicked towards me. I picked it up, like you said, and made off. But I didn't know it had killed anyone. I just thought it was a good knife, too good to waste, so I took it with me. Then on the moors, I saw there was blood on it, so I flung it away. That's how it happened."

"You're a bloody liar," Burgess said. "Do you think I'm an idiot? Is that what you take me for? I might be a city boy, but even I know there aren't any lights on the fucking moors. And even you're not stupid enough to lie there in the street, boots flying all around you, police everywhere, and think, 'Oh, what a pretty blood-stained knife. I must take it home with me!' You've been talking cobblers." He turned to Banks. "That's what you get for being soft with them, see. Spin you a yarn a bloody mile long."

Swiftly, he grasped the back of Paul's neck and squeezed hard. Paul hung on to the edge of the desk and struggled, almost upsetting his flimsy chair. Then, just as abruptly, Burgess let go and leaned casually against the wall.

"Try again," he said.

Paul massaged his neck and looked pleadingly at Banks, who remained impassive.

"It's true, I tell you," Paul said. "I, swear it. I never killed him. I just picked up the knife."

"Let's assume we believe you," Banks said. "That still leaves us with a problem, doesn't it? And that problem is: why? Why did you pick up the murder weapon and sneak it away from the scene of the crime? See what I mean? It doesn't add up."

Paul shifted in his seat, casting nervous glances at Burgess, who stood just within his peripheral vision. "I didn't even know there was a crime," he said.

"Who are you protecting, Paul?" Banks asked.

"Nobody." But Paul had answered so quickly and loudly that even the most gullible person in the world would have known he was lying. Recognizing his slip, he turned red and stared down at his knees.

"The people at Maggie's Farm took you in and cared for you, didn't they?" Banks said. "They were probably the first people who ever did. You were lost, just out of jail, no job, nowhere to go, at the end of your tether, and then you met them. It's not surprising you'd want to protect them, Paul, but can't you see how transparent you're being? Who do you suspect?"

"I don't know. Nobody."

"Osmond, Tim Fenton, Abha Sutton? Would you go out of your way to protect them?"

Paul said nothing.

Burgess slapped the metal table. "Tell him!"

Paul jumped, startled by the sound. "I might," he said, glaring at Burgess. "I might protect anyone who killed a pig."

Burgess backhanded him across the face. Paul went with the blow and almost fell out of his chair.

"Try again, dick-head."

Banks grabbed Burgess by the elbow and led him over to the window. "Don't you think," he said between gritted teeth, "that you'd do better using your brains instead of your bloody fists?"

"What's wrong with you, Banks? Gone soft? Is that why they sent you up here?"

Banks jerked his head towards Paul. "He's used to hard knocks. They don't mean anything to him, and you bloody well ought to know that. You're satisfying your sadistic urges, that's all."

Burgess sniffed and turned back to Paul, who sat wiping the blood from his mouth with the back of his hand, sneering at both of them. He had overheard, Banks realized, and he probably thought the whole scene was staged just to throw him off balance. "You admit that when you found the knife on the ground you recognized it, right?" Banks asked.

"Yes."

"And you didn't want any of your friends at the farm to get into trouble."

"That's right."

"So you took it and threw it away."

"Yes. I went back on the moors to look for it a few times. I knew it was stupid just to throw it away without wiping it or anything, but I panicked. I should've taken it back to the farm and cleaned it up again, just like new. I know that now. I walked miles and miles looking for the bloody thing. Couldn't find it anywhere. And then that shepherd bloke turned up with it."

"So who did you think you were protecting?"

"I don't know." Paul took out a crumpled Kleenex and dabbed at the thin trickle of blood at the corner of his mouth. "I've already told you, I didn't see who took the knife and I didn't see who used it."

"We'll leave it for now, then." Banks turned to Burgess. "What do you think?"

"I still think he's lying. Maybe he's not as thick as he looks. He's trying to put the blame on his mates, subtle like."

"I'm not too sure," Banks said. "He could be telling the truth. Problem is he's got no proof, has he? I mean, he could tell us anything."

"And expect us to believe it. Let's lock him up for a while, anyway. Let him cool his heels. We'll question him again later and see if everything tallies."

Paul, who had been glancing from one to the other with his mouth open, let out a cry. "No! I've told you, it's the truth. What more do you want me to do?"

Burgess shrugged and leaned back against the wall. Banks reached for a cigarette; his pack was empty. "Well, I'm inclined to believe him," he said. "At least for the time being. Are you sure you didn't see who took the knife, Paul?"

"No. It could've been anyone."

"That gives us seven suspects, am I right?" Banks counted them off on his fingers. "Seth, Rick, Zoe, Mara, Osmond, Tim and Abha. Was anyone else up there during the week before the demo? Anyone we don't know about?"

"No. And Mara wasn't there."

"But the others all were? Zoe was?"

He nodded.

"Did any of them have a reason for killing PC Gill?" Banks asked. "Anyone know him? Had a run-in with him before?"

Paul shook his head. "Maybe the students. I don't know."

"But I don't think you'd go out of your way to protect them, Paul, I really don't. Was Gill mentioned that afternoon?"

"Not that I heard."

"You see, it still doesn't ring true," Banks said. "Someone picking the knife up on purpose like that and taking it along, as if whoever did it knew he was going to do it. Premeditated, that is."

"I don't know what you mean."

"Oh, I think you do." Banks smiled and stood up. "I'm just off for some cigarettes," he said to Burgess. "I doubt that we'll get much more out of him."

"Maybe not," Burgess agreed. "Pick me up a tin of Thumbs, will you?"

"Sure."

"And give my love to Glenys."

Banks was grateful for the cool fresh air outside the station. He stood for a moment, breathing in and out deeply, then crossed Market Street to the Queen's Arms.

"Twenty Silk Cut and a tin of Tom Thumbs, please, Cyril," he said.

"These for that mate of yours?" Cyril asked, slapping the cigars on the counter.

"I wish you'd stop calling him my mate. You'll be getting me a bad name."

"Well, my Glenys has been acting a bit funny lately. She's an impressionable lass, if you know what I mean, and headstrong. Gets it from that bloody mother of hers. It's just little things, things only a husband notices, but if I find that your mate's behind it, I'll ... Well, I needn't spell it out for you, need I, Mr Banks?"

"Not to me, Cyril, no. Better not. I'll inform him of your concern."

"If you would."

Back outside, Banks noticed that the light had gone out in his office window. No doubt they'd sent Boyd down to the cells and gone for coffee. As he crossed the street, he heard a scream. It came from above, he was certain of that, but he couldn't pin-point it exactly. Apprehensive, he hurried back upstairs and opened the door. The office was dark, but it wasn't empty.

When he flicked on the fluorescent light, Banks saw that Sergeant Hatchley had been sent away and only Boyd and Burgess remained. The slats on the venetian blind had been completely closed, shutting out all the light from the street, a feat Banks himself had never been able to manage in all the time he'd been in Eastvale.

Boyd was whimpering in the chair, sweating and gasping for breath. He looked up in terror when Banks came back. "He turned the lights off," he said, struggling to get the words out, "and closed the blinds, the bastard."

Banks glared at Burgess, who simply flashed him a "who, me?" look and said, "I think he was telling the truth. At least, if he wasn't, he's just given the most convincing performance of his life."

"Under duress." Banks tossed him the cigars. Burgess caught the tin deftly, unwrapped it and offered Banks one. "Celebrate with me?"

"I prefer these." Banks lit a Silk Cut.

"You can have a smoke now if you want, kid," Burgess said to Paul. "Though with a breathing problem like yours, I'd watch it."

Paul lit up and coughed till he was red in the face. Burgess laughed.

"So, what now?" Banks asked.

"We lock him up and go home." Burgess looked at Paul. "You're going to have plenty of time for long chats with the prison shrink about that claustrophobia of yours," he said. "In fact, you could say we're doing you a favour. Don't they say the best way to deal with a phobia is to confront it? And the treatment's free. What more could you ask for? You'd have to wait years on National Health for that kind of service."

Paul's jaw slackened. "But I didn't do it. You said you believed me."

"It takes a lot more than that to convince me. Besides, there's tampering with evidence, accessory after the fact of murder, wasting police time, resisting arrest. You've got a lot of charges to face."

Burgess called downstairs and two constables came to escort Paul to the cells. He didn't struggle this time; he seemed to know there was no point.

When they were alone in the office, Banks turned to Burgess. "If you pull a stunt like that on my patch again," he said, "I'll kick your balls into the middle of next week, superintendent or no fucking superintendent."

Burgess held his gaze, but Banks felt that he took the threat more seriously than he had Rick Trelawney's.

After the staring match, Burgess smiled and said, "Good, I'm glad we've got that out of the way. Come on, I could murder a pint."

And he put his arm around Banks's shoulder and steered him towards the door.

ELEVEN

I

The rattle of the letter-box and the sound of mail slapping against the hall mat woke Banks early on Saturday morning. His mouth tasted like the bottom of a bird cage, and his tongue felt dry and furry from too many cigarettes and too much ale. He and Burgess had murdered more than one pint after Boyd's interrogation. It was getting to be a habit.

Banks still wasn't used to waking up alone in the big bed. He missed Sandra's warm body stirring beside him, and he missed the grumbles and complaints of Brian and Tracy getting ready for school or for Saturday morning shopping expeditions. But they'd all be back in a few days. With a bit of luck, the Gill case would be over by then and he would be able to spend some time with them.

Over coffee and burnt toast—why the toaster only burnt toast when *he* made it, Banks had no idea—he examined the mail: two bills, a letter and a new blues-anthology tape from Barney Merritt, an old friend on the Met, and, finally, just what he'd been waiting for—the package from Tony Grant.

The information, which Grant had copied in longhand from PC Gill's files, made interesting reading. Ever since picket-control duty at the Orgreave coking plant during the miners strike in 1984, Gill had volunteered for overtime at just about every demonstration that had come up in Yorkshire: protests outside U.S. missile bases, marches against South Africa, National Front meetings, anything that had seemed likely to turn into a free-for-all. Gill certainly wasn't the only one, but he seemed to have been the kind of person who graduated from school bully to legalized goon. Banks wouldn't have been surprised if he had carved notches in his truncheon.

There were complaints against him, too, generally for excessive use of force in subduing demonstrators. However, there were surprisingly few of these, and no action had been taken on them, except perhaps a slap on the wrist now and then. The most interesting complaint came from Dennis Osmond, charging Gill with using unnecessary violence during a local demonstration in support of the Greenham Common women about two years ago. Another familiar name on the list was Elizabeth Dale, who had accused Gill of lashing out indiscriminately against her and her friends during a peaceful anti-nuclear march in Leeds. Banks couldn't immediately place her, as she didn't seem to belong to the pattern that included Paul Boyd and Dennis Osmond, but he knew the name. He made a note to check it in his files, then read carefully through the rest of the material. No other names stood out.

But the most important piece of information Banks gleaned from the files had nothing to do with Gill's behaviour; in fact, it was so damn simple he cursed himself out loud for not seeing it sooner. He always thought of his colleagues by name, even the uniformed men. Most policemen did—especially plain-clothes detectives. But it was a different matter for others. How could a member of the public name a particular police officer in a complaint, or even in a letter of commendation? He couldn't. That's why the numbers were so important. Called "collar-numbers" because they originally appeared on the small stand-up collars of the old police uniform, the metal numbers are now fixed to the officer's epaulettes. And there was Gill's number staring him right in the face: PC 1139.

He remembered driving back from the Black Sheep after his lunch-time chat with Mara. He had been listening to Billie Holiday and wondering what it was he'd said that should have meant more than it did. Now he knew. He had mentioned Gill's name and, in his next question, the number. They had almost leaped together to complete the circuit, but not quite.

Banks put the papers away, grabbed his coat and hurried out to the car. It was a beautiful morning. The wind still blew cool, but the sun shone in a cloudless sky. After the miserable late-winter weather they'd been having recently, the smell of spring in the air—that strange mixture of wet grass and last autumn's decay—was almost overwhelming. As the pipes on Keats's Grecian urn appealed not to the "sensual ear" but played "spirit ditties of no tone", so this smell didn't so much titillate the sensual nose as it exhaled a scent of promise, a special feeling of anticipation, and a definite quickening of the life force. It made him want to slip the Deller Consort recording of Shakespeare's songs into his Walkman and step lightly to work. But he would need the car for the visit he had to make later in the day. Still, he thought, no reason why he shouldn't follow the musical impulse where it led him, especially on a day like this, so he made a special trip back inside and found the cassette to play in the car.

It was after nine when he got to the office. Richmond was playing with the computer, and Sergeant Hatchley was struggling over the *Daily Mirror* crossword. There was no sign of Dirty Dick. He sent for coffee and went to peer out of the window. The good weather had certainly enticed people outdoors. Tourists drifted in and out of the church, and some, wearing anoraks over warm sweaters, actually sat on the worn plinth of the market cross already eating KitKats and drinking tea from Thermos flasks.

Banks spent an hour or more staring out on the busy square trying to puzzle out why PC Gill's number had turned up in Seth Cotton's old notebook. Had it even been Cotton's handwriting? He examined the book again. It was hard to tell, because only the faint imprint remained. The numbers were exaggeratedly large, too, unlike the smaller scrawl of most of the measurements. Carefully, he rubbed a soft pencil over the page again, but he couldn't get a better impression.

He remembered Mara Delacey telling him that Paul spent a lot of time working with Seth in the shed, so the number could just as likely have been written down by him. If so, that implied premeditation. Boyd's name hadn't appeared on Grant's list of complainants, but that didn't mean they hadn't come into conflict before. A kid with a record, like Paul, would hardly walk into the nearest police station and lodge a complaint.

The only thing of which Banks could be sure, after two cups of coffee and three cigarettes, was that somebody at Maggie's Farm knew of PC Gill before the demonstration and expected him to be there. The number had been written down hard enough to press through, and that indicated some degree of passion or excitement. Who had a grudge against Gill? And who had access to Seth Cotton's notebook? Anybody, really, as he never locked the shed. Boyd was the best candidate, given the evidence against him, but Banks had a nagging suspicion that he'd been telling the truth, especially when he stuck to his story after Burgess had put the lights out on him. But if Boyd was telling the truth, who was he more likely to be protecting than Seth, Mara, Rick or Zoe?

And where, Banks asked himself, did that leave Osmond, Tim and Abha?

Tim and Abha had so far been the only ones to admit to knowing of PC Gill's existence, which probably indicated that they had nothing to hide. Banks doubted, in fact, that they had anything to do with the murder. For a start, they had no real connection with the farm people other than a mutual interest in wanting to save the human race from total obliteration.

Osmond, however, was a friend of Rick, Seth and the rest. He had been up to the farm often, and he knew Gill's number all right, because he had used it on his complaint. Perhaps he had written it in the notebook himself, or had seen it there and recognized it. Paul Boyd may have been telling the truth about not killing PC Gill, but had he been an accomplice? Had there been two people involved?

Like so many of Banks's thinking sessions, this one was raising far more questions than it answered. Sometimes he thought he could solve cases only after formulating a surfeit of questions; he reached saturation point, and the overflow produced the answers.

Before he did anything else, though, he needed something to stop the growling in his stomach. Burnt toast wasn't sufficient fuel for a detective.

On his way out to the Golden Grill for elevenses, he bumped into Mara Delacey entering the station.

"I want to see Paul," she said, brandishing the morning paper. "It says here you've caught him. Is it true?"

"Yes."

"Where is he?"

"Downstairs."

"Is he all right?"

"Of course he is. What do you think we are, the Spanish Inquisition?"

"I wouldn't put anything past Burgess. Can I see Paul?"

Banks thought for a moment. It would be unusual to grant such permission, and Burgess wouldn't like it if he found out, but there was no reason Mara shouldn't see Boyd. Besides, it would give Banks the opportunity to ask him a couple of questions in Mara's presence. Through body language and facial expressions, people often gave more away than they intended when friends or enemies were nearby.

"All right," he said, leading the way down. "But I'll have to be there."

"As you can see, I've not brought him a birthday cake with a file in it."

Banks smiled. "Wouldn't do him much good anyway. There aren't any bars on the window. He could only escape to the staircase and walk right up here."

"But his claustrophobia," Mara said, alarmed. "It'll be unbearable for him."

"We got a doctor." Banks relished his small victory over Burgess's callousness. "He's been given tranquillizers, and they seemed to help."

The four cells were the most modern part of the building. Recently overcrowded with demonstrators, they were now empty except for Paul Boyd. Mara seemed surprised to find clean white tiles and bright light instead of dark, dank stone walls. The only window, high and deep-set in the wall, was about a foot square and almost as thick. The cells always made Banks think of hospitals, so much so that he fancied he could smell Dettol or carbolic every time he went down there.

Boyd sat on his bunk and stared out through the bars at his visitors.

"Hello," Mara said. "I'm sorry, Paul."

Boyd nodded.

Banks could sense tension between them. It was due in part to his being there, he knew, but it seemed to go deeper than that, as if they were unsure what to say to each other.

"Are you all right?" she asked.

"I'm okay."

"Will you be coming back?"

Paul glared at Banks. "I don't know. They're determined to charge me with something."

Banks explained the procedure.

"So he might still be arrested for murder?" Mara asked.

"Yes."

There were tears in her eyes. Paul stared at her suspiciously, as if he wasn't sure whether she was acting or not.

Banks broke the tense silence. "Does the number 1139 mean anything to you?" he asked Boyd.

Paul seemed to consider the question, and his answer was an unequivocal no. Banks thought he was telling the truth.

"What do you know about that old notebook Seth kept in his workshop?"

Paul shrugged. "Nothing. It was just for addresses, measurements and stuff."

"Did you ever use it?"

"No. I was just an assistant, a dogsbody."

"It wasn't like that, Paul," Mara said. "And you know it."

"It doesn't matter now, does it? Except maybe it'll get me a job in the prison workshop."

"Did anybody else ever use it, other than Seth?" asked Banks.

"Why should they?" Paul was obviously puzzled by the line of questioning. "It wasn't important."

"Do you know who took the knife?"

Paul looked at Mara as he answered. "I've already told you I don't, haven't I?"

"I'm giving you another chance. If you really aren't responsible for PC Gill's death, any help you give us will count for you."

"Oh, sure!" Paul got to his feet and started pacing the narrow cell. "Why don't you just bugger off and leave me alone? I've nothing more to tell you. And tell the quack to bring me another pill."

"Is there anything we can do, Paul?" Mara asked.

"You can leave me alone, too. I curse the day I met you and the rest of them. You and your bloody protests and demonstrations. Look where you've got me."

Mara swallowed, then spoke softly. "We're still on your side, you know. It wasn't anything to do with me, with any of us, that you got caught. You can come back to the farm whenever you want."

Paul glared at her, and Banks could sense the questions each wanted to ask and the answers they hoped for. But they couldn't talk because he was there. Mara would implicate herself if she assured Paul she hadn't tipped the police off about the warning, the money and the clothes she'd given him. Paul would incriminate her if he thanked her or questioned her about these things.

"Come on." Banks took Mara's arm gently. She shook his hand off but walked beside him back upstairs. "You've seen that he's all right. No bruises."

"None that show, no."

"How did you get here?" Banks asked as they walked out of the station into the glorious day.

"I walked over the moors."

"I'll give you a lift back."

"No. I'm happy walking, thanks."

"No strings. I'm going up there anyway."

"Why?"

"Just a few questions for Seth."

"Questions, bloody questions."

"Come on."

Mara got into the Cortina beside him. She sat in silence with her hands on her lap as Banks pulled out of the car-park and set off up North Market Street for the Swainsdale road. They passed the Community Centre steps, where Gill had been stabbed. The spot looked as innocent as everywhere else that day; no signs of violence and bloodshed lingered in the grey stone. Banks pushed the tape in and the Deller Consort sang "It Was a Lover and His Lass." Mara managed a weak smile at the hey-noni-nos, peering curiously at Banks as if she found it hard to connect him with the music he played.

A couple of fishermen sat under the trees in the river-meadows, and there were more walkers on the road than Banks had seen since the previous October. Even the wind chimes up at Maggie's Farm seemed to be playing a happier tune, despite the misfortune that had befallen the place. But nature is rarely in harmony with human affairs,

Banks thought. It follows its predetermined natural cycles, while we fall victim to random, irrational forces, thoughts and deeds. It's natural to identify with the rain and clouds when we feel depressed, but if the sun shines brightly and we still feel depressed, we don't bother bringing the weather into it at all.

Banks found Seth in his workshop. Wearing his overalls, he was bent over the bench, planing a long piece of wood. Shavings curled and fell to the floor, releasing the clean scent of pine. Noticing his guest, he paused and put down his plane. Banks leaned against the wall near the dusty bookcase.

"What is it now?" Seth asked. "I thought you'd got your man."

"It does look like it. But I'm the kind who likes to tie up loose ends."

"Unlike your friend."

"Superintendent Burgess doesn't concern himself overmuch with little details," Banks said. "But he doesn't have to live up here."

"How is Paul?"

Banks told him.

"So, what are your loose ends?"

"It's that number in your book." Banks frowned and scratched the scar by his right eye. "I've found out what it means."

"Oh?"

"It was PC Gill's number. PC 1139."

Seth picked up his plane and began to work slowly at the pine again.

"Why was it written in your notebook?"

"It's quite a coincidence, I'll admit that," Seth said without looking up. "But I told you, I haven't got the faintest idea what it meant."

"Did you write it down?"

"I don't remember doing so. But pick any page of the book and the odds are I'd hardly have it ingrained deeply in my memory."

"Did you know PC Gill?"

"I never had the pleasure."

"Could anyone else have scribbled it down?"

"Of course. I don't lock the place up. But why should they?"

Banks had no idea. "Why did you tear the page out?"

"I don't know that I did. I don't recall doing so. Look, Chief

Inspector—" Seth put his plane aside again and leaned against the bench, facing Banks—"you're chasing phantoms. Anybody could have jotted that number down, and it could mean anything."

"Like what?"

"A phone number. They still have four digits around here, you know. Or it could be part of a measurement, a sum of money, almost anything."

"It's not a phone number," Banks said. "Do you think I haven't checked? It is PC Gill's number, though."

"Coincidence."

"Possibly. But I'm not convinced."

"That's your problem." Seth picked up the plane again and began working more vigorously.

"It could be your problem, too, Seth."

"Is that a threat?"

"No. I leave those to Superintendent Burgess. What I mean is, it would be very convenient if someone else had killed Gill—you, say—and Paul Boyd took the blame. He really doesn't have a leg to stand on, you know."

"What do you mean?" Seth paused again.

"I mean the odds are that he'll go down for it."

"Are you saying he's confessed?"

"I'm not free to talk about things like that. I'm just saying it looks bad, and if you know of anything that might help him you'd better tell me pretty damn quick. Unless it's to your advantage that Boyd gets charged with murder."

"I don't know anything." Seth bent over the length of pine and caressed the surface. His voice was tight, and he kept his face averted.

"I can understand it if you're protecting someone," Banks went on. "Like Mara tried to protect Paul. But think about what you're doing. By covering for someone else, you almost certainly condemn Paul. Does he mean so little to you?"

Seth slammed down the plane. He turned to face Banks, his face red and eyes bright. The vein by his temple throbbed. "How can you talk like that?" he said in a shaky voice. "Of course Paul means a lot to us. He's not been tried yet, you know. It's only you bastards who've convicted him so far. If he didn't do it, then he'll get off, won't he?"

Banks lit a Silk Cut. "I'm surprised you've got such faith in justice, Seth. I'm afraid I haven't. The way things are these days, he may well be made an example of."

Seth snorted. "What would you do? Fix the jury?"

"We wouldn't need to. The jury's made up of ordinary men and women—law-abiding, middle-class citizens for the most part. They'll take one look at Boyd and want to lock him up and throw away the key."

"He'll manage. And we'll stick by him. We won't let him down."

"Admirable sentiments. But it might not be enough. Where did you live before you bought this place?"

Surprised, Seth had to think for a moment. "Hebden Bridge. Why?"

"Where did you get the money from, for the farm?"

"If it's any of your business, I saved some and inherited a little from a dotty aunt. We...I also had a small business there, which I sold—a second-hand bookshop."

"What kind of work did you do?"

"This kind." Seth gestured around the workshop. "I was a jack-of-all-trades, showed the true Thatcherite entrepreneurial spirit. I made good money for good work. I still do."

"Who ran the bookshop, then?"

"My wife." Seth spoke between his teeth and turned back to his wood.

"There was some kind of accident, wasn't there?" Banks said. "Your wife?" He knew some of the details but wanted to see how Seth reacted.

Seth took a deep breath. "Yes, there was. But it's still none of your business."

"What happened?"

"Like you said. I had a wife. There was an accident."

"What kind?"

"She was hit by a car."

"I'm sorry."

Seth turned on him. "Why? Why the bloody hell should you be sorry? You didn't even know Alison. Just get the fuck out and let me get on with my work. I've nothing more to say to you."

Banks lingered at the doorway. "One more thing: Elizabeth Dale. Is that name familiar to you?"

"I know someone called Liz Dale, yes."

"She's the woman who ran off from the mental hospital and ended up here, isn't she?"

"Why ask if you know already?"

"I wasn't sure, but I thought so. Do you know anything about a complaint she made against PC Gill?"

"No. Why should I?"

"She used his number: 1139."

"So?"

"Bit of a coincidence, that's all: her complaint, his number in your notebook. Could she have written it?"

"I suppose so. But so could anyone else. I really don't know anything about it." Seth sounded tired.

"Have you seen her recently? Has she been up here in the past few weeks?"

"No."

"Do you know where she is?"

"We've lost touch. It happens."

Seth bent over the pine again and Banks left, avoiding the house by using the side gate. In the car, he contemplated going to the barn to talk to Rick and Zoe. But they could wait. He'd had enough of Maggie's Farm for one day.

II

Burgess winked at Glenys, who smiled and blushed. Banks was the only one to notice Cyril's expression darken. They carried their drinks and ploughman's lunches back to the table.

"How's Boyd?" Burgess asked.

"He's all right. I didn't know you cared."

Burgess spat the remains of a pickled onion into his napkin: "Bloody awful stuff. Gives me heartburn."

"I wouldn't be surprised if you're developing an ulcer," Banks said, "the way you go at life."

Burgess grinned. "You only live once."

"Are you going to stick around and see what happens?"

"I'll stay a few more days, yes." He eyed Glenys again. "I'm not quite finished up here yet."

"Don't tell me you're getting to like the north?"

"At least the bloody weather's improved, even if the people haven't."

"Friendliest lot in the country, when you get to know them."

"Tell me about it." Burgess shoved in a chunk of Wensleydale and washed it down with Double Diamond.

Banks grimaced. "No wonder you get heartburn."

Burgess pushed his plate aside and lit a cigar. "Tell me honestly, Banks. What do you make of Boyd? Guilty or not?"

"He's obviously involved. Deeply involved. But if you're asking do I think he killed Gill, the answer's no, I don't."

"You could be right. He certainly stuck to his guns under pressure, and I don't think he's that tough." Burgess prodded the air with his cigar. "Personally, I don't give a damn what happens to Boyd. I'd rather see him go down for it than no one at all. But give me some credit. I'm not a bloody idiot, and if I'm not satisfied everything's wrapped up I like to know why. I get nagging feelings like every copper."

"And you have one about Boyd?"

"A little one."

"So what are you going to do?"

"Consider the alternatives. You heard what he said last night, about the others going up to the farm on Friday afternoon. That covers just about everyone we've had our eye on since this business started. Who do you reckon?"

Banks sipped some beer to wash down his lunch. "It depends," he said. "Any of the people Boyd mentioned could have got access to the knife, and so could anyone else who went up there a few days before the demo. Nobody had noticed whether it was missing or not—at least, nobody admits to noticing. If you're convinced it was a terrorist act, then obviously you're best starting with the most politically active of them: Osmond. Trelawney and the students. On the other hand, if you accept that there could have been some other motive, then you have to rethink the whole thing in more human terms: revenge, hatred, that kind of thing. Or maybe someone was trying to put the blame on the farm people, someone who had a reason to hate them or want them off their land."

Burgess sighed. "You make it sound so bloody complicated. Do you really think that's where the answer lies?"

"It's possible, yes." Banks took a deep breath. "Gill was a bastard," he said. "He liked thumping people, bashing heads. He's volunteered for more crowd control duties than I've had hot dinners. And another thing: Osmond made an official complaint about him for using undue force in another demo a couple of years back. So did a woman called Elizabeth Dale, in a separate incident. And she's got some connection with the farm crowd."

Burgess drank some more beer and sucked his lips. "How do you know?" he asked quietly.

Banks had been expecting this. He remembered Burgess's order not to look into Gill's record. "Anonymous tip," he said.

Burgess narrowed his eyes and stared as Banks took out a cigarette and lit it.

"I don't know if I believe you," he said finally.

"It doesn't bloody matter, does it? It's what I'm telling you that counts. Do you want to get to the bottom of this or don't you?"

"Go on."

"I'm saying we've got two options: terrorism or personal motive. Maybe they're both mixed up as well, I don't know."

"And where does Boyd come in?"

"Either he did exactly as he told us, or he was an accomplice. So we dig deeper into his political background. Richmond's doing all he can at the computer, checking people Boyd knew in jail and any others he hung about with when the local police were keeping an eye on him. He spent some time in Ireland, which is where he was heading when we caught him, and some of the people he knew had connections with the IRA. We can't prove it, but we're pretty damn sure. We also have to consider the personal motive. Gill was the kind of person to make enemies, and it looks like Osmond was one of them."

"In the meantime," Burgess said, "we hang onto Boyd."

Banks shook his head. "I don't think so."

"Let him go?"

"Yes. Why not?"

"He scarpered last time. What's to stop him doing it again?"

"I think he found out that he'd nowhere to go. If you let him out, he'll go back to the farm and stay there."

"But why let him out at all?"

"Because it might stir something up. If he's not guilty, there's still a chance he might know who is. He might slip up, set something moving."

Burgess swirled the beer in his glass. "So we charge him with tampering with evidence, wasting police time, and let him out. Is that what you're suggesting?"

"For the time being, yes. Have you got a better idea?"

"I'm not convinced," Burgess said slowly, "but I'll go along with it. And," he added, poking his cigar in Banks's direction, "on your head be it, mate. If he buggers off again, you'll answer for it."

"All right."

"And we'll keep him in another night, just so he gets the message. I'll have another little chat with him, too."

It was a compromise. Burgess was not the kind of man to give way completely to someone else's idea. It was the best deal he would get, so Banks agreed.

Burgess smiled over at Glenys. Down at the far end of the bar, a glass broke. "I'll go get us a couple more, shall I?"

"Let me." Banks stood up quickly. "It's my round." It wasn't, but the last thing they needed was a lunch-time punch-up between the landlord of the Queen's Arms and a detective superintendent from Scotland Yard.

"I'll take Osmond again, too," Burgess said, when Banks got back. "I don't trust you when that bird of his is around. You go all gooey-eyed."

Banks ignored him.

"Can I take DC Richmond with me?" Burgess asked.

"What's wrong with Sergeant Hatchley?"

"He's a lazy sod," Burgess said. "How he ever made sergeant I don't bloody know. Every time he's been with me he's just sat there like a stuffed elephant."

"He has his good points," Banks said, surprised to find himself defending Hatchley. He wondered if the sergeant really had been nurturing a dream of Burgess's inviting him to join some elite Yard squad just because they both believed in the privatization of everything and in an England positively bristling with nuclear missiles. If he had, tough titty.

The difference between them, Banks thought, was that Hatchley just assumed attitudes or inherited them from his parents; he never thought them out. Burgess, on the other hand, really believed that the police existed to hold back the red tide and keep immigrants in their place so that the government could get on with the job of putting the Great back in Britain. He also believed that people like Paul Boyd should be kept off the streets so that decent citizens could rest easy in their beds at night. It never occurred to him for a moment that he might not pass for decent himself.

Banks followed Burgess back to the station and went up to his office. He had a phone call to make.

TWELVE

I

South of Skipton, the landscape changes dramatically. The limestone dales give way to millstone grit country, rough moorland for the most part, bleaker and wilder than anything in Swainsdale. Even the drystone walls are made of the dark purplish gritstone. The landscape is like the people it breeds: stubborn, guarded, long of memory.

Banks drove through Keighley and Haworth into open country, with Haworth Moor on his right and Oxenhope Moor on his left. Even in the bright sun of that springlike day, the landscape looked sinister and brooding. Sandra hated it; it was too spooky and barren for her. But Banks found something magical about the area, with its legends of witches, mad Methodist preachers and the tales the Brontë sisters had spun.

Banks slipped a cassette in the stereo and Robert Johnson sang "Hellhound on My Trail." West Yorkshire was a long way from the Mississippi delta, but the dark, jagged edges of Johnson's guitar seemed to limn the landscape, and his haunted, doom-laden lyrics captured its mood.

Dominated by mill-towns at the valley bottoms and weaving communities on the heights, the place is a product of the Industrial Revolution. Majestic old mills with their tall chimneys of dark, grainy millstone grit still remain. Many have now been scoured of two hundred years' soot and set up as craft and antique markets.

Hebden Bridge is a mill-town turned tourist trap, full of bookshops and antique shops. Not so long ago, it was a centre of trouser and corduroy manufacturing, but since the seventies, when the hippies from Leeds and Manchester invaded, it has been more of a place for arts festivals, poetry readings in pubs and other cultural activities.

Banks drove down the steep hill from the moors into the town itself. Rows of tall terraced houses run at angles diagonally along the hillside and overlook the mills at the valley bottom. They look like four-storey houses, but are actually rows of two-storey houses built one on top of the other. You enter the lower house from a street or ginnel at one level, and the upper from a higher one at the back. All of which made it very difficult for Banks to find Reginald Lee's house.

Lee, Banks had discovered from his phone call to PC Brooks of the Hebden Bridge police, was a retired shop owner living in one of the town's two-tiered buildings. Just over three years ago he had been involved in an accident on the town's busy main street—a direct artery along the Calder valley from east to west—which had resulted in the death of Alison, Seth Cotton's wife.

Banks had also discovered from the police that there had been nothing suspicious about her death, and that Mr Lee had not been at fault. But he wanted to know more about Seth Cotton's background, and it seemed that the death of his wife was a good place to start. He was still convinced that the number written so boldly in the old notebook was PC Gill's and not just part of a coincidentally similar calculation. Whether Seth himself had written it down was another matter.

Lee, a small man in a baggy, threadbare pullover, answered the door and frowned at Banks. He clearly didn't get many visitors. His thinning grey hair was uncombed, sticking up on end in places as if he'd had an electric shock, and the room he finally showed Banks into was untidy but clean. It was also chilly. Banks kept his jacket on.

"Sorry about the mess," Lee said in a high-pitched, whining voice. "Wife died two years back and I just can't seem to get the hang of housework."

"I know what you mean." Banks moved some newspapers from a hard-backed chair. "My wife's been away at her mother's for two weeks now and the house feels like it's falling apart. Mind if I smoke?"

"Not at all." Lee shuffled to the sideboard and brought an ashtray. "What can I help you with?"

"I'm sorry to bring all this up again," Banks said. "I know it must be painful for you, but it's about that accident you were involved in about three years ago."

Lee's eyes seemed to glaze over at the mention. "Ah, yes," he said. "I blame that for Elsie's death, too, you know. She was with me at the time, and she never got over it. I retired early myself. Couldn't seem to ..." He lost his train of thought and stared at the empty fireplace.

"Mr Lee?"

"What? Oh, sorry, Inspector. It is Inspector, isn't it?"

"It'll do," Banks said. "The accident."

"Ah, yes. What is it you want to know?"

"Just what happened, in as much detail as you can remember."

"Oh, I can remember it all." He tapped his forehead. "It's all engraved there in slow motion. Just let me get my pipe. It seems to help me concentrate. I have a bit of trouble keeping my mind on track these days." He fetched a briar from a rack by the fireplace, filled it with rubbed twist and put a match to it. The tobacco flamed up and blue smoke curled from the bowl. A child's skipping rhyme drifted in from the street:

> *Georgie Porgie, pudding and pie,*
> *Kiss the girls and make them cry.*

"Where was I?"

"The accident."

"Ah, yes. Well, it happened on a lovely summer's day. The sixteenth of July. One of those days when you can smell the moorland heather and the wild flowers even here in town. Not a cloud in the sky and everyone in that relaxed, dozy mood you get in summer. Elsie and I were going for a ride to Hardcastle Crags. We used to do a lot of our courting up there when we were youngsters, like. So whenever the weather was good, off we went. I wasn't doing more than thirty—and I hadn't a drop of drink in me, never touch the stuff—when I came upon this lass riding along on her bicycle on my inside." He faltered, sucked at his pipe as if it were an oxygen mask, and carried on. "She was a bit wobbly, but then a lot of cyclists are. I always took special care when there were cyclists around. Then it happened. My front wheels were a foot or two away from her back.

She was over by the kerb, like, not directly in front of me, and she just keeled over."

"Just like that?"

"Aye." He seemed amazed, even though he must have told the story dozens of times to the police. "As if she'd hit a jutting stone. But there wasn't one. She might have bounced off the kerb or something. And she fell right in front of the car. I'd no time to stop. Even if I'd only been going five miles an hour I wouldn't have had time. She went right under the wheels. Keeled over, just like that."

Banks let the silence stretch. Tobacco crackled in the pipe bowl and the repetitive chant continued outside. "You said she was wobbling a bit," he asked finally. "Did she seem drunk or anything?"

"Not especially. Just like she was a learner, maybe."

"Have you ever come across a policeman by the name of Edwin Gill. PC 1139?"

"Eh? Pardon me. No, the name and number aren't familiar. It was PC Brooks I dealt with at first. Then Inspector Cummings. I don't remember any Gill. Is he from around here?"

"Did you ever meet Seth Cotton?"

"Yes," Lee said, relighting his pipe. "I plucked up the courage to go and see him in the hospital. He knew all the details and said he didn't blame me. He was very forgiving. Of course, he was in a shocking state, still beside himself with grief and anger. But not at me. I only went the once."

"In hospital? What was he doing there?"

Lee looked surprised. "I thought you'd have known. He tried to kill himself a couple of days after the hospital phoned him about the accident. Slit his ankles. And they say he smashed the phone to bits. But someone found him before it was too late. Have you seen the lad lately?"

"Yes."

"And how is he?"

"He seems to be doing all right." Banks told him about the farm and the carpentry.

"Aye," Lee said. "He mentioned he were a carpenter." He shook his head slowly. "Terrible state he were in. Bad enough losing the lass, but the baby as well...."

"Baby?"

"Aye. Didn't you know? She were pregnant. Five months. The police said she might have fainted, like, had a turn, because of her condition...."

Lee seemed to drift off again, letting his pipe go out. Banks couldn't think of any more questions, so he stood up to leave. Lee noticed and snapped out of his daze.

"Off, are you?" he said. "Sure you won't stay for a cup of tea?"

"No, thank you, Mr Lee. You've been very helpful. I'm sorry I had to put you through it all again."

"There's hardly a day goes by when I don't think on it," Lee said.

"You shouldn't keep torturing yourself that way," Banks told him. "Whichever way you look at it, no blame can possibly attach itself to you."

"Aye, no blame," Lee repeated. And his piercing inward gaze put Banks in mind of the actor Trevor Howard at his conscience-stricken best. There was nothing more to say. Feeling depressed, Banks walked back out to the street in the chilly spring sunshine. The children paused and stared as he passed by.

It was after five o'clock and the people down in the town were hurrying home from work. All Banks had to look forward to was a tin of ravioli on toast—which he would no doubt burn—and another evening alone.

Looking up the hillside to the west, he thought of Heptonstall, a village at the summit. He'd heard that the pub there served Timothy Taylor's beer, something he'd never tried. It had been a wasted and depressing afternoon as far as information was concerned, so he might as well salvage it somehow.

Alison Cotton's death had obviously been a tragic accident, and that was all there was to it. She had either rubbed against the kerb and lost her balance, or she had fainted, perhaps due to the effects of her pregnancy. Banks could hardly blame Seth for not wanting to talk about it.

He got in his car and drove up the steep hill to Heptonstall. It was a quiet village at that time of day: narrow winding terraces of small dark cottages, many with the tell-tale rows of upper windows where weavers had once worked.

He lingered over his food and beer in the window seat of the

Cross Inn, planning what to do next. The Timothy Taylor's bitter was good, smooth as liquid gold. Shadows lengthened and the fronts of the gritstone houses over the narrow street turned even darker.

It was late when he got home—almost ten—and he'd hardly had time to put his slippers on and sit down before the phone rang.

"Alan, thank God you're back. I've been trying to call you all evening." It was Jenny.

"Why? What's wrong?"

"It's Dennis. His flat has been broken into."

"Has he reported it?"

"No. He wants to see you."

"He should report it."

"I know, but he won't. Will you go and see him? Please?"

"Was he hurt?"

"No, he was out when it happened. It must have been sometime earlier this evening."

"Was anything taken?"

"He's not clear about that. Nothing important, I don't think. Will you see him? Please?"

Banks could hardly refuse. In the first place, Jenny was clearly distraught on Osmond's behalf, and in the second, it might have a bearing on the case. If Osmond refused to come to him, then he would have to go to Osmond. Sighing, he said, "Tell him I'll be right over."

II

"You don't like me very much, do you, Chief Inspector?" said Osmond as soon as Banks had made himself comfortable.

"I'm not bowled over, no."

Osmond leaned back in his armchair and smiled. "You're not jealous, are you? Jenny told me how close you two got during that Peeping Tom business."

She did, did she? Banks thought angrily. Just how much had she told him? "Could you just get on with it, please?" he said. "I'm here, at Jenny's request, to investigate a break-in you haven't reported officially. The least you can do is stop trying to be so fucking clever."

The smile disappeared. "Yes, all right. For what good it'll do me."

"First off, why didn't you report it?"

"I don't trust the police, certainly not the way I've been treated since the demonstration. Burgess was around here again this afternoon tossing insults and accusations about. And I don't want my apartment done over by a bunch of coppers, either."

"Why not? What have you got to hide?"

"Nothing to hide, not in the way you mean it. But I value my privacy."

"So why am I here?"

Osmond crossed his legs and paused before answering. "Jenny persuaded me."

"But you don't really want to talk about it?"

"What's the point? What can you do?"

"We could do our job if you'd let us. Check for fingerprints, interview neighbours, try to get a description. Was anything stolen?"

"A book."

"What?"

"A book. Most of my books were pulled off the shelves, scattered on the floor, and I noticed when I put them back that one was missing."

"Just one?"

"That's right. Marcuse's *One Dimensional Man*. Do you know it?"

"No."

Osmond smiled smugly. "I didn't think you would. It doesn't matter. Anyway, that's all."

"That's all that was taken?"

"Yes."

"How did they get in? The lock doesn't seem broken."

"It's easy enough to open. They probably used a credit card or something. I've had to do that myself more than once."

"And it works?"

"Yes. Unless the catch is on from the inside. Obviously, as I was out at the time, it wasn't."

"Then I'd suggest the first thing you do is get a new lock. Preferably a deadlock."

"I've already called the locksmith. He's coming on Monday."

"Did you get the impression that they were looking for something? Or was it just vandalism?" Banks had his cigarette packet in his hand without thinking before he realized Osmond was a rabid non-smoker.

"Oh, go on, Chief Inspector." Osmond allowed himself another superior smile. "Pollute the atmosphere if you must. You're doing me a favour; it's the least I can do in return."

"Thanks, I will." Banks lit up. "What might they have been looking for? Money?"

"I don't think so. There was a little cash in the dresser drawer, but they left it. There was also some quite valuable jewellery—it used to be my mother's—and they left that, too. The only things disturbed were the books and some papers—nothing important—but there was no damage. I don't think it was vandalism."

"But it was clear they'd seen the money and jewellery?"

"Oh, yes. The drawer was open and the contents of the jewellery box were spilled on the bed."

"What do you think they were looking for?"

Osmond scratched his cheek and frowned. Noticing Banks's half inch of ash, he fetched an ashtray from the kitchen. "In case of emergencies," he said. "Stolen property, I'm afraid. Courtesy of the Bridge, Helmthorpe."

Banks smiled. Having got over his initial nervousness that, as with so many people, manifested itself in the form of rudeness, Osmond was making an attempt at least to smooth the waters. He still wasn't comfortable around the police, but he was trying.

"Would you like a drink?"

"Scotch, if you've got it." Osmond was prevaricating, making time to think. That meant his answer would be at best a blend of truth and falsehood, and it would be damn difficult for Banks to sort out which was which. But there was no point pushing him. Osmond liked being in control, and any challenge at this point would just make him clam up. Best wait for a gap in his defences and leap right through. Let him take his own sweet time.

Finally, drink in hand, Banks repeated his question.

"I don't want to appear unduly paranoid, Chief Inspector," Osmond began slowly, "but I've been involved with the CND and a number of other organizations for some years now, so I think I can speak from experience. I take it you know, of course, that I once made a complaint against the policeman who was killed?"

Banks nodded. "You'd have saved us a lot of trouble if you hadn't lied in the first place."

"That's easy for you to say. Anyway, your charming superintendent knew. He wouldn't let it drop. So I assume you know about it, too. Anyway, we come to expect that kind of thing. The CND doesn't take sides, Chief Inspector. Believe it or not, all we want is a nuclear-free world. But some members bring along strong political beliefs, too, I won't deny it. I'm a socialist, yes, but that doesn't have anything to do with the CND or its aims."

He paused and fingered his small gold crucifix. As Banks looked at him slouching on the sofa with his long legs crossed and his arms spread out along the back, the word languid came to mind.

"Have you noticed how things seem to come in packages?" Osmond went on. "If you're anti-nuclear, people also expect you to be pro-choice, pro-union, pro-gays, anti-American, anti-apartheid and generally left wing. Most people don't realize that it's perfectly possible to be, say, anti-nuclear and anti-apartheid without being pro-gay and pro-choice—especially if you're a Catholic. Oh, the permutations might differ a bit—some packages are more extreme and dangerous than others, for example—but you can pretty well predict the kind of things our members value. The point is that what we stand for is politically hot, and that draws attention to us from all sides. The government thinks we're in league with the Russians, so they raid our offices periodically and go over our files. The communists think we're allies in overthrowing a decadent capitalist government, so they woo us and infiltrate us with their own. It's a bloody mess, but we manage, through it all, to stick to our aims."

"Are you saying you think the break-in was politically motivated?"

"That's about it." Osmond lifted the Scotch bottle and raised his eyebrows. Banks held out his glass. "And the theft of the book was a sort of calling card, or warning. So do you see what I mean about not expecting much help from the police? If Special Branch or MI5 or whoever are involved, you'd get your wrists slapped, and if it's the other side, you'd never catch them anyway."

"But what were they looking for?"

"I don't know. Anyway, I don't keep my files here. Most of the important ones are at the CND office, and some of the stuff is at work."

"The Social Services Centre?"

"Yes. I've got an office there. It's convenient."

"So they didn't find what they were looking for because they didn't look in the right place."

"I suppose so. The only current thing is the inquiry I'm making into the demo. I've already told you about that—and Superintendent Burgess, too. I've talked to quite a lot of people involved, trying to establish exactly what happened and how it could have been avoided. Tim and Abha are helping, too. They've got most of the info at their place. We're having a meeting up at the farm tomorrow to decide what to do about it all. Ever since your boss was taken off the job, we've been carrying on for him, and our results will be a hell of a lot less biased."

"You're wrong," Banks said, lighting another cigarette. "The trouble with people like you, despite all your talk about packages, is that you tar everyone with the same brush. To you, all police are pigs. Superintendent Gristhorpe would have done a good job. He wouldn't have swept it all under the carpet."

"Maybe that's why he was taken off," Osmond said. "I read in the paper that they were going to appoint an impartial investigating commission—which, I suppose, means a bunch of high-ranking policemen from somewhere other than Eastvale—but most of us think they're just going to forget about the whole embarrassing affair. Once the killer is convicted—and it looks like you're well on your way to doing that—the anti-nuke lefties will be shown up for exactly what you all think we are—a gang of murderous anarchists—and the police will gain a lot of very useful public sympathy."

Banks put his empty glass down and walked over to the window. "Tell me about Ellen Ventner."

Osmond paled. "You certainly do your homework, don't you?"

"Ellen Ventner."

"If you think I'm going to admit to those ludicrous charges against me, you must be crazy."

"Much as it saddens me to say so, I'm not here to investigate those old charges. So you like to beat up women. That's your privilege."

"You bastard. Are you going to tell Jenny?"

"I honestly don't know. Ellen Ventner didn't pursue the charges. God knows why, but a lot of women don't. Maybe she thought you were still a really sweet fellow underneath it all. But that doesn't alter what happened. You might think you're a very important man in the political scheme of things, but personally I doubt it. On the other hand, a woman you once assaulted might bear a grudge."

"After four years?"

"It's possible."

"Forget it. She wouldn't. Besides, she emigrated not long after we split up."

"I can understand why she might have wanted to get as far away from you as possible. Just checking all the angles."

Osmond glared, then looked into his glass and started to fiddle with his crucifix again. "Look, it was only the once.... She...I was drunk. I didn't mean to ..."

Banks sat down opposite him again and leaned forward. "When you made your complaint about PC Gill," he asked, "how did you do it?"

Osmond floundered. It was so easy, Banks thought. Stir up a man's emotions then change the subject and you're in control again. He'd had enough of Osmond's lectures and his arrogance.

"What do you mean, how did I do it? I wrote a letter."

"How did you refer to him?"

"By his number. How else?"

"1139?"

"Yes, that's it."

"You still remember it?"

"Obviously."

"So how did you know his name?"

"Look, I don't—"

"When I first asked you if you knew Gill, you said no. I didn't use his number, I used his name, and you recognized it when you lied to me."

"He told me," Osmond said. "When I tried to stop him from hitting a woman at a demo once, he pulled me aside and told me to keep out of it. I told him I'd report him, and he said go ahead. When I looked at his number, he told me his name, as well. Spelled it out, in fact. The bastard was proud of what he was doing."

So Osmond defended women in public and only hit them in private. Nice guy, Banks thought, but he kept his questions factual and direct. "When you were up at Maggie's Farm on the afternoon of the demonstration, did you mention that number to anyone?"

"I don't know. I can't remember."

"Think. Did you write it in a notebook, or see it written in a notebook?"

"No, I'd remember something like that. But I might have mentioned it. Really, I can't say."

"How might you have mentioned it? Just give me a sense of context."

"I might have said, 'I wonder if that bastard PC 1139 will be out tonight.' I suppose I'd have warned people about him. Christ, you can't be involved in demos around this part of the world and not know about PC bloody 1139."

"So I gather." Banks remembered what Tim and Abha had told him.

There was nothing more to ask. Banks said good night and Osmond slammed the door behind him. In the corridor, he decided to try the flats on that floor to see if anyone had noticed the housebreaker. There were only ten—five on each side.

At the third door, a man who had been nipping out to the off-licence at about a quarter to eight said he'd seen two men walking along the corridor on his way back. They had seen him, too, but had made no move to run off or turn away. The description was average—most people are about as observant as a brick wall, Banks had discovered over the years—but it helped.

They were both tall and burly, and they both wore dark-blue pants, a bit shiny, probably the bottom part of a suit; one had on a black overcoat, fake leather, while the other wore a light trench coat; one had black hair, the other none at all; and neither wore a hat or glasses. About facial features, the man remembered nothing except that both men had two eyes, a nose, a mouth, and two ears. They had walked confidently and purposefully, as if they knew where they were going and what they were about, not furtively, as he imagined criminals would have done. So, no, he hadn't seen any need to call the police. He was sorry now, of course. His speech was slurred, as if he'd already drunk most of what he'd bought at the off-licence. Banks thanked him and left.

Over the next four doors, Banks found himself told to piss off by a writer whose concentration he had disturbed and asked in for a cup of tea by a lonely military-type who wanted to show off his medals. As yet, there had been no temptress in a négligé.

It wasn't until the ninth door that he found anyone else who knew anything. Beth Cameron wore tight, checked slacks, which hardly flattered her plump hips and thighs, and a maroon cardigan over a shiny white blouse. Her curly brown hair showed traces of a recent perm, and she had the most animated face that Banks had ever seen. Every comment, every word, was accompanied by a curled lip, a raised eyebrow, a wrinkled nose, a deep frown or a mock pout. She was like one of those sponge hand-puppets he remembered from his childhood. When you put your hand inside it, you could wrench the face into the most remarkable contortions.

"Did you see anyone coming in or out of Mr Osmond's flat this evening?" Banks asked.

"No, no, I can't say I did. Wait a minute, though, I did notice *something* odd. Not up here but down in the garage. It struck me as a bit strange at the time, you know, but I just brushed it off. You do, don't you?"

"What did you see?"

"A blue Escort. And it was parked in Mr Handley's spot. He's often out during the evening—he's the entertainment reporter for the Eastvale *Gazette*—but still, I thought, that's no reason to steal the man's parking spot, is it? See, there's places for visitors outside. We don't encourage non-residents to park underground. It could lead to all sorts of trouble, couldn't it?"

"What time was this?" Banks asked.

"Oh, about eight o'clock. I was just bringing Lesley—that's my daughter—back from her piano lesson."

"Did you see if there was anyone in the car?"

"Two men, I think. Sitting in the front."

"Did you get a good look at them?"

"No, I'm sorry. They looked big, but I mean, you just don't look at people, do you? Especially not in places like that. It doesn't do to make eye contact with strangers in an underground garage, does it?"

"No," Banks said, "I don't suppose it does. You didn't recognize either of the men, then?"

"No. Whatever happened, anyway?" Mrs Cameron suddenly frowned. "There wasn't nobody assaulted, was there? I've been saying all along that place is too dark. Just asking for trouble it is."

"Nobody was hurt," Banks assured her. "I'm just interested in that Escort. Have you ever noticed it before?"

"No, never. I did think of calling the police, you know. It did cross my mind they might be up to no good. But you don't want to cause a fuss, do you? It might all be perfectly innocent and there you'd be with egg on your face looking a proper fool. But I'd never forgive myself if someone got hurt."

"Don't worry, it's nothing like that. You didn't get the number, by any chance?"

"No." She laughed, then put her hand to her mouth. Her finger-nails were painted pale green. "I'm sorry, Mr Banks, but I always think it's so funny when the police go asking people that on telly. I mean, you don't go around collecting car numbers, do you? I don't think I even know my own."

"Is there anything else you can think of?" Banks asked, without much hope.

Beth Cameron chewed her lower lip and frowned for a moment, then shook her head. "No. Not a sausage. I didn't pay it much mind, really. They weren't doing nothing. Just sitting there like they were waiting to leave. . . . Wait a minute!" Her eyebrows shot up almost to her hairline. "I think one of them was bald. There was a light on the pillar by the car, you see. Dim as can be, but I could swear I saw a bald head reflecting the light." Then her lips curved down at the edges. "I don't suppose that's much help, though, is it?"

"Everything helps." Banks closed his notebook and put it back into his inside pocket. At least he was certain now that the two men in the blue Escort were the same two who had been seen in the corridor near Osmond's flat. "If you see the car again," he said, handing her a card, "would you please let me know?"

"Yes, of course I will, Mr Banks," she said. "Glad to be of use. Good night."

At the last door Banks turned up nothing new. It had been a long time since he'd made door-to-door enquiries himself, and he had enjoyed it, but now it was going on for half-past eleven and he was tired. Outside, the crisp, cold air woke him up a bit. He stood by his car for a few moments and smoked a cigarette, thinking over what had happened that evening.

However much he had ridiculed the man's pretensions, he had to admit that Osmond was the type who made waves politically. Banks had a lot of sympathy for the CND and its goals, but he knew that, like so many peace-loving, well-meaning groups, it sometimes acted as a magnet for dangerous opportunists. Where there was organization there was politics, and where there was politics there was the aphrodisiac of power. Maybe Osmond *had* been involved in a plot to do with the demonstration. Perhaps his masters didn't trust him to keep his trap shut, and what had happened this evening had been intended as a kind of warning.

Banks found it hard to swallow all the cloak-and-dagger stuff, but the mere possibility of it was enough to send a shiver of apprehension up his spine. If there really was anything in the conspiracy theory, then it looked like these people—Russian spies, *agents provocateurs*, or whoever they were—meant business.

If that was true, Osmond might get hurt. That didn't concern Banks very much, but it did cause him to worry about Jenny. It was bad enough her being involved with a man who had beat up a previous girl-friend, but much worse now there was a strong possibility that some very dangerous and cold-blooded people were after him too. None of it concerned Jenny directly, of course; she was merely an innocent bystander. But since when did governments or terrorists ever give a damn about innocent bystanders?

THIRTEEN

I

Maybe it was the spring weather, but the toasted teacakes in the Golden Grill tasted exceptionally good to Banks on Sunday morning. Burgess chose a doughnut filled with raspberry purée and dusted with icing sugar, which he dipped into his coffee. "A taste I developed in America," he explained, as Banks watched, horrified. "They've got a place there called Dunkin' Donuts. Great."

"What's happening with Boyd?" Banks asked.

"I had another chat with him. Got nowhere. Like you said, I let him go this morning, so we'll see what turns up now."

"What did you do? Torture him again?"

"Well, there's not many can keep on lying when faced with their greatest fear. The way things stand now, I think we could get a conviction on Boyd, no problem, but we'd probably get chucked out of court if we tried to fit one of the others up—Osmond, for example. I say if we turn up nothing more in a couple of days, let's just charge Boyd with murder and I'll bugger off back to the Smoke a happy man."

"What about the truth?"

Burgess treated Banks to a slit-eyed glance. "We don't know Boyd didn't do it, do we? The Burgess Test notwithstanding. It's not infallible, you know. Anyway, I'm getting a bit sick of your moralizing about the truth all the bloody time. The truth's relative. It depends on your perspective. Remember, we're not judge and jury. It's up to them to decide who's guilty and who's not. We just present the evidence."

"Fair enough, but it's up to us to make a charge that sticks, if only to stop us looking like prize berks in court."

"I think we're solid on Boyd if we need to be. Like I say, give it a couple of days. Find anything interesting on the funny-farm lot?"

"No."

"Those students puzzled me. They're only bloody kids—cheeky bastards, mind you—but their little minds are crammed full of Marx, Trotsky, Marcuse and the rest. They even have a poster of Che Guevara on the wall. I ask you—Che fucking Guevara, a vicious, murdering, mercenary thug got up to look like Jesus Christ. I can't understand what they're on about half the time, honest I can't. And I don't think they've got a clue, either. Pretty gutless pair, though. I can't see either of them having the bottle to stick a knife between Gill's ribs. Still, the girl's not bad. Bit chubby around the waist, but a lovely set of knockers."

"Osmond's place was broken into yesterday evening," Banks said.

"Oh?"

"He didn't report it officially."

"He should have done. You talked to him?"

"Yes."

"Then you should have made a report. You know the rules." He grinned. "Unless, of course, you think rules are only for people like me to follow and for Jack-the-lads like you to ignore?"

"Listen," Banks said, leaning forward, "I don't like your methods. I don't like violence. I'll use it if I have to, but there are plenty more subtle and effective ways of getting answers from people." He sat back and reached for a cigarette. "That aside, I never said I was any less ruthless than you are."

Burgess laughed and spluttered over a mouthful of recently dunked doughnut.

"Anyway," Banks went on, "Osmond didn't seem to give a damn. Well, maybe that's too strong. At least, he didn't think we would do anything about it."

"He's probably right. What *did* you do?"

"Told him to change his lock. Nothing was stolen."

"Nothing?"

"Only a book. They'd searched the place, but apparently they didn't find what they were looking for."

"What was that?"

"Osmond thinks they might have been after some papers, files to do with his CND stuff. He's got a touch of the cloak-and-dagger about him. Anyway, he keeps most of his files at the local office, and Tim and Abha have all the stuff on the demo. It seems they're having a meeting up at the farm this afternoon to plan their complaint strategy. It looks like the thieves wasted their time, whoever they were."

"Who does he think it was? KGB? MI5? CIA?"

Banks laughed. "Something along those lines, yes. Thinks he's a very important fellow does Mr Osmond."

"He's a pain in the ass," Burgess said, getting up. "But I'll trip the bastard up before I'm done. Right now I'm off to catch up on some paperwork. They want everything in bloody quadruplicate down at the Yard."

Banks sat over the rest of his coffee wondering why so many people came back from America, where Burgess had been to a conference a few years ago, full of strange eating habits and odd turns of phrase—"pain in the ass" indeed!

Outside on Market Street tourists browsed outside shop windows full of polished antiques and knitted woollen wear. The bell of the Golden Grill jangled as people dropped in for a quick cup of tea.

Banks had arranged to meet Jenny for lunch in the Queen's Arms at one o'clock, which left him well over an hour to kill. He finished his drink and nipped over to the station. First, he had to enlist Richmond's aid on a very delicate matter.

II

Mara was busy making scones for the afternoon meeting when Paul walked into the kitchen. Her hands were covered with flour and she waved them about to show she'd embrace him if she could. Seth immediately threw his arms around Paul and hugged him. Mara could see his face over Paul's shoulder, and noticed tears in his eyes. Rick slapped Paul on the back and Zoe kissed his cheek. "I did the cards," she told him. "I knew you were innocent and they'd have to let you go." Even Julian and Luna, caught up in the adults' excitement, did a little dance around him and chanted his name.

"Sit down," Seth said. "Tell us about it."

"Hey! Let me finish this first." Mara gestured at the half-made scones. "It won't take a minute. And it was your idea in the first place."

"I tell you what," Paul said. "I could do with a cup of tea. That prison stuff's piss-awful."

"I'll make it." Seth reached for the kettle. "Then we'll all go in the front room."

Mara carried on with the scones, readying them for the oven, and Seth put the kettle on. The others all wandered into the front room except for Paul, who stood nervously behind Mara.

"I'm sorry," he said. "You know . . ."

She turned and smiled at him. "Forget it. I'm just glad you're back. I should never have doubted you in the first place."

"I was a bit . . . well, I did lie. Thanks for tipping me off, anyway. At least I had a chance."

The kettle started boiling, and Seth hurried back in to make tea. Mara put the tray of scones in the oven and washed her hands.

"Right," she said, drying them on her apron. "I'm ready." They sat down in the living-room and Seth poured tea.

"Come on, then," he urged Paul.

"Come on, what?"

"Tell us what happened."

"Where do you want me to start?"

"Where did you go?"

Paul lit a Player's and spat a strand of loose tobacco from his upper lip. "Edinburgh," he said. "Went to see an old mate, didn't I?"

"Did he help you?" Mara asked.

Paul snorted. "Did he fuck. Bastard's changed a lot. I found the building easy enough. It used to be one of those grotty old tenements, but it's all been tarted up now. Potted plants in the stairwell and all that. Anyway, Ray answers the door, and he doesn't recognize me at first—at least he pretends he doesn't. I hardly knew him, either. Wearing a bloody suit, he was. We say hello and then this bird comes out—hair piled up on top of her head and a black dress slit right down the front to her belly button. She's carrying one of those long-stemmed wineglasses full of white wine, just for the effect. 'Who's this, Raymond?' she says, right lah-de-dah, like, and I head for the stairs."

"You didn't stay?" Mara said.

"Are you joking?"

"Do you mean your old friend wouldn't let you in?"

"Gone up in the world has old Raymond. Seems he was entertaining the boss and the wife—he's in computers—and he didn't want any reminders of his past. Used to be a real wild boy, but...Anyway, I left. Oh, I reckon he might have let me in if I'd pushed hard enough, stuck me in the cupboard or somewhere out of the way. But I wasn't having any."

"So where did you go?" Seth asked.

"Just walked around for a while till I found a pub."

"You didn't walk the streets all night, did you?" Mara asked.

"Like hell. It was colder than a witch's tit up there. This is bloody Scotland we're talking about. First thing the next morning I bought myself a duffle coat just to keep from freezing to death."

"What did you do then, after you left the pub?"

"I met this bloke there," Paul said, reddening. "He said I could go back to his place with him. Look, I know what you're thinking. I'm not a fucking queer. But when you're on the streets, just trying to survive, you do what you have to, right? He was a nice enough bloke, anyway, and he didn't ask no awkward questions. Careful, he was, too, if you know what I mean.

"Next day I was going to head for Glasgow and look up another old mate, but I thought fuck that for a lark, best thing to do is get straight to Ireland. I've got mates there, and I don't think they've changed. If I'd got to Belfast, *nobody* would have found me."

"So what went wrong?" Seth asked.

Paul laughed harshly. "Bloody ferry dock. I goes up to this shopbloke to buy some fags and when I walk away he shouts after me. I can't understand a bleeding word he's saying on account of the Jock accent, like, but this copper sees us and gives me the look. I get nervous and take off and the bastards catch me."

"Did the shopkeeper recognize you?" Mara asked. "Your picture was in the papers, you know."

"Nah. I'd just given him too much bloody money, that's all. He was shouting he wanted to give me my fucking change." Paul laughed and the others laughed with him. "It wasn't so funny at the time," he added.

"What did the police do?" asked Rick.

"They've charged me with being an accessory. I'll have to go to court."

"Then what?" Mara asked.

Paul shrugged. "With my record I'll probably end up doing porridge again. That copper with the scar seems to think I might get off if they get a sympathetic jury. I mean, sometimes you respect people for standing by their mates, right? He says he might be able to get the charge reduced to giving false information and wasting police time. I'd only get six months max, then. But the other bloke tells me I'm looking at ten years. Who do you believe?"

"If you're lucky," Mara said, "Burgess might be gone by then and Banks'll take it easy on you."

"What's wrong with him? He soft or something?"

Seth shook his head. "Somehow I don't think so, no. He just has a different technique."

"They're all bastards when you get right down to it," Rick added.

Paul agreed. "So what's been happening here?" he asked.

Seth filled him in on the police visits. "Apart from that, not much really. We've all been worrying about you most of the time." He ruffled Paul's hair. "Glad you're back, kid. Nice new haircut, too."

Paul blushed. "Fuck off. Anyway, nothing's changed, has it?"

"What do you mean?" Mara asked.

"Well, they still don't have their killer and they're not going to stop till they do. And if they don't get someone else, I'm still their best bet. That Burgess bastard made that quite clear."

"Don't worry about it," Seth said. "We won't let them blame it on you."

Paul looked at his watch. "Nearly opening time," he said. "I could do with a pint and some nosh."

"We'll have to eat at the pub today, anyway," Mara said. "I've not made any dinner. What with that meeting and all. . . ."

"What meeting?" Paul asked.

"We're getting together to talk about the demo this afternoon," Rick said. "Dennis is bringing Tim and Abha up about three. We want to look over statements and stuff to prove police brutality."

"Well you can count me out," Paul said. "I've had enough of that bleeding demo, and those fucking do-gooders. Sod 'em all."

"You don't have to stick around," Mara told him. "Not if you don't want."

"I think I'll go for a walk," Paul said, calming down. "Being cooped up in that cell hasn't done my head much good."

"And I've got work to do," Seth said. "I've got to finish that bureau today. It's already overdue."

"What's this?" Rick said. "Is everybody copping out on us?"

"I'll put my two penn'orth in, first, don't worry," Seth said. "Then I'll get some work done. As for now, I think Paul's right. They do a nice Sunday lunch at the Black Sheep and I'm starving."

Seth put his arm around Paul. The others stood up and went for their coats. In the fresh spring air, the seven of them walked down the track to Relton, happy together for the last time.

Except for Mara. The others might realize it, too, she thought, but nobody's saying anything. If Paul isn't guilty, then someone else here is.

III

Jenny was already waiting when Banks came into the Queen's Arms at lunch-time. Hungry, he arranged with Cyril for a few slices of roast leg of lamb. Glenys wasn't around, and Cyril, though he said nothing, seemed distracted.

"So," Jenny said, resting her elbows on the table and cupping her chin in her hands, "what's new? Dennis told me you dropped by. Thanks for going."

"*He* didn't thank me."

Jenny smiled. "Well, he wouldn't, would he?"

"You didn't tell me it was you who persuaded him to talk to me in the first place."

The lines around her eyes crinkled. "Didn't I? Sorry. But did you find anything out?"

"Not really."

"What does that mean?"

"It means no, I suppose. Have you ever noticed a blue Escort with two burly men in it hanging around Osmond's place?"

"No. Haven't you got *any* ideas, Alan?"

"Maybe one. It seems a bit far-fetched, but if I'm right...."

"Right about what?"

"Just an idea, that's all."

"Can you tell me?"

"I'd rather not. Best wait and see. Richmond's working on it."

"When will you know?"

"Tomorrow, I hope."

The food arrived. "I'm starving," Jenny said, and the two ate in silence.

When he'd finished, Banks bought another round of drinks and lit a cigarette. Then he explained his doubts about Paul Boyd's guilt.

"Are you any closer to catching the real killer?" Jenny asked.

"It doesn't look like it. Boyd's still the closest we've got."

"I can't believe that Dennis is a murderer, you know."

"Are you speaking as a psychologist?"

"No. As a woman."

"I think I'd trust that opinion more if it came from a professional."

Jenny arched her eyebrows. "What do you mean by that?"

"Don't bristle, it doesn't suit you. I mean that people—men and women—tend to be very protective about whoever they get involved with. It's only natural—you know that as well as I do. And not only that, but they deliberately blinker themselves sometimes, even lie. Look what Boyd did. If he really is innocent of murder, then he sure as hell risked a lot. And think about how Mara behaved. Whichever way you look at it now, it comes down to Seth, Rick or Zoe—with Mara, Tim and Abha, *and* your Dennis running close behind."

"All right. As a professional, I don't think Dennis did it."

"Just how much do you know about him?"

"What do you mean?"

"Never mind."

"What? Come on. Out with it. If there's something I should know, tell me."

Banks took a deep breath. "Would you say Osmond is the kind of person to hit women?"

"What?"

Haltingly, Banks told her about Ellen Ventner. The more he said, the paler she became. Even as he told her, Banks wasn't sure of his motives. Was he doing it because he was worried about her association with Osmond, or was it out of pure vindictive jealousy?

"I don't believe it," she whispered.

"Believe it. It's true."

"Why are you telling me this?"

"I didn't want to tell you. You pushed me into it."

"It was you who made me push you. You must have known how bloody humiliated it would make me feel."

Banks shrugged. He could feel her starting to turn her anger against him. "I'm sorry, that's not what I intended. He could be dangerous, Jenny. And I don't know about you, but I have problems understanding a person who rescues defenceless women from police brutality in public and beats them up in private."

"You said it only happened once. There's no need to go making him into a monster. What do you expect me to do? Chuck him over just because he made a mistake?"

"I expect you to be careful, that's all. Osmond hit a woman once, put her in hospital, and he's also a suspect in a murder investigation. In addition, he seems to think the CIA, the KGB and MI5 are all after him. I'd say that merits a little caution, wouldn't you?"

Jenny's eyes glittered. "You've never liked Dennis right from the start, have you? You've never even given him a chance. And now as soon as you find a bit of dirt on him, you sling it at me. Just what the bloody hell do you hope to achieve, Alan? You're not my keeper. I can take care of myself. I don't need a big brother to look out for me."

She picked up her coat and swept out of the pub, knocking over her glass as she went. Faces turned to stare and Banks felt himself flush. Good one, Alan, he said to himself, you handled that really well.

He followed her outside, but she was nowhere in sight. Cursing, he went back to his office and tried to occupy his mind with work.

After a couple of false starts, he finally got through to Rick's wife's sister at her home in Camden Town. She sounded cagey and Banks first had to assure her that his call had nothing at all to do with the custody battle. Even then, she didn't sound as if she believed him.

"I just need some information about Rick's wife, that's all," he said. "Were you always good friends?"

"Yes," the sister answered. "Our ages are close, so we always supported one another, even after she married Rick. I don't want you to think I've anything against him, by the way. He's selfish and egotistical, but then most men are. Artists even more so. And I'm sure he's a good father. Pam certainly wasn't capable of taking care of Julian when they split up."

"And now?"

"She's getting there. It's a long road, though, alcoholism."

"Did Pam ever have any connections up north?"

"Up north? Good Lord, no. I don't think she's ever been farther north than Hendon."

"Not even for a visit?"

"No. What's there to visit, anyway? It's all canals and slag heaps, isn't it?"

"So she's spent most of her life in either London or Cornwall?"

"Yes. They had a few months in France some years ago. Most painters seem to gravitate towards France at one time or another. But that's all."

"Have you ever heard her mention a policeman called Gill—PC Edwin Gill, number 1139?"

"I've never heard her mention any policemen. No, I tell a lie. She said the local pub in Cornwall stayed open till all hours when the bobby was there. But I don't think that'd be your PC Gill."

"No," Banks said, "it wouldn't. Did she ever attend political demonstrations—Greenham Common, the Aldermaston march, that kind of thing?"

"Pam's never been very political. Wisely so, if you ask me. What's the point? You can't trust one lot more than the other. Is that all, Chief Inspector?"

"Is she there? Can I talk to her?"

There was a short pause and Banks heard muffled sounds from the other end of the line. Finally, he could hear the phone changing hands and another voice came on—husky and weary, as if doped or ill.

"Yes?"

Banks asked her the same questions he'd asked her sister, and the answers were the same. She spoke hesitantly, with long pauses between each sentence.

"Are the police involved in this custody battle?" Banks asked.

"Uh, no," she answered. "Just...you know...lawyers."

Naturally, Banks thought. "And you've never heard of PC Gill?"

"Never."

"Has your sister visited Yorkshire recently?" Banks asked the question as soon as it came to him. After all, the sister might have got herself involved somehow.

"No. Here...looking after me. Can I go now? I've got to...I don't know anything."

"Yes," Banks said. "That's all. Thanks for your time."

He hung up and made notes on the conversation while it was fresh in his mind. The one thing that struck him as odd was that neither of the women had asked about Julian, about how he was. Why, he wondered, did Rick's wife want custody if she didn't even care that much about the child? Spite? Revenge? Julian would probably be better off where he was.

Next he called the Hebden Bridge police and asked for PC Brooks.

"Sorry to bother you again, Constable," he said. "I should probably have asked you all this before, but there's been rather too much going on here. Can you tell me anything about Alison Cotton, the woman who was killed in the car accident?"

"I remember her all right, sir," Brooks said. "It was my first accident and I...well...I, er..."

"I know what you mean. It happens to us all. Did you know her before the accident?"

"Oh, aye. She'd been here a few years, like, ever since the artsy types discovered us, you might say."

"And Alison was artsy?"

"Aye. Helped organize the festival, poetry readings, that kind of thing. She ran the bookshop. I suppose you already know that."

"What kind of a person was she?"

"She were a right spirited lass. Proper bonny, too. She wrote things. You know, poems, stories, stuff like that. I tried reading some in the local paper but I couldn't make head nor tail of it. Give me 'Miami Vice' or 'Dynasty' any day."

"Was she ever involved in political matters—marches, demos, things like that?"

"Well," PC Brooks said, "we never had many things like that here.

A few, but nowt much. Mostly 'Save the Whales' and 'Ban the Bomb.' I don't know as she was involved, though she did sometimes write bits for the paper about not killing animals for their fur and not making laboratory mice smoke five hundred fags a day. And about them women outside that missile base."

"Greenham Common?"

"That's the one. When it comes down to it, I dare say she was like the rest, though. If some bandwagon came along, they jumped on it."

"Ever heard of a PC Gill, 1139, from Scarborough?"

"Only what I've read in the papers, sir. I hope you catch the bastard who did it."

"So do I. What about a friend of Cotton's called Elizabeth Dale? Heard of her?"

"Oh, aye. Liz Dale hung around with the Cotton crowd all right. Thick as thieves. I felt sorry for her, myself. I mean it's like a sickness, isn't it, when you get so you need something all the time."

"Was she a registered addict?"

"Aye. She never really gave us any trouble. We just like to keep an eye on them, that's all, make sure they're not selling off half their prescriptions."

"What kind of person is she?"

"Moody," Brooks said. "She got off drugs, but she were never really right afterwards. One day she'd be up, the next down. Right bloody yo-yo. But there was a lass with strong political opinions."

"Liz Dale was political?"

"Aye. For a while, at least. Till she got it out of her system. Like I said, bandwagon."

"But she was keener than the rest?"

"I'd say so, yes. Now Seth, he was never much more than partly interested. Rather be slicing up a piece of wood. And Alison, like I said, well, she had a lot of energy and she had to put it somewhere, but she was more your private, artistic type. But Liz Dale, she was up to her neck in everything at one time."

"Were Liz Dale and Alison Cotton especially close?"

"Like sisters."

Banks thought of the complaint Dale had made against PC Gill. From that, he already knew she had attended at least one demonstration and come across him. Perhaps there had been others, too. Alison Cotton could have been with her. Perhaps this was the link he was looking for. But so what? Alison was dead; Reginald Lee had run her over by accident. It still didn't add up, unless everyone was lying and Liz Dale *had* been at Maggie's Farm and at the Eastvale demonstration. Banks didn't know her, but if she did have a history of drug abuse, there was a chance she might be unbalanced.

"Thanks a lot," Banks said. "You've been a great help."

"I have? Oh, well—"

"Just one more thing. Do you know where Liz Dale lives?"

"Sorry, I can't help you there, sir. She's been away from here a few years now. I've no idea at all."

"Never mind. Thanks anyway."

Banks broke the connection and walked over to the window. At the far side of the square, just outside the National Westminster bank, a rusty blue Mini had slammed into the back of a BMW, and the two drivers were arguing. Automatically, Banks phoned downstairs and asked Sergeant Rowe to send someone over. Then he lit a cigarette and started thinking.

He certainly needed to know more about Liz Dale. If he could prove that she had been in the area at the time of the demo, then he had someone else with a motive for wanting to harm Gill. The Dale woman could easily have visited the farm one day earlier that week and taken the knife—Mara said that no one paid it any mind as a rule. If nobody had seen her, perhaps she had walked in and taken it while everyone was out. But was she at the demo? And why use Seth's knife? Did she have some reason other than revenge for wanting Gill dead? Obviously the best way to get the answer to that was to find Dale herself. Surely that couldn't prove too difficult.

As PC Craig approached the two drivers in the market square, Banks walked over to his filing cabinet.

IV

Mara stood inside the porch with Rick and Zoe and waved goodbye to Dennis Osmond and the others as they drove off. The sky was darkening in the west, and that early-evening glow she loved so much held the dale in its spell, spreading a blanket of silence over the land- scape. Flocks of birds crossed the sky and lights flicked on in cottages down in Relton and over the valley in Lyndgarth.

"What do you think?" she asked Rick, as they went back inside. The evening was cool. She hugged herself, then pulled on a sweater and sat in the rocking chair.

Rick's knees cracked as he knelt at the grate to start the fire. "I think it'll work," he said. "We're bound to get the newspapers inter- ested, maybe even TV. The police might try and discredit us, but people will get the message."

Mara rolled a cigarette. "I'll be glad when it's all over," she said. "The whole business seems to have brought us nothing but trouble."

"Look on the bright side," Rick said, turning to look at her. "It's a blow against the police and their heavy-handed tactics. Even that woman from the Church for Peace group has started calling them pigs."

"Still," Mara said firmly, "it would have been better for all of us if none of it had ever happened."

"Everything's all right now," Zoe said. "Paul's back, we're all together again."

"I know, but..."

Mara couldn't help feeling uneasy. True, Paul's return had cheered them up no end, especially Seth, who had been moping around with a long face the whole time he'd been away. But it wasn't the end. The police weren't going to rest until they'd arrested someone for the murder, and they had their eyes on the farm. Paul might still end up in jail as an accessory, a serious charge, Mara now realized. She won- dered if Banks was going to charge her, too. He wasn't stupid; he must know she had warned Paul about Crocker's finding the knife. Everything felt fragile. There was a chance she might lose it all, all the peace of mind and stability she had sought for so long. And the children, too. That didn't bear thinking about.

"Cheer up." Rick crawled over and tilted her chin up. "We'll have a party to celebrate Paul's release. Invite everyone we can think of and fill the place with music and laughter, eh?"

Mara smiled. "I hope you're right."

"Where is Paul, anyway?" Zoe asked.

"He went walking on the moors," said Mara. "I suppose he's just enjoying his freedom." She almost added "while it lasts," but decided that Rick was right; she at least ought to try to enjoy herself while things were going well.

"Seth didn't want much to do with us this afternoon, either," Rick complained.

"Don't be like that, Rick," Mara said. "He's been getting behind in his work. This business with the police has been bothering him, too. Haven't you noticed how upset he's been? And you know what a perfectionist he is, what he's like about deadlines. Besides, I think he's just relieved Paul's back. He's as fed up of the aftermath of this bloody demonstration as I am."

"We have to try and bring some good out of it," Rick argued, placing the coal on top of the layered newspaper and wood chips. "Don't you see that?"

"Yes, I do. I just think we all need a rest from it, that's all."

"The struggle goes on. There is no rest." Rick lit the fire in several places and stood the piece of plywood in front of the fireplace to make it draw. Behind the board the flames began to roar like a hurricane, and Mara could see red around the edges.

"Be careful," she said. "You know how wildly it burns with the wind up here."

"Seriously," Rick said, keeping an eye on the plywood shield, "we can't stop now. I can understand your lack of enthusiasm, but you'll just have to shake yourself. Seth and Paul, too. You don't get anywhere against the oppressors by packing it in because you're fed up."

"I sometimes wonder if you ever get anywhere," Mara muttered.

She was aware that now she had found her home, Maggie's Farm, she was less concerned about the woes of the world. Not that she didn't care—she would be quite happy to write letters for Amnesty International and sign petitions—but she didn't want to make it her whole life, attending rallies, meetings and demonstrations. Compared to the farm, the children and her pottery, it all seemed so distant and pointless. People were going to go on being as cruel to one another as they always had been. But here was a place where she could make room for love. Why should it be contaminated by the sordid world of politics and violence?

"Penny for them?"

"What? Oh, sorry, Zoe. Just dreaming."

"It's okay to dream."

"As long as you don't expect them to come true without hard work," Rick added.

"Oh, shut up!" Mara said. "Just give it a rest, can't you, Rick? Let's pretend everything's all right for a few hours at least."

Rick's jaw dropped. "Isn't that what I said at first?" Then he shook his head and muttered something about women. Mara couldn't be bothered to take him to task for it.

Just then, the kitchen door flew open and Paul stood there, white and trembling. Mara jumped to her feet. "Paul! What is it? What's wrong?"

At first he couldn't speak. He just leaned against the door jamb and tried to force the words out. Rick was beside him by then, and Zoe had reached for his hand.

"What is it, Paul?" she asked him softly. "Take a deep breath. You must try to tell us."

Paul followed her advice and went to slump down on the cushions. "It's Seth," he said finally, pointing towards the back garden. "I think he's dead."

FOURTEEN

I

Banks and Burgess rushed through the dark garden to Seth's work-shop, where a bare bulb shone inside the half-open door. Normally, they would have been more careful on their approach to the scene, but the weather was dry and a stone path led between the vegetable beds to the shed, so there was no likelihood of footprints.

Burgess pushed the door open slowly and they walked in. Mixed with the scents of shaved wood and varnish was the sickly metallic smell of blood. Both men had come across it often enough before to recognize it immediately.

At first, they stood in the doorway to take in the whole scene. Seth was just in front of them, wearing his sand-coloured smock, slumped over his work-bench. His head lay on the surface in a small pool of blood, and his arms dangled at his side. From where Banks was standing, it looked as if he had hit his head on the vice clamped to the bench slightly to his left. On the concrete floor over in the right-hand corner stood a small bureau in the Queen Anne style, its finish still wet, a rich, glistening nut-brown. At the far end of the workshop, another bare light bulb shone over the area Seth used for office work.

It was only when Banks moved forward a pace that he noticed he had stepped in something sticky and slippery. The light wasn't very strong and most of the floor space around Seth was in semi-darkness. Kneeling, Banks saw that what he had first taken for shadow was, in fact, more blood. Seth's feet stood at the centre of a large puddle of blood. It hadn't come from the head wound, though, Banks realized, examining the bench again. There hadn't been much bleeding and none of the blood seemed to have dribbled off the edge. Bending again, he caught sight of a thin tubular object, a pen or a pencil, perhaps, half-submerged in the pool. He decided to leave it for the forensic team to deal with. They were on their way from Wetherby and should arrive shortly after Dr Glendenning and Peter Darby, the young photographer, neither of whom had as far to travel.

Leaving the body, Banks walked cautiously to the back of the workshop where the old Remington stood on its desk beside the filing cabinet. There was a sheet of paper in the typewriter. Leaning forward, Banks was able to read the message: "I did it. I killed the policeman Gill. It was wrong of me. I don't know what came over me. I'm sorry for all the trouble I caused. This is the best way. Seth."

He called Burgess over and pointed out the note to him.

Burgess raised his eyebrows and whistled softly between his teeth. "Suicide, then?"

"Looks like it. Glendenning should be able to give us a better idea."

"Where the hell is this bloody doctor, anyway?" Burgess complained, looking at his watch. "It can't take him that long to get here. Everywhere's within pissing distance in this part of the country."

Burgess and Glendenning hadn't met yet, and Banks was looking forward to seeing Dirty Dick try out his aggressive arrogance on the doctor. "Come on," he said, "there's nothing more to do in here till the others arrive. We'll only mess up the scene. Let's go outside for a smoke."

The two of them left the workshop and stood in the cool evening air. Glendenning, Banks knew, would smoke wherever he wanted and nobody had ever dared say a word to him, but then he was one of the top pathologists in the country, not a lowly chief inspector or superintendent.

From the doorway of the shed, they could see the kitchen light in the house. Someone—Zoe, it looked like—was filling a kettle. Mara had taken the news very badly, and Rick had called the local doctor for her. He had also phoned the Eastvale station, which surprised Banks, given Rick's usual hostility. Still, Seth Cotton was dead, there was no doubting that, and Rick probably knew there would be no way of avoiding an investigation. It made more sense to start out on the right foot rather than have to explain omissions or evasions later. Banks wondered whether to go inside and have a chat with them, but decided to give them a bit longer. They would have probably got over the immediate shock by the time Glendenning and the scene-of-crime team had finished.

At last, the back door opened and the tall, white-haired doctor crossed the garden, a half-smoked cigarette hanging from the corner of his mouth. He was closely followed by a fresh-faced lad with a camera bag slung over his shoulder.

"About bloody time," Burgess said.

Glendenning gave him a dismissive glance and stood in the doorway while Darby did his work. Banks and Burgess went back into the workshop to make sure he photographed everything, including the blood on the floor, the pen or pencil, the Queen Anne bureau and the typewriter. When Darby had finished, Glendenning went in. He was so tall he had to duck to get through the door.

"Watch out for the blood," Banks warned him.

"And there's no smoking at the scene," Burgess added. He got no answer.

Banks smiled to himself. "Ease up," he said. "The doc's a law unto himself."

Burgess grunted but kept quiet while Glendenning felt for a pulse and busied himself with his stethoscope and thermometer.

About fifteen minutes later, while Glendenning was still making calculations in his little red notebook, the forensic team arrived, headed by Vic Manson, the fingerprints man. Manson was a slight, academic-looking man in his early forties. Almost bald, he plastered the few remaining hairs over the dome of his skull, creating an effect of bars shadowed on an egg. He greeted the two detectives and went inside with the team. As soon as he saw the workshop, he turned to Banks. "Bloody awful place to look for prints," he said. "Too many rough surfaces. And tools. Have you any idea how hard it is to get prints from well-used tools?"

"I know you'll do your best, Vic," Banks said. He guessed that Manson was annoyed at being disturbed on a Sunday evening.

Manson snarled and got to work alongside the others, there to take blood samples and anything else they could find.

Banks and Burgess went back outside and lit up again. A few minutes later, Glendenning joined them.

"What's the news, doc?" Burgess asked.

Glendenning ignored him and spoke directly to Banks. "He's dead, and that's about the only fact I can give you so far."

"Come on, doc!" said Burgess. "Surely you can tell us more than that."

"Can you ask your pushy friend here to shut up, just for a wee while?" Glendenning said to Banks in a quiet, nicotine-ravaged voice redolent of Edinburgh. "And tell him not to call me doc."

"For Christ's sake." Burgess flicked the stub of his cigar into the vegetable patch and stuck his hands deep in his pockets. He was wearing his leather jacket over an open-necked shirt, as usual. The only concession he had made to the cold was a V-necked sweater. Now that darkness had come, their breath plumed in the air, lit by the eerie glow of the bare bulb inside the workshop.

Glendenning lit another cigarette and turned back to Banks, who knew better than to rush him. "It doesn't look to me," the doctor said slowly, "as if that head wound was serious enough to cause death. Don't quote me on it, but I don't think it fractured the skull."

Banks nodded. "What do you think was the cause?" he asked.

"Loss of blood. And he lost it from his ankles."

"His ankles?"

"Aye," Glendenning went on. "The veins on the insides of each ankle were cut. I found a blade—most likely from a plane—lying in the blood, and it looks like it might have been used for the job. I'll have to make sure, of course."

"So was it suicide?" Burgess asked.

Glendenning ignored him and went on speaking to Banks. "Most suicides with a penchant for gory death," he said, "slit their wrists. The ankles are just as effective, though, if not more so. But whether he inflicted the wounds himself or not, I canna say."

"He's tried that way before," Banks said. "And there was a note."

"Aye, well, that's your department, isn't it?"

"Which came first," Banks asked, "the head wound or the cut ankles?"

"That I can't say, either. He could have hit his head as he lost consciousness, or someone could have hit it for him and slit his ankles. If the two things happened closely in succession, it won't be possible to tell which came first, either. It looks like the head wound was caused by the vice. There's blood on it. But of course it'll have to be matched and the vice compared with the shape of the wound."

"How long has he been dead?" Banks asked. "At a guess."

Glendenning smiled. "Aye, you're learning, laddie," he said. "It's always a guess." He consulted his notebook. "Well, rigor's not much farther than the neck, and the body temperature's down 2.5 degrees. I'd say he's not been dead more than two or three hours."

Banks looked at his watch. It was six o'clock. So Cotton had probably died between three and four in the afternoon.

"The ambulance should be here soon," Glendenning said. "I called them before I set off. I'd better just bag the head and feet before they get here. We don't want some gormless young ambulance driver spoiling the evidence, do we?"

"Can you do the post-mortem tonight?" Banks asked.

"Sorry, laddie. We've the daughter and son-in-law down for the weekend. First thing in the morning?"

Banks nodded. He knew they'd been spoiled in the past by Glendenning's eagerness to get down to the autopsy immediately. It was more usual to be asked to wait until the next day. And to Glendenning, first thing in the morning was probably very early indeed.

The doctor went back inside, where Manson and his team were finishing up. A short while later, the ambulance arrived, and two white-coated men bearing a stretcher crossed to the workshop. Seth looked oddly comical now, with his head in a plastic bag. Like some creature out of a fifties horror film, Banks thought. The ambulance men tagged him, zipped him into a body bag and laid him on the stretcher.

"Can you leave by the side exit?" Banks asked, pointing to the large gate in the garden wall. "They're shook up enough in the house without having to see this."

The ambulance men nodded and left.

Manson came out five minutes later. "Lots of prints," he grumbled, "but most of them a mess, just as I thought. At first glance, though, I'd say they belong to only two or three people, not dozens."

"You'll get Seth's, of course," Banks said, "and probably Boyd's and some of the others. Could you get anything from the blade?"

Manson shook his head. "Sorry. It was completely covered in blood. And the blood had mixed to a paste with the sawdust on the floor. Very sticky. You'd have to wipe it all off to get anywhere, and if you do that..." He shrugged. "Anyway, the doc's taken it with him to match to the wounds."

"What about the typewriter?"

"Pretty smudged, but we might get something. The paper, too. We can treat it with graphite."

"Look, there's a handwriting expert down at the lab, isn't there?"

"Sure. Geoff Tingley. He's good."

"And he knows about typewriting, too?"

"Of course."

Banks led Manson back into the workshop and over to the old Remington. The suicide note was now lying beside it. Also on the desk was a business letter Seth had recently written and not posted. "Dear Mr Spelling," it read, "I am most grateful for your compliments on the quality of my work, and would certainly have no objection to your spreading the word in the Wharfedale area. Whilst I always endeavour to meet both deadlines and quality standards, I am sure you realize that, this being a one-man operation, I must therefore limit the amount of work I take on." It went on to imply that Mr Spelling should seek out only the best jobs for Seth and not bother him with stacks of minor repairs and commissions for matchbox-holders or lamp stands.

"Can you get Mr Tingley to compare these two and let us know if they were typed by the same person?"

"Sure." Manson looked at the letters side by side. "At a pinch I'd say they weren't. Those old manual typewriters have all kinds of eccentricities, it's true, but so do typists. Look at those 'e's, for a start."

Banks looked. The 'e's in Seth's business letter had imprinted more heavily than those in his suicide note.

"Still," Manson went on, "better get an expert opinion. I don't suppose his state of mind could be called normal, if he killed himself." He placed each sheet of paper in an envelope. "I'll see Geoff gets these first thing in the morning."

"Thanks, Vic." Banks led the way outside again.

Burgess stood with his hands still in his pockets in the doorway beside Peter Darby, who was showing him the polaroids he'd taken before getting down to the real work. He raised his eyebrows as Banks and Manson joined him. "Finished?"

"Just about," Banks said.

"Time for a chat with the inmates, then." Burgess nodded towards the house.

"Let's take it easy with them," Banks said. "They've had a hell of a shock."

"One of them might not have had, if Cotton was murdered. But don't worry, I won't eat them."

In the front room, Zoe, Rick, Paul and the children sat drinking tea with the doctor, a young female GP from Relton. A fire blazed in the hearth and candles threw shadows on the whitewashed walls. Music played quietly in the background. Banks thought he recognized Bach's Third *Brandenburg* Concerto.

"Mara's under sedation," Rick said. "You can't talk to her."

"That's right," the doctor agreed, picking up her bag and reaching for her coat. "I just thought I'd wait and let you know. She took it very badly, so I've given her a sedative and put her to bed. I'll be back in the morning to check."

Banks nodded, and the doctor left.

"How about some tea?" Burgess said, clapping his hands together and rubbing them. "It's real brass-monkey weather out there."

Rick scowled at him, but Zoe brought two cups and poured the steaming liquid.

Burgess smiled down at her. "Three lumps and a splash of milk, love, please."

"What happened?" Zoe asked, stirring in the sugar. Her eyes were red and puffy from crying.

"That's for you to tell us, isn't it?" Burgess said. He really was being quite polite, Banks noticed. "All we know is that Seth Cotton is dead and it looks like suicide. Has he been depressed lately?" He took a sip of tea and spluttered. "What the fuck is this?"

"It's Red Zinger," Zoe said. "No caffeine. You shouldn't really have milk and sugar with it."

"You're telling me." Burgess pushed the tea aside. "Well, was he?"

"He was upset when Paul was in jail," Zoe answered. "But he cheered up this morning. He seemed so happy today."

"And he never said anything about ending it all?"

"Never." Zoe shook her head.

"I gather you had some kind of meeting this afternoon," Banks said. "Who was here?"

Rick eyed him suspiciously but said nothing.

"Just Dennis Osmond, Tim and Abha, that's all," Zoe answered.

"What time were they here?"

"They arrived about half-two and left around five."

"Were you all present?"

Zoe shook her head. "Seth stayed for a few minutes then went to . . . to work."

"And I went for a walk," Paul said defiantly. "I needed some fresh air after being cooped up in your bloody jail for so long."

"Not half as long as you will be if you don't knock off the cheek, sonny," said Burgess.

"Was it you who found the body?" Banks asked.

"Yes."

"Don't be shy. Tell us about it," Burgess prompted him.

"Nothing to tell, really. I just got back from my walk and decided to look in on Seth and see how he was doing. I helped him, you know. I was sort of an apprentice. When I opened the door—"

"The door was closed?" Burgess asked.

"Yes. But it wasn't locked. Seth never locked it."

"And what did you see?"

"You know what I saw. He was sprawled out on the bench, dead."

"How did you know he was dead? Did you feel his heart?"

"No, of course I didn't. I saw the blood. I called his name and he didn't answer. I just knew."

"Did you touch anything?" Banks asked.

"No. I ran in here and told the others."

"Did you go near the typewriter?"

"Why should I? I didn't even notice the bloody thing. All I saw was Seth, dead."

It was hard to know whether or not he was telling the truth.

The shock of what he'd seen made his responses vague and defensive.

"So you left everything just as you found it?" Banks said.

"Yes."

"This afternoon, during the meeting," Burgess asked, "did anyone leave the room for any length of time?"

"We all left at one time or another," said Zoe. "You know, to go to the toilet, stretch our legs, whatever."

"Was anyone gone for a long time?"

"I don't know. We were talking. I don't remember."

"So someone could have been away for, say, ten minutes?"

"I suppose so."

"I know you were all busy playing at being concerned citizens," Burgess said, "but surely one of you must have noticed if anyone was gone too long?"

"Look," Rick cut in, "I thought you said it was suicide. What are you asking these questions for?"

"I said it *looked* like suicide," Burgess answered coldly. "And I'll ask whatever bloody questions I think necessary, without any comments from you, Leonardo, thank you very much."

"Did any of you hear the typewriter at any time this afternoon?" Banks asked.

"No," Zoe answered. "But we wouldn't anyway. The walls are thick and the workshop's right at the far end of the garden. Well...you've seen where it is. We were all here in the front room. We could never even hear Seth sawing or using his drill from here."

Banks glanced at Burgess. "Anything else?"

"Not that I can think of right now," the superintendent said, subdued again after his exchange with Rick. "I don't want any of you buggering off anywhere, hear me?" he added, wagging his finger and giving Paul a particularly menacing look. "There'll be more questions when we've got the results of the post-mortem tomorrow, so be available, all of you."

Banks and Burgess left them to their grief. Down the valley side, the lights of Relton looked inviting in the chilly darkness.

"Pint?" Burgess suggested.

"Just what I had in mind," said Banks. They got into the Cortina and bumped away down the track towards the Black Sheep.

II

The pillow felt like a cloud, the bed like cotton wool. Mara lay on her back, drifting, but not quite asleep. When she had first heard the news, she had lost control completely. The tears seemed to spurt from her eyes, her heart began to beat wildly, and the breath clogged in her throat. But the doctor's injection had taken care of all that, trading spasms and panic for clouds and cotton wool.

She could hear the muffled voices downstairs, as if from a great distance, and they made her think of those times when Seth and Liz Dale had stayed up late talking. How jealous she had been then, how insecure. But Liz was long gone, and Seth, they told her, was dead.

Dead. The thought didn't register fully through the layers of sedative. She thought she should still be crying and gasping for breath, but instead her body felt as heavy as iron and she could hardly move. Her mind seemed to have a life of its own, wandering over events and picking them out like those miniature mechanical cranes that dipped into piles of cheap trinkets and sweets at seaside arcades. You put your penny in—a real penny, large and heavy—and off the crane went, with its articulated grip, inside the glass case. You held down a button to make it swing over and pressed another to make it drop onto the heap of prizes. If you were lucky, you got a chocolate bar, a cigarette lighter or a cheap ring; if not, the metal claw came up empty and you'd wasted your money. Mara had never won anything. Just as well, her father had always said: chocolate is bad for teeth; you're too young to smoke and those rings will turn your finger green inside a week.

But her mind felt like one of those machines now, one she could not control. It circled her life, then swooped and snatched up the memory of the first time she and Seth had met. Just out of the ashram and eager to escape London, Mara had taken on a friend's flat in Eastvale when the friend emigrated to Canada.

She needed a job and decided to seek craft-work before falling back on her secretarial skills, which were pretty rusty by then. Luckily, she heard of Elspeth's shop in Relton and went out to see her. Dottie had just become too ill to work—the pottery workshop was hers—and Mara got the job of helping out in the shop and the use of the facilities. It didn't bring in much money, but it was enough, along with the commission on the pottery. Her rent wasn't very high and she lived cheaply. But she was lonely.

Then one day after work, she had dropped in at the Black Sheep. It was pay-day and she had decided to treat herself to a glass of lager and a cheese-and-onion sandwich. No sooner had she started to eat than Seth walked in. He stood at the bar, tall and slim, his neatly trimmed dark hair and beard frosted with grey at the edges. And when he turned around, she noticed how deep and sad his eyes were, how serious he looked. Something passed between them—Seth admitted later that he'd noticed it, too—and Mara felt shy like a teenager again. He smiled at her and she remembered blushing. But when he came over to say hello, there was no phoney coyness on her part; there were never any silly games between them.

He was the first person she'd met in the area with a background similar to her own. They shared tastes in music and ideas about self-sufficiency and the way the world should be run; they had been to the same rock festivals years ago, and had read the same books. She went back with him to the farm that night—he was the only one living there at that time—and she never really left, except to give her notice to her landlord and move her meagre belongings.

It was a blissful time, a homecoming of the spirit for Mara, and she thought she had made Seth happy, too, though she was always aware that there was a part of him she could never touch.

And now he was dead. She didn't know how, or what had killed him, just that his body had ceased to exist. Her spiritual beliefs, which she still held to some extent, told her that death was merely a beginning. There would be other worlds, other lives perhaps, for Seth's spirit, which was immortal. But they would never again drink wine together in bed after making love, he would never kiss her forehead the way he did before going to the workshop, or hold her hand like a boy on his first date on the way down to the Black Sheep. And that was what hurt: the absence of living flesh. The spirit was all very well, but it was far too nebulous an idea to bring Mara much comfort. The miniature crane withdrew from the heap of prizes and held nothing in its metal claw.

Downstairs, the voices droned on, more like music, a *raga*, than words with meaning. Mara felt as if her blood had thickened to treacle and darkened to the colour of ink. Her body was getting heavier and the lights in the glass case were going out; it was half in shadows now, the prizes indistinguishable from one another. And what happens when the lights go out in the fun-house? Mara began to dream.

She was alone on the moors. A huge full moon shone high up, but the landscape was still dark and bleak. She stumbled over heather and tussocks of grass, looking for something.

At last she came to a village and went into the pub. It was the Black Sheep, but the place was all modern, with video games, carpets and bare concrete walls. A jukebox was playing some music she didn't understand. She asked for the farm, but everyone turned and laughed at her, so she ran out.

This time it was daylight outside, and she was no longer in Swainsdale. The landscape was unfamiliar, softer and more green, and she could smell a whiff of the ocean nearby.

In a hollow, she saw an old farmer holding wind chimes out in front of him. They made the same music as the jukebox and it frightened her this time. She found her voice and asked him where Maggie's Farm was. "Are you the marrying maiden?" he asked her, smiling toothlessly. "The basket is empty," he went on, shaking the wind chimes. "The man stabs the sheep. No blood flows. Misfortune."

Terrified, Mara ran off and found herself in an urban landscape at night. Some of the buildings had burned out and fires raged in the gutted shells; flames licked around broken windows and flared up high through fallen roofs. Small creatures scuttled in dark corners. And she was being followed, she knew it. She hadn't been able to see anyone, just sense darting movements and hear rustling sounds behind her. For some reason, she was sure it was a woman, someone she should know but didn't.

Before the dream possessed her completely and turned her into one of the scavengers among the ruins, before the shadow behind tapped her on the shoulder, she struggled to wake up, to scream.

When she opened her eyes, she became conscious of someone sitting on the bedside pressing a damp cloth to her forehead. She thought it must be Seth, but when she turned and looked closely it was Zoe.

"Is it morning?" she asked in a weak voice.

"No," said Zoe, "it's only half-past nine."

"He really is dead, isn't he, Zoe?"

Zoe nodded. "You were having a nightmare. Go to sleep now." Mara closed her eyes again. The cool cloth smoothed her brow, and she began to drift. This time there was only darkness ahead, and the last thing she felt before she fell asleep was Zoe's hand gripping hers tightly.

III

"Anything wrong?" Larry Grafton asked, pulling Banks a pint of Black Sheep bitter.

Banks glanced at Burgess, who nodded.

"Seth Cotton's dead," he answered, and felt ears prick up behind him in the public bar, where most of the tables were occupied.

Grafton turned pale. "Oh no, not Seth," he said. "He was only in here this lunch-time. Not Seth?"

"How did he seem?" Banks asked.

"He was happy as a pig in clover," Grafton said. "That young lad was back and they all seemed to be celebrating. You're not telling me he killed himself, are you?"

"We don't know yet," Burgess said, picking up his pint of Watney's. "Anywhere quiet the chief inspector and I can have a little chat? Police business."

"Aye, you can use the snug. There's no one in there."

The snug was aptly named. Hidden away behind a partition of smoked glass and dark wood, there was room for about four people, and even that would be a tight squeeze.

Banks and Burgess made themselves comfortable, both of them practically draining their drinks before even reaching for smokes.

"Have a cigar," Burgess said, offering his tin.

"Thanks." Banks took one. He didn't enjoy cigars as a rule, but thought that if he tried them often enough he might eventually come to like them.

"And I think I'd better get a couple more drinks in before we start," Burgess said. "Thirsty work, this."

He was back in a moment carrying another pint of bitter for Banks and, this time, a pint of draught Guinness for himself.

"Right," he said, "I can tell you're not happy about this. Don't clam up on me, Banks. What's bothering you?"

"Let's take it at face value, for a start," Banks suggested. "Then maybe we can see what's wrong."

"Suicide?"

"Yes."

"But you don't think so?"

"No. But I'd like to play it through and see if I can pin down my ideas."

"All right. Cotton murdered Gill, then he was overcome with remorse and slit his ankles. Case closed. Can I go back to London now?"

Banks smiled. "But it's not as simple as that, is it? Why would Cotton murder PC Gill?"

Burgess ran a hand through his greying, Brylcreemed hair. "Bloody hell, I thought we'd been through all this before. We're talking about a political crime; call it an act of terrorism. Motive as such doesn't apply."

"But Seth Cotton was perhaps the least political of the lot of them," Banks argued. "Except maybe for Mara, or Zoe Hardacre. Sure, he was anti-nuclear, and he no doubt believed in social equality and the evils of apartheid. But so do I."

Burgess sniffed. "You might be the murder expert around here, but I know about terrorism. Believe me, anyone can get involved. Terrorists play on people's ideals and warp them to their own ends. It's like the brainwashing religious cults do."

"Do you think Gill's death was calmly planned and executed, or was it a crime of passion?" Banks asked.

"A bit of both. Things aren't so clear-cut in this kind of crime. Terrorists are very emotional about their beliefs, but they're cold and deadly when it comes to action."

"The only thing Seth Cotton cared passionately about was his carpentry, and perhaps Mara. If he did commit suicide, I doubt it was anything to do with politics."

"We have his note, don't forget. It's a confession."

"Let's leave that for later. Why did he kill himself? If he's the kind of person you're trying to make out he is, why would he feel remorse after succeeding in his aim? Why would he kill himself?"

Burgess doodled in the foam of his Guinness. "You expect too many answers, Banks. As often as not, there just aren't any. Can't you leave it at that?"

Banks shook his head and stubbed out the cigar. It tasted like last week's tea-leaves. He swigged some more Black Sheep bitter to get rid of the taste and lit a Silk Cut. "It's because there's too many questions," he said. "We still don't know much about Cotton's political background before he came to the farm, though if there'd been any subversive activity I'm sure Special Branch would have a record of it. And what about his behaviour over the last few days? How do you read that?"

"They said he seemed happy when Boyd was released. Is that what you mean?"

"Partly."

"Well, of course he'd be happy," Burgess said. "If he knew the kid wasn't guilty."

"Why should he care? It'd be better for a cold-blooded terrorist to let someone else go down for what he'd done. So why kill himself?"

Burgess shrugged. "Because he knew we'd get to him soon."

"So why didn't he just disappear? Surely his masters would have taken care of him in Moscow or Prague or wherever."

"More likely Belfast. But I don't know. It's not unusual for suicides to appear happy once they've decided to end it all."

"I know that. I'm just not sure that he was happy because he'd decided to kill himself."

Burgess grunted. "What's your theory, then?"

"That he was killed, and it was made to look like a suicide."

"Killed by who?"

Banks ignored the question. "We won't know anything for certain until the doc does his post-mortem," he said, "but there's a few things that bother me about the note."

"Go on."

"It just doesn't ring true. The damn thing's neither here nor there, is it? Cotton confesses to killing Gill, but doesn't say why. All he says is, 'I don't know what came over me.' It doesn't square with what we know of him."

"Which is?"

"Precious little, I admit. He was a closed book. But I'd say he was the kind who'd either not bother with a note at all, or maybe he'd explain everything fully. He wouldn't come out with such a wishy-washy effort as the one we saw. I think he'd have used Gill's number, too, not his name. And I don't know if you had a good look, but it seemed very different from that business letter on the desk. The pressure on the characters was different, for a start."

"Yes," Burgess said, "but don't forget the state of mind he must have been in when he typed it."

"I'll grant you that. Still...and the style. Whoever wrote that suicide note had only very basic writing skills. But the business letter was more than competent and grammatically correct."

Burgess slapped the table. "Oh, come on Banks! What's the problem? Is it too easy for you? Business letters are always written in a different style; they're always a bit stuffy and wordy. You wouldn't write to a friend the same way you would in a business letter, would you, let alone a suicide note. A man writing his last words doesn't worry about grammar or how much pressure he puts on each letter."

"But that's just it. Those things are unconscious. Someone used to writing well doesn't immediately become sloppy just because he's under pressure. If anything, I'd have expected a more carefully composed message. And you don't think about how each finger hits the keys when you're typing. It's something you just do, and it doesn't vary much. Why leave it over in the typewriter, too? Why didn't he put it on the bench in front of him?"

"And what I'm saying," Burgess argued, "is that his state of mind could account for all your objections. He must have been disturbed. Contemplation of suicide has an odd effect on a man's character. You can't expect everything to be the same as usual when a bloke's on the verge of slitting his bloody ankles. And remember, you said he'd tried that before."

"That is a problem," Banks agreed. "Whoever did it must have known about the previous attempt and copied it to make it look more like a genuine suicide."

"That's assuming somebody else did it. I'm not sure I agree."

Banks shrugged. "We'll see what forensic say about the note. But I'm not happy with it at all."

"What about the bureau?"

"What about it?"

"He'd obviously just finished it, hadn't he? The coat of varnish was still fresh. And he'd moved it to the corner of the workshop. Doesn't that imply anything?"

"That he was tidying things up behind him, you mean? Tying up loose ends?"

"Exactly. Just like a man on the point of suicide. He finished his last piece of work, put it carefully aside so he wouldn't get blood all over it, then he slit his fucking ankles. When he got weak and passed out, he hit his head on the vice, accounting for the head wound."

Banks stared into the bottom of his glass. "It could have happened that way," he said slowly. "But I don't think so."

"Which brings us back to the big question again," Burgess said. "If we're to follow your line of reasoning, if you *are* right, then who killed him?"

"It could have been any of them, couldn't it? Zoe said as much."

"Yes, but she might have said that to get herself and her mates off the hook. I'm thinking of one of them in particular."

"Who?"

"Boyd."

Banks sighed. "I was afraid you'd say that."

"I'll bet you bloody were." Burgess leaned forward so suddenly that the glasses rattled on the table. Banks could smell the Guinness and cigar smoke on his breath. "If we play it your way, there's no getting around the facts. Boyd was missing all afternoon, unaccounted for. We only have his word that he was walking on the moors. I shouldn't think anybody saw him. It would have been easy for him to get in by the side gate and visit Seth while everyone in the house was wrapped up in their own little games. Nothing odd about that. He helped Seth a lot, and the shed would be full of his fingerprints anyway. They talk, and he kills Seth—pushes his head forward to knock him out on the vice, then slits his ankles." Burgess leaned back again, satisfied, and folded his arms.

"All right," Banks said. "I agree. It fits. But why? Why would Boyd kill Seth Cotton?"

Burgess shrugged. "Because he knew something to link Boyd to Gill's murder. It makes sense, Banks, you know it does. Why you're defending that obnoxious little prick is beyond me."

"Why was Cotton so miserable when Boyd was in jail," Banks asked, "and so happy when he came out?"

Burgess lit another Tom Thumb. "Loyalty, perhaps? He knew something and was worried he might be called on to give evidence. He wasn't sure he could carry on with his lies and evasions under pressure. Boyd gets out, so Cotton feels immediate elation. They talk. Cotton tells Boyd what he knows and how glad he is he won't have to testify under oath, so Boyd gets worried and kills him. Remember, Boyd knew he wasn't quite off the hook, whatever Cotton might have made of his release. And you know how terrified the kid is of enclosed spaces. He'd do anything to avoid a life sentence."

"And the note?"

"Let's say you're right about that. Boyd typed it to clear himself, put the blame on someone who isn't able to defend himself. It's a cowardly kind of act typical of someone like him. That explains the pressure on the keys and the literacy level. Boyd wasn't very well educated. He was spending most of his time on the streets by the time he was thirteen. And he couldn't explain anything about Cotton's motives because he killed Gill himself. So," Burgess went on, "even if we see it your way, I still come out right. Personally, I don't give a damn whether it was Boyd or Cotton. Either way, we've cracked it. Which way do you want to go? Toss a coin."

"I'm still not convinced."

"That's because you don't want to be."

"What do you mean by that?"

"You know damn well what I mean. You've argued yourself into a corner. It was your idea to let Boyd out and see what happened. Well, now you've seen what's happened. No sooner is he out than there's another death. That makes you responsible."

Banks took a deep breath. There was too much truth for comfort in what Burgess was saying. He shook his head. "Somebody killed Seth," he said, "but I don't think it was Boyd. For all the kid's problems, I believe he genuinely cared. The people at Maggie's Farm are the only ones who have ever done anything for him, gone out on a limb."

"Come off it! That sentimental bullshit doesn't work on me. The kid's a survivor, an opportunist. He's nothing more than a street punk."

"And Cotton?"

Burgess sat back and reached for his glass. The chair creaked. "Good actor, accomplice, innocent bystander, conscience-stricken idealist? I don't bloody know. But it doesn't matter now, does it? He's dead. It's all over."

But Banks felt that it did matter. Somehow, after what had happened that afternoon, it seemed to matter more now than it ever had before.

"Is it?" he said. Then he stubbed out his cigarette and drained his glass. "Come on, let's go."

FIFTEEN

I

Eastvale General Infirmary stood on King Street, about half a mile
west of the police station, not far from the comprehensive school.
Because the day was warming up nicely, Banks decided to walk. As he
left the station, he turned on his Walkman and listened to Muddy
Waters sing "Louisiana Blues" as he made his way through the warren
of narrow streets with their cracked stone walls, gift shops and over-
priced pubs.

The hospital itself was an austere Victorian brick building. About
its high draughty corridors hung an air of fatalistic gloom. Not quite
the hospital I'd choose if I were ill, Banks thought, fiddling with the
Walkman's off-switch in his overcoat pocket.

The mortuary was in the basement, which, like the police station's
cell area, was the most modern part of the building. The autopsy
room had white-tiled walls and a central metal table with guttering
around its edges to channel off the blood. A long lab bench, complete with Bunsen burners and microscopes, stretched along one wall,
with shelving above it for jars of organs, tissue samples and prepared
chemical solutions.

Fortunately, the table was empty when Banks entered. A lab
assistant was in the process of scrubbing it down, while
Glendenning stood at the bench, a cigarette dangling from his
mouth. Everyone smoked in the mortuary; they did it to keep the
stench of death at bay.

The lab assistant dropped a surgical instrument into a metal kidney bowl. Banks winced at the sound.

"Let's go into the office," Glendenning said. "I can see you're a bit pink around the gills."

Glendenning's office was small and cluttered, hardly befitting a man of his stature and status, Banks thought. But this wasn't America; health care was hardly big business, despite private insurance plans. Glendenning took his white lab coat off, smoothed his shirt and sat down. Banks shifted some old medical journals from the only remaining chair and placed himself opposite the doctor.

"Coffee?"

Banks nodded. "Yes, please."

Glendenning picked up his phone and pressed a button. "Molly, dear, do you think you could scrape up two cups of coffee?" He covered the mouthpiece and asked Banks how he liked his. "One black no sugar, and the usual for me. Yes, three sugars, that's right. What diet? And don't bring that vile muck they drink at reception. What? Yes. I know you'd run out yesterday, but that's no excuse. I haven't paid my coffee money for three weeks? What is this, woman, the bloody Inquisition?" He hung up roughly, ran a hand through his white hair and sighed. "Good help is hard to find these days. Now, Mr Banks, let's see what we have here." He riffled through the stack of papers on his desk.

He probably knew it all off by heart, Banks thought, but needed the security of his files and sheets of paper in front of him just as Richmond always liked to read from his notebook what he knew perfectly well in the first place.

"Seth Cotton, aye, poor chappie." Glendenning took a pair of half-moon reading glasses from his top pocket and held the report at arm's length as he peered down his nose at it. Having done with that, he put it aside, took off his glasses and sat back in his chair with his large but delicate hands folded on his lap. The coffee arrived, and Molly, giving her boss a disapproving glance on the way, departed.

"Last meal about three hours before death," Glendenning said. "And a good one, too, if I may say so. Roast beef, Yorkshire pudding. What better meal could a condemned man wish for?"

"Haggis?"

Glendenning wagged his finger. "Dinna extract the urine, Mr Banks."

Banks sipped some coffee. It was piping hot and tasted good. Clearly it wasn't the "vile muck" from reception.

"No evidence of poisoning, or indeed of any other wounds bar the external. Mr Cotton was in perfectly good health until the blood drained out of his body."

"Was that the cause of death?"

"Aye. Loss of about five pints of blood usually does cause death."

"What about the blow to the head? Was it delivered before or after the cuts to the ankles?"

Glendenning scratched his head. "That I can't tell you. The vital reaction was quite consistent with a wound caused before death. As you saw for yourself, there was plenty of blood. And the leucocyte count was high—that's white blood cells to you, the body's little repairmen. Had the blow to the head occurred some time after death, then of course there would have been clear evidence to that effect, but the two wounds happened so closely together that it's impossible to say which came first. Cotton was certainly alive when he hit his head—or when someone hit it for him. But how long he survived after the blow, I can't tell. Of course, the head wound may have caused loss of consciousness, and it's very difficult to slash your ankles when you're unconscious, as I'm sure you're aware."

"Could he have hit his head while bending down to make the cuts?"

Glendenning pursed his lips. "I wouldn't say so, no. You saw the blood on the bench. None of it had trickled onto the floor. I'd say by the angle of the wound and the sharp edges of the vice that his head was resting exactly where it landed after the blow."

"Could someone have come up behind him and pushed his head down onto the vice?"

"Now you're asking me to speculate, Mr Banks. All I can tell you is that I found no signs of scratching or bruising at the back of the neck or the head."

"Does that mean no?"

"Not necessarily. If you come up behind someone and give his head a quick push before he has time to react, then I doubt it would show."

"So that means it must have been someone he knew. He'd have

noticed anyone else creeping up on him. Whoever did it must have
been in the workshop already, someone he didn't mind having around
while he carried on working."

"Theories, theories," Glendenning said. "I don't know why you're
not satisfied with suicide. There's absolutely no evidence to the
contrary."

"No medical evidence, perhaps."

"I'm sorry," said Glendenning. "I'd like to be able to help you more,
but those are the facts. While the blow to the head may well have
caused complications had Mr Cotton lived, it was in no way responsible for his death."

"Complications? What complications?"

Glendenning frowned and reached for another cigarette from the
box on his desk. It looked antique, and Banks noticed some words
engraved in ornate italics on the top: "To Dr C.W.S. Glendenning, on
Successful Completion of . . ." He couldn't read the rest. He assumed
it was some kind of graduation present.

"All kinds," Glendenning answered. "We don't know a great deal
about the human brain, Mr Banks. A lot more than we used to, of
course, but still not enough. Certain head wounds can result in effects
far beyond the power of the blow and the extent of the apparent
damage. Bone chips can lodge in the tissue, and even bruising can
cause problems."

"What problems?"

"Almost anything. Memory loss—temporary or permanent—
hearing and vision problems, vertigo, personality change, temporary
lapses of consciousness. Need I go on?"

Banks shook his head.

"But in the case of Mr Cotton, of course, that's something we'll
never know."

"No." Banks got to his feet. "Anyway, thank you very much, doctor."

Glendenning inclined his head regally.

On the way back to the station, Banks hardly heard Muddy
Waters. According to Glendenning, Cotton could have been murdered, and that was enough for Banks. Of course, the doctor wouldn't
commit himself—he never did—but even an admission of the

possibility was a long way for him to go. If Burgess was right, there was a good chance Boyd had done it, and that left Banks with Seth's blood on his hands.

As if that weren't enough, something else nagged at him: one of those frustrating little feelings you can't quite define, like having a name at the tip of your tongue, or an itch you can't scratch. He didn't want to be premature, but it felt like the familiar glimmer of an idea. Disparate facts were coming together, and with a lot of hard thinking, a bit of help from the subconscious and a touch of luck, they might actually lead to the answer. He was still a long way from that as yet, and when Muddy Waters started singing "Still a Fool," Banks believed him.

It was after eleven o'clock, according to the church clock, and Burgess would be out questioning Osmond and the students. In his office, Banks called the forensic lab and asked for Vic Manson. He had to wait a few minutes, but finally Vic came on the line.

"The prints?" Banks asked.

"Yes. Four sets. At least four identifiable sets. One belongs to the deceased, of course, another to that Boyd character—the same as the ones we found on the knife—and two more."

"They'll probably be Mara's and one of the others'." Banks said. "Look, thanks a lot, Vic. I'll try and arrange to get the others finger-printed for comparison. Is Geoff Tingley around?"

"Yep. Just a sec, I'll get him for you."

Banks could hear distant voices at the end of the line, then someone picked up the receiver and-spoke. "Tingley here. Is it about those letters?"

"Yes."

"Well, I'm almost positive they weren't typed by the same person. You can make a few allowances for changes in pressure, but these were so wildly different I'd say that's almost conclusive. I could do with a few more samples of at least one of the writers, though. It'll give me more variables and a broader scope for comparison."

"I'll see what I can do," Banks said. There were probably other examples of Seth's typing in the filing cabinet. "Would it do any good if we got a suspect to type us a sample?" he asked.

"Hmmm. It might do. Problem is if he knew what we were after it wouldn't be too difficult to fake it. I'd say this chap's a plodder, though. You can tell it's been pecked out by the overall high pressure, each letter very deliberately sought and pounced on, so to speak. Hunt-and-peck, as I believe they call the technique. The other chap was a better typist, still two fingers, I'd say, but fairly quick and accurate. Probably had a lot more practice. And there's another thing, too. Did you notice the writing styles of the letters were—"

"Yes," Banks said. "We spotted that. Good of you to point it out, though."

Tingley sounded disappointed. "Oh, it's nothing."

"Thanks very much. I'll be in touch about the samples and testing. Could you put Vic on again? I've just remembered something."

"Will do."

"Are you still there?" Manson asked a few seconds later.

"Yes. Look, Vic, there's a couple more points. The typewriter for a start."

"Nothing clear on that, just a lot of blurs."

"Was it wiped?"

"Could have been."

"There was a cloth on that table, wasn't there? One of those yellow dusters."

"Yes, there was," said Manson. "Do you want me to check for fibres?"

"If you would. And the paper?"

"Same, nothing readable."

"What about that pen, or whatever it was we found on the floor. Have you had time to get around to that yet?"

"Yes. It's just an ordinary ball-point, a Bic. No prints of course, just a sweaty blur."

"Hmmm."

The pen had been found in the puddle of blood, just below Seth's dangling right arm. If he was right-handed, as Banks thought he was, he could have used the pen to write a note before he died. It could have just fallen there earlier, of course, but Seth had been very tidy, especially in his final moments. Perhaps he had written his own note, and whoever killed him took it and replaced it with the second version. Why? Because Seth hadn't murdered Gill and had said so clearly in his note? That meant he had committed suicide for some other reason entirely. Had he even named the killer, or was it an identity he had died trying to protect?

Too many questions, again. Maybe Burgess and Glendenning were right and he was a fool not to accept the easy solutions. After all, he had a choice: either Seth Cotton was guilty as the note indicated and had really killed himself, or Paul Boyd, fearing discovery, had killed him and faked the note. Banks leaned closer towards the second of these, but for some reason he still couldn't convince himself that Boyd had done it—and not only because he took the responsibility for letting the kid out of jail. Boyd certainly had a record, and he had taken off when the knife was discovered. He could be a lot tougher and more clever than anyone realized. If he was faking his claustrophobia, for example, so that even Burgess was more inclined to believe him because of his fear of incarceration, then anything was possible. But so far they had nothing but circumstantial evidence, and Banks still felt that the picture was incomplete. He lit a cigarette and walked over to look down on the market square. It brought no inspiration today.

Finally, he decided it was time to tidy his desk before lunch. Almost every available square inch was littered with little yellow Post-it notes, most of which he had acted on ages ago. He screwed them all up and dropped them in the waste basket. Next came the files, statements and records he'd read to refresh his memory of the people involved. Most information was stored in the records department, but Banks had developed the habit of keeping brief files on all the cases he had a hand in. At the top was his file on Elizabeth Dale. Picking it up again, he remembered that he had just pulled it out of the cabinet, after some difficulty in locating it, when Sergeant Rowe had called with the news of Seth Cotton's death.

He opened the folder and brought back to mind the facts of the case—not even a case, really, just a minor incident that had occurred some eighteen months ago.

Elizabeth Dale had checked herself into a psychiatric hospital on the outskirts of Huddersfield, complaining of depression, apathy and general inability to cope with the outside world. After a couple of days' observation and treatment, she had decided she didn't like the service and ran off to Maggie's Farm, where she knew that Seth Cotton, an old friend from Hebden Bridge was living. The hospital authorities informed Eastvale that she had spoken about her friend with the house near Relton, and they asked the local social services to please check up and see if she was there.

She was. Dennis Osmond had been sent to the farm to try to convince her to return to the hospital for her own good, but Ms Dale remained adamant: she was staying at the farm. Osmond also had the nerve to agree that the place would probably do her good. In anger and desperation, the hospital sent out two men of its own, who persuaded Elizabeth to return with them. They had browbeaten her and threatened her with committal, or so Seth Cotton and Osmond had complained at the time.

Because Elizabeth Dale also had a history of drug addiction, the police were called out when the hospital employees said they suspected the people at the farm were using drugs. Banks had gone out there with Sergeant Hatchley and a uniformed constable, but they had found nothing. Ms Dale went back to the hospital, and as far as Banks knew, everything returned to normal.

In the light of recent events, though, it became a more intriguing tale. For one thing, both Elizabeth Dale and Dennis Osmond were connected with PC Gill via the complaints they had made independently. And now it appeared there was yet another link between Osmond and Dale.

Where was Elizabeth Dale now? He would have to go to Huddersfield and find her himself. He'd learned from experience that it was absolutely no use at all dealing with doctors over the phone. But that would have to wait until tomorrow. First, he wanted to talk to Mara again, if she was well enough. Before setting off, he considered phoning Jenny to try to make up the row they'd had on Sunday lunch-time.

Just as he was about to call her, the phone rang.

"Chief Inspector Banks?"

"Speaking."

"My name is Lawrence Courtney, of Courtney, Courtney and Courtney, Solicitors."

"Yes, I've heard of the firm. What can I do for you?"

"It's what I might be able to do for you," Courtney said. "I read in this morning's newspaper that a certain Seth Cotton has died. Is that correct?"

"That's right, yes."

"Well, it might interest you to know, Chief Inspector, that we are the holders of Mr Cotton's will."

"Will?"

"Yes, will." He sounded faintly irritated. "Are you interested?"

"Indeed I am."

"Would it be convenient for you to call by our office after lunch?"

"Yes, certainly. But look, can't you tell me—"

"Good. I'll see you then. About two-thirty, shall we say? Goodbye, Chief Inspector."

Banks slammed the phone down. Bloody pompous solicitor. He cursed and reached for a cigarette. But a will? That was unexpected. Banks wouldn't have thought such a nonconformist as Seth would have bothered making a will. Still, he did own property, and a business. But how could he have had any idea that he was going to die in the near future?

Banks jotted down the solicitor's name and the time of the meeting and stuck the note to his desk. Then he took a deep breath, phoned Jenny at her university office in York, and plunged right in. "I'm sorry about yesterday. I know what it must have sounded like, but I couldn't think of a better way of telling you."

"I over-reacted." Jenny said. "I feel like an idiot. I suppose you were only doing your job."

"I wasn't going to tell you, not until I realized that being around Osmond really might be dangerous."

"And I shouldn't have mistaken your warning for interference. It's just that I get so bloody frustrated. Damn men! Why do I never seem able to choose the right one?"

"Does it matter to you, what he did?"

"Of course it matters."

"Are you going to go on seeing him?"

"I don't know." She affected a bored tone. "I was getting rather tired of him, anyway. Have there been any developments?"

"What in? The break-in or the Gill murder?"

"Well, both, seeing as you ask. What's wrong? You sound a bit tense."

"Oh, nothing. It's been a busy morning, that's all. And I was nervous about calling you. Have you read about Seth Cotton?"

"No. I didn't have time to look at the paper this morning. Why, what's happened?"

Banks told her.

"Oh God. Poor Mara. Do you think there's anything I can do?"

"I don't know. I've no idea what state she's in. I'm calling on her later this afternoon. I'll mention your name if you like."

"Please do. Tell her how sorry I am. And if she needs to talk... What do you think happened, or can't you say?"

"I wish I could." Banks summed up his thoughts for her.

"And I suppose you're feeling responsible? Is that why you don't really want to consider that Boyd did it?"

"You're right about the guilt. Burgess would never have let him go if I hadn't pressed him."

"Burgess hardly seems like the kind of man to bow to pressure. I can't see him consenting to do anything he didn't want to."

"Perhaps you're right. Still... it's not just that. At least, I don't think so. There's something much more complex behind all this. And don't accuse me of over-complicating matters—I've had enough of that already."

"Oh, we are touchy today, aren't we? I had no such thing in mind."

"Sorry. I suppose it's getting to me. About the break-in. I've got something in the works and we'll probably know by tonight, tomorrow morning at the latest."

"What's it all about?"

"I'd rather not say yet. But don't worry, I don't think Osmond's in any kind of danger."

"Are you sure?"

"Absolutely."

"If you're right?"

"Am I ever wrong? Look, before you choke, I've got to go now. I'll be in touch later."

Though where he had to go he wasn't quite certain. There was the solicitor, but that wasn't until two-thirty. Feeling vaguely depressed, he lit another cigarette and went over to the window. The Queen's Arms, that was it. A pie and a pint would soon cheer him up. And Burgess had made a tentative arrangement to meet there around one-thirty and compare notes.

II

Banks found the offices of Courtney, Courtney and Courtney on Market Street, quite close to the police station. Too close, in fact, to make it worthwhile turning on the Walkman for the journey.

The firm of solicitors was situated in what had once been a tea-shop, and the new name curved in a semicircle of gold lettering on the plate-glass window. Banks asked the young receptionist for Mr Lawrence Courtney, and after a brief exchange on the intercom, was shown through to a large office stacked with legal papers.

Lawrence Courtney himself, wedged behind a large executive desk, was not the prim figure Banks had expected from their phone conversation—three-piece suit, gold watch chain, pince-nez, nose raised as if perpetually exposed to a bad smell—instead he was a relaxed, plump man of about fifty with over-long fair hair, a broad, ruddy face and a fairly pleasant expression. His jacket hung behind the door. He wore a white shirt, a red and green striped tie and plain black braces. Banks noticed that the top button of the shirt was undone and the tie had been loosened, just like his own.

"Seth Cotton's will," Banks said, sitting down after a brisk damp handshake.

"Yes. I thought you'd be interested," said Courtney. A faint smile tugged at the corners of his pink, rubbery lips.

"When did he make it?"

"Let me see.... About a year ago. I think." Courtney found the document and read off the date.

"Why did he come to you? I'm not sure how well you knew him, but he didn't seem to me the kind of person to deal with a solicitor."

"We handled the house purchase," Courtney said, "and when the conveyance was completed we suggested a will. We often do. It's not so much a matter of touting for business as making things easier. So many people die intestate, and you've no idea what complications that leads to if there is no immediate family. The house itself, for example. As far as I know, Mr Cotton wasn't married, even under common law."

"What was his reaction to your suggestion?"

"He said he'd think about it."

"And he thought about it for two years?"

"It would appear so, yes. If you don't mind my asking, Chief Inspector, why all this interest in his reason for making a will? People do, you know."

"It's the timing, that's all. I was just wondering why then rather than any other time."

"Hmmm. I imagine that's the kind of thing you people have to think about. Are you interested in the contents at all?"

"Of course."

Courtney unfolded the paper fully, peered at it, then put it aside again and hooked his thumbs in his braces. "Not much to it, really," he said. "He left the house and what little money he had—somewhere in the region of two thousand pounds, I believe, though you'll have to check with the bank—to one Mara Delacey."

"Mara? And that's it?"

"Not quite. Oddly enough he added a codicil just a few months ago. Shortly before Christmas, in fact. It doesn't affect the original bequest, but merely specifies that all materials, monies and goodwill relating to his carpentry business be left to Paul Boyd, in the hope that he uses them wisely."

"Bloody hell!"

"Is something wrong?"

"It's nothing. Sorry. Mind if I smoke?"

"If you must." Courtney took a clean ashtray from his drawer and pushed it disapprovingly towards Banks. Undeterred, Banks lit up.

"The way I see things, then," Banks said, "is that he left the house and the money to Mara after he'd only known her for a year or so, and the carpentry business to Paul after the kid had only been at the farm for a couple of months."

"If you say so, Chief Inspector. It would indicate that Mr Cotton was quick to trust people."

"It would indeed. Or that there was nobody else he could even consider. I doubt that he'd have wanted his goods and chattels to go to the state. But who knows where Boyd might have got to by the time Cotton died of natural causes? Or Mara. Could he have had some idea that he was in danger?"

"I'm afraid I can't answer that," Courtney said. "Our business ends with the legal formalities, and Mr Cotton certainly made no mention of an imminent demise. If there's anything else I can help you with, of course, I'd be more than willing."

"Thank you," said Banks. "I think that's all. Will you be informing Mara Delacey?"

"We will take steps to get in touch with beneficiaries in due course, yes."

"Is it all right if I tell her this afternoon?"

"I can't see any objection. And you might ask her—both of them, if possible—to drop by the office. I'll be happy to explain the procedure to them. If you have any trouble with the bank, Chief Inspector, please refer them to me. It's the National Westminster—or NatWest, as I believe they call themselves these days—the branch in the market square. The manager is a most valued client."

"I know the place." Know it, Banks thought, I practically stare at it for hours on end every day.

"Then goodbye, Chief Inspector. It's been a pleasure."

Banks walked out into the street more confused than ever. Before he got back to the station, however, he'd managed to put some check on his wild imaginings. The will probably didn't come into the case at all. Seth Cotton had simply had more foresight than many would have credited him with. What was wrong with that? And it was perfectly natural that, with his parents both dead and no close family, he would leave the house to Mara. And Paul Boyd was, after all, his apprentice. It was a gesture of faith and confidence on Seth's part.

Even if Mara and Paul had known what they had coming to them, neither, Banks was positive, would have murdered Seth to get it. Life for Mara was clearly better with Seth than without him, and whatever ugliness might be lurking in Boyd's character, he was neither stupid nor petty enough to kill for a set of carpenter's tools. So forget the will, Banks told himself. Nice gesture though it was, it is irrelevant. Except, perhaps, for the date. Why wait till two years after Courtney had suggested it before actually getting the business done? Procrastination?

It also raised a more serious question: had Seth felt that his life was in danger a year ago? If so, why had it taken so long for the danger to manifest itself? And had that fear somehow also renewed itself around Christmas time?

Before returning to his office, he nipped into the National Westminster and had no problem in getting details of Seth's financial affairs, such as they were: he had a savings account at £2343.64, and a current account, which stood at £421.33.

It was after three-thirty when he got back to the station, and there was a message from Vic Manson to the effect that, yes, fibres matching those from the duster had been found on the typewriter keys. But, Manson had added with typical forensic caution, there was no way of proving whether the machine had been wiped before or after the message had been typed. The pressure of fingers on the keys often blurs prints.

Banks's brief chat with Burgess over lunch had revealed nothing new, either. Dirty Dick had seen Osmond and got nowhere with him. Early in the afternoon he was off to see Tim and Abha, and he was quite happy to leave Mara Delacey to Banks. As far as Burgess was concerned, it was all over bar the shouting, but he wanted more evidence to implicate Boyd or Cotton with extremist politics. Most of the time he'd had his eye on Glenys, and he'd kept reminding Banks that it was her night off that night. Cyril, fortunately, had been nowhere in sight.

Banks left a message for Burgess at the front desk summarizing what Lawrence Courtney had said about Seth's will. Then he called Sergeant Hatchley, as Richmond was busy on another matter, to accompany him and to bring along the fingerprinting kit. He slipped the Muddy Waters cassette from his Walkman and hurried out to the car with it, a huffing and puffing Hatchley in tow. It was time to see if Mara Delacey was ready to talk.

"What do you think of Superintendent Burgess?" Banks asked Hatchley on the way. They hadn't really had a chance to talk much over the past few days.

"Off the record?"

"Yes."

"Well..." Hatchley rubbed his face with a hamlike hand. "He seemed all right at first. Bit of zip about him. You know, get up and go. But I'd have thought a whiz-kid like him would have got a bit further by now."

"None of us have got any further," Banks said. "What do you mean? The man's only flesh and blood after all."

"I suppose that's it. He dazzles you a bit at first, then..."

"Don't underestimate him," Banks said. "He's out of his element up here. He's getting frustrated because we don't have raving anarchists crawling out of every nook and cranny in the town."

"Aye," said Hatchley. "And you thought I was right wing."

"You are."

Hatchley grunted.

"When we get to the farm, I want you to have a look in Seth's filing cabinet in the workshop," Banks went on, pulling onto the Roman road, "and see if you can find more samples of his typing. And I'd like you to fingerprint everyone. Ask for their consent, and tell them we can get a magistrate's order if they refuse. Also make sure you tell them that the prints will be destroyed if no charges are brought." Banks paused and scratched the edge of his scar. "I'd like to have them all type a few lines on Seth's typewriter, too, but we'll have to wait till it comes back from forensic. All clear?"

"Fine," Hatchley said.

Zoe answered the door, looking tired and drawn.

"Mara's not here," she said in response to Banks's question, opening the door only an inch or two.

"I thought she was under sedation."

"That was last night. She had a good long sleep. She said she felt like going to the shop to work on some pots, and the doctor agreed it might be good therapy. Elspeth's there in case...just in case."

"I'll go down to the village, then," Banks said to Hatchley. "You'll have to manage up here. Will you let the sergeant in, Zoe?"

Zoe sighed and opened the door.

"Are you coming back up?" Hatchley asked.

Banks looked at his watch. "Why not meet in the Black Sheep?"

Hatchley smiled at the prospect of a pint of Black Sheep bitter, then his face fell. "How do I get there?"

"Walk."

"Walk?"

"Yes. It's just a mile down the track. Do you good. Give you a thirst."

Hatchley wasn't convinced—he had never had any problems working up a thirst without exercise before—but Banks left him to his fate and drove down to Relton.

Mara was in the back bent over her wheel, gently turning the lip of a vase. Elspeth led him through, muttered, "A policeman to see you," with barely controlled distaste, then went back into the shop itself.

Mara glanced up. "Let me finish," she said. "If I stop now, I'll ruin it." Banks leaned against the doorway and kept quiet. The room smelled of wet clay. It was also hot. The kiln in the back generated a lot of heat. Mara's long brown hair was tied back, accentuating the sharpness of her nose and chin as she concentrated. Her white smock was stained with splashed clay.

Finally, she drenched the wheel-head with water, sliced off the vase with a length of cheese-wire, then slid it carefully onto her hand before transferring it to a board.

"What now?" Banks asked.

"It has to dry." She put it away in a large cupboard at the back of the room. "Then it goes in the kiln."

"I thought the kiln dried it."

"No. That bakes it. First it has to be dried to the consistency of old cheddar."

"These are good," Banks said, pointing to some finished mugs glazed in shades of orange and brown.

"Thanks." Mara's eyes were puffy and slightly unfocused, her movements slow and zombie-like. Even her voice, Banks noticed, was flatter than usual, drained of emotion and vitality.

"I have to ask you some questions," he said.

"I suppose you do."

"Do you mind?"

Mara shook her head. "Let's get it over with."

She perched at the edge of her stool and Banks sat on a packing crate just inside the doorway. He could hear Elspeth humming as she busied herself checking on stock in the shop.

"Did you notice anyone gone for an unusually long time during the meeting yesterday afternoon?" Banks asked.

"Was it only yesterday? Lord, it seems like months. No, I didn't notice. People came and went, but I don't think anyone was gone for long. I'm not sure I would have noticed, though."

"Did Seth ever say anything to you before about suicide? Did he ever mention the subject?"

Mara's lips tightened and the blood seemed to drain from them. "No. Never."

"He'd tried once before, you know."

Mara raised her thin eyebrows. "It seems you knew him better than I did."

"Nobody knew him, as far as I can tell. There was a will, Mara."

"I know."

"Do you remember when he made it?"

"Yes. He joked about it. Said it made him feel like an old man."

"Is that all?"

"That's all I remember."

"Did he say why he was making it at that time?"

"No. He just told me that the solicitor who handled the house, Courtney, said he should, and he'd been thinking about it for a long time."

"Do you know what was in the will?"

"Yes. He said he was leaving me the house. Does that make me a suspect?"

"Did you know about the codicil?"

"Codicil? No."

"He left his tools and things to Paul."

"Well, he would, wouldn't he. Paul was keen, and I've got no use for them."

"Did Paul know?"

"I've no idea."

"This would be around last Christmas."

"Maybe it was his idea of a present."

"But what made him think he was going to die? Seth was what age—forty? By all rights he could expect to live to seventy or so. Was he worried about anything?"

"Seth always seemed...well, not worried, but preoccupied. He'd got even more morbid of late. It was just his way."

"But there was nothing in particular?"

Mara shook her head. "I don't believe he killed himself, Mr Banks. He had lots to live for. He wouldn't just leave us like that. Everyone depended on Seth. We looked up to him. And he cared about me, about us. I think somebody must have killed him."

"Who?"

"I don't know."

Banks shifted position on the packing crate. Its surface was hard and he felt a nail dig into the back of his right thigh. "Do you remember Elizabeth Dale?"

"Liz. Yes, of course. Funny, I was just thinking about her last night."

"What about her?"

"Oh, nothing really. How jealous I was, I suppose, when she came to the farm that time. I'd only known Seth six months then. We were happy but, I don't know, I guess I was insecure. Am."

"Why did you feel jealous?"

"Maybe that's not the right word. I just felt cut out, that's all. Seth and Liz had known each other for a long time, and I didn't share their memories. They used to sit up late talking after I went to bed."

"Did you hear what they were talking about?"

"No. It was muffled. Do smoke if you want."

"Thanks." She must have noticed him fidgeting and looking around for an ashtray. He took out his pack and offered one to Mara.

"I think I will," she said. "I can't be bothered to roll my own today."

"What did you think about Liz Dale?"

Mara lit the cigarette and inhaled deeply. "I didn't like her, really. I don't know why, just a feeling. She was messed up, of course, but even so, she seemed like someone who used people, leaned on them too much, maybe a manipulator." She shrugged wearily and blew smoke out through her nose. "She was Seth's friend, though. I wasn't going to say anything."

"So you put up with her?"

"It was easy enough. She was only with us three days before those SS men from the hospital took her back."

"Dennis Osmond came up first, didn't he?"

"Yes. But he was too soft, they said. He didn't see why she shouldn't stay where she was, especially as she hadn't been committed or anything, just checked herself in. He argued with the hospital people, but it was no good."

"How did Osmond and Liz get along?"

"I don't know really. I mean, he stuck up for her, that's all."

"There wasn't anything between them?"

"What do you mean? Sexual?"

"Anything."

"I doubt it. They only met twice, and I wouldn't say she was his type."

"And that was the first time Seth met Osmond?"

"As far as I know."

"Did you get the impression that Osmond had known Liz before?"

"No. I didn't. But impressions can be wrong. What are you getting at?"

"I'm not sure myself. Just following my nose."

"Mr Banks," Mara whispered suddenly. "do you think Dennis Osmond killed Seth? Is that it? I know Seth couldn't have done it himself, and I...I can't seem to think straight...."

"Steady on." Banks caught her in his arms as she slid forward from the stool. Her hair smelled of apples. He sat her on a stiff-backed chair in the corner, and her eyes filled with tears. "All right?"

"Yes. I'm sorry. That sedative takes most of the feeling out of me, but..."

"It's still there?"

"Yes. Just below the surface."

"We can continue this later if you like. I'll drive you home." He thought how pleased Hatchley would be to see the Cortina turning up again.

Mara shook her head. "No, it's all right. I can handle it. I'm just confused. Maybe some water."

Banks brought her a glass from the tap at the stained porcelain sink in the corner.

"So are we," he said. "Confused. It looked like a suicide in some ways, but there were contradictions."

"He wouldn't kill himself, I'm sure of it. Paul was back again. Seth was happy. He had the farm, friends, the children...."

Banks didn't know what to say to make her feel better.

"When he tried before," she said, "was it because of Alison?"

"Yes."

"I can understand that. It makes sense. But not now. Someone must have killed him." Mara sipped at her water. "Anyone could have come in through the side gate and sneaked up on him."

"It didn't happen like that, Mara. Take my word for it, he had to know the person. It was someone he felt comfortable with. Have you seen or heard anything from Liz Dale since she left?"

"I haven't, no. Seth went to visit her in the hospital a couple of times, but then he lost touch."

"Any letters?"

"Not that he told me about."

"Christmas card?"

"No."

"Do you know where she is now?"

"No. Is it important?"

"It could be. Do you know anything about her background?"

Mara frowned and rubbed her temple. "As far as I know she's from down south somewhere. She used to be a nurse until . . . Well, she fell in with a bad crowd, got involved with drugs and lost her job. Since then she just sort of drifted."

"And ended up in Hebden Bridge?"

"Yes."

"Did you see her do any drugs at the farm?"

"No. And I'm not just saying that. She was off heroin. That was part of the problem, why she was unable to cope."

"Was Seth ever an addict?"

"I don't think so. I think he'd have told me about that. We talked about drugs, how we felt about them and how they weren't really important, so I think he'd have told me."

"And you've no idea where Liz is now?"

"None at all."

"What about Alison?"

"What about her? She's dead."

A hint of bitterness had crept into her tone, and Banks wondered why. Jealousy? It could happen. Plenty of people were jealous of pre-

vious lovers, even dead ones. Or was she angry at Seth for not making her fully a part of his life, for not sharing all his feelings? She
unfastened her hair and shook her head, allowing the chestnut tresses
to cascade over her shoulders.

"Can I have another cigarette?"

"Of course." Banks gave her one. "Surely Seth must have told you
something," he said. "You don't live with someone for two years and
find out nothing about their past."

"Don't you? And how would you know?"

Banks didn't know. When he had met Sandra, they had been
young and had little past to talk about, none of it very interesting. "It
just doesn't make sense," he said.

The shop bell clanged and broke the silence. They heard Elspeth
welcoming a customer, an American by the sound of his drawl.

"What are you going to do now?" Banks asked.

Mara rubbed her eyes. "I don't know. I'm too tired to throw
another pot. I think I'll just go home and go to bed early."

"Do you want a ride?"

"No. Really. A bit of fresh air and exercise will do me good."

Banks smiled. "I wish my sergeant felt the same way."

"What?"

Banks explained and Mara managed a weak smile.

They walked out together, Banks collecting a sour look from
Elspeth on the way. Outside the Black Sheep, Mara turned away.

"I am sorry, you know, about your loss," Banks said awkwardly to
her back.

Mara turned around and stared at him for a long time. He couldn't
make out what she was thinking or feeling.

"I do believe you are," she said finally.

"And Jenny sends her condolences. She says to give her a call if
you ever need anything . . . a friend."

Mara said nothing.

"She didn't betray your confidence, you know. She was worried
about you. And you went to her because you were worried about
Paul, didn't you?"

Mara nodded slowly.

"Well, give her a call. All right?"

"All right." And tall though she was, Mara seemed a slight figure walking up the lane in the dark toward the Roman road. Banks stood and watched till she was out of sight.

Hatchley was already in the Black Sheep halfway through his second pint, judging by the empty glass next to the half-full one in front of him. Banks went to the bar first, bought two more and sat down. As far as he was concerned, Hatchley could drink as much as he wanted. He was a lousy driver even when sober, and Banks had no intention of letting him anywhere near the Cortina's driving seat.

"Anything?" the sergeant asked.

"No, not really. You?"

"That big bloke with the shaggy beard put up a bit of an argument at first, but the little lass with the red hair told him it was best to cooperate."

"Damn," Banks said. "I knew there was something I'd forgotten. Mara's prints. Never mind, I'll get them later."

"Anyway," Hatchley went on, "most of the letters in the cabinet were carbons, but I managed to rescue a couple of drafts from the waste bin."

"Good."

"You don't sound so pleased," Hatchley complained.

"What? Oh, sorry. Thinking of something else. Let's drink up and get your findings sent over to the lab."

Hatchley drained his third pint with astonishing speed and looked at his watch. "It's going on for six-thirty," he said. "No point rushing now; they'll all have buggered off home for the night." He glanced over at the bar. "Might as well have another."

Banks smiled. "Unassailable logic, Sergeant. All right. Better make it a quick one, though. And it's your round."

III

At home, Banks managed to warm up a frozen dinner—peas, mashed potatoes and veal cutlet—without ruining it. After washing the dishes—or, rather, rinsing his knife and fork and coffee cup and throwing the metal tray into the rubbish bin, he called Sandra.

"So when do I get my wife back?" he asked.

"Wednesday morning. Early train," Sandra said. "We should be home around lunch-time. Dad's a lot better now and Mum's coping better than I'd imagined."

"Good. I'll try and be in," Banks said. "It depends."

"How are things going?"

"They're getting more complicated."

"You sound grouchy, too. It's a good sign. The more complicated things seem and the more bad-tempered you get, the closer the end is."

"Is that right?"

"Of course it is. I haven't lived with you this long without learning to recognize the signs."

"Sometimes I wonder what people do learn about one another."

"What's this? Philosophy?"

"No. Just frustration. Brian and Tracy well?"

"Fine. Just restless. Brian especially. You know Tracy, she's happy enough with her head buried in a history book. But with him it's all sports and pop music now. American football is the latest craze, apparently."

"Good God."

Brian had changed a lot over the past year. He even seemed to have lost interest in the electric train that Banks had set up in the spare room. Banks played with it himself more than Brian did, but then, he had to admit, he always had done.

To keep the emptiness after the conversation at bay, he poured out a glass of Bell's and listened to Leroy Carr and Scrapper Blackwell while he tried to let the information that filled his mind drift and form itself into new patterns. Bizarre as it all seemed, a number of things began to come together. The problem was that one theory seemed to cancel out the other.

The doorbell woke him from a light nap just before ten o'clock. The tape had long since ended and the ice had melted in his second Scotch.

"Sorry I'm so late, sir," Richmond said, "but I've just finished."

"Come in." Banks rubbed his eyes. "Sit down. A drink?"

"If you don't mind, sir. Though I suppose I am still on duty. Technically."

"Scotch do? Or there's beer in the fridge."

"Scotch will do fine, sir. No ice, if you don't mind."

Banks grinned. "I'm getting as bad as the Americans, aren't I, putting ice in good Scotch. Soon I'll be complaining my beer is too warm."

Richmond fitted his long athletic body into an armchair and stroked his moustache.

"By the way you're playing with that bit of face fungus there," Banks said, "I gather you've succeeded."

"What? Oh, yes, sir. Didn't know I was so obvious."

"Most of us are, it seems. You'd not make a good poker player—and you'd better watch it in interrogations. Come on then, what did you find?"

"Well," Richmond began, consulting his notebook, "I did exactly as you said, sir. Hung around discreetly near Tim and Abha's place. They stayed in all afternoon."

"Then what?"

"They went out about eight, to the pub I'd guess. And about half an hour later that blue Escort pulled up and two men got out and disappeared into the building. They looked like the ones you described. They must have been waiting and watching somewhere nearby, because they seemed to know when to come, allowing a bit of a safety margin in case Tim and Abha had just gone to the shop or something."

"You didn't try to stop them from getting in, did you?"

Richmond seemed shocked. "I did exactly as you instructed me, sir, though it felt a bit odd to sit there and watch a crime taking place. The front door is usually left on the latch, so they just walked in. The individual flats are kept locked, though, so they must have broken in. Anyway, they came out about fifteen minutes later carrying what looked like a number of buff folders."

"And then what?"

"I followed them at a good distance, and they pulled into the car-park of the Castle Hotel and went inside. I didn't follow, sir—they might have noticed me. And they didn't come out. After they'd been gone about ten minutes, I went in and asked the desk clerk about them and got him to show me the register. They'd booked in as James Smith and Thomas Brown."

"How imaginative. Sorry, carry on."

"Well, I rather thought that myself, sir, so I went back to the office and checked on the number of the car. It was rented by a firm in York to a Mr Cranby, Mr Keith J. Cranby, if that means anything to you. He had to show his licence, of course, so that's likely to be his right name."

"Cranby? No, it doesn't ring any bells. What happened next?"

"Nothing, sir. It was getting late by then so I thought I'd better come and report. By the way, I saw that barmaid, Glenys, going into the hotel while I was waiting outside. Looked a bit sheepish, she did, too."

"Was Cyril anywhere in sight?"

"No. I didn't see him."

"You've done a fine job, Phil," Banks said. "I owe you for this one."

"What's it all about?"

"I'd rather not say yet, in case I'm wrong. But you'll be the second to find out, I promise. Have you eaten at all?"

"I packed some sandwiches." He looked at his watch. "I could do with a pint, though."

"There's still beer in the fridge."

"I don't like bottled beer." Richmond patted his flat stomach. "Too gassy."

"And too cold?"

Richmond nodded.

"Come on, then. We should make it in time for a jar or two before closing. My treat. Queen's Arms do you?"

"Fine, sir."

The pub was busy and noisy with locals and farm lads in from the villages. Banks glanced at the bar staff and saw neither Glenys nor Cyril in evidence. Pushing his way to the bar, he asked one of the usual stand-in barmaids where the boss was.

"Took the evening off, Mr Banks. Just like that." She snapped her fingers. "Said there'd be three of us so we should be able to cope. Dead cagey, he was too. Still, he's the boss, isn't he? He can do what he likes."

"True enough, Rosie," Banks said. "I'll have two pints of your best bitter, please."

"Right you are, Mr Banks."

They stood at the bar and chatted with the regulars, who knew better than to ask too many questions about their work. Banks was beginning to feel unusually pleased with himself, considering he still hadn't found the answer. Whether it was the chat with Sandra, the nap, Richmond's success or the drink, he didn't know. Perhaps it was a combination of all four. He was close to the end of the case, though, he knew that. If he could solve the problem of two mutually exclusive explanations for Gill's and Seth's deaths, then he would be home and dry. Tomorrow should be an interesting day. First he would track down Liz Dale and discover what she knew; then there was the other business.... Yes, tomorrow should be very interesting indeed. And the day after that, Sandra was due home.

"Last orders, please!" Rosie shouted.

"Shall we?" Richmond asked.

"Go on. Why not," said Banks. He felt curiously like celebrating.

SIXTEEN

I

Dirty Dick was conspicuous by his absence the following morning. Banks took the opportunity to make a couple of important phone calls before getting an early start.

Just south of Bradford, it started to rain. Banks turned on the wipers and lit a cigarette from the dashboard lighter. On the car stereo, Walter Davis sang, "You got bad blood, baby, / I believe you need a shot."

It was so easy to get lost in the conurbation of old West Yorkshire woollen towns. Built in valleys on the eastern edges of the Pennines, they seemed to overlap one another, and it was hard to tell exactly where you were. The huge old textile factories, where all the processes of clothes-making had been gathered together under one roof in the last century, looked grim in the failing light. They were five or six storeys high, with flat roofs, rows of windows close together, and tall chimneys you could see for miles.

Cleckheaton, Liversedge, Heckmondwike, Brighouse, Rastrick, Mirfield—the strange names Banks usually associated only with brass bands and rugby teams—flew by on road signs. As he drew nearer to Huddersfield, he slowed and peered out through his rain-spattered windscreen for the turn-off.

Luckily the psychiatric hospital was at the northern end of the town, so he didn't have to cross the centre. When he saw the signpost, he followed directions to the left, down a street between two derelict warehouses.

The greenery of the hospital grounds came as a shock after so many miles of bleak industrial wasteland. There was a high brick wall and a guard at the gate, but beyond that, the drive wound its way by trees and a well-kept lawn to the modern L-shaped hospital complex. Banks parked in the visitors' lot, then presented himself at reception.

"That'll be Dr Preston," said the receptionist, looking up Elizabeth Dale in her roll file. "But the doctor can't divulge any information about his patients, you know."

Banks smiled. "He will see me, won't he?"

"Oh, of course. He's with our bursar right now, but if you'll wait he should be finished in ten minutes or so. You can wait over in the canteen if you like. The tea's not too bad."

Banks thanked her and walked towards the cluster of bright orange plastic tables and chairs.

"Oh, Mr Banks?" she called after him.

He turned.

She put her hands to the sides of her mouth and spoke quietly and slowly, mouthing the words as if for a lip-reader. "You won't wander off, will you?" She flicked her eyes right and left as if to indicate that beyond those points lay monsters.

Banks assured her that he wouldn't, bought a cup of tea and a Penguin biscuit from the pretty teenage girl at the counter and sat down.

There was only one other person in the canteen. A skinny man with a pronounced stoop and hair combed straight back from his creased brow, he was dressed as a vicar. Seeing Banks, he brought his cup over and sat down. He had a long, thin nose and a small mouth. The shape of his head, Banks noticed, was distinctly odd; it was triangular, and the forehead sloped sharply backwards. With his hair brushed straight back, standing at forty-five degrees, he looked as if his entire face had been sculpted by a head-on wind.

"Mind if I join you?" he asked, smiling in a way that screwed up his features grotesquely.

"Not if you don't mind my smoking," Banks replied.

"Go ahead, old chap, doesn't bother me at all." His accent was educated and southern. "Haven't seen you here before?"

It should have been a comment, but it sounded like a question.

"That's not surprising," Banks said. "I've never been here before. I'm a policeman."

"Oh, jolly good!" the vicar exclaimed. "Which one? Let me guess: Clouseau? Poirot? Holmes?"

Banks laughed. "I'm not as clutzy as Clouseau," he said. "Nor, I'm afraid, am I as brilliant as Poirot and Holmes. My name's Banks. Chief Inspector Banks."

The vicar frowned. "Banks, eh? I haven't heard of him."

"Well, you wouldn't have, would you?" Banks said, puzzled. "It's me. I'm Banks. I'm here to see Dr Preston."

The vicar's expression brightened. "Dr Preston? Oh, I'm sure you'll like him. He's very good."

"Is he helping you?"

"Helping me? Why, no. I help him, of course."

"Of course," Banks said slowly.

A nurse paused by the table and spoke his name. "Dr Preston will see you now," she said.

The vicar stuck out his hand. "Well, good luck, old boy."

Banks shook it and muttered his thanks.

"That man back there," he said to the nurse as she clicked beside him along the corridor, "should he be wandering around freely? What's he in for?"

The nurse laughed. "That's not a patient. That's the Reverend Clayton. He comes to visit two or three times a week. He must have thought *you* were a new patient."

Bloody hell, Banks thought, you could soon go crazy hanging around a place like this.

Dr Preston's office lacked the sharp polished instruments, kidney bowls, hypodermics and mysterious odds and ends that Banks usually found so disconcerting in Glendenning's lair. This room was more like a comfortable study with a pleasant view of the landscaped grounds.

Preston stood up as Banks entered. His handshake was firm and brief. He looked younger than Banks had expected, with a thatch of thick, shiny brown hair, a complexion as smooth as a baby's bottom, and cheeks just as chubby and rosy. His eyes, enlarged behind spectacles, were watchful and serious.

"What can I do for you, er, Chief Inspector?" he asked.

"I'm interested in an ex-patient of yours called Elizabeth Dale. At least, I think she's an ex-patient."

"Oh, yes," Preston said. "Been gone ages now. What exactly is it you wish to know? I'm sure you realize that I'm not at liberty to—"

"Yes, doctor, I understand that. I don't want the details of her illness. As I understand it, she was suffering from depression."

"Well—" The doctor unbent a paper-clip on his blotter "—I suppose in layman's terms... But you said that's not what you came about?"

"That's right. I just want to know where she is. Nothing confidential about that, is there?"

"We don't usually give out personal information."

"It's important. A murder inquiry. I could get a court order."

"Oh, I don't think that will be necessary," Preston said quickly. "The problem is, though, I'm afraid we don't know where Miss Dale is."

"No idea?"

"No. You see, we don't keep tabs on ex-patients as a rule."

"When did she leave here?"

Preston searched through his files. "She stayed for two months." He read off the dates.

"Is that usual? Two months?"

"Hard to say. It varies from patient to patient. Miss Dale was... well, I don't think I'm giving too much away if I tell you she was difficult. She'd hardly been here a couple of days before she ran off."

"Yes, I know." Banks explained his involvement. "As far as I understand, though, she admitted herself in the first place, is that right?"

"Yes."

"Yet you treated her as if she had escaped from a high-security prison."

Preston leaned back in his chair and his jaw muscles twitched. "You have to understand, Chief Inspector, that when anyone arrives here, they are given a whole range of tests, and a complete physical examination. On the basis of these, we make a diagnosis and prescribe treatment. I had examined Miss Dale and decided she required treatment. When she disappeared we were naturally worried that she.... Well, without the proper treatment, who knows what might have become of her? So we took steps to persuade her to come back."

"Doctor knows best, eh?"

Preston glared at him.

"How was she when she'd completed her treatment?" Banks asked.

"Given your hostile attitude, I don't know that I care to answer that."

Banks sighed and reached for a cigarette. "Oh, come on doctor, don't sulk. Was she cured or wasn't she?"

Preston passed an ashtray as Banks lit up. "That'll kill you, you know." He seemed to take great pleasure in the observation.

"Not before I get an answer from you, I hope."

Preston pursed his lips. "I imagine you know about Elizabeth Dale's drug problem?"

"Yes."

"That was part of the cause of her mental illness. When she came to us she said she'd been off heroin for about a month. Naturally, we're not equipped to deal with addicts here, and if Miss Dale had been still using drugs we would have had to send her elsewhere. However, she stayed, on medication I prescribed, and she made some progress. At the end of two months, I felt she was ready to leave."

"What did *she* feel?"

Preston stared out of his window at the landscaped garden. A row of topiary shrubs stood close to the building, cut in the shapes of birds and animals.

"Miss Dale," Preston started slowly, "was afraid of life and afraid of her addiction. The one led to the other, an apparently endless circle."

"What you're saying is that once she'd got used to the idea she'd have been happy to stay here forever. Am I right?"

"Not just here. Any institution, anywhere she didn't have to make her own decisions and face the world."

"And that's the kind of place I'm likely to find her in?"

"I'd say so, yes."

"Can you be any more specific?"

"You might try a DDU."

"DDU?"

"Yes. A Drug-Dependency Unit, for the treatment of addicts.

Elizabeth had been in and out of one a couple of times before she came to us."

"So she hadn't been cured?"

"How many are? Oh, some, I agree. But with Elizabeth it was on and off, on and off. The cure worked for a while—Methadone hydrochloride in gradually decreasing doses. It's rather like chewing nicotine gum when you're trying to stop smoking. Helps with some of the severe physical symptoms, but—"

"That's not enough?"

"Not really. Many addicts get hooked again as soon as the opportunity for a fix arises. Unfortunately, given the network of friends they have, that can be very soon."

"So you think this DDU might have Liz as a patient, or might know where she is?"

"It's likely."

"Where is it?" Banks slipped out his notebook.

"The only local one is just outside Halifax, not too far away." Preston continued to give directions. "I hope she's not in any trouble," he said finally.

"I don't think so. Just need her to help us with our inquiry."

Preston adjusted his glasses on the bridge of his nose. "You do have a way with words, you policemen, don't you?"

"I'm glad we've got something in common with doctors." Banks smiled and stood up to leave. "You've been a great help."

"Have I?"

Banks beat a hasty retreat from the hospital back onto the rain-swept roads and headed for Halifax. He soon found the DDU, using the Wainhouse Tower as a landmark, as Dr Preston had suggested. Originally built as a factory chimney, the tall, black tower was never used as one and now stands as a folly and a lookout point, its top ornamented in a very unchimneylike pointed Gothic style.

Banks found the DDU up a steep side street. It was set back from the road at the top of a long sloping lawn and looked like a Victorian mansion. It also had an eerie quality to it, Banks felt. He shivered as he made his approach. Not the kind of place I'd want to find myself in after dark, he thought.

There were no walls or men at the gate here. Banks walked straight inside and found himself standing in a spacious common room with a high ceiling. On the walls hung a number of paintings, clearly the work of patients, dominated by an enormous canvas depicting an angel plummeting to earth, wings ablaze and neck contorted so that it looked straight at the viewer, eyes red and wild, raw muscles stretched like knotted ropes. It could have been Satan on his way to hell. Certainly the destination, impressionistically rendered in the lower half of the painting, was a dark and murky place. He shuddered and looked away.

"Can I help you?" A young woman came up to him. It wasn't clear from her appearance whether she was a member of staff or a patient. She was in her early thirties, perhaps, and wore jeans and a dark-brown jacket over a neck-high white blouse. Her long black hair was plaited into wide braids and pinned at the back.

"Yes," Banks said. "I'm looking for Elizabeth Dale. Is she here, or do you know where I can find her?"

"Who are you?"

Banks showed her his identification.

The woman raised her eyebrows. "Police? What do you want?"

"I want to talk to Elizabeth Dale," he repeated. "Is she here or isn't she?"

"What's it about?"

"I'm the one who asks the questions," Banks said, irritated by her brusque, haughty manner. Suddenly, he realized who she must be. "Look, doctor," he went on, "it's nothing to do with drugs. It's about an old friend of hers. I need some information to help solve a murder case, that's all."

"Elizabeth's been here for the past month. She can't be involved."

"I'm not saying she is. Will you just let me talk to her?"

The doctor frowned. Banks could see her brain working fast behind her eyes. "All right," she said finally. "But treat her gently. She's very fragile. And I insist on being present."

"I'd rather talk to her alone." The last thing Banks wanted was this woman watching over the conversation like a lawyer.

"I'm afraid that's not possible."

"How about if you remained within calling distance? Say, the other end of this room?" The room was certainly large enough to accommodate more than one conversation.

The doctor smiled out of the side of her mouth. "A compromise? All right. Stay here while I fetch Elizabeth. Take a seat."

But Banks felt restless after being in the car. Instead, he walked around the room looking at the paintings, almost all of which illustrated some intense level of terror: mad eyes staring through a letterbox; a naked man being dragged away from a woman, his features creased in a desperate plea; a forest in which every carefully painted leaf looked like a needle of fire. They sent shivers up his spine. Noticing plenty of pedestal ashtrays around, he lit up. It was warm in the room, so he took off his car-coat and laid it on a chair.

About five minutes later, the doctor returned with another woman. "This is Elizabeth Dale," she said, introducing them formally, then walked off to the far end of the room, where she sat facing Banks and pretended to read a magazine. Liz took a chair on his left, angled so they could face one another comfortably. The chairs were well-padded, with strong armrests.

"I saw you looking at the paintings," Elizabeth said. "Quite something, aren't they?" She had a melodic, hypnotic voice. Banks could easily imagine its persuasive powers. He had a feeling, however, that it would probably become tiresome after a while: whining and wheedling rather than beautiful and soft.

Elizabeth Dale smoothed her long powder-blue skirt over her knees. Her slight frame was lost inside a baggy mauve sweater with two broad white hoops around the middle. If she was Seth's contemporary, that made her about forty, but her gaunt, waxy face was lined like that of a much older woman, and her black hair, hacked, rather than cut, short was liberally streaked with grey. It was a face that screamed of suffering; eyes that had looked deep inside and seen the horror there. Yet her voice was beautiful. So gentle, so soothing, like a breeze through woods in spring.

"They're very powerful," Banks said, feeling his words pathetically inadequate in describing the paintings.

"People see those things here," Elizabeth said. "Do you know what this place used to be?"

"No."

"It was a hospital, a fever-hospital, during the typhoid epidemics in the last century. I can hear the patients screaming every night."

"You mean the place is haunted?"

Elizabeth shrugged. "Maybe it's me who's haunted. People go crazy here sometimes. Break windows and try to cut themselves with broken glass. I can hear the typhoid victims screaming every night as they're burning up and snapping bones in convulsions. I can hear the bones snap." She clapped her hands. "Crack. Just like that."

Then she put her hand over her mouth and laughed. Banks noticed the first and second fingers of her right hand were stained yellow with nicotine. She rummaged inside her sweater and pulled out a packet of Embassy Regal and a tarnished silver lighter. Banks took out a cigarette of his own, and she leaned forward to give him a light. The flame was high and he caught a whiff of petrol fumes as he inhaled.

"You know," Elizabeth went on, "for all that—the ghosts, the screaming, the cold—I'd rather be here than . . . than out there." She nodded her head towards the door. "That's where the real horror is, Mr Banks, out there."

"I take it you don't keep up with the world, then. No newspapers, no television?"

Elizabeth shook her head. "No. There is a television here, next door. But I don't watch it. I read books. Old books. Charles Dickens, that's who I'm reading now. There's opium-taking in *Edwin Drood*, did you know that?"

Banks nodded. He had been through a Dickens phase some years ago.

"Have you come about the complaint?" Elizabeth asked.

"What complaint?"

"It was years ago. I made a complaint about a policeman for hitting people with his truncheon at a demonstration. I don't know what became of it. I never heard a thing. I was different then, things seemed more worthwhile fighting for. Now I just let them go their way. They'll blow it up, Mr Banks. Oh, there's no doubt about it, they'll blow us all up. Or is it drugs you want to talk about?"

"It's partly about the complaint, yes. I wanted to talk to you about Seth Cotton. Seth and Alison."

"Good old Seth. Poor old Seth. I don't want to talk about Seth. I don't have to talk to you, do I?"

"Why don't you want to talk about him?"

"Because I don't. Seth's private. I won't tell you anything he wouldn't, so it's no good asking."

Banks leaned forward. "Elizabeth," he said gently, "Seth's dead. I'm sorry, but it's true."

At first he thought she wasn't going to react at all. A little sigh escaped her, nothing more than a gust of wind against a dark window. "Well, that's all right, then, isn't it?" she said, her voice softer, weaker. "Peace at last." Then she closed her eyes, and her face assumed such a distant, holy expression that Banks didn't dare break the silence. It would have been blasphemy. When she opened her eyes again, they were clear. "My little prayer," she said.

"What did you mean, poor Seth?"

"He was such a serious man, and he had to suffer so much pain. How did he die, Mr Banks? Was it peaceful?"

"Yes," Banks lied.

Elizabeth nodded.

"The problem is," Banks said, "that nobody knew very much about him, about his feelings or his past. You were quite close to Seth and Alison, weren't you?"

"I was, yes."

"Is there anything you can tell me about him, about his past, that might help me understand him better. I know he was upset about Alison's accident—"

"Accident?"

"Yes. You must know, surely? The car—"

"Alison's death wasn't an accident, Mr Banks. She was murdered."

"Murdered?"

"Oh yes. It was murder all right. I told Seth. I made him believe me."

"When?"

"I figured it out. I used to be a nurse, you know."

"I know. What did you figure out?"

"Are you sure Seth's dead?"

Banks nodded.

She eyed him suspiciously, then smiled. "I suppose I can tell you, then. Are you sitting comfortably? That's what they say before the story on 'Children's Hour,' you know. I used to listen to that when I was young. It's funny how things stick in your memory, isn't it? But so much doesn't. Why is that, do you think? Isn't the mind peculiar? Do you remember Uncle Mac and 'Children's Favourites'? 'Sparky and the Magic Piano'? Petula Clark singing 'Little Green Man'?"

"I'm sorry, I don't remember," Banks said. "But I'm sitting comfortably."

Elizabeth smiled. "Good. Then I'll begin."

And she launched into one of the saddest and strangest stories that Banks had ever heard.

II

What Liz Dale told him confirmed what he had been beginning to suspect. His theories were no longer mutually exclusive, but he felt none of his usual elation on solving this case.

He drove back to Eastvale slowly, taking the longest, most meandering route west through the gritstone country away from the large towns and cities. There was no hurry. On the way, he listened to scratchy recordings of the old bluesmen: gamblers, murderers, ministers, alcoholics, drug addicts singing songs about poverty, sex, the devil and bad luck. And the signs flashed by: Mytholmroyd, Todmorden, Cornholme. In Lancashire now, he skirted the Burnley area on a series of minor roads that led by the Forest of Trawden, then he was soon back in Craven country around Skipton, where the grass was lush green with limestone-rich soils.

He stopped in Grassington and had a pub lunch, then cut across Greenhow Hill by Pateley Bridge and got back to Eastvale via Ripon.

Burgess was waiting in his office. "You owe me a flyer," he said. "A couple of glasses of Mumm's and she was all over me."

"There's no accounting for taste," Banks said.

"You'll have to take my word for it. I'm not crass, I don't go in for stealing knickers as a trophy."

Banks nodded towards the superintendent's swollen, purplish cheek. "I see you've got a trophy of a kind."

"That bloody husband of hers. Mistrustful swine." He fingered the bruise. "But that was later. He's lucky I didn't pull him in for assaulting a police officer. Still, I suppose he deserved a swing at me, so I let him. All nice and quiet."

"Very magnanimous of you." Banks pulled a five-pound note from his wallet and dropped it on the desk.

"What's wrong with you today, Banks? Sore loser?" Burgess picked up the money and held it out. "Fuck it, you don't have to pay if you're that hard up."

Banks sat down and lit a cigarette. "Ever heard of a fellow called Barney Merritt?" he asked.

"No. Should I?"

"He's an old friend of mine, still on the Met. He's heard of you. He's also heard of DC Cranby. Keith J. Cranby."

"So?" The muscles around Burgess's jaw tightened and his eyes seemed to turn brighter and sharper.

Banks tapped a folder on his desk. "Cranby and a mate of his—possible DC Stickley—rented a blue Escort in York a couple of days ago. They drove up to Eastvale and checked into the Castle Hotel—the same place as you. I'm surprised you didn't pass each other in the lobby, it's not that big a place."

"Do you realize what you're saying? Maybe you should reconsider and stop while the going's good."

Banks shook his head and went on.

'The other day they broke into Dennis Osmond's flat. They didn't find what they were looking for, but they took one of his political books to put the wind up him. He thought he had every security force in the world after him. Yesterday evening they broke into Tim and Abha's apartment and took away a number of folders. That was after I told you where the information they'd collected on the demo was kept."

Burgess tapped a ruler on the desk. "You have proof of all this, I suppose?"

"If I need it, yes."

"What on earth made you think of such a thing?"

"I know your methods. And when I mentioned the Osmond break-in you didn't seem surprised. You didn't even seem to care very much. That was odd, because my first thought was that it might have had a bearing on the Gill case. But, of course, you already knew all about it."

"And what are you going to do?"

"I just don't understand you," Banks said. "What the bloody hell did you hope to achieve? You used the same vigilante tactics they did in Manchester after the Leon Brittan demo."

"They worked, though, didn't they?"

"If you call hounding a couple of students out of the country and drawing national attention to the worst elements of policing good, then yes, they worked."

"Don't be so bloody naïve, Banks. These people are all connected."

"You're paranoid, do you know that? What do you think they are? Terrorists?"

"They're connected. Union leaders, Bolshy students, ban-the-bombers. They're all connected. You can call them misguided idealists if you want, but to me they're a bloody menace."

"To who? To what?"

Burgess leaned forward and gripped the desk. "To the peace and stability of the nation, that's what. Whose side are you on, anyway?"

"I'm not on anyone's side. I've been investigating a murder, remember? A policeman was killed. He wasn't a very good one, but I don't think he deserved to end up dead in the street. And what do I find? You bring your personal bloody goon squad from London and they start breaking and entering."

"There's no point arguing ethics with you, Banks—"

"I know—because you don't have a leg to stand on."

"But let me remind you that I'm in charge of this case."

"That still doesn't give you the right to do what you did. Can't you bloody understand? You with all your talk about police image. This vigilante stuff only makes us end up looking like the bad guys, and bloody stupid ones at that."

Burgess sat back and lit a cigar. "Only if people find out. Which brings us back to my question. What are you going to do?"

"Nothing. But you're going to make sure those files are returned and that the people involved are left alone from now on."

"Am I? What makes you so sure?"

"Because if you don't, I'll pass on what I know to Superintendent Gristhorpe. The ACC respects his opinion."

Burgess laughed. "You're not very well-connected, you know. I don't think that'll do much good."

"There's always the press, too. They'd love a juicy story like this. Dennis Osmond has a right to know what was done to him, too. Whatever you think, I don't believe it would do your future promotion prospects much good."

Burgess tapped his cigar on the rim of the ashtray. "You're so bloody pure of heart, aren't you, Banks? A real crusader. Better than the rest of us."

"Don't come that. You were out of line and you know it. You just thought you could get away with it."

"I still can."

Banks shook his head.

"You're forgetting that I'm your superior officer. I can order you to hand over whatever evidence you've got."

"Balls," said Banks. "Why don't you send Cranby and Stickley in to steal it?"

"Look," Burgess said, reddening with anger, "you don't want to cross me. I can be a very nasty enemy. Do you really think anyone's going to take any notice of your accusations? What do you think they'll do? Kick me off the force? Dream on."

"I don't really care what they do to you. All I know is that the press will make a field-day of it."

"You'd be sawing off the branch you're sitting on. Think about where your loyalty lies. We do a difficult enough job as it is without taking an opportunity to set everyone against us. Have you considered that? What effect it would have on you lot up here if it did get out? I don't have to live here, thank God, but you do."

"Damn right I do," said Banks. "And that's the point. You can come here and make a bloody mess then bugger off back to London. I have to live and work with these people. And I like it. It took me long enough to get accepted as far as I have been, and you come along and set back relations by years. Take it or leave it. Give back the files, call off your goons, and it's forgotten, another unsolved break-in."

"Oh, what a bleeding hero we are! And what if I put on a bit more pressure, got a couple of higher-ups to order you to hand over your evidence? What then, big man?"

"I've already told you," Banks said. "It's not me you need to worry about, it's the press, Osmond and the students."

"I can handle them."

"It's up to you."

"That's it?"

"That's it. Take your pick."

"Who's going to believe a couple of loony lefties anyway? And everyone knows the press is biased."

Banks shrugged. "Maybe nobody. We'll see."

Burgess jerked to his feet. "I won't forget this, Banks," he snarled. "When I make my report on this investigation—"

"It's over," Banks said wearily.

"What is?"

"The investigation." Banks told him briefly about his conversation with Elizabeth Dale.

"So what happens now?"

"Nothing. Except maybe you piss off back home."

"You're not going to go blabbing the whole bloody story to the press?"

"No point, no. But I think Mara and the others have a right to know."

"Yes, you would." Burgess strode over to the door. "And don't think you've won, because you haven't. You won't get out of it as easily as all that."

And he left, the threat hanging in the air.

Banks stretched out his hands in front of him and noticed they were shaking. Even though the office was cool, his neck felt sweaty under the collar. His legs were weak, too, as he found out when he grabbed another cigarette and walked over to the window. It wasn't every day you got the chance to be high-handed with a senior officer, especially a whiz-kid like Dirty Dick Burgess. And it was the first time Banks had ever seen him ruffled.

Maybe he *had* made a dangerous enemy for life. Perhaps Burgess had even been right and he was overplaying the crusader role. After all, he played it a bit close to the edge himself sometimes. But to hell with it, he thought. It wasn't worth dwelling on. He picked up his coat, pocketed his cigarettes and set off for the car-park.

III

The rain had stopped and the afternoon sun was charming wraiths of mist from the river-meadows and valleysides. Banks's Cortina crackled up the track and pulled up outside the farmhouse.

Mara answered the door on his second knock and let him in.

"I suppose you want to sit down?" she asked.

"It might take a while." Banks made himself comfortable in the rocking chair. The children sat at the table colouring, and Paul slouched on the beanbag cushions reading a science-fiction book.

"Where are Rick and Zoe?" Banks asked.

"Working."

"Can you go get them, please? I'd like to talk to all of you. And would it be too much to ask for some tea?"

Mara put the kettle on first, then went out to the barn to fetch the others. When she came back, she saw to the tea while Rick and Zoe sat down.

"What the bloody hell is this?" Rick demanded. "Haven't we had enough? Where's your friend?"

"He's packing."

"Packing?" Mara said, walking in slowly with the teapot and mugs on a tray. "But—"

"It's all over, Mara. Almost over, anyway."

Banks poured himself some tea, lit a cigarette and turned to Paul. "You wrote that suicide note, didn't you?"

"I don't know what you're talking about."

"Come off it, the time for messing around is over. The pressure on the keys was different from that on the letters Seth typed, and his style was a hell of a lot better than yours. Why did you do it?"

"I've told you, I didn't do anything." They were all staring at him now and he began to turn red.

"Shall I tell you why you did it?" Banks went on. "You did it to deflect the blame from yourself."

"Wait a minute," Mara said. "Are you accusing Paul of killing Seth?"

"Nobody killed Seth," Banks said quietly. "He did it himself."

"But you said—"

"I know. And that's what we thought. It was the note that confused me. Seth didn't write it; Paul did. But he didn't kill anyone. When Paul found him, Seth was already dead. Paul just took the opportunity to type out a note of confession, hoping it would get him off the hook. It didn't seem like such a bad thing to do, I'm sure. After all, Seth was dead. Nothing could affect him any more. Isn't that right, Paul?"

Paul said nothing.

"Paul?" Mara turned to face him sternly. "Is it true?"

"So what if it is? Seth wouldn't have minded. He wouldn't have wanted us to go on being persecuted. He was dead, Mara. I swear it. All I did was type out a note."

"Had he written anything himself?" Banks asked.

"Yes, but it said nothing." He pulled a scrap of paper out of the back pocket of his jeans and passed it over. It read, "Sorry, Mara." Just that. Banks passed it to Mara, and tears filled her eyes. She wiped them away with the back of her hand. "How could you, Paul?" she said.

Paul sat forward and hugged his knees. "It was for all of us," he said. "Can't you see? To keep the police off our backs. It's what Seth would have done."

"But he didn't," Banks said. "Seth had no idea that Paul would forge a note. As far as he was concerned, his suicide would be accepted for what it was. He'd never imagined that we'd see it as murder. If his death led us to the truth, so be it, but he wasn't going to explain. He never did while he was alive, so why should he when he was about to die?"

"The truth?" Mara said. "Is that what you're going to tell us now?"

"Yes. If you want me to."

Mara nodded.

"You might not like it."

"After all we've been through," she said, "I think you owe it to us."

"Very well. I think Seth killed himself out of shame, among other reasons. He felt he'd let everyone down—including himself."

"What do you mean?"

"I mean that Seth stabbed PC Gill and he couldn't live with what he'd done. Paul had already suffered for it. Seth would never have let him take the blame. He'd have confessed himself rather than that. When Paul was released, he was happy for him. What it meant for Seth, though, was that the police would get even closer to him now. It was just a matter of time. I'd already seen PC Gill's number in his notebook, and those books in his workshop. I knew it was his knife, too. I'd asked him about Elizabeth Dale, and he knew how unstable she was. All I had to do was find her and get her to talk. Seth knew all this. He knew it would soon be all over for him."

Mara was pale. Her hands trembled as she tried to roll a cigarette. Banks offered her a Silk Cut and she took it. Zoe went around and poured tea for everyone.

"I can't believe this, you know," Mara said, shaking her head. "Not Seth."

"It's true. I'm not saying that he intended to kill PC Gill. He couldn't be sure that the demo would turn nasty, even though Gill was supposed to be there. But he went prepared. He knew very well the kind of things that were likely to happen if Gill was around. That's why I asked you if you'd heard anyone mention Gill's number that afternoon. Someone had it in for him and knew he'd be there."

"I thought it sounded vaguely familiar," Mara said, speaking quietly as if to herself. "I was in the kitchen, I think, with Seth."

"And Osmond mentioned the number."

"I...It could have been like that. But why Seth? He wasn't like that. He was a gentle person."

"I agree, on the whole," Banks said. "But the circumstances are very unusual. I had to find Liz Dale to put it all together. She told me a very curious thing, and that was that Alison, Seth's wife, was murdered. Now that didn't make sense to me, because I'd spoken to the local police and to the man who ran her over. It was an accident. He hadn't killed her deliberately. It had ruined his life, too.

"Seth tried to commit suicide after Alison's death, but he failed. He got on with his life but he never got over his grief, and that's partly because he never expressed it. You know he didn't like to talk about the past, he kept it all bottled up inside, all those feelings of grief and guilt. We always blame ourselves when someone we love dies, because maybe, just in a fleeting moment, we've wished them dead, and we tell ourselves that if things had been just a little different—if Seth had ridden to the shops that day instead of Alison—then the tragedy would never have happened. Liz was the only one who really knew about what went on, and that was only because she was a close friend of Alison's. According to the Hebden Bridge police, Alison was more outgoing, spirited and communicative than Seth. Because he was the 'strong silent type,' everyone thought he was really in control, calm and cool, but he was torturing himself inside."

"I still don't see," Mara said. "What does all this have to do with that policeman who got killed?"

Banks blew gently on the surface and sipped some tea. It tasted of apple and cinnamon. "Liz Dale filed a complaint about PC Gill's vicious behaviour during a demo she went to with Alison Cotton. Seth hadn't been there himself. During the demo, Liz told me, Alison was struck a glancing blow on her temple by Gill. It was just one of many such incidents that afternoon. Alison didn't want to make a fuss and attract police attention by making a complaint, but Liz was far more political at that time. She made a complaint about Gill's behaviour in general. When nothing came of it, she didn't pursue it any further. She'd lost interest by then—heroin made her forget politics—and like you, she assumed that the police wouldn't listen to someone like her."

"Can you blame her?" Rick said. "They obviously didn't, did they? It hardly seems that—"

"Shut up," Banks said. He spoke quietly, but forcefully enough to silence Rick.

"Over the next few months," he went on, "Alison started to show some unusual symptoms. She complained of frequent headaches, she was becoming forgetful, and she suffered from dizzy spells. Shortly afterwards, she became pregnant, so she put her other troubles out of her mind for a while.

"One time, though, she really scared Seth and Liz. She started speaking as if she were a fourteen-year-old girl. Her family had been on holiday in Cyprus then, staying with an army friend of her father's who was stationed there, and she started describing a warm evening walk by the Mediterranean in Famagusta in great detail. Apparently, even her voice was like that of a fourteen-year-old. Finally she snapped out of it and recalled nothing. She just laughed when the others told her what she'd been talking about.

"But that did it as far as Seth was concerned. He was worried she might have a brain tumour or something, so he insisted she tell the doctor. According to Liz, the doctor had nothing much to say except that pregnancy can do strange things to a woman's mind as well as her body. Alison told him that the symptoms started *before* she got pregnant, but he just said something about people having funny spells, and that was that.

"A few weeks later, she went to the local shop one evening and got lost. It was about a two-minute walk away, and she couldn't find her way home. Seth and Liz found her wandering the streets an hour later. Anyway, things didn't get much better and she went to see the doctor again. At first, he tried to blame the pregnancy again, but Alison stressed the terrible headaches, lapses of memory, and slipping in and out of time. He said not to worry, but he arranged for a CAT scan, just to be on the safe side. Well, you know the National Health Service. By the time her appointment came around, she was already dead. And they couldn't do a proper autopsy later because of the accident—her head was crushed.

"Seth had his breakdown, attempted suicide, put himself back together and bought the farm, where he lived in isolation for a while—until you came along, Mara. He proved himself capable of moving on, but he carried all the weight of the past with him. He was always a serious person, a man of strong feelings, but there was a new darker dimension to him after the shock of Alison's death."

"It doesn't make sense," Mara said. "If all that's true, why did he wait so long before doing what you say he did?"

"Two reasons really. First, he wasn't convinced until about a year ago. That's around the time he made his will. According to Liz, about eighteen months ago he'd read an article in a magazine about a similar case. A woman showed symptoms like Alison's after receiving a relatively mild blow to the head, and she later crashed her car. Just after he'd read this and started thinking about the implications, Liz ran off from the hospital and came to stay. He talked to her about it, and she agreed it was a definite possibility. After all, Alison's attacks only began to occur shortly after the demo. Liz hadn't been a very good nurse—not good enough to come up with a diagnosis at the time—but she knew something about the human body, and once Seth had put the idea into her head, she helped to convince him."

"That's when they were up talking all the time," Mara said. "Is that what they were talking about?"

"Mostly, yes. Next, Seth went on to study the subject himself. I even saw two books on the human brain in his workshop, though I'd no idea what significance they had. One was called *The Tip of the Iceberg*. Seth just left them there; he never really tried to cover his tracks at all. And then there was PC Gill's number in his notebook. Liz said she wrote it down for him the last time she was here. He must have torn it out in anger after he'd heard Gill would be at the demo."

"You said there were two reasons he didn't act straight away," Mara said. "What's the other one?"

"Seth's character, really. You know he wasn't normally quick-tempered or impatient. Far from it, he needed lots of patience in his line of work. He wasn't the type to go out seeking immediate vengeance, either. And remember, he'd never really got over his grief and his guilt. I imagine he repressed his anger in the same way, and it all festered together, under the surface, and finally turned into hatred— hatred for the man who had robbed him of his wife and child. And it wasn't just a man, it was a policeman, an enemy of freedom." He glanced at Rick, who was listening closely and sucking on a strand of his beard.

"But there was nothing he could do. It had happened so long ago, and there was no evidence—even if he had believed that the police would listen to his story. I don't think he really considered revenge, but when Osmond mentioned the number that afternoon, something gave. The whole business had been eating away at him for so long, and he felt so impotent.

"He snatched up the knife, expecting trouble. I shouldn't imagine he really believed he would kill Gill, but he wanted to be prepared. When he dropped the knife later and it got kicked away, he must have been surprised to find no blood on him. Most of Gill's bleeding was internal. So he kept quiet. There were over a hundred people at that demo. As far as Seth was concerned, that seemed to mean we hadn't a snowball in hell's chance of finding the killer. Besides, we'd be after the politicos, and he wasn't especially active that way." Banks paused and sipped some more tea. "If Paul hadn't taken the knife and thrown it away, we might never have known where it came from. None of you would ever have told us it was missing, that's for certain. Liz had described Gill to him as well—a big man with his teeth too close to his gums—and he was easy to spot up there on the steps. That's where the most light was, above the doors. And Seth was near the front of the crowd. When they got close in the scuffles, Seth saw the number on Gill's epaulette and—"

"My God!" Zoe said. "So that's it!"

"What?"

"When the police started to charge, I was next to Seth, right at the front, and the first thing that policeman did was lash out at a woman standing on my other side. She looked a bit like you, Mara."

"What happened next?" Banks asked.

"I didn't really see. I was frightened. I got pushed away. But I looked up at Seth and I saw an expression on his face. It was...I can't really describe it, but he was pale and he looked so different...so full of hate."

They all remained silent as they digested what Zoe had said. She couldn't have known at the time, but what Seth was seeing was a replay, an echo of what happened to Alison. Given that, Banks thought, what Seth had done was even more understandable. He had been pushed far beyond breaking point.

"Liz Dale told you all about his background?" said Mara finally.

"Yes. Everything else made sense then: Seth's behaviour, the knife, the number, the books."

"If...if you'd found her earlier, talked to her, would that have saved Seth?"

"I don't think so. It's not as easy as that. It was actually carrying out the crime that finished him. He'd spent all his hate and anger, and he felt empty. He might have committed suicide sooner if he hadn't been lucky and got away from the demo clean. I imagine he thought he could live with what he'd done at first, but as the investigation went on, he realized he couldn't. I don't think he could have faced prison, either, and he knew that we'd find him. All that talking to Liz Dale has done is put things in perspective and make the motive clear.

"And Liz is a difficult person. Her grasp on reality is pretty tenuous, for a start. She knew nothing of the demo or of Gill's murder. And I honestly don't think she'd have told me about Seth unless I'd told her he was dead. I probably wouldn't even have known the right questions to ask. I'm not making excuses, Mara. We make mistakes in this job, and usually someone suffers for them. But the rest of you lie, evade and treat us with hostility. There's good and bad on both sides. You can't look back and say how things might have been. That's no good."

Mara nodded slowly. "Do you think Seth was right?"

"Right about what?"

"About Gill being responsible for Alison's death."

"I think there's a good chance, yes. I've spoken to the police doctor about it, too, and he agrees. But we'll never know for sure. Liz Dale was wrong, though—Alison wasn't murdered. Gill might not have been a good policeman, but he didn't *intend* to kill her.

"But look at it from Seth's point of view. He'd lost everything he valued—in the most horrible way—and he'd lost it all to a man who abused the power the state gave him. Seth came of age in the late sixties and early seventies. He was anti-authoritarian, and he lost his wife and unborn child to a representative of what he saw as oppressive authority. It's no wonder he had to hit back eventually, especially considering what Zoe just told us, or go mad. That's why he made the will when he did, I think, because knowing what had happened to Alison—knowing the real cause of her death—changed things, and he wasn't sure he could be responsible for his actions any more. He wanted to make certain you got the house."

Mara covered her face with both hands and started to cry. Zoe went over to comfort her and the children looked on, horror-stricken. Paul and Rick seemed rooted where they sat. Banks rose from the chair. He'd done his job, solved the crime, but it didn't end there for Mara. For her, this was only the beginning of the real pain.

"But why couldn't he be happy here?" she cried from behind her hands. "With me?"

Banks had no answer to that.

He opened the door and late-afternoon sunshine flooded in. At the car, he turned and saw Mara standing in the doorway watching him, arms folded tightly across her chest, head tilted to one side. The sunlight caught the tears in her eyes and made them sparkle like jewels as they trickled down her cheeks.

All the way home through the wraiths of mist, Banks could hear the damn wind chimes ringing in his ears.